READER'S DIGEST

CONDENSED BOOKS

FIRST EDITION

THE READER'S DIGEST ASSOCIATION LIMITED
25 Berkeley Square, London W1X 6AB

**THE READER'S DIGEST ASSOCIATION
SOUTH AFRICA (PTY) LTD**
Nedbank Centre, Strand Street, Cape Town

Printed in Great Britain by Petty & Sons Ltd, Leeds and Varnicoat Ltd, Pershore

Original cover design by Jeffery Matthews M.S.I.A.

For information as to ownership
of copyright in the material in this book see last page

ISBN 0 340 23409 1

Reader's Digest
CONDENSED BOOKS

JAWS 2

A completely new novel by Hank Searls,
based on a screenplay by **Howard Sackler** and **Dorothy Tristan,**
inspired by **Peter Benchley's** *Jaws*

A DANGEROUS MAGIC

Frances Lynch

THE FOREST DWELLERS

Stella Brewer

TALK DOWN

Brian Lecomber

COLLECTOR'S LIBRARY
EDITION

In this volume

JAWS 2 (p.9)

*A completely new novel by
Hank Searls,
based on a screenplay by
Howard Sackler and Dorothy Tristan,
inspired by Peter Benchley's Jaws*

Four years ago a great white shark
terrorized the summer resort of
Amity, Long Island. Now, when
tranquillity seems restored, two deep-
sea divers vanish, a boat explodes.
The menace is back; but this time it
is a pregnant female shark, ravenous
with hunger and ready to destroy
anything within range. . . .

This galvanizing sequel to *Jaws* is
soon to be released as a major film.

A DANGEROUS MAGIC
by Frances Lynch (p. 149)

There is a sinister secret hidden in the
long life of Lady Otranta Tantallon.
To someone in her household it
presents a desperate threat, so when
young Bridie comes to the gloomy
castle on the Firth of Forth to help
her great-aunt write her memoirs
she finds her path beset with
frightening surprises.

What is old Peggy, a relic of Lady
Otranta's theatrical past, trying to
hide? What strange part does the
taciturn estate manager play? And
can Bridie trust her three attractive
cousins?

Brilliant period detail highlights
the mystery and romance of this
enthralling story.

THE FOREST DWELLERS
by Stella Brewer (p. 297)

The Brewer family home in West Africa overflowed with animals: there were dogs and cats, hyenas and antelopes, tiny monkeys and even a python.

When seventeen-year-old Stella first cared for a sick baby chimpanzee she did not realize that this was only the beginning of an exciting project to rehabilitate captive chimps. To train her delightful companions to be independent, Stella camped with them in the remote forests of Senegal and shared the adventures and dangers of their new life. The story of her courageous experiment is one of humour and heartbreak, struggle and success.

TALK DOWN *by Brian Lecomber* (p. 381)

With appalling suddenness Ann Moore finds herself in charge of a small plane 4,000 feet above the English countryside. Beside her the pilot lies unconscious. When a flying instructor picks up her terrified screams on his cockpit radio, a nationwide emergency operation is mounted.

The author, a skilled instructor himself, brings a stunning authenticity to this tale of suspense.

JAWS 2

A condensation of
a completely new novel by
HANK SEARLS
based on a screenplay by
HOWARD SACKLER and
DOROTHY TRISTAN
inspired by **PETER BENCHLEY'S** "Jaws"

illustrated by Harry Schaare
to be published by Pan Books

The great white shark was dead. Again and again, that nightmarish summer, the deadly jaws had struck at the beaches of Amity, Long Island. In an epic battle Police Chief Martin Brody had confronted the fish—and won.

Now, four years later, Amity is emerging from The Trouble. Tourism is up, and the construction of a gambling casino promises new life for the town's economy.

Then a spate of accidents begins: two divers disappear, a boat explodes for no apparent reason. As Brody grapples with these emergencies, a niggling suspicion takes root. Murder? Or something worse. . . .

Based on the Universal screenplay, here is the exciting sequel to the best-selling book *Jaws*. A story of driving action and relentless suspense.

PART ONE—Chapter 1

A FLATTENED, blood-red sun rose dead ahead.

The white Hatteras powerboat, *Miss Carriage*, out of Sag Harbor, slithered around Montauk Point. She emerged from Long Island Sound and rose to the swell of open ocean. The two half-suited scuba divers high on her flying bridge took wider stances.

The taller of the two, a Long Island obstetrician, flicked off the running lights. The shorter was a Manhattan attorney. The two had little in common except an interest in diving, diminishing as they aged, and a partnership in the boat. They almost never met except on summer weekends.

Every spring the physician dreaded the first few scallop dives. Equipment always felt strange at first. The water would be cold and cloudy. And here, off Amity Township, lurked a ghost.

The beast was dead. The doctor had all but forgotten the stories in the *Long Island Press*. The Manhattan lawyer seldom thought of the pictures in the *Times*. But a secret halftone specter swam in the subconscious of each.

The doctor was suddenly cold. He glanced at the Fathometer tracing the depth. They were searching for a clump of bottom rocks they knew, but the graph on the instrument was still as flat as the trace of a terminal patient in intensive care. The doctor pictured mud below, and silt.

He shivered and swung down the flying-bridge ladder. He tugged his neoprene upper suit from behind a tank rack in the cockpit, and squirmed into it. He had put on weight.

9

Even after he smoothed it on, he was still shivering. He stepped into the cabin. Crossing to the stainless galley stove, he took two cups from a rack. He poured a double slug of Old Grand-Dad into his cup and a single into his partner's, then filled the cups with coffee from the stove. He sat down at the lower steering station to sip the stronger one.

The ground swell, which was making him queasy, told him they were paralleling the beach too closely. He gazed through binoculars out the starboard window. The gray summer cottages of Napeague, Amagansett, East Hampton, and Sagaponack slumbered less than half a mile away. A child poked along the tideflats, teased to run by a huge woolly dog. The doctor found a strange comfort in the cottages and decided not to ask his partner to move farther out.

The sound of the engines suddenly diminished. Obviously, the first trace of the Fathometer had sprung to life.

The doctor hesitated, then slugged down the drink he had intended for the man topside. He went forward and dangled a stainless Danforth anchor until he felt the bottom some thirty feet below. As his partner backed slowly, he paid off chain and line. Finally he snubbed the line on a bow cleat, and signaled his partner that the hook was properly set.

Sidling aft along the narrow deck outboard of the cabin, he glanced at the shoreline. All the shoulder-to-shoulder communities lining Long Island dunes had always looked the same to him, but he was pretty sure he had anchored on the doorstep of Amity.

THE great white shark swam south, twenty feet below the surface, leaving Block Island to her right. She turned, dead on course for Montauk Point.

She was gravid with young and her hunger overwhelming. She had fed last evening off Nantucket on a school of cod and all night long she had held course southwest along the coast of Rhode Island. Her six-foot-high tail propelled her bulk with stiff, purposeful power.

Before her, an invisible cone of fear swept the sea clean from bottom to surface. For a full mile ahead the ocean was emptying of life. Seals, porpoises, whales, squid, all fled. All had sensors—electromagnetic, aural, vibratory, or psychic—which were heralding her coming. As she passed, the Atlantic refilled in her wake.

Man would have ignored such sensors, if he still had them, in favor of intelligence. But man was not her normal prey.

To overcome the clairvoyance of her quarry, she was ordinarily swifter than whatever animal she pursued. Her food included almost any creature of worthwhile size that swam, floated, or crawled in the ocean. But she had become so large, near term, that her speed was down.

She grew more ravenous with every mile that passed.

HALFWAY down the anchor line the doctor paused. His panting, amplified in his regulator, was earsplitting. He was sure his partner, descending in a green flowering of bubbles ten feet below him, could hear every gasp. Clinging to the half-inch rope, he tried to relax. If he could not slow his breathing, he would be out of air and forced to surface in ten or fifteen minutes. He could not understand the apprehension that was making him pant.

When his respiration eased, he resumed his descent. Visibility was better than he had expected—fifteen feet or more. When he reached the bottom, he found the lawyer in a cloud of silt, trying to bury the Danforth against the outgoing tide. He assisted in this and finally they had the anchor flukes buried.

The lawyer glanced at his wrist compass, jerked his thumb toward the north, and began to swim, searching for the clump of rocks. The doctor followed, cruising five feet above the bottom and off his partner's left hip. He began to feel at home again. His three-shot breakfast was working through his system, calming him wonderfully.

Swimming along, he glanced at his partner and found himself smiling. The little attorney was burdened with all the equipment that money could buy. His mask was prescription ground so that he needed no glasses. He wore a pressure-equalizing vest. This was its maiden voyage, and he kept climbing and descending as he tried to regulate it.

On the lawyer's left wrist was the compass, and on his right an underwater watch. From his neck dangled a Nikonos underwater camera. He looked, thought the doctor, like Dustin Hoffman in *The Graduate,* hiding from the festivities, at the bottom of his parents' swimming pool.

11

Dawn had begun to shimmer faintly down to her as she passed Montauk. Her eyes were black, flat, and unblinking, giving her an air of profound wisdom. She had excellent vision even in this dim light. But she continued to navigate as before, blindly and mindlessly as a computer would, using the electro-receptor ampullae that covered her head.

Two years before, not far from here, she had been hit by a male not much smaller than she. Despite her superior strength, he had somehow borne her to the muddy bottom. There, passive and supine, she had received both of his yard-long claspers into her twin vents.

Even before her pregnancy she had outweighed any creature in the sea except for some cetaceans and her own relatives, the basking shark and whale shark. At thirty feet and almost two tons, she was longer than a killer whale and heavier by half.

Now, near term, her girth was enormous. In her left uterus squirmed three young. In her right lived five, three females and two males. The smallest was a little over three feet long and weighed only twenty-two pounds. Nevertheless, he had survived *in utero* for almost two years, eating thousands of unfertilized eggs and, with his remaining brother and sisters, some thirty weaker siblings.

He himself was not out of danger yet, especially from his sisters, who—typical of their sex—were uniformly larger than males. If the mother hunted successfully for the next few days, her egg production would satisfy his siblings and he would probably live.

The doctor almost overran the lawyer, who had slowed and was pointing to the left. The doctor turned his head. He saw a shape, not the clump of rocks they had dived last year. It was abrupt, angular, man-made.

Excitedly, his partner swam toward it. The doctor followed. The stern of a wrecked fishing boat loomed from the murk. She was an immensely rugged old craft. The barnacle growth on her twisted planks told them that she had been here for several years.

The doctor spotted a heavy hawser lying along the sand. It ran below the half-buried quarter of the wreck. He rounded the stern to see where it led. The lawyer porpoised along beside him, trying to adjust his buoyancy.

The doctor found the other end of the rope. Secured to it by a giant shackle, a fifty-five-gallon iron drum bumped restlessly against the hull. It was crushed and dented, but the remains of yellow paint showed that it had once been a float.

The current swept it suddenly against the boat with a mournful clang. The Old Grand-Dad left the doctor's veins in a rush. He was very cold.

The lawyer was rubbing at the sea-grass whiskers growing on the stern. He yanked his scallop iron from its scabbard on his leg and chiseled off half a dozen barnacles, loosening a mist of mud. When the water cleared, the doctor could read, in faint orange letters, the name *Orca*. The name chorded some deep memory.

Suddenly the lawyer jammed a fist into a palm. Excitedly, he pointed at the name on the shattered stern. Then he took both hands, fingers clawed like teeth, and swept them through the motion of huge jaws closing.

The doctor understood. The half-forgotten story, read in the *Long Island Press*, of a shark fisherman, a tank-town police chief, and some oceanographic expert surfaced in his mind.

He discovered that he did not like it here. They were after scallops, not wrecks, and anything of souvenir value must have been salvaged long ago. He found, in fact, that he was no longer even interested in the scallops. His breath was rasping again and his heart hammering.

He pointed to the surface, but his companion shook his head, tapped the camera, and drew him to a position by the stern. Then the lawyer backed off, camera to faceplate.

The doctor pointed obediently at the orange letters, smiling idiotically around his mouthpiece. The strobe light fired, turning everything momentarily white.

All at once he heard a sound like a subway train, fast approaching from his rear. His partner, swaying on sand as he tried to balance in the current, wound his camera, then stopped. He stared at something approaching from above and behind the doctor. His mouthpiece fell from his face.

The doctor, startled, began to turn but instinctively hunkered down, clinging to a broken plank. His eyes were riveted on his companion. A great bubble soared from his partner's mouth. The lawyer threw up an arm to protect himself. The camera strap fouled and the strobe fired again, making the doctor feel naked.

The green surface light faded. An enormous bulk swept by, a foot above the doctor's head, blotting out the dancing sunlight. It seemed to pass forever. The last of the shape became a tail, towering taller than himself. It swished once, almost sweeping him loose and blotting his view of his partner in a cloud of bottom silt and mud.

There was silence. The barrel clanged.

The doctor clung to the plank, peering into the murk. One of his partner's diving fins bounced past, heading to sea on the tidal current. He could have reached out and touched it. He did not budge from the stern.

It was fear that finally drove him from shelter. He became more frightened of dying where he was with an empty tank than of discovery. Tentatively, he moved a few feet and waited. Nothing happened. In a burst of courage, he kicked off.

He remembered to rise no faster than his bubbles, remembered to kick slowly and steadily without panic—for whatever it was would be attuned to panic—remembered, when he surfaced into golden sunlight, to shift his mouth from regulator to snorkel. And he remembered, for a while, to kick with a careful, pedaling motion so as not to splash the surface with his fins.

He eased his head from the water. The Hatteras powerboat slapped at anchor hardly a hundred feet away. A rush of joy that it was he who had survived warmed his veins. Carefully, he slithered toward the boat. He hardly broke the water. Once he stopped and gazed straight down. He saw nothing but shafts of emerald light lancing the depths.

He raised his head. A thousand yards beyond the boat slept the houses by the dunes. Two tiny figures raced along the tide line. It seemed an eternity since he had seen them from the Hatteras' cabin, but it was the same child, same woolly dog.

He shivered suddenly. Deep in his soul he felt another onrush of terror. He quickened the beat of his fins. One of them plopped loudly, and then the other, but he had less than thirty feet to go. He could no longer stand the dragging pace. With twenty feet to go, he was sprinting, thrashing recklessly.

All at once, ten feet from the boat, he felt a firm grasp on his left femur, some three inches above the knee. It was surprising, but not at all violent. His first thought was that his partner had somehow survived, caught up with him, and plucked his thigh for attention. He dipped his mask, looking down.

He was amazed to see half a human leg, swathed in neoprene, tumbling into the depths. He observed that, though fully detached from the upper femur, it exhibited little bleeding, though a cloud of blood from somewhere else was forming quickly. Whoever had amputated had performed neatly: the incision was scalpel clean.

He was filled with sudden lassitude. He floated, fascinated by the leg spinning into the depths. He had the sense of something vast moving below the limb, out of his zone of visibility. The leg rose as if bumped, and disappeared.

His left side was weak. He wondered if he had had a stroke. He was getting too old to dive. He might even sell his share in the boat. He began feebly to swim again.

He heard the faint subway roar. He did not care. He stopped moving. He was too tired to fight his sleepiness, though the boat was only a few feet away.

Then he was borne aloft. He sensed that his ribs, lungs, spleen, kidneys, bowels, duodenum, were being squeezed firmly together as if in a giant hydraulic press.

He felt no pain at all.

Chapter 2

CHIEF Martin Brody of the Amity police sat at his desk and watched the clock on the wall. It jerked to noon, croaked for an instant, and subsided. A light on his desk phone began to flash. He glared across the office at old Polly Prendergast, dominating the switchboard. She was supposed to *hold* lunch-hour calls. He stared her down, refusing to reach for the phone.

"Who is it?" he demanded.

"Nate Starbuck," she announced. "Parking."

"Damn," he breathed. To frustrate her, he continued to ignore the phone. "Tell him," he said, "I'll drop by the drugstore on the way home for lunch."

It suddenly struck him that he had not had a parking complaint in over a year. "*Parking?* Things must be looking up."

He took a book of traffic tickets and emerged from Town Hall into the bright spring sunshine. It was just like Polly to come up with something to turn him around when he was homeward bound. Senile, like the town she served. But the town was being reborn. There was no rebirth in sight for Polly.

He slid behind the wheel of Car Number 1 and drove down Main, almost deserted, toward Water Street. Four years before, there would have been cars lining both sides of the street, even this early in June. Today, though it was Saturday, there were not half a dozen vehicles slanted into the meter spots.

As he approached the center of town his spirits were buoyed by the construction he saw. Chase Manhattan had bought out Amity Bank and Trust, and the facade of the new branch was getting a coat of white paint. What was more, they were building a drive-in teller's window, on Saturday overtime, and there were contractors' trucks scattered all over the bank's parking lot.

He parked in the red zone in front of Martha's Dresses and stepped into the dim coolness of Starbuck's Pharmacy. Even Starbuck's seemed to be coming back to life. Nate had come very close to bankruptcy during The Trouble, as Amity called it. He had laid off his own nephew, who had handled the photo processing in the rear, and fired the delivery boy and the girl behind the old-fashioned fountain. For over a year Nate had developed film between prescriptions, refused to deliver, and let his scrawny wife, Lena, jerk the sodas behind the marble counter.

Now, Brody observed, at least he had hired a new fountain girl: Jackie Angelo, the fifteen-year-old daughter of one of his own patrolmen. She was a great improvement on Lena. Jackie had sky-blue North Italian eyes, and honey hair. She seldom smiled. When she did, her eyes danced, her nose crinkled, and her hand flew to her mouth to hide the most blatant braces in town.

Starbuck, lank survivor of a line of Bedford whaler merchants, was standing behind the prescription window typing out a label. He was right off a Norman Rockwell cover, green celluloid visor and all. And despite what seemed to be a minor renaissance in his business, he remained as sour as ever.

"Morning, Nathanial," murmured Brody.

Starbuck did not look up. He plastered the label carefully onto a bottle and put the vial on the counter. "Your wife phoned yesterday. Her thyroid pills."

"What's the parking problem?"

Starbuck jerked a thumb toward his side door. "Casino del Mar." He pronounced it distastefully, with the accent on the *Cas*, as if to show his scorn for foreign names. "Next to my delivery truck. Saw Peterson park it. He's in the bank." He stared at Brody. "On a Saturday."

"You think he's trying to rob it?"

"Shouldn't wonder, but not with a gun. Bank don't open for *me* on Saturday."

"Maybe you don't owe them enough money."

Starbuck's eyes went cold. "Don't everybody? Except them as sold their property."

"Just about *everybody* sold, Nate. Look, Peterson couldn't park in the bank's lot. It's full of trucks. Yours is empty, what difference does it make?"

Starbuck's lips grew thinner. "Township ordinance, ain't it? *Pharmacy* customers only? You afraid to ticket him?"

Brody spun on his heel and strode through the side door. Peterson's Monaco, with New Jersey plates and CASINO DEL MAR gilded discreetly on the doors, was parked next to Starbuck's delivery van. He glanced up at the wall of the building. No out there. The sign, PHARMACY CUSTOMERS ONLY: VIOLATORS WILL BE TOWED AWAY, had been freshly repainted. Starbuck's contribution to the general face-lifting.

He was starting to write the ticket when he saw Peterson, a slight, intense man built like a bantamweight, approaching.

"Is Amity *that* broke?" Peterson grinned.

"Look, Pete, go in and buy something from the old buzzard. A piece of bubble gum, or something?"

Peterson thanked him and entered the store. Brody put his citation book away and went back to Car Number 1. He surveyed the street again.

It was really looking pretty good. If the gambling law passed, if Amity became another Atlantic City and downtown property came back, then this man, Peterson, would have saved the town, and idiots like Starbuck didn't even seem to know it.

He'd forgotten Ellen's pills, but it was too nice a day to face Starbuck twice.

He climbed in his car and drove home to lunch.

"SEAN," SIGHED ELLEN, "are you going to finish your succotash?"

Brody tilted back his chair and observed his younger son's plate across the table. Eleven limas, in shotgun offense, were lined up in the shadow of their own goalposts. Eleven corn kernels, the Jets, opposed them in a 4-3-3-1 formation. Obviously, Buffalo was in deep trouble. But not for long.

Fascinated, Brody watched O. J. Simpson slice off tackle, propelled by a single tine of Sean's fork. The deep safety seemed about to get him when the point, flashing from nowhere, impaled him. O.J. sped for the edge of the dish.

"Way to go," murmured Brody.

Ellen was not amused. "If he's through, I'd like to wash his plate." She whisked the dish away, over Sean's protests. "Don't forget to talk to Mike," she reminded Brody.

He hadn't forgotten, just put it off. Mike had conned his mother into serving on the Amity Boat Club Junior Race Committee. He had got his younger brother all steamed up about crewing for him in next Sunday's regatta. And then Mike had apparently quit cold. His rigging needed tuning, he had a rip in his mainsail, and he hadn't run the course to Cape North light since last summer.

Heavily, Brody stood up. Sean stood, too. Brody eased his belt. So did Sean. Brody squatted suddenly, eye level to his son. "Hey, Spud, how about a little swim tonight, off the casino?"

Sean grinned. He was missing a tooth. Even the hole was beautiful. "No way," said the little boy, pretending a bite. Suddenly, impulsively, he kissed Brody and scampered out the door.

At least, thought Brody, there's that. Reluctantly, he climbed the stairs.

Brody stood at Mike's desk by the bedroom window. He leafed through *Skin Diver Magazine* while he gave his angry son, lying on his bed, time to cool off.

So helping him buy a boat, then, hadn't done the trick, Brody thought.

The magazine was the top issue of a pile a foot high. Brody stopped at a two-page ad from U.S. Divers, full color. A macho diver dripped with seawater and gleaming new equipment. A model, who looked as if her rubber suit had been sprayed onto her, gazed at him wet-eyed with lust. The creeps, he thought. Money-grabbing creeps . . .

18

"What are you going to do, burn them?" complained Mike, addressing the ceiling. "It's not *porn!*"

Brody regarded his older son. Mike looked tired. He had skipped lunch, not only today, but yesterday, too. The hunger strike revolved around the permission form that his friend Andy Nicholas had picked up at the Aqua Sport Diving Center and given to Mike. Andy's father had signed his, and Andy was presumably deep into a scuba-diving course. It would be a cold day in hell before Brody signed his son's.

"Take it easy, Mike," he said. "Look, if you want to swim, use Town Pool. Your baby brother's got more sense than you. And *he* was on the beach four years ago. You were in the *ocean!*"

"In the ocean," squeaked Mike. "For the last time! I can swim like an eel! I live on an island! And I'm not allowed to—"

"You can sail!"

"And *that* took like an act of Congress! I'm tired of the dumb Laser—"

"You're the best sailor in town!"

"Look, I want to be the best scuba diver instead, OK? It's *my* life! I'm sick of your hang-up. Sick of Spitzer."

"Who's Spitzer?"

"Mark Spitzer." Mike was crying now. "Great Olympic . . . swimmer. 'Hey, Spitzer, come on down to the beach, you won't get wet. . . .' 'Gimme a swimming lesson, Spitzer. . . .' 'Spitzer, hey, move your towel, man, tide's coming in.'" He drew in a great shuddering sigh. "*I'm* Spitzer."

"Mike—" Brody began helplessly.

"Dad, *the shark is dead.*"

Brody reached out and brushed his son's hair from his eyes. He nodded. "The shark is dead."

He talked Mike into going down for a sandwich.

Then he folded the permission form, slid it into his jacket pocket, and left the house.

THE fat little girl was digging a hole to China in the sand. Next to her the lean, hard-muscled man she called Daddy—but she was sure he was not really her father, or else how could she be so fat—seemed to be sleeping behind his mirrored sunglasses.

He was not. "You see Uncle Brian lately?" he asked suddenly.

Her mommy had told her not to answer such questions, but if she did not, he might get mad and take her back early.

"No," she lied. "Look, Daddy, an ant fell in the hole!" There was no ant, but she had to say something, and she wasn't supposed to talk about Uncle Brian, or Uncle Jerry, or Flip, or just about anybody else.

Her father turned over and inspected the hole. "Ant?"

She reddened. "Well, there was. Daddy? There *was!*"

He grunted and turned back. "So what have you and Mommy been doing? Same baby-sitter?"

A trap. She nodded. She did not feel like digging anymore. She began to watch a flock of five pelicans, rare this far north, diving for fish very close to the beach.

"Look at the pelicans, Daddy!"

He did not stir, only muttered that yes, he had seen them before. She waited for the next question. She was following the leader of the flock, plummeting like a diving plane on TV. He smacked the water in a splatter of spray.

"She take you to the dentist, like I said?"

"Yes." She felt her teeth. "Yuk!"

An outright lie. She concentrated on the reappearance of the pelican, who had not yet risen from the depths. If she could just get him interested in the diving birds, he might forget about it. "Daddy! They're going to eat all the fish!"

"Everybody's got to live. Any cavities?"

Now she had done it. How could she know if she had cavities, when her mother, with her own help, had forgotten to take her? "Daddy, the pelican didn't come *up!*"

"Maybe a fish ate *him.* Any cavities, honey?"

"No." Now she was truly concerned about the pelican. "How long can they stay under?"

"Beats me. A long time, I guess." He looked at his watch and her throat tightened. Not yet, not yet . . .

He rolled over on his tummy. She relaxed. That was all it was, time to roll over.

The pelican must have come up somewhere else, where she wasn't looking. She counted the birds skimming the surf line. Four left. Another dropped for the surface. She stood to see better.

That one didn't come up, either. "Daddy? *Daddy!*"

He was asleep, or pretending to be. He wouldn't believe her anyway.

Angrily, she kicked sand into her hole to China. If there *had* been an ant, he was sure dead now.

BRODY parked outside Amity Aqua Sports, Inc., a new store housed in a huge green structure half a block from Town Dock. All winter long Tom Andrews had sawed and hammered inside. Now the place glistened under dark green paint. Behind its new plate-glass windows, around an old-fashioned copper diving helmet, were grouped scuba tanks, water skis, and wind surfers, which Andrews hoped to popularize off the breezy sands of Amity.

Brody had met him only once. He was a Californian bucking the normal east-west tide of migration. Whatever his plans, they expressed vast financial faith in the future of Amity. Brody liked him more and more.

He entered the building. Andrews had just sold a water-ski flag to a cheerful young couple. When they left, Andrews extended a hand the size of a catcher's mitt.

"Hi," he grinned. His eyes twinkled from between rolls of fat, but even the fat looked muscular. Brody decided that the bearded proprietor weighed three hundred pounds.

"What can I do for you, Chief?" the giant asked.

"Skip the 'Chief,' Tom. Makes me feel like a navy lifer or something. And my whole department is just me and three other klutzes. Martin, or just Brody, OK?"

"Check. What's up?"

Brody produced Mike's form. The effect was startling. Andrews rounded the counter, moving like an athlete. He flung an arm like a tree limb around Brody's shoulder and squeezed.

"Great! Just great! How'd he do it?" He was beaming.

Brody looked at him, shocked. "Look, I haven't signed the thing; I just wanted to talk to you about it."

Some of the exuberance left Andrews' face. He moved back behind the counter and began to disassemble a diving regulator. "All right," he said. "The course for juniors is four weeks. They graduate with a full-fledged diving card. No dive shop will fill your tank without it, so it means something to them."

He told Brody that the schedule was two hours Saturday and

two hours Sunday. Basic testing of swimming ability, skin diving with a snorkel, basic introduction to scuba equipment, buddy breathing, emergency ascents.

"In the Town Pool?" Brody asked. His mouth was dry.

"Everything, so far. Then comes a written exam on theory." Andrews tapped a pile of texts on his workbench. "Permissible bottom time, decompression curves, nitrogen effect in the bloodstream. One hundred percent is passing."

Brody felt hope. Mike might swim like an eel, but he'd never concentrate long enough to pass the technical exam. OK, he'd sign. At least it would be off his back. He reached for the pen as Andrews' voice went on. "Then a final checkout. For the first class it's tomorrow. In the ocean."

His hand began to tremble. Stupid, stupid, stupid. Still, he could not sign, and he put down the pen.

"How much . . . How much does it run?"

Andrews smiled. "For Mike, nothing."

"Come *on*, Tom!" As police chief, he was uncomfortable when offered a favor, although at his salary they needed every cent they could save. "You can't do that."

The giant was reassembling the regulator. "Actually, I've done it already."

"What?"

Andrews opened a file drawer, pulled out a folder, and extracted an exam. Mike's name was printed at the top, much more neatly than on any school paper he'd ever brought home. Brody read a few of the questions: "State Boyle's law. . . ." "What is the percentage of nitrogen in the air?" Across the top Andrews had scrawled, "100%." This, from a kid who couldn't pass Algebra I?

He felt a flash of anger. "Why does he want me to sign? He seems to have done all right without me!"

Andrews faced him, speaking softly. "I started the class last month. Twelve kids. Signed forms in their hands. All suited up and jumping with joy. And one kid in a bathing suit at the other end of the pool—man, it was cold. No wet suit. But listening. Pretending he wasn't. After the class he tells me you've got this hang-up, and why. He's not allowed in the ocean. But could he kind of listen in, at the pool? He's saved enough money if I want it."

Andrews shrugged. "I figured, what the hell, I'm probably not liable if it's for free, and maybe he can talk you into it before the ocean dive, and he's looking at me with those big blue eyes . . ."

"OK," Brody said abruptly. "OK!"

He was angry, not at Andrews, or even Mike, but at himself, for forcing his son into this charade. People dived the Amity coast all year round. They swam and sailed and water-skied and surfed, and no one got a scratch. The Amity shark was dead. Statistically, there'd never be another. Not in his lifetime, or probably Mike's either.

He thanked Andrews. He bought Mike a wet suit, and Sean a jackknife to balance it. Finally he faced the form. He took out his pen. This time his hand shook hardly at all.

That afternoon Brody quit five minutes early. He was on his way home when he spotted Sean sprinting up Water Street in a dead run for home. He stopped and opened the car door.

The little boy tumbled in. "Fish! Going home to get my pole! There's cod all over the harbor. *Big* ones!"

Brody glanced down Water Street. It was true. There were more people on Town Dock than he ever remembered seeing. Half of them had poles already, and the rest were queued in front of Hyman's Bait & Tackle, trying to rent more.

"Daddy! Let's *go!*" Sean was bouncing up and down.

"Fasten your belt."

Sean groaned and clicked the latch. "Use your *siren!*"

"No siren." He pulled away, and glanced back at the dock in his mirror.

Strange. He had never heard of a cod run in Amity.

BRODY had intended to lecture Mike on evasion and dissembling. But he had broken no family law by swimming in the Town Pool. And, watching TV, his face was so sad that Brody could not let him suffer anymore. Ellen, who seemed relieved that the no-ocean edict had passed, gift wrapped the wet suit in the kitchen. Sean had departed for Town Dock, staggering under a pole three times longer than he.

Brody poured his evening belt and walked into the living room. Ellen, behind him, bore the gift. Mike turned away from the TV. "What gives?"

"We do," grinned Ellen.

"It's your birthday," explained Brody. "We've never told you, but you were born twice."

Mike took the box. A year ago he would have torn into it like a dog at a rabbit hole. Now he untied the ribbon carefully, unfolded the wrapping, and froze.

"Aqua Sports," he breathed. "Aqua Sports? Dad?"

He took the top off the box. He did not remove the suit. He stroked it for a second. All at once he was in Brody's arms, face pressed against his stubble. Sean kissed his father all the time, but it had been ten years since Brody felt his older son's cheek. Embarrassed, Mike pulled away.

"For tomorrow," Brody said softly.

"You signed it!" whispered Mike.

"Try it on," said Brody. "Let's see it."

Mike dropped his pants and squirmed in.

He was fifteen years old, but, like a little boy, he ate dinner in the wet suit, just the same. And passing his room to go to bed that night, Brody glimpsed him inside, preening before the mirror.

For a happy kid his eyes seemed strangely haunted. It must have been a trick of the light.

Chapter 3

AT SEVEN a.m. the young engineer pushed his bright yellow ski boat from Town Dock, climbed aboard, and took the wheel from his wife. He eased the throttle forward and came left to avoid a towering Hatteras cabin cruiser under Coast Guard tow. Then he poured on the coal.

His bow came up, his stern squatted, a nearby dinghy almost capsized, and they were bound for open ocean. Only then did he breathe deeply. It was good to get away from the smell of cod and creosote and into the cool sea air.

"Skis checked?" he asked his tawny, long-limbed wife.

"Checked, Commodore," she sighed. "Life vests aboard, warning flag stowed, flares and Very pistol—"

"Look," he yelled above the engine's howl, "this isn't just crap. The engine quits, or something, you'll be glad we do it."

She began to rub Coppertone onto her forehead. "What'd I leave out, Commodore?"

"The radio check." He was assistant head of quality control at Grumman Aerospace. He never forgot anything.

She reached under the foredeck, drew out the microphone, and intoned: "Coast Guard Radio Shinnecock. This is *Overtime*. Radio check. Over."

Shinnecock Bay crackled back instantly. "Loud and clear, *Overtime*, good morning. Shinnecock out."

He relaxed, letting the bow leap across the dawn-flat water. He had the best boat in the world, the best woman, and a two-week vacation. It was good to be alive.

"If it was the fish," Sean wanted to know, "why aren't I sick, too?"

Brody looked down at his older son, lying on the fake-leather couch in the solarium. "It was the fish, all right," groaned Mike. "It was your damned little minnow—"

"Mike," warned Brody, voice rising. "Knock it off!"

Mike tried to get up, but another cramp seized him, and he lay back, shivering. "Why'd he have to catch the thing? And why'd she have to cook it? For *breakfast!*"

"It was a regular-sized fish! And it didn't make me sick, or Dad, or Mom!" Sean marched off, head high.

Ellen arrived, professional as always in the face of crisis, shaking down a thermometer. She poked it into Mike's mouth and felt his pulse. He mumbled something, mouth closed.

"Pulse is eighty. That's high for him," Ellen said. "He wants to know what time it is."

Brody looked at his watch. "Nine twenty."

Mike sat up as if galvanized. The thermometer fell from his lips. "Nine twenty? I got to be at Town Dock at ten! Suited up!"

Gently, Brody pushed him back. "You aren't going anywhere, Cousteau. Not with cramps *already*."

The phone rang. It was Len Hendricks, who took Polly's place at the dispatch desk on Sundays. "Chief?"

"Brody," sighed Brody. "Or Martin. Or Marty."

"Sorry, Chief. We got a problem."

"At nine twenty, on a Sunday?"

"That's *it*. The nine-thirty ferry's due in ten minutes. And there's a big yacht blocking Town Dock."

Brody's temple began to throb. "Tell them to move it."

"That's our problem, Chief. There's no one aboard."

A deep bellow sounded across Amity Sound. He looked out the window. The Amity Neck ferry churned toward him from Cape North, on schedule for the first time in living memory.

"Len?"

"Yeah?"

"*You* want to be chief?"

"Come on!" muttered Len hopefully. "You kidding?"

Brody hung up. During The Trouble, everyone had wanted him to quit when he tried to close the beaches. Even Ellen had wanted him to quit, and still did.

"What did Len say to *that?*" Ellen demanded. "*Does* he want to be chief?"

"I think he does," murmured Brody.

Hendricks was stupider than he'd thought.

THE young engineer waited until his wife gave him the thumbs-up signal, checked that the warning flag in the stern was erect, and eased the throttle forward until the slack was out of the ski line. He glanced ahead to clear their track and gave the boat full throttle. His wife rose gracefully in his wake, like a mermaid from the deep, riding one ski.

The water was still glassy, with the slightest suggestion of swell. She was weaving from one side of the wake to the other, over-confident as usual. Impishly he threw the wheel over, half stopping the boat, slowing her, then jerking her ahead as he took off in a new direction. She survived that one, gyrating wildly, but he got her with the next one. She crashed in a sheet of spray. He wheeled to starboard, slowed, and dragged the line close to her. He had her set up again, and she was nodding, when he suddenly tensed.

A hundred yards behind her an enormous, lazy fin was beckoning. She did not see it, and while he stood frozen in horror, it began to move, in a leisurely manner, up their trail.

His first thought was that it was a killer whale; did orcas attack humans? Then he remembered the Amity shark, but it couldn't be, that shark was dead. . . .

"Dee!" he screamed.

She smiled at him over the water and took a hand off the tow

27

bar, waving him ahead. The fin was coming up on her now, weaving across their dying wake. It was simply gigantic.

He jammed the throttle forward, way too fast, catching her off-balance. She lost the smile, shaking her head in irritation. For a moment he was afraid that she would pitch headfirst into the wake when she rose, but if he eased the throttle to take tension off the line, she might overcompensate. Just leave it, he thought, and pray that she'd get up; once he had her *up* he could outrun any fish that swam.

She was squatting, half erect, and then pitching. The fin was faster than he had estimated, but not that fast. She was on the ski now, and rising. . . .

"Weight back!" he shrieked, but of course, over the howl of the engine she would hear nothing.

She made it, and signaled him OK with thumb and forefinger. She favored him with her most forgiving smile.

He stood erect, searching their wake for the fin. The thing must have dived, that was it, he had fooled it. Now, all he had to do was head for the beach. She was capable, when he signaled her, of riding her ski onto dry sand.

He scanned the beach for a safe place. Where they were building the casino there were people, and suddenly he wanted to be where there were people. But there was a more gentle slope of beach in front of an old weather-beaten cottage farther from the town.

His eye on his wife, he began a sweeping curve toward the cottage. She was weaving again, jumping the wake each time, exuberantly. He signaled her to take it easy, simply to ski, finally slowed the boat so that she couldn't weave, and then saw the fin again, coming up fast astern.

He found that his hand was so wet he could hardly hold on to the throttle. But he eased it forward, again, and the fin disappeared. She began to weave once more, port to starboard, head back and golden hair flying. "Dee," he croaked. "No, no!"

He remembered the radio. He lunged for it, but the boat, without his hand on the wheel, slued sideways, almost spilling her.

His mind raced. He could probably tug her off, make a violent turn and a fast run up, and yank her from the water.

He didn't dare. Whatever it was, orca or shark, if it was fast enough to keep up with the boat, it was fast enough to beat him

back. He looked aft. She was doing well now, maybe tiring enough
to simply ski until he had her safe. Please, honey, he prayed. No
more hotdogging, just ski.

He headed dead for the weather-beaten house on the beach.
Two miles away, maybe less. Not all that far.

Suddenly he froze. Halfway between him and the beach was
the fin. He couldn't understand it. He was making twenty knots
easily; could the damn thing make thirty? He curved back out to
sea. The fin disappeared.

He was an engineer. There had to be a way. He had it. He would
stop, put slack in the line, warn her of her danger, haul her in, and
when she was close enough, drag her into the boat.

But not now. The fin reappeared, still a football field behind
her. He would have to wait until it disappeared before he stopped.
The throttle was against the stops already, but he found himself
shoving anyway. Suddenly it came off in his hand. "No!" he wailed.

No slowing now. No stopping, either. So much for hauling her in.
He headed back for the house on the beach. He looked at his wife.
"Don't!" he bellowed.

She had not tired, had only been thinking, probably, in the cautious, lip-nibbling way she had. Tentatively, she was trying something. By the set of her body he guessed what it was.

He had learned to turn and ski backward. It had taken him
three summers to do it, and she'd so far been unable to. Now she
was trying it again.

"No, Dee, no!" he howled. She seemed to hear him, turned her
head, almost fell. He shut up.

The fin was back in their wake. It was a hundred yards astern
of her. And coming up, surely coming up.

His wife teetered, made the move, and turned. She had done it!
She was skiing backward, and if she could just get herself turned
around again . . .

The fin was gaining. Her body went suddenly rigid. She had
seen it. Somehow she whipped around without falling. Now her
face was a mask of horror. She was yelling, and wobbling . . .
Steady, Dee, steady. Not far to the beach.

As if she heard him, she seemed to relax. Carefully, she skied
out from the wake into smooth water. The fin disappeared. He
chanced a look at the beach. Half a mile. A white speck on the

weather-beaten porch, a person, someone to care for her when she sliced to the beach. And he'd be OK. Without her drag, no fish in the sea could catch *Overtime*. . . .

But when he looked back he knew that they had lost. The fin was closing fast. In seconds it was towering above her. Instinctively, he grabbed the flare pistol, jammed a cartridge into it, fired it into the air. It rose in a gentle arc, burning with a feeble orange light hardly noticeable against the glaring sky. He would need help, fast: medical help, even if the best happened and she survived the first attack.

"*Dee!*"

A leviathan snout broke water ten feet behind her. He could not credit its size. A hideous maw ringed with white opened behind her, twisted sideways, closed on her, shook her once, tossing her as it reared in a froth of blood and flesh and the long, tawny hair. And then she was gone.

He ripped at the ignition harness. The engine quit instantly, hurling him forward. He reloaded the flare pistol. "Come on, you bastard!" he shrieked.

The snout rose, heading for the boat. Lurching back, pistol at the ready, he stumbled and discharged it. For an awful instant he knew. He had fired straight into the spare gas tank.

His world went up in a dull orange boom.

Half a mile away, Minnie Eldridge, Amity's ancient postmistress, stopped her rocker. She spilled her Siamese off her lap, set aside the Sunday *Times*, and peered seaward. Behind the gentle surf blossomed a dirty pall of smoke.

She hobbled inside to phone.

HAULING on lines from the dock, Brody and his patrolman Dick Angelo got the Hatteras cruiser snugged closely enough to the quay to allow the ferry to make her slip.

"Coast Guard dumped her," volunteered Yak-Yak Hyman from the bait shop. Last night's windfall of cod had made him positively garrulous. He'd even said good morning.

"Just *dumped* her?" demanded Brody.

Yak-Yak simply looked at him. That's right, Brody thought. You already told me that. Sorry, Yak-Yak.

"Coast Guard say when they'd be back?"

Yak-Yak shook his head. Not too much—you had to be quick to see it—but a little. Brody walked to Starbuck's Pharmacy and telephoned Shinnecock Bay.

The Coast Guard, said the Shinnecock duty officer, had noticed the yacht yesterday, anchored over the *Orca* wreck. No anchor light last night, a lobsterman had almost run her down. The Coast Guard had stood by for an hour this morning, in case divers, if any, reappeared. Then they'd buoyed the site and towed her to the nearest harbor.

They'd just contacted the wife of one of the yacht owners. She was on her way. They'd launch a chopper search later, do everything they could, but Brody was the closest law enforcement officer. He'd have to send down divers and handle the paperwork—

"Wait a minute," begged Brody. "I *got* no divers!"

"Look, we just got another call. A speedboat blew up. You got a question, call the district commandant."

Now Brody's whole head was aching. He stepped back into sunlight. He looked toward Town Dock at the gleaming cruiser. On a fancy plastic stern board he read *Miss Carriage,* out of Sag Harbor. It seemed a sad name for so expensive a yacht.

He walked over to it and climbed aboard. Divers had been here, for sure. There was a rack of tanks in the cockpit. Nothing on the flying bridge but a pair of sunglasses behind the binnacle, a sweater slung on the wheel. He swung below, entered the cabin. Wall-to-wall carpeting, stereo speakers, another steering location. In case it rained? A bottle of Old Grand-Dad and two coffee cups. He picked up one of the cups and sniffed. He smelled whiskey. He smelled the other. It seemed even stronger.

Well, there was no law against drunken diving, so far as he knew. Except the law of survival.

He returned to the dock. Down the length of it, heading for Tom Andrews' boat, *Aqua Queen*, staggered a procession of teenagers in wet suits: Andy Nicholas, Chip Lennart, Larry Vaughan, Jr., the mayor's son. Leading the troop was the bearded giant, Andrews. Brody tensed. Tagging last was Mike, looking very white.

He got whiter when he saw his father. "No temperature," he explained quickly. "Mom said—"

Brody ignored him and caught up with Andrews at the *Aqua Queen*. "Tom, what's your time worth?"

The township emergency fund was low, but Brody could fight it out for him later before the selectmen. He explained the situation, booze and all.

"Liquor," Andrews groaned. "Damn! Happens all the time. No charge, Brody. Let's go."

"Hey," Larry squealed. "What about—"

Andrews held up his hand. "Next Saturday, troops," he growled. "Same time, same channel. Tanks back to the shop."

Everybody groaned, including Mike, but for some reason the color was back in his cheeks.

THE fat man woke up again to a madhouse.

He was paying a bundle a week for the cottage. It was Sunday, and the dog was barking and his son screaming on the beach.

A jungle, a stupid jungle by the sea . . .

He swung his feet over the side of the crummy bed and rubbed his head. The inside of his mouth tasted of whiskey, stale beer, and the old lady's idea of a Saturday night special: knockwurst and sauerkraut.

He longed for their flat in Queens and the soothing growl of the Main Street bus.

"Shut up!" he bellowed.

His wife rolled over like a dead whale. That would be the next thing, probably—a dead whale.

Potbelly hanging over his pajamas, he charged out the cottage door, over the scrubby sand, and down to the surf.

It was another seal, backed to the water, its tail wet by every lapping roller. King, their shabby sheep dog, was yelping at it from twenty feet away. When he perceived reinforcements, he moved six inches closer.

The seal swung its soft brown eyes at him.

"Split!" The gentle eyes infuriated him. He kicked its side as hard as he could, stubbing his bare toes. The seal only shook its head, showering him with water. He spotted a stick of driftwood the size of a baseball bat. He picked it up and advanced.

The seal sighed, backed up, and turned. It flounced into the shallow water, wheeled once reproachfully, then wallowed away into the surf.

He was breathing hard. Cardiac City. "Next time," he told his son softly, "next time, tie up the dog. And come and wake me up. Real quiet."

"What are you going to do?"

"I'm going to *shoot* the son of a bitch!"

He clumped back across the sand. He had been sentenced to Amity for years, every summer, two weeks. He had never in all the dreary summers seen a seal on the beach. There had been two yesterday, and this was the second today.

BRODY ignored the radio on Andrews' boat, concentrating on the bubbles he was trying to follow. He was standing on the helmsman's seat, to better see them, steering with his foot. He wondered how it was, skimming the murky bottom. He could hardly conceive of any man brave enough to enter such a hostile environment. When he himself swam, he couldn't even put his face down.

They had left Amity Harbor to look for the buoy that the Coast Guard had left. It was supposed to be very close to the wreck of the *Orca*. So they had churned along south-southeast from Amity. Finally, to Brody's regret, Andrews turned over the wheel to him and began to don his equipment.

Brody had found the orange buoy, and now Andrews was below. Brody hated it here, but he had swallowed his discomfort and cut the throttle.

"Just follow my bubbles," Andrews had ordered. "I'll start at the wreck and swim north, then east, then west, then south. Then out a little and the same thing again. Dig?"

He dug. And now, daydreaming, he had lost the track. He ran to the side of the boat and searched the water desperately. Where the hell *was* he?

He heard a sound behind him and almost fell off the boat. He whirled. Andrews was standing on the rear diving platform. He held out a small black camera with a very large strobe light. "Sorry," he said. "Spooked?"

Brody took the camera. His hand was shaking. "Yeah."

"Bad vibes down there, too." He took off his mask and shook it. "Funny . . ." His deep-set eyes were troubled. "I found the camera right away. Ten yards off the stern of the *Orca*."

"Nothing else?"

Andrews shook his head. "They're gone, man. Booze, nitrogen narcosis, 'rapture of the deep.' I don't know."

Brody felt seasick. He wanted to get home. "Worth another search?" he asked. "More divers, I mean?"

Andrews shrugged. "If they're on the bottom, they're long dead." He swept his hand seaward. "And if they're out *there*, they're dead, too. Sixty-degree water. Hypothermia. Eight hours max, wet suit or not."

They contacted Shinnecock Coast Guard by radio. Brody reported the dive. "Thanks, Chief," Shinnecock crackled. "We got another problem. . . ." An idiot blew up his speedboat, said Shinnecock, off South Amity Beach. He'd been towing a skier. Would Brody check it out?

Brody moaned. "OK, OK."

They churned back to Town Dock. Andrews, who seemed to know everything, had inspected the camera, announced that two pictures had been shot, and carefully removed the film. Brody dropped it at Starbuck's Pharmacy.

There might be a clue on the film to what happened. For the next of kin.

HE PULLED the department dune buggy to the rear of Minnie Eldridge's house and moved along the flagstone walk, between the miraculous rows of roses that she managed to grow by burying soil boxes in the sand. Beyond her house a Coast Guard chopper was thrumming wildly up and down the surf line.

Knowing that it was no use, Brody banged on the kitchen door. Finally he walked in. Her kitchen was immaculate, as always. Just being there made him hungry. He thought he could actually smell the brownie scent from the oven.

"Minnie!" he called. No answer.

He stepped into the living room. She was sitting at her window, enjoying the aerial activity she had brought to her isolation. She still did not know he was there. Her Siamese stared at him.

"Minnie!" he shouted.

She turned, twirled her hearing aid, and regarded him wryly. She looked at her cuckoo clock, ticking in the corner beside a framed letter from Postmaster General Farley thanking her for twenty years of faithful service. It was dated 1940.

"Good thing somebody wasn't drowning; maybe they were. Now, before you start trying to be a TV policeman, you go out there and look in the upper left-hand corner of the cupboard, the cookie corner, and—"

"I can't, Minnie. There's just too much going on."

"In Amity?" She settled herself as he took out his report book. "Len logged your call at ten thirty-five. Was that when you heard the explosion?"

It was. And it checked out with the Sunday watchman at the casino building site, who had seen nothing, but heard a boom at about that time, while brewing coffee in his shack. He'd thought it was a navy jet from Quonset. The explosion must have been tremendous, to break through to Minnie's private world.

Brody shut his book, accepted a cookie, took a second one for the road, and finally a bagful for the boys. Then he climbed into the dune buggy, jammed it into four-wheel drive, skirted her house, and rocketed to the hard sand below to search for debris.

He dreaded finding anything. He had always hated looking for floaters, even before The Trouble.

The Trouble was over, though.

Nothing he would find today would be as bad as *that*.

THE fat man had not been able to get back to sleep. He lay tensely in the canyon he made in the flabby mattress, listening to the rumble of his wife's snoring.

Next year, he promised himself, no Amity! He even hated the name of the town—too like the pardon Carter gave the longhairs. He'd rather be down at the precinct locker room, telling lies.

Roughly, he shook his wife. "Look, you going to sleep all day? I'm near starved."

The big cow eyes opened reproachfully. "Huh?"

"Huh, hell. It's damn near noon, and the seals have been stirring up the dog and the kid, and you just sleep—"

"Seals?" she repeated.

"Seals! Next year, so help me, I go deer hunting with the commissioner! You and the kid can go to Coney Island!"

The big brown eyes filled with tears, giving her that certain passive appeal that only inflamed him. The dog began to yelp on the beach. The bedroom door creaked and the little boy tiptoed in.

"There's another seal!"

The man hit the deck and stumbled to the closet. "Where's my gun?"

He thrashed through the mess inside, threw five rounds of Hi-Speed ammunition into the Savage rifle, grabbed the boy by the wrist, and headed out the door.

His wife was howling behind them. She probably thought he was going to murder the kid.

BRODY stopped the dune buggy and squinted into the dazzle of the surf. Whatever it was that was tumbling in the foam was yellow and looked like part of a boat. He pulled the buggy away from the tide, took off his shoes and socks, unholstered his gun, and laid it on the passenger seat.

He walked to the edge of the water. He heard a mighty thumping approaching. The Coast Guard chopper, hardly higher than his head, reared to a stop over the surf, whipping up a minor typhoon. It hovered for a moment. Then the pilot shrugged regretfully and soared, sandblasting Brody as he spiraled away over the beach.

Brody swore until he felt better, and plodded into the surf. He plucked from the wavelets a shard of fiberglass and trudged back to dry land. A passing gull jeered at him. He stood for a moment, intending to let his feet dry before he put on his socks.

Pang . . . Pang-pang . . . Three shots, very loud and close, sounded from behind the western dunes.

Still barefoot, he dived behind the wheel, jerked ahead toward the sound. He soared over the nearest dune, jammed on the brake, and almost landed on a fat man and a boy.

The man was kneeling on a knoll, ready to fire again. The boy stood behind him, fingers to his ears, while a shaggy dog cringed. On the beach, a little pile of beige fur barked plaintively.

The man half turned, swinging a rifle. Brody found himself standing in the jeep, forefinger leveled, gun forgotten on the seat beside him. "Drop it!" he ordered.

The man did not drop the rifle, but he cradled it under his arm. "Hi," he said. He extended his hand. "Charlie Jepps. Sergeant. Fourth Precinct, Flushing."

Brody reached down, yanked the rifle away, and tossed it into the rear. He jerked his thumb toward the seat beside him, remembered his revolver was still there, and holstered it. "Sit there!" He ordered. "You're under arrest."

"Whadda ya mean, 'under arrest'?"

"Township ordinance, for openers." He jumped from the buggy and raced for the water. A baby harbor seal stared up at him in wonder. Blood oozed from a wound at the base of its tail. It coughed politely, great liquid pupils glazed with pain.

All eyes and agony and a long way from momma . . .

He scooped it into his arms, staggered back to the buggy, and laid it in the rear. The man had still not climbed in.

Brody drew his gun. "In," he yelled. "Get in the buggy!"

"You don't figure," the fat man suggested, "you better call your chief?"

Brody, for the first time in his life, pointed a loaded weapon at another human being. Nothing happened.

He cocked it.

The boy wailed, the dog barked, and from the porch of the gray house a blowsy woman began to bellow.

The fat man got in. He smelled of whiskey and beer.

Chapter 4

BRODY tried to sort out the chaos that had fallen on his office while the fat man, seated in his pajamas in front of Brody's desk, glared at him.

They had turned the township jail cell, over the years, into a storage room for school board records, and Henry Kimble was clearing it out now. Brody moved to the dispatch desk, where Hendricks was leafing through a tattered copy of the federal wildlife statutes.

Hendricks pointed out a paragraph. "Once he's booked, I don't think Norton *can* set bail. That is, not without a federal attorney being here."

"Good." Willy Norton was justice of the peace. Brody turned to Dick Angelo. "Snap it up, Dick. OK?"

Dick Angelo had found the fingerprint cards. Now he settled himself under the picture of Mayor Larry Vaughan to study the directions. Did he have to learn it here, in front of the suspect?

"*I'll* print him, Dick. Go tell Henry to get a necktie. I want him to be bailiff at the hearing." Brody sat down and inserted an arrest form in his typewriter.

"The animal was attacking my dog," said the fat man.

"What's your permanent address, Sergeant?"

The fat man spit out an address in Flushing. He continued in a monotone. "I was trying to scare it off. I'm an expert rifleman. Check with the Flushing P.D. If I'd *wanted* to kill it, I coulda blown its head off!"

"Too bad you couldn't *miss* it. Local address? Never mind, the Smith place."

"You can't hold me! You never *seen* me shoot it!" He added that when the state police commission heard about this, which would be tomorrow at nine, Brody would be lucky to get a job *feeding* seals at the Bronx Zoo.

Brody smiled at him. "It's a *federal* charge, friend. Under the Marine Mammal Protection Act of 1972. A year and twenty grand. The little guy's a harbor seal, not a tin can."

That shook the fat man not at all. The cold monotone never changed: his kid used that beach, *babies* played on that beach. Seals had teeth, didn't they?

"Not very long teeth, not this one," said Brody. "The vet says he's about three weeks old."

Hendricks was trying to get his attention from the dispatch desk. "Chief?" He mouthed. "Miranda? *Miranda!*"

He'd forgotten to read his rights! Quickly he did so, from a card in his wallet.

Hendricks came to his desk. "Doc Lean called. Seal's all right, but he's driving the dogs up the wall. He says we got to go get it. Just listen."

Amity Animal Clinic, a block away, was sounding like the hound chorus from *Uncle Tom's Cabin*. The seal was legal evidence, but obviously they couldn't leave it there. Brody called Ellen and told her to pick it up and put it in their garage.

"OK, you *hear* that," observed the fat man reasonably. "Now, how are you supposed to sleep? What am I supposed to do, shoot my dog? Third seal this morning."

"*Third* seal?"

"Third today. Two yesterday."

Lying creep. Amity Beach never had seals. They stayed offshore, barking and laughing at the summer people. This one was a lost pup, obviously, maybe caught by a wave. . . .

Or shot offshore and swept in by the surf?

He chilled, struck by an unspeakable suspicion.

He turned back to the arrest report in his typewriter. His hands were shaking. "You shoot at the others?" he asked, pretending faint interest. "Yesterday?"

"No."

"Funny you didn't. Guy likes to shoot seals, seems he'd do it any chance he got. Shoot 'em in the water, even. Why let them *get* ashore?"

The little green eyes flashed hate, but the fat man did not answer. Brody swung away from the machine.

"A little target practice, yesterday, from the porch?" His voice rose. "You're an expert, you told me. And experts *hit*, man. How's your eyesight? Good enough to tell a seal from a diver in a hood?"

The green eyes widened. "You got me shooting divers?"

"I don't know." He arose, shaking. "If they're there, we'll find them. And if we do, we'll send you up for so long you'll *never* come down!"

The man pointed at the phone. "I get to make a call."

Brody shrugged. "Go ahead."

The sergeant phoned his wife. "Get the commissioner. Tell him to find me the best lawyer in New York State." He paused, smiled coldly. "Don't *worry* who pays for it. There's a jerk right here's going to pay for it." His little eyes met Brody's. "He just don't seem to know it yet."

THE seal weighed almost two hundred pounds. She craned her neck from the water, searching the beach. She had been there for almost an hour, though some visceral instinct impelled her to be somewhere, anywhere, else.

She watched the shaggy dog, sniffing near the edge of the water. Her whiskers quivered, but she was safe, here behind the surf line. Safe from anything *ashore* . . .

Every now and then a tiny moan would escape her. She barked once, inquiringly. She sensed somehow that it had not been from seaward that her pup had been snatched. He must have caught her fear and floundered up on the sand, while she, thinking him near her, had paralleled the surf, making for the breakwater where he would be secure.

She was a harbor seal. Three weeks ago she had borne her pup away from land. She had nursed him far from her fellows, romped with him alone, and taught him to dive and pluck crabs and lobsters from the bottom. She had cradled him in her flippers when he tired, though her own feeding suffered, for she could submerge for forty-five minutes and he only fifteen.

A female seal of another family, like the fur seal or the sea lion, might have abandoned him now, knowing the risk and sensing, too, that perhaps in a few weeks she could find an orphan to mother, northward in the summer rookery. But this one had never seen a rookery. To her he was the only pup in the ocean. And when he had not come to the breakwater, she slid back into the water, although she knew it was far too soon for her own safety.

The signs, to seaward, of a fast white death were still very close. She had ignored them and swum back along the beach, stroking strongly with her flippers and steering with her tail.

When she had come at last to this place, she knew it was the spot where he had landed.

The dog was still scrabbling in the sand. The seal backed her flippers and shot ten feet offshore.

She could not see the beach well, in the dazzle of the setting sun. She waited, listening for the pup's cry.

THE preliminary hearing, held in the mayor's office because Amity had no courtroom, was over. Willy Norton, justice of the peace, sat back in the mayor's executive chair.

"OK, Brody," he said. "He'll probably be out tomorrow, but you did it."

There was a metallic clang from across the hall as the cell door was slammed. Brody's stomach was jumping. Suppose he'd acted too quickly? "*We* did it," he reminded him.

"I don't think you can sue a JP," mumbled Norton. He led the Cub pack, was on the chamber of commerce, headed the PTA. He was a young service-station operator on his way up.

"Nobody's suing anybody," said Brody, rising. "He broke the township firearms ordinance and a federal statute! How the hell can he sue?"

40

Brody wished that he felt as sure as he sounded.

He locked up the rifle for evidence, strolled to the cell door for a last look at the prisoner. As Willy Norton said, he would probably be out tomorrow, when he got a lawyer. There must be something more they could do to wreck his weekend.

Suddenly he remembered that he had forgotten to inform the Amity *Leader* of the arrest. He glanced at his watch. Harry Meadows, whose gluttony for food was only exceeded by his appetite for work, would be there now, laying out tomorrow's issue. Brody dialed the paper. Speaking loudly, so that Sergeant Jepps could worry about the wire services picking up the feature, he briefed Harry on the first police story of the summer.

"That's all he hit, a seal?" Meadows sounded disappointed.

"A *baby* seal," urged Brody. "Look, Harry, you sobbed for half a page Monday about people taking baby *clams!*"

"Nothing else *happened* Monday. Now we got two divers drowned and a ski boat blown up, plus three columns on how we got to let the Brownies race in the regatta next Sunday, or your wife says she'll never speak to me again—"

"Suppose," Brody suggested, "the divers and the ski boat got blasted by the same idiot?"

That got his interest. There was a long silence. "Have you *got* something?" Meadows finally asked.

He heard Jepps rise and move to the cell door.

"Well," said Brody, "a pretty good suspicion."

"Can I quote you?"

Brody drummed his fingers. He wished he knew more about libel law and slander. "Say it's under investigation."

"Good enough," said Meadows, and hung up.

Brody smiled sweetly at Jepps, who was simply staring at him, zapping him with animal hatred.

THE seal was in Brody's garage. His name was Sammy. Sean was already his playmate and mentor. He had a bowl of canned sardines and a pot of milk spread out before his charge. He was cradling the seal, who must have weighed forty pounds, on his lap.

"Daddy, he's *crying* all the time. Look at his eyes!"

Sean was right. The big brown eyes were wet with tears. "I'll check it out with Doc Lean," Brody promised.

"And he won't leave the bandage on."

"Nature knows best." Brody's nose twitched. "What the heck . . ."

Sean rose, red-faced. "It wasn't his fault, Daddy. He just hasn't learned yet!"

"You are covered, my friend," murmured Brody, "with seal turd." He found a clean place at the tip of his son's nose, bent, and kissed him on it. "Dump your clothes at the kitchen door and take a bath."

Sean scurried off.

Brody filled a bucket and began to wash down the garage. Sammy floundered across to him, drank him in with the moist brown eyes. Sammy got hosed down, too.

Brody hoped the fat sergeant drew life.

Later that evening, Ellen Brody opened the door between the kitchen and the little utility room that Brody had built on the back porch. The clothes dryer was still groaning away, patiently tumbling Sean's clothes. She thought she could still catch Sammy's musty, fishy scent, but she was not sure.

She stopped the machine and took out Sean's faded jeans. She sniffed. She heard her husband at the door.

"All gone?" he asked.

She shrugged. "It's relative. They never did smell like English Leather."

"Sean's sorry," he proposed hopefully.

"Wasn't his fault."

"So's Sammy."

"Wasn't his either."

"*I'm* sorry," said Brody.

"Are you?"

"Look, Ellen, the seal's evidence."

"Then the township ought to keep him."

"Where?"

"In the high school gym, in the municipal pool, in Larry Vaughan's bathtub," she flared. "I don't care. They can't turn my house into a zoo!"

She was being awful, just awful. She liked the seal. He was beautiful and heartbreaking, and she was pleased that Sean had taken to him so quickly and that the seal seemed to regard Brody as its mother. Maybe that was what was wrong. The seal, like Mike and Sean and everything else Brody touched, fell in love with Brody, and she was left out in the cold.

"I'll ask Doc Lean about moving him," promised Brody.

"Oh, never mind. Sean's involved." Now *she* was sorry, and looked into his face for forgiveness. "It's just that *you* didn't have to rinse his clothes and wash them, then do it all again to kill the smell."

"I will next time."

No, he wouldn't. Some town problem would come up, or one of the boys would want him for something more important, like painting a boat or buying a wet suit.

"OK, Brody," she said gently. "I seem to be all uptight."

He helped her unload the dryer. They left the clothes on the ironing board and started upstairs hand in hand. She knew what awaited her and felt a pleasurable rush. At least that, which had once gone bad, was all right now.

Slipping off his shirt, Brody snapped his fingers. "Oh, hey, Sean told me to ask you—"

Warning flags. "What?"

"About the Brownie thing . . ."

"Stay out of it," she warned. "The Brownies *are* getting a canoe for the regatta. And that's *it!*"

"Look, *I* gave in on the Moscotti kid. . . ."

"With reason." Johnny Moscotti was the lonely little son of a Queens mobster who summered at Amity. Brody, visiting the sins of the father on the son, had wondered if it was wise to let him into Sean's Cub pack. He had tried to argue that the Moscottis were summer visitors and the pack was for permanent kids. She still got angry when she thought of it.

"You talk about *unconstitutional!*"

"The Brownie thing is different. Sean thinks—"

"The Brownies are going to race," she stated. "In a Cub Scout canoe!"

"Sean thinks—"

"He's a male chauvinist piglet." The injustice of it brought her voice up an octave. "The Cubs get everything from the Giants' games to open house at Quonset Point, and the Brownies sit home and make cookies. I'm sick of it, and if the Cubs race, the Brownies race, too!"

"And if they don't," finished Brody, "neither does Den Three?"

"You got it, Brody," she said.

Silently, he stripped and got into bed.

She turned her back and pretended to go to sleep.

NATHANIAL Starbuck's wife knocked at the darkroom door. It had taken thirty years, he reflected, but at least she'd learned that. "Yeah, yeah, light's on," he called.

She entered. "Nate? Cod cakes are ready."

"Wait a minute," he murmured. "Film's ready to hang."

"Is that Brody's?" asked Lena. "What is it?"

He glanced at the envelope he'd taken it out of. It was the Amity P.D.'s—rush—and he hadn't even noticed. If Brody was right, these were the last pictures some dead diver had ever taken. Curious, he grabbed the bottom of the strip, pulled it over so that the light would shine through it, and shook his head. "Nothing. Never shot anything."

"Wait! By your fingers!"

He looked down. She was right. The first two frames were exposed. He reversed the film and inspected the transparencies. Suddenly he adjusted his glasses.

The first shot was of a scuba diver, underwater, posing by the *Orca* wreck. He squinted at the other.

He could hear the water dripping from his wash bath. From upstairs he heard the jounce of Lawrence Welk. "Lena," he said hoarsely, "magnifying glass? Over the print tray?"

She handed it to him. He inspected the picture again, but he already knew. He just wanted to be sure. It was incredible, but he had to be sure.

"Nate," his wife cried. "What is it?"

The picture canted crazily and was underexposed, as if the camera had been moved. The letters on the *Orca*'s stern were red where they should have been orange, and the monster's teeth were gray where they should have been white.

"*Nate?*"

The thing was still off Amity. They had not killed it; Brody had lied. The Trouble was back, had never left.

He thought he was going to be sick.

And though Brody might have lied when he said they'd killed

it, he had not lied about its size. It was the biggest damn white any man had ever seen.

He lifted the filmstrip to let her see. She peered at it for a long moment. She swung her eyes to him. They were wild with fear. "Oh, God," she moaned. "What'll we do?"

He managed a smile. "Sell," he shrugged. "Shut up and sell. What else?"

PART TWO — Chapter 1

THE white had cruised last night from Amity to Fire Island light. She had taken a young bull seal off Sagaponack and hit a school of sea bass off Great South Beach. During the night she had consumed three hundred pounds of living protein, but by dawn, back off Amity, she was ravenous again.

She had driven a school of cod into Amity Harbor two days before, and now she found another and herded it into Amity Sound. She was homing in on its greatest mass when a rhythmic *chung . . . chung . . . chung . . .* from the eleven-thirty Amity Neck ferry confused her sensors and dispersed the school. She was so hungry by then that she very nearly went for the strange, angular shadow passing above her, but she sheered off at the last moment.

She was seen by no one aboard, although the captain's dog, Williwaw, perched on the main deck ahead of the load of six cars, began to bark excitedly.

In her right uterus the smallest of her brood turned on the largest of his squirming sisters and fought her off.

BRODY parked the dune buggy above the high-water mark, near where he'd found Sammy the seal. On the porch of the Smith house the sergeant's fat wife glared at him for a moment, then disappeared inside, dragging the little boy. Brody helped Tom Andrews into his diving gear.

The bearded giant had agreed to accept pay for looking for the demolished ski boat. He pulled on his flippers, then strode to the water, using enormous, exaggerated steps to keep from tripping in the sand. He looked like the Jolly Green Giant in black. When he reached the water, he turned and walked backward into the surf.

Brody picked up his microphone. "Car Three. I'm on Smith's beach, Polly."

"Roger, Chief," said Polly. "Ellen called. She said bring home evaporated milk for Sammy."

He wrote it down in his ticket book. Sammy had thrown up Sean's morning offering, adding the finishing touches to his previous night's work on the garage. What the poor thing needed was a mother's care, and mother was out there somewhere, probably, waiting to provide it. He decided to photograph the wound, for evidence, so that they could turn Sammy loose when he was well enough to swim. It would break Sean's heart.

Phil Hoople's taxi jounced along Beach Road. It was Jepps returning to his rented home. A rumpled law clerk from Flushing had arrived this morning and left the Township of Amity five hundred dollars bail. Now Jepps, leaving the cab, saw Brody in the dune buggy, stiffened, and moved thoughtfully into the house.

For half an hour Brody waited for Andrews. He was glancing more and more at his watch, overcome by a feeling of apprehension, when the shaggy dog burst over the eastern dunes. Jepps followed, his gut overhanging a wisp of a swimming suit. He approached the dune buggy, smiling, though his eyes were as cold as ever.

"Look, Brody," he began, "I'm up here for a vacation. This town needs all the summer trade it can get—"

"Not to shoot up our beach."

"I was *wrong*, Brody! I'm trying to tell you."

Brody pointed out that he didn't *have* to tell him that, he had a guy on the bottom right now trying to find out just how wrong he was. They looked to sea. Andrews was growing from the surf, like some prehistoric monster. In his hand he carried what looked like the remains of a shattered gas tank. It was red.

He clomped ashore, pulled off his fins, and put the tank on the hood of the dune buggy. "No divers. But I found this."

Brody studied the gas tank. He was no explosives expert, but this tank was very odd indeed. One side was blown completely out; the other had a gaping hole, as if struck by a projectile. He glanced at Jepps.

The fat man was staring at the tank. His eyes bulged. A tiny muscle in his jaw began to work. He swung his eyes toward Brody.

"OK, Chief. I know when somebody's trying to set me up." He tapped the tank. "Go ahead with *this* and we'll have your butt!" He wheeled and walked away.

"What was *that?*" rumbled Andrews.

Brody picked up the tank. It reeked faintly of gasoline. "He must have got drunk for the weekend," he mused. "He used our beach for a shooting gallery. He got more ducks than he planned." Angrily, he tossed the tank into the rear of the buggy.

NATE Starbuck sneaked a glance out the prescription window. His wife was still dusting the cosmetics counter. She had been at it for fifteen minutes, with a vacuous look on her face. She was wasting time, and her thoughtfulness made him uncomfortable.

"Lena! Come here!"

He led her back to the darkroom, flicking the red "keep out" light. "Lena, what's biting you? Forget you ever saw it!"

"I *did* see it. And so did you." She looked him full in the face. "Somebody *else* could get killed!"

"I hope it's Brody."

"Nate!"

"Except," he continued viciously, "he don't go near the water, does he? He or his kids."

"*He* never did. Even before!"

He ignored her. "And he got to be a hero!" He began to stride back and forth. He had already told her all that last night. She just couldn't seem to get it through her stupid head.

It was a plot, by the ins, against the outs. Mayor Larry Vaughan must have known, and Willy Norton, the great justice of the peace, and the selectmen. Knowing the shark still lived, they had taken Peterson and his syndicate for plenty on the casino deal. Well, he'd sell, too, before it was too late.

"I don't want to sell!" Lena murmured.

"Well, we're *going* to. For as much as we can, as quick as we can, and move as far as we can from Amity."

"We never found a buyer during The Trouble."

"*During* The Trouble? The Trouble never left! And The Trouble never will!"

There was no use explaining it to her. She knew nothing about sharks or the sea. But his great-grandfather, who had lived to eighty-nine, had told Nate his tales of the whaling days. And Nate had listened, not with his ears—for he'd heard the stories from infancy—but with the pores of his skin.

A great white off Sydney, Australia, had hit one of the old man's whaleboats in 1897 and very nearly capsized it. The same shark attacked a flensed carcass in 1899, half a mile away. For the white *lived* there.

A white off Tonga had turned the water red with the blood of a sperm they'd taken in 1896, and the same shark had hit another in 1898. Same place.

Sharks were jealous of their waters. And they didn't leave. If they found a feeding ground to their taste, why would they?

"Suppose we can't sell?" she whispered. "Suppose nobody wants to buy it?"

Nate smiled thinly. "I think somebody'll want it."

When he had her calmed down, he opened a brand-new roll of film. He felt funny exposing it under the bright light. It seemed wasteful. But it was only $1.30 dealer price. With the whole drugstore at stake, what difference did $1.30 make?

He developed it blank and hung it up to dry.

BRODY found a break in the sand cresting South Amity Beach, downshifted the dune buggy, went into four-wheel drive, and ground to the top of the knoll, heading for Beach Road. He felt Andrews' hand on his arm. "Wait . . ."

Brody stopped and followed his gaze. Far down the beach a group of lanky teenagers had spread towels on the deserted sand. Most of them were in wet suits, probably kids from the scuba class. Andrews watched them. "Just wanted to make sure nobody got hold of a diving tank somewhere, to beat the gun. Let's go."

"Hold it . . ." said Brody. His eyes were on the closest boy. It was Mike. He was wearing his suit. Farther along, Larry Vaughan, Jr., the mayor's son, sprang from a towel, raced into the water, and flung himself into an oncoming wave.

Mike watched it come, squatted, and let shallow waters rise to his hips. Larry beckoned him from beyond the surf line. He waved back, took a few steps out, yawned self-consciously. Suddenly he grabbed his leg and hobbled from the water.

48

The big man regarded Brody. "He subject to cramps?"

"He'll be OK," said Brody tightly. He was not going to apologize for Mike to anyone, for anything.

Or tell him, since Mike obviously hadn't, of what, once, the poor kid had seen.

BRODY faced the druggist across the counter. "What do you mean, you screwed up?"

Nate regarded him with pale blue eyes. "Well, it wasn't me, exactly. Lena opened the darkroom door."

"*Nothing* left on the film?" Brody couldn't believe it.

Starbuck opened a drawer, took a roll of film from a yellow envelope marked RUSH: AMITY P.D. He held it up. It was clear from one end to the other.

"Damn," breathed Brody.

"Probably nothing on it *before*. Hear they were drunk."

"And now we'll never know, will we? Damn it, Nate, it's the last picture the guy ever took! What do I tell his wife?"

Starbuck shrugged. He seemed to be undergoing a mental struggle. Suddenly, as if he had resolved a painful dilemma, he reached into the film rack.

"Tell her we're giving her a fresh roll of film."

Brody looked into the blue Yankee eyes, vacant as the sea. "I'll *tell* her you said you were sorry. You can *shove* the film!"

BY NOON the seal was skirting the Amity beachline. She had spent most of the night off the spot at which she had lost her pup. Finally she had trundled ashore, despite the dog smell. There she sensed that she was very close to where her pup had been. She nosed the dry sand. The scent of his blood excited her greatly.

But he was there no longer, and at dawn she had reentered the water. She floated offshore for an hour indecisively. Then she paralleled the beach until she reached the Amity breakwater. She heaved herself up on the rocks, safe from the terror which she still sensed to seaward.

She was basking under the sun, overcome by a tight feeling of loneliness, when some force impelled her back into the water. She swam across the harbor entrance, around the point, and turned up into Amity Sound.

49

This was confining and unfamiliar territory. But she felt that her pup was somewhere near, so she stopped a hundred yards from a white clapboard house, floating and letting his closeness comfort her. She did not see, smell, or hear him, but she sensed that he was not far away. And so she stayed.

BRODY sipped his luncheon beer, watching his sons finish their sandwiches. Sean was scowling at the Amity *Leader* spread before him. Suddenly he thrust it at his father.

"Read it to me, Dad," he demanded. "It's about Sammy."

Brody shook his head. "*You* read it to *me*." Sean hated to read. Sean frowned, but began in schoolroom monotone:

"Amity—A vacationing police officer was arrested yesterday for allegedly shooting and wounding a baby seal on Amity Beach. He was reportedly charged with . . . vilation?"

"Violation," Mike interrupted. He craned to see, grabbed the paper, and commenced, staccato:

"He was reportedly charged with violation of the Marine Mammal Protection Act and a municipal ordinance against discharging firearms in the town limits. The suspect was identified as Sergeant Charles Jepps, 54, of the Flushing Police Department. He is a summer resident at Smith's Sandcastle, West Beach Road.

"Chief Martin Brody said the victim was a three-week-old harbor seal. Brody says he is conducting a further investigation to determine whether shootings by the accused are connected with two missing divers and a boat explosion off Amity Beach."

"Boy," groaned Ellen, "you don't mind sticking your neck out, do you?"

"No sweat," Brody said, trying to project confidence. "He *did* shoot the seal."

"And you put him in jail, right?" Sean prompted.

"He wants to get it straight," Mike sighed. "He's bringing Sammy up to date."

Brody nodded. "Yes, I put him in jail, Sean. But he's out now. On bail."

Sean's eyes widened. "That isn't fair! Just one night?"

"Tell Sammy I'll do my best to put him back."

50

Sean shot off to the garage. Brody studied his older son. Mike had stayed irritable, jumpy, with the same haunted eyes he had shown for days. Brody decided to take him aside, for he had a good idea why.

Four years before, when The Trouble had hit, Mike and Sean had been as amphibious as frogs. The first few shark attacks had not had the slightest effect on either: it had been all he could do to keep them out of the ocean. He had ordained that they swim only off the muddy shore that bordered their backyard on Amity Sound.

At the height of the panic, while Mike swam in a tidal pond and Sean played in the sand nearby, the white had slithered under the railroad bridge and struck a man basking on a rubber raft not fifty feet from Mike.

The effect on Mike had been catastrophic. He had been carried from the water in shock, without a scratch on his body, but with a deep and jagged wound on his soul.

They had never spoken afterward of the attack.

After lunch, Brody drew Mike to the solarium and they sat on the back steps, gazing across the water at the minute daytime flicker of Cape North light, far across Amity Sound. Mike's Laser sat stranded and forlorn on its rack above high water.

"You going to win Sunday?" asked Brody.

Mike shrugged. "If I race."

"Hey, you promised Sean! You can't just *dump* it!"

"OK, I'll go, I'll go! No big deal."

Brody faced him. "You got a problem, Mike?"

"Problem?" Mike would not meet his eyes. He craned to look at Brody's watch. "What time is it? Jackie—"

"Forget Jackie. I think we ought to talk about your swimming off the beach. Have you been doing it?"

Mike shrugged. "Tried out my suit this morning."

"Keep you warm?"

Mike's eyes shifted. "Fantastic."

"Nice to get back in the ocean? No . . . worries?" Brody's voice trailed off. These were grounds full of land mines.

"No!" Mike faced him fiercely. "Look, you *hate* the water! But I *like* it! You think I'd worry?"

From the garage came a piercing bark, followed by a yell from Sean. Brody and Mike moved swiftly across the lawn.

The garage still smelled horribly of seal. Sean was locked in struggle with Sammy, who was escaping out the door. Boy and seal were yelling hysterically.

Brody squatted in front of the seal, who shook his head and tried to nudge him out of the way. The three of them managed to ease him back into the garage. The seal was barking plaintively, his eyes still wet with tears. It would be impossible to keep him here much longer. It would be equally impossible, when he left, to console Sean.

"We were just playing," the boy explained, "and he tried to split."

Brody led Sean out and closed the door. "Give him a rest." Regretfully, he looked at his watch. In the winter his sons were in school, and in the summer there was never enough time for them. He had an appointment at the Suffolk County Crime Lab in Bay Shore in half an hour. He turned to Mike. "So what'll you do this afternoon?"

Mike shrugged. "Fool around with Jackie; it's her day off. Maybe take her for a swim."

His son looked suddenly taller, lankier, and wiser. And Jackie was certainly beautiful, behind her braces.

He found himself hoping that Jackie would keep Mike out of the water altogether. But that was stupid. The Trouble was over.

LARRY Vaughan, mayor of Amity and president of Vaughan & Penrose Realty, liked no one to discuss real estate in his Town Hall office. Clients were to be referred to his clapboard realty shack on Scotch Road. He was afraid that if he used his official quarters for personal gain, the selectmen would refuse to pay Daisy Wicker, his secretary.

But Starbuck had somehow bulled past Daisy and was staring at him across the mayor's desk.

"Sell the drugstore?" Vaughan repeated incredulously. He searched for the druggist's true reason, not being disposed to take another's stated reason—especially in business—as true.

"Yup," said Starbuck. "That's what I aim to do."

"Well, Nathanial," Vaughan said slowly, "I'm shocked, but of course I'll handle it. Your price seems high, but maybe in a month or so, if the gambling law passes—"

"I'm not talkin' about a month or so. I want to sell now."

An alarm bell jingled in Vaughan's head. Though reasonably he knew that Vaughan & Penrose and Amity Township itself faced a vista of unprecedented growth and prosperity, The Trouble had sensitized his antennae. Why did Starbuck want to bail out now? Perhaps receipts were down.

He tapped a pencil on the desk. "Nathanial, let's not discuss price right now. What shocks me, there's been a Starbuck handling the town's pharmaceutical needs for, what is it, three generations? So you can see—"

"Health," said Starbuck. His eyes did not flicker. "Lena. Cancer."

Vaughan chilled. Almost forty years ago, Lena, then a thin teenager with buckteeth, had been his baby-sitter. She had been warm and friendly and had taught him double solitaire. "No!" he exclaimed. "Not Lena!"

"She'll have to go to New York—Memorial Hospital. Sixty, a hundred a day at least, for who knows how long."

Vaughan drummed his fingers. Starbuck's property was the choicest downtown lot. When the casino was finished and the law passed, anything south of Scotch Road would be worth a bloody fortune. It was possible that Starbuck had no idea of his lot's future value. He wanted fifty thousand dollars; Vaughan was sure that he could sell it for seventy-five. Or buy it himself and wait . . .

"Tell her I'm sorry, Nathanial. And I'll list the pharmacy at fifty. I'm sure we can sell it."

"I'm sure you *better*," said Starbuck. He arose, placed his hat squarely on his head, and left.

Now what the hell had he meant by that? Strange man.

Vaughan decided to let him dangle for a week, offer thirty-five for Lena's sake, and buy the place himself.

The phone on his desk began to flash. It was Clyde Bronson, the state legislator representing Amity's district in Albany. He had just had a visit from the state police commissioner, who had had a visit from an attorney representing a police sergeant named Jepps, currently charged with a firearms offense and a federal wild-life violation by the Amity police.

The state police commission, explained Clyde, were anti-gambling anyway. If Vaughan thought that ticking *them* off was going to help the gambling bill pass, Vaughan just thought wrong. "Do you get my message, Larry?"

He could hear the legislator breathing strenuously. Vaughan told him that yes, he'd got the message.

He replaced the phone and lumbered across the hall to the police department. Brody's desk was empty.

"Where is he?" he asked Polly.

"Suffolk County Crime Lab. Is something wrong?"

"Nothing firing your boss won't cure."

"You can't," she said primly. "We're civil service."

Chapter 2

BRODY parked Car Number 1 outside the Suffolk County police headquarters and gathered up the Savage rifle, the paper bag with the ammunition he had found in its magazine, and the ski boat's shattered gas tank. He felt silly, carrying the weapon and the other evidence, as if he were playing Sherlock Holmes.

The young desk sergeant made him sign the visitors' book, turned the desk over to another officer, and took him upstairs. Brody dipped in his memory for the young man's name, remembering him as a lecturer on police administrative procedures. That was it: Sergeant Pappas.

They walked down corridors buzzing with activity. Uniformed, plainclothes, and civilian personnel moved purposefully through the hallways. Radios crackled, telephones jangled.

"Rat race," muttered the sergeant. "Do you need another man out there?"

"They'd make you chief," said Brody, "and you'd starve on my salary."

"Try me," murmured Pappas. He led Brody into the crime lab, where he signed in the gun and ammunition and gas tank, then moved through a cluttered room to a door marked BALLISTICS LAB.

Across a wall hung a collection of weapons, from dainty handbag automatics to a machine gun Brody recognized from GI days as a fifty-caliber Browning. Above the collection was printed COMPARATIVE BALLISTICS TEST SECTION.

On the adjoining wall was mounted another collection—of Saturday night specials, brass knuckles, and sawed-off shotguns. Above the second collection, in gold Gothic script, was painted THE RIGHT OF THE PEOPLE TO BEAR ARMS SHALL NOT BE INFRINGED.

A pretty young black woman, with a triumphant burst of hair, was peering at a pair of bullets through a binocular-microscope. She swung on her stool when she heard them approaching.

"Brody," said the young sergeant, "this is the pride of Suffolk County. Lieutenant Swede Johansson. Lieutenant, this is Chief Brody of Amity P.D."

She groped for something in her memory. "Amity . . ."

"The next Las Vegas East," Brody suggested.

She shook her head. "No. That's not it."

"Late hometown of the great white shark," Brody confessed. He hated this, and ran into it all the time. The pall of The Trouble seemed to persist forever.

The lieutenant snapped her fingers. "Ri-i-ight," she drawled. "And *you* were the shark bait?"

"I was there," admitted Brody.

The young woman shivered. "You must have been out of your mind!"

"Out of my element anyway," said Brody, holding out the rifle. "Like now."

"That's refreshing," she said, glancing at the weapon. "You're the first cop who's walked in here in a year who didn't claim to know more ballistics than me."

"He wants to know," the sergeant said, putting the shattered gas tank, the bullets, and the rifle on her table, "did this cannon and these rounds make *this* hole? Full report. And an estimate of your time and charges."

Brody felt uncomfortable. Amity, theoretically, had to pay for Suffolk County police services when they were required. But there was no budget he could tap.

He licked his lips. "I thought maybe you could just, well, as a matter of professional courtesy . . ."

The lieutenant smiled. "Lunch sometime," she proposed. "Department cafeteria? Dollar-thirty-five blue plate, and apple pie à la mode?"

"You're on."

Swede turned back to the microscope. "I'll have a prelim by Wednesday. Give me a call."

"Thanks, Lieutenant," said Brody.

"There are *seven* lieutenants," she said. "Ask for Swede."

AT SIXTEEN HUNDRED hours the U.S. destroyer *Leon M. Cooper* was rattling southwest of Block Island. The j.g.—lieutenant junior grade—on the starboard wing of her bridge passed the watch to his relief, the gunnery officer. As the j.g. turned over the duty, he saluted. The gun boss, a full lieutenant, did not salute back.

Sloppy, thought the j.g. He was Annapolis '73, and he was irritated that things on this ship seldom went as he had been taught to expect.

The j.g. was combat information center officer, and at least he had his own shop squared away. He decided to visit the CIC now, to see if they had studied tonight's exercise, which was to find, if they could, the U.S. submarine *Grouper*, sneaking about in all the vast water to seaward.

Before he stepped into the darkened, fluorescent coolness of the CIC, he glanced to starboard. It was hazy, but he could dimly discern Montauk off the bow. For a moment he let his mind drift into a familiar dream. A carrier would loom out of the mist, dead on a collision course with the *Cooper*. Everyone else would miss it. The j.g. would race to the bridge, grab the wheel, slam it over, and save the ship by inches as the skipper tumbled from his cabin wet-eyed with gratitude.

Or perhaps he would spot a Russian torpedo snaking from the deep. . . .

He'd simply been born too late, even for Nam.

For a while he observed the helicopter, their partner in the hunter-killer team, dipping its sonar ball a hundred yards off their port quarter. It was too early to hear the *Grouper;* he must be only testing his gear.

He stepped inside and stood behind the radarman for a moment to see that he was logging contacts. He could see Montauk on the screen, and pointed it out. That woke up everyone else. The sonarman turned on his sonar, though it was an hour before he could expect the sub. The air-plot man began to pencil planes out of Naval Air Station Quonset. The radioman began to warm up the short-range radio.

"Sir?" called the sonarman. "Submarine contact, two-two-zero. Range six miles. Closing."

The j.g.'s heart leaped. Too early for the *Grouper,* and he knew of no other sub in the zone. No other *U.S.* sub . . .

He took the sonarman's earphones. He could follow the beat of the chopper off their quarter, an underseas pounding so loud that it was sometimes supposed to attract sharks. In counterpoint to it he could hear the familiar *ping* of their own transducer. *Ping* . . . and then the fainter echo, *ping. Ping* . . . *ping*.

Closing indeed. And fast. Too fast for a school of fish. Too fast for anything but, perhaps, a *Keshnov*-class sub, sent to spy. To spy, or worse.

"Bass, sir?" asked the sonarman.

"Too big for a school of bass," the j.g. said. He took off the headset and reached for the bridge phone. "Bridge from CIC!" Nobody answered. That figured, on this turkey.

The sonarman had put on the headset again. "It's too early for the *Grouper*. Too big for *anything*," he puzzled. Suddenly he snapped his fingers. "Whale! Finback whale! Heard the same echo in sonar school. It's duller than a sub."

"Whale?" Indecisively, the j.g. stood, bridge phone in hand.

"Whale," repeated the sonarman with conviction.

"CIC from bridge," the loudspeaker said finally. "You call?"

The j.g. hesitated. He took back the headset and listened. The contact was moving toward the beach. It had to be a whale. He was covered, anyway, by his sonarman's evaluation. He was an officer and gentleman, not a sonar expert.

"Never mind," he told the bridge. "Belay it."

When he left CIC to wash up for dinner, he saw the chopper chomping off toward shore.

HUNGER had again driven her, during the morning, into Amity Sound. She had done her best to clean it of everything that moved. She had consumed perhaps a hundred pounds of mackerel off Amity Neck. She skirted the breakwater and headed for open ocean. She found nothing until, as the sun slanted westward and the light at five fathoms began to dim, she felt the slow pounding, far away, of a low-flying helicopter. *Thump* . . . *thump*, and behind it, much less exciting, a feeble, rhythmic *ping*.

Blindly, she headed for the thumping. The sound, as with any rhythmic vibration, triggered her digestive juices. She became more ravenous with every sweep of her tail. She followed the pounding of the helicopter toward the beach.

57

LARRY VAUGHAN, JR., HAD stopped his moped on Beach Road when they spotted the bikes chained to a fence post. Andy Nicholas, Amity's fat boy, climbed off the postilion seat. His tail ached and the road dust, he feared, was bringing on his asthma.

"Man, let me drive home. *You* sit back there."

Larry turned off the ignition. "You'd bust the fork, chubby-cheeks." He considered the bikes. "That's his, all right. But who's the girl's?" He began looking for a name under the bar of the girl's bicycle. "Mary Detner? Sue Jacobs?" He studied the bike. "Hey! Jackie Angelo? I bet it's the silver-toothed devil herself."

"You think?" asked Andy with some interest.

"Old Angelo will have a fit," promised Larry, "he ever finds out. He'll shoot him with that cannon he carries."

"Naw," said Andy. "They're swimming, is all. He's trying to show off in his wet suit."

Larry shook his head. "Not Spitzer. That's the ocean out there, not the Town Pool."

He scrambled up the sandy bank and began to reconnoiter the beach from the hummocks along the crest. Andy followed, making too much noise. Larry motioned him down. The fat boy dropped to his hands and knees, although he was afraid the sand would complete the job on his asthma. Cautiously, the two scanned the ocean and the dunes.

Banks of summer fog were gathering on the southeastern horizon. Andy felt Larry poke him. His freckled brow was furrowed. When Andy listened, he could hear a low murmur from the hollow behind the nearest dune. He could make out Mike's voice, and a throaty chuckle he recognized as Jackie's.

His blood began to warm, but he felt a shiver go up his back. Mike was thirty pounds lighter than he, but sinewy, fast, and strong. "Let's split," he whispered.

Larry glanced at him incredulously. "You crazy, man?"

Pulling his body forward on his elbows, Larry began to slither down the slope. Andy hesitated. Then, drawn by some irrepressible force, he began to snake down the hillock himself.

He was breathing heavily. At the bottom of the slope he paused. Above him, Larry was climbing to the top of the dune hiding the couple. Sand slid into Andy's eyes, but nothing on earth could have stopped his progress now.

MIKE BRODY SHIFTED HIS weight on Jackie's beach towel. He stared into the angel face only six inches from his own. Two heavenly dimples appeared at the corners of the most desirable mouth in the world. Tentatively, he reached out a finger and brushed a strand of shimmering hair from a perfect ear.

He began to tickle the lobe. Did that arouse women? She was nice. He just wanted to be here with her, drinking in her beauty forever. He even loved the silver braces.

"Mike, that . . . kind of tickles." She put out her own hand and began to play with the lobe of his ear.

It tickled, all right, and did more than that. It sent arrows of pleasure and longing through him. He couldn't stand it if she kept it up, but he couldn't bear it if she stopped.

"I love you," he blurted.

She removed her hand and sat up.

Now why had he said *that?* He'd blown it for sure.

But he *did* love her, more than his mother, even, or his dad, and a lot more than Sean.

She was gazing out over the ocean. "Foggy, pretty soon," she said softly. "We could get lost going home."

"Jackie," he muttered bleakly, "you don't want to go *home?*"

She smiled down at him. "I don't *ever* want to go home."

He took her in his arms.

CHIEF Brody wiped his forehead. It was hot in the Vaughan & Penrose Realty office.

"Drop the case?" he repeated incredulously. "What do you mean, '*drop*' it?"

Vaughan arose, red-faced, and moved to the county map dominating his tiny shack. He tapped the casino site and turned back to Brody.

"Drop it, or we'll lose the casino. It's that simple."

"What's Jepps got to do with the *casino?*"

"He's got to do with a state police commissioner—"

"He *says,*" Brody interjected.

"He does, all right. The commissioner got to Clyde Bronson. Bronson got to me, and I'm getting to you."

Bronson was not only their representative in Albany, he was also the co-sponsor of the state gambling law.

"Damn it," Brody growled. "This guy's a suspect for *manslaughter!*"

"Drop it," sighed Vaughan. "The charge won't stick without a body," the mayor pointed out. "Just drop it."

Brody felt his temper rising. Bitterly, he murmured, "This remind you of something, Larry?"

"What?" Vaughan looked uncomfortable.

"The start of The Trouble? When the girl got hit? And I tried to close the beaches? And nobody in town would talk to me, or Ellen, or Mike, or even Sean? And the Kintner kid got killed, and it turned out I was right? We closed the beaches then—when it was too late."

Vaughan returned to his desk, sat down heavily. "There's a difference. The shark didn't have a single friend in Albany. I'm telling you, Brody! *Drop* it!"

Brody met the mayor's eyes. They were red-rimmed, from lack of sleep or from booze. But they did not shift or look away. He slammed his hand on the mayor's desk.

"Not this time, Larry. Not in a million years!"

He left the shack and walked into sunlight. Fog would be drifting in soon, he could feel it. So could the horn on the end of the Amity breakwater, which let out a sudden blast.

He loved Amity. If he had to leave here, he'd have no place to go. But he was damned if he'd fold again.

ANDY Nicholas lay in agony next to Larry Vaughan, Jr., behind a bush at the crest of the dune. Dust from the bush was searing his chest and closing his throat. He knew that he had better escape before he began to wheeze, but he could not tear himself away. Oh, Jackie's soft, warm body.

"*Do* it, Spitzer!" he heard Larry whisper.

"Shut up," mouthed Andy. If Mike heard them, it was he who would suffer, not Larry, who could do the hundred in ten flat. Larry would escape and Andy would end up in the sand.

His breath began to come in familiar, strangled gasps. He would have to slither back down the dune and split, now or never. He risked one last glance.

He felt Larry clutch his elbow. "Shut up," Larry whispered in horror. "Shut the hell up!"

Andy shook his head helplessly. A red, familiar tide was engulfing him. He sounded like a leaky radiator, a winded horse. . . .

The tableau below him froze. For an instant it was stop-motion, like the replay of a close call on TV. Then it all exploded into action. Mike was scrambling up the side of the hollow, Larry was on his feet, and Jackie was screaming angrily. Andy rolled in the dust, trying to get to his feet.

Mike reached the summit, somehow slung Larry seaward down the hill toward Jackie, and drew back his bare foot.

Andy took it full in the stomach. Between the asthma and the foot in the gut, he thought he would die. His vision darkened. When he could see again, he found Jackie on her knees beside him, patting his cheeks, but none too gently.

"You OK, Andy?"

He managed to nod.

She got to her feet and looked down on him fiercely. "You crummy little creeps," she said.

She gazed out to sea. He followed her glance. At the edge of a fogbank a navy helicopter was dangling something into the water. He let his eyes fall closer to the shoreline.

If Spitzer was scared of the ocean, as Larry Vaughan always claimed, he had got over it in a hell of a hurry. Larry was splashing to sea, fifty yards past the surf line. But thirty yards astern was Mike, gaining fast.

"He'll kill him," Jackie said desolately, "and they'll send him to Juvie Hall. He'll *drown* the creep!"

She was probably right. Andy guessed he ought to be out there, trying to save him. But Mike, once he took care of Larry, might drown him, too. He decided to walk home instead.

THE great white circled aimlessly. The rhythmic thumping of helicopter vanes which was exciting her had also jammed her computer. She could ordinarily home precisely on a vibrating body. The beat she followed now seemed to be everywhere and nowhere. The hunt for its source was fruitless, but she was unable to break from its fascination. Once she swerved to scoop up a giant squid, but mostly she wound in a pointless figure eight.

Always she stayed as close to the source as she could, though it moved toward the shore and the shallows.

THE NAVY CHOPPER PILOT glanced seaward at the fogbanks and then shoreward at the dunes. His orders were to plug the space between water too shallow for the *Grouper* and the zone that the *Leon M. Cooper* was patrolling to seaward.

He looked at the clock on his instrument panel. The *Grouper* was presumably well out of New London by now, submerged, and heading into the exercise zone. If she didn't hurry, he'd have to abort his mission and haul back to Quonset before the fog caught him.

It didn't seem a bad idea. There was still time to make Happy Hour at the club. He looked, almost furtively, at his young sonarman. "Too foggy," he proposed.

"Doesn't look so bad to me, sir," the sonarman said.

The pilot sat back. The kid had seemed so eager and interested in the patrol that he had let him dip the sonar gear early to test it. But now the pilot was getting bored with the whole operation. The young man was an impediment.

"How you doing?" he asked the boy.

"Mackerel, pistol shrimp, the usual. I hear everything but the *Grouper*. Let's drag it a little farther inshore."

The pilot nodded, eased the stick forward. He felt the sonarman's hand on his arm. "Sir? Hold it! I heard a yell, somebody in the water yelling."

They scanned the ocean ahead. Suddenly the pilot spotted them. "You see two kids, off the surf line?"

"Yes, sir. Hey, one's drowning, or they're fighting."

"Up gear," ordered the pilot. He heard the winch whine for a moment, checked the panel, and swooped ahead toward the pair.

SHE had been swimming northeastward at five fathoms, hypnotized by the thumping from above, and utterly famished. She would have struck at a boat, a bottle, or a lobster buoy if she had sensed one. There was nothing, so she glided haphazardly.

Suddenly, beyond the thumping, she heard a surface splashing that galvanized her senses. It was as if two large fish were fighting, or two seals mating at the surface.

A chord was struck. She wheeled, tossing her gravid belly upward, and doubled back. The mysterious thumping was far outweighed by this new and more exciting signal.

MIKE BRODY, ENRAGED, allowed Larry Vaughan, Jr., to surface, but kept his hold. "Mike!" screamed Larry. "You turd, you're outta your mind!"

Mike, treading water, stared into the tear-streaked, freckled face. He must have damn near drowned him. It was time to quit, but he had shown them that when chased by Mike Brody, the ocean was no sanctuary.

He shoved Larry roughly away, turned on his back, and floated. "Pervert," he spat. "Crummy pervert!"

The two lay panting, drifting apart in the ground swell. Mike let his eyes stray to a navy chopper speeding toward them. The chopper reared, quivered, and finally lowered a black ball into the water. Listening for subs from New London, he knew.

A great elation surged through him. He could be that chopper pilot if he wanted, or one of the men on the sub he was looking for, or a U.S. marine.

He knew no fear of the ocean or anything else.

THE pilot yawned. The sonarman said, "They're just kids, sir, horsing around."

And the pilot had waved at them and eased back on the stick, stopping the chopper in midair. "What say we secure for the day?" he suggested to the young man.

"Whatever you say, sir," his companion said, but he looked disappointed and, what the hell, the kid had probably never had a sub contact in his life and the *Grouper* was due any minute.

"Dangle your gear a while more," he capitulated.

The sonarman grinned, dropped it again, and adjusted his headset. The pilot sat back and yawned.

SHE was not far behind the thumping, but it was the surface targets that occupied her now.

Her smallest male squirmed in her right uterus. Deprivation of food for a few more hours would turn his stronger sisters upon him, and he somehow knew it and eased his body around in the packed organ to a better fighting position. As if she knew his danger, the mother increased her speed.

Ahead of her, under the pervasive thumping, she heard a sudden *plop*. In the dim light she glimpsed a black shape descending. She

63

rolled, snapped open her mouth, and snatched it between row upon row of serrated teeth. There was a moment of wild resistance from above. Then she had it free, crushed it between her jaws, and spit it out in a cloud of teeth, wires, and mangled metal.

She coasted for a moment.

She heard no more thrashing from the surface, and even the thumping was receding. She turned and headed to sea to hunt.

THE sonarman was still quaking and the pilot himself was shaky on the controls. He took it out on the sonarman. "How deep did you *have* the damn thing?"

The boy shook his head helplessly. "Ten, twelve feet deep at the most, sir."

The pilot climbed. He had only one desire, to get high enough to autorotate in case the incredible strains on the chopper proved fatal. At sixty feet they were dead ducks if the structure collapsed or a vane began to flutter. He had never sustained, in twenty-five years and eight thousand hours, a jerk on a cable as violent as the one they had just survived.

As he ascended, he listened for the telltale blade dissonance that would spell fuselage or engine failure. No, everything seemed all right.

"You dragged the bottom," he insisted.

"No, sir!" the sonarman protested. "That ball never got within twenty-five feet of the bottom! You can hear it when it's dragging the bottom. This was something else. I heard a kind of swishing, like, I don't know. You think we fouled a bat ray or a giant squid or something?"

"No," scoffed the pilot. "You hung it too low. We snagged a reef or a wreck!" He continued to climb, not leveling off until he was at two thousand feet. All seemed OK, but he was still not happy.

"Damn it, son, you know what those balls cost?"

"Twelve thousand dollars." The kid looked as if he were about to cry.

"That's not counting whatever we did to the aircraft," muttered the pilot. He heard a high-pitched, rhythmic squeaking from the rotor-blade assembly. He didn't like it at all. He pressed the throat-mike button to call the *Leon M. Cooper,* describe his problem, and punch out from his patrol. Before he could call, the

stick began to vibrate in his hand. He should have ditched the chopper the instant he had felt that tug.

"Pan! This is a pan call." Pan was a step below Mayday. "*Leon M. Cooper* from navy chopper one-four-seven-eight, aborting. Returning to—" He suddenly felt it coming. . . .

As a young man in Korea he had snatched wounded marines from the peaks above Pyongyang. Ten years ago he had plucked navy pilots from the Gulf of Tonkin. He knew suddenly that after all the danger, it might end here, off a stupid little beach town whose name he could never remember.

He pressed the button again. "Mayday! Mayday! Navy one-four-seven-eight, calling Mayday! I'm five miles south of . . ." It came to him suddenly—the shark place—"Amity. Amity, Long Island. I'm going to lose a blade. Commencing descent."

The vane left with a twang like a broken guitar string. He caught a glimpse of it in metallic sunlight, spinning a lazy arc down to the silver sea. The chopper canted crazily, flipped, and his world turned upside down. He saw the fogbanks through the bubble canopy, between his feet. He heard the sonarman scream. And then he could only hang on.

BRODY sat in a rickety aluminum chair on his front porch and watched his son cycling up Bayberry Lane. When he got closer and parked the bike, it was like seeing a new boy. Mike's shoulders were back, his eyes were steady, and a hint of a secret smile played on his lips.

"Good day?" Brody asked.

"Went swimming with Jackie," he grinned.

Brody looked into his boy's eyes. "*Swimming?*"

Mike colored. "Look, Dad, she's a nice girl."

"I know that. What are you so uptight about?"

"*You're* uptight, not me. Just because I take a girl for a swim, do we have to be making it?"

But something had happened. A weight had been lifted from Mike's soul.

For a moment the two were locked in total eye contact. The moment passed. The Amity foghorn blasted and behind it a cacophony of lesser horns. Mike looked puzzled. He obviously hadn't heard the news. His father told him. "A chopper went down in the fog. Dick Angelo's out there now. And half of Quonset Point. Hate to think of Dick ghosting along between warships on a foggy night."

Mike was listening to the foghorns, thoughtfully. "I wonder. There was a chopper, when Larry and I were swimming; we were kind of wrestling around outside the surf line."

Brody knew he should be glad. If Mike had breasted the surf, the phobia was dead. Now, if only he didn't get carried away and try to swim to Nova Scotia. . . .

"The pilot kind of made a run on us," Mike said. His voice trembled oddly. "I could see him, right through his windshield. Maybe he thought we were in trouble, you know, drowning or something, and he came over to see."

Brody shrugged. "Maybe."

"And then he waved. Dad, you suppose he got *killed?*"

Brody was sure of it, from what they had told him of the man's last transmission, but there was no use stirring up the kid. He pulled him close and squeezed his shoulders.

"He waved, and dropped that thing they drag around, you know, to listen for subs. . . ." Mike grimaced, thinking. "Funny. Do they leave it in the water when they go?"

Brody shook his head. "I don't think so."

"This guy did. I could see the line he was hanging it from. Just swinging, you know, nothing on it?"

That seemed odd, but maybe they *did* leave the units and come back later. Or maybe Mike was mistaken. They went in to dinner.

ELLEN Brody was, as usual, the only den mother who had come to the pack meeting. She squirmed in her seat in Miss Fairleigh's sixth-grade classroom. The desks were too small for adults. Willy Norton, justice of the peace, president of the PTA, and Cub master, had the only decent seat—behind Miss Fairleigh's desk.

The ambience made her feel tiny. She found herself waving her hand for attention like an eight-year-old. "Mr. Norton? Willy? The regatta?"

The chair recognized her reluctantly, as if Norton had been down this road before and had no desire to travel it again. Behind her she heard Sean's warning stage whisper. "Moth . . . er!"

"Yes, Ellen?" Norton said wearily.

"It has to do with Martha Linden's Brownies," she began. Behind her erupted a Greek chorus of sighs, wails, and boos.

Willy Norton held up his hand. "Pipe down, gang! Ellen, we took a vote last week. Only three canoes and three dens, right? And I think we decided to lend the Brownies the canoes before the den race, or after, or whatever. Equal rights."

"They want to *compete* with the boys. For the cup!"

"Then they ought to get their own canoe," piped someone.

"That's right," Sean seconded.

Ellen swung around and glared at him, subduing him temporarily. The time had come to yank off the velvet glove of reason. She turned back. "There's only one problem, Willy. I'm treasurer of the United Fund. And if the Brownies are restricted from the canoe race, I can't ethically release the regatta hot dog money. No hamburgers, no Cokes. No Hostess Ding-Dongs," she added brutally.

Willy Norton was only a service-station operator. But he was a politician, too. He knew when he was licked, and how to divert the attention of the mob. "Let's go, gang," he said, glancing at the clock above the blackboard. "Half an hour on the basketball court, Pack One against Two, and the winner plays Three. The two best get canoes Sunday. The other den gets to cheer."

There was a howling rush to the door, and the two were alone.

"Sorry, Willy," Ellen said. "I know I'm stupid to make an issue of it—"

"No," he shrugged, "and you win." He seemed preoccupied. "Now, your *husband's* issue, that's another matter."

She asked him what he meant.

"Jepps." He sat back, studying her. "That Jepps thing is getting out of hand."

"Out of hand?" she flared. "Look, the *least* that idiot did was shoot a helpless baby seal. And he just might have killed those divers and blown up a boat—"

" 'Might have' isn't enough." Willy Norton sighed. "It seems every time this town starts moving, it stumbles on the chief of police."

"What do you mean?" she demanded. "A shark starts chewing up swimmers and he closes the beach until he can kill it. A maniac starts shooting up the beach and he puts him in jail! *That's* making the town *stumble?*"

She stared at him, but he didn't look away. "Brody was right to try to close the beach. Everybody knows that," Willy Norton said. "He's right wanting to prosecute Jepps, probably. But if he does, there'll be no gambling, and they'll have our butts. Brody's butt, and probably mine, too, for putting Jepps in jail."

"*Who* will?"

He smiled sadly. "The casino."

"Peterson is Brody's friend."

"Peterson's a *front*."

"No!" She stared at him numbly. "He owns it all."

Norton wanted to tell her something, but seemed afraid to speak. Finally he said, "You'd find out from Brody. So I'll tell you." He lowered his voice. "Behind Peterson stand some of the best Families in New York."

"Well, good," she said, relieved.

"Tuciano," he said sickly. "Di Leone, and our little friend's daddy, Moscotti—"

"Moscotti!" she muttered. By local legend, Shuffles Moscotti was the most vicious Mafia don on Long Island.

She was still staring at Norton when the troops returned.

BRODY arose and took Pete Peterson's empty glass to the kitchen, where he poured them both another Scotch. Then he took the drinks back into the living room.

"Pete," he said carefully, "I'm sorry. I like you. I like what the casino's doing for the town. But tearing up a parking ticket outside Starbuck's is one thing. Withdrawing these charges is another."

Peterson shifted his body minutely. Brody did indeed like him, though he was always a little too perfectly conditioned, too graceful, and too much onstage. Now his face was tense and his gray eyes steady.

"Brody, I'm underfinanced."

"Aren't we all?"

"*You* can get a loan."

"That's a matter of conjecture," Brody murmured. He got the drift suddenly. "You mean *you* can't?"

"Not from the bank. No more collateral."

Brody was shocked. His visions of the rebirth of Amity faded. "You're going to quit construction?"

No, he'd made certain arrangements. But if gambling hit a snag, the arrangements would fail. "And apparently, if you don't drop charges, it'll snag."

Brody studied his face. The man had come in from New Jersey—quiet, diffident, with a record as clean as the Pope's. Brody knew, because he had checked it out with Trenton and the state police records and identifications sections. It had taken three days, and he'd felt like Dick Tracy all the time.

"Well, I can't drop charges, Pete. I just can't."

Peterson looked embarrassed. He obviously did not like his role. "You're a good man," he said softly. "That's why I'm going to give you some facts." He moved to the solarium window. Brody followed. "I've taken in a few partners," Peterson said.

Brody stiffened. "What partners?"

Peterson seemed to be having trouble getting it out. "I *said* I had no more collateral. What partners do you think?"

Brody's heart was pounding. "Sharks?"

Peterson nodded.

"Who?"

"Di Leone, Tuciano." Brody had never heard of them. "And Moscotti," added Peterson quickly.

"*Moscotti?*" groaned Brody. Shuffles Moscotti was the only don he had ever seen in the flesh, an immense, quiet capo with bat-wing ears and a flashing gold tooth. He'd had a summer home on Vista Knoll for years, a storm-beaten mansion that had formerly belonged to the town physician. When Clyde Bronson had proposed the gambling law, Moscotti had almost bought the Amity Inn through Vaughan. Brody had yelled until Vaughan stopped the deal. Outside of that, and letting his little boy join the Cub Scouts, Moscotti had so far stayed as remote from Amity's real pulse as any other summer visitor. That was how it must remain.

"Why are you telling me now?"

Peterson looked into his eyes. "Because I like you. I like Ellen. If gambling doesn't pass— Damn it, Brody, *drop* it!"

"Meaning if I don't, we might get hurt?"

Peterson did not flinch. "I don't know."

Brody heard Ellen park the station wagon, heard Sammy yelp happily, heard Sean bounce into the garage. "Get out," he murmured. "Get out of my house!"

Brody opened the solarium door, grabbed his arm, and shoved. Outside, Peterson turned, his face shadowed. "Please, Brody. Drop it?"

"Move!"

He returned to the living room to find Ellen standing tensely at the kitchen door. "Where'd he go?"

She'd seen Peterson's car in front. "Out. The back way. Ellen, there's something to tell you."

"The Mafia? Norton already did. Oh, Brody, what's going to happen? You'll have to resign. Tomorrow!"

She sat down on the couch and covered her face. He sat beside her. Clumsily, he put his hand around her shoulder.

"Ellen, don't cry."

"You won't be able to handle this! You don't have the training, or the men, or the—"

"Guts?" he asked softly.

"You've got guts! But not the instinct for the jugular."

He felt sick. She was right. "Well, I'm not Serpico—"

"I don't want Serpico! I want you, in one piece!"

"Look, Moscotti's lived here for years. Nothing happened when I blew his deal with the inn—"

"Nothing *had* to happen! He knew he'd slide in. Now you're *really* in the way!" She wiped her eyes. "Over a seal!"

"And a trigger-happy bull who might have killed two divers and a couple of nice young people."

"'*Might* have killed,'" she repeated.

"Well, we ought to know Wednesday."

SHE had found the searching warships as evening fell and the depths turned inky.

Devoid of fear, without even the mechanism for it, she was impelled to remain in the area. In mammalian terms she might have been thought of as curious, but she was not: the eons had simply taught her that where there was action there was food.

At five fathoms, under the crisscrossing screws of searching destroyers and the higher whine of patrolling launches, she made her giant figure eights. Every few moments the blast of a vessel's foghorn would penetrate to her depths. She ignored such distractions, as she ignored the churning propellers above, but the

71

horns added to the general din and furor which glued her to the locale.

Her flat ebony eyes were highly sensitive in dim light, but it was pitch-black now, and her ocular inputs had been cut off by nightfall. However, they were the least of her sensory aids. Her ampullae of Lorenzini—tiny vials of a clear liquid, spaced around her head—could receive electromagnetic energy emitted by her smallest quarry. Sensitized now by need for food, the ampullae were processing every frequency through which she passed.

Her hearing was exquisite. Though her ears were only tiny ducts, they were, after millennia of development, perhaps the most efficient listening organs on earth. In the low-frequency range her hearing was better than the sonar operating on the great ships thrashing above.

But all of her receptors together could not equal her sense of smell. Seventy percent of her computer brain was devoted to olfactory functions. When she caught a whiff of blood, her brain instantly analyzed the speed and direction of the flow that was carrying it to her, and she homed without thought at its source.

She had been holding at five fathoms and a steady three knots for the last half hour. Suddenly a shiver passed down her length. She peeled off and commenced a gentle climb.

THE young aviation sonarman was fading fast. When he had heard the first faint sounds of search, he had wasted his voice uselessly.

He had no memory of the actual crash, just a kaleidoscopic recollection of spinning clouds, a whirling ocean, and the sound of his own screams. He had no idea what had happened to the gray-haired pilot.

He had found himself clear of the fuselage, hidden in fog. His right arm was lacerated. Automatically, he had inflated his life vest. And then had come hope, with the foghorns blasting everywhere, and despair as they moved away.

He had turned on his life-jacket light at dusk, and he still had the whistle attached to his vest; and his arm, though torn and bleeding, had gone numb, and that was a relief.

He had heard a helicopter beating somewhere above the fog. It did not cheer him. He remembered reading that the low-frequency sound of a chopper attracted sharks. He felt vulnerable from below. And when finally the sound of the vanes retreated, he felt more relieved than abandoned.

Now, suddenly, he heard a foghorn much closer than the others. He fumbled for the whistle and began to shrill with all his might.

THE j.g. stood on the starboard wing of the *Leon M. Cooper*, staring into misty blackness. He hoped that the skipper had seen him there, for it was not his watch, and he was the only junior officer who had felt obliged to come topside during the search.

He had begun to regret it almost immediately, when the chill penetrated his flimsy summer khakis. But he wanted to be sure he was noticed, so he stayed.

The foghorn twenty feet from his head cut loose with a gut-jarring blast. He thought of the risk of collision with the *Pritchett*, the *Kane*, or any of the other destroyers searching to port or to starboard. He shivered. A horrible thought struck him. If the *Pritchett*, for instance, loomed out of the fog and struck them, could he be held responsible even though off watch?

It was something to consider, and he was about to desert the bridge when he heard the faint shrill of a whistle.

He burst into the pilothouse. The skipper, coffee in hand, was sitting on his throne in the red glow of the binnacle light, peering out at the fog. The j.g. reported the shrilling, and the captain ordered all engines stopped. They returned together to the bridge. This time they both heard it, faintly, far off the starboard bow.

"Searchlight!" shouted the skipper at the signal bridge.

The light went on with a whine, but only showed a wall of blinding fog. "Searchlight off," the captain yelled.

They had wrecked their night vision, so they could only stand and listen. They heard nothing more.

THE young sonarman in the water had heard the engines stop, far away. He sensed from a rushing bow wave somewhere beyond the fog that he was very close to rescue. He whistled again, wildly. Adrenaline pumped through his veins, cutting his lassitude.

He saw a white glow a few hundred yards away through the fog. He raised his hand to wave and felt a piercing pain from his right elbow, where something jagged in the chopper had torn his flesh. His wound was bleeding faster. Thank God they were so close. He would not last long.

An awful conviction that he was exposed from below, from all sides, struck him. The ocean turned malevolent. He looked around wildly.

Then he lay back. This was not the time to panic. He would be safe within minutes.

A monstrous force tore him out of the water, tossed him high, arms and legs flailing.

He had a vision of himself, as if from above, enveloped by a dark shadow from the sea. No thought of a shark entered his consciousness; he'd offended somewhere, this was the hand of God. Mangled and torn, he knew nothing else.

THE j.g. pulled aside the wardroom curtains and stepped into the lounge. The launches and the captain's gig, dropped to search for the source of the whistling, were still out, inching through fog.

He'd done his part when he heard the whistle; he'd risk no mistakes by staying topside.

He went to his stateroom, undressed, and crawled into the upper bunk.

The stupid chopper pilot had screwed up the whole exercise by crashing, so he might as well get his sleep.

Chapter 3

MAYOR Larry Vaughan got up quickly from behind his desk and closed the door to his office. "Brody, you don't give a damn what you say, or who hears you, do you?"

Brody shrugged. "I figured everybody knew anyway."

"*I* didn't know, Brody. I resent the—"

"Cut it, Larry. If I hadn't screamed so loud, you'd have sold the inn to Moscotti two years ago."

"Well, I didn't know about *this*."

Not true, thought Brody.

To test the theory, he said, "I want you to suspend Peterson's building permit."

Vaughan snorted. "You're off your rocker!"

74

"Cancel his permit, or I'll go to the selectmen."

"The selectmen of this town," said Vaughan slowly, "are not going to flush it down the drain because a minor public servant doesn't think he can handle a small-time hood!"

"Well," Brody said edgily, "I can't."

"Maybe they'll want to find somebody who can."

Brody had a sudden inclination to rip off his badge and slap it on the mayor's desk. It would make Ellen very happy.

"Sure," he said. "Maybe you can hire Jepps . . . when I let him off the hook."

"Which, from what you've told me, better be pretty soon."

Before Brody could ask Vaughan what he meant, Len Hendricks knocked and entered. He saluted the chief like a Fort Benning recruit. A navy helicopter had landed a block away, in Town Square. Wasn't that illegal, or something?

Brody left to check it out.

At least for now he hadn't given up his badge.

BRODY pushed through the crowd surrounding an ungainly blue-gray chopper squatting on the grass. It had just destroyed half a row of azaleas that Minnie Eldridge had planted in the spring of 1956. He confronted a curly-haired navy pilot. On the collar of his khaki shirt were a pair of gold oak leaves.

Brody shook his head. "Look, Major, or whatever—"

The pilot stretched out a hand. "Lieutenant Commander Chip Chaffey, helicopter safety officer, Quonset Point."

Brody ignored the hand and asked why he thought he could land in the middle of Town Square.

"It's official business with your department and—"

"Would you land in Central Park if you wanted to see the N.Y.P.D.?"

"No, sir."

A certain pecking order having been established in front of the peasants, Brody decided not to arrest him.

The commander requested a police beach patrol to look for the bodies of the two chopper men lost the day before.

Brody pointed out that the officer was looking at fifty percent of the Amity Police Department, right now, in the persons of himself and Officer Hendricks, and anyway, wouldn't it have been just as easy to telephone as to blow down half the shrubbery in the only Town Square they had?

"Sorry, sir," said the pilot, disarming him further. "But I want to try to find somebody who might have seen the chopper from the beach, before the accident."

"My son did," volunteered Brody.

He sent the commander with Len Hendricks to see Mike, and left in the dune buggy to sweep the beach for chopper victims, diving victims, explosion victims, or whatever.

It might turn out to be a bloodier summer than the year with The Trouble.

ELLEN Brody, serving coffee in the living room to Commander Chaffey and Len Hendricks, caught her older son's eye. He looked away. Strange. She was certain that Mike was hiding something from the jovial man with the golden leaves.

"No, Mike," the pilot said. "I doubt if just horsing around with your buddy would have brought him closer. Unless he figured one of you was drowning or something."

"That will be the day," Ellen scoffed. "They're born with gills and they swim before they walk."

The commander glanced at her. He was attracted; she had sensed it from the moment he and Len Hendricks had arrived. She was used to that, but it was always nice to know that someone was out there looking.

"So just you and this Larry dude," said the commander, "you're the only guys who saw him?"

Mike colored. "Well, Andy Nicholas . . ."

"And Jackie," Ellen urged him.

"Jackie Angelo, I forgot," muttered Mike. "Her dad's a cop."

"Police officer," Ellen said automatically. She glanced at Mike curiously. Was he afraid of Jackie's father? Wasn't she supposed to go swimming? What had they been doing out there anyway?

But the commander seemed satisfied. "We won't bother them." He closed his notebook. "Mike, you know where the wreck of the *Orca* lies?"

"Does he ever!" breathed Ellen.

"My dad was aboard," Mike said proudly, "when she sank."

The commander had a theory. The missing pilot had been his

shipmate in Nam. He was a good pilot. The sonarman was inexperienced. If the crewman had goofed and dragged his gear too low, it could have snagged on the *Orca*, the only wreck around.

To find the sonar pack and try to decide what had snagged it might someday save another pilot's life.

Mike's face lighted up. He told the commander about their diving class. Andrews, the instructor, might let them search the wreck.

Commander Chaffey shook his head. Balanced on the verge of laughter, he said no, they'd use a UDT team from Quonset.

Ellen saw him to the front porch. When she asked if he thought the crew had survived, he said flatly, "No. Not anymore. Too long in the water, even if we find them."

And so the friendly wave from the pilot to Mike had been his final communication with the living world. Perhaps that was what was bugging Mike.

As Len drove the commander off, Mike appeared on the front porch, munching an apple. "What's a UDT team?" Ellen asked.

"Underwater demolition," he explained condescendingly. He was staring down Bayberry Lane. "Wow!"

Ellen followed his gaze. A low yellow sports car, mirror sleek and lethal-looking, drew to a stop at their curb.

"Ferrari Two Forty-six," pronounced Mike. "That's twenty thousand bucks' worth of wheels!"

Protruding from the car's passenger window was a familiar fishing pole. Her younger son popped into view, pulling the pole free. As she stared, the driver's door opened and a broad-shouldered, massively paunched figure in Bermuda shorts slid from behind the wheel.

It was a moment before Ellen realized who was shuffling up her front walk, with the strange, punchy gait that gave him his name.

Sean ignored her, dropping the pole on the scrubby lawn and heading straight for Sammy in the garage. Mike deserted her for a closer look at the car. The man kept coming.

"Mrs. Brody?" He smiled, baring yellowed teeth, punctuated by one golden canine. It was Moscotti. He held out a hand. Automatically, she took it and found herself staring into the man's flat black eyes, like a rabbit confronting a serpent.

"The chief in?" he asked.

"No. Yes. He's coming back any minute."

"Yeah. Me and Sean, we had a nice ride. Talked about Cub Scouts, the regatta, you know, town things."

She managed to draw her hand away. It felt dirty.

He chuckled, watching her. "Just wanted to tell your husband something, give him some advice. When I stopped, Sean, he climbed right in. Don't let your kids take rides."

Sean knew that, he *knew* it. He would never have let it happen if he hadn't been dazzled by the car.

"They don't," she managed. "They aren't allowed to."

"That's nice," he smiled. "Makes me feel I ain't such a stranger in town." He turned, joined Mike at the car, playfully punched his arm, and slid into the seat. He closed the door, stuck his massive face through the window, and said, more loudly, "You never know *who* might pick them up."

He pulled the car from the curb and took the corner at a good forty miles an hour as smoothly as a model racer.

It all came out. "Sean!" she shrieked. "Come here!"

He appeared at the garage door, bucket in hand, looking scared. He knew.

She met him at the side of the porch. "Don't you ever, *ever—*"

"I *forgot*," he whined.

She slapped him, hard, on the face. He had never been slapped on the face in his life, and he stared at her in silent shock. Then he whirled and went pounding to the rear of the house, heading for the mud flats. Mike approached the porch cautiously, as if she had gone mad.

She ran inside and up to the bathroom. She could hardly recognize her face in the mirror. She began to wash Moscotti's touch from her hand.

YAK-YAK Hyman checked the live bait in his shop and decided to replenish it, in case the cod ran again. He walked toward the bait cages sloshing at the foot of the pilings on Town Dock. Abreast of the police launch, he glanced down at Dick Angelo, working on the engine. Angelo looked up. "Hi, Yak-Yak."

Yak-Yak considered a nod. He decided against it. It could lead to Angelo's coming by the shop to pass the time of day, which could lead to his asking for a beer, or even one of the crabs that he suspected Yak-Yak took in illegal pots off the end of the pier.

Forget Angelo. Forget cops. Laboriously, he started down the rough wooden rungs to his live-bait cages. Halfway, he paused, staring. The neatly severed head and gills of a sleek fat cod was floating in on the flood. He leaned far out and snagged it with his bait scoop.

He climbed back up the pilings, walked to the end of the dock, and glanced surreptitiously around. He found a yellow line he had wedged in a piling, and pulled from the bottom a crab trap dripping mud and muck.

It was empty, so far, but the bait was so rotten he doubted any crab would touch it. He regarded the severed corpse in his scoop. Almost fresh enough to eat himself, but it would rot soon enough. He tossed it in the trap and lowered it to the bottom.

Some fisherman with a very sharp knife had chopped the body in two, for bait, maybe, or for cooking. And this half had slipped off his fantail.

Somebody's loss was always someone's gain; that was the ocean.

BRODY parked the dune buggy in front of his house and spotted his young son sitting dejectedly on the front porch. He had found no bodies on the beach, thank God. The chopper crew must have sunk or drifted out to sea.

Sean, who would ordinarily have been piping the news of the day by now, looked up resentfully.

"What's wrong, Spud?" Brody asked him.

Sean jerked his head toward the door. "Ask *her!* Dad, can she just *belt* a guy?" His voice was choking.

Brody smiled. "I guess she can. What'd you do?"

Sean raised his eyes, and they were without hope. Suddenly he jumped to his feet and ran to the garage. Puzzled, Brody entered the house.

Ellen was sitting at the bedroom window, looking out over Amity Sound. "What's going on here?" he asked.

She turned. Her eyes were bleak. "Did he tell you?"

He put an arm around her shoulder. "Oh, come on, Ellen. You've paddled him before."

"I slapped him. On the *face*. Like a damn fishwife!"

He couldn't believe it. "What did he do?"

She told him. Brody felt his legs go weak.

79

"A threat? You think?" he muttered.

She stared at him. "Last night Peterson warned you. Today the only hood this side of Flushing picked up Sean. Of course it's a threat!"

He looked out across Amity Sound. The sun was setting on his favorite view. The sand on the flats glowed golden. The cross on the spire of St. Xavier's, last point in town to see the sun, was getting its good-night kiss.

Well, the gun on his belt wasn't wooden and the badge on his shirt wasn't tin. No two-bit hood was scaring him, or anyone else in Amity.

He whirled, left the room, and flew down the steps.

MINUTES later Brody was parked in front of Shuffles Moscotti's sprawling home. He pressed the bell. The door opened and a boy of about ten, with Moscotti's broad mouth, but with soft Latin eyes, looked up at him. It had to be Johnny, of the Amity Cubs. Brody was surprised. He had expected to be greeted by half the Mafia of Queens. The boy smiled, and it was not a bad smile. "He's watching TV. You want to come in?"

The Moscottis had left Doc Ruskin's furniture, old leather easy chairs and worn rattan, as they had found it. A dowdy woman in an expensive black slack suit was curled in front of a stereo, selecting records. She got up awkwardly. "Chief Brody! Would you like to sit down?"

Brody shook his head, told her that he was not here socially, and would like to see her husband.

Moscotti, apparently, did not bring his office problems home, or she would have known why he was here.

Moscotti opened the door of what had been old Ruskin's surgery. He motioned Brody inside. The gangster had turned the room into a den. Books lined the walls, a massive desk glowered near the window, and a TV faced an overstuffed easy chair.

Drawn next to the easy chair was a smaller one, and on it sat a hulking, fresh-faced youth of perhaps twenty-five. He wore a flowing mustache. He seemed delighted at Mike Douglas, guest gushing on his show.

Moscotti turned down the volume. The youth seemed not to notice. "Dummy," Moscotti explained. "Nephew from Palermo.

80

Don't speak Italian, don't speak English, don't hear either, nobody told me." He shrugged. "Family. What am I gonna do?"

"Keep your rotten hands off my kid!" blurted Brody.

The gangster's eyes widened. He sat behind his desk and smiled, gold tooth flashing, but his eyes were rock hard. "Hell, I thought you come up here to thank me. Poor little guy, carrying that pole. Just thought I'd be neighborly."

"How long you summered here?" lashed Brody.

"Three years," grinned Moscotti.

"And after three years, the night after you find out your casino might not get to *be* a casino—"

"*My* casino? Hey, I ain't got a casino."

"—might not *be* a casino because I'm stirring up heat in the legislature, *then* you get neighborly? Bull!"

"Funny thing," Moscotti ruminated. "Everybody told me Amity was *for* a casino."

"Backed with Chase Manhattan's money. Not yours."

"Hey!" Moscotti began to laugh. He slid open his drawer and drew out a stack of hundred-dollar bills bound in a paper collar. On the collar was printed CHASE MANHATTAN BANK. "Hey, this *is* Chase Manhattan's. See?"

"It's dirty."

Moscotti picked up the stack and pretended to look at it. "I don't see no dirt." He tossed it across the desk. "You see dirt? Take it home, look at it good."

"You lousy punk," said Brody. "*You* take it home to Queens. *We don't want it here.*"

"Who's this 'we'?"

"Amity."

"Amity? You know what Amity is?" Moscotti stretched and yawned. "A mayor that can't make up his mind if he wants to be straight or a two-bit scam artist. Half a dozen selectmen you wouldn't hire to run a funeral parlor. And a couple hundred more yucks that know if the casino *don't* come in, they'll be digging clams in a month."

"This town," grated Brody, "beat a shark. It beat more hurricanes than you got soldiers on the streets. And it'll beat you, Moscotti."

"That's nice," murmured Moscotti. "That all you come up here to say?"

"No. Don't let my kids even *see* you again." Brody leaned on the desk. "Do you read that? Loud and clear?"

The black eyes studied him. "Hey, Brody?"

"What?"

"You don't have no other summer kids in the Cub Scouts. Who let Johnny in?"

"What's the difference—"

"Your wife, right?"

"She couldn't see why a kid should get hurt—"

"And what did *you* have to say?"

"I didn't like it. All right. About *that*, I was wrong."

Moscotti smiled. "Ain't fair, take it out on a kid. Very happy you figured that out. You should be happy, too. Very happy." He got up. "Don't push your luck."

BRODY sat opposite Harry Meadows in Cy's Diner and watched the fat editor drown his after-breakfast cigar in his half-filled coffee cup. "They're in, Harry," Brody told him. "The Families are in. And you and me have to get them out."

"I heard about Moscotti." Harry belched. "So what else is new?" He shifted, making the table between them screech. "Hey, you like Danish pastries? Try the bearclaws here."

"No thanks, and you better not either." Brody regarded the remains of fried eggs on Harry's plate, shoestring potatoes, ham, and cream cheese left from a bagel. "You're killing yourself."

Meadows speared a potato. "There are worse ways to go. You could strangle in the trunk of your car. You could blow up with the morning paper."

"Has Moscotti been talking to you?"

"He doesn't have to. And he knows it." Meadows signaled the waitress and ordered two bearclaws. He smiled at Brody. "You just *got* to try one of these, with butter, lots of butter."

"No thanks. Harry?"

"Um?"

"Print it."

"There's no *story*. Peterson needed money. He had to go to the Families. It isn't *news!*"

The waitress returned and set a warm bearclaw before Meadows and another before Brody. Meadows picked his up. "If you're going to have gambling, you're going to have gambling money, and that's Mafia money. The town should have known that going in."

"*I* didn't."

"Well, *I* did. And Vaughan did, you can bet."

"Then block the gambling law!"

"It looks like *you* will, if you just keep rousting Jepps." Meadows noticed that Brody was not eating his bearclaw. He slid it onto his own plate. "And how *is* your homicide investigation? What did you have on him anyway?"

Brody told him. Meadows sat, fork suspended. "That's all?"

Brody nodded. "Enough."

"No! To go to county ballistics, maybe. But not to get me to go to *press!* You ever hear of *libel?*"

Brody nodded tiredly. "Since you ask, noble scribe, yes, I have."

He left the diner. He had never seen Meadows more serious.

LIEUTENANT Commander Chip Chaffey, helicopter safety officer at Quonset Point, braced himself on the minuscule bridge of the aviation rescue boat that was anchored over the *Orca* wreck. He was nauseated from the ground swell. Years of shore duty had lost him his sea legs.

He accepted another cup of coffee from the skipper of the divers, a big, broad-chested ensign in a wet suit. The ensign had been sulking from the beginning.

"You know, Commander, how very futile this is."

Chaffey flinched. "*You* think it's futile. But those guys you got over the side, and your friend the porpoise, you got *them* thinking it's futile?"

"The men, frankly, don't care. It's bottom time, and they need it. But yes, they think it's futile. They know the ball will roll, and they know the currents. It's been twenty-four hours."

"And what about the porpoise?"

"Well, he wasn't exactly eager, was he?"

The team had managed to launch the porpoise, pride of their unit, at ten a.m. His name, imaginatively, was P-19. He was a Pacific bottlenose, trained to locate lost torpedoes, sunken subs, and stray bombs from plane crashes.

From the moment they anchored, P-19 had been an unenthusiastic participant. He had struggled as they eased him from his tank into his sling, chattering peevishly at his keeper. And when finally he had been winched into the water, he had refused to leave his padded cocoon.

There had been great puzzlement. His keeper had explained to Chaffey that P-19 was a perfect porpoise—trustworthy, loyal, obedient. He had once found a practice warhead in forty fathoms off Norfolk, and a ditched fighter off Key West. Last week he had followed the submarine *Growler* all night long, surfacing every quarter hour to beep his location to the pursuing forces.

Chaffey had stared down at the reluctant animal. He was nuzzling the side of the rescue boat as if it were his mother. "Maybe he wants a better pension plan."

Everyone had smiled, though thinly. His handler, circling in a rubber raft with an outboard engine, had finally pried him loose with an oar. Slowly rolling away from the sling, P-19 had tossed his flukes high and disappeared.

No one had seen him since, though he was supposed to surface every fifteen minutes. Now the handler was charging desperately back and forth between the rescue boat and the beach, stopping every few moments to shrill on a whistle. As Chaffey watched, the keeper zoomed up abeam.

"Sir," he yelled to the ensign. "He's twenty minutes over!"

"He's gone," muttered the ensign. To the handler he said, "Give him another five minutes. We'll call in and secure." He tossed a lighted cherry bomb into the water to recall his divers. "Damn!" he moaned. "You wouldn't believe the paperwork I'll have to do."

"They split very often?" asked Chaffey.

The ensign shrugged. "Sometimes. Not this one, though."

Chaffey tossed the contents of his cup over the side. The hell with it, for today. The pilot was gone, and if he had to depend on the underwater demolition team, they would never know why. But he was damned if he'd give up. He'd somehow get Disbursing to post a reward for finding the sonar gear. His heart sank at *that* paperwork, but he owed it to the lost chopper pilot.

THE porpoise had been ten miles to sea, and now, sensing that he had lost the shark, he was streaking back to land. He scanned the world ahead as he went, using his high-pitched clicking voice to envision the shoreline and the wreck of the *Orca*. Half a mile in front of him he sensed that the vessel carrying his keeper, who was also his god, was departing.

He had been born in a tank and all of his friends were men. He loved to swim with them and to find their toys on the bottom when they lost them. He was a sensitive, impressionable animal, and at present a little confused.

He had sensed a shark while he was still on the boat. He had squirmed under the gentle hands of his trainer, picking up vibrations of danger through the hull of the vessel, or from the air. He had no real fear of sharks. But into him had been trained a desire to warn divers when one was about. This he would have liked to do on the boat. But there was no way he could warn them until he was launched. So finally, after protesting every way he knew, he had permitted himself to be slung and hoisted.

Ordinary sharks avoided him. Instinctively, if he had sensed one near a school of dolphin with young in their midst, he would have attacked with the rest, snout centered on one of the soft shark targets, the ventral zone. His friends had not taught him to attack sharks, only to play at assaulting the gigantic steel toys he shadowed when they failed to beep properly. His brain began to marry the unprogrammed instinct to the learned program.

Suddenly, as he vacillated next to the boat, he caught the shark echo loud and clear. It imprinted on his massive cerebellum so monstrous a picture that none of the rules applied. For a moment he was immobile with fright.

It was approaching very swiftly. He knew instantly a good deal about the fish. He knew her sex, that she was feeding and desperate and would attack anything that moved—his own kind or his friends when they plunged in. He had pressed for a moment close to the hull, chattering cries for help. No one had understood. Then he heard the *klunge . . . klunge . . . klunge* of his friends as they dropped into the water, and knew he must act.

So he had taken a last look at the keeper, gulped a deep breath, and dived. He computed a course straight for the oncoming white. She sensed him coming, and he sensed that he had her complete attention.

By the time he had glimpsed her bulk, a hundred feet away and closing fast, he knew that she was not going to flinch like a normal shark to present a target.

86

In a flash she was on him. Unthinkingly, he twisted, spun, and felt the lash of her tail, lacerating his dorsal with its deadly little skin teeth. He had headed seaward.

Now he was crying in alarm, shrieking for other dolphins, men, anything to help him. He had no more thought of attack. He had no idea where she was, and was afraid to try to find out. Dead aft, he was almost deaf and could not echolocate, but he was afraid to turn to bring his sonar into play, for fear she would gain.

He bore seaward for ten minutes, starved for air but afraid to climb. Finally, five miles from the beach, he broached, taking a sonar reading. She was a full minute behind him. He lengthened his lead and began to curve toward shore, half afraid that his friends would leave without him, half afraid to draw the white death into their midst. But by the time he was fully headed in, she was six minutes astern and losing.

He skimmed past the *Orca* wreck on the bottom. His own boat was gone. His god had left. Confused, he circled. He had an excellent sense of direction and no fear that he could not overtake the vessel. He let his sonar rove for a moment, disappointed that his friends had left. With his echolocator he caught something lying on the bottom, and zeroed in on it.

A hundred yards toward the beach from the wreck lay a battered metal object caught in a rocky crevice. He broached, glimpsed the distant, departing boat, and dived for the plaything.

It was the toy they had come to find. He nuzzled it but could not move it. Now he was puzzled, with the boat gone, how to announce to his keeper that he had found what they were looking for. He paused, drifting and entranced.

First he would catch up with the boat. . . .

In his last moment he realized that he had been caught from astern. He knew an instant very much like regret as he twisted and tried to surface.

He wished they knew he had come back.

BRODY seated Lieutenant Swede Johansson across the table from him in a quiet little restaurant in Bay Shore. When he had seen the thickness of the file she had prepared on the Savage rifle and the blasted gas tank, he had refused, blue-plate special or not, to take her to the department cafeteria.

The file sat on the table between them now as they sipped martinis. He ordered a club sandwich for her and a hamburger for himself. It had been years since he had taken any woman but Ellen to a restaurant.

"So, what have we got?" He lifted the file.

Her amber eyes twinkled in the darkness. "Drink up while we're still friends."

He chilled. "Is it that bad?"

She nodded at the file. "I did a complete ballistics." She had test-fired three rounds from the Savage into the lab water barrel, and another two into a replica of the gas tank. The entry holes on the duplicate tank had shown a diameter thirty percent smaller than the entry on the exhibit.

He rubbed his temple. "Suppose what I brought you is an *exit* hole. Wouldn't that be bigger?"

"It's not an exit, it's an entry," she said simply. "I'm sorry, pal. It's no soap."

Brody stabbed viciously at the olive in his drink. What had done it, then? "*Something* blew up the tank!"

She asked him how much he knew about the water-skiers.

"The guy was an engineer from Grumman. They say he was very competent, a quality-control type. Wife was a secretary there. Just a nice young couple, is all."

He paused, remembering something. "You know, I saw them the day before? They were buying a ski flag at the aqua center."

"Why?"

"A safety device. You're supposed to fly it when you're towing, so nobody cuts too close astern. Nobody bothers to fly it much around Amity."

"But this guy did."

The waitress brought their lunch. Swede was deep in thought now, her coffee-colored brow furrowed. "You find any flares?" she asked suddenly.

"*Flares?* No."

"A man that careful, he might have had flares." She sat back. "Brody, the spectrograph analysis showed it first. Whatever hit that can was *loaded* with magnesium."

Brody regarded his hamburger. He didn't feel like eating it. "Tracers, maybe, from the Savage?"

"I checked the barrel. Every groove from muzzle to breech. There's no trace of magnesium in the *rifle*. Brody, it came from a flare pistol." She placed a hand on his. "A standard navy Very pistol, probably surplus."

He studied her face. She was dead certain.

"And why," he demanded, "would a man fire a flare into his own gas tank?"

She shrugged. "That's not ballistics. That's a field problem. You're the guy in the field."

"Yeah."

"You better start over, my friend."

He paid the bill, returned with her to the lab, and picked up his useless evidence. They'd forgotten, she reminded him, the pie à la mode.

"Next time," he said. "And speaking of forgetting, I'll drop my manslaughter charge on this suspect, of course. But I'll still look awfully stupid. Do you think you might . . ."

"You have the original," she grinned. "I'll lose our copy. We can't tarnish the image of the Amity chief of police."

He signed the rifle, ammunition, and gas tank out with the young sergeant at the desk. The sergeant asked him again if there was a vacancy at Amity.

"There just might be, if this leaks out."

Chapter 4

LIEUTENANT Commander Chip Chaffey wandered up to the officers' club bar at NAS Quonset Point. In the breast pocket of the worn green aviation uniform that would probably get him kicked out of the club if the duty officer happened in, rested a report on the chopper crash. It was a nothing report. He knew as little about what had caused his old shipmate to die as when he had started.

He sipped at a vodka and ginger beer. He was a bachelor, divorced. Like his old shipmate, he was one of a vanishing, hard-drinking breed who would never get any farther in the navy and had no desire to do so. His future stretched interminably. Countless hours aloft until, perhaps, a random engine failure or a fatigued engine bolt would strike him down. Or whatever had happened to his friend.

He scanned the bar. Two lone navy wives sat together. Their husbands were probably at sea on the *Grouper* or one of the tin cans. The hell with them. Navy wives seemed to get more faithful every year.

He decided to buzz over to Amity tomorrow. The police chief's wife had been cute. Anyway, he'd find the chief's kid or his diving instructor, and try to scratch up some enthusiasm for another search for the sonar pack.

He slugged down his drink. Next to the report in his pocket was a letter from Disbursing. He had asked for a two-thousand-dollar reward for anyone finding the gear; they had, predictably, authorized him to promise one thousand dollars. Well, that ought to stir interest in Amity.

BRODY awoke at seven to the blast of the Amity Neck ferry leaving her slip on the other side of Amity Sound. Since it was running so early, he knew instantly that today was Saturday. Summer and Saturday. For a long moment he lay still, certain that this day would not be a good one, not at all.

First, the damn ballistics report. He would simply let the whole thing slide. The problem would drift away if no one rocked the boat, and he still had the federal and local charge.

He stirred, unwilling to get up. Today Mike joined the muscular, seal-skinned ranks he saw in the pages of *Skin Diver Magazine.* He did not like the image, and turned restlessly.

The last of today's problems would be that of Sammy the seal. The wound was healed. He and Ellen had decided that this was the time to pry him loose, send him back to the ocean if he seemed capable, or to the Bronx Zoo or Woods Hole institute if he didn't.

He glanced at Ellen. She was snuggled into a ball. A bronze strand of hair shivered in the breath from her nose. He brushed it aside with his finger.

The telephone rang. *Damn!* He stumbled to the desk by the window. "Brody! Yeah?"

"Good morning," said Harry Meadows. He sounded edgy. "Look, can you come up to my office?"

"Do you know," Brody asked sweetly, "what time it is?"

"Seven oh eight," Meadows said. "We're in trouble."

"Who's 'we'?"

"Mostly you," Meadows said tiredly. "Just get down here, OK?"

"Maybe." Brody hung up. He slipped back into bed, slid a hand under the cover, and let his fingers trail along Ellen's thigh. Her eyes bounced open. She smiled.

The alarm blasted by his bed. In the next room Mike's transistor awakened, blaring. Outside the open window he heard Sean yelling at something. He gave up, tousled Ellen's hair, and arose for good. "I'll get your breakfast," she murmured, and plopped back to sleep.

He turned off the alarm and leaned out the window. Sean was hurling rocks at the water. "Hey, Spud, what do you think you're doing?"

Sean spun guiltily. "Nothing. Just . . . skipping rocks."

Brody, puzzled, dressed and went down to feed himself.

HARRY Meadows' tiny cubicle at the Amity *Leader* smelled of the salami-infested hero sandwiches he had sent up from Cy's Diner when he was hard pressed on a deadline. Their odor seemed to have penetrated the woodwork. As Brody entered, the editor swiveled his oversize chair, which shrieked in agony.

"What's the flap?" asked Brody. "I'm supposed to open shop at nine—"

"You may not *have* a shop," Meadows growled, "unless you can think of some way to get the *Leader* off the hook."

Brody was tired of people threatening to get him fired, and told him so. "To start with, outside of Hendricks, you'll never find anybody else stupid enough to take this job."

"Don't count on *that*," Meadows said. "When gambling comes in here, every vice squad dick in Manhattan will be crying for a job just to get in on the ice."

If Moscotti had truly bought casino control, he was probably right. "OK, Harry," he muttered. "What have you got?"

Meadows flicked a sheaf of papers across his desk. Brody recognized it instantly as a copy of the confidential ballistics report. "*How'd* you get this?" he demanded. "It's confidential! Why'd you *want* it?"

"It's the *last* thing I wanted. Did you ever meet Hollerin' Halloran? Counselor-at-law?"

Brody winced. "Jepps's lawyer?"

"You better believe it. Well, he brought me this. Suffolk County police sent it to him. Yesterday."

"I don't believe it," murmured Brody stiffly. He felt as if someone had pulled his seat out from under him.

"He *didn't* shoot at anybody, did he?" the editor asked.

"Just the seal."

Meadows sat back. "Thanks. You're the stubbornest SOB . . ."

"OK. What's the hassle?"

"Libel."

"It's not libel, Harry. All you said was I was investigating it. And I was! Where's the libel?"

Meadows shook his head sadly. "I'm not saying I'd *lose!* I'm saying I can't afford to fight! From my point of view, and the paper's, which as you know is all I've got, libel means bankruptcy."

Brody moved to the window, looked out at the street. Yak-Yak Hyman was leaving the diner, heading for Town Dock. To Brody's surprise he saw Nate Starbuck, who should have been opening the pharmacy, parking his delivery truck in front of Town Hall. A license fee to complain about? No, this was Saturday. Another parking complaint, maybe.

Brody looked at his watch. It was time to finish here, visit the aqua center, and then go to his office to await the blows of a summer Saturday.

He turned back to Meadows and asked him what he wanted him to do. Meadows rolled a story from his typewriter. He slid it across to Brody.

POLICE SERGEANT CLEARED

Amity Police Chief Martin Brody revealed today that his investigation into manslaughter charges against Flushing Police Sergeant Charles Jepps revealed no evidence of a connection between the inadvertent discharge of weapons by Sergeant Jepps on the beach and the disappearance of two scuba divers and a boating couple last weekend.

Ballistics tests on debris recovered from the ski boat proved conclusively that the explosion off Amity Beach last Saturday was the result of a flare gun fired into a gas tank, apparently by one of the occupants of the boat.

"Evidence exonerates Sergeant Jepps," Brody said. "All charges have been dropped."

"Did I say this?" Brody asked.

"Just initial it, huh?" Meadows handed him a pencil.

Brody tapped the pencil on the desk. " 'Inadvertent discharge'?" he complained. "No!" He crossed out "inadvertent," drew a line through the last paragraph, and wrote in, "Federal wildlife and firearm misdemeanor charges still remain." He signed his name and tossed the story back to Meadows.

"I was afraid of that," Meadows said miserably. "You're going down the drain for a stupid seal?"

"I got a couple of kids," said Brody, "who wouldn't understand it any other way."

MAYOR Larry Vaughan looked up into the gaunt New England face. He groaned inwardly. Starbuck had called three times in the last three days.

"Damn it, Nathanial," Vaughan exploded, "I've asked you not to bug me here. This is a township office."

"I pay township taxes," shrugged Starbuck. "Any offers on the pharmacy?"

Starbuck's cold blue eyes made Vaughan uncomfortable. He toyed with the idea of making his own offer now, just to get the old buzzard out of his office. But no, let Lena's illness back him farther into a corner. "I have some feelers out," he said. "I know it's urgent, Nate. How is she?"

Nate waved his hand. "Worse. Don't worry about that. Just sell it. 'Mayor' . . ."

There were quotes around the title as he said it, and a threat behind the bland face. It was time to drag out into the open whatever Starbuck thought he had. Vaughan was suddenly sure that he knew. The old jerk must have found out about Moscotti. Approaching things backward, as always, Starbuck must have perceived the gangster's involvement in the casino as a threat to business, instead of the opposite. And he must have thought of it as a secret, which it was not, that would embarrass Vaughan, lose him the next election, perhaps.

He sat back. "When's Lena scheduled to go into Memorial? *If* she is?" he asked slyly.

"Never mind. She ain't. Sell the drugstore for me, or you'll wish you had."

So he was right. Starbuck thought he had something on him. Vaughan relaxed. "And why's that, Nathanial?" he asked easily.

Starbuck smiled. He moved to the leather couch Vaughan used for afternoon naps and settled himself. "Maybe there's people in this town don't know everything you and Brody, and maybe some others, know about this rebirth we been waitin' for. Maybe they'd *like* to know. Maybe guys like you and Brody would like me out of town before it hits the fan, as they say."

A little brainwashing was obviously necessary. At that Vaughan considered himself a master. "Nathanial," he said heavily, "you're right. Unfortunately. About what may happen. I don't know how you found out about Moscotti, but—"

"I didn't say anything about Moscotti," said Starbuck.

Vaughan studied him, puzzled. Well, you couldn't figure out Starbuck. "He's got us *all* scared," Vaughan conceded. "He may save the casino. But," he lied, "it's not going to help legitimate business one bit. Trouble is, word's going to get around—"

"About Moscotti," Starbuck interjected thoughtfully. "You mean about Moscotti? Getting into the casino?"

Vaughan nodded. "When *everybody* knows, there *might* be a selling panic. You're right."

Starbuck made no comment. He seemed almost to have lost interest. A strange man . . .

Vaughan went on. "Well, even if Lena's all right, I know you want to sell. *I'm* willing to bet on Amity. Nobody from the outside is likely to make that bet, after the shark thing."

"The shark thing," Starbuck repeated sarcastically. "Right. Let's not forget the shark thing, Larry."

Well, if Starbuck thought the taint of the shark still lingered, fine. Vaughan sat back, contorting his face in thought. He drummed his pencil. He made notations on a sheet of paper, pretending to add numbers.

Starbuck sighed. "Cut the bull. What's your bid?"

Vaughan looked up, as if hurt. "Twenty-five," he said. "Thirty . . . I can maybe go thirty."

"The price is fifty," said Starbuck tartly. "And I wonder if Moscotti knows *everything?* He still vacation up here?"

"What do you mean, 'everything'?"

"He still in the Ruskin place?"

94

"Yeah. Look, Nate, you aren't going to offer it to *him?* Don't quote me," Vaughan said cautiously, "but having him in the casino is one thing. Selling him the town *drugstore* is another. I mean, narcotics and all? He finds a crooked pharmacist . . ."

"Maybe I won't *have to*," Starbuck said mysteriously. "Might be I can sell him something else instead." Again, there was a threat in his voice.

"What are you trying to say?"

Starbuck only shook his head and left. Vaughan watched him go. The hell with him.

The buzzer on his desk hummed. "Mr. John Halloran, attorney-at-law," Daisy announced. "Representing Sergeant Jepps."

Vaughan groaned and flipped the switch. "Send him in, Daisy. And get Brody."

BRODY parked his car outside the aqua sports diving center and walked in. No one was visible, but he heard voices in the rear. They came from an open door marked AIR—NO TANKS FILLED PAST PURGE DATE. He went in.

Tom Andrews towered over a fifty-five-gallon topless drum filled with water, set next to a whirring air compressor. Ringed around him were Mike, Andy Nicholas, Larry Vaughan, Jr., and half a dozen other potential mermen. They looked at Brody in alarm, afraid, no doubt, that he was going to throw another wrench into their dive.

Brody asked Andrews whether he had sold any flare guns since he opened up shop. Yes, he had. To whom? He'd have to check his records. He pulled out a Diners Club draft. "Last Saturday, to R. L. Heller, 1433 Myrtle, Lynbrook—"

"That's it," said Brody. He explained that the shattered gas tank he'd found had been torn by a flare, and Andrews winced.

"So it wasn't that cop?"

Brody shook his head. "But he still shot a seal."

The door jingled. Ellen walked in with Commander Chip Chaffey, the helicopter safety officer. Surprised, Brody introduced them to Andrews.

"He turned up in Hoople's taxi," Ellen volunteered, "so I brought him down."

She said it a little too quickly. Brody felt a stab of jealousy.

He stifled it quickly. During The Trouble, there had been a thing, maybe, with a young shark expert, but Brody had been too distracted by the shark to go into it.

"Mr. Andrews," announced Chaffey, "there's a thousand-dollar reward for finding that navy ball."

"Wow!" yelled Mike. "We'll look. There're thirteen of us. . . ."

Andrews glared at him. "You look," he promised, "you try *anything* but exactly what I tell you and it's your last dive. I'll tear up that exam you took and you won't get your card. The *navy* can't find it, and you guys want to try?"

Mike blushed. Brody felt the need to protect him. "It isn't the money, Tom. He was the last guy to see the chopper."

"It's the money, with *me*," Andrews told the commander. "I'll take a look next week."

Chaffey apologized for bringing the matter up in front of the class, and Ellen volunteered to drive him back to his chopper, which this time he had landed well out of town, on the abandoned airstrip between Amity and Montauk.

"I'll take him," Brody said, too quickly.

Rumbling through Amity with the commander, Brody rationalized. He hadn't been jealous. He just had a feeling that between Jepps, Moscotti, and the Amity *Leader,* the longer he stayed away from his office the better.

SINCE striking the porpoise the day before, the white had circled in a triangle formed by Block Island, Fishers Island, and Montauk Point.

She was patrolling the northeastern entrance to Long Island Sound. She was within a day or two of bearing her young. Her hunger—which would cease instantly when she birthed, to protect her offspring from her appetite—was flaring once more.

As she glided off Montauk Point for another sweep near Amity, a remora fastened itself by its suction-cup mouth to her lower jaw, hanging like a living whisker and nearly driving her into a frenzy.

Unsuccessfully, she had tried to scrape it off on an underwater rock. Now it hung listlessly, still alive and irritating her, but lost in her tunnel-vision need for food.

By the time she was off Amity, her young were squirming to be free of each other, and of her. The remora sucked relentlessly. Her hunger was white-hot, searing.

She was ready to explode on anything that moved.

HOLLERIN' Halloran was, at first, soft-spoken. He seemed simply a gnome with a bald head and thick bifocals. Brody wondered, for the first three minutes in Mayor Vaughan's office, where the little lawyer had picked up his nickname.

He did not have to wonder long. "So, Chief," Halloran smiled, "have I described the situation? That you didn't *see* the shots fired? You only heard them over the dunes?"

Brody pointed out that he'd arrived on the scene within seconds, had spotted the accused kneeling and ready to fire again, with his little boy holding his ears and his dog cowering behind him. "It's all in my report," said Brody.

"But there are two reports," murmured Halloran, more softly. "One from Suffolk County, a ballistics report. Ordered by you. Now, did you *see* my client fire at a skin diver?"

"Of course not."

A little louder. "A ski boat?"

"Nope."

"Anybody *else?*" A bark, with overtones of hysteria.

"Look, Mr. Halloran. This isn't a courtroom! When I'm a sworn witness, you can pull this stuff. Not now!"

Halloran gave no sign that he heard. "If you didn't see him shoot at anybody, then why did you call the Amity *Leader* with this?" From his briefcase he yanked the previous week's *Leader* and poked it into Brody's face.

"I told them I was investigating," said Brody, fighting for his cool. "And that's what they printed."

"That's what you *asked* them to print." The little man was bellowing now. "What you actually said—and my client heard you—was 'I got a pretty good suspicion that the divers and the ski boat got blasted by the same idiot!' Do you deny that?"

Brody was silent. "Good," said Halloran softly. He grinned. "That's slander. When he printed it, it became libel. The question is, why did you volunteer that? There has to be a reason."

"Your client was shooting up our beach. I like to let people know the police department doesn't approve."

"Look, Brody," cautioned Vaughan, "I don't think you ought to get in any deeper—"

"He is in deeper," yelled Halloran at full volume. "Your whole town's in deeper. You know why Brody slandered my client?"

Vaughan stared at Halloran dumbly, as if hypnotized.

Halloran leveled a skinny forefinger at Brody. His voice fell dramatically. "Gambling's coming in. Or was, until your boy here fouled it up. It'll be a gold mine for an ambitious chief of police. Jepps has summered here for years. He retires from the Flushing P.D. next year. You couldn't *find* a better chief. Brody knows it. Your two-bit local boy is afraid for his job. *That's* why!"

Brody found himself gaping at the little lawyer. "Say again?" he asked weakly.

Behind the thick glasses Halloran's eyes shone triumphantly. Despite himself Brody took a step toward him.

"Brody!" warned Vaughan. "Watch it!"

The mayor looked uncomfortable. He addressed Halloran. "Listen, Mr. Halloran, if Chief Brody can be persuaded to drop the federal charges—"

"It's too late," said Halloran. "The damage was done with the newspaper article. My client's a very angry man. I doubt if I could turn him around."

"Let's try," begged Vaughan. "Right, Brody?"

Brody looked into Vaughan's face. For a moment the mayor's eyes held his own. Then they dropped.

"No," Brody said quietly. He turned on his heel and left.

ANDY Nicholas looked like a fat sausage in his wet suit and knew it. He was always the last to succeed in cramming his porcine flesh into the tight neoprene pants. Now he had one leg encased, and the other foot jammed halfway down the vise-tight rubber. He looked helplessly around the *Aqua Queen*. Larry Vaughan, Jr., was busy brownnosing Tom Andrews, probably asking to dive with someone other than him. Larry always put you down. He glanced at Mike Brody, who was ready, as usual.

"Hey, Mike?"

Mike flopped over to him in his fins. He didn't seem to be sore anymore at the stupid spying on the beach. He grabbed Andy's foot and by sheer sinewy strength pulled it through the pant leg.

Mike was worth three Larry Vaughans. He had sure scared Larry that day. "You want to pair up today?" Andy begged.

"If you'll keep your eyes open for that thing," Mike murmured. "The sonar gear, you know?"

Andy nodded, although he had grave doubts whether he'd be able to keep his eyes on anything but the closest human form.

"Pair up," Andrews said. "And one last time. What do we do going down?"

"*Breathe,*" everyone chorused. "*In and out!*"

"And what do we do coming *up?*"

"Breathe *out, out, out!*"

"And how fast do we rise?"

"*As slow as our slowest bubble!*"

Andrews stuck up a thumb, looked around, and, God, thought Andy, he was going to pick Mike and him first.

"Brody and Nicholas, in the drink!"

They switched on each other's air valves, wheezed into their regulators to test them, and spit into their masks to clear them. Suddenly, Mike twisted and dropped into the water. Heart pounding, Andy shut his eyes and followed.

The world before his mask was a smeary jungle of bubbling green. He heard his strangled breath in his regulator. Suppose he had an asthma attack down there? He couldn't see. What was wrong? Then he remembered. He let water into his mask, deliberately swirled it around by shaking his head, expelled it through his nose valve.

Life turned brilliant. Mike Brody, already spiraling into the emerald void, jumped into clear focus in a storm of dancing bubbles. Mike paused, looked up, and beckoned.

Andy followed.

THE seal had spent most of the last five days bobbing helplessly in the placid waters of Amity Sound, off the mud flats, for she sensed her pup's presence nearby. When the wind turned southeast, she could actually smell him. She had eaten very little. The catch was scarce in the Sound at all times; she knew this. Had the pup been with her, she would have been far to the north by now, away from the white death which she felt always.

Devoted as she was, there came finally a time when her hunger simply impelled her to head to sea and hunt. So, this morning, she had barked farewell and broken away, skirting the shoreline of Amity Sound. She saw no cod, no haddock. This was strange, and could mean that the white was closer than she had felt.

She doubled and headed back to Cape North, where nervousness impelled her to beach herself. Here she rested for a while. But she still had not eaten, and finally hunger drove her again into the water. She sped to the place she had first lost her pup, but now she was intent upon only one thing. Food.

She was in the middle of a fifteen-minute dive along the bottom when she surprised a school of mackerel darting seaward. She took the largest fish she could see through the murky water, sensed a lightning communal decision of the school to turn north. She cut across its path and took two more. Appetite sated, she began to ascend.

All at once she felt great danger. She had got too far from land. She turned shoreward. Looking back, she craned to see if the white death was close.

She saw nothing, but all of her instincts drove her toward shore. She shot for the surface, gulped a huge breath of air, and dived again. She was faster underwater than on the surface.

This time, when she craned back, it was there, a dim gray shape homing on her, matching her speed.

Knowing in her core that it was no use, that it was all too late, she tore onward. Somewhere ahead she heard the strange, rasping man sound of divers.

Having no fear of them, she shot toward the sound.

ANDY Nicholas was ecstatic. Trailing Mike Brody's left hip, matching him kick for kick as their great flat flippers sped them along the bottom, he knew suddenly that he had found his world.

No asthma here, no dust, only pure air from the tank on his back. His breath was steady and easy. A fat boy could swim as well as a skinny one down here, more comfortably, perhaps, warmer under the layers.

He took his eyes off Mike and began to look around. The Long Island shoals were not the sort of thing you saw in *Skin Diver Magazine*. No reefs or waving coral. Mostly mud, with only a few dead shells to break the monotony.

100

A brief flash at the edge of his vision sent a thrill through him. It was a stingray. He moved closer to Mike, but he was losing ground. He turned on every bit of speed he had, and found that he was hardly keeping up. Damn it, they were supposed to stay together. Slow down, he protested silently.

Suddenly, off to the left, he spotted an oblong, man-made object on the bottom. He knew immediately that he had found the chopper ball, though he could not really credit it, not a thousand dollars' worth, not found by him when so many others had failed!

Buddy system forgotten, Andy swam to the thing. That was it, all right, black, mashed, with wires protruding. He was poking at it cautiously when he sensed a shape approaching. For a moment he thought Mike was returning. He had a flash of jealousy: the thing was his discovery, and now Mike would get half the credit and half the reward. Well, he didn't care. They'd end up friends and partners for life. The shape took form. It was not Mike. Astonished, he saw that it was a seal hurtling toward him. He cowered. Did seals attack humans?

It was almost on him. He waved it ineffectually away. It passed within five feet. He glimpsed a soft brown eye flicking toward him, had the strange impression that the seal itself was frightened. Of him, or something else?

He peered into the murk. What he saw sent a shock of terror through his nervous system, overwhelming his training, purging him of all but the simple instinct to leave.

A mammoth shark was tearing toward him out of the murk. He had a flash of an ebony eye, profoundly unthinking, and great tail lashing dimly.

He squeezed his own eyes shut, gulped in a great breath of air, held it, and shot for the surface. His lungs grew larger, as if asthma had cut off his larynx. There was something he was supposed to do. . . . He was supposed to breathe *out*, that was it. . . .

Before he broke the surface he knew certainly that the shark had been after the seal, had not even seen him, and he knew that whatever he had done to his body—embolism, bends, or paralysis—had been done for nothing.

Surfacing, he exhaled. But by that time it was too late. He tasted blood. The world went dim, and then black.

Mike Brody turned. He could not believe his eyes. Andy had been practically fastened to his leg not two minutes before. Now he had disappeared.

His first thought was that he must find him before he surfaced, or they would both lose their diving cards for not having stayed together. He tried to retrace his path, but he was completely disoriented. There was no way to tell, in the featureless waste, which was north, south, landward, or seaward.

He seached for perhaps three minutes; then, truly concerned, he rose slowly to the surface, breathing out, out, out. The water around him blended from brown to jade to aqua, and suddenly he broke into daylight.

He craned around. He spotted the *Aqua Queen* not fifty yards away. And all at once he saw his partner, ten yards off. "Andy!" he called, not too loudly. "Where the hell—"

He stared. Andy's nose was streaming blood. His eyes were closed. Mike swam over and grasped him. Blood from his left ear was oozing around the jawline of his wet-suit hood.

He arched himself from the water like a broaching marlin, shrieking for Andrews. He saw the giant run forward, slash his anchor line, and hurtle aft to start the engine. There was a thunderous roar as it caught.

Within a minute Andrews was plucking Andy from the sea like an air-filled rubber doll. Mike scrambled aboard. They roared home, with Andrews on the radio demanding a Coast Guard chopper to fly the victim to the decompression chamber in New London.

Brody sat frozen with fear at his desk. Shinnecock Bay Coast Guard did not know the name of the diving victim.

He hung up, rushed from the office, and rocketed down Main to Water, siren yowling. He skidded onto Town Dock. *Aqua Queen* was tying up. Everyone in wet suits looked the same. Andrews rose from a knot of divers in the stern, carrying a body.

But . . . a fat body. Brody almost collapsed with relief. A fat, sausage body, not Mike's. Andy Nicholas'.

He cleared his throat. "Get him in my car," he told Andrews. "Chopper will land in Town Square."

"Convulsion," grunted Andrews as they swept down Main,

siren wailing. His agonized eyes met Brody's in the rearview mirror. "Air bubble must have hit his brain."

They reached Town Square. The chopper was spiraling down over the homes on Amity Knoll. As Brody helped remove the body, Andy's eyes flicked open and met his. Brody reached out and brushed back a strand of hair.

"OK, Andy, OK, son . . ."

The boy seemed to try to talk. His mouth opened, his tongue worked. Brody bent close. "Yes, Andy? What happened?"

Andy's eyes filled with tears. He tried again. "S . . . awk . . ."

All at once the body went stiff, writhed, and convulsed. When the spasm passed, Andy grew limp.

They loaded him into the chopper. Andrews climbed in beside him. In minutes the whirring blades had disappeared.

Brody drove back to Town Dock. Mike was handing up tanks to the wharf. When he saw his father, he scrambled ashore.

"What happened, Mike?" asked Brody.

Mike made a move as if to come into his arms, then remembered the watching kids. "I was with him," he muttered. *"Dad, I was his buddy!"*

"What happened?"

"I *lost* him. How do I know what happened?"

"I have to tell his folks."

"Tell them their son couldn't keep up with the local Spitzer. Way it goes, tell 'em." Fighting tears, Mike stooped, heaved a tank to his shoulder, and started down the dock.

Chapter 5

NATE Starbuck parked his delivery van behind Moscotti's Ferrari on the sweeping drive of the mansion. He still thought of the gray, crumbling place as Doc Ruskin's. Years ago, when the old doctor had had his offices here, Starbuck had made deliveries often. Looking at the immense building, which must be worth a hundred thousand, he felt apprehension.

There were supposed to be hoods and bodyguards all over a mobster's home, from what he had seen on TV. Suppose, instead of paying for Starbuck's information, Moscotti simply had him killed? Bumped off?

Starbuck took a deep breath and jabbed the doorbell. In a moment a little boy opened the door. A tall, broad-shouldered young man with a flowing mustache towered behind him. He had a pleasant smile. He looked nothing like a TV mobster.

"Want to see Moscotti," Starbuck said. "Shuffles Moscotti." *Why* had he added that? "*Mr.* Moscotti," he amended.

Apparently, he need not have worried. The young man pointed to his ears, his lips, and shook his head. Starbuck could hear the mumble of voices behind the door to old Doc Ruskin's surgery.

Mrs. Moscotti, whom he recognized from her drugstore visits, appeared from the kitchen, wiping a plate. She smiled. "Well, but Moscotti, he is not in."

He *was* in, or someone was.

"I have something to tell him. It can save him a lot of money. It can maybe *make* him a lot of money."

"He will be in town tomorrow. I can ask him to see you."

For a moment he stood irresolute. The deaf-mute stood smiling. "He better come down," Starbuck said, feeling foolish. "I'll be in the store all day. Important."

The door closed gently as he left. He turned and glared at it. No-good foreigners.

He opened the door of his truck, stood lost in thought for a moment. He had given up on selling the store. He was sure that Vaughan was playing with him, letting him dangle. When the next swimmer got hit, the mayor would try to pick up the pharmacy for a song. But Moscotti would pay his way to Florida, and more.

Whatever he had in the casino, it would be worth lots to him to get it out. Nate had been going to ask ten thousand dollars for the picture.

On second thought, he'd ask fifteen.

SHUFFLES Moscotti leaned back in his swivel chair and studied the thin face of Hollerin' Halloran, then glanced at Jepps.

He had heard of the heat in Albany and he had expected this meeting, down deep. He had paid enough ice over the years to cops like Jepps. He expected no pig to miss an opportunity, nor a shyster like Halloran to dissuade a client from a blackmail attempt.

Amused, he lighted the jet on his desk lighter, played it over

104

the coarse tobacco in his pipe bowl. "Let's say," he puffed, "I *did* lend Peterson some money. X dollars, say." He loved the phrase. It made him sound like a government economist. "X dollars," he repeated. "Then I find out I ain't got nothin' for collateral because a tank-town cop stirs up Albany, so there ain't going to be no gambling after all."

"What tank-town cop you talking about?" growled Jepps.

"Take your choice, Sergeant," smiled Moscotti. He knew precisely what was coming and how he would deal with it.

The door opened and his nephew came in, heading for the TV set as if there were nobody there at all. Moscotti beamed at him. The young man lived in innocence behind his veil of silence. Moscotti was beginning to love him like a son.

He caught his eye, pantomimed whiskey pouring from a bottle. Instantly all three were sipping bourbon. Then the hulking youth settled himself in front of a Saturday night movie, volume off.

But the young man bugged Halloran. "He's staying?"

"He's a dummy," scoffed Jepps. "Can't you see that?"

"No," Moscotti said softly. "Exceptional. You understand?"

His eyes met Jepps's little green ones. The guy even *looked* like a pig, behind the folds of fat. "So get it off your chest," Moscotti yawned. "I want to go to bed."

Halloran explained that his client was facing a possible federal term and a fine. If he had a defense fund of, say, twenty thousand dollars, he'd be inclined to go to trial—to risk the fine and even federal prison—and not to rock the boat in Albany further.

"Bull," grinned Moscotti. "He ain't going to jail. Shooting a seal? And the fine ain't going to be nothing." The whole charade was suddenly boring.

Halloran's voice began to rise. "I can state categorically that unless the charges are dropped, which nobody seems to be able to accomplish . . ."

"That's interesting that you should bring that up. I was just thinking. . . . If Brody's the *only* one wants to press charges, there's a cheaper way to protect my collateral."

Halloran stood suddenly. "I don't want to hear about it. Neither does my client."

"Don't be too sure," muttered Jepps.

Moscotti sucked on his pipe. "Tell me, fat boy, what'd you like better? Twenty big ones for your 'defense fund,' or Brody goes up in smoke?" He caught a speculative gleam in Jepps's eye.

"Good question. Your problem, not mine," Jepps said.

Moscotti·put down his pipe, shuffled to the door of his den. "I'll give the 'problem' everything I got."

He watched his wife see them out the front door, stumbled back to his desk. He sketched a rough map of South Amity Beach, placed on it a mark for Smith's Sandcastle, and, offshore, inscribed an X. He shot a rubber band at his nephew's hulking back. The boy was at his desk in a flash.

He handed him the map and the keys to the Ferrari. He swiveled and drew from a file cabinet a twelve-gauge shotgun with a foot-long sawed-off barrel.

He pantomimed a beer belly, pointed to the door through which Jepps had left. He put a thumbnail to his teeth and shot it toward his departed guests in a vicious motion.

It was the first real task that Moscotti had entrusted to the boy. Tears of gratitude gathered in his nephew's eyes. Impulsively, he bent and kissed Moscotti's cheek, and then he was gone.

Maybe it wasn't the safest solution, reflected Moscotti. The death of a Flushing police sergeant would cause more heat than the death of the Amity chief of police.

But Brody's wife had let Johnny join the Cubs.

BRODY stopped Car Number 1 halfway up his driveway, switched off the ignition, and sat for a moment gathering strength. He had broken the news of Andy to Phil and Linda Nicholas, had detailed Dick Angelo to speed them across Long Island Sound to New London in the police launch, saving hours of driving.

Brody expected his own house to be in emotional shambles, with Mike's guilt and Ellen's preparations for tomorrow's regatta. Then there was the impossible task of reconciling Sean to Sammy's banishment.

He slid from behind the wheel and moved reluctantly through the side door. He built himself a blast of Scotch. He carried it into the living room. Mike sat in front of the TV, staring blankly at the tube.

"You tell them?" the boy muttered hopelessly.

Brody nodded. "They were OK," he lied.

"They sore at me?"

Brody shook his head. "Nobody is. But you."

"I don't want to race tomorrow."

"Sean hopes you will. *I* hope you will. OK?"

Mike finally nodded. "Is he going to die?"

"He'll be fine." He wished he felt as confident as he sounded.

"Dad, I think he saw the ball."

"Why?"

Mike shrugged. "He'd have kept up with me, you couldn't have *tore* him loose, if he hadn't seen *something*."

Something . . . Brody looked into his son's eyes. Did the kid, scarred like himself by The Trouble, think of sharks when he was in the ocean?

To ask him would start the whole lousy scene again. It was better for Mike and for himself to leave it alone.

Drink still in hand, he headed for the garage, where Sean was trying to teach Sammy to sit up and beg. But the seal was listless, dispirited.

"He's tired," Sean said. "He's happy here, now, though."

"He tried to break loose all week," Brody reminded him.

"That was before— No, he likes it here now."

Something was going on with Sean and Sammy, and it had to do with the tideflat waters below. "Spud, what were you throwing rocks at this morning?"

Sean's lower lip came out. "Just . . . throwing."

"Cub's honor?" He held up his fingers in the Scout sign.

Sean couldn't do it. His eyes skittered away.

"Another seal?" Brody murmured. "His mother?"

"I don't know," squeaked his son. "A seal, is all."

"And you threw rocks at it?" Brody said quietly. "Hey, Spud . . . that wasn't right!" His son was suddenly in his arms, crying. He patted his head. "Sean, tomorrow, before the regatta, we have to let him go. OK?"

"Suppose she's gone?"

"She'll find him."

His son pulled away. "You think?"

Brody nodded. "I promise."

Sean looked suddenly older, like a smaller Mike.

"OK."

Sergeant Charlie Jepps lay in bed, eyes bleary and open, listening to the hated boom of the surf on the beach. He belched. He had had bourbon at Moscotti's, and then had sat alone for hours at his kitchen table drinking beer. Every night since Brody had arrested him, it had been harder and harder for him to forget Brody's lean Boy Scout face and to drop off to sleep. And his wife compounded his insomnia. She snored every few minutes all night long.

From the beach below, the sound of a breaker began, with a distant ripping sound, building, building, then ending in a crash. His wife snorted like an anxious mare. The Amity foghorn bellowed. Cape North horn groaned back, far away. The dog began to howl at the flitting moon. Damn . . .

He rolled over, tried to sleep, rolled back, and stared into the night. At least the Moscotti thing looked good. He thought of Brody stuffed into an oil drum or sprawled in a Suffolk County ditch, and his spirits rose.

He was drifting off to sleep, despite the cacophony of surf, foghorns and wife, when the dog, chained outside, began to yelp. Another seal? Or a prowler?

He scooped his thirty-eight from the bedside table, grabbed the flashlight next to it, and padded onto the sagging porch. Still half drunk, he banged his shin on a beach chair. He dropped the flashlight, cursing, grabbed his leg.

The porch creaked behind him. All at once he knew that he had blown it. After thirty years he had let down his guard. Habit took him into a combat crouch, his gun instantly cocked. He was too late.

The muzzle pressed behind his left ear told him that he had walked into the valley of death. A long arm reached around him, almost gently, and removed his revolver. An enormous paw urged him from the steps.

Enormous? *The dummy!*

Prodded from the porch, he stumbled onto the sand. He almost fell. His assailant grabbed him. Jepps smelled Aqua Velva and mouthwash.

"Look, paisano . . ." he began uselessly.

He tripped again, on a scrub-crested hummock halfway from the porch to the pounding surf. He fell to his knees. The gun barrel

108

jabbed him. Somehow he scrambled up. "Hey," he choked. His tongue was thick. "Come on, lay off."

His mind was clearing. He knew they were plodding through hard, wet sand. The disembodied figure behind him crunched inexorably toward the water. Jepps's pajamas grew wet at the cuffs with the last retreating wave. What was he doing? Why couldn't he fight? He was leaving life like a pig trussed for the knife.

His limbs were limp. Everything moved slowly. He felt the rising water. He could hear his murderer splashing behind him. Now was the time, *now.* . . .

To seaward a giant comber was gathering in the moonlight. So apparently the dummy understood sound, was waiting for the boom of surf to drown the sound of his weapon, and the wave was growing, combing, reaching. . . .

The breaker collapsed with a roar like a thirty-seven-millimeter howitzer. His brain met the sound in a red-orange blast that, for him, would span eternity.

THE great white cruised north, gliding through ebony waters at the six-fathom mark. Her passion for food ebbed and flowed. Her young squirmed more and more violently to be free. When they were active enough, her appetite left, as it would leave at the instant of birth, to protect them from herself. When the furor subsided, she was famished again.

Off South Amity Beach, where she had earlier in the day taken the big female seal, she scented a trace of human blood.

She banked and turned, slashing through the surf for its source. When she found it, some subtle signal told her that the meat, though fresh, was already dead. By then she had severed a haunch and taken part of the abdomen.

Her hunger left. Tonight, carrion did not interest her. She shook loose the body in a cloud of viscera and swam on.

BRODY had been trudging the moonlit edge of Amity Sound for half an hour, barefoot. He had done this during The Trouble, for he had found ease from the pressure here, when he was the town villain for closing the beaches.

At the tip of Amity Point he found a boulder he remembered, and sat down. Five miles away he could see the Cape North light.

In three hours or so the tide here would be in raging battle with the sea, all the way across the entrance of Amity Sound to the great tide rip off Cape North. But now the tide was slack and tranquil.

The urge to be here seemed somehow tied in with The Trouble. He tried to dredge the problem to the surface of his mind. All afternoon it had slipped away when he had grappled with it.

Now he saw himself bending over Andy Nicholas, as the vanes on the helicopter beckoned impatiently. Whatever Andy had tried to say, he was *not* reporting that he had spotted the navy's ball.

"S . . . awk." Sawk? Sock? *Shark?*

Ridiculous. The shark was dead. If another had come, they would have known by now.

He started home. Low scud was suddenly racing in from seaward. There would be fog by dawn.

When he reached his house, he was tired. But he had a feeling that he could not sleep yet. He went inside, walked upstairs to his desk, and drew a book from a pile above it. Then, because he didn't want to awaken Ellen, he took the book below to the dining-room table, popped a beer can, and sat down.

It was *The Shark Book* by Richard Ellis. It had cost him a fortune: $17.50, discounted at Amy's Book Nook, during The Trouble. It was so beautifully illustrated that he had kept it, though he got rid of everything else that reminded him of those frantic days.

He leafed through it, looking for a painting of the great white he remembered. When he found it, enormous and chilling in pursuit of a sea lion, he tensed.

A few clippings soared from the pages. Most were from the Amity *Leader*, first vilifying him for closing the beaches, then extolling him as Amity Man of the Year when the shark was destroyed. There was another clipping somewhere, from the Sunday *Times*. . . . He flipped through the pages, finally found it—a yellowing, brittle feature.

GREAT WHITE SHARK TERRITORIAL?

WOODS HOLE, Mass., Aug. 15—Dr. Harold Lamson, chief of the shark statistical section of Woods Hole Oceanographic Institution, reported today at a symposium on shark behavior that recent findings cast doubt on the migratory habits of *Carcharodon carcharias*—the great white shark.

110

"Tagging of this species off the Great Barrier Reef of Australia, North Island of New Zealand, and Catalina Island off southern California is making us take a second look," Dr. Lamson said.

Lamson reported that while certain individuals were observed to stray as much as 1,000 miles from areas where they had been tagged, others seemed to remain near reefs and shoals where there was a good food supply. "They seldom leave it, and even, possibly, protect it from other predators."

The shark was dead. He had seen it die.

But if he had *not*, himself, seen it killed, what would he be thinking now? In seven days two divers had disappeared, a ski-boat skipper had apparently panicked and blown up his craft, something had snagged the dangling gear of a navy helicopter hard enough to structurally damage it, cod had run for the first time in Amity Harbor—for refuge?—seals had begun to crawl onto dry land, despite dogs and man.

If he'd not seen the shark killed, he'd have thought it back.

He turned at a movement behind him. Ellen, sleepy and provocative in a shorty nightgown, stood looking down at him from the steps. "Brody?"

"Yeah?"

"What you reading?"

"Just browsing." He closed the book carefully, on sharks and other nightmares.

There *were* no sharks. The shark was dead.

PART THREE—Chapter 1

BRODY awakened reluctantly to the sound of Sean's outraged voice drifting up from the kitchen. He looked at the clock. Seven fifteen. Ellen lay coiled beside him, smiling in her sleep. He kissed her, got up, looked out the window.

Already the night fog had burned away. It seemed that the regatta would be on.

He went downstairs. He spotted *The Shark Book* on the dining-room table. But the dark thoughts of the night before were gone.

The shark was dead. They were territorial. When you killed the one you had . . . you were safe.

He stuffed the book in a bookcase, under a pile of paperbacks.

Sean wandered from the kitchen and confronted him. "Daddy, he wants to take Jackie!"

"I'm *taking* Jackie," called Mike from the kitchen. "If Sean wants to tend the sheets, OK."

Sean's voice trembled. "She weighs a thousand pounds!"

Brody reminded him that the captain's word was law. "And don't forget, today's the day we launch Sammy."

He led the boy to the garage, tried to gather Sammy in his arms, and could hardly budge him. The seal must have gained twenty pounds. He straightened. "Go get Mike."

Sean shook his head. "Sammy!" he called.

The seal shot Brody a look of scorn and floundered toward the boy. Sean flipped him a mackerel from a bucket filled yesterday at Amity Market. The seal caught it expertly. In Brody's mind a cash register rang up eighty cents a pound. Sammy gulped, reared his body, and clapped his flippers modestly.

"Cute," said Brody. "But let's go, chum."

Sean's china-blue eyes pleaded for a moment with his own. Then the boy capitulated. Taking the bucket of fish, he led the way. Sammy wallowed after him—down the bluff, across the hard sand, and to the water's edge. To Brody's surprise, Sean was right. The seal didn't want to go in.

He heard Ellen calling him from the bedroom.

"Brody! Len Hendricks. Morning emergency!"

Brody ran toward the house. "Leave him," he called back to Sean. "He'll go." His anger rose with every step. Poor Sammy, Sean's agony, their stinking garage, were all Jepps's fault. He picked up the downstairs phone. "Yeah, Len?"

"Missing person. Wife just called."

Len couldn't handle *that*? "Who?"

A pause. "Charlie Jepps."

Brody moaned.

SHUFFLES Moscotti watched as his son and nephew lifted Johnny's Laser off the trailer behind his Ferrari. They carried it together down the Amity Boat Club ramp and launched it. He noted

112

a gay little power cruiser tied to the dock, festooned with pennants. On it a banner read COMMITTEE BOAT—FINISH LINE.

Little girls—the Brownies, he assumed, that Johnny had complained of—were paddling a canoe. They had just lost a race to a canoe full of boys—Johnny's Cub Scout pack.

When the boys saw Johnny, they waved. Moscotti glowed. His boy had no friends in Queens, but Amity was another matter, and he felt a surge of affection for the town.

He noticed Ellen Brody at the end of the dock, dressed in a den-mother uniform. *Bellissima!* Great hips. Long legs. He moved to where she stood talking to another woman. Ellen shot him a startled glance. Her eyes grew hard. She turned away.

He should have been angry, but instead found himself amused. He had a crazy inclination to tell her he had just spared her husband's life and murdered Brody's enemy.

He grinned widely, glanced at a row of trophy cups glittering on a weathered bench. He took a fifty from his wallet, dropped it into the largest cup. "Bonus. Maybe Johnny'll win."

"Amateur race," Mrs. Brody said grimly, plucking it out.

"For hot dogs, then?"

"Come on, Ellen," pleaded the other woman.

Mrs. Brody colored. "OK," she said finally. "Thanks."

He shuffled back up the dock. Amity was good to him, he was good to Amity. He climbed into his car to wait for the start. After a while he dozed in the misty sunlight.

TOM Andrews had spent the night in the decompression chamber with Andy Nicholas. The boy was paralyzed, conscious, but couldn't articulate. There were two air bubbles in his brain.

It brought to mind another night, years before, when Tom's abalone partner had died screaming in a tank in Port Hueneme, California, driving him east to forget. Now, bare-chested and still wearing wet-suit pants, he stood with the Nicholases in the X-ray lab and watched Andy wheeled from the room.

The tall, white-haired neurosurgeon was supposed to be the best in Connecticut. Stepping to the viewer, he radiated confidence. He wanted to enter the frontal lobe and relieve the pressure on the left hemisphere that was caused by one of the two air bubbles. The trouble was, it was a high-risk procedure.

114

. He went on paternally, speaking as if to children and only occasionally falling into medical jargon. "The circulation to the *motor* cortex seems to be improving. Meaning that this *upper* bubble is resorbing. It's the pressure of this *lower* embolus here"—he pointed—"embarrassing circulation to the Wernicke area—his *speech*—that concerns me. I think we have to relieve it."

"Will it work?" begged Linda Nicholas.

"It's our best shot," the doctor said simply. "Aphasia is living death."

"We're not wealthy," blurted Andy's father. "You should know that—"

"I can help," cut in Andrews. "I'm closing up, but I've got stock. If I have to, I'll dive scallop."

Linda's eyes filled with tears, and before she could thank him, he left the room. He wanted to say good-by to Andy and, if he could, lend him strength.

ELLEN Brody joined Willy Norton, race committee chairman, at the end of the boat club dock.

He was studying the haze to seaward. The committee boat was returning from Cape North light, having anchored the racing buoy in the shallows of Amity Sound, a quarter mile off the lighthouse.

Ellen had made the orange pennants for the buoys, and she squinted into the distance to see whether her flags showed through. It was too far away. Even the Cape North light seemed dwarfed, but maybe younger eyes in the dinghies and Lasers could make out her work better.

"I don't know," Willy said doubtfully. He turned and scanned the spectators. He spotted Yak-Yak Hyman, chewing on a hot dog at the refreshment stand.

"Yak-Yak," he called, "we going to have fog?"

Yak-Yak looked at him in amazement. To expect a man of his dignity to reply in public at such distance was almost more than reason could bear. He shrugged, shook his head in disgust.

"Going to get foggy?" Willy asked Harry Meadows.

The editor smiled kindly. "I don't know. I never read the paper."

"Oh, Willy," exploded Ellen. "You've lived in Amity all your life! Can't *you* decide?"

Willy looked at her reproachfully. He turned and surveyed the dinghies, Lasers, Flying Dutchmen, and classless vessels jostling the pilings below. There were fifteen entries, Ellen noted, and Larry Vaughan, Jr., was going to win. He sailed alone, and handled his craft like a pro, as Mike could do when he wanted.

Her eyes fell on Mike's poor *Happy Daze,* burdened with Sean and Jackie. "Sean," she called, as quietly as she could over the water, "ask Larry if he'll take you to crew. You guys are going to *sink!*"

"Tell *her.* I earned a spot on this boat."

Jackie grinned up at her in a flash of silver bands. Lithely, the girl rose and grasped the mast. She seemed ready for sacrifice. "I'll watch, Mrs. Brody. I don't want to—"

Mike reached up and grabbed the seat of her shorts. "You stay," he said. "Nerdhead can go if he wants."

Sean, insulted, looked around wildly and asked Johnny Moscotti if he could sail with him. Johnny nodded, brought his boat alongside, and Sean leaped in with a wild, froggy movement that almost capsized them both.

"Is it yes or no?" Ellen demanded of Willy.

Reluctantly, he nodded. Through a bullhorn borrowed from Brody, he lined up the crazy armada below.

The one-minute warning blew, then the thirty-second warning, then the flag and the cannon, and they were off. Incredibly, Mike took the lead. But Larry Vaughan, Jr., was in hot pursuit.

ANDY Nicholas lay in the dreamy haze of a strange, foggy coma. He could think quite clearly sometimes, recognize mother, father, and Tom Andrews by sight, although he had forgotten everyone's name and even the words for what they were.

He could not move anything but his left hand. And he could not talk. This he had realized almost from the first. He could not understand why.

What he heard made sense for an instant and then disappeared forever just as he was beginning to understand.

But he could recall his dive with perfect clarity. He had been following Mike through the green murk, and he could see Mike's bubbles now. The bubbles had soared away to the surface, and then he had seen the oblong, beat-up object on the bottom, with its rows of scratches—scratches he associated with the horror he

116

had seen later—but which he could not name. And the terrified thing like a dog with flippers—he could not remember what it was called. And then . . .

Andrews was looking down into his face. Andy wanted to tell him what he had seen. He tried to remember what the things were called—the sonar ball, the seal, the shark. What were their names? What was his own?

The bearded man wiped Andy's mouth with a Kleenex. Andy peered into his eyes. He knew that he had failed the giant, as he had failed in everything all his life. He wanted to explain that anybody, *anybody* would have panicked. . . .

The thing had been as big as an airplane, and coming just as fast. He tried to say it with his eyes: the gaping mouth, full of gleaming teeth. . . . "Tee . . ." he managed.

Andrews stared, grinned suddenly. Excitedly, he pushed a button hanging from the bed. A nurse came in. In a daze Andy heard him ask if he could have tea.

No, no, whatever that was, it wasn't what he'd meant.

The nurse shook her head. "Preop. Nothing." She looked startled. "He *asked* for it?"

"I think so."

"Wonderful!" she cried, and left.

Andy tried again. It wasn't fair.

"Baa . . ." he gasped.

Andrews leaned closer. "Baa . . . ?"

Andy lifted his left hand. He tried to form it into a round thing like a . . . a *what*? Already he had forgotten.

"Ball?" yelled the giant. "The sonar ball, Andy?"

Andy felt faint. He could not think, could not remember.

The giant stood up. "I'll dive on it. I'll find it for you."

Andy's mind drifted back suddenly. Dive? No! Danger there, the thing with teeth. . . . *Shark?*

He had the word on the tip of his tongue, fumbled with it, and lost it. Then he floated into sleep.

Tom Andrews stared down at the chubby, whitened face. He had no idea what the operation would cost, but the thousand bucks should help.

He called Chip Chaffey at NAS Quonset Point. The least the navy could do was fly him home to dive for its stupid ball.

For half an hour Ellen Brody had been sitting at the commodore's desk in the boat club shack. She had totaled receipts at the hot dog stand and sent three honest teenagers to the deli with Moscotti's fifty dollars to buy hamburger meat and rolls.

When she finished, she looked out the window and chilled. She could still see the sails bobbing toward Cape North light. But behind the cape the ocean blended imperceptibly with a gray pall that meant, to her at least, that fog would shortly be oozing into the mouth of Amity Sound.

She wandered outside to look for Willy Norton. She found him drinking a beer with Larry Vaughan and drew their attention to the haze forming to seaward.

"Hell, Ellen," Larry Vaughan said, "nobody gets lost in Amity Sound!"

"The tide's starting out," she reminded him.

"It does that," he admitted, "twice a day."

She deferred to male insouciance and had herself one of Moscotti's hamburgers.

But when she went back to the boat club shack, she surprised Willy Norton, who was on the phone calling Shinnecock for the Coast Guard forecast. He hung up.

"Well . . . it's iffy." He moved to the window. "They say if the temperature goes down, we'll have fog. If the sun heats things up, we're home free."

"Remarkable," Ellen said dryly. "Are you going to recall them?"

"They're halfway across. We'd have to send a boat. They'd never hear the cannon now."

"So what are you going to do?"

He looked at his watch. "We'll give it another half hour."

Brody hung up the phone on his desk. He had already cruised along the beach, checking every dune and hillock. Unable to find Sergeant Jepps, he had become more and more concerned. Finally he had called in everything but federal troops.

He'd heard the cannon shot that signaled the start of the sailboat race, and he was angry at life for keeping him from seeing it.

Len Hendricks was exultant. "Solves our problem, right, Chief? I mean, if he took off? Fugitive, federal warrant! Maybe he left the state!"

118

"Suppose he got wasted," remarked Brody, "as you war heroes put it."

"Solves it even better!"

"Does it, Len?" Brody asked heavily. "Does it really?" He heard a loud thrumming, suddenly, outside. He threw open the window and saw a navy chopper suspended over Town Square.

Damn! He moved swiftly to Car Number 1 and drove three blocks. The chopper had already landed, destroying three of Minnie's five remaining azaleas. Out of the door dropped Tom Andrews, still in a wet suit.

Brody confronted him. "How's Andy?"

Andrews gave him the news, not all bad, but bad enough. And he wanted to dive as soon as possible: nobody could tell how the navy's ball would wander on the bottom. Chaffey emerged from the hatch behind him, apologizing again for landing in Town Square.

Brody regarded the huge craft. It was gathering a crowd of tourists. Even spectators from the boat club dock were wandering up to look. Well, it was in a good cause.

The commander was looking past him eagerly. Brody turned. His wife was moving through the gathering throng.

"I thought you were counting sailboats," Brody said.

She told him that the fog was coming in, you couldn't see the sails anymore, and the committee boat wouldn't start. She seemed genuinely worried, and now he was, too. He glanced seaward. The soup would be coming in, all right, and they ought to be recalled. How? The Coast Guard? Maybe. Or . . .

He turned to Chaffey. "You got a PA system?"

"I'll recall them." Chaffey nodded, then turned to Andrews. "Can you dive it alone?"

"I'll follow his bubbles," said Brody. "I've done it before."

Chaffey climbed into his craft. The chopper burst into whirling life. In a few moments it was aloft.

So much for the last of Minnie's azaleas, Brody reflected, driving Andrews to the *Aqua Queen*.

MIKE Brody trimmed his sail and brought the boat more tightly on the wind. Jackie moved her bare feet—the most beautiful feet in the world—under the hiking strap which ran along the length of the cockpit. She leaned far to windward, helping him stiffen the boat against the wet rising breeze. She was strong, he reflected, for a girl, and had all the right moves on a boat.

At least he had got rid of Sean, always restless and erratic, scrambling port and starboard. Sean, with the Moscotti kid, was somewhere in the crowd of sails behind him.

And somewhere ahead, hidden by the belly of his own sail, was Larry Vaughan, Jr. Mike dropped his head to peer under the boom. He spotted Larry in the hazy sunlight. He tried to gauge whether they were gaining. He thought so. And with Jackie helping him stiffen the boat, he had a better chance than Larry of pointing high enough to round the racing buoy anchored off the tide race at Cape North.

Jackie turned aft, grinning, her braces forgotten. "Mike doll, this is it!" She reached over and ran her finger down his leg.

She was torturing him! The boat wandered to windward, luffed, and he lost fifty feet on Vaughan.

The Cape North horn groaned mournfully, two miles ahead. Fog approaching? Turn back? No, never. Not the famous Spitzer of Amity Beach.

He had no fears for themselves. Only for Sean and the Moscotti kid. He didn't think they could find their butts with both hands in clear weather; what they'd do if the fog rolled in, he hadn't the slightest idea.

YAK-YAK Hyman wandered back from the crowd around the boat club. He looked at the lonely length of Town Dock with distaste. His bait shop was deserted. The regatta had taken away the fishermen he might have expected this morning. Damn fool kids, and their parents . . .

He moved to the end of the pier, checking to make sure that Dick Angelo was not back from New London. Then, furtively, he pulled up the illegal trap.

No crabs had crawled in to investigate the half a cod he had placed in it for bait. He lowered it again, spitting in the water for luck.

He suddenly noticed, bumping the pilings, a submerged but solid shape three or four feet under the oily water. At first he thought it was a bale of engine-room rags, lost overboard from a passing freighter.

120

Curiously, he half descended the wooden rungs in the pilings. In the hazy sunlight, the water, under its sheen of oil, shimmered with dancing colors, just enough in the ebbing tide to obscure the object.

He climbed down three more rungs to get a better view.

SHUFFLES Moscotti awakened in the driver's seat of his Ferrari. He had dozed and missed the start of the race.

He glanced at his nephew, sitting in silence, dark eyes peaceful and half lowered. No ulcers there, no heart attack. The kid would live forever.

The race would take two hours. Moscotti decided to find out what the local druggist wanted. He checked for Brody's squad car, made a fast U-turn, and minutes later was leaning on the pharmacy counter.

Starbuck's lean horseface twisted into a smile. "No, Mr. Moscotti. It ain't got to do with narcotics. I'm a reputable licensed pharmacist."

"So why am I here?" Moscotti asked, pleasantly enough. He would make friends with these people or die trying.

Starbuck seemed to come to a conclusion. "They tell me you got a piece of the casino."

Moscotti simply stared at him. The druggist's face, as he had known it would, turned red.

"I heard it's a big piece. So anything hurts tourism," said Starbuck, "will hurt you, too. Me, Larry Vaughan, even Brody. Anyone who owns land. Willy Norton—we're all in the same boat."

Enough of this, Moscotti decided abruptly. "You told my old lady you had something to say. What is it?"

Starbuck rubbed his hands across the keys of the oldest typewriter Moscotti had ever seen. The druggist said, "I'm giving you a chance to get off the boat first. It's going to sink. You remember The Trouble?"

"You had a *shark*. Say shark. What's this 'Trouble' bull?"

"Suppose it was back?"

Moscotti hoped it was. A *pack* of sharks might be a good thing, to keep the sheep at the tables, where they belonged. "If your shark don't shoot craps, what do I care?"

Starbuck looked shocked. "You got a *hotel* there, too, people going to swim, kids want to play in the water. Only they ain't. Shark never left!"

"It was killed. I read it."

"Brody *said* it was killed."

Moscotti wondered what the idiot expected to get for a rumor.

Starbuck went on. "I ain't told anybody else. Prices are up, now. If I tell Harry Meadows, at the *Leader* . . . property prices'll go . . . wham!"

"*I* don't believe your shark."

Starbuck's mouth worked nervously. "I got a picture."

"Let's see it," Moscotti suggested, mildly interested.

Starbuck began to sweat. "It's worth money."

Moscotti grinned. He took a bottle from the counter and hurled it across the store at his nephew's back. The boy was instantly at his side. Moscotti pointed to a row of patent medicines. The boy kicked the shelf under them. They crashed satisfyingly. Starbuck yelped as if in pain. Moscotti nodded again. The kid overturned a perfume case. The scent of a thousand roses filled the store. Moscotti turned back to Starbuck. "Picture worth *that?*"

Starbuck gulped like a landed fish. "Lena? *Lena!*"

Mrs. Starbuck appeared at the back doorway. She was a skinny old bag, and terrified.

"The picture?" Moscotti proposed pleasantly.

Starbuck's lips pursed. "No!"

Moscotti flicked his eyes at his nephew. A stubby thirty-eight appeared in the boy's hand.

"The safe," Starbuck croaked. "We got to open the safe."

Yak-Yak Hyman, suspended over water, stepped down another rung in the pilings. Whatever was in the water floated upward. He swung away from the pilings, reached out a rubber boot, and prodded it. It broke surface. He almost let go. He heard someone screaming, and realized that it was himself.

Below, breaking the surface, was the headless torso of a man. Bits of flesh streamed from what had been the jaw and upper neck. A huge whitened cavity gaped where the chest had been. The right leg hung from a band of flesh, as if suspended from a rubber band, and from it, streaming seaward, hung a striped pajama leg.

Still shouting, he scrambled up the pilings, looked around wildly.

Dick Angelo, returning from New London, was rounding Amity Light, a good half mile away. He yelled at him. Too far.

Chattering incoherently, he sprinted for Starbuck's.

MOSCOTTI waited as Starbuck fumbled with the combination to the safe. The druggist was too nervous to open it. Moscotti shoved him away. The safe was an old Sentry, and tumbled in thirty seconds.

Moscotti stepped politely back and motioned Starbuck. The druggist shambled over, dropped to his hands and knees, and pulled out a long envelope. From that he pulled a strip of film. Moscotti took it to the light. It had two pictures at the end. He gaped, felt for his glasses, and inspected it more closely.

His heart began to pound.

He had not really understood. He had seen sharks when he took his son to Sea World, but they were tearing at hunks of meat for the tourists. They bore no relation to the monster on the film. "My God . . ." he gasped.

Above a cowering scuba diver loomed an enormous shadow, blending into a mammoth mouth studded with gray-white teeth. In the murky background he sensed the sweep of a tail that was as tall as his nephew.

A chill began in his gut, spread to his legs and arms. *Johnny* was on the ocean, and the shark could still be there.

"When?" breathed Moscotti. Suddenly, viciously, he kicked the kneeling, cringing Starbuck in the groin. The tall man hugged his knees, whimpering. "When was it here? Who took this?"

"Divers . . . Last week," moaned Starbuck.

Moscotti felt a rage take hold of him greater than any anger he had known. And fear, more fear than he had ever felt, because it was not for himself, but for Johnny.

The monster on the film could smash a boat like his son's to powder, razor his boy in half with a flick of the tail, grind his flesh to pulp.

He looked down at Starbuck. He did not see him groveling on the floor; he saw him lying in a deserted quarry near Queens, a wire trussed from his neck in a way he knew, to backward-bent legs, feet upturned, head thrown rearward, writhing as he tried to ease the pressure, legs straining for slack, hour after hour. . . .

And the old lady, she'd known, too; she would be watching him die and wondering if she was next. . . .

"*Shark!*" someone screamed from the drugstore door. "Shark's back! There's a *man-eater* out there, somewhere."

Moscotti swung around. It was the fish guy from the pier. "Where?"

"There's a body in the harbor," the man chattered. "Telephone! Brody . . . Nothing hardly left."

"A *kid's* body?"

The man, babbling hysterically, was trying to dial the phone. "No head. All chewed up—" He got through. "Brody? Len?"

Moscotti was filled with sudden calm. It *couldn't* be Johnny. There hadn't been time. It was probably Jepps. Sure, Jepps, who else? But what now? The shark and Johnny were still out there, somewhere. . . .

The fear returned, tenfold, and a rage that turned to ice. He'd kill them all on the spot, the witness, too, and let Brody try to prove it. He turned to the druggist. "A week?" he murmured. "You said last week?"

Starbuck didn't answer. Moscotti turned to his nephew. Slowly, ceremoniously, he put his thumbnail into his teeth, jerked it away.

"No!" the woman screamed.

The gun was blasting, again and again and again, while Moscotti watched, deep in a prayer that his son was safe. . . .

"Drop it!" someone screamed from the door. Moscotti whirled. The Italian cop. Angelo? Angelo fumbled with his gun as he stared wide-eyed at the shambles. "I said drop the gun!" he yelled again, uncertainly. Moscotti's nephew did not turn, only fired once more at Starbuck.

"He can't hear!" yelled Moscotti.

Angelo's gun sounded like a cannon in the little shop. The boy's knees buckled. He looked at his uncle in astonishment as a great red stain spread across his white shirt. But the gun was still in his hand, and he glimpsed his assailant and leveled it.

"No!" howled Moscotti. He dived for his nephew. There was a roar behind him. The boy rose, spun, jerked in slow motion toward the wall, slammed into it, and lay like a huge bleeding scarecrow yanked from its vineyard post.

The man at the phone had dropped the instrument and was babbling again. The old lady drew in a breath and began to scream, far, far away. Moscotti clasped his nephew's head, closed the staring eyes, and wept.

Chapter 2

BRODY leaned on the rail of the *Aqua Queen*. They had moored on chain, using Andrews' immense storm anchor, because he'd sacrificed his other yesterday to get to Andy quickly.

Brody had checked his watch when Andrews slid into the water. Fifteen minutes gone.

He looked into the dark green water. Andy might have tried to say "ball" to Andrews, but he had certainly tried to say "shark," or something like *that,* to Brody. But when he had reported this to the diver, Andrews had simply shrugged. "Maybe he saw a sand shark. They're all over."

Brody slipped into the little cuddy forward, found a can of warm beer, cracked it, and returned topside.

The shoreline was clear. Amity was perfectly visible, but he could not see the lighthouse on Cape North, and the horizon to seaward had disappeared.

He shivered. Hell of a day for a race.

He was glad Chaffey was leading it home.

LIEUTENANT Commander Chip Chaffey, cruising at fifty feet above the fogbank, dipped into the rolling clouds, straining for a look at the ocean. Twenty minutes before, he had caught up with the stragglers, three little dinghies, far to the rear of the invisible armada ahead.

He had announced on his PA system that the race was over, they must return, feeling as always like the voice of God when he saw the startled faces flip skyward.

He had had to intone it three times before they admitted they heard him. Then they waved resignedly. Presumably, they were halfway home now, racing the incoming scud.

The problem of the main body of the fleet was something else. It was below him, somewhere, under the white blanket. He had flicked on his radar, but the boats were wooden or plastic and he got no mark at all on his scope.

He cursed silently. He was suddenly in thick fog, and there was no up, down, or sideways. Automatically, he shifted to instruments, climbed out of the damp white mist, and got his bearings. If he didn't spot them soon, they might be in more trouble than anyone thought.

Tom Andrews was skimming the muddy bottom at five fathoms. Stuffed under his weighted belt was a balloon and a long light line. If he found the sonar gear, which weighed too much to lift, he would buoy it, blowing some of his regulator air into the balloon and letting it float to the surface. Then he would rise, reanchor the boat nearby with Brody, and hoist the prize aboard.

He was snaking along, unable to penetrate the cloudiness by more than eight or ten feet, when he glimpsed the black object ahead. His heart soared. Their luck had changed.

In a moment he was inspecting it. It was half crushed. As he watched, it teetered in the muck, feeling the tug of tidal current sweeping out of Amity Harbor. He could not understand what had flattened it.

He grew suddenly alert. There were scrapes and dents along the top, as if it had been battered by the tines of some giant rake. Studying the strange serrations, he shivered. He was feeling odd.

He had never feared the bottom. He had endured the agony of anoxia and the bliss of nitrogen narcosis. He had watched his last partner writhing in the scuppers of an abalone boat, racing, too slowly, for the California coast. But until *this* moment he had never felt real apprehension below. And now he could not explain it, only overcome it as best he could.

So he shook off the nameless dread and tied the buoy line to the cable projecting from the sonar pack. He removed the mouthpiece of his regulator and blew the balloon half full. It would fully inflate on the way up, as the outside pressure eased.

He let the balloon go, and again he inspected the ball. The marks on it were more like teeth marks than anything else. . . .

Teeth marks? For a moment the ghost of the Amity shark hovered closely.

Bull. No great white he had seen, in movies or in books, could have encompassed this pack, much less have torn it loose from the chopper. Slowly, he began to rise, slanting in the direction of the *Aqua Queen,* and when he surfaced he was only a hundred yards from his boat. Through his water-smeared mask he could see Brody lounging on the taffrail, drinking a beer, and gazing toward Cape North. A good man, even if timid of the water.

"Brody," he called. His voice was high, almost tremulous in his own ears. "Over here!"

Brody jumped and began to search the water.

"Found it!" called Andrews. "Start hauling up the—"

Brody leaped suddenly, as if galvanized, pointing somewhere behind him. Andrews whirled in the water.

A bolt of terror ripped him. A hundred yards away, not far from the bright red balloon bobbing over the sonar pack, an enormous tail waved languorously.

His instinct was to jettison his gear and sprint for the boat, but he had read of the great white's speed. He could never make it.

On the surface, he was vulnerable from below, would have no chance at all. Below, at least he could try to hide.

He swished his fins silently, jackknifed, and dived for the bottom. He left hardly a ripple behind.

Above him, Brody was in a state of shock. He had the nightmarish feeling that he was back on the *Orca* four years before, with the Amity shark slinking nearby.

Another shark?

He tried to radio for help, fiddled with the "squelch" knob, heard only a high-pitched blast of static. No time to dope it out now.

What good would the Coast Guard do anyhow? The shark was here, with Andrews, and so was he. His place was as near to the diver as possible.

So he abandoned the radio, jumped to the forepeak, and hauled fathom after fathom of barnacled chain aboard, leaving it jumbled on the fo'c'sle. He found himself sobbing with frustration, or exertion, or fear.

Why had Andrews dived?

By sheer strength Brody pulled the boat directly over the anchor. It was fouled somehow below. He gave a final mighty heave, timing it to the slope of an oncoming wave. His back exploded in a jolt of pain. The anchor gave way. All at once he could pull it up easily. He got it over the gunwale and limped aft to try to start the engine.

He had no idea how to do it. There was no ignition key, just a row of buttons and knobs. Helplessly, he looked to port. Nothing but the silly red balloon dancing on the water, a rising sea, and snowy banks of incoming fog.

The race! The kids had no right to be in the same ocean with the monster whose tail he had seen.

He calmed himself. Chaffey had found the sailboats long ago, turned them around. The kids were safe ashore, stuffing themselves with hot dogs.

The danger was here, not in Amity Sound.

If Andrews still lived, his life depended on Brody's being near the balloon when he surfaced. The boat, once free, had already drifted past it, heading seaward. He should have tried to start the engine first, *then* pulled up the anchor.

He pushed a promising button on the dash. It was the horn. He pulled a knob. The bilge pump started. His fingers were trembling, his heart pounding. He flicked every switch, pulled every knob. Nothing happened. He peered under the panel.

There was a red button hiding there. He pushed it. The starter whined, groaned, faltered. He tried again. Suddenly the engine roared. He jammed the throttle forward and began a wide turn back to the spot where the bearded giant had dived.

Tom Andrews moved silently along the bottom, keeping his breathing slow so that the rasping of his regulator would not attract the fish. He finally found, growing from a barnacle-covered rock, a six-inch tuft of eelgrass.

He grasped it and rested, conserving air. He had forty minutes left if he could keep his nerves in check. If the shark did not sense him by whatever means it hunted, he would wait until his air was exhausted and slip quietly for the surface. Perhaps by then the shark would have left.

Suddenly he heard a noise and stiffened. Brody had started the engine. Getting ready to pick him up when he surfaced?

Or bailing out? Panicked? Bolting?

No way. Too solid a man for that. . . .

But suppose Brody had broken under the strain? Thought he'd been killed already? He suddenly remembered the sailboat race. *Both* Brody's boys were in it.

He could not risk it. He let go the eelgrass and floated toward the surface, silent as a rising bubble.

Fifteen feet toward sunlight he knew that Brody was not leaving. The boat was very near, and closing. For a moment he thought of descending again, giving the shark another half hour.

But the *Aqua Queen* whined closer. It would be stupid not to try for it.

And then he saw it, blocking his ascent, drifting as he was, tail disappearing into the jungle-green murk, moving idly. A remora swung from its lower jaw.

The shark's black, staring eyes seemed careless of his presence. For a moment he had hope. Then he saw that it was turning its body from right to left, slowly, doggedly, sparring for an opening.

In a swift motion he doubled, drew the knife from the holster at his left calf. *Come on, bastard,* he screamed silently.

He charged, knife thrust out like a lance. The shark met him head-on. The knife flashed, plunged briefly into an ebony orb.

And then Andrews, clasped between enormous jaws, was rising, rising, rising into sunlight. He glimpsed the boat, ten feet away. Brody, his mouth a screaming void, was drawing his gun. Then Andrews was torn downward into oblivion.

BRODY leaned trembling by the wheel of the *Aqua Queen,* still holding his gun. He had hit the sinking tail, but it had not even quivered. For a long while he circled the red balloon, searching the rising swells for a trace, any trace, that would show him that he had not dreamed it all.

He had found nothing, but the reddened water told him it was not a dream.

He tried the radio again. He heard the same squawk, but now, faintly, he could hear Shinnecock Bay Coast Guard, apparently talking to one of its cutters.

"Navy chopper is looking for them. . . . He has sent three sail-boats home so far . . . find the others due to fog."

Brody chilled. Hadn't Chaffey found them *yet?*

He fought down his terror. Cape North was a long way off. His job was to report the attack, to call Coast Guard cutters to the spot to search for Andrews' body. He pressed the mike button and called. No answer, only bits and pieces of the faint cold voice:

129

"Pilot reports . . . ceiling less than thirty feet . . . trying to find the racing buoy they were heading for. . . ."

Brody hung up the mike. Staying here was stupid. Andrews was gone forever. His place was at Cape North, looking for the living.

MIKE Brody had lost sight of the Cape North racing buoy ten minutes ago. He was trying now to keep the hazy sun on precisely the same bearing from his bow. Jackie, standing at the mast, was shivering. "Hey, you suppose we missed the buoy?"

"We'll run her up on Cape North," said Mike, trying to sound as if he knew where they were, "and spend the night ashore."

"You may have to marry me."

She turned back to search. Mike ran his eyes along the curve of her hips and the gentle sweep of her waist. It wouldn't be a bad idea at that. How old did you have to be?

Somewhere above the clouds a helicopter was thrumming. He was comforted by the beat.

They were lost, but not the only people in the world.

THE shark swept northward. She was within hours of birthing. The flashes of her hunger peaked less frequently. She had ingested nothing of the diver, simply worried him along the bottom and left his torn carcass bouncing seaward.

Her young were more active by the minute. Their constant squirming had killed her hunger. She was hunting now, not for food, but for a peaceful place to bear them. Once born, they would be, as always, safe from all but their own species. But programmed into her slender brain was a knowledge that others of her kind could destroy them.

Until they were safely launched, she would eliminate anything threatening that ventured into range.

Along the strip of coast she had annexed last week, she had been dangerous only when hungry.

Now she was simply dangerous.

Cruising hurriedly at five fathoms, she banked toward the water spilling from Amity Sound, her destination. As she turned, her ears, ampullae, and lateral lines picked up a rising crescendo of information. The strange thumping she had followed before was somewhere ahead.

Once she had tailed it from hunger. Now it was a predator intruding on her world.

It was over the spot she had chosen to birth.

MIKE Brody luffed into the breeze to slow his progress. Over the drumming of the sail he thought he heard a yell. He tightened the mainsheet to quiet the Dacron and yelled into a curtain of mist. "Ahoyyy . . ."

"Brody?" he heard faintly. "That you?" It was Larry, from somewhere ahead in the whiteness.

"You find the buoy?" Mike shouted.

"Hanging on it!" called Larry. He sounded frightened.

Suddenly he was in sight, a hundred feet ahead. His sail was unfurled and he was kneeling in his fo'c'sle clinging to the float, the orange pennant slapping him in the face in the gusty wind.

The buoy lay flat, tugged by the seaward rush. All the water in Amity Sound was trying to get through the neck to Cape North tide race at the same time.

Mike rounded into the wind, intending to raft alongside Larry.

"No!" yelled Larry. "You'll pull me loose."

"Shut up and grab," Mike ordered. He dropped his sail and tossed the line to Larry. Fumbling from cold or fright, Larry tied a knot on the buoy, took a turn around his mast, and got the rest back to Mike. The mayor's son sank back. "Man! That tide!"

Mike couldn't answer. He was afraid his voice would break. They were safe, but what about Sean?

He scrambled to the stern, sat disconsolately. His hand fell on the tiller. Rough, a really crummy paint job, but the kid had worked on it for a week. For what? To be swept to sea on another boat. He was close to tears.

Jackie sensed it. "I'm *sorry* I came, but he'll be all right."

"Not your fault," he mumbled. He took a deep breath, got it all together, and made Larry and Jackie join him in yelling for the other boats.

SEAN Brody huddled miserably over the tiller of Johnny Moscotti's Laser. Johnny had already abandoned his captaincy and was scrunched trembling in the shallow cockpit.

Ape Catsoulis, who was over sixteen, was intermittently in sight ahead, and it was on Ape's dinghy that Sean placed his trust. Ape was not the sailor that Mike was, but at least he was someone to follow.

Sean half stood, peering wildly forward. Ape had disappeared again, was lost somewhere. They would float out to sea, and he would never see Mike or his mother or his father again.

"Ape!" he piped.

Moscotti looked up at him reproachfully. "I coulda kept up, alone."

The heck with him. City jerk. He was not about to let him see the tears in his eyes. "Shut up! Hey, *Ape!*"

Ape didn't answer, but the fog lifted and Sean could see the ghostly outline of his sail.

He hung on to its shadow like grim death.

ELLEN Brody could no longer stand the strain in the boat club shack. She left Willy Norton on the telephone, and walked along the flats of Amity Sound to clear her head.

Where was Brody?

The last half hour had been unmitigated hell. Nate Starbuck was dead. Lena was hysterical. The young deaf-mute's body lay next to Nate's and the Flushing sergeant's lacerated remains in the Amity Funeral Home.

Dick Angelo had held himself together long enough to get Moscotti in custody. Then he had collapsed into a black depression and would speak to no one.

And all the time Len Hendricks, a babbling idiot at the instant of his greatest opportunity, was at her. Where was Brody? Why had he gone diving? When would he be back?

Where the hell *was* Brody?

She had wandered as far as her house. It seemed suddenly shabby and very empty in the fog. She heard a muffled bark and looked down. Sammy, forgotten in all the excitement, regarded her with moist reproachful eyes. She rubbed his head.

"OK," she muttered to the seal, "stay until he comes back."

He shook himself, showering her with gray tidal mud, tossed his head disdainfully, and flopped into the water.

She watched him swim away.

Then she returned to the boat club dock.

MARTIN BRODY HATED the ocean. He had hated it all his life. Now, creeping through the gray waters toward Cape North horn, he had no need to wonder why.

Any sane man would hate it. It was a cold surging hell.

Twilight was creeping in. He wondered if he would be able to see, through the fog, the 1,300,000-candlepower Cape North light, before he ran Andrews' boat onto some hidden rock. He thought he could hear surf ahead, but he was not sure. And always there was the chomping of the helicopter above. He tried again to call. "Navy helicopter, navy chopper, this is Brody, on the *Aqua Queen*. Do you hear me?"

This time, at least, he got an answer, from the Coast Guard. "Station calling chopper on Channel Sixteen. . . . Say again?"

He tried it once more, and again, and when he got no answer, hung up the mike.

He put the Cape North horn on his starboard beam, as nearly as he could judge, and began cautiously to grope west, against the current.

THE boats had drifted toward them out of the fog, one by one.

Mike Brody counted the craft, which had tied to each other, rafting against the pull of the current, and all hanging on to the straining buoy. Ten. Too many for the little mushroom anchor on the bottom. The thing was bound to drag, might be dragging now, and they'd soon be past the shelter of Amity Sound, in open ocean.

There had been fifteen in the race. Five were still missing. Sean was on one of them. If he hadn't turned back, he was in trouble.

The horn blasted and everyone yelled for the umpteenth time. From the fog another dinghy took shape. Mike recognized Ape Catsoulis standing in the cockpit, tense with the strain of his passage. "You see Sean?" Mike called.

Across fifty feet of water he could see Ape shake his head. "Not for half an hour. Boy, am I glad to—"

Ape suddenly straightened, staring back into the mists from which he'd emerged. All at once he screamed in terror.

Mike found himself on his feet. He had the impression of a towering fin, a rolling white belly, a jagged white mouth, and all at once Ape's dinghy hurtled end over end.

Ape, tumbled aloft, hit the water swimming.

And then he was gone, as if he had fallen into a hole in the surface of the sea. Fog drifted over the spot.

For a long moment there was silence. Gradually, Mike heard a rising howl of fear behind him.

Then, suddenly, he found Jackie was in his arms.

"Mike, Mike, *Mike!*"

He fought down the hysteria plucking at his throat.

On Amity Sound, four years ago, the man on the rubber raft had died near him, shouting, and all had gone mercifully black. He felt himself slipping away now.

He must not let himself go.

IN LESS energy-conscious days the Lighthouse Service had advertised that the Cape North light drew more power in one day than the whole of Amity in a week.

Now, with luminescent flashes, it was lighting the whole sky to the north, seeming to penetrate the mist more thoroughly with every sweep of its giant orb.

The daylight was waning fast, but the fog was lifting. Brody eased the throttle forward. Every four seconds he was lighted by the sweep of the searchlight.

The thumping of the chopper above grew louder. He still could not see it.

The radio crackled into life. The Coast Guard sounded excited. "Navy chopper four-five-three-one-two . . . Shinnecock Bay Coast Guard . . . a report from Amity police . . ."

Brody stiffened and turned up the volume.

". . . a body . . . floating near Amity Dock . . . apparent shark attack."

Thank God they knew. . . . But whose body? Andrews'? No, too far from Amity Beach, too soon.

". . . draw your attention to danger of helicopter rescues in shark-infested waters . . . evidence blade vibration draws sharks. Suggest you terminate search."

Brody froze. It was a nightmare. "Draws sharks?" *Get out,* he begged the chopper. *Get away from here.*

All at once he heard the chopper's blades increase their beat. The thing was climbing; Chaffey had heard. In a few moments the sound was gone.

THE CHOPPER HAD GIVEN up, apparently, and left them to die. Mike Brody found himself staring wildly into the night, squeezing Jackie's hand, and waiting.

The first two attacks had been on the outside boats. Mike had seen the fin, dimly in the dusk, weaving from right to left, and screamed a warning to those on the perimeter. They scrambled across the hulls to safety in other boats.

It was Bob Burnside's catboat that the shark hit. It went skyward in a froth of foam, came down capsized, and lay with a broken painter, drifting swiftly out to sea. "Oh, God," Mike heard Bob Burnside breathe.

They were forgetting to yell. "Hey!" bellowed Mike. "Hey, Sean!"

Not a sound, except Larry cursing steadily.

"Brody, the buoy's dragging."

Mike disengaged his hand from Jackie's and crawled into Larry's boat. He snaked forward to the fo'c'sle and touched the line. He could feel the tremors, and visualized the mushroom anchor dragging along the bottom.

"Here it comes!" Jerry Norton yelled. The JP's son was braced in his dinghy, immobile with fright.

"Move!" yelled Mike. "Come here!"

But Jerry simply cowered, and the great snout appeared, and the belly flashed in the moonlight. The astonishing jaws encased the stern of the dinghy, jamming Jerry into the debris like a giant winepress. Mike glimpsed a slate-black eye, oozing blood and utterly unconcerned.

Marcie Evans, in Bugeye Richard's Flying Dutchman, began to scream.

Larry Vaughan, Jr., got up, braced at his mast, and stared down at Mike in the moonlight. His face was twisted and his eyes were wide with hate.

"Your old man said he'd killed him!"

Mike did not believe his ears. "It's *another one!*"

"Bull!"

Mike gathered himself for the charge. "You're going *in,* Vaughan."

"Try it, Spitzer!" Larry lifted a foot, clinging to the mast. "Just try it."

"We're loose!" cried Tommy Carroll, pointing at the Cape North light. "We're moving out to sea!"

"Later," Mike promised Larry. He was ready to jump to his own boat to cast off from the rest when he saw the dark shadow easing in from seaward. He yanked Jackie into Larry's boat, shielded her with his body, and waited.

The snout rose again, so close he could have jammed an oar into the black oozing eye.

The shark crushed his Laser, tore it loose from the rest, and tugged it below.

Its rudder, torn loose, floated away, with Sean's painted tiller pointing straight up, white in the moonlight. When the yelling had died down, Mike could hear the surf crashing on the Cape North rocks. The rip was running full force, and from the sound of it less than a quarter mile away. Sucked into its vortex, they would be dead ducks, shark or not.

136

THE MOON WAS HIGH in the east, teasing Brody from behind the rearguard wisps of fog. He throttled back, turning shoreward toward Cape North light. So far as he knew, he was near the spot where each year they planted the racing buoy. He could not understand why it wasn't in sight. Perhaps it had been swept to sea, and the racers had taken shelter on the granite shore.

He moved the boat in close, searching the little sand coves behind the swirling rocks. He saw nothing, except the sign under Cape North light: CABLE CROSSING: DO NOT ANCHOR. So he headed away from the shore, cutting toward the Cape North tide race.

In the old days, there had been a lighthouse keeper, who might have known whether the boats had passed below.

But now it was all automated.

He was getting too close to the rocks, so he turned away, fighting the current, half sick from the jolting maelstrom. The great light approached, caught him, traveled off, touching, he thought,

137

a whitened mass to starboard. He found himself on the gunwale, craning.

There was something there. A raft? No. Boats, many boats, undulating as they swept toward the Cape North rip.

He jammed the throttle forward. He had found them, then; they were safe. It was not until he was within twenty-five yards that he saw that everyone was huddled on the seaward three boats.

The Cape North light swept past again, catching the monster like a flashbulb as it tore at a bright green catboat.

Brody sheared away, in shock. A bright white belly shone in the glare, and the shark was gone. He circled the mass of boats until he reached the kids.

MIKE Brody worked fast. He recognized the *Aqua Queen*, was puzzled that it was his father at the wheel, not Andrews, but there was no time to ask about that.

His father tossed him a hawser. The line slithered from his grip. He made a last quick clutch and grabbed it. Quickly, he took a turn around a mast.

"Drop your anchor," he yelled.

His dad leaped to the bow, tossed over Andrews' big storm anchor. Mike heard its chain clatter through the hawsepipe.

The anchor dragged, then held. The crazy hodgepodge strung out a hundred yards: taut anchor chain, the *Aqua Queen*, a hundred feet of hawser, rafted boats at the end of the tether, behind them all, the Cape North rip.

The kids began to haul on the hawser. Imperceptibly, they tugged the floating mass to the stern of the *Aqua Queen*. When they had the mass snugged tightly, they scrambled aboard the boat in seconds. Mike was the last over.

Brody moved through the milling kids. "Sean?" he murmured. "Where's Sean, Mike?"

Mike felt like crying. "Out there, somewhere."

His father moved faster than Mike had ever seen him. He was on the fo'c'sle, had the anchor chain in his hands, was tugging at it. Mike moved forward to help him. Larry took the throttle, powered ahead to ease the strain.

A tiny white sail grew from the moonlight. Mike grabbed his father's arm and pointed.

138

"Sean?" bellowed Brody. "Sean! Here!"

Sean's faint voice came back. "I'm trying!"

The searchlight swept past, and they could see Moscotti's Laser, a hundred yards away, two figures huddled in the stern.

If the anchor chain had been rope, they could have cut it and been free to pick them up. For Mike knew instantly that there was no way his brother could angle the tide to make the *Aqua Queen*. But chain was another matter.

Brody, still tugging at the chain, also sensed that the Laser, clawing against the tide, would fall far short of their stern.

"Line, Dad!" Mike yelled in his ear. "Heaving line?"

Brody, afraid to lose the progress they had made, continued to haul on the chain. "Don't know where . . . he'd stow it. Too far to heave it . . . anyway."

Mike shook his head. Out of the corner of his eye Brody saw him scrabbling in the cockpit, tossing life vests and pillows aside. Brody's grip was failing on the slimy links of chain. What the hell had snagged it below? But snagged it was. . . .

He whirled and dropped into the cockpit just in time to see Mike, with a fluid, sidearm grace, send a yellow line looping into the moonlit night. It snaked through the air and dropped across the bow of the Laser.

Johnny Moscotti sat dully by the mast and let it slither away. Everyone yelled, too late.

Mike jumped to the rail. Instinctively, Brody grabbed his leg, gripped the wetness, and lost him.

Mike split the water in a silent, arrow dive. Brody heard Jackie scream in protest. And then he had dropped his gun belt and belly flopped into the water himself. He kicked off his shoes and began tracking his son in the strange, jerky style that he had never improved, nor until this moment wanted to.

Ten yards short of the Laser he bumped blindly into his son. Mike had stopped, searching for the line he had thrown, floating somewhere in the chop.

"Get back on that boat!" Brody gasped. "Now!"

"No!" Their eyes met.

Suddenly Brody felt something. It was rough and coarse, twining around his body. It was the line. He glanced ahead. He could never get it to the Laser in time. He handed it to Mike.

"OK. Try."

His son churned off in a froth of foam. Brody turned and began to struggle back to the *Aqua Queen*.

He heard Jackie scream, and then the others. The rising crescendo told him that the kids had sighted the shark again.

And so, finally, a shark would get Mike, as one had got the swimmer close to him that day. Fate had simply put off the moment for four years, and it would end the same after all.

But the monster need not get them both.

Brody began to beat the water, begging for the beast's attention, not even close to fear.

The screams from the *Aqua Queen* rose in pitch. He sensed that he had done it, baited the monster away from his sons, and struck out again for the stern of the motorboat.

But now the fear came in a rush. Some grinding instinct told him that he had succeeded too well, that from somewhere below the white was rushing him, and very, very close.

He twisted in panic, knotting himself into a cringing ball. He felt a crushing blow on his hip, found himself half rolled above the surface, tossed toward the *Aqua Queen*. He felt the sandpaper rasp of the mammoth snout, glimpsed the gleam of a black eye, and heard Larry's voice, screaming into his very ear. He looked up.

Half a dozen slender arms reached down for him. He found himself yanked from the water as it erupted again. He felt the scrape of sharkskin on his bare toes, and crashed into the cockpit on his shoulder. He fought to his feet and looked back.

Mike had made the Laser. He had carried the line, too; he was in the craft, pulling frantically to the *Aqua Queen*. But the great black fin was weaving back to the tiny boat. Brody groped on the cockpit deck for his gun belt, drew his thirty-eight, and thudded three quick shots point-blank at the water close to the stern.

The triangular black blade seemed to hesitate. "Oh, God," moaned Brody. "Send it *here!*"

The white belly glistened in the moonlight and the shark reversed. "Get clear!" he screamed, leading the rush forward.

There was a moment of silence.

And then it hit, somewhere astern, with a shuddering crash that knocked down half the kids and sprung planks enough to start a hissing leak. He heard someone yell, "We're sinking!"

He went back to the anchor chain. He heaved, and heaved again, breath rasping and blood from his lacerated toes splattering the deck. Larry and three others joined him. The anchor was snagged on a rock below, or something.

"Pull!" he groaned. "Damn it, pull!"

Imperceptibly, it gave. It was straight up and down now.

The shark hit again. This time they did not see it, only felt it, as it launched itself from somewhere in the depths, tossing the stern high, spilling everyone in the cockpit.

Incredible. Not a living creature . . . A force of nature . . .

Brody was overcome by the futility. The shark would simply sink them where they were, as the other had the *Orca*, and destroy Mike and Sean and everyone else afterward. Nothing could kill it. It was invulnerable, would be here when all he knew had left.

"It's coming," Jackie said behind him. Her voice was without hope, factual, cool. "It's coming up again."

The shark struck, this time to starboard, and Brody heard Mike yell from the cockpit. "Bail! *Bail.* Hands, hats, anything!"

So Mike had got his brother and the Moscotti boy back, just in time to sink with the rest. Even that had been in vain.

The anchor appeared as they pulled, glowing phosphorescent in the moonlight, fouled in something from below. The Cape North light impaled them all briefly. Brody snubbed the chain on the bitts, bent over the bow to see what the anchor had snagged.

It looked like a giant sea serpent, entangled in the anchor flukes. It was black, shiny, and as thick as his upper leg. How he and a few teenage kids had got it from the bottom, he had no idea.

But he had no time to think of that. The shark had circled for a run on their bow, and was growing and growing, the great wide jaws studded with curved and angry teeth. He caught a glimpse of the flat black eye, and shrank back, knowing that the beast had won, and wishing that Ellen could know how hard he had tried.

He glimpsed the huge white belly upthrown in an arc, had a nightmarish vision of a smaller replica squirming from it, screamed as the jaws opened on the bow, encompassing rails, anchor, and the strange serpentine line.

The jaws ground shut in a rending crash.

There was an instant of silence. Then the bow lighted in a blue electric glow.

He smelled ozone, burning insulation, and a raw acrid odor he could not place.

Then he knew.

The teeth had cut the power line to the lighthouse on the point.

The Cape North light went out.

The great fish, as long as the boat, seemed to grow before his eyes. It snapped suddenly bone rigid, danced across the water on its tail, emitting a pale blue luminescence, weightless and graceful as a vision in a dream.

By moonlight he saw the shark, belly up, slithering into the depths.

He crawled back to the cockpit and sat down in water six inches deep beside Sean, who was weeping. He squeezed his shoulders, looked up into Mike's sky-blue eyes.

"OK," he told Mike. "Let's go home."

Chapter 3

MARTIN Brody stood up at his desk. His office was crowded with Flushing and Suffolk County homicide men, and he intended to leave Moscotti to them.

He had called New London. Andy Nicholas had survived the operation, and the bubble of air had been relieved.

Brody waited until Lieutenant Swede Johansson had signed her report on Jepps, and took her to her car.

"Very succinct evaluation," he remarked, opening the door. "I just hope you're not *assuming* that shark couldn't have mutilated his head the same way."

"I'm not assuming anything. A twelve-gauge shotgun did it, and *then* the shark got him."

"What makes you so damn sure?" Brody asked.

"Because I'm a lieutenant," she said. "And sharp, right? How could a black girl get to be a lieutenant unless she was sharp?"

He looked into her lively amber eyes. "By turning over ballistics reports to politicians? Handing them over to the defense before the investigator even sees them?"

Her eyes fell. "Do you think I did that?"

"I know it, Swede."

She climbed into the car. "You're quite a guy, Brody. From what

I hear, you're Amity's chief for life, if you want it. I can tell you that. And I will."

"What do you mean by that?"

She grinned. "There's a guy down there in the crime lab wants your job. Name of Sergeant Pappas. Next time you want a *private* report, bring the evidence to me. Direct. All right?"

"I'll be damned," he breathed. "OK."

He watched her drive down Main and turn onto County Road Five. He felt years younger suddenly. He climbed into his car.

The lights at home were out. He noticed Ellen in the solarium, gazing out at the moonlit water. He poured a drink for both of them, and joined her.

"Andy's going to be all right," he reported.

"Did you tell Chip Chaffey?"

He stiffened. "No. Why?"

"I'll call him, tomorrow."

"*I'll* call him," Brody said tensely.

"I thought you would," she giggled, and moved closer. "There's nothing there, Brody. It's just that . . ."

"It's just that nobody looks at you that way anymore."

"How did you know?" she murmured.

"I've been watching."

"I noticed."

He leered at her, putting everything he had into the longing in his eyes, and when she had enough of that, he pursed his lips like a barroom Lothario and kissed the air. "I'm looking at you. That way. OK?"

"You nut," she said. "You know, it works?"

They went upstairs to bed.

Epilogue

THE seal had cruised Amity Sound for hours, seeking his mother. He had not heard or sensed her off the tideflats for days, but when he had flounced into the water, some thinking memory had been triggered which gave him hope.

Now he had lost it. He skirted the breakwater, surprised a school of haddock, took one and missed another before he had to surface.

The Amity bell buoy clanged. There were harbor seals riding it, like him, but adult, and he was too small to lift himself out beside them.

So he swam slowly along the breakwater, lolling in the moonlight. He longed for his kind.

He became suddenly nervous. There were emanations around him, like those his mother had feared, and deep down, they made him uncomfortable.

He dived.

The vibrations were even stronger there. He surfaced quickly. He headed for the breakwater. Not knowing why, he swam very swiftly, increasing the beat of his flippers. Finding surface swimming too slow, he dived again.

He twisted his neck, searching to the rear. A flash of white, a perfect little replica of the white death his mother had dodged, sent him into a blind, panicky dash for the rocks. He sensed danger overtaking him, descended, doubled, caught a flash of white, grinning teeth and black saucer eyes already the size of scallops.

The shark nearly missed him, grazing his soft belly with its thrashing tail, slashing fur, and tearing flesh from his right flipper.

The seal found a surge of energy. He spurted for the rocks and floundered out, cutting himself on the barnacles.

For a long while he lay panting on the seawall. He heard a furtive bark, and inched higher.

The seal was female, bigger than his mother, and quite old. She was not his mother at all, but he felt comfort in her presence.

After a while he slept.

Hank Searls

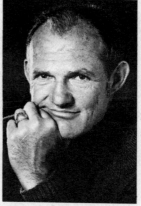

Hank Searls has had more experience than most novelists with sharks and the sea. A naval officer in World War II, he lives in Malibu, California—where he had his first encounter with a shark. "I was off the beach in about forty feet of water when I saw it, a blue, maybe twenty feet below me. I panicked and shot to the surface and into kelp, which is like coming up in the tentacles of an octopus. There I was, trapped, wearing a tank on my back. Fortunately a neighbour, a retired lifeguard, was out fishing in a big, heavy boat. He saw me thrashing around, and he pulled me out."

So much depends on your mood, Searls says. The next time he met a shark it was a different story. He was diving around a World War II wreck in a lagoon at the Pacific island of Guam. "The guy I was diving with was well checked out in those waters, the visibility was great, and we spotted some sharks. We had absolutely no fear, and since we had underwater cameras, we chased them, and they took off. But," he adds quickly, "I don't want to be known as the guy who goes around chasing sharks. I have a lot of respect for them. A third of all the authenticated white shark attacks in the world have occurred right here off the California coast."

Searls has been described by novelist Morris West as "a man who has really experienced the wonders of the Lord in the great deeps." A three-year cruise from San Diego to New Zealand in a forty-foot ketch was the background for Searls's last novel, *Overboard*, a Reader's Digest Condensed Books selection. His crew was his wife, Bunny, who also dives, skis, motor-cycles, and flies with him. They have another cruise in mind, two books from now.

A DANGEROUS MAGIC

a condensation of the book by

FRANCES LYNCH

Illustrated by George Sharp
Published by Souvenir Press

In a gloomy castle on the Firth of Forth, Lady
Otranta Tantallon is writing her memoirs.

Her great-niece Bridie, sent north to help her,
soon discovers that this formidable widow, once
the intimate friend of the late Queen Victoria,
was not always so respected a personage. Scottish
society had frowned on her early career as a
conjurer's assistant, and somewhere in her long
life is concealed a terrible secret.

In an atmosphere of mystery, menace and
romance, Bridie herself now faces danger as she
attempts to unravel the past. Clearly there is
someone who will stop at nothing to prevent the
publication of the memoirs.

But who can it be? Surely not one of Lady
Otranta's two handsome sons, or her unassuming
stepdaughter? Surely not one of her devoted
servants? Or is it that all of them are caught up
equally in the dangerous magic of illusion, in a
train of deception with its beginnings far back
in Lady Otranta's theatrical past. . . .

ONE

*I*t's no use at all, sitting down to write one's memoirs, and then trying to fudge them. One must be prepared to be utterly truthful. Of course, the truth is often painful—both to oneself and to those others, possibly near and dear to one, whom it may affect. But truthfulness is still absolutely essential, especially when, as in my own case, one has reached the age of sixty—if one's mirror is to be believed, seventy-five at least—and has decided it's high time the record be set straight on any number of important particulars. Not, you understand, simply in order that one's soul may be purged but rather so that justice may finally be done.

The lie I have lived has gone on long enough. The purpose of these memoirs is that it should be ended, once and for all.

I was twenty-nine when I consented in church to become the wife of Sir James Tantallon. For Sir James to give his name and high social position to a young woman only recently come from twice-nightly performances on the stage of Edinburgh's Empire Theatre was both brave and extraordinarily generous. I shall be grateful for his generosity, and for the twenty-eight happy years he gave me, for the rest of my life.

Even in these enlightened Edwardian times I fear that the variety theatre is still hardly considered a respectable calling. Mind you, I wouldn't want it thought that I'm ashamed of my former occupation.

My fame had been worked for honestly. Thanks to my dear friend and mentor, the great illusionist, Professor Henri Salvador, I was then at the top of my profession. The Incredible Madame Otranta had performed, as the saying goes, before all the crowned heads of Europe. But this was scarcely a recommendation when I was later striving for social acceptance as the wife of a member of Queen Victoria's most intimate circle.

The Queen herself, God rest her, had her own problems. Not the least . . . but I run ahead. The gentleman who has consented to publish these memoirs would, I feel sure, prefer me to keep any revelations concerning the poor late Queen until their proper place in my narrative. . . .

The momentous letter from her great-aunt's publisher arrived one morning in late August. Young Bridie Tantallon, running down the stairs and across the dingy oilcloth of Mrs. Bartlett's hall, was in such a hurry that she might easily have missed it.

She'd given up expecting letters. Indeed, in the months following her father's death and her subsequent move from their pleasant rooms in Maida Vale, she had given up expecting very much of anything—except the doubtful, twentieth-century pleasures of being an independent young woman, with the poverty and loneliness that this seemed to involve. She would, therefore, probably not have seen the letter at all, had she not paused anxiously to survey herself in the umbrella-stand's lozenge-shaped mirror.

Her haste was on account of being on her way to yet another interview—this time with the Black Diamond Shipping Company in Horseferry Lane—and, although she had little hope that it would come to anything (there were, by all accounts, already a full seven thousand girls in London quite as expert on the typewriter as she) she was nevertheless determined to be punctual. And to create at least a passable first impression.

Having satisfied herself that her heavy coils of auburn hair were still more or less where they ought to be, and jammed her straw boater firmly down on top, she was about to turn away when the letter, propped up on the umbrella stand, caught her eye. Typewritten—which suggested a business communication. She stuffed the letter into her handbag and hurried out.

Not until she had boarded the omnibus taking her down to the West End, did she open the letter. It was from Mr. Pugh-Hennessy, her father's publisher.

"I would be very grateful," he wrote, "if you could visit me at your earliest convenience here in my offices in Covent Garden. The matter will, I believe, be to our mutual advantage. It concerns the memoirs of your great-aunt, Lady Otranta Tantallon."

Mr. Pugh-Hennessy was the nearest Bridie had to a friend—they had known each other almost for as long as she could remember, ever since he had first consented to publish her father's virtually unsaleable musical biographies. Mr. Pugh-Hennessy's loyalty and faith in Professor Tantallon had seen Bridie and her father through many lean months—as the younger son the Professor had, under Scottish law, received nothing of the substantial family estates—and it was Mr. Pugh-Hennessy who had sorted out the Professor's affairs after his sudden death.

Bridie did not make friends easily. Her mother had died when she was twelve, leaving her the sole companion and helpmeet of her father, who himself had suffered from a progressive affliction of the eyes that had cruelly brought him total blindness for the last years of his life. His courage and unfailing good spirits had been a source of constant inspiration to her—but the sad fact was that they had left her now, at nineteen, quite without friends of her own age and far too shy to make any quickly.

She read the letter again. Lady Otranta's *memoirs?* What could Mr. Pugh-Hennessy possibly expect her to know about Lady Otranta? She and her great-aunt had never even corresponded, let alone met. In fact, the two sides of the Tantallon family had not been on speaking terms these thirty-odd years.

All the same, if Mr. Pugh-Hennessy wanted to see her, she'd go. But, should she go now, or after her interview? She stared again at the letter. Interviews terrified her. And besides, dear, kind old Mr. Pugh-Hennessy had asked her to come at her "earliest convenience". So surely it wouldn't be civil to keep him waiting?

She made her decision. Somehow the summons from the Black

Diamond Shipping Company drifted down onto the crowded pavements of the Tottenham Court Road. She herself left the omnibus rather more decorously in the Strand, and made her way briskly towards Covent Garden.

A SIMPLE AND REASONABLE decision, she had thought. . . . One, however, that less than a week later she found herself regretting intensely. For, as a direct result, she was by then irrevocably committed to the Flying Scotsman and well on her way up to Castle Tantallon. Which was, of course, her great-aunt's home near Kincardine, on the shores of the Firth of Forth, across the water from the ancient city of Edinburgh.

She still didn't quite know how it had happened. Distractedly she peered out of her first-class carriage window. How fast the train was going—with the next stop York, the journey was already almost half over. By nightfall she'd be at the castle and face-to-face with the fearsome Lady Otranta.

She'd tried to explain to Mr. Pugh-Hennessy that even the simplest conversation with strangers threw her into a ridiculous panic. But Mr. Pugh-Hennessy's mind was quite made up. He'd commissioned memoirs from Lady Tantallon, and now the old lady was apparently unwilling to go through with them. Bridie was just the person to go up and help her, reason with her, persuade her.

"Lady Otranta won't *eat* you, my dear. After all, you *are* a member of the family. And she *has* written to say she'll have you. . . ."

As she sat dismally watching the golden harvest fields of the Midlands hurry by, Bridie shivered. The whole idea was preposterous.

"We've never been exactly close," she told Mr. Pugh-Hennessy. "Why, my grandfather was her brother-in-law, and he refused even to go to her wedding."

"But that's an *ancient* quarrel. *Quite* over and done with." Mr. Pugh-Hennessy hoisted himself to his feet and moved to the open window. He was a fusty person, tall and thin, with steeply-sloped eyebrows, a profusion of dark, greying hair, and lugubrious false teeth. "Believe me, child, in polite society today the question of

152

Lady Tantallon's—ah—*unorthodox* beginnings is long forgotten. She is undoubtedly a *most* remarkable woman. And she has some . . . er . . . remarkable things to tell. . . . Otherwise you may be *sure* I would never have commissioned the book in the first place."

He flashed her his rather over-furnished smile. "I have no doubts at all that the two of you will get on excellently. . . ."

The train entered a cutting and thick white smoke funnelled down beside the carriage. Bridie closed her eyes. So polite society had quite forgotten her great-aunt's beginnings, had it? For her father, at any rate, everything about the good lady had been faintly ridiculous, if not downright disgraceful. *The Incredible Madame Otranta*, indeed! A wretched young woman who earned her living telling fortunes and being sawn in half twice nightly.

In the circumstances, Bridie thought, it was hardly surprising that her side of the family had opposed Sir James's remarriage so bitterly, and the first Lady Tantallon scarcely twelve months departed this life. Could such a quarrel really be so quickly forgotten, she wondered?

Not that Bridie herself cared a fig for the Lady Otranta's origins. And besides, within a very few years of her marriage the second Lady Tantallon had become accepted by Scottish society. And her elder son, from what Mr. Pugh-Hennessy had said, was a worthy successor to his father's title and estates.

On the other hand, the old lady's evident eccentricity and the prospect of a houseful of total strangers, with two sons, a step-daughter, and heaven knows what else, terrified Bridie. If only Mr. Pugh-Hennessy had been willing to listen to her. . . .

"But . . . but I still believe you would be better advised to send someone with a little more experience. By your account, sir, Lady Otranta is a somewhat difficult person, and I—"

"Difficult? Of course she's *difficult*, like most old people. I'm difficult meself." He returned to his desk and began to rummage among the papers on its littered surface. "An outline she sent us. Promising the most astounding revelations. An *excellent* outline— I have it here somewhere. . . ." His telephone lurched on its stand; Bridie darted forward and caught it. The old man sighed, and gave up the search.

153

"She sent it *four* months ago. Since then, nothing but letters full of *ridiculous* excuses."

He peered up at Bridie through the tangled hedges of his brows. "Which is precisely why I'm sending *you,* my child, and not one of the fellows upstairs. Your work with your father has given you *literary* skills. And besides, with the Lady Tantallons of this world, it's *breeding* that counts. And you have it."

He took her by the arm and led her firmly to the door. "You see—I have faith in you. So run along now to Mr. Thwaite, there's a good child. He will see to your travel arrangements." He opened the door and thrust her through. "You'll do a good job, Bridie. I *know* you will. . . ."

The train lurched, and began to slacken speed. Brought back to the present, Bridie looked out upon a jumble of smoky grey rooftops, with the tall tower of a cathedral rising massively in its midst. York Minster. A moment later the train entered the station and stopped with a juddering of brakes.

Steam billowed up past her carriage window. Through it she watched absently as people hurried to and fro on the platform. Briefly her attention was caught by a broad, bearded figure in a tartan kilt. His hair was wild, and of a fiery ginger. For a moment it seemed that he was gazing intently in her direction. Their eyes met, then the steam thickened, and when it drifted away the man in the kilt was gone.

Bridie let the fringed velvet curtain fall across the window and turned towards the compartment's interior. For most of the journey she had had the compartment to herself, for which she was profoundly grateful, but now, alas, the door opened and an elderly manufacturing gentleman with a large rose in his buttonhole entered, followed by a motherly person in blue bombazine, clearly his wife. When they had settled themselves, they turned to her with friendly curiosity.

"It's a grand day, is it not?" the gentleman's wife suggested.

"Yes," Bridie agreed, blushing deeply.

"I see from the label on your box you're for Edinburgh. It's a fair flower of a city. Och, you're in for a fine treat, I'm thinking. Is she no, Angus?"

"Aye, she is that, my dear." The manufacturing gentleman

154

rubbed his hands with great heartiness. "The fairest city in all the land."

Bridie shuffled her feet and wished that the red plush seat would open and swallow her. At that moment, mercifully, the train jerked violently, and they were on their way again. Bridie turned to the window and watched as the city of York disappeared into the summery haze behind her.

She knew it was foolish to be so shy. Ridiculous, even. But that was the way she was. Her father had understood her difficulty, that the modern "small talk" expected of young women now that Edward VII was on the throne left her blushing and wordless. And so often she was afraid, when there was absolutely nothing to be afraid of. Unlike her father. . . . Even after his sight had failed him completely he'd refused to be afraid. "The world out there is for living in," he'd told her. "And the people, they're for talking to, for getting to know. . . ."

And he'd been right. Even though his determination to be fully a part of the world had led him finally to a wretched death beneath the hooves of a panic-stricken dray horse. Even then he'd been right. The world *was* for living in.

Just then the dining-car attendant approached, announcing the second sitting for luncheon. She stood up to tidy herself in the bevelled mirror above the seats. A reasonable face, she decided. Too square perhaps for real beauty, but with eyes of an unusual golden-brown, and a mouth that was really quite adequate when it smiled. Her hair though—anxiously she licked her palms and pushed ineffectually at its heavy auburn coils. Somehow it just would not get used to the idea of being *up*. She frowned at it, put on her straw hat with the pink daisies and went out into the corridor, a slim little figure looking considerably more determined than it felt.

The dining car had ornate plush chairs with buttoned backs, and cut-glass panels set into the mahogany partitions. Bridie waited nervously by the door till an attendant came and showed her to a table for two.

"Madam is travelling alone? She would perhaps prefer to take her luncheon undisturbed?"

She nodded. At once the chair opposite her was borne away.

She ordered her meal: onion soup, to be followed by fillet of sole, roast duck *à l'orange*, and *bombe glacé*. And, by the time she was halfway through her fish, even the prospect of her coming meeting with Lady Otranta seemed no longer quite so daunting.

Suddenly, a shadow fell across the table. She looked up into a pair of piercing blue eyes deep set beneath beetling ginger eyebrows above a positive entanglement of ginger beard. Her fork clattered noisily onto her plate. It was the man in the kilt she had seen staring at her from the platform at York.

He bowed stiffly. "Mistress Bridie Tantallon?" he inquired.

She licked her lips nervously. "I think you have the advantage of me, Mr.—"

"Duncan Symonds." He bowed again and held out his hand. She shook it timidly. "I serve your great-aunt, you see," he went on. "I'm the factor on the Tantallon estate. I've been in York on business. It was Sir Andrew's idea that I keep an eye open for you on the train."

Sir Andrew—that would be her great-aunt's elder son. "That . . . that was very kind of him," she stammered. "But I really—"

"He was feared that I might not know you. But he needna' have fashed hissell. The Tantallon features are no easily mistaken. And you have them to perfection, Miss Bridie. I knew it the moment I first set eyes on you in York."

She found his directness disconcerting, yet oddly in no way disagreeable. "If I didna' approach you at once," he continued, "it was because I chose to make gey certain. So I checkit in all the first-class carriages before I came here. And there wasna' a body as came anywheres near you."

"You . . . you knew I'd be travelling first class, then?" she queried.

He nodded. "It was a' laid out in yon Pugh-Hennessy's letter. And Sir Andrew had a fair suspicion his telegram wouldna' meet with much of a reception."

"Telegram? What telegram was that?"

Mr. Symonds smiled quizzically down at her. "Aye . . . weel, I'm no honestly surprised your employer kept it from you." Before Bridie could press him further, Mr. Symonds had caught the sleeve of a passing waiter. "I'd take it kindly if you'd bring us another chair, laddie. Miss Tantallon and I have important matters to discuss, y'ken."

His confidence astounded her. Inviting himself to her table as if they were old friends. And yet, when the waiter turned a questioning eye in her direction she helplessly nodded her agreement.

The chair was brought and Mr. Symonds seated himself opposite her. His elbows on the table and his bearded chin upon his knuckles, he gazed affably across at her.

"I've no put you off your food, I hope. It's plain fare we have at the castle, so I'd make the most of it."

She fumbled with her knife and fork and captured a small piece of fish. Seeing her awkwardness he clucked sympathetically. "I'll warrant it's as cold now as a herring on a marble slab." He raised his voice the merest shade. "Miss Tantallon will have her next course now," he announced.

Like magic, her plate was whisked away, and the duck appeared in front of her. Bridie found herself almost enjoying the sense of friendly importance Mr. Duncan Symonds gave her.

"Are you no taking wine wi' the duck?" he murmured. "And if you had a wee half bottle I'm no saying as I wouldna' join you in a glass."

To her own astonishment, she heard herself ordering a half bottle and two glasses. When the wine was brought it was he, reassuringly, who tasted it and approved. "I'm thinking this is your first visit to Scotland," he observed.

She nodded. "Yes. And I'm much looking forward to it." Her own words surprised her. Certainly she hadn't been looking forward to her visit half an hour before.

"Aye . . . weel, you'll be seeing us at our best the noo. It gets gey dismal come October. But you'll awa' back to the south well afore that, I reckon."

"I don't think so, Mr. Symonds." She frowned. Already it was the first week of September. "Surely Mr. Pugh-Hennessy explained that I'd be with you for five or six weeks at least? Lady Otranta's memoirs, you know—there's a great deal of work to be done on them."

For a moment he didn't answer. Then he settled himself in his

157

seat. "Mebbe I should tell you something of Castle Tantallon," he said. "It was built some forty years ago, y'ken, when the old Queen, God rest her, was still discovering the wonders of the Highlands. Sir Jamie was appointit steward of her Stirling estates. He was a kinsman o' the Douglas, so when he built himself the castle he named it after their fine old ruin near Dunbar—that being his own name too, for by. Then he marrit the first Lady Tantallon. The Lady Margaret was daughter to the provost of Edinburgh, and—"

But Bridie was tired of not receiving direct answers to her questions. "Is this why my cousin asked you to meet me? So that you could acquaint me with the family history?" She waited, suddenly horrified by her boldness.

Mr. Symonds, however, seemed in no way put out by her tart reminder. "The fact is, Miss Bridie," he said, scratching the side of his nose, "Sir Andrew asked me to put it to you—in the kindest fashion, mind—that you'd be far better staying the night in Edinburgh and taking the morning train back down to London. That Castle Tantallon was, in short, no place for you."

Bridie stared at him incredulously. "But that's absurd! Mr. Pugh-Hennessy made all the arrangements. I have Lady Otranta's personal invitation."

"Sir Andrew kens that weel. He also understands your employer's difficulty concerning the memoirs. Which is why he was feart that his telegram might have little effect. So he askit—"

"Telegram?" Bridie was angry now. "That's the second time you've mentioned it. What exactly was in this telegram?"

Mr. Symonds spread his hands. "Words . . . just words."

"If your instructions were to send me back to London, how is it that you've been so reluctant to carry them out?"

Suddenly her companion was serious. "Because one look at you told me you were a Tantallon to the verra tips of your fingers. So I'll just ask you this: now that I've told you Sir Andrew doesna' want you at the castle, are you likely to be away at once, back down to London?"

"Certainly not!"

His seriousness dissolved into the broadest of smiles. "Then you've answered your own question," he said.

158

"But how could I go back?" Bridie insisted crossly. "I have my employer to think of. And besides, Lady Otranta is relying on me to—" She broke off. Wasn't this just the excuse she'd been looking for? Not to have to face her alarming great-aunt? And yet . . . she was hardly one to shirk her duty at the very first hint of opposition. "And besides," she repeated, glaring obstinately across at Mr. Symonds, "Lady Otranta is relying on me to help her with the writing of her memoirs."

Mr. Symonds rubbed his hands. "You see? It isna' only the Tantallon face you've been gifted wi'. You have their spirit too." He tilted his head. "And their pig-headed obstinacy as well, I wouldna' be surprised."

His complacency infuriated her. "How dare you!" she said.

Abruptly his smile faded. He leaned forward and put his hand gently on her arm. "There now, Miss Bridie. I fear I've preachit at you, which was never my intention. Can you forgive me?"

Her heart was touched by his warm simplicity. "Don't let us talk of forgiveness, Mr. Symonds. Let us say instead that we understand each other a little better now."

He nodded, then lifted his glass. "To your stay at Castle Tantallon," he said. "And may it be a happy one."

She joined him gladly in the toast, then cleared her throat. "Though I really don't see that my stay can be happy if Sir Andrew is so determined to make me unwelcome," she said. "What are his reasons for this?"

For once Mr. Symonds appeared in some difficulty. "That's . . . weel, that's something I'd rather you found out for yourself, Miss Bridie. It may be that they're nobbut a fret about next to nothing. In which case you'd be better not knowing. . . . I'd just have you mindful of this, though—she's a remarkable old wumman, the Lady Otranta. I'd do anything in the world for her."

He began to talk about the people she would meet at her destination. He was always carefully circumspect and loyal, she noticed, and never more so than when speaking of Lady Otranta's elder son, Sir Andrew. From which she was able to deduce his secret disapproval.

"He works himself into the ground, that man. Out in a' weathers. Forestry, sheep-herding, the sawmills—I've never seen

159

anyone more eager to learn. And he's no afraid to get his hands dirty. Next month he'll be there with the rest of us, juicing the sheep. It's no his fault if—"

"Juicing the sheep?" Bridie laughed. "What on earth is that?"

"It's a dip the shepherds use to keep the poor beasts healthy. Tobacco and soapy water boiled up in a cauldron . . . Aye, it's no the Laird's fault if the men think him a wee bit interferin'."

And not only the men, Bridie decided. "And what of his brother?" she asked.

"Young Mr. Robert?" Duncan Symonds stroked his beard thoughtfully. "He's a second son a' ower, if y'ken what I'm saying. . . . But he'll find his place in the world soon enough. You'll get on with him fine, I'm thinking."

Which was clearly more than could be said for the older brother. But they had to break off then, for the dining-car attendant was hovering with the bill. When it was paid, Mr. Symonds accepted Bridie's invitation to return with her to her compartment. The manufacturing gentleman and his wife were sleeping soundly, and neither stirred as she and Mr. Symonds settled themselves by the window.

"There's an older half-sister, isn't there?" Bridie now asked. "And not married, I understand?"

Mr. Symonds frowned. "Weel now, she's the strange one, yon Mistress Melissa. Over thirty, aye, and still no marrit . . . and no for want of suitors either." He pulled at his beard. "She's aye gadding about on one of them bicycles—and she's a great one for what she calls 'the rational dress'. Yon baggy trouser things." He brightened. "But she's a good-hearted body, and you'll get on fine wi' her, too."

After a short pause he went on, "And then there's old Peggy. Herself is the one you'll be needing to be on good terms with. They're as close as twa corbies, her and my lady. A fair old tyrant, if you want the truth, Miss Bridie. . . . She workit for my lady as a dresser back in her theatre days, old Peggy did."

Bridie was quiet for a time, then a thought came to her. "Mr. Symonds—you told me that you were employed by Lady Otranta."

"Aye. The estate needs a manager, y'ken."

160

Manager—so at least the unfamiliar word *factor* was now explained. "If your employer is Lady Otranta," Bridie insisted, "then how can it be that Sir Andrew would send you on a mission so completely contrary to his mother's wishes?"

"That's no a verra great problem," he said imperturbably. "First point—it's no for a man in my position to take sides in every wee family difference that may come along. And second point—I kenned weel that you'd no be a true Tantallon if you took heed of a single word I said." He smiled. "So where was the harm in it?"

Mr. Symonds was, she saw now, a man of rare diplomacy. "And I'd say you're a fair bit wiser for the chance of this wee talk it's given us," he concluded. "If I've helpit you, I'm glad. For it's no an easy household you'll be going into."

She nodded slowly. The picture Duncan Symonds painted was hardly reassuring. On top of all her other forebodings, to discover that she was entering a divided family, unwanted by at least one of its members. . . . In her present situation she could only be profoundly grateful that the amiable Scotsman opposite her seemed willing to give her his support and friendship.

TWO

I must begin at the beginning, then, with a brief account of my true origins. Contrary to the more exotic versions later in circulation, I was born in Dulwich of honest and industrious parents, my father being a senior accounting clerk in the City.

My parents shared the standards of the nobility sufficiently for the career I chose to be a source of real distress to them—distress that I'm sorry to say was never eased by pride in my later successes, since they were both killed in a gas-main explosion shortly after my eighteenth birthday.

The news was brought to me by a young constable just as I was about to go on at the Chiswick Empire. At that time I was manipulating cages of singing birds for an aged Doctor Melodious who paid me three and sixpence a week, all found.

I took the young constable's news bravely, and went on all the same. My parents might be dead, but Doctor Melodious was not, and he needed me.

A sensible enough reaction. But I was showing, I see now, the sturdy heartlessness that was to stand me in good stead in my future life. There would soon be times when an iron will and a brisk lack of sentiment were all that lay between me and disaster. When the life and happiness of the man I loved rested in the balance. When it was up to me alone to act, and act decisively. . . .

"Wait 'ere, please, miss. Madame Otranta will see you in a minute."

Old Peggy followed these words with a disparaging sniff, then shuffled from the room. Lady Otranta's intimidating personal servant was a short and immensely fat old woman, encased in a huge brown garment the front of which was liberally equipped with rows of pins, lengths of ribbon and dangling elastic, and a large pair of dressmaker's scissors suspended from a cord about her neck.

Bridie sat down by one of the narrow windows to wait. The room she had been shown to by an elderly manservant called Meredith, somewhat toothless but with impressive Dundreary whiskers, was small and octagonal, presumably set into one of the pointed turrets she had seen at the corners of the castle's main block. This much she had been able to glimpse of Castle Tantallon and very little else, for the motor car bringing Mr. Symonds and her from the steamship landing stage at Kincardine —a buttercup-yellow Argyll he drove expertly—had scarcely left the surrounding pine trees and negotiated a steep little stone hump-backed bridge before it was clattering over a massive wooden drawbridge and entering the castle's inner courtyard.

From the deep slit of a window she could see little except treetops and the distant silvery waters of the Firth of Forth. The crossing by paddle-steamer from Leith had been uneventful. Nevertheless, she'd been glad of Duncan Symond's company, for the tramway ride before it from Edinburgh's Waverley station to the Albert Dock at Leith had been five miles of such a lurching, clattering progress, along cobbled streets thronged with honking motor taxis and with such a mass of cheerful, inquisitive people all talking at the tops of their voices, that it had seemed far longer than all the four hundred up from London put together.

Seldom had Bridie felt so alone and vulnerable as, abandoned by Mr. Symonds at the castle door, she had been welcomed by none other than the man who had tried to stop her coming at all, Sir Andrew Tantallon.

He had come towards her down the wide staircase and across the dark, stone-flagged entrance hall, limping slightly, his hand outstretched. He wore a high-lapelled dark green jacket over narrow tartan trousers. He was tall and lean, with neatly-cut hair and moustaches of a surprising silvery fairness, and piercing blue eyes that looked down at her from deep sockets, dark-rimmed perhaps from some anxiety. He was clearly an outdoor man, someone at home out on the wild hillsides surrounding Castle Tantallon, yet he had an easy grace and most courteous manner.

To her astonished relief he greeted her warmly, and seemed, indeed, unsurprised to see her.

"My dear cousin—you've got here safely. I'm so glad. I trust the journey wasn't too arduous?" His accent was slight, but unmistakably Scots.

She shook his offered hand. "Not at all, thank you." She tried bravely to sound self-possessed and easy.

"I'm delighted to hear it. Well, Meredith will show you to your room. And take you afterwards to my mother's quarters. She's sure to be expecting you." Sir Andrew frowned briefly, as if in some doubt. He limped a pace or two away, then turned. "Forgive me, cousin. I must speak with the kitchen." He took out his watch and consulted it elaborately. "There was, you understand, no great certainty as to whether you would arrive in time for dinner."

His words were bland enough but the meaning they cloaked was rather less pleasant: there had been no great certainty as to whether she would arrive at all.

He bowed then and went away quickly, down the echoing length of the entrance hall, past dismal suits of armour, a massive pipe organ, and through a green baize door at the far end. All his movements, Bridie saw, were strangely jerky and ill-controlled, as if he were suffering some great inner tension.

The ancient butler, Meredith, conducted her up the stairs and around a gallery to her room, carrying with him the smaller of her portmanteaux. The gallery was hung with stags' heads and formidable cudgels, spears and barbaric leather shields. And her room was hardly more welcoming. In the centre of the floor, surrounded by deerskin rugs, stood a vast four-poster bed. The sunset striking in through the leaded panes of the deeply-mullioned windows cast a menacing crimson light on the heavy furniture and low beamed ceiling, making the room grotesquely gloomy. Bridie's spirits—already low—plummeted still further.

When Meredith had gone, Bridie crossed to the wash-stand and splashed ice-cold water upon her face. The shock revived her a little.

So this was Castle Tantallon. She didn't know whether to laugh or cry. Certainly nothing on earth would make her stay here. She must go and tell Sir Andrew at once of her decision. At least he, for one, would be delighted to hear it.

At that moment Meredith returned, bringing the second of her cases. He put it on the bed and leaned upon it, wheezing faintly. "My lady will see ye now, Mistress Bridie," he said, his voice a gentle sing-song.

"No," she said firmly. "No—first I must talk to Sir—"

"If they've told ye the old one's something to be afeared of, Mistress Bridie, that's nobbut their nonsense. She'll like ye fine." He touched her arm. "Ye canna' disappoint her. Och, she's talked of little else but your coming this week and more."

There was something irresistible in his appeal. Bridie hesitated, then nodded. After all, there'd be plenty of time for her to talk about leaving later.

The whiskers on Meredith's face spread into a toothless smile. "I was sure ye'd see it. My lady's a puir lonely soul. Nobbut a puir lonely soul since Sir Jamie's going. . . ."

A *puir lonely soul* . . . ? Yet Duncan Symonds called her *a remarkable wumman*. And Mr. Pugh-Hennessy had labelled her *difficult*. Could all of these really be the same person?

Meredith led her, at his own snail-like pace, down a succession

164

of echoing passages till finally they came to a small octagonal room. And now, here Bridie was, sitting nervously by the arrow-slit of a window, waiting for her summons.

"Madame Otranta will see you now, miss." Fat old Peggy had reappeared in the doorway. "And jus' you see you watch your p's and q's, mind!"

Bridie nodded meekly, and walked into the room beyond.

"Your great-niece, Madame," Peggy intoned majestically behind her. "Jus' arrived up from London." So saying, she closed the door firmly.

For a moment Bridie stood spellbound. The room, curtained and dimly lit with flickering candles, was in dramatic contrast to the rest of the castle. It was, for one thing, unbearably hot. Also, its air was heavily laden with the smoke from sticks that smouldered aromatically in oriental vases. Thick Chinese carpets lay upon the floor, cluttered with quantities of ornate furniture. Opposite the windows a huge log fire burned beneath a fringed and much-mirrored overmantel. While to one side of the fire sat a swarthy turbanned Turk, his back to her, hunched forward over what appeared to be a chessboard.

"Come forward, child, so that I can see you."

Her great-aunt, Bridie saw now, was on the far side of the fire, dressed entirely in black and sitting upon a sombrely upholstered high-backed chair, so that principally only her pale hands and face were visible, floating in the shadows.

"No, child—on second thoughts it would be better if you drew the curtains."

Obediently Bridie moved towards the nearest window. Her great-aunt's voice was husky, yet magnetic. Now it took on a slightly ironic note. "Candlelight is kind to a woman such as myself, no longer in . . . shall we say the first flower of her beauty. . . ?" A faint dry laugh disturbed the incense-laden air. "But you, my child, are no ordinary visitor. It is better that we should see each other as we really are."

Bridie drew back the curtains and turned to face her great-aunt. What she saw was a pale, gaunt woman, bright areas of rouge lying uneasily upon haggard cheeks beneath an elaborate coiffure of hair improbably black, regarding her intently through jet-framed lorgnettes. A long silence ensued, broken only by the soft shifting of the logs in the hearth.

Suddenly her great-aunt let the eye-glasses fall. "Well, child?" she demanded, "Is the spectacle much what you expected?"

"I—I did not come expecting anything in particular," Bridie blurted, blushing deeply. "I'm sorry if I seemed to stare, Great-aunt. But everything here is so very strange to me."

"So." For a moment longer Lady Otranta watched her forbiddingly. Then she turned slowly away. "Bridie . . . Bridie my dear," she said, her voice suddenly gentle, "have you never wondered why it is that the old like to torture the young?" She paused. "Might it not be because they are jealous of youth, of its courage and beauty?" She sighed and closed her eyes.

Bridie took an anxious step forward, then stopped, her attention abruptly drawn to the dark-skinned Turk sitting across the fireplace from her great-aunt. The light from the windows glinted in his eyes as if in two cold, hard jewels. Bridie stood transfixed, then, all at once, she relaxed. "Why, he's a dummy!" she cried, in sudden absurd relief.

Lady Otranta opened her eyes. "Az Rah?" she said. "A dummy? I tell you, my child, in his time poor Az Rah has defeated the finest chess players in all the courts of Europe."

Though Bridie had never seen the illusion, she had heard of it many times. "Was it you," she asked, fascinated now, her shyness forgotten, "who hid inside him and controlled his movements?"

Her great-aunt sat up straight again. "Use your eyes, child. Where would there be space within poor Az Rah for such as myself?" He was indeed exceedingly small and slender, hunched over a cabinet the doors of which stood open to reveal an array of cogs and levers. The old lady rose unsteadily and stooped to place a pine log upon the fire. "Tell me, my child," she said, "what room has my son put you in to sleep?"

The sudden change of subject surprised Bridie into frankness. "To be honest, Great-aunt, not a nice room at all. A huge draughty cave of a place, with a big four-poster bed, and—"

Lady Otranta clicked her tongue irritably. "I imagine he thinks to make you so uncomfortable you will not stay. You see, he does not want you here."

166

Bridie hesitated. "Great-aunt . . . Why does he not?"

"You must ask him that yourself, my dear," the old lady said. "Though you will discover for yourself soon enough that I am not . . . I am not always as you now see me."

She rose and walked slowly and stiffly round the room, extinguishing the candles while Bridie watched her, taking in only dimly the extraordinary items of furniture between which she moved. There were cabinets clearly theatrical in purpose, and a strange crystal casket upon spindly legs, and a screen from which knives projected in the outline of a human body.

Lady Otranta completed her circuit. "On the subject of your room," she said, "you shall have quarters in my own part of the castle. Those old four-posters were never comfortable—I used to tell my Jamie he'd been swindled by the man he bought them from." She sighed. "This whole castle, come to that, was built simply to humour the old Queen, God rest her. She had a fancy, you see, for what she thought of as *Scottish* architecture. . . ."

Bridie couldn't help smiling. "You knew Queen Victoria quite well, I believe."

Thoughtfully Lady Otranta placed a cone of silver cardboard over a wine bottle standing on a side table. When she lifted the cone again the wine bottle was gone, replaced by a vase of paper flowers.

"I knew the Queen as well as anyone could—who wasn't a servant, that is," she murmured.

The trick had been simple enough, the flowers concealed within the shell of the fake bottle which was lifted off inside the cone. But the old lady's reply to Bridie's question . . . why, that remained baffling.

Lady Otranta laid the cone down. "All this," she said, gesturing around her, "the maestro left to me when he died. The great Professor Salvador . . . and he really was great, you know. He left me all his secrets . . ." she sighed again. "You'll think me foolish to have kept them."

"Not at all, Great-aunt."

"But so I am. Old and foolish . . ." Then she brightened. "But now, child, you shall tell me about your father." She seated herself and indicated a nearby chair for Bridie. "I understand he was

168

blind, poor man, in his later years. You must tell me everything—
unless, of course, it will pain you to speak of him?"

"Not to you, Great-aunt."

Certainly Bridie's memories of her father were still sharp and
full of the pain of loss. But there was about the old lady a warm
understanding that overcame the girl's uncertainties. She poured
out her story. . . .

When it was finally done Lady Otranta sat for a time in
thoughtful silence. Then, "Clearly, child, you are a determined
and courageous person," she said. "And it cannot have been easy
for you to come here alone, simply at the whim of that wretched
Mr. Pugh-Hennessy." She sighed. "He's an impatient man. He
will not understand the difficulties that surround me. . . ."
Suddenly she leaned forward and took Bridie's hand. "You must
not be disheartened, my dear, if your work here with me does not
progress as rapidly as you would wish."

Her grip on Bridie's hand tightened as she pulled herself
laboriously to her feet. "There now, child—they'll be serving
dinner soon. You must go and change. And Bridie . . . ask that
dreadful Peggy to come in to me, will you? She's as crotchety as
a Musselburgh fishwife, but if I talk to her nicely she'll see that
your things are moved to another room."

Bridie thanked her, then rose and made her way cautiously out
of the room in the last of the fading light. She found old Peggy,
a lamp lighted now, bent over an enormous and unidentifiable
piece of purple needlework. She passed on her great-aunt's
message.

"Huh!" Peggy got up, peered suspiciously over her spectacles,
her bright black eyes sly above the prodigious curves of her
cheeks. "A word from *Madame* and I'm supposed to come
running." She jerked her head in the direction of the next room.
"You bin a long time in there. On her best behaviour, was she?"

"Lady Otranta was very kind to me," Bridie said, puzzled.

The old servant looked Bridie up and down. "Ho yes—*Madame*
can be kindness itself when she's a mind to. . . . But jus' you
remember, my pet—things ain't always sunshine here, not by a
long chalk. And when they ain't, well, it's old Peggy as gets to
bear the brunt of 'em, like as not."

As Bridie approached the gallery above the entrance hall, the sound of an organ came to her. Somebody was playing Bach, with enthusiasm if not with total accuracy. . . . When she emerged from the final archway, the music burst over her in a flood of sound. Intrigued, she went to the gallery rail and peered down.

Seated at the keyboard of the organ was a man she took at first, from his head of silver-blond hair, to be her cousin Andrew. Then, abruptly, as if her presence above him had caught his eye, the music stopped and he turned to look up at her.

She saw the Tantallon features, the square brow above deep eye-sockets, the straight nose, the angular jaw-line . . . but somehow blurred a little, with a mouth wider and more sensual. The face was clean-shaven, and the hair far longer and more unruly than Sir Andrew's. This, then, must be the younger brother, Robert.

"Well, well, well—here's the brave little cousin from the big city!" he cried. His fingers broke into a few deafening bars of music, then he stopped. "Don't mind me," he said. "I'm supposed to be the artistic member of the family. The name's Robert. Welcome to Castle Tantallon, Bridie. You play the organ and the piano yourself, if my spies are to be believed."

Bridie hated to be patronized. "By 'your spies' I presume you mean Mr. Pugh-Hennessy," she said primly, descending the staircase.

Robert swivelled to face her. "Pugh-Hennessy?" he repeated, mimicking her tone. "Now, isn't that the hoitiest-toitiest name you could possibly imagine? *Puuuugh-Hennnnessy.* . . ."

He looked so ridiculous that she couldn't help but laugh. At which his mood changed abruptly and he became exaggeratedly solemn. "Now *that*, dear cousin Bridie, is *it*. Laughter. The only way to make life in this ghastly mausoleum of a place even remotely bearable."

As she reached the bottom of the stairs he rose and came to her side. She saw now that, although not as tall as his brother, he was still a good half-a-head taller than herself.

"It certainly doesn't seem to be a very cheerful place," she admitted.

"And thereby hangs a tale, little coz." He took her arm

170

conspiratorially and led her into a corner. "You've been closeted with our honoured mama," he murmured in her ear. "Tell me now, how was the Incredible Madame Otranta? Drunk, of course. But doubtless, in your honour, not yet entirely incapacitated?"

"*Drunk?*" Bridie recoiled. His joking had gone too far. "Of course she wasn't . . . d-drunk."

Suddenly her companion shed his flippancy and looked at her with genuine sadness. "Well, that makes a nice change, at any rate. But I'm afraid there's no 'of course' about it. That's what the joss-sticks are for—to cover the powerful reek of spirits . . ." He said ruefully. "If only mama's drinking made the old girl happy, I wouldn't mind so much."

Bridie was speechless. Until, incongruously, her cousin burst out laughing, and kissed her lightly upon the forehead. "Which is why," he said, "I do my best to keep the flag flying, old dear. And now, heaven be praised, I've got you here to help me."

Help him? Instinctively Bridie pulled away, her mind vigorously rejecting what he had told her. He had to be lying to her for some unimaginable reason. He *had* to be.

And yet. . . . Sentences began to return unbidden to her. Old Peggy: *On her best behaviour, was she?* Lady Otranta herself: *I am not always as you see me now. . . .*

Explained also was her aunt's apparent inability to get on with her memoirs. . . . Oh, the poor, poor woman! It was no wonder, indeed, that Sir Andrew had wished to keep Bridie from the castle.

Through all this silent agonizing her cousin Robert stood watching her. "I wasn't serious about your helping me," he now said coldly. "It's nothing to do with you. After all, she's not *your* mother."

He went slowly away, up the wide staircase. On the gallery he paused, cheerfulness regained. "They'll be tonking the dinner gong in fifteen minutes or so," he called down. "And I warn you, brother Andrew's a great one for punctuality. So I wouldn't blot your copybook with him—not on your first evening."

Bridie looked up. His smiling face seemed deathly pale in the candlelight. "Thank you for the warning," she said. Briefly she hesitated. "And I'd like to help you. If I can."

THREE

I often wish that my father had lived long enough to see me settled. And I regret very much the pain that my running away from home must have caused him.

He was a simple man, and good-hearted. Oddly enough, it was his addiction to reading that I have to thank for the uniqueness of my name; it derives from the title of his favourite book, "The Castle of Otranto" by Horace Walpole. Poor man! Had he guessed how well it would look in later years on the playbills, he would certainly have bowed to my mother's wishes and called me something less romantic.

As for my mother, she was neither simple nor good-hearted. She was obsessed with a determination that I should "better" myself, meaning, of course, that I should marry a man my social superior. The first stage of her plan for my betterment had been a young ladies' academy overlooking Dulwich Park. There I learned my letters, some genteel needlework and water-colouring, and the multiplication tables—these last, later, to be of the greatest use to me.

The second stage of her plan involved my induction into high society, which in Dulwich meant tea parties with the wife of the local sanitary inspector and visits to improving lectures.

I was sixteen and a half when I ran away. I had never actually been inside a theatre, of course, but I had learned enough from the playbills outside the Town Hall to know what I wanted to do. I was going to be a famous actress. . . .

Dinner at Castle Tantallon was served in an impressively baronial hall. Faded banners hung from a high ceiling, a forest of antlers decorated the walls, to one side of the tomblike fireplace stood an enormous stuffed bear, and a short distance behind the chair at the head of the table, mounted upon an easel, was a portrait of the late Sir James Tantallon in full Scottish garb.

Bridie thought that of all the people assembled around one end of the long table only her great-aunt had stature enough for the room. Still dressed in rustling black, her haggard face painted like a doll's, she managed nevertheless to radiate an unquenchable vigour . . . until, that is, the wine, which she drank in large quantities, began to take effect.

For the rest, Sir Andrew, tall and handsome in superbly tailored dinner clothes, appeared muted, while Robert, in spite of a flow of nonsensical conversation, seemed but little more than a boy, whistling impertinently in the caverns of his ancestral home.

Melissa, their older half-sister, came in late, muttering something about a broken chain on her bicycle. Briskly introducing herself to Bridie, she sat down opposite and set to work on her food. Her face, though not at all of the Tantallon cast—being oval, with a longish nose and drooping eyebrows beneath fine black hair pulled back in an uncompromising bun—was decidedly attractive, for all its air of strenuous commonsense.

Bridie herself, although just come from the largest city in the world, had to admit she herself did not sparkle with worldly sophistication. Her blue cotton frock with the pie-frill collar and little puff sleeves was badly crumpled. Her cousins carefully chose topics they thought of interest to a young woman-about-town, and consequently she had barely opened her mouth the whole spartan meal. She had been warned by Mr. Symonds to expect plain fare—but would that often mean, as it had this evening, three courses all of which were principally *oatmeal?* Oatmeal soup, lightly flavoured with celery, followed by a brown oatmeal concoction called haggis, and a mixture of oatmeal and unsweetened rhubarb to finish. . . .

She noticed her cousins Robert and Melissa put all away with seeming gusto. And if Sir Andrew ate almost as sparingly as she, this was certainly on account of his anxious preoccupation with his mother, who ate scarcely at all, but drank copiously. Repeatedly he contrived to move the old lady's glass beyond her reach, only for her to lean firmly forward and retrieve it.

Never before had Bridie so longed for a meal to end. Yet the end, when it came, took her by surprise. They had only just embarked upon the cheese when Lady Otranta suddenly rose from her chair and stood, swaying slightly, her hands gripping the table's massive edge.

"We are forgetting our manners, Andrew," she said, enunciating each word with exaggerated precision. "There is a guest here this evening. We must open a bottle of the Boy with which to toast your cousin."

"Champagne, Mama?" Her son caught the butler's eye and shook his head minutely. "If you say so, Mama."

"Certainly I say so." The old lady staggered, and momentarily closed her eyes. "I . . . I fear I am not very well. Another time, perhaps . . . If my niece will forgive me I think it would be better after all if I went to my room." Making a great effort, she straightened her back. "Will you kindly ring for Peggy?"

The fat old dresser appeared with such promptness that Bridie supposed she had been waiting behind the door, and led her mistress away. When she was almost out of the room, Lady Otranta paused, and turned.

"Bridie, my dear. . . ." She frowned as if she had forgotten what she had intended to say. "Bridie my dear, may I commend you to your Bible? 'Judge not, that ye be not judged.'" She swayed and would have fallen had not Peggy taken her firmly by the arm. And together, precariously, the two old women vanished from sight.

For a long moment no one moved or spoke. Then Robert seated himself with elaborate nonchalance. "Well, at least she made it under her own steam," he murmured.

Andrew cleared his throat and moved to the head of the table. "You will understand now," he said, addressing Bridie, "why I tried to discourage you from coming here. I wanted to spare you, I wanted to spare us all."

Bridie flushed. "I came here to help," she replied hotly. "It seems now that my help is needed even more than I thought."

Her cousin frowned. "Poor Mama is . . ."

But he got no further, for there was a sudden commotion as Melissa scrambled to her feet. "If there's to be another family discussion," she cried, "you can count me out, Andy!" And, upsetting her chair, she stumbled away, banging the door behind her.

Robert clicked his tongue. "Poor 'Lissa," he said. "She does take these *contretemps* to heart so."

"And so do you, Robert," his brother admonished him sharply. "In your own way, if only you'd admit it."

In the silence that fell again, Bridie was made powerfully aware of the bond that existed between the brothers: Sir Andrew standing stiffly in his mother's place; Robert, leaning negligently back in his chair, his face uncertain. Unlike as these two were, they both cared deeply, for each other and for their mother.

Slowly Andrew relaxed. He seated himself, turned to Bridie. "You spoke of helping Mama," he said gently. "I wish I thought that were possible. But we have all tried. Even Dr. Macnab—it's a pretence really that he comes all the way from Edinburgh just to treat her for her arthritis—he has tried also."

"Macnab's not a bad old stick," Robert affirmed. "He's got no time for most of the so-called 'cures' you hear about. There are powders one can put into wine for example—they may put a person off drinking for a while, but they're full of antimony and terribly dangerous."

Bridie leaned forward. "But might not a complete outsider like me stand a better chance of helping?" she said. "Could I not, for instance, perhaps get her interested again in her memoirs? Keep her busy?"

"Those memoirs? Positively not." Andrew's sudden vehemence was alarming. "Those wretched memoirs—I swear they're in some way at the root of all the trouble."

"What Andy means," Robert put in, "is that up until Mama started committing herself to paper she was as right as rain."

Sir Andrew nodded. "I blame myself, of course. When she suggested writing the story of her life, you see, I thought it would give her an interest. And she'd had such an extraordinary life, its story would surely be worth telling. . . . How was I to know?"

He sighed. "I even gave her the name of the man she should contact in London, Pugh-Hennessy. His family had rented an estate up here once—not that he and Mama had ever met, you understand, but I thought the coincidence might take his fancy. And it did, it did . . . How was I to know what misery my encouragement would bring in its wake?"

"But," Bridie wrinkled her forehead, "how could just writing some memoirs bring about such a . . ."

175

"According to Macnab," Robert said, "the writing of these memoirs has forced Mama to remember certain things best forgotten. Possibly it's making her face secret truths about herself that she'd managed to ignore for many years."

Andrew banged the table. "That idea's quite ridiculous, of course. A woman like Mama, conscientious, loving, virtuous—what secrets could she possibly have?"

Robert shrugged his shoulders. "Anyway," he concluded, "if Mama does indeed have secrets, I vote she be allowed to keep them. If she wants to go no further with her memoirs then that's her business. Convince her of that, and maybe we could all get back to normal again."

Possibly he was right. In which case, Bridie wondered, where did that place *her*? One thing was certain—her position in the Tantallon household was turning out far more complicated than she could ever have imagined.

FOUR

I called myself Lucy London when I first ran away from home, and sometimes, even after all these years, I wonder who I really am. Little Lucy London who couldn't dance and couldn't sing but tramped month after month from theatre to theatre, trying to convince producers that she could do both? Or Madame Otranta, successfully deceiving audiences night after night with the oldest tricks in the business? Or Lady Tantallon, living perhaps the greatest lie of all. . . ?

Once these memoirs are done—if they are ever done—perhaps I shall know the answer.

I went to Bristol first, to the Hippodrome and then the Theatre Royal. In neither case did I get past the stage doorkeeper. I went up through the Midlands, my tiny savings dwindling all the time, until, one rain-drenched afternoon in Leeds, I was actually allowed inside a theatre. And I was introduced to Captain Sawbright and his troupe of child acrobats.

It would be nice to say that he engaged me because he thought

176

me talented. Or pretty. Or <u>something</u>. But I was given the job solely because I was there, and because the only available costume—which had previously been worn by a girl at that moment quite blotto in the corner of the orchestra pit—fitted me perfectly.

I don't recall minding. A job was a job. And after three months on the road one wasn't too fussy. I've always been a pragmatist, I think, making the best of the various bad jobs life offered me. Not, please understand, that I lump Sir James in under that heading. He was the grand exception. He and my charming, handsome, <u>intolerable</u> children. . . .

Next morning Bridie woke to the steady drip of rain on the window of the neat little chintz-curtained room to which she had been moved.

To her relief, her cousin Andrew had approved of the move.

"The fault was mine for pre-judging you," he told her frankly. "I thought you would be a very *London* sort of person, and a proper blue-stocking too, to work for someone like Mr. Pugh-Hennessy." He smiled shamefacedly. "Hence the Baronial Bedroom, kept specially for unwanted guests. But I was quite wrong. You're just like one of us, really."

And there was nothing he could have said that would have pleased her more.

For a while she lay in bed, listening to the rain and remembering his words. Remembering also his face as he had spoken them, his smile warm and his eyes gentle for all the dark lines of worry that encircled them. A sudden wish had come over her to smooth those lines away, a wish so powerful that her pulse quickened even at the memory of it.

She threw back the bedclothes, and went to the window. Her room faced a wooded hillside up which a broad track wound to disappear into layers of low-lying mist. Nothing stirred in the still, dank air, not a blade of grass. Bridie shivered, and turned back to the room.

Just as she was finishing at the wash-stand a knock upon the door heralded the arrival of breakfast, brought to her by a young

177

chambermaid called Agnes who curtsied nervously and scuttled out again before Bridie could think of anything to say.

She ate her breakfast slowly, at a little table by the window—porridge, of course, and tea, and two bantams' eggs boiled as hard as little bullets—turning over in her mind all that she had learned since coming to the castle. Clearly she must talk to her great-aunt as soon as possible—if the old lady's memoirs were really to be abandoned then Mr. Pugh-Hennessy must be told at once, and given reasons. But what reasons? The truth? That Lady Otranta was habitually too drunk to complete them? It was a cruel thing to say of any person. Besides, Bridie wasn't even sure that it was so.

Her breakfast done, she rose briskly from the table, paused at the dressing table to confirm her businesslike appearance—plain white blouse with a small cameo brooch at the high neck, above a floor-length, dark grey woollen skirt—and then made her way purposefully in the direction of her great-aunt's room.

"What's this, then? Where ezzackly d'you reckon you're orf to, miss?" Old Peggy, like an irritable watchdog, was lurking by her mistress's door.

Bridie squared her shoulders. "Good morning, Peggy," she said, pleasantly but firmly. "I have important matters to discuss with my great-aunt."

"Not now, you 'aven't." Peggy sniffed indignantly. "Nobody discusses nothing with Madame—not before noon, they don't."

"But that's ridic—" Bridie stopped herself. Perhaps it wasn't so ridiculous, not if one remembered the night before.

"Nobody's to disturb 'er, y'see." Peggy explained, unbending a little. "Not even me. Every morning it's the same—I takes in her breakfast around nine, and she swears at me a bit, and I pushes orf again." Peggy tweaked at her cap ribbons. "I mean . . . it's only natural, I mean, when a person's not been well the night before she needs her beauty sleep."

Not been well—it seemed an evasion more humiliating even than the truth.

"You don't have to pretend with me," Bridie said briskly. "I saw my great-aunt. I know she was d . . . drunk—" Bridie's tongue tripped over the unfamiliar word. "And—"

178

"Drunk?" Peggy threw back her head and cackled raucously. "If you think that's drunk, you should just see Madame sometimes."

Bridie hung her head. She realized how pompous she must have sounded. "I'll . . . I'll come back in the afternoon then," she muttered. "Perhaps we can work on the memoirs after lunch."

"After lunch? I doubts it, miss." The old woman clutched Bridie's arm. "If you ask me, them memoirs is a lot of wicked nonsense. There's some things as is better not told."

What things? Did the old dresser know, or was she simply guessing? "You may be right," Bridie said guardedly. "But it really depends on what you mean by—"

At that moment the door to her great-aunt's room opened and, to Bridie's astonishment, Mr. Duncan Symonds came through, a business-like folder labelled *Accounts* under his arm. He closed the door behind him, then politely inclined his head.

"A verra good morning to you, Miss Bridie," he said.

"And the same to you, Mr. Symonds." Then, addressing him but staring hard at old Peggy, "And how did you find my great-aunt this morning?"

Mr. Symonds frowned. "And how should I be finding her ladyship? A wee bit tired, y'ken, but. . . ." He hesitated. "Weel, mebbe after the way she was last night you know full weel just how I found her. But the affairs of the estate have to go on, for a' that." He paused, cleared his throat. "I'm thinking I'd best be awa' about my business. . . ." He went slowly out of the room.

"You didn't tell me the truth," Bridie accused Peggy. "You said nobody was allowed in to see my great-aunt before noon."

Peggy leaned forward, her eyes venomous. "Not Mr. Duncan flamin' Symonds. He's the flamin' hexception. A regular little John Brown, he is. Treats her like she was the old Queen. *And* she lets him. I tell you, it's history repeating itself." She lowered her voice. "And what I'd like to know is, where does that leave poor Sir Andrew? Out in the cold, that's where—just like Prince Edward. Out in the cold, I tell you."

Bridie was silent. She had wondered about her cousin Andrew's position in the household. Now it was clear: like the Prince of Wales, now King Edward, he was under the thumb of a mother

179

who would give up none of her authority. And like the old Queen who had had her faithful Scottish servant John Brown to dance attendance upon her, Lady Tantallon had Duncan Symonds.

Yet there was a difference. The Prince, in his frustration, had turned to fast living. . . . Her great-aunt's words returned to her: *a bottle of the Boy*—it was Prince Edward's partiality for champagne and his frequent cries for the boy to bring him another bottle that had caused his friends to give it that nickname. Whereas Sir Andrew had stayed decently by his mother's side. She thought, too, of his touching concern for his mother. And how, according to Mr. Symonds himself, he worked himself into the ground.

Old Peggy straightened her back. "Mind you," she wheezed, "I'm not saying anything I haven't already said to Madame a thousand times. Not that it makes no difference. But we understands each other, Madame and me." Suddenly her sharp little eyes misted over. "If only she'd listen . . . but I just can't somehow get through to her. And I know she's keeping somethink from me. . . ."

There was anger in her sorrow, frustration at events she could no longer control, no longer even understand. Her sudden helplessness was pitiful. Bridie put an arm round her shoulders.

"Dear Peggy . . . we'll think of something. You'll see. It'll come out all right."

The old woman blew her nose on a grubby handkerchief, and reached for her needlework. Softly then, Bridie left her. *We'll think of something*, she'd said. Easy words. Think of something . . . but what?

As she started slowly down the stairs, a voice called up to her from the hall below.

"Care for a walk?" It was Melissa. "You'll have to get used to walking—if you're here any time, that is. There's precious little else to do."

"I . . . I'd like that very much," Bridie replied, hurrying down. "But isn't it raining?"

Melissa laughed. "This is Scotland, my dear. If we waited till it wasn't raining we'd scarcely budge outside the front door." She was wearing a tailored coat and skirt made of heather-coloured

180

tweed, a tam-o'-shanter pulled rakishly over her dark hair. "As a matter of fact, though, we're in luck. It seems to have blown over for the moment. But you'll need a cloak. And what about your shoes?" She lifted her own skirt to reveal neat black galoshes. "Don't worry—we're sure to have something to fit you."

From a low cupboard inside the porch, Melissa fitted out Bridie with a pair of Wellington boots. Then she handed her a tweed cloak and strode out through the huge, iron-studded doors. Bridie followed her at a trot.

"I was wrong, actually, when I said there was nothing to do," her cousin called back over her shoulder. "I was forgetting the sheep-juicing. You couldn't have come at a better time, really. After it's over we have a bit of a do for everyone on the estate. Not forgetting the local gentry. It's the nearest we get to a harvest y'see. A feast, dancing, what we call a *ceilidh* in Scotland. It's nothing very grand," Melissa went on. "Just a lot of hopping about. Can you dance a reel?" She didn't wait for an answer. "It doesn't matter if you can't, there's time enough to put you in the way of it. The party's not for ages yet."

They were out of the main archway by now and on the drawbridge, its massive planks wet and slippery beneath their feet. All at once there came a loud warning cry from the courtyard. Bridie looked back, then froze idiotically in her tracks.

The big yellow Argyll that had met her at the ferry was bearing fast down the courtyard's steady incline, pilotless, through the archway and out onto the drawbridge. Bridie stood, paralysed by terror, directly in the runaway vehicle's path.

It was Melissa's screams that broke the spell. Bridie saw her cousin sprawled upon the wet planks, tearing frantically at the cumbersome folds of her skirt. In an instant Bridie was at her side, pulling her clear—while in a silent rush the Argyll surged past them, towering overhead, close enough for Bridie to see the mud-flecked underside of its running-board, past them and down onto the drive.

It rolled on, slowing now, and came to rest in a thicket of rhododendrons. And behind it, in the middle of the drawbridge, nearly cut in two, Bridie saw one of her cousin's galoshes, the imprint of the motor car's tyre vivid on its shiny black rubber.

181

Bridie leaned, gasping, on the drawbridge's low parapet. Footsteps approached at a run. She closed her eyes as a strong arm came round her shoulders.

"I shouted . . . I tried to warn you. . . . Thank God you're both safe." It was Robert.

She gave way then, and drifted off into unconsciousness.

FIVE

*W*hen I first met Sir James Tantallon he was dying. He didn't know it, though, and neither did I. I simply saw a tall, distinguished gentleman standing in the door of my dressing room, leaning lightly on a gold-mounted malacca cane. I suspected that he was ill, however, for he was painfully thin, and his fine patrician's face was pale and haggard. But hardly dying. . . .

He'd spoken to me earlier that evening, he said, across the footlights. I'd been on the point of telling him the inscription inside his watch when he'd suddenly had to leave the auditorium. Perhaps I remembered?

I did remember. It had been a great relief to me. The inscription had been giving me a lot of trouble, as inscriptions always did. Yet Professor Salvador refused to give them up, and he was quite right. It was on feats like that that my reputation as a mind-reader mostly depended.

Anyway, Sir James had come to apologize. He'd been taken with a sudden spasm of sickness, he said. And he wanted me to know his departure had had nothing to do with my performance, which he'd found fascinating.

And so he should have too! It had taken us long enough to work up, the Professor and I. It was Henri Salvador who had rescued me from Doctor Melodious's miserable little birds. He'd offered me fame—and five shillings a week—in exchange for a few simple mental exercises, and I'd leapt at the chance. God knows, if I'd guessed what he meant by "a few simple mental exercises" I might have thought twice. They turned out to be a thousand times worse than anything the young

*ladies' academy, for all its multiplication tables, had ever come up
with. Still they sharpened my mind. And, while they were being
painfully mastered, my body came in for some honing, too.*

*It was, for example, the legs of the girl he sawed in half twice
nightly. I was a slender and supple young woman, yet the constrictions
of the space into which I had to fold myself for that performance
never ceased to amaze me. I was also expected to disappear from the
stage in at least seven different ways, all of which needed near-
miraculous agility.*

*It was all, I suppose, undignified, but it was honest toil. And the
time was to come when I would thank the Professor for this early
training. When it would be all that stood between me and certain
death. . . . I couldn't have known that then, of course, so I longed for
the day when I would put the gymnastics behind me and emerge
seductive and sphinx-like, as Madame Otranta.*

*It was as Madame Otranta that James first saw me. And he fell
in love with me, so he told me later, on that very first evening. . . .*

Bridie remained unconscious for no more than a few seconds.
Then she opened her eyes, discovered that she was sitting
ungracefully propped up against the parapet, and scrambled at
once to her feet. Melissa sat on the ground a few feet away, nursing one ankle, while Robert leaned solicitously over her.

He looked up at Bridie. "You're all right then—thank God for
that." His face was deathly pale, his eyes dark with shock. "What
can I say? You . . . you saved 'Lissa's life. It was like a nightmare.
I saw it all—I was just coming across from the stables. I shouted—
I ran as fast as I could—but I could do nothing. You saved 'Lissa's
life."

Bridie felt embarrassed. "The stupid car went nowhere near us,"
she muttered.

"You're sure you're all right?"

She nodded. Melissa stood up slowly, leaning on Robert's arm,
and hobbled to her side. "No great harm done then," she said
gruffly. "I'm grateful, though. . . ."

Both her cousins were badly shaken. "I—I wonder how it happened?" Bridie said, hoping to divert them. "I mean, motor cars don't usually run away like that, do they?"

"The hand-brake must have slipped. I'm always telling Duncan he should leave wedges under the back wheels," Robert said angrily.

He went to pick up Melissa's mutilated galosh from the middle of the drawbridge. He stared at it in horror for a moment, then flung it into the encircling pine trees. It was as if he was ridding himself of the terrible possibilities it represented.

He turned back to them and gave his arm to Melissa, whose ankle was obviously still paining her, and together the three of them made their way in through the archway and across the cobbled courtyard. Robert left them and went on ahead to a patch of dry cobbles away in the corner, presumably where the Argyll had been parked. Bridie saw him stare thoughtfully at two small objects on the ground. Then he came back.

"The wedges are there, all right." His voice was uneasy. "I really don't see what can have happened. It's . . . it's almost as if they've been moved on purpose."

In the silence that followed Bridie felt the cold touch of terror. "But why?" she faltered.

Again silence pinned them there until at last Melissa spoke brusquely. "Lot of nonsense. The things could easily have slipped —the ground's wet enough. Besides—who'd want to give us a scare like that?" She laughed scornfully, and hobbled in through the castle door, calling "Meredith! *Meredith*—ah, there you are. Tell Duncan his precious machine's gone galloping off down the drive all on its own. . . ."

Robert tentatively took Bridie's hand. "'Lissa's quite right, of course. Trust me to dramatize things. The wedges slipped—they *must* have."

She managed a reassuring smile, and let him lead her in. In the doorway, however, she glanced back over her shoulder. What she saw confirmed her worst suspicions. The ground where the wedges lay wasn't in the least wet or slippery. And it seemed to her that the motor car must have been aimed with great care—otherwise it would have crashed into the archway.

She sat down just inside the door to remove the borrowed boots. It was impossible, surely, that anyone could seriously have wanted to harm her and Melissa. What then? Could it possibly have been a warning, aimed at her alone? Connected with her great-aunt's memoirs? A warning—with the clear implication that if she persisted in the task Mr. Pugh-Hennessy had set her there would be worse to follow?

"Why so thoughtful, fair coz?" Robert said, smiling down at her.

"You'd be thoughtful too, if your shoes had buttons like mine," she said lightly and stood up, dusting the mud off her skirt as best she could. Could she trust him? Could she trust anybody?

They retired to a small sitting room on the right of the entrance hall where Melissa was already resting, and had coffee brought to them which Robert laced with brandy.

Melissa stirred her cup. "Where's Andrew got to?" she asked. "I'm surprised he didn't hear all the commotion."

"He mentioned something about going up to the sawmill with Duncan. . . ." A thought struck Robert. He hesitated, then shook his head, as if brushing an unwelcome idea away. "The big saw-blade has buckled," he said with some emphasis. "Andy wanted to see if there's something wrong with the alignment."

Bridie made no comment. If Duncan Symonds was with Andrew then that exonerated both of them. Which left only one of the castle servants as a possible culprit. No—Robert had been quite right, the whole idea was ridiculous.

Shortly afterwards the rain came down torrentially, so they went to the library, a comfortable, leather-smelling place with a brisk log fire, and there her two cousins showed her some of its treasures—in particular two volumes of the Highland diary Queen Victoria had published, with an inscription in the Queen's own hand to old Sir James. There had been, so Robert said, a third volume planned, dealing with Victoria's years with her trusted servant John Brown, but her advisers had warned against its publication. Brown had been very unpopular with the Queen's English subjects at the time—she allowed him to be too familiar, they thought. And hinted at even harsher objections. So the manuscript was suppressed, and had never been heard of since.

At noon Bridie excused herself and went nervously upstairs to Lady Otranta's quarters.

This time the octagonal room was empty. Bridie crossed to her great-aunt's door and timidly knocked upon it. Peggy's voice, somewhat faint, called for her to go in. The room was empty, but through yet another door Bridie could see into Lady Otranta's bedroom. She crossed the cluttered sitting room and went to stand at the foot of her great-aunt's magnificent bed. Like the rest of the bedroom furniture it was done in Chinese red lacquer, with intricate landscapes and golden dragons rioting over every possible surface.

"Well, child?" Lady Otranta was sitting forward while Peggy plumped up the pillows behind her. Her black hair hung down thick and straight on either side of her heavily made-up face. "Have you lost your tongue again," she asked waspishly, "or did you really only come in order to gape at me?"

Bridie jumped. What a change this was from their previous afternoon's conversation.

"Good morning, Great-aunt," Bridie began. "I hope I find you—"

"You find me very well indeed," Lady Otranta's words were slightly slurred. "Or at least I will be, as soon as this fumbling nincompoop finishes whatever it is she thinks she's doing." On the bedside table stood a glass and a half-empty whisky bottle.

Quickly Bridie looked away. "I'm glad you're feeling well," she said brightly. "Because, you see, I'd very much like to talk to you about. . . ." She hesitated. Clearly now was hardly the best time for a serious discussion. But if not now, when? She battled on. ". . . To talk to you about your memoirs. Mr. Pugh-Hennessy has asked me to—"

"That man!" Her great-aunt flung herself back on her pillows. "Doesn't he know what it is to be a writer, an *artist*?"

Peggy stepped back from the bed. "Ain't the gent down in London dealing with writer folks every blessed day of his life? Don't you reckon he knows what he's doing?"

Bridie held her breath, waiting for the inevitable blast. None came. Instead, the old lady sagged down in the bed and closed her eyes. "Dear Peggy," she murmured, "whatever would I do without you to remind me of my manners?"

"Huh!" The fat old dresser moved to Bridie's side. "Madame'll behave herself now, I reckon," she said, making no attempt to lower her voice. "And if she don't, you just call me. I'll only be in the next room."

Her words were brusque enough. Only her eyes pleaded with Bridie not to judge her great-aunt too harshly.

Lady Otranta waited until the bedroom door closed. "You see now what I have to put up with, my dear." She paused, tweaked at the sleeves of her crimson silk nightdress. "What we both have to put up with. . . . But enough of all that." She patted the bed close beside her. "Come and sit here, child, and tell me all about your Mr. Pugh-Hennessy."

Bridie seated herself where she was bidden. A dusty scent of attar of roses came from the old lady, strongly overlaid with raw spirits. "Mr. Pugh-Hennessy," she began, "is very concerned that you should complete your memoirs, Great-aunt. He believes they will attract a great deal of interest."

"He also has a not inconsiderable sum of money already invested," put in her great-aunt.

"That too," Bridie conceded. "But all the same, if you truly do not wish to proceed any further might it not be better if Mr. Pugh-Hennessy cancelled the contract? If you are unwell, then I'm sure he'd understand."

"No!" Her great-aunt clutched her arm. "No! The memoirs shall be written. I promise you that. But in my own time. . . ."

Confused and embarrassed, Bridie looked away, her eyes inexorably drawn to the bottle on the bedside table. She resolved on one last attempt to make her great-aunt see reason.

"Both your sons," she said, "believe that this writing distresses you. It worries them a great deal to see you so . . . so upset."

"Let us call things by their proper names, child!" Lady Otranta lifted her head. "It worries the boys to see their mother so *drunk*. And do you not think, Bridie my dear, that it worries me also?"

The words were wrung from her painfully, as if in a sudden moment of agonizing self-awareness. "If you only knew, child . . . if you only knew how beset I am. . . ."

Instinctively Bridie put her arm round the old lady's shoulders, pathetically thin beneath the gaudy nightdress. "Then why don't

187

you let me help you?" she whispered. "Together we can surely—"

Suddenly Lady Otranta relaxed, resting in Bridie's gentle embrace, and the room was silent.

Then she raised her head. "Don't leave us," she begged. "Don't go back to London. Perhaps one day I shall explain to you . . . when the moment is right. But you must stay here at the castle. It—it won't be for long, I promise you."

And Bridie hugged her close and whispered that of course she'd stay, and the two of them remained huddled together on the bed in the dim, watery light. Until abruptly there came a sharp tap upon the door.

Bridie got up and moved away, to stand by a dying, yellow-leafed aspidistra on a table in the window embrasure, while her great-aunt called "Come in."

Old Peggy entered and folded her arms impressively across her considerable bosom. "There's a something for you outside, Madame," she announced enigmatically.

Lady Otranta clicked her tongue. "Not now, Peggy. I can't be bothered with all that. Just tell me who or what it is, and be done with it."

"A *something*, Madame," Peggy insisted. "Surely Madame can discover it for herself?"

Bridie stared, bewildered. Had the woman gone quite out of her mind? Her great-aunt, however, sighed resignedly and turned to Bridie. "I'm supposed to read the poor old thing's mind," she explained. "Mind-reading was my speciality back in the old days. A pretty enough illusion. But—"

"Come along now, Madame." Peggy wagged a minatory finger. "You know how you enjoys showing off your powers. And we mustn't keep the young lady waiting. Come along now," she repeated, "we mustn't keep—"

"Don't nag me, dear." Lady Otranta rebuked her mildly. "It's all a question of getting into the mood. . . ." She closed her eyes and began to smooth her forehead with the tips of her fingers. Then she frowned. "You must try to concentrate, dear. The pictures are all confused."

Peggy sidled over to Bridie and nudged her delightedly. "She's off now, and no mistake," she whispered.

"*Concentrate*. You really must concentrate. . . ." Suddenly Lady Otranta's hands were still, her fingertips pressing hard against her temples. "I see a man. There's a man waiting in the next room."

"That's better." Old Peggy was positively hugging herself. "And what's this man's name?"

Lady Otranta's frown deepened. "It's my son . . . Andrew."

"Better and better." Peggy jogged up and down excitedly. "Now then, tell us what he's holding in his hand?"

"It's a . . . a piece of paper."

"Right first time," Peggy told her. "Next thing is, what's on this piece of paper?"

"I . . . I can't quite see." The old lady's breath was coming in short gasps. Then suddenly she smiled. "What a lot of trouble for really so very little," she said. "It's a list—a list of guests for our coming festivities. And the name at the top of the page is Spiller. That'll be the Spillers from over near Alloa."

Fat old Peggy ran forward and hugged her. "I knew you could do it, Madame. I just *knew* you could do it."

"Of course I could do it." Though clearly much pleased with her success, Lady Otranta made a great show of shrugging Peggy off.

Bridie had to admit that it was most impressive—always assuming, of course, that what her great-aunt had predicted turned out to be correct. And she had little doubt but that it would. All the same, she decided to check with her cousin Andrew later—solely in the interests of scientific accuracy—and discover if in truth he had been expected that morning, with a list of party guests headed by the name Spiller. For she had, it must be said, little faith in the genuinely supernatural powers of theatrical performers, even those as successful as the Incredible Madame Otranta.

SIX

We got on at once, Sir James and I. He did not often come to the theatre, he explained, but he had been in business in the city that day, and a storm had blown up during the afternoon to prevent him going home. He lived across the Firth, and didn't care to risk a *rough steamship crossing. His wretched recent illness—not even the best doctors in Edinburgh seemed able to cure it.*

Left therefore with the evening to fill before he could reasonably retire to his club, he had spotted one of Professor Salvador's play-bills and taken a chance.

He visited me again a few days later and again the following week. To be honest, he fascinated me. He was gentle, and a little shy—and he was modest. He didn't tell me in our first three or four meetings that he was steward to the Queen's Stirlingshire estates. Neither, less admirably, did he tell me that he was married. But, when he did finally make that admission, I have to say that I was past caring. I was in love.

He was older than I by fifteen years. He was a baronet. And he was married. He had a baby daughter. But none of that mattered, nor that his marriage was unhappy. Divorce, anyway, was out of the question—his position alone saw to that. We would be discreet, I told him, and snatch what happiness we could before my season at the Empire ended and I went back to London. In those early innocent days I was content with very little. We both were.

But shadows were gathering. My Jamie's illness, his refusal to take it seriously, was bad enough. And the suspicion growing in my mind that there was a pattern in his attacks. A pattern that started me thinking the unthinkable. . . .

How much simpler my life would be—and the life of the one who I'm afraid would rather see me dead than see this work completed—if I gave up these memoirs here and now. Yet to stop would be cowardice. And, whatever else I've been, I don't think I've ever been a coward.

There was no need for Bridie to ask Andrew if either he himself or his list had been expected. One short minute's conversation between him and his mother convinced Bridie that they were not.

Respectfully, he limped into the old lady's bedroom, holding the expected sheet of paper. She glanced at him, then attacked.

"I'd have expected you to know better," she slurred, "than to come pestering me about the shepherds' party. It's no concern of yours. I shall discuss it in detail with Duncan Symonds when the time is right."

He flushed. "Since when has Duncan had anything to do with the guest list? Always it was Papa who—"

"Your father is dead." The words fell coldly, bitterly, killing all further discussion.

Andrew hesitated, then turned wretchedly away. Bridie, hurt by his humiliation, longed to go after him.

When the door had closed behind him her great-aunt turned to her. "I suppose you think I was unfair."

Bridie swallowed nervously. "Yes, Great-aunt, I'm afraid I do."

"I thought as much." Lady Otranta nodded. "At least you're honest with me, child." Suddenly her face crumpled. "Oh, he's so like his father. Sometimes—I know it's terrible to say this—but sometimes I can hardly bear to have him in the room with me."

Bridie struggled with the shock of this admission. "Have you ever tried to explain that to him?" she asked softly. "Or would you like me to try?"

"Yes. . . . No. . . ." Lady Otranta flapped her hands in distress. "Oh, go to him—tell him what you will. Tell him I'm sorry. And that if he were to bring his list of guests to me again when I'm . . ." she tensed against what seemed a twinge of pain ". . . when I'm more myself, then perhaps we could discuss it together sensibly."

Gratefully taking her at her word, Bridie hurried along the twisting passages into the entrance hall. She caught sight of Meredith, just going through the green baize door, and asked him if he had seen Sir Andrew.

The old man pointed to an arched doorway. "The Laird went into the study a few minutes since," he told her.

She tapped on the door, lifted the heavy iron latch and entered. Andrew was standing by the window in a large, oak-panelled office, with large-scale maps pinned on the walls and a swivel chair in front of a massive roll-topped desk. The unfortunate guest list was a crumpled ball in his hand.

"Bridie, my dear—come in." He came quickly forward. "Sit you down." He swept untidy stacks of papers from a chair. "And what can I do for you?"

Bridie looked up at him. "Your mother—" she began.

"Shall we not talk of my mother?" He turned away, his hands clenched behind his back.

"She misses your father very much."

"Do not we all?" He swung round on her. "I tell you, it's more than two years now since Papa died, yet still I sometimes cannot believe it."

"You're very like your father," Bridie said. "Physically, I mean. It must be hard for your mother to . . . to . . ." She hesitated, hoping Andrew might fill in her meaning for himself.

For a long moment he stared down at her, then understanding did indeed come and he relaxed, sighing deeply.

"Isn't it sad," he murmured, "the way people can blind themselves to the obvious. Poor dear Mama—if only I'd realized before what pain I must be giving her."

He sat down at the desk, and smiled wryly at her. "You sit there so quietly, like a . . . like a small brown dormouse. And yet . . . you're as wise as you're bonny, little Bridie. And I'm truly grateful to you."

She blushed. "I—I was only passing on your mother's message," she stammered. "Lady Otranta asked me to tell you she was sorry she'd been so abrupt. And to ask you to bring the guest list to her again when she's more herself."

Bridie's thoughts wandered to the morning, and Andrew's absence when the car had run away.

"Is it a long way up to the sawmill?" she asked. "You've been up there with Mr. Symonds all morning, haven't you?"

A shifty look came over his face. "As a matter of fact . . . I was too busy to go. Important matters came up that . . . that had to be attended to. So I decided to go this afternoon instead."

"I see." She felt sure he was being less than honest with her. Slowly she got up and moved towards the door.

He called after her. "I tell you what, Bridie. Why don't you come with me?"

She paused, her hand on the door latch. Well, if an act of faith were needed, she'd make it gladly.

"Thank you very much," she said. "I've never seen a sawmill before. I'd like that enormously."

SEVEN

Sir James took to staying in Edinburgh for several days at a stretch.
His wife didn't seem to mind this—by then they were hardly
on speaking terms anyway. We'd meet in the late morning—walk a
little, and then take lunch in some small eating house up in the Old
Town, where he wasn't likely to be recognized.

Or rather, it was I who took lunch while he simply toyed with a
glass of milk. I had noticed, as I have already said, that there was a
pattern to his sickness. Each time he arrived from Castle Tantallon
he'd be a pitiful wraith of a man, unable to keep down even the
blandest of food. His condition would then improve steadily, so that
towards the end of a two- or three-day visit there'd be colour in his
cheeks and he'd be eating almost normally.

I was badly worried. The implication—to me at least—was as
clear as day. . . . And so, one afternoon, as casually as I could, I
mentioned how strange it was that his health seemed to get better the
longer he stayed away from his home.

At first he didn't take me seriously. Then, when I insisted, he
offered his improvement as proof that my company was better than
any amount of doctor's physic.

It was a pretty explanation, and I loved him for it. The truth,
though, as I saw it was rather less charming. . . . But I didn't argue
with him—the explanation I had in mind wasn't one to be presented
lightly. Proof was essential.

And proof, for my lover's sake, was what I was determined to
find.

After accepting Andrew's invitation to go up to the sawmill with
him that afternoon, Bridie went to her room to tidy herself for
lunch. Arriving in the dining room early, she found only Robert
there, deep in a dramatic pantomimed conversation with the stuffed
bear which stood beside the fireplace.

As *some* reaction to the ludicrous performance seemed expected of her, Bridie applauded loudly. Robert bowed low, then suddenly abandoned his play-acting.

"Well?" he demanded, almost fiercely. "What did she say?"

"What did *who* say?"

"Come along, coz." He frowned impatiently. "You've been to see Mama, haven't you? Is she keeping on at her memoirs or isn't she?"

Bridie took a deep breath, only now catching up with the abrupt change in his manner. "Your mother . . . insists that she must go on with the work. But she won't let me help her. And without my help I really can't see her making very much progress."

"I see." Her cousin was thoughtful. "How far d'you think she's got?"

Clearly the matter was important to him. "If you want my opinion," she said carefully, "I'd say your mother hasn't even started. And to be honest, seeing the way she is, I don't think she ever will."

"No. . . ." Robert's mood lightened as suddenly as it had darkened. "That doesn't mean our city cousin will be haring off back to London, I hope?"

Bridie shook her head. "Your mother seems to want me to stay, so I'll stay—as long as Mr. Pugh-Hennessy lets me, of course."

"Of course Mama wants you." He came to her then and put a friendly arm round her shoulders. "We all want you. You're our little ray of sunshine."

Laughing companionably together, they moved to one of the high stone-mullioned windows, beyond which the rain still fell in a steady downpour.

"Just look at it," Robert exclaimed. "I bet poor Andy's glad he had that dust-up with Duncan. Otherwise he'd be trekking down from the sawmill at this very minute, and getting soaked to the skin for his pains."

Bridie pricked up her ears. "What dust-up was that?"

"Poor chap—it was all quite horribly humiliating. All the same—" he lowered his voice. "Well, it seems there's been some breakdown up at the mill, and my brother said he'd go up with Duncan this morning to look at it. At which friend Duncan ups and says Sir James always trusted him to do what was best—and there's no

194

need for my brother to concern himself in the matter." Robert sighed. "Which is fair enough, in its way. But it's frustrating for Andy—to be continually kept out of things."

"So Mr. Symonds went up to the sawmill alone?" Bridie queried.

"Don't ask me," Robert shrugged and as, at this point, Melissa came in, the question of Andrew's "dust-up" with the estate manager was tactfully abandoned. But Bridie was profoundly glad it had been mentioned, for it explained Andrew's earlier evasiveness: he would hardly have wished to share still another humiliation with her.

After lunch, therefore, she set off with him, her mind perfectly easy. They went up the steep track through the wood, walking mostly in silence. The rain had stopped, the sky was clearing, and shafts of sunlight struck down between the tall columns of trees.

The pace Andrew set, in spite of his limp, was brisk enough to have Bridie soon breathless. At last he stopped on a stretch of level track, and turned to look down on the castle spread out below them and beyond it the white-flecked waters of the Firth.

He wiped his forehead with a red bandanna. "I've hurried you," he said. "It's this wretched foot of mine," he went on quickly. "It seems I always have to be proving it doesn't make me any . . . any less than the next man."

She felt a sudden flood of sympathy for him. "Anyone who thought that," she said stoutly, "would be a fool."

"I got it in a shooting accident, you know. When I was fifteen. In the gun-room at the castle." He gestured down at the turrets and battlements below. "What a ridiculously pompous place it is, to be sure."

Yet the sprawling, mock-medieval hulk of the castle generated a strange aura of power. It crouched in a hollow among the trees, almost like a great rocky outcrop of the hill itself.

Andrew started up the track again, Bridie following him. After he had gone a few paces he stopped. "By the by," he threw back over his shoulder, "you may well hear unkind gossip about what happened when my foot was injured. 'Lissa was there, you see. . . ." He lowered his head. "But that's all nonsense, of course. I was actually holding the gun when it happened. She had nothing whatever to do with it. It was all a stupid accident."

He swung round on her, fixed her with his piercing gaze. "I wouldn't want you to feel uneasy with poor 'Lissa. She's the dearest, kindest person." He smiled then, and held out his hand. "Shall we be on our way, then? I'm afraid the track gets steeper now."

She took his hand. It was broad and strong, and its touch warmed her. They began to climb again. And they chatted together now, easily, openly.

"Your mother has asked me to stay," Bridie told him.

"Excellent. I would have asked you myself otherwise." He

paused, helped her round a deep rut in the track. "And what of the memoirs?"

She told him what she had told his brother. He asked her then about her employer down in London, how long she thought he'd let her stay.

"Oh, for a good while yet," she told him, pretending a greater confidence that she felt.

"Oh, splendid. Excellent . . . !" He swung her hand. Then added hastily, "I know 'Lissa will be delighted to hear it. She'll want you to accompany her when she sings at the party. The last

197

time Robert did it he played faster and faster till she lost her temper and hit him with her music stand and stormed away up to her room." He checked himself. "I shouldn't laugh. It was heartless of him—inexcusable, really."

But the story was irresistibly comic. So that, try as she might, Bridie could not but laugh aloud as she climbed hand-in-hand with her cousin Andrew, and he laughed with her. Only the day before he had seemed such a distant and threatening figure, and now she felt as if she had known him all her life.

The sky was blue now, the sun warm on their backs, the air soft with the scent of pine needles. They came to a rushing mountain stream, tumbling between mossy boulders, and crossed it by a broad timbered bridge. The stream came from the tiny loch up among the hills that fed their mill-wheel, he told her.

The track swung across the hillside, then, without warning, ended on a wide ledge cut out of the forest, a ledge carpeted with aromatic golden sawdust. To the rear of the ledge stood the mill-house, a long stone building with a water-wheel towering beside it. Three massive timber wagons were drawn up nearby, their shafts empty. The mill-wheel was stopped now, and the only sound was the tumultuous murmuring of water, close at hand yet unseen and mysterious.

Her companion paused at the edge of the surrounding trees. "When the mill-leet is closed," he explained, indicating a built-up stone channel on a level with the top of the wheel, "the water from the loch is drawn off through an underground passage. It surfaces a hundred feet or so farther down the hill."

The sound of voices came from the mill, followed by clanging hammer-blows. "They're fitting the new saw-blade." Andrew took an uncertain pace forward. "I only hope they're getting it properly aligned this time," he said. "No doubt Duncan knows his business well enough, but . . ."

He tailed off. Bridie realized that he felt a trespasser here too, as he seemed to in his father's study. She stepped onto the soft carpet of sawdust and her cousin followed her. Clear of the trees now, she could see the gleaming Firth, and a steamer, tiny and toy-like, coming down on the tide.

"That'll be one of Galloway's excursions," Andrew murmured.

198

"Papa, of course, couldn't bear the sight of those steamers. But then, that's hardly surprising."

Bridie was puzzled. "Why was that?" she asked.

"Did they not tell you?" Her cousin frowned. "It was from just such a ship as that that Papa's first wife, Melissa's mother, fell to her death."

"How dreadful!" Bridie shuddered. "What a terrible way to die. How did it happen? Was there no handrail?"

"Certainly there was a handrail. It's a bit of a mystery really. An eye-witness said the wind seemed to catch at her hat, and she lurched out to reach it."

"What did your father do?"

"He was not with her. He was in some other part of the ship."

The words were spoken firmly, a sharp denial of whatever Bridie might have been tempted to suspect. And yet, why should she be expected to think such a thing? She caught her breath. "I didn't mean to suggest—"

He swung round on her. "The rest of the world did, though. . . ." He took her hands in his. "Forgive me, dear Bridie. It's a sore subject. They weren't happy, you see, Papa and the first Lady Tantallon. And there was talk he'd been seen with Mama—a vulgar music-hall performer—in the weeks before his wife's death. The talk may even have been true, for all I know. Papa's marriage *was* miserable, and he and Mama certainly adored one another. But that does not mean. . . ."

He shook his head sadly. "How cruel people are. Even your grandfather, Papa's own brother. . . . And it was all so unfair! Papa was nowhere near the platform—a dozen witnesses said so."

In his anguish he was crushing her hands in his. Then, gradually, he relaxed his grip. "But it's all ancient history now. Over and done with. I should never have mentioned it. I'm sorry."

"Of course you should have mentioned it," Bridie said earnestly. "If it concerns you, then it concerns me also." The words, sincere, impetuous, unconsidered, were out before she could stop them. And she was glad.

For a moment her cousin was disconcerted. Then he lifted her hands to his lips and gently kissed them. "Bless you, Bridie," he said. "I should have known you'd feel like that." He released her.

199

"After all, you're one of the family," he went on briskly. "You're a Tantallon through and through."

Did he really not know, she wondered wistfully, that that was not what she had meant at all?

At that moment, however, she heard a shout and a black and white collie dog came bounding down the path. Duncan Symonds was standing in the big open double doors of the mill building.

"Noble, come here," he called. "Come here, sir, you devil!"

Then, seeing Andrew and Bridie, he came forward. "Is it you then, Sir Andrew?" He snapped his fingers and the dog came to heel, to sit quietly at his master's feet.

"The repairs are progressing?" Andrew asked.

"Fine. . . . Aye." Symonds stroked his beard thoughtfully. "Though now that you're here, sir, I'm thinking that you might be able to gi'e us a wee bit advice. We canna' get the main pulley to run true."

Bridie stared at him, amazed. Duncan Symond's behaviour to her cousin now was in surprising contrast to what it must have been earlier in the day.

Andrew excused himself politely, and together the two men disappeared into the sawmill. The dog Noble, having sniffed Bridie's skirt in mild curiosity, trotted off.

For a time Bridie wandered about the clearing, then approached the open doors of the mill itself and looked inside.

The sight that met her eyes was impressive indeed. In the centre of the floor, mounted upon well-greased iron rails, she saw a huge metal-topped table. A slot ran the length of the table, through which projected a great jagged-toothed saw-blade. Other machines, equally menacing, were positioned to one side of the table, all connected via great swooping lengths of loops and pulleys to a series of overhead shafts. In the midst of which, spanning the entire building, was a heavy girder bridge, also running on rails, and hung with grapnels like the claws of some gigantic iron bird, a monster powerful enough to lift even the biggest tree trunk as if it were a matchstick.

The men—Andrew, Mr. Symonds and another—were up on the gantry, deep in conversation. Tentatively, Bridie moved farther into the building, and was about to call out to them when Mr.

Symonds appeared to glance down at her. Abruptly he stooped, and pulled a lever. She waited, puzzled. For a moment nothing happened. Then slowly, with a silken rustling, the wheels about her began to move, gathering speed until, in a matter of twenty seconds the entire building was filled with a nightmare chaos of sound and movement.

Bridie covered her ears, and cried out shrilly, cowering back against the wall as the giant saw-blade, now only a few inches from her face, its thousand iridescent teeth spinning faster and faster, began to keen an hypnotic lament.

Bridie was drawn towards it as if mesmerised, already she felt the wind of its passing cool upon her cheek. She was hardly aware of the change when, her cries heard by the men above, the machinery began to slow. Footsteps clattered down the iron ladder from the gantry.

"Bridie! Bridie! For God's sake, are you all right? Are you hurt?" Andrew was close beside her, his face pale.

She leaned back against the wall, shaking her head weakly. "No, not hurt. Only—"

His arm was about her waist. "You must never—you must *never* enter this mill without letting the foreman know you are here. Can't you see how dangerous it is?" He shook her, half angrily. "With these long skirts of yours, you might easily have been. . . ."

He didn't need to finish. She found she was trembling. "I'm truly sorry, Andrew. Could I sit down a minute, please?"

"Of course. Of course." He led her into an office, sat her down and poured her a glass of water.

She drank it gratefully. "It was silly of me to get upset," she stammered. "I was really in no danger—no danger at all."

What else could she say? If she claimed that Mr. Symonds had known she was there, he would surely deny it. And besides, had he really known? He was her friend. What reason could he possibly have had to place her in such peril? She closed her eyes. The entire episode was no one's fault but her own. It *must* have been. . . .

"Well, well—" Andrew relented. "It's over now, and no harm done. We were testing the overhead pulleys, you see, and they seem to be running fine."

She opened her eyes and looked up at him again. On the wall

201

behind him hung a portrait of the old Queen above a large green-painted safe. There were wooden filing cabinets also, and samples of planking, all carefully varnished and labelled.

"Did you fix them?" she asked him. "The pulleys, I mean?"

Andrew appeared doubtful. "I *checked* them . . . gave a grub-screw an extra turn here and there. Anyway, if they weren't running true before, they certainly are now. So I must have done *some* good, I suppose."

All the same, Bridie wondered, recalling the "dust-up" Robert had described between his brother and Mr. Symonds, it was strange that the estate manager should have asked for Andrew's help in what now appeared to have been such an unimportant matter. Unless of course the request had been intended as a peace offering. . . . It was almost as if there had been some reason why Duncan Symonds hadn't wanted her cousin up at the sawmill that morning—a reason that no longer applied. Duncan was clearly a man rather less straightforward than her first impressions of him had suggested.

EIGHT

*T*he proof I needed was come by all too easily. And my theory wasn't wrong.

First of all I found a chemist willing to do what I wanted and ask no questions. He was a man used to the secrecy of us theatricals— Professor Salvador regularly bought spirits of mercury for a trick that involved turning water into something that looked like wine. Next I discreetly obtained samples of Sir James's vomit and took them to this chemist for analysis. The results the next afternoon confirmed my worst suspicions.

He found poison. To be exact, he found antimony—and in such quantities as to suggest that, since the patient was still alive, the poor fellow had developed a partial immunity to it. He wasn't at all surprised that the patient was being sick. Antimony worked that way. In his opinion, the patient was being systematically done to death.

I had already asked Jamie to meet me after the performance that night. To say what must be said would be the most difficult thing I had ever attempted.

A growler was waiting at the stage door. I asked the driver to take us to Arthur's Seat, a prominent local landmark. Time enough, I thought, for all that had to be said between us. Jamie was waiting for me inside the carriage. We kissed as it lurched away beneath the flickering gas-lamps.

Then I disengaged myself. I told him I had something very difficult and upsetting to say to him. Naturally he jumped to the wrong conclusion. "Your season at the theatre here is ending," he said wretchedly. "You have to go back to London."

I shook my head. "I'm to be here until the end of September. That's six weeks off." I'd promised myself I'd stay calm but I couldn't bear it. I burst into tears and blurted out what I had discovered.

When I had done, he sat in silence for a long time, while the growler creaked and swayed through the steep dark streets. Then he sighed.

"Antimony, you say? But how could it be got hold of?"

So his first question had been how rather than who.

I dried my tears. "First," I said. "I'm going to ask you a question. And you must answer it truthfully. Tell me, James, when you're at home, are you a drunkard? So that someone who lived with you would be justified in trying to cure you?"

He turned to me. I remember clearly how the fusty horsehair seat squeaked beneath him. "I swear to you, Otranta, never more than a glass or two of wine. And the malt at bedtime. But a drunkard— never! Why do you ask?"

"Because antimony is in the powders you can buy by post from a certain English doctor. It's put in small quantities into the wine of an excessive drinker to make him sick, and thus cure him of his habit."

"I see." He seemed to draw away from me. For a time neither of us spoke. Then, "You've given me a great deal to think about," he said at last. "I'm not sure that I thank you for it."

I watched him sadly, realizing that he had never, in all the time

203

since we had first met, been as far from me as he was then. Shut away from me by what we both knew.

"This English doctor," he said at last. "Would he be a Doctor Smithson of Brighton, by any chance?"

I was wary. "That is the man's name, I believe."

"Aye. . . . Aye, I thought as much." He passed his hand wearily across his eyes. "I—I saw the name on a packet at the back of my wife's bureau. A matter of two or three weeks ago. I asked her what the packet might be, and she said it was medicine for her migraine. I asked her then what was wrong with our local doctor's medicine, and she flew into a rage. . . ."

He spoke levelly, listlessly. "I believed her. I had no reason not to, you see." He stopped, and all at once began to sob uncontrollably. I moved towards him, and touched his hand. At last he came to me, and I comforted him as best I could.

It wasn't easy to have given a man the knowledge that his wife was a would-be murderess. All I could think was that I loved him, and he loved me. The future remained dark and impenetrable. . . .

Mr. Symonds had joined Bridie and her cousin in the office. "They tell me the new Argyll nearly ran you down, you and Mistress Melissa," he said concernedly. "They're treacherous things, these motors." He paused. "I'd like you to know, Mistress Bridie, that the blocks were secure beneath its wheels when I left it. I wouldna' have you thinking I do not know my responsibilities."

His eyes were guileless in his handsome, bearded face. How could she doubt him? Either in this or in the matter of the mill machinery? "Of course not," Bridie said firmly. "The blocks must have slipped on the wet cobbles. It wasn't anybody's fault." And now, as the event receded in her memory, she believed her words.

Later, on their way down from the mill, Andrew wanted to know what Duncan had been referring to. She realized that at lunch Robert and Melissa had chosen to talk of other things—possibly so as not to add to Andrew's other worries. She described briefly what had happened.

He was horrified. "What a terrible thing! In future the Argyll shall always be left at the lower end of the courtyard, facing the wall." He took her arm. "You've had quite a day, my dear. I wouldn't want you to think life at the castle is always so perilous."

She laughed then, and they walked in companionable silence down the track until they reached the stream. Here they leant on the rail of the wooden bridge, looking down into the rushing water. She sensed there was something he wanted to say to her.

At last he spoke. "My mother. . . ." Frowning, he cleared his throat. "What do you really think of her? Is Robert right? Does she really possess some terrible secret?"

Bridie paused. She did not want to answer hastily. "Lady Otranta is a very unusual woman. . . . She has suffered a tragic bereavement. But that, I think, is not all that is troubling her. It is as if there were indeed some hidden torment, something she dare not speak of—scarcely dare even *think*. . . ."

Silence fell between them, strained and unhappy, broken only by a wood pigeon murmuring gently to itself in a nearby tree. All at once Andrew relaxed, held up one finger. "Listen to that bird. Mama used to tell us a story about a wood pigeon when we were children. Dearest Mama, what *fun* she used to be." His grip on her hand tightened. "And will be again, Bridie—I swear it."

He quickened his pace, and she with him, running through the shadowy, pine-smelling woods. She knew it was a promise he was making—a promise to his mother, and to her also.

They came to the castle. She left him then and climbed to her room with a light heart. Her hand on the door-latch, however, she changed her mind. She would go and cheer up her great-aunt, take to the old lady all the hope and determination that had come to her and Andrew up on the summer hillside.

The sitting room was empty. Bridie crossed it, tapped upon the closed bedroom door, waited a moment, then burst impatiently in.

And froze. Appalled.

Old Peggy was seated on the edge of the bed, her glasses knocked crooked on her nose, propping up Lady Otranta where she lay, sprawled across the heavy crimson covers. The old lady's head lolled, her eyes gaped sightlessly at the opposite wall, while from her grotesque, painted-doll mouth there issued unmistakable snoring.

Bridie's horror lasted only a moment. Then she started forward, filled with compassion.

Only to be brought up short by Peggy's harsh words. "For Gawd's sake, ain't there *no* bloody privacy left in this rotten world?" She hugged the old, unappealing body to her. "We managed right enough before she come, didn't we, my pet?" she crooned. "And we'll manage right enough after she's gone, too." She glared at Bridie. "Which can't 'appen too soon for my liking, neither!"

Silently Bridie backed from the room. Her resolve to help her great-aunt had not weakened, but there were areas where she dared not trespass.

NINE

*O*bviously I've reached the ugliest part of my story. One to which the reader already knows the beginning (that Sir James was being systematically poisoned by his wife) and the end (that he and I were eventually joined in what some might call unholy matrimony) but not the middle. Now, if I'm ever to find peace of mind, it must be faced.

I've already stated that there's one who I believe would do just about anything to stop me finishing these memoirs. How then, you may well ask, do I dare to go on? And the answer has to be, by deceit.

It's hardly the first deceit in my life, and certainly not the worst. Put baldly, my deceit is to pretend drunkenness. These days my entire household, save one whom I think I can trust, believes me a helpless alcoholic. Day after day I act the drunkard, seeing all the time the misery my squalid performance is causing to those I love. But the sad fact is that I haven't been able to think of another that would work even half as well.

Mine isn't a large household. Most of the time we've a pretty good

206

idea what each one of us is doing. So the only way I can think of to get some time to myself is to pretend to be badly the worse for drink. It's a repugnant business. But at least it allays the suspicions of the one above all whose suspicions <u>must</u> be allayed.

Do ends ever justify means? I hope so. Certainly common justice demands that my story be told. And not only the story of James and myself and his wife Margaret either. There are things about the late Queen also that need bringing out into the open before the myths surrounding Victoria become too firmly entrenched. And I have documentary proof. I'm not promising scandal, but, rather, unique insights into a sensitive and much-misunderstood woman.

But I'm straying from the point. Which for the moment must be the situation facing Sir James and myself in that August of the year 1875. . . .

The weather was fine that August. It mocked our misery, Jamie's and mine. He'd returned to the castle the day after our midnight cab-ride. And he'd already told me he wasn't going to challenge his wife with what we'd discovered. Not until he'd decided what he was going to do about it.

For myself, I'd have gone straight to the police. I hated the woman. I'd never met her, never even seen her. I knew nothing of her, or of her reasons. But nothing in the world could have excused what she was doing.

James got away from the castle again as soon as he could. We sat and talked in a quiet corner of the Princes Street Gardens.

The police, he told me, must be a last resort. Apart from anything else, he blamed <u>himself</u> for his wife's monstrous behaviour. I knew the true reason had to be that woman's twisted mind, but, he said, if he'd been anything of a husband to her, she'd never have been driven to such desperate straits. He'd been neglectful, he said. Then again, there was his baby daughter. He'd wanted a son, and his wife knew it. Perhaps she'd felt he didn't care enough for the child. . . .

Round and round he went, trying to find an excuse for murder. In some strange way he still felt a loyalty towards the wretched woman.

*While I hated her all the more. And made my plans . . . she deserved
death. She was a monster.*

*Strong words. But I believed them, and I believe them still. She
can't be harmed by them now, of course, being dead.*

For Bridie life at Castle Tantallon quickly settled into a predictable routine. The middle two hours of each day, when Lady
Otranta had recovered from her excesses of the night before, were
the best time for her to visit the old lady. She was good company
then, reminiscing about Sir James's proud years in the old Queen's
service, but when Bridie led the conversation round to the problem of the memoirs, always her great-aunt gently evaded her.

She reported as much to Robert one day. She'd found him—as
he was most often to be found—seated at the organ, a Bach fugue
on the music stand. Music, Bridie had soon discovered, was Robert's
passion. He had facility and talent, but not the genius he craved.
And because he could not excel as he wished, he made light of his
ability, as he did of most things. For the rest, although he occasionally accompanied Andrew on his rounds of the estates, he
seemed a young man with little to do but "buzz" about the
neighbourhood in the Argyll.

He listened to her as she described her most recent conversation
with Lady Otranta. "It must be difficult for you," he said. "After
all, if this goes on long enough, she may give up the idea of the
book altogether."

Apart from the two hours or so spent each day with her great-
aunt, Bridie's time was her own. Frequently she was racked with
guilt at her idleness, which she assuaged in long letters to her
employer, hinting at the difficulties facing her, and offering to
return to London. His letters in reply she opened fearfully, terrified that he might take her at her word. But he was always patient
and encouraging, begging her to persist.

For the rest, she was busy enough, walking in the woods with
Andrew, going on bicycle rides with Melissa, playing the organ,
or the piano in the long, oak-galleried music room, practising
accompaniments for the songs Melissa would sing at the coming
party, or jaunting with Robert in the motor car along the shore of

208

the Firth of Culross, from where the stupendous Forth Bridge could be viewed.

Inevitably there were interruptions in her routine. One of these came on the Monday of her second week at the castle, when the yellow Argyll, driven by Duncan Symonds and bearing a portly stranger in a wide-awake beaver, clattered past her and Melissa as they were returning on their bicycles from a morning ride.

Melissa wobbled dangerously and put her foot down, as clouds of dust and smoke billowed in the car's wake. "That horrible Macnab—looking as pleased with himself as ever, I see! Duncan will have been down to meet him from the ferry. Such a performance! As if the local Alloa doctor wasn't good enough for Mama."

Tentatively Bridie suggested that perhaps an Edinburgh doctor was better versed in difficult cases such as Lady Otranta's.

Melissa snorted. "He'd have you think that, of course. . . . But I mustn't be uncharitable. Anything that might help my poor stepmother is worth trying." She edged her bicycle a little closer to Bridie's and lowered her voice. "But I do wish he wasn't just back from Vienna, and so full of peculiar stories. There's some German doctor there, he says, with the most curious theories concerning the affections between the sexes. He would have us women believe we're all in love with our fathers. An odd idea, wouldn't you say? If not positively disgusting?"

Bridie considered. She remembered with painful clarity the depth of her affection for her own dear father. "I don't know," she ventured, then glanced sideways. "Your father now, weren't you perhaps just a little in love with him?"

"In love with Papa?" Melissa hunched her shoulders. "Yes, perhaps I was . . . at least, when I was little."

She stared at the ground. "But not . . . not afterwards. I blamed him. It wasn't fair, I knew, but somehow I decided it was all his fault. The letter. Everything. Even my mother's—" She broke off.

"What letter was that? Did you blame him for your mother's death?" They were friends enough to be frank with each other, Bridie thought.

Her cousin looked up sharply. "Good Lord, no," she said. "My mother's death was an accident. Everybody knows that. But by all accounts she wasn't an easy woman. And perhaps, if Papa had been a little firmer. . . ." She shook her head, then hoisted herself back onto the saddle. "Anyway, I wasn't a bit in love with Papa. But I *was* frightened of him, I think—which probably amounts to almost the same thing."

So saying, she pedalled off in the direction of the castle, leaving Bridie thinking that she had just heard the most extraordinary definition of being "in love" she had ever come across. It seemed to explain just why her cousin was still unmarried.

Up at the castle the family was gathered in the small sitting room, waiting for the result of Dr. Macnab's examination of the old lady. When he came to them, he appeared irritatingly self-satisfied. Considering, that is, what they all knew about the condition of his patient.

Andrew leapt to his feet. "Well, doctor?"

Macnab clasped the lapels of his jacket with fat pink hands. "As well as can be expected, Sir Andrew."

"And what does that mean?" Robert demanded.

"It means that your mother's arthritis is incurable. The most we can hope to do is slow its progress. Which we appear to be doing quite satisfactorily."

"But Mama doesn't even *have* arthritis." Robert swung round. "Does she?"

Dr. Macnab positioned himself at the empty fireplace as if warming the backs of his legs at the non-existent flames. He was nearly bald, with the sort of ruddy, well-polished complexion that betokened years of good living. "You must have seen for yourself that the patient suffers almost continual discomfort," he said. "I've prescribed laudanum, of course, but I've had to warn her of its addictive properties. If she prefers to resort to alcohol I for one cannot wholly blame her."

Andrew sank wretchedly into a chair. "I don't understand," he said. "Last time you were here you had a different theory. You talked about the memoirs Mama was writing, and—"

"Ah yes, those memoirs. . . . In view of what I have learned today I suspect they may have been something of a red herring."

"I'm glad to hear it." Andrew looked up. "But what has made you change your mind?"

"Naturally my conversations with the patient are confidential.

But I think I may safely say that the memoirs are not significant. The patient has given up all idea of ever writing them."

Bridie stared at him incredulously. "Are you sure?"

Dr. Macnab appeared to see her for the first time. "We haven't been introduced, I believe. You must be Miss Bridie. How d'you do?" He bowed.

"The patient has spoken of you most highly," the doctor continued. "She hopes that you may be persuaded to extend your visit. To be honest, I hope so too."

Bridie blushed. "I . . . I'll stay as long as I'm needed," she said. Though how she could square that with Mr. Pugh-Hennessy if her great-aunt had really decided not to write her memoirs she couldn't imagine. She'd stay on anyway, she decided—even if he chose to dispense with her services.

"I'm delighted to hear it." Dr. Macnab beamed. "The patient has need of all the support she can get. . . . And now, if you don't mind, I'd best be on my way." He produced an enormous gold watch from his waistcoat pocket. "The next ferry leaves in forty minutes, I believe."

Andrew rang for Meredith. Duncan was to bring the car to the main entrance. He turned back to the doctor, and they talked for a few moments longer. Then the clatter of the approaching Argyll was heard through the open windows. Dr. Macnab moved quickly to the door.

"Now, don't any of you disturb yourselves. Naturally you will have things to discuss. If Miss Bridie would kindly escort me. . . ?"

She followed the doctor out into the hall. She didn't mind him treating her like a sort of poor relation. After all, that was what she was, more or less. On the steps outside Dr. Macnab paused.

"You must forgive me for that little ruse, Miss Bridie. But I wanted a word with you alone." He lowered his voice. "You see, I have to admit that there are things about your great-aunt's condition that I do not altogether understand. And since she seems to be particularly fond of you, I was wondering if—"

"What sort of things don't you understand, doctor?"

He frowned. "It would be better, I think, if I did not lead you. Rather let me say that if there's anything that does not seem to you to . . . as it were, to make *sense*, then I'd be most grateful

211

if . . ." He tailed off, rummaging in one of his waistcoat pockets.

"A lot of the things my great-aunt does don't seem to make much sense," Bridie said sharply. Did he want her to be a spy?

"Ah yes, but mostly they do, you know. If you think about them." Suddenly his tone was utterly serious. "Which is why this . . . this other matter is so puzzling to me."

He presented a card to her. "Believe me, I have Lady Otranta's interest deeply at heart. And I certainly would not ask you to betray any confidence. But if you *did* happen upon anything that you thought might be helpful. . . ." He prodded at the card. "You know now where to find me." He took her hand and squeezed it. "I'd be really most grateful."

He went away then, down the steps. On the cobbles he turned back. "She trusts you, you know. And now that I've met you I think I can understand why. You've a wise head on your shoulders, and you're outside all . . ." he gestured with his hat ". . . outside all this."

She watched him climb into the motor car, and a moment later it was gone in a fine haze of smoke. She looked down at the card in her hand: *Reginald Macnab MD. 12, St. George's Square, Edinburgh.* She wasn't at all sure what he expected of her. A wise head on her shoulders? She very much doubted it. But she did care what happened to her great-aunt. And she *was* outside the various undercurrents of life at the castle. . . .

She was to be forcibly reminded of just those undercurrents the very next day when, on her way to visit her great-aunt, she was brought up short just outside the open sitting room door by the sound of raised voices. Suddenly, to her astonishment, she realized that it was Robert, easy-going Robert, who was haranguing Lady Otranta. And in terms so violent as to suggest that the old lady might need Bridie's protection. So she returned to the open doorway and looked in. Robert was leaning over his mother in her high-backed chair, shouting into her face, almost beside himself with rage. As Bridie watched, he stooped and shook his mother's shoulders.

"A millstone round your neck," he shouted. "Round all of our necks. And for what? Out of loyalty? To *'Lissa?*"

Her great-aunt remained astonishingly calm. "Be quiet,

Robert," she said coldly. "You just have to live with the fact that your father loved her. Jealousy is hardly—"

"Jealousy? *Jealousy?*" Robert swung away. "My dear Mama, what a ridiculous—" He caught sight of Bridie standing in the doorway and stopped abruptly. She saw his expression change to its habitual mask of mocking indifference.

She went bravely forward into the room. "I'm sorry," she said. "I didn't mean to eavesdrop. But the door was open, and I. . . ."

"It really doesn't matter." Her cousin folded his arms. "You'd have to find out sooner or later. . . . The thing is, you see, poor 'Lissa's been up here again, ranting on at poor Mama about those rotten memoirs. We all know what a horror she has of them, although she tries to keep it to herself. And I honestly can't imagine why. Can you, fair coz?"

She met his gaze. "No, I can't. And to be frank, I don't believe it."

"Oh, Bridie, Bridie. . . ." He smiled at her sadly. "How little you know about us. We Tantallons are a nasty twisted lot beneath our smiling exteriors." He moved closer, and lowered his voice. "Be nice to poor Mama. I know I've behaved disgustingly. But . . . well, I hate to see her taken advantage of." He looked charmingly apologetic. "You're thinking it's 'Lissa I should have bullied. And you're quite right. But she takes these things to heart so. And she's so . . . vulnerable."

A millstone round our necks . . . was that really the way the family thought of Melissa? If so, then it was no wonder she took things to heart so. Robert went away then, and Bridie stared after him, wretched that such jealousy and unhappiness could exist in any family.

"People seem to think that because I'm old I'm deaf." Her great-aunt's brisk voice roused her. "But I'm not, you know. And you mustn't take Robert too seriously. He has all of his father's temper, but none of his father's self-control."

Bridie turned back into the room. Lady Otranta had moved across to the fireplace in which a log fire was burning and had positioned herself beside the dummy chess player.

"Come and sit down, child. It's high time Az Rah and I told you about some of the tricks we got up to with the great Professor

213

Salvador." The old lady poured herself a drink from a bottle on the mantelpiece, then came round in front of the cabinet on which Az Rah's chessboard was laid out, and began opening the various doors. "Watch closely, my dear, and I'll show you how the trick was accomplished. . . ."

Bridie watched, and nodded her head in obedient amazement. It was almost as if the old lady were trying to take Bridie's mind off Robert's behaviour. Which of course made the girl all the more determined to get to the truth.

By three o'clock Lady Otranta's frequent visits to the bottle on the mantelpiece were obviously taking effect, so Bridie was able to tuck her drowsily up in her chair and make her escape.

She went at once in search of Melissa, finding her cousin seated at the piano, picking out the tune of a mournful Scottish folk song. She looked up as Bridie came in.

"I can't seem to get the stupid thing right," she called. "Do come and play it for me." She stood up and Bridie took the piano stool, poising her hands nervously above the keys as she wondered how to lead up to the question she had to ask.

She lowered her hands again to her lap. "These memoirs," she said boldly. "I didn't think you minded very much whether Lady Otranta finished them or not."

Her cousin's eyes widened angrily. "You've been listening to Robert, of course—what exactly has the little swine been saying?"

"Only that you didn't want the memoirs finished." Already Bridie felt ashamed. "I . . . I have to know, you see. After all, I'm supposed to be helping her with them. I'm sure not a single word's been written in the two weeks I've been here, but I wouldn't want you to—"

"Why can't Robert mind his own business? He doesn't really know anything—not a bloody thing!"

Her cousin's bad language shocked Bridie. But it convinced her more than anything else that there was indeed something to know. . . . She got up from the piano. "I'm sorry I poked my nose in, 'Lissa. It's really nothing to do with me."

"No, it's not." Melissa swung round on her. Then, suddenly, all her anger melted away. "Oh Bridie, Bridie—how rotten life is. We shouldn't be quarrelling, not you and I."

214

There were tears in her eyes. Bridie moved forward impulsively and put her arms about her cousin. "It's not important 'Lissa."

"But it is, it *is*. . . ." Melissa's shoulders were shaking uncontrollably. "Oh God, if only I could tell just *somebody*. . . ."

Bridie hugged her closer. The music room seemed vast and threatening about them. "Here—I'll play that tune for you now. *Ye banks and braes*, wasn't it?"

Her cousin straightened her back. "Oh, to hell with it," she said, giving her short, sharp laugh. "Robert's quite right, of course. He doesn't know why, though. But my stepmother knows very well. Still, it won't be the end of the world, I suppose, if she puts it all down in this rotten book of hers. One day I'll tell you all about it, but not now. . . ."

Then, quite suddenly, Bridie thought she knew what was worrying Melissa. The accident in the gun-room that had maimed her half-brother, Andrew: perhaps her part in it had not after all been entirely blameless. She'd know she could rely on Andrew's discretion—Bridie remembered how guarded he had been on the subject. But if Lady Otranta knew the truth also. . . .

Not for the first time Bridie wished devoutly that she'd never even heard of the confounded memoirs. She smiled at Melissa reassuringly, then bent over the piano keys.

TEN

To be frank, Jamie's indecision infuriated me. I had a matinée to do that day, so I was forced to leave him shortly after one. But I promised to meet him again that same night, after the evening show. I was deeply worried for him—he looked so utterly wretched, sitting there in the sun on that bench in the Princes Street Gardens. . . .

He met me at the stage door. We walked. If there was danger in Edinburgh's darkened streets at that time of night, we didn't think of it. We had other problems. He told me he'd decided not to go to the police. There was his daughter to think of—how could he

215

*have her growing up knowing her mother was a murderess? And
as for himself, the scandal would certainly ruin him.*

*His reasoning didn't convince me. I asked him—I had to—did he
still love his wife? He stopped beneath a street lamp and turned to
me. I remember his face to this very day. And his words also.*

*"I loved her once. Perhaps I always will. But I hate her too, and
all the more because of that love. . . . Do you think you can understand that, Otranta?"*

*I couldn't. But it didn't matter. If he said that was how he felt,
then I had to believe him. "Jamie . . . Jamie, what are we to do
now?" I said.*

*He didn't answer. As we walked on again he was taken suddenly
with a horrible spasm of pain. He leaned against some railings,
retching dryly. I held him tight. Dear God, how the poison
lingered.*

*When the worst of the agony was passed he lifted his head. "I
wish she was dead," he whispered. "God forgive me, Otranta—
I wish she was dead."*

*I helped him back through the streets to the door of his club.
Little else was said between us. But the seed was sown. And at last
he and I were in total agreement. . . .*

The castle had a garden, a place of bright lawns—one set out
for croquet—and roses and lavender, with paved paths thick
with fragrant alyssum, and a fountain playing in the middle of a
lily pond. Sheltered on all sides by high stone walls, to the east
an arcaded terrace had been built, with teak seats and great stone
tubs of hardy escallonia.

It was to this sunny corner that Bridie often came in the late
afternoon. It was her "thinking place", where she could sit quietly
and review the events of the day, and it was here, one afternoon a
few days later, that she found Andrew, staring at the fountain with
unseeing eyes. He did not hear her approach, until she kicked a
pebble across the grey paving stones. At the sound he stiffened,
and turned warily. Seeing her, he relaxed.

216

"Bridie my dear, forgive me—I'm afraid I'm intruding on your private corner."

"It's hardly *my* private corner. It was here a long time before me and I'm sure it'll be here a long time after."

Andrew looked away. "But you've made it yours," he murmured. "Certainly I shall always think of it as yours."

She didn't know how to answer. Suddenly there was tension between them. By what means did he know how often she came there? He had seemed so absorbed in the affairs of the estate recently, almost as if he was avoiding her.

"I've got that guest-list sorted out now," Andrew said. "I went over it with Mama yesterday evening before dinner. She was . . . well, surprisingly coherent."

Bridie hesitated. If he wanted to talk about his mother, then they would. "I think she's getting better," she said.

"Do you? Do you really?" He turned to her, then all at once straightened up, and limped away down the terrace. He stopped by a pillar. "You know, this is not what I wanted to say at all." His back was turned to her. "I wanted to tell you . . . oh, so many things. But. . . ."

He swung slowly round. "Bridie, dear, you must try to understand. I'm not my own man. You'll think me weak, perhaps, not to stand up to her. But I—"

"Not weak, Andrew." It took great strength—and love—to bear all that he bore so patiently. "Your mother's ill. Naturally your first thought must be for her."

Despairingly he ran his fingers through his hair. "One day, maybe, when all this is over . . . yet who can say when that will be?" He beat his fist against the pillar's side. "I have so little to offer, Bridie. A nightmare. Nothing more."

Her eyes blurred. "It won't go on for ever," she whispered.

"But what about you? What about *your* feelings? I haven't even asked—oh God, I'm doing this so badly." Returning, he took her arm and drew her down beside him onto one of the benches. "Look—I'd better begin again properly. I . . . I care for you very much, Bridie. You're good and beautiful and true. You're—"

She put up her hand to cover his mouth. "Please, Andrew—please don't."

He grasped her hand and kissed it. "How long have you been here—three weeks? It might as well have been a lifetime. I *know* you, Bridie."

Her heart was pounding. "And I know you too, Andrew."

He let go her hand. "But what do you know? A limping wreck of a man, with a troubled household and . . . a mother who—it's impossible. How can I talk like this when there are so many problems?"

She cradled his face in her hands. "I don't mind waiting," she said.

"Oh, Bridie. . . ." He kissed her, lightly at first, then as his passion grew, so hers grew to match it. Until suddenly, breathless and more than a little afraid at the powerful, unfamiliar urgings of her body, she thrust him away.

"No, Andrew," she gasped. "No. . . ."

He stared anxiously into her face. "I love you, Bridie. Should I not have kissed you, my dearest?"

"Oh, *yes.*"

He smiled, then pressed her closely to him, her head against his breast. "I was afraid I'd been too bold. And clumsy perhaps."

"Clumsy? Oh no, not clumsy." She relaxed into his arms, feeling their strength. He smelt deliciously of tweed and camomile soap.

"I have a confession to make," he told her. "I've been avoiding you. I'd made up my mind never to tell you how I felt, you see. I had so little to offer—it wouldn't be fair, I thought." He lifted her chin with his fingers and stared into her eyes. "But then, this afternoon, my love got the better of me."

"Things won't always be like this," she said earnestly. "Your mother *will* get better."

"Do you honestly believe that?"

Thoughts fluttered in her mind like imprisoned moths. No, she did not believe it. "I know *something* will happen," she cried. Then an idea came to her. "Perhaps Lady Otranta would be happier, perhaps she'd see things differently if we were to—" She broke off then, horrified at what she'd nearly said.

But he'd guessed her meaning. "If we were to be married?" Suddenly his face was radiant. "You care for me enough for that, Bridie?"

She hesitated, seeking the right words, and as she hesitated, his elation died and he released her.

"But it wouldn't work, Bridie. You've seen how Mama treats me. I'm denied even the smallest authority. I tell you, I couldn't endure her scorn, the cruel things she'd say to us both."

"That's not true!" Bridie was near to tears. "You sound as if you think she's wicked."

"Not wicked. Only sick—and desperately unhappy." He stopped speaking, looking over her shoulder, back along the terrace. Standing on the path not twenty feet away was Peggy, her bright button eyes behind the thick lenses of her spectacles screwed up against the late afternoon sun, her whole attitude one of sly outrage.

Andrew got to his feet. "Well, Peggy?" he demanded brusquely.

"Well what?" the fat old dresser returned. "A person can walk in the garden, can't she? It's a free country, innit?"

Andrew folded his arms. "Well, you can get on with your walk now, Peggy."

"That's as may be. Knowing what I knows, I might well say as a word of kindly warning's called for. You see there's no future in it, not for neither of you. When Madame's bloody memoirs is done it'll mean ruin for the lot of yer." She smacked her fat lips. "Ruin, I say. Out and out ruin."

"Peggy," Bridie said carefully, "what exactly do you know about Lady Otranta's memoirs?"

"What I knows?" Peggy thrust her head pugnaciously forward. "I'm not stupid. I can put two and two together. If Madame writes the whole truth about what she done like what she's threatening, then it's ruin for the lot of yer."

Andrew laughed. "How melodramatic you are, Peggy."

But Bridie could see he was worried. She glanced calmly at her watch, not wanting to give old Peggy the satisfaction of seeing their distress. "Dinner in a quarter of an hour," she said. "You'll excuse us, Peggy, I'm sure."

Andrew took her arm and they walked together up the path between the long beds of dusty pink roses, through the low arched doorway and into the garden room. As they were about to part,

Andrew hesitated. "D'you think that she really knows anything?"

"Of course she doesn't." He looked so distressed that Bridie quickly kissed him. "You don't honestly think your mother has some terribly guilty secret?"

"I don't know," he murmured. "The thing is, Bridie, *I just don't know*. She's such an extraordinary woman—she might have done anything, anything at all. . . ."

ELEVEN

I thought then, and I still think now, that Jamie's wife deserved to die. If we take the wish for the deed, the woman was already many times a murderess, in her own heart . . . having sought, day after day, the death of another; I have always thought the difference the law makes between murder and attempted murder is totally misguided.

That Jamie's wife should die, therefore, was not only necessary but just. That, and the exact method, never worried me. As far as James and I were concerned, the only problem was how to say the words.

If it was up to me to play Lady Macbeth's part, then so be it. I spent the rest of that sleepless night formulating a plan. And I broached it to him the very next morning.

We were in the gardens again, sitting upon the same discreet bench. He refused my plan pointblank, of course. He had to. Apart from anything else, there was danger to myself in it. We argued for a long time, but finally I persuaded him there was no other way. He wept then, the tears streaming unheeded down his cheeks.

I did not weep. I knew I had to be strong enough for the two of us. And there was much to be arranged.

I hope I will be forgiven now if I cheat a little. For to divulge the details of my plan at this stage would be to rob my story of half its momentum. And I wasn't Professor Salvador's assistant for nothing. I still know the value of keeping a trick or two up my sleeve. . . .

A *Dangerous Magic*

Bridie had hoped to spend the next morning with Andrew, but he'd gone out early with the head shepherd, up onto the hill pastures to check the arrangements for the sheep-juicing, now less than a week away.

So she sought out Robert instead. She'd seen little of him since their stormy meeting in her great-aunt's room, and she was afraid she might have misjudged him.

She discovered him at last on his back under the motor car, tinkering with its insides. But he wriggled out readily enough when she spoke to him, and hurried away to wash hands and face in one of the stables. He emerged a moment later, shirtless, drying himself vigorously on a coarse striped towel.

"I say, coz—how about a game of croquet? Usually the lawn's like a bog, but I wouldn't be surprised if this spell of fine weather's dried it out."

She laughed. "I'm afraid I'll give you a rotten game. I haven't played since my school days."

"Doesn't matter in the least. Do say you'll play."

She nodded.

He put on his shirt and they went to the small summerhouse to haul out the croquet equipment and set up the game. He played well, but he fooled around so much that Bridie was able to keep up.

As time went on they played less, and chatted more. He was full of the coming party. One of the shepherds was a master fiddler, and there'd be Highland dancing. Bridie was reminded that Melissa had promised to teach her the reels, but that somehow nothing had come of it.

"Pooh on that," he said. "I tell you, all they do is prance round and round in ever decreasing circles."

He grabbed her hands and revolved with her faster and faster until he caught his foot in a croquet hoop and fell sprawling. He sat on the grass looking up at her, suddenly serious. "You know," he said, "that brother of mine's a jolly lucky fellow."

She blushed, not quite sure if he meant what she thought he did.

"Oh, come now," he said, getting slowly to his feet. "You'd

221

not expect that abominable old Peggy to keep a little titbit like that to herself, now would you?"

She blushed still deeper. "Then it's . . . it's all round the castle?" she faltered. "What about your mother?"

"I've no idea. She might jump any way, or no way at all. I'm not saying she will, mind, but she *might* just try to fill you up with stories about Andrew. . . ." Briefly his eyes flickered. "If she does, be sure you take them with a good big pinch of salt, eh?"

A shadow seemed to have fallen over the sun-warmed garden. Bridie clenched her hands together. "What sort of stories? Please, Robert—you must tell me."

He shrugged. "No one's perfect, not even Andy. Anyway—what if he hasn't always been quite the sober, self-controlled chap you see today?" His expression was uncharacteristically determined. "I'll say no more, fair coz. If Andy's declared himself to you, then it must mean he's put the past firmly behind him. And so must you. If Mama tries to dig it all up again, then don't listen."

He picked up the mallets, handed her one. "We were playing croquet, I fancy. And you were about to consign my ball to that farthest rose bed." She let the matter drop, and they got on with the game, but his words had taken all the fun out of it for her. No one was perfect, he'd said. But it wasn't true. Andrew was perfect. And he loved her.

When the game was finally over she went to her room. There, to settle her mind, she typed a short letter to Mr. Pugh-Hennessy, telling him she honestly believed now that he was wasting his money on her services. Lady Otranta would never write her memoirs—even her doctor said so. She was willing to return to London to report to him in person if he so wished, but that otherwise she would be staying on at Castle Tantallon for—her fingers hesitated, then rapidly tapped out the rest of the sentence —for a few weeks longer as a guest.

Bridie took her letter down to the box for out-going mail in the entrance hall, and tucked it through the slot with a sigh of relief. That was one at least of her worries dealt with. Now it was past midday, and time for her to go and see Lady Otranta. Robert's warning she cared not a fig for. But in deference to

Andrew's fears she would proceed cautiously with the old lady.

Her great-aunt was waiting for her, the inevitable bottle and glass on a table at her elbow, a book open upon her knee.

"Come in, child, come in. I was beginning to think you had abandoned me."

"Not at all, Great-aunt." Bridie sat down close to the old lady. "It was just that I had a letter to—"

"It's no matter. You're here now. And I have come to a most important decision." She closed the book on her knee with a snap. "I have decided to let you into the secrets of mind-reading. . . . Not that they're exactly secrets—this book, by Robert Houdin, explains everything for those who care to read it. But it's not a volume in general circulation—and anyway, I understand that people these days use some completely different system. But this was the one Professor Salvador and I employed, and you've seen it in action yourself."

Bridie couldn't believe her ears. Mind-reading? What on earth was her great-aunt thinking of? Had Peggy then said nothing to her of what she had seen yesterday down in the garden?

"I've felt a bit guilty," Lady Otranta went on, "ever since that little demonstration. You're very dear to me, and it didn't seem fair to leave you possibly believing in mystical powers that I certainly don't possess. Mystical powers, no. An excellent memory and a head for figures, yes."

Bridie had to stop the old lady. "Forgive me, Great-aunt, but just before you tell me about the mind-reading, I wonder if I could—"

But Lady Otranta, once launched, was virtually unstoppable. "Later, dear, later. . . ." she murmured, then returned to the attack. "There are what are called *trigger phrases*, you see. Twenty-six of them. One for each letter of the alphabet and for twenty-six groups of words also—colours, shapes, materials, and the sort of items that might reasonably be in the pockets of a member of the audience. There are twenty-six words in each group—that's six hundred and seventy-six words to be memorized, and in their correct order too."

She peered at her great-niece. "You appear muddled, child," she accused. "It's really very simple. Take any trigger phrase you like. *Come along now:* well, that's an easy one. It's the first one on the list, so it stands for the first letter of the alphabet. Old Peggy used it, you may remember, when she asked me who was waiting outside. *Come along now,* she said, so I knew at once that it must be someone whose name began with A. Therefore, Andrew."

In spite of herself, Bridie was intrigued. "What if there'd been two people whose names began with A?"

"Then Peggy'd have gone on to give me the next letter in the name. And the next after that, if necessary. *Hurry up,* she'd have said. Now that's the fourteenth trigger phrase. And the fourteenth letter of the alphabet is N. For D she'd have given me *Try harder*—that's the fourth trigger phrase. And so on. . . ."

"And there really are twenty-six of these phrases?"

"Certainly there are." The old lady closed her eyes and began to rattle them off. "*Come along now; Do your best; Now then; Try harder; I want to know; Concentrate; We want to know; We'd like to know. . . .*"

The words ran together insanely in Bridie's ears. "But surely," she interrupted, "you can't spell out everything? It would take too long. And someone might notice."

"Aha!" Lady Otranta opened her eyes. "That's where the lists come in. Phrase number one, for example, *Come along now*—that refers to list number one also, which is colours and shapes, twenty-six of them. Yellow, green, blue. . . . I needn't go on. First you're given your list number, then the number of the word upon that list. You understand?"

"It sounds like an awful lot to remember."

"And so it is, child. But I've never forgotten them, and neither has Peggy. She helped me learn them, you see. Anyway, the phrases and words are all here in Houdin's book." She held it up. "He should never have written it of course. But then, as I've said, it's all old stuff now. Now, child, we'd better put the book away safely. You're privileged, my dear. I've never before let anyone— not even the boys—into my little secret."

She poured some whisky and drank it; "Take the book, Bridie, and put it in the drawer over there." She pointed to a little shallow glass specimen cabinet with solid sides, standing on four

224

spindly legs. Bridie stared at it—the cabinet had a glass top and front and back, and there was no sign of a drawer, nor room for one. But she carried the book over to it all the same—she'd learned enough in earlier visits to know that little in that room was what it seemed to be.

And indeed the cabinet, on close inspection, proved to be yet another cunning deception. Inside, at the bottom of its glass front, a mirror sloped up diagonally to the back top corner, beautifully fitted against the solid sides and perfectly reflecting the triangular inside of the cabinet above it so that the space appeared both rectangular and perfectly transparent. While behind and beneath the mirror, as Bridie saw when she went round to the back of the cabinet, there was room for a tapering drawer big enough to accommodate the book. Bridie put it in and closed the drawer with a click.

"Well done, child. We'll make a magician of you yet." Lady Otranta nodded approvingly. "But now, my dear, if you don't mind, I'm a little tired. Perhaps you would be good enough to call Peggy for me."

Bridie realized unhappily that she was being sent away. "But *please*," she protested, "please let me stay just a bit longer. There's something very important I have to tell you—I . . . I love Andrew. And he loves me. And we—"

"Indeed?" Lady Otranta stared at her coldly. "I was afraid you were trying to tell me some such nonsense. And I did my best to spare you. Spare us both. . . ." She groped for her stick and began pounding on the floor. "Peggy? *Peggy?* Where are you, you great fat, idle creature?"

Bridie felt wretched, understanding now what all that talk of mind-reading had really been about. The old lady had made it as plain as she could that she didn't want to discuss the matter of herself and Andrew.

Abruptly Lady Otranta paused in her pounding, and fixed Bridie with a blurred, uncertain eye. "You'll be hurt, m'dear. Give up the whole ridiculous notion—now, while there's still time. Go back to London and try to forget you ever met the accursed Tantallons."

She began to pound again and call for Peggy. Bridie was

225

utterly bewildered by the sudden change that had come over her. At last the fat old Peggy sailed imperturbably in.

"Now, what's all this, *Madame?* Did I hear a little birdie singing?"

"God Almighty, woman, you did *not.*" Lady Otranta flailed the air unsteadily with her stick. "You heard your wretched employer shouting herself hoarse for the want of a little simple attention."

Peggy removed the stick from the old lady's grasp. "Well, old Peggy's here now, so we won't be needing that, now will we?" She leaned it beside the fireplace. "And there's no call to get all aeriated. You're upsetting Miss Bridie there."

Peggy looked across at Bridie, and nodded in the direction of the door. As Bridie backed from the room her great-aunt was being hoisted gently to her feet.

Outside in the octagonal room Bridie paused. If she hadn't actually seen Lady Otranta's rapid deterioration with her own eyes she would never have believed it possible. How much had the old lady drunk—half a tumblerful? Hardly more. It struck her that her great-aunt might almost have been putting on that pitiful performance as a way of getting rid of her.

Slowly Bridie made her way back to her room. She sat on the bed, staring unhappily at her neat button boots. She didn't know which was better—to believe her great-aunt's drunkenness an act, or to believe it genuine.

At least, however, drunk or not, the old lady hadn't tried openly to defame Andrew's character. . . . Bridie lifted her eyes, idly took in her typewriter on the table by the window. It was *not* as she had left it. There was a piece of paper now wound crookedly onto the roller.

With a curious sense of foreboding she rose and went to the table. An uneven line of words was spelled out on the paper. She wound the paper out of the machine and stared at it. The message was clear, and unpleasant.

a word from a freind. go back to london. youll be sorry if you dont. i mean it.

She crumpled the paper into a tight, angry ball. A friend, indeed! She was trembling all over, both from fury and from a

226

profound sense of shock. Who disliked her enough to play this
sort of cheap, cruel trick?

Everybody knew she visited her great-aunt at midday.
Everybody knew her room would be empty then. Robert, Melissa,
Duncan Symonds, Peggy, even dear old Meredith . . . it could be
any one of them. Slowly she tore the paper into small pieces and
threw them into her wastebasket.

It could have been any one of them. Just as it could have
been any one of them, she realized, who had staged the episode
of the runaway car. But it couldn't have been any one of them up
at the sawmill—only Duncan Symonds had been there then.
Duncan Symonds? No, it wasn't possible. That episode at least had
been no more than an unfortunate mistake. And Duncan, of all
people, was the least likely to have stooped to this latest,
despicable stratagem.

Anyway, she couldn't honestly believe she was in any real
danger. Whoever it might be simply wanted to frighten her. Well,
they'd failed. She wasn't going to give in and go running back
to London. Lady Otranta needed her. And so, she believed, did
Andrew.

Distantly she heard the sound of the gong for lunch. She went
to the wash-stand, splashed water in her face, and dried it.
Someone, perhaps, would be watching to see how well their evil
trick had succeeded. She tidied her hair, thrusting pins into it
with savage determination. Come what may, she'd show them she
wasn't a Tantallon for nothing.

TWELVE

*O*n *Thursday the twenty-eighth of August the three-thirty ferry
from Kincardine across the Firth of Forth to Leith, was a little late
in leaving. The delay was caused by the arrival on the jetty at the
very last minute of Sir James Tantallon's carriage. Sir James being
steward to Her Majesty's Stirlingshire estates, mere ferry steamers
were proud to suffer some slight delay.*

So the man at the gangplank of the "Lord Morton" waited

respectfully. He saw Sir James and Lady Margaret descend from the carriage. He was to concede later that he had been surprised at this for, like most locals, he was well aware that Lady Margaret had not been seen abroad in the company of her husband for several months. He was not to know, of course, that the entire enterprise was the result of a long and painful confrontation between Sir James and his wife the previous evening, and that, as Lady Margaret came towards him up the gangplank on the arm of her husband, her lowered face and the copious veiling about it were also the outcome of that same confrontation. Lady Margaret had been first outraged and later ashamed and distressed by what Sir James had said to her. She was distressed still, and in fact near to weeping.

Their original intention, it seemed, had been to travel by train to Stirling and then on down to Edinburgh, on account of Sir James's increasing ill health and consequent dislike of the ferry crossing. Reaching the nearest station to Castle Tantallon, however, they had apparently changed their minds and made post haste for the jetty at Kincardine instead. Upon being pressed in court to give a reason for this, Sir James had said the decision had been entirely his: since the weather was so exceptionally fine and calm he had chosen to spare his wife the tedious train journey and go by boat after all.

This explanation was generally accepted to be a thoroughly gentlemanly attempt to add nothing further to his wife's already considerable reputation for selfishness and ill-humour.

At the Kincardine jetty the couple went quickly aboard the "Lord Morton" and retired at once to her first-class main saloon, while the ship began to reverse away from the jetty.

The next person to report seeing Sir James Tantallon and his wife was the first-class saloon steward. He brought the couple tea at approximately four o'clock. There were no other first-class passengers taking tea in the saloon and he noticed nothing out of the ordinary.

It was as the paddle steamer was skirting the rocky islet of Inch Garvie that several people reported seeing Sir James Tantallon and
228

his wife walking together upon the upper promenade deck. The water was calm, and they seem to have stayed there for most of the rest of the voyage. At one moment, when the ship was nearing her destination, it is thought that Lady Margaret went briefly below decks. But she quickly returned, and the reason for her going was discreetly not inquired into. The ladies' rest room was just aft of the main companionway.

The next time the couple's whereabouts could reliably be established was when the "Lord Morton" was backing up in the deep water outside Leith docks. By then they were separated, Sir James being on the promenade just forward of the wheelhouse, while his wife was out on the observation platform above the starboard paddle casing. This was an unusual position, since the "Lord Morton" had by then turned her port side to the Leith shore, and most passengers therefore tended to crowd to that side of the ship. No satisfactory explanation was ever found for Lady Margaret's going out onto the observation platform.

Suddenly a scream was heard, even above the pounding of the "Lord Morton's" engines. Many pairs of eyes turned at once in its direction, in time to see Lady Margaret totter precariously over the rail, hesitate for one breathtaking moment, and then disappear from sight. A gasp of horror went up from all the onlookers. As one man they rushed across to the starboard side, while the master in his wheelhouse frantically rang down to stop the engines, and the "Lord Morton" slowed to a halt.

Afterwards at least a dozen witnesses were prepared to swear that nobody had been within a good thirty feet of Lady Margaret at the moment of her falling, certainly not Sir James—the ship's master himself could vouch for that, since the nobleman had been clearly in sight in front of his wheelhouse for around a quarter of an hour before the catastrophe.

As to the reason for Lady Margaret having fallen, the theory was put forward at the inquest that the wind had caught her elaborate hat and veil, and in reaching for them she leaned out too far and over-balanced. But since nobody could be found who had

229

actually been watching her before the moment of her scream, this remained no more than a plausible theory.

Within a few seconds of her screaming, however, at least a hundred people were leaning over the "Lord Morton's" starboard rail, staring avidly down into the murky water, expecting to see the mutilated corpse of the poor woman, for the paddles of the ship had been backing up on maximum power at the time of the tragedy. In the event they saw nothing but her hat and cloak floating on the turbulent waters. Her body had disappeared completely, drawn down, no doubt, by the powerful currents prevailing in the Firth at that stage of the tide.

Rowing boats put out from the harbour, and the search for the body was continued unsuccessfully for several hours. A watch was kept along the shores for many weeks, but the remains of Lady Margaret were never recovered. This was not an unusual circumstance. The tides were strong, and the currents unpredictable. Many poor souls had been lost that way, and their bodies denied a decent, Christian burial.

It was suggested at the inquest that the behaviour of Sir James Tantallon immediately following the accident had hardly been as grief-stricken as might have been thought suitable. But that is neither here nor there. He behaved, in fact, with complete propriety, going into full mourning for a twelvemonth and receiving the sympathetic understanding not only of his friends but of Queen Victoria herself. . . . Admittedly, no more than another two months after the end of the mourning period, he remarried—and chose for the second Lady Tantallon a young person with the most disreputable theatrical connections. . . .

In the days that immediately followed her finding the message on the typewriter, Bridie was wary. But as time went by and nothing out of the ordinary occurred, she began to recognize that her anxiety had been overdone—even ridiculous. Life at the castle went on just as before, growing slowly in momentum as it built up to the party being held on the Saturday night after the last of the Tantallon flocks had been dipped. Happy hours were spent in the music room with Melissa, learning the complex patterns of the reels, and menus and decorations were discussed.

Meanwhile, Mr. Pugh-Hennessy had answered Bridie's letter. She mustn't give up. The Tantallon memoirs were important to him. He had, he confessed vaguely, a certain *personal interest* in them. She must persevere with her great-aunt. She had read the letter hurriedly, then put it aside.

Bridie had told nobody of the threatening message, but she *had* described to Andrew his mother's reaction to the news of their love for one another. "It could have been a great deal worse," he told her. "If we bide our time and play things carefully, she's sure to come round before very long. And then—oh, Bridie, the life we'll have. So much to do, so much to show you. Scotland's a wonderful country, my love."

He kissed her then and she clung to him, forgetting everything in the excitement and magic of him.

Even the weather remained kind to the lovers, an Indian summer rare in those stormy northern regions. The first day of the sheep-juicing dawned bright and clear. Soon after breakfast Bridie, with Robert and Melissa, walked up the short way over rising ground behind the castle. This route was difficult and steep, but they soon came out on an open hillside, divided into fields by snaking walls of massive black, wind-scoured stones. It was a high, wild place, and today noisy and crowded.

Sheep covered the hillside in a great shifting carpet, restless as treetops in a summer wind. Among them men and dogs moved ceaselessly, funnelling them down from field to field, then on through a narrowing pathway of hurdles to where the long wooden sheep trough waited. A gigantic cauldron bubbling over a fierce wood fire close by sent out powerful fumes of boiling soap and tobacco.

Duncan Symonds stood at one side of the trough, Andrew at the other, their sleeves rolled up, heaving the sheep in one by one, then urging them on their way to a lower paddock. Already both men were sodden and muddy, their voices hoarse as they shouted and prodded at the struggling animals.

Bridie watched entranced, proud to see how Andrew—Sir Andrew, Laird of Tantallon—laboured willingly alongside his men, and was accepted by them.

Robert touched her arm. "There's true glory for you," he said, pointing. "There's what it is to be a real man, not just a posturing aesthete like me." There was only unashamed admiration in his expression.

"Then why not take off your jacket and join them?" she teased.

He laughed. "What—and end up with a smudge on my nose and blisters? No, thank you!" Affectionately he nudged Melissa. "Mind you, that's what 'Lissa here would do, if she were a man. Wouldn't you, 'Lissa?"

His half-sister's eyes were bright with the day's excitement. "Maybe I would! But it'd be a dull old world if we were all the same. And you can't talk—you don't mind what sort of a state you get yourself into, tinkering with that rotten motor car."

He put a brotherly arm round her waist, smiled across at Bridie. "The thing is, fair coz, to know your limitations. I know mine. And the really manly stuff I leave to Andrew. He's so good at it, you see."

She turned back to the hectic scene round the sheep trough. Yes, she thought joyfully, he *was* good at it. Remembering his fear that she might think him weak she knew now, more than ever, how foolish that had been. He was *strong*—as strong as he was gentle.

At eleven the men broke for bread and cheese, and a great brew of scalding, milkless tea. Andrew came over to join them, but he didn't linger. "It's hot, wet work," he said, cheerfully wringing out his shirt tails, "and I'm not really fit for the fine company. . . ." And he was off again, taking with him a powerful stench of drenched fleeces and tobacco water.

And so it went on every day that week, Andrew out on the high hillside from dawn to dusk, and Bridie trudging, alone now, up the alternative, easier path through the woods with the stout ash staff he had provided for her, and watching quietly from the edge of the trees, until only two more days of the sheep-dipping remained.

232

That evening she lingered on till dusk before regretfully waving to Andrew and Duncan and turning to make her way back down the path through the wood. Andrew would take the shorter route down later, after he had seen the last of the men off to their homes.

She walked on, singing quietly to herself one of the songs Melissa would sing at the party in two days' time: *Gin a body meet a body, comin' through the rye.* . . . Suddenly she broke off, hearing away to the left, a faint rustling sound. She stopped, hoping to see some animal, a badger perhaps. But the brushwood here was thick and she could not see for more than a few feet into the undergrowth. She was about to walk on when the rustling began again. And this time accompanied by other sounds. Human sounds, she was sure. Muffled groaning. And then, unmistakably, a pathetic, faltering cry for help.

Her heart began to pound. Cautiously she advanced along a track, thick with dead leaves, heading away from the main path in the direction of the sounds. As she hesitated, the cry for help was repeated. The skin at the back of her neck prickled. "What is it?" she called. "Where are you? What's the matter?"

No answer came, only a renewal of the dry scrabbling, and heavy, painful breathing. She moved on, her stick held protectively in front of her. The track straightened and in the rapidly gathering dusk she saw on the ground, some four yards ahead, a dark form. Nothing moved. The woods were silent save for that rasping breath.

Pity overcame her fears, and she started forward. Her foot caught in a root and she staggered, groping wildly with her stick, dropping it and falling finally on her knees. And in the same instant there came a sudden convulsive eruption of the leaves in front of her, and a grinding snap as two great rows of rusty teeth burst out and fastened with horrible finality on the stick that had triggered them.

For a moment she stared down at the iron jaws in horror. Then she screamed, and screamed again, her voice pitifully small in the cathedral stillness of the trees. The man-trap had been meant for her. Another step forward and it would have been her own leg, rather than the stick, lying splintered in its grip.

It was some seconds before her terror was penetrated by sounds of violent movement. Looking up, she saw that the dark shape on the ground was gone. Its monstrous plan to lure her forward thwarted, only the noise of its headlong flight remained.

She got to her feet, and stood for a while in the thickening shadows, gazing fearfully down at the shattered remains of the stout ash staff Andrew himself had cut for her and realizing with a new, cold certainty that her former innocent confidence had been dangerous folly: she had under-estimated her enemy. Whoever had devised this latest horror wanted far more than simply to frighten her.

And what, she wondered, if the plot had succeeded? Would the perpetrator still have fled, leaving her to a bleak and bloody vigil till the inevitable search party from the castle found her? Or would he have stayed and . . . and dealt with her while she lay trapped and helpless, contriving no doubt to make it seem all part of the same unfortunate accident? A foolish girl had strayed from the beaten track and blundered to her death. . . .

She shuddered. The idea was vile, the work of a madman. Yet that, she now knew, was what she was up against. A lunatic and a *man*. For had not the figure on the ground been. male? She believed so, but could not be certain. In all honesty, though, could any woman have contrived and carried out a scheme so fiendish?

With stumbling footsteps she returned to the path and started the weary walk back to the castle. It took a long time, for it was now nearly dark. When finally she staggered into the castle courtyard Andrew was there, still in his work clothes, a lantern in his hand.

"Bridie my dearest—thank God you're safe." He caught her in his arms. "Where have you been? You had us worried out of our wits."

Haltingly she poured out her terrible story. He led her gently in, seated her by the fire in the small drawing room and brought her brandy.

"A man, you say, lying on the ground?"

"I . . . I think it was a man. It was dark beneath the trees. So dark. . . ." She shuddered again at the memory.

"So dark, perhaps, that you might have mistaken a fallen log or a pile of leaves for—"

"No, Andrew. No!" She clutched at his arm. "He moved—he breathed—he called for help."

"His voice, then—did you not recognize his voice?"

"It was a whisper . . . no more than a whisper." Dear Heaven, he didn't believe her. "The trap is there, Andrew. It's *there* . . . And I'm sure you could see, if you looked, the marks in the leaves where he lay."

She was weeping now and he kneeled beside her, his arm about her shoulders. "Hush, my dear. You're safe now. And of course I'll look—in the morning, when there's light enough." He held her till she was calm again. Then gently he released her. "Early to bed, I think. You've had a shocking experience. Agnes shall bring you supper, and something to help you sleep."

He went with her to the door of her room, then kissed her tenderly on the forehead. "To save any awkward questions I shall tell the others you may have caught a chill up on the high pasture. And we'll talk again tomorrow." He left her then.

She undressed and got into bed. Agnes came, bringing her food on a tray, and a concoction in a medicine glass which she drank obediently. Soon she began to feel pleasantly drowsy. She slept, not hearing when Agnes came to remove the supper tray.

When she woke Andrew was standing by her bed. The curtains were drawn back and sunlight streamed in through the windows.

"Forgive me, my love. I should not have roused you."

The events of the previous night flooded back. Anxiously she reached for his hand, holding it tight. "You've been up to the woods?"

He nodded. "I found the trap, just as you described. A terrible thing. We used them once, but haven't for many years." He hesitated. "It *is* possible, though, that one or two are still around, overlooked when my father forbade their use."

She understood at once what he was suggesting. "No, Andrew —it was placed there deliberately. Could you not see?"

He moved away to the window. "I have to be honest with you, my love. For all I could see, the thing might have been there since God knows when. Nor did I find any trace of the man you

236

believed you saw. Leaves had been disturbed, certainly, but who could tell by what, or how recently?"

The image of a dark shape huddled on the ground was vivid in her mind. "Then you don't believe me."

"I did not say that. Simply that I found no clear proof." He returned to her bedside. "What can I do, my dearest? If we go to the police with your story they will say the same as I. Besides, who do you think could have done such a wicked thing, or for what reason?"

Resignedly she lay back on the pillow. "It was dark among the trees," she conceded. "Perhaps you are right. Perhaps I *was* mistaken." Already the horrible certainty in her mind was fading. Perhaps that dark shape had been a fallen log or some woodland animal, and the cry the call of a night bird. . . .

He kissed her cheek. "You're so precious to me," he whispered. "So precious. . . ." Sighing deeply, he moved to the door, then paused. "It won't be necessary, I think, to tell poor Mama what has happened. As for Robert and Melissa, I shall leave it to you to do as you think fit."

She smiled. He still loved her. That was all that mattered. "I really don't think I could bear any more questions. I'd much rather it was kept just between the two of us."

"It would be the wisest thing, I'm sure." He fidgeted with his watch chain. "I wish I could stay with you, my love. But I'm expected up on the sheep pasture. There's the Milbrannon flock still to be dipped. And we must be finished by lunchtime tomorrow, so that all can be made ready for the party." He blew her a kiss, and was gone.

Whatever had or had not happened the previous night, Andrew loved her and would see in future that no harm befell her. That much was certain. And now there was the party to look forward to. . . . She leaped out of bed and was dressed and waiting impatiently by the time Agnes arrived with her breakfast. Soon afterwards Melissa came knocking on her door with anxious inquiries for her health. She also wanted to talk about what the two of them were to wear the following evening. They needed to be sure, she explained, that they neither "clashed" nor went in anything too similar.

237

Bridie could have hugged her, since she recognized the excuse for what it was—the dearest, most tactful way of offering assistance. She herself had been quite resigned to wearing her single evening dress—the one with the pie-frill collar and little puff sleeves—yet again, but Melissa must have suspected from its regular appearances that it was the only one she possessed. And have determined, therefore, discreetly to do something about it.

Bridie admitted happily to her predicament. Melissa whisked her off at once to her own room, where the two of them spent a very pleasant hour sorting through clothes.

"I know I'm taller than you," Melissa admitted, "and a bit more up and down. But once we've chosen something, old Peggy'll fix it. She's a positive wizard when it comes to giving a little and taking a little." She broke off, staring round rather shamefacedly at all the dresses spread out on the furniture. "Goodness knows what I ever thought I needed all this stuff for," she muttered. "Mama *would* get them for me . . . why, some of these must date right back as far as—" She stopped abruptly, then recovered herself. "Oh, fourteen years at least," she finished, with an attempt at lightness.

For a moment Bridie was thoughtful. Fourteen years ago her cousin would have been only eighteen—and it had been then, she suddenly realized, that the accident to Andrew's foot had occurred in the castle gun-room. This must be the secret in Melissa's life that made her so afraid of her stepmother's memoirs —she had in some tragic way been responsible for Andrew's injury, and the old lady knew it.

Bridie looked up, came near to speaking. But the moment slipped by. Her cousin's past was anyway none of her business.

From all the dresses they chose finally a pale green shot silk trimmed with a darker green velvet that would go well with Bridie's rich auburn hair and pale complexion, while her dark-haired cousin would wear a striped maroon and gold taffeta. They took Bridie's dress along to Peggy and cajoled the old woman into making the necessary alterations.

She stood Bridie up on a stool and slashed at the dress with tailor's chalk. "Needed termorrer, is it?" she snorted, her mouth full of pins. "Fat chance of that, I must say."

"Oh, Peggy dear, it only needs the tiniest bit doing," Melissa wheedled. "And Mama's always saying how clever you are with your needle."

Peggy glared at her over her spectacles. "I'll have you know, Miss Melissa, as how flattery won't get you nowheres."

It did, however. In the end it got old Peggy to promise to have the dress ready for a fitting that same night. Hardly had Bridie finished changing back into her skirt and blouse before Duncan Symonds came through from Lady Tantallon's room, the accounts folder as usual under his arm. She was horrified—a moment earlier and he'd have caught her in her chemise and petticoat. Not, she decided, that he was a man to make much of such an unexciting spectacle. He was far too wise and avuncular for that. And to think that occasionally she had suspected he might wish her harm. . . .

But she knew very little about Mr. Symonds's private circumstances. When he had left she turned to Melissa. "Is Duncan married?" she asked.

"Good Lord, no." Melissa gave one of her short, sharp laughs. "He's the born bachelor, I'd say. Lives over the stable block. Keeps his place as clean as a pin."

Old Peggy looked up sharply. "Mind you, there's them as would say he *was* married, though. In all but name, that is. To Madame Otranta."

There was a shocked silence. Melissa was the first to break it, frowning coldly. "What a disgraceful thing to say, Peggy. I suppose it's all that John Brown nonsense Mama's been filling you up with. Once and for all, Peggy, Mama is *not* Queen Victoria, and Duncan is *not* John Brown."

"Nonsense, is it?" The old woman tugged angrily at her needle. "You've not seen what I have. The actual diaries. Folks said as they was destroyed, and destroyed they should of been too. Let 'em both rest in peace, the poor souls—that's what I say."

Melissa frowned again. "What diaries are these? Mama's? Are you talking about her *memoirs?* Do explain yourself, for goodness' sake."

"Not me. I knows what I knows. And I reckon I've said a deal too much, as it is." She bent over her work, refusing to say another word.

With an effort Melissa controlled her temper and turned to Bridie. "I do hope you know Mama well enough not to believe—"

"Of course I do." Bridie patted her cousin's arm. "Anyway, your mother'll be expecting me about now. Why don't we go in together?"

Lady Otranta was still in bed, sitting up among all the elaborate oriental furnishings, her pale face flushed, her eyes bright as if with some secret excitement. "*Two* visitors? Come in, come in. What a pleasant surprise."

"Melissa's lent me a dress for tomorrow," Bridie said. "We've just been persuading Peggy to alter it a bit."

"That was thoughtful of you, Melissa. . . . But then, you always were a thoughtful girl. And such a help when the boys were little, and Robert such a trial to us all." She patted the heavy crimson covers on the bed. "Come here where I can see you, and tell me about the dress you've chosen for your city cousin."

Melissa obeyed, and Bridie wandered away to the window, pleased to see Lady Otranta and her step-daughter getting on so well together. The aspidistra on the table close beside her caught her eye. It was looking really quite sickly. Absent-mindedly she felt the soil—perhaps it wasn't getting enough water. No, the soil felt moist enough. . . . She took out her hand-kerchief and wiped her fingers. Then she stared at the grains of soil upon the linen. A faint but most curious smell was rising from them. She sniffed her handkerchief. Then she dug down into the pot, brought more soil out, and sniffed again.

There could be no doubt about it. The soil in the pot positively reeked of whisky.

She stepped back a pace, bewildered. Behind her the voices of her cousin and great-aunt rose and fell peacefully. She peered at the plant—clearly it was no wonder that the poor thing was dying. But why *whisky*, of all things?

Until suddenly, astonishingly, the answer became clear. If a person wished to appear to be drinking far more than she actually was, there were only a limited number of places in which to dispose of the surplus spirits. The fire was one, of course. But what if, as in the mornings recently, the fire was not yet lighted?

240

Where then could a person go to tip a glass or two, when she was sure no one was looking?

Always assuming, of course, that any person would be eccentric enough to wish to create an impression of excessive drinking in the first place. . . .

THIRTEEN

I have cheated in my story, of course. By describing the events on board the "Lord Morton" that afternoon in August 1875 principally from the point of view of the world at large, I have managed to tell rather less than half the truth.

The story in fact begins two days earlier, on Tuesday the twenty-sixth of August. On that day I took a first-class return journey across the Firth on the "Lord Morton". My plan needed testing. I spent a long time upon each of the observation platforms above the "Lord Morton's" paddle casings, staring apprehensively down the ship's side at the frothing water below. Eventually I decided that my plan was feasible, if only just. And I reported as much to a haggard Sir James that same evening.

On Wednesday Jamie, poor man, faced his wife with what he had discovered, and laid the alternatives for her future clearly before her. Either she fell in with his wishes or he went straight to the police. Needless to say, after a predictable amount of bluster and weeping, she agreed to the former.

Early on Thursday morning, wearing a light grey travelling cloak and a saucy boater, I took another return ticket on the "Lord Morton", booking a first-class cabin at the same time. I went ashore at South Queensferry, walked to the railway station there, boarding the eleven thirty-seven train bound for Stirling, which I left at Alloa. A short walk around that town to purchase a newspaper, and two o'clock found me again at the station, buying a second-class ticket to Aberdeen. I then repaired to the Ladies' Waiting Room, removed my cloak and hat, and placed both, together with the ticket to Aberdeen, on a bench just inside the door. Thereafter I sat down behind my newspaper in the farthest corner and did not look

up when the waiting-room door banged open, and certain small rustlings took place. I had no wish to see Sir James's wife -and I imagine she felt the same about me.

Only when the door had banged shut again did I lay down my newspaper and move to the bench on which I had left my cloak and hat and ticket. In their place lay a cloak of far richer material, blue, and a broad hat with a great deal of veiling. Stifling my disgust, I put them on. They smelt of _her_. It was, I swear, the hardest part of the whole enterprise.

Tying the veils firmly about my face, I left the waiting room. James was ready for me a short distance off, while away down at the far end of the platform stood a passable imitation of myself, in light grey cloak and saucy boater, her back turned upon us both.

The rest is obvious. James and I hurried back to the coach. I climbed in, my head averted, while James shouted instructions to the coachman. It was I, therefore, who accompanied Sir James onto the "Lord Morton", and not his wife. She, the wretched woman, was by then well on her way to Aberdeen, to a new identity and a new life. It was I who took tea with Sir James in the first-class saloon. It was I who stood with him by the starboard rail. And it was I who climbed up onto the observation platform as the ship approached Leith Harbour.

A small technical digression is now necessary. The observation platforms on the "Lord Morton" overhung the paddle casings by perhaps three feet. Beneath them the sides of the hull swelled to a broad strip called, I believe, a rubbing strake. Above this strake, and some five feet below the platform, were the port-holes to the first-class cabins.

I had previously, in the person of myself, secured the cabin immediately below the platform. And I had also, during the crossing with Sir James, slipped below briefly to make sure that the parcel I had hidden on the earlier crossing was still there, and that the cabin port-hole was firmly open. It was a fitting nearly two feet in diameter —a squeeze, certainly, but for a slim young woman with Professor Salvador's training behind her, no very serious problem.

The rest, as they say, is history. There was a nasty moment, admit-

242

tedly, when the heavy stuff of my borrowed cloak encumbered my legs so that I almost missed my footing as I "fell". But I overcame that, cowered briefly on the rubbing strake beneath the platform, just long enough to shed both cloak and hat into the water below, and then dived precipitately head first through the open port-hole and onto the bunk within. . . . I lay there, panting. Images passed before my eyes, images of knife-edged paddle blades that flashed by only inches from my feet. Images of what would have happened had I slipped. . . . But I had not slipped.

Briskly I got to the floor and tidied myself. I put on the shawl and hat from my parcel, then left the cabin, and unobtrusively joined the people hurrying to see what had become of the poor woman who had just fallen to her death from the starboard observation platform.

It must be said, of course, that had the question ever been asked whether or not I, in the person of myself, had ever actually boarded the "Lord Morton", nobody would have been able to give a definite answer, such were the crowds and the general commotion.

And as for the light grey travelling cloak and saucy boater in which I had set out that morning—and which by then were well on their way to Aberdeen—who in the world was likely to ask after them? Except dear Peggy. And she, the pet, would believe just about anything I told her. . . .

Green shoes. If Bridie's evening ensemble were to be complete, this was the one thing she must have. . . . No—if one wanted an excuse to go to Edinburgh, and nowhere else would do, then green shoes were a positive brainwave.

The thought of going to Edinburgh had not come to Bridie at once. She had stood in her great-aunt's bedroom quite paralysed, listening to the inconsequential chatter of her cousin and the old lady, staring blankly at the grains of whisky-sodden earth still clinging to her fingers. And she had watched without comment while Lady Otranta went through the now familiar ritual of filling her glass, drinking from it (quite moderately, in fact), and becoming progressively more incoherent.

243

Finally, Bridie made her escape and in her bedroom was able to think more clearly. She thought, almost at once, of Dr. Macnab. He'd asked her to go to him. *If there's ever anything that does not seem to you to . . . as it were, to make sense,* he'd said. And this latest discovery made no sense at all. She must confide first in Dr. Macnab, then, armed with his expert opinion, she would go to Andrew.

The doctor's card was in a drawer. She got it out and stared at it. How to find an excuse for going alone to Edinburgh? It was then, with the gong sounding for lunch, that inspiration came to her. The party . . . her dress . . . the green shoes she'd need to go with it. Shoes from one of the smart Edinburgh shops.

Bracing herself, she raised the question of her shoes at lunch, and the journey was fixed, by the eight-thirty ferry next morning. She'd still get back in plenty of time for the party.

Duncan Symonds drove her to the ferry. At the jetty he stopped and pointed across at the dark clouds massing above the distant shore line. "Yon marks the end o' the fine weather, I'm thinking." He reached behind the front seat and produced a large umbrella. "You'd best be taking this, Mistress Bridie. When the wet comes down it'll be no wee bit drizzle."

Bridie thanked him and took the umbrella. The dog, Noble, sitting on the floor between them, whined and placed his head upon Bridie's knee. Absentmindedly she patted his head. The *Stirling Castle* was waiting at the jetty, a ship very similar, she thought, to the one from which Lady Margaret Tantallon had fallen.

"I'll be here to meet the two o'clock from Leith," Mr. Symonds told her. "So you mind you're on board her."

Throughout the crossing the sky darkened and the wind grew stronger. But the waves were still short, and the *Stirling Castle* rode them easily. At the Leith West Pier Bridie took a horse cab direct to Dr. Macnab's address. The fare would be more than she cared to afford, but the time saved would be worth it. She had a lot to get through if she was to see the doctor and also buy the shoes.

Jolting along cobbled streets, they came at last to Edinburgh, to the staid black terraces and crescents she remembered from her previous journey. The cab turned up a steep incline to St. George's Square, just as the first large drops of rain were spotting the pavement. Bridie paid off the cab at the door of number twelve, knocked and was admitted. She gave her name to the uniformed maid and was shown into a vast and empty waiting room, its heavy mahogany table set neatly with staggered yellowing rows of *Punch* and the *Illustrated London News*.

When her name was called she followed the maid down a corridor and into Dr. Macnab's consulting room.

"Mistress Bridie Tantallon," the maid announced, then departed. Bridie stood, fidgeting nervously and wishing she hadn't come.

The doctor rose majestically from his desk, and progressed towards her across the faded carpet. "Miss Tantallon—I'm truly delighted to see you. Sit you down." He held a chair for her, then returned to his desk. "And what can I do for you now, Miss Tantallon? Is it on your own account you've come?"

She shook her head. "You . . . you asked me to come if . . . if. . . ."

"Ah yes, Lady Otranta." He leaned back in his chair and blandly steepled his fingers. "She's an extraordinary woman, you know."

Bridie did know. And even if she hadn't, that was really all that anybody ever said about her great-aunt. The doctor was a fool. She should have trusted her first impression of him.

But she hadn't come all that way only to give up at the last minute. Clenching her hands in her lap, she told Dr. Macnab about her suspicions concerning her great-aunt's drunkenness, and about the proof of them that she had discovered the previous afternoon.

Dr. Macnab sighed. "I'm afraid this doesn't really surprise me," he said.

"You mean you've suspected something of the sort all along?"

"Unfortunately not. The signs were there, I'm sure, but I was blind to them." Such a frank admission warmed her to him. "There was something, though, that I could not exactly put my finger upon. . . . I take it you've mentioned nothing of this to anybody at the castle?"

Bridie shook her head.

"Very wise. I said you were a wise young woman, and now there's proof of it." He turned and moved away to the window, tucking his hands thoughtfully up beneath the tails of his morning coat. "I'm going to tell you something, Miss Tantallon, that nobody else in the whole world knows. It's a breach of professional etiquette, but I believe you will handle the knowledge wisely." He swung round. "Which means you will tell it to nobody. And you will not allow it to affect your behaviour in the smallest particular."

She shrank down in her chair. "What use will this knowledge be to me, then?"

The doctor came to stand beside her, his hand on her shoulder. "Understanding, Miss Tantallon. To be truly wise you must first of all understand." He paused. Then, "This arthritis your great-aunt is suffering from. What do you think of it?"

"What should I think of it?" Bridie racked her brains. "That it is progressive, and—"

"The disease Lady Otranta is suffering from is undeniably progressive. But it is *not* arthritis. Your great-aunt is dying, child. Rapidly." His grip on her shoulder tightened. "She is being consumed from within. Nothing anyone can do can save her."

"How . . . how long?"

Dr. Macnab discreetly gave her his own silk handkerchief. "A month?" he said. "A week? A day . . . ? Every time I visit her I am astonished at her powers of survival."

Bridie stared at the handkerchief in her hand. He was expecting her to cry. But she had seldom felt less like crying. The doctor's news was far too terrible for that. "It's my great-aunt's wish that her family shouldn't know of this?"

"Her wish." He smiled gently. "She's a brave woman. The only thing she said she couldn't endure was to see them suffer with her. For her . . . And besides, there was something she needed to accomplish. I never discovered exactly what. But. . . ."

Bridie stared up at him. "Her memoirs? But you told us—last time you came to the castle, you told us. . . ."

". . . That she'd given up all idea of completing them?" He smiled again. "That is correct. In the past she'd always seemed worried about them, so that I'd suspected some psychological cause. We all have things in our lives we're ashamed of. But the last time I spoke to her she seemed more than worried—she seemed afraid. She told me that she'd abandoned the memoirs."

"Did you believe her?"

"Not . . . entirely. But to set her mind at rest I promised to pass the information on to her family."

Bridie was thoughtful. "But what then of the pretended drunkenness?"

Dr. Macnab looked down at his pointed shoes. "A ruse, would you not say? A way of convincing whoever might be interested that the all-important memoirs were not being worked upon?"

"While in fact they were? And still are?"

"Who can say?" The doctor hesitated, shrugged. "But I doubt if it matters. If they're not finished soon, they never will be. . . . And you must be very brave now, Bridie. Your great-aunt will need your strength. And her family will too . . . afterwards."

Bridie bent her head then and the tears flowed.

FOURTEEN

*S*ir James and I did not meet for many weeks after his wife's "death". This separation was, of course, an essential part of our plan, so that no suspicion should fall upon either of us. I even returned to London with Professor Salvador at the end of our season at the Empire without seeing him.

I wonder if my readers were expecting to be told how Sir James and I had committed murder? Did they really believe us capable of that?

Sir James was so loyal to his wife that, in spite of all she had done, he not only spared her the indignity of imprisonment but in all her future wanderings—and she wandered far, settling at last in a Continental watering place—sent her an allowance. This he paid, faithfully, in expiation of whatever wrongs he felt he might have done her, until the day of her death, from natural causes, some twenty-five years later.

It hardly needs be said that she kept her side of the bargain, changing her name, never contacting her daughter, never exposing the trick she had been a party to. Admittedly a word from her would have ruined us all, a fact that James and I lived with all our days together. Ruined us all, I say. And with good reason. James, and myself, and in due course our two sons. Our two bastards. For it must be obvious by now that the marriage ceremony James and I went through was illegal. He was a bigamist, and I his knowing accomplice. And our two children therefore illegitimate.

The true inheritor of the Tantallon estate is Melissa Tantallon, the daughter of Jamie's only legal marriage.

There. It's done. At long last the record is put straight. James, right up to the moment of his death, had insisted that for my sake the truth be concealed. But it needed to be told.

It'll be hard on the boys, of course. But life will deliver them harder knocks than this, surely, before it's finally done with them. I love them both dearly. And my belief is that, when they think upon it seriously, they will see how wrong it would have been for them to continue to enjoy privileges rightfully belonging to Melissa. . . .

For Bridie the journey back across the Firth of Forth was a nightmare.

She had left Dr. Macnab in a daze. He would have called her a taxi to take her back to Leith, but even in her trance-like state she remembered the shoes—she dare not return to the castle without them. She insisted upon walking the short distance down to the shops on Princes Street and reluctantly he let her go.

"Not a word of this, now," he called after her. "For your great-aunt's sake, not a hint in word or gesture!"

The rain was now torrential from a sky that seemed to rest, dark and menacing, close upon the very chimney pots. When she reached Princes Street the pavements were deserted. Somehow she found a shoe shop, took the first green pair that fitted her, paid over an unconscionable amount of money and went out again into the street. And it was then, her spirits at their lowest ebb, that fate thrust yet another puzzle in her path.

As she stood in the arcade outside the shoe shop, staring out at the rain, a motor taxi splashed slowly by. Suddenly it was hailed from a shop entrance not ten feet away from her, and a man hurried out across the pavement to it, an elderly man, tall, with sloping eyebrows beneath his high-crowned hat. He stood for a moment, the rain dripping from his hat-brim, while he gave the driver his instructions. Then he got into the taxi, and it drove away.

The entire commonplace episode had taken perhaps thirty seconds. And Bridie had watched it in silent astonishment. For the elderly man had been her London employer, Mr. Pugh-Hennessy.

What in God's name was he doing in Edinburgh? His most recent letter had made no mention of coming north. Instinct told her that he was here in the city without her knowledge because that was his intention. His reasons were obviously secretive, and therefore not to her liking.

The time was nearly one. Scarcely more than an hour remained before the ferry left Leith for Kincardine. And she knew the wretched shoes had so far depleted her purse that a taxi all the way was out of the question. In desperation she set forth beneath Duncan's large umbrella, and from a policeman found that North British Railway trains left from the Haymarket station for Porto-bello and Leith. He pointed the way to the Haymarket station. It was, he said, a goodly walk for a young lady.

She made it, or most of it, at a goodly run.

Miraculously there was a train waiting that got her to Leith within ten minutes of the ferry's sailing. And so to the ferry, and to the unhappiest and most frightening journey of her life.

A full gale was blowing. The steamer lurched like a mad thing while Bridie, with eight or ten other ill-advised passengers, cowered in the main saloon, its windows totally obscured with rain and breaking water, her thoughts as tumultuous as the elements about her, the soggy little package containing her new shoes pressed tightly to her bosom.

Her great-aunt had pretended drunkenness. Her great-aunt was dying. Her great-aunt had been working surreptitiously upon her memoirs. Mr. Pugh-Hennessy had come secretly to Edinburgh. Her great-aunt was dying. . . . Round and round the thoughts went. And round and round went her stomach also.

She scarcely noticed when the ship's motion eased, and they arrived at Kincardine. Not a word, Dr. Macnab had said, not a hint in word or gesture. She only hoped that such a thing were possible.

Duncan Symonds was waiting in the car, just as he had promised. "You got what you went for, then?" he asked.

She nodded. The first of many bitter lies. What she had really got she had certainly not gone for. "How is Lady Tantallon?" she asked suddenly.

"Her Ladyship? Fine, fine. . . . And out about the castle too, here and there and everywhere, seeing to the preparations."

The *party*—the only reason for the shoes, yet somehow she had completely forgotten it. Then she remembered Mr. Pugh-Hennessy. "Mr. Symonds—has there been a letter for me today? Or a telegram?"

He glanced at her as the car lurched through rain-filled potholes on the approach to the narrow stone bridge. "Not that I've heart of, Mistress Bridie. You were expecting something?"

"Not really. It doesn't matter." Another lie. It mattered very much. Even Mr. Pugh-Hennessy, now, couldn't be wholly trusted.

The castle was in turmoil. The huge table in the dining hall had been pushed back against the wall and a buffet laid out upon it. In the music room chairs were being set out for the entertainment, while the entrance hall and the main drawing room were being cleared for dancing. Servants hurried in with kegs of strong beer and bundles of branches for the decorations.

The first person Bridie met was Lady Otranta, storming across the entrance hall, waving her stick. "Not the *crystal* punch glasses," she was shrieking, apparently to no one in particular. "It's not the Queen we're entertaining, I tell you!"

Seeing Bridie, she paused in mid-stride. Her face was pale, her eyes unhealthily bright. "Ah, there you are. The *King* I meant, of course. It's so easy to forget." Briefly she leaned on her stick. "You got back safely then. Didn't have to swim for it, I see."

"No, Great-aunt, I—"

But the old lady was already away again, crying hoarsely, "Not the *crystal* ones, you idiot!"

Bridie leaned for a moment against the newel post at the bottom of the stairs and closed her eyes. Knowing what she did, she could not bear to see Lady Otranta push herself so. Surely . . . ? She

250

opened her eyes and pulled herself upright. Only five minutes in the castle, and already she was giving way to anxiety. Firmly she lifted her sodden skirts and made her way to her bedroom.

The family—including Lady Otranta—had high tea in the small drawing room. Then, on her way back up to her room to change for the party, Bridie was joined on the stairs by Andrew. She took his hand, trying to seem carefree and gay. But, miserably, she felt the secrecy that Dr. Macnab had imposed upon her loom darkly between them.

Absorbed in thoughts of his own, he didn't notice her preoccupied air. At the door to her room he hesitated. "May I come in, Bridie? There's something I have to say to you."

Instantly alarmed she led him through the door and he closed it behind them. Suddenly she remembered the trap laid for her in the woods. He had promised he would make inquiries. She felt a coldness in her bones. "You have news for me, Andrew? There really was a man that night? You have discovered something?"

For a moment he stared at her blankly. Then, "No . . . no, nothing. There was nobody, my dear. Truly there was nobody."

"Then what—?"

"I had to see you. I had to. . . ." He held out his arms and she went to him. "Oh, Bridie. . . ." He kissed her passionately, so that she forgot everything—her great-aunt, Mr. Pugh-Hennessy, everything but the wonder of their love. "Bridie . . . my dearest, to go on like this is folly."

Her heart was pounding. "But Andrew, your mother—"

"Listen to me, my love. I want us to be married—and you want that too, Bridie?"

"You . . . you know I do."

"Then may I announce our engagement tonight? At the party? May I tell the whole world that you've consented to become my wife?"

The cosy little room reeled about her. "But Andrew—we've been through this before. You—"

"You're thinking of Mama. But in this I *am* my own man, Bridie. And I love you. I cannot live my entire life under Mama's shadow. Marry me, my dear. Let me make the announcement tonight."

She stared at him. Her whole being cried out yes.

"Don't say a word." He walked her to the window seat and pressed her gently down. "There's something perhaps I should not say to you. But Mama is sick—we all know that. Possibly, though, we don't know just *how* sick. . . ."

She looked away. Outside the rain fell in an unrelenting downpour. How near he was to the truth.

"It may be," he went on, "that she does not have long to live. I've watched her—she's thinner, weaker, every day." His voice broke, but he struggled to continue. "And I know that in her heart she wants me to be happy. I want her to live to see our joy, yours and mine. I want her to understand, and be happy too. For us."

She could resist no longer. "If you really want to marry me, Andrew, then you may make the announcement."

She was in his arms again. The decision was made. And in all her life she knew she'd never regret that moment.

FIFTEEN

*T*wo *months after his mourning period was up, James and I were married. It was a November ceremony, and as quiet as we could make it. He'd been down in London for a time before, and I travelled up with him at the end of October to meet his little daughter, his younger brother David and his family.*

Both David and his wife opposed the match. I had expected that, if not the full violence of their opposition. David was a lawyer of rigid Presbyterian principles, living in Glasgow with his wife Mary and an earnest, bespectacled son called Arthur. The son was to lose his sight in later years, poor man, and to father in his turn the most delightful, intelligent, daughter. . . . But David and Mary did everything they could to prevent Jamie's marrying me, a gold-digger, a cheap little nobody. When they saw they had failed, they stormed from the castle, never to return.

Originally dear faithful Peggy had gone north with me simply to act as chaperone before my marriage. But when the nurse to Sir James's little daughter departed (in righteous indignation at the coming introduction into the household of anyone as lowly as my-self), Peggy insisted on staying to help me with the child. In the event, caught at first between resentful servants and local neighbours who studiously ignored me, I was very grateful. And the child was en-chanting, so spontaneously open-hearted that we soon became very close. In fact, we stayed that way right up to her eighteenth birth-day. . . . Since the tragedy, I regret to say, things have never been quite the same between us. Guilt, perhaps? I don't know. Certainly I never blamed her for what happened. How could I, when I never even discovered what it was? My son Andrew, who might have told me, remained impenetrably discreet. . . .

It was around eight when the guests started arriving. Andrew stood with his mother at the foot of the great staircase to wel-come them, while Melissa and Robert hovered on one side, ready to help. The champion fiddler had come early—a tiny, bow-legged Scotsman in full tartan regalia—and was already scraping cheer-fully away in the dining hall.

Bridie knew very few of the guests, of course, and indeed, after half an hour or so of watching the arrivals, it seemed to her that literally everybody living within a thirty-mile radius of the castle had been invited.

She remarked on this to Robert when he drifted briefly into earshot. He laughed. "At least we're not snobs," he said. "A laird and his people are one, you see." He spoke, she thought, with some pride and little of his usual mockery.

At that moment Andrew, one pair of guests safely despatched, lifted his head in her direction. As he stood there in his kilt and white frilled shirt and dress sporran, she was reminded of the tall, commanding figure of his father in the portrait. He was his own man, he'd said. Old Sir James had been his own man also. . . . Their eyes met above the crowd. She blushed, pressing her clasped hands tightly against her breast.

In the big drawing room couples were being made up for an eightsome reel, and at that moment a young farmer came shyly to claim Bridie as his partner. She accepted gladly, safe in the knowledge of Andrew's love, afraid of nothing—not even the intricacies of the eightsome reel.

From that moment on, until the concert began at ten, she was never still. Mr. Pugh-Hennessy . . . the memoirs . . . all was forgotten. The green silk whirled and the green shoes hopped and capered. It was the first real dance of her life. Yet even the excitement of that was eclipsed in the breathless expectation of what was to come.

Twice Andrew partnered her. In a lull he whispered in her ear, "Midnight, my love. At midnight I'll make the announcement."

Briefly, in spite of herself, she looked round, afraid that her great-aunt might have overheard his words. But the old lady was sitting on the far side of the room, watching the dancing.

If Andrew dominated the proceedings that night by his handsome stature and boundless energy, his mother in her own way dominated them also—by the sheer magnetism of her presence. Although she moved slowly, leaning upon her stick, and sat often, she commanded respectful attention wherever she went.

At ten the haggis was piped in with full Gaelic ceremony. Then, with forks and steaming plates in their hands, everyone went into the music room and settled down for the concert, an entirely informal affair, one performer bobbing up from the audience and coming forward as soon as another was done. By the time Bridie's turn came to accompany Melissa, she had quite forgotten to be nervous. They were all friends there, every one of them.

At last, the entertainment ended, dancing was resumed, now to the music of the piper. Robert came forward, and danced between two swords crossed upon the floor, his hands held high, leaping and skipping. All evening he had been laughing, flattering, tossing his silvery hair, bewitching surely a dozen hearts with his outrageous charm. Never in all her life had Bridie been present at such a joyful gathering. As midnight approached she began to look round for Andrew. She left the dancing and wandered from room to room, finding him at last, sitting on the edge of the stage in the almost deserted music room. His face had a sickly greenish tinge and he was hunched forward, staring morosely into his empty wine glass. Her heart sank: obviously he had taken a great deal too much wine.

"Come along now, my dear." She helped him to his feet. "It's so hot in here—perhaps a little fresh air would. . . ."

She tried to lead him away but he resisted, swaying as he pushed his face down at her. "Kiss me, Bridie. Kiss me—"

Dear God, was this mouthing lout her Andrew? Desperately she looked round for help—but the room was empty save for a couple leaning on the piano with eyes for no one but each other.

"No, Andrew. No—not now. I—I think you should go upstairs. Lie down for a while. Until you're . . . better."

"Lie down. . . ." He seemed to think this a good idea and started away across the room, leaning heavily upon her arm. Suddenly he stopped and began to fumble feverishly for his watch. "I'm not late, am I? The announcement—I'm not late, am I?"

He'd got his watch out and was peering at it. "There's a . . . a minute to go, Bridie. You must help me, my dear. I feel so strange, so unsteady. . . . I doubt if I can make it without your help."

"No, Andrew." She spoke sharply, but near to tears. "I shall not help you. You're in no fit state."

He broke away, suddenly angry. "Then I'll manage on my own, by God!"

He squared his shoulders and made his faltering way to the music room door. She ran after him, trying to hold him back. But he thrust her aside.

"The announcement—you gave me your word. You shall not go back on it now. You gave me your word, Bridie."

She watched in despair as Andrew stalked blindly between the dancing couples in the entrance hall. At the foot of the stairs he paused and beckoned a servant to him, and they conferred briefly.

Bridie saw the servant look anxiously round, then nod and move away. She caught sight of Robert and his mother standing in the door to the dining hall, and began to ease her way towards them. But she was only halfway across when the sound of the great bronze dinner gong rose deafeningly above the piper's music. The bagpipes died with a discordant groan. The dancers stopped, looking round in bewilderment to their host where he stood upon the broad sweep of the stairs. Silence descended.

"Ladies and gentlemen . . ." Andrew swayed, then recovered himself. "My lords, ladies and gentlemen . . ."

Bridie stared in helpless fascination at the lurching drunken stranger who was her Andrew.

"My lords, ladies and gentlemen, *friends* . . . I shall not take up much of your time. . . . You are all of you my guests, and I welcome you."

He stood for a moment in silence. He seemed to have forgotten what he had planned to say next. Several of the dancers began to clap half-heartedly. The noise roused him. "I have an important announcement to make, you see. A very important announcement. . . ."

Bridie saw Lady Otranta imperiously forcing her way towards the staircase as her son looked out across the heads of the people, and repeated, "A very important announcement, and a proud one, also—"

Abruptly he broke off, his eyes turning up in their sockets till only the white showed. He stood a moment longer, then crumpled sideways, falling against the rail and tumbling slowly forwards down the stairs.

Someone laughed. It was a sound quickly stifled. With great presence of mind the piper began to play again as the guests drifted away in small embarrassed groups.

When Bridie reached the foot of the stairs Robert and his mother were there also. Andrew lay on the flagstones at their feet, dead to the world.

"See to Mama, will you?" Robert whispered urgently. "I'll deal with Andrew."

The old lady leaned on her stick, staring down at her son, breathing in fast, shallow gasps. Bridie put her arm about her waist. A moment later Melissa arrived, accompanied by Gordon Craig, a neighbour with whom she had been dancing. Together the two men lifted Andrew and began to carry him up the stairs.

"You go with him," Melissa said. "I'll look after Mama."

Bridie hesitated, then did as she was told, catching up with them as they shuffled along to Andrew's door, Gordon Craig puffing slightly, Robert cursing all the way under his breath. They went in and laid Andrew on the bed. Mr. Craig discreetly disappeared. Bridie wetted a towel from the water jug and began to bathe Andrew's forehead.

256

"You're wasting your time," Robert said savagely. "He's done this before. He'll be out till morning."

She didn't believe him. Was this then the truth he'd hinted at, that day on the croquet lawn? "What d'you mean?" she demanded.

"Forget I ever spoke, dear coz," he whispered. Then he reached down and loosened his brother's collar with rough affection. "And forget all this too, if you've any sense."

She laid the towel gently across Andrew's forehead and backed from the room. The last she saw of him was one of his hands trailing lifelessly from the bed as Robert began to remove his shoes.

Downstairs Lady Otranta had rallied miraculously and was circulating among the crowd, offering dignified words of apology for her son's behaviour. But the guests began to leave soon after—the evening was ruined.

It wasn't until the very last of them had gone, and her great-aunt was safe in old Peggy's care, that Bridie could go to her room and find release for all the pent-up misery within her. Andrew—oh, *Andrew. . . .* She cried herself to sleep that night.

SIXTEEN

O bviously there are people who would prefer that these memoirs so far had not been written. People who fear for Sir James's reputation, or for his wife's reputation, or even (bless them) for my own reputation. Not to mention those who stand to lose materially by what I have revealed.

As to the rest of these memoirs, there will be other people anxious to prevent <u>their</u> publication. The man, for example, who helps me every day. He's a good man, an honest man. Yet I've had to make him swear never to read a single word of what I write—for I know he'd move heaven and earth to stop me if he guessed the nature of what I am about to reveal. His overriding loyalty, you see, would be to what he thinks of as the late Queen's memory. By which he means the myth of her inhumanly faultless propriety. His affection for her is such that he even owns, to this very day, a collie dog called Noble, just as she once did.

While I myself, on the other hand, have evidence written with her own pen that she was blessedly neither more nor less human than the majority of her subjects. . . . But I anticipate. There's the episode of my miraculous acceptance into the Queen's circle first to be described. It came on a day in early spring, when. . . .

For three days after the party Lady Otranta held her own. Dr. Macnab was sent for and departed smiling blandly. On the fourth day, however, he was sent for again. And this time, when he came to the family where they waited in the small drawing room, his smile was gone.

"I have grave news," he said. "Lady Otranta's condition is very serious." He paused. "I fear she may not last the night."

Bridie closed her eyes. She had seen the change for herself, the gathering in of the old lady's resources, the strange new quality of peace. . . .

Melissa stifled a sob. Robert leaped to his feet, his fists clenched. "You're wrong, I say. I was with Mama last night, and I tell you she was better. *Much better.*"

"Please, Robert. . . ." Andrew had not risen. Now he leaned forward. "Does Mama know she's—she's dying?" he asked.

Dr. Macnab cleared his throat. "Yes. She knows." He hesitated. "I think she's known for a long time."

"Which is more than *you* have, you blundering idiot!" Robert leaned his head against the mantelpiece and wept.

Andrew seemed about to say something, then changed his mind. Helplessly Bridie watched his quiet anguish across the gulf which —since the night of the party—had separated them. He had come to her the very next morning, disdaining apology for his behaviour, simply in quiet, formal tones releasing her from their engagement. And she, distressed and uncertain, had accepted her release without argument.

Yet she had seen it simply as a way of gaining breathing space. She knew she still loved him. But his behaviour at the party had terrified her. She needed time. . . . And since then, Lady Otranta's condition had become so desperate. Events crowded in upon them both.

"Is there anything we can do?" Melissa asked. "Should we get a nurse over from Edinburgh?"

"There's no need." Dr. Macnab went to the window, and stared out at the rain that by then had been falling continuously for four days. "Lady Otranta is comfortable. Nothing else remains to be done. And now, if you don't mind, I'd like to get back to my patient." At the door he paused. "Lady Otranta has accepted the truth. She's a very courageous woman. But she needs the support of every single one of you. The time for grieving will be later." Then he left the room.

Bridie hurried after him, catching him on the stairs. "Why did you not defend yourself?" she whispered. "Why did you not tell them that—"

"Hush, my dear." He put a finger to his lips. "Your great-aunt knows her own mind. And things are bad enough for her family without them also having to know, and be grateful for, the many months of misery she's spared them."

Bridie thoughtfully retraced her steps back to her three cousins.

As she entered the room Robert was facing the door. "What's this, then?" he demanded loudly. "Secrets, is it? Secrets between our little Bridie and the good doctor?"

Bridie lowered her head in confusion. Andrew rose and limped across to his brother. "Don't bully her, Robert. We've troubles enough without that."

"But—"

"Don't *bully* her, I said."

For a moment the two men glared at each other. Then Robert subsided. "Well," he said bitterly, "at least if Mama dies now it'll solve a lot of our problems."

Andrew grabbed angrily at his arm. "What exactly do you mean by that?"

"You know very well what I mean."

"I do not."

"Then I'm not going to tell you."

It was Melissa who broke the impasse. "We've none of us very much to be proud of," she said coldly.

"That's true enough!" Robert wrenched his arm from Andrew's grasp and strode away. "We're a pretty lot, we Tantallons."

259

Bridie watched, horrified. For her great-aunt to be dying was bad enough. But for the old lady's family to wrangle so was past all endurance.

She ran to her room, flung herself upon the bed, and wept. How long she lay there she didn't know, but she was roused at last by a gentle tap at the door.

"Bridie, my dear. . . . Bridie, it's Andrew."

Instantly, fearing bad news, she leaped up and flung the door wide.

"I just wanted a word with you."

She stepped back, weak with relief, and let him in. He went to the window seat, his head averted.

"When . . . when all this is over," he began, "there'll be nothing to keep you here. You'll be going back to London, to your old life there. . . . But I just wanted you to know that I love you, Bridie."

He turned to look at her and his eyes pleaded for an answer. But the time was wrong. She couldn't concentrate on such matters, couldn't make decisions, not now.

She lowered her tear-smudged face, avoiding his gaze. "Is there . . . is there more news of your mother, Andrew?"

"A little. Dr. Macnab says it's all right for us to go to her. Robert and Melissa have just been."

Her great-aunt's room was silent save for the busy ticking of the clock. By the foot of the bed old Peggy sat as still as a statue. Lady Otranta too was motionless, propped up on a great mound of pillows, but her lizard eyes were open, and the deep lines of pain gone from her face.

"Don't just stand there," she said, echoing her usual sharpness with gentle self-mockery. "Come in, both of you. And sit where I can see you."

They moved forward, one to each side of the bed. Andrew stooped and kissed her cheek. "How are you feeling, Mama?"

She smiled. "What would Macnab say? 'As well as can be expected'?" She struggled into a more upright position. "The man's a fool—d'you know that? Bundling me up like this, just because he says I'm dying! Queen Elizabeth, now—she refused pointblank even to go to bed. But then, she was a queen, so I suppose people had to give in to her. Nobody gives in to me. Never have and never will."

Andrew straightened her sheet. "You know, Mama, I'd say you were one of the most given-in-to women in all of Scotland."

"You would, would you?" She glared at him. Suddenly her mock indignation faded. "Perhaps you're right, boy. And perhaps it would have been better otherwise. . . . You've been a good son to me, Andrew. And in return I've treated you abominably."

Down at the foot of the bed old Peggy snorted.

The old lady ignored her. "How sad it is," she went on, "that we never manage to learn from the mistakes of others. I was jealous of my own son, you see, determined that he should never, *could* never take his father's place—just as Victoria had been jealous of poor Edward. And I'd seen the petty indignities she heaped upon him, and the harm they did . . . yet *still* I could not help myself."

She reached for one of Andrew's hands and held it tight. "Your father was a fine brave man, Andrew. Sometimes, when I look at you, it's as if my Jamie were standing there again. . . . But I want to tell you this, my dear—you have something he never had. You have humility. And the strength that only true humility brings."

The old lady patted his hand, then released it, and turned to Bridie, mischief in her eyes. "Well now, child, I've done with pretty speeches. But what about you? I take it you agree with me about this dear, silly son of mine?" Bridie nodded cautiously. "In that case, my girl, just when exactly are you going to bring yourself to marry him?"

"Marry . . . ?" The abrupt onslaught left her bewildered. Then she pulled herself together. "To be honest, Great-aunt, the last time I talked to you about this I got the impression that—"

"Oh, I know I said you'd get hurt. We all get hurt, one way or another. But that never stops us making fools of ourselves over the right man. . . . Well, child? I asked you a question."

"I—I'm not sure I can answer it, Great-aunt." She knew the answer very well. But she didn't like being rushed.

"Not answer it? Why not, pray? Because the foolish man drank too much at the party? That worried me too, I agree. But I've been known to do the same myself just now and then, you know."

The old lady flashed a sly glance round the room. "Though not perhaps quite so often as certain people might imagine."

"I know that, Great-aunt." If this was a time for being truthful, then so be it. "I've seen that poor aspidistra in the window."

"Have you, now?" Lady Otranta regarded her great-niece through half-closed eyes. "You're shrewder even than I thought. And more discreet. . . . So much the better. You'll know how to cope with my idiot son's manifold deficiencies."

"Honestly, Mama—" Andrew's laughter was now a little forced "—you know as well as I do that I've never been drunk before in my life. You mustn't speak as if I make a habit of it."

Briefly Robert's words flashed across Bridie's mind: *He's done this before*. Which one of them, she wondered, was lying?

"Be quiet, I say!" The old lady didn't even turn in her son's direction. "Well, child? Are you going to marry him?"

For Bridie the whole world seemed suddenly to stand still, waiting for her answer. She glanced across at Andrew, his eyes pleading. She took a deep breath. "I am," she said quietly. "If he'll have me, that is."

From Andrew, a great sigh of relief.

Her great-aunt closed her eyes, and her head slumped sideways on her pillow. In an instant old Peggy was at her side, feeling the old lady's pulse. Then she relaxed.

"I do wish you wouldn't do that, *Madame*," she chided. "Frightenin' us all so." She gestured Andrew and Bridie to the door. "But then, that's you all over," she went on. "No consideration for others at all. . . ."

They left, but not before Lady Otranta had opened one bright eye and winked at them. She was biding her time. She'd go when she was good and ready.

In the little octagonal room Andrew pulled Bridie close. "Is it wicked to be so happy?" he murmured. "So happy, while Mama is. . . ."

She hugged him. "Your mother's happy too."

They went to sit in the library, talking a little, reading when they could. Dinner time came and went. No one ate. Shortly after eleven o'clock, when the family were all gathered in the small drawing room, Dr. Macnab came in.

"I think you should go up now."

Andrew put aside his book. "All of us?"

The doctor nodded. "Be very quiet, though."

Bridie went up the stairs last of all. Suddenly she felt an intruder. Although she had come to love her great-aunt she had known her for such a short time.

Lady Otranta was lying propped up on pillows as before, her eyes closed. As they entered the room however, she stirred, and looked about her.

"All the Tantallons," she said, her voice still surprisingly strong. "That's nice."

Her children separated, Robert going to the fireplace, Melissa to the window, Andrew staying by the foot of the bed. Bridie lingered just inside the door. Beyond the heavy curtains the wind rushed and battered. Suddenly old Peggy, who had been fussing with the bedside lamp, gave a strangled sob, and stumbled from the room.

Andrew lifted his head. But his mother spoke first. "You'll look after that abominable old creature, I know. She's been with me longer than any of you . . . she'll still need a home."

"She'll never be without one, Mama. Bridie and I—"

"I hoped you'd say that. But things aren't going to be easy." She smiled wryly. "I've been a troublesome old woman. And a troublesome young one. You're going to find out soon just how troublesome. . . ."

Robert stepped forward. "I wish you wouldn't talk like that, Mama."

She held out a hand to him and he took it. "They do say that confession is good for the soul, Robert." A sudden spasm shook her. When it passed she was noticeably weaker.

"Bridie? Is that you, Bridie, over by the door?"

Bridie moved to her bedside, opposite Robert. "I'm here, Great-aunt."

The old lady reached out her other hand and took Bridie's arm firmly. "The memoirs, child—I want you to listen to me carefully."

Andrew stepped round the foot of the bed. "You're confused, Mama. There are no memoirs."

"So you say, my son. But Bridie here knows better, I think." Another spasm took her, and Bridie felt her great-aunt's fingers bite into her arm like claws. "Listen to me carefully, child. . . . Come along now and concentrate. . . . I'd like to know. . . ." She shook her head from side to side. "It's really not difficult. Not if you do your best. Just be quick, my dear. It's really not difficult. . . ."

Bewildered, Bridie looked up, and caught Andrew's eye. He shook his head infinitesimally. "I'm sure Bridie understands you, Mama. Of course it's not difficult."

"Do you, child? *Do you?*"

And suddenly Bridie did. She nodded, closing her eyes and repeating Lady Otranta's words to herself, fixing them in her memory.

"Excellent, my dear. Excellent. . . . I was sure you would. . . . They're a prickly lot, my little family. But I love them all very dearly."

The old lady's hand fell from her arm. She released Robert also.

"You know," she said, "there really are times when to be tired is the most delightful feeling in all the world. That, and an easy conscience."

She sighed then, and became still. But with a different stillness.

For a while all was silent in the room, save for the wind and the ticking of the clock. Then, softly, Melissa began to cry. Andrew went to call the doctor, who was waiting outside, and returned to put his arm about Melissa's shoulders. They stayed in the room while Dr. Macnab removed the pillows from behind Lady Otranta's head and closed her eyes and placed two silver crowns upon them. Then Andrew led his half-sister out, Robert and Bridie following behind.

Her thoughts were in a turmoil. She felt grief certainly. But for herself and the others, rather than for her great-aunt who was now at peace. The old lady had placed a terrible responsibility upon her. And why? With all the others in the room, why had Lady Otranta chosen her? Had there really been those of her closest family whom she could not trust? Robert? Melissa? Even Andrew?

They passed old Peggy weeping uncontrollably among the bizarre furnishings of the sitting room. Robert would have spoken to her, but she shook him off. They left her to grieve alone, and went wearily downstairs.

Dr. Macnab came down soon after. He took Bridie on one side. "I think someone should go up to Peggy," he murmured. "She's deeply distressed."

Bridie slipped away. As she approached her great-aunt's quarters she heard a terrible commotion and began to run. In the doorway she stopped short, horrified.

The place was in ruins. Cabinets lay on their sides, panels smashed in. Broken glass was scattered everywhere. In the midst of it all old Peggy continued her work of destruction, flailing about her with a poker. As Bridie watched she turned upon colourful little Az Rah, ripping his body from the chess board and flinging it savagely onto the fire, where the silken garments flared into flames.

Then she caught sight of Bridie. "Secrets as the Perfessor worked on all his life," she cried defiantly. "Well, no one's having 'em, see?" She began beating at Az Rah's cabinet till the doors splintered.

Bridie hesitated, appalled by such wanton destruction. The poor woman must be stopped somehow.

"Peggy," she cautiously began, "I—I wonder if you could help me. Lady Otranta's memoirs, I think they're hidden somewhere after all, and I'm sure you could help me find them."

"Help you?" The fat old woman paused, hands on hips, panting. "Oh, I suspected what she was up to, all right. Though I never did catch her at it. . . . But as for helping you, I'd rather die first." She returned to her battering. "All the Perfessor's secrets . . . they should of died with him. . . ."

Bridie waited her opportunity, then caught Peggy's wrist and held on to it. For a moment they struggled, then, suddenly, the old woman collapsed into Bridie's arms, sobbing bitterly.

"Dear Gawd,—what's to become o' me?"

Bridie led her to one of the few chairs remaining upright. "Hush now. There'll always be a place for you here."

Sobbing still, Peggy surveyed the wreckage around her. "I'd do it again, mind," she muttered. "And as for helping you—never! Them memoirs . . . I'm not daft, you know. I can add up two and two. And she never did tell me what became of that nice travelling cloak and her best straw boater. . . ." Slowly she grew calmer, and Bridie helped her to her room, then went downstairs.

She sought out Andrew and told him what had happened. He shook his head in tired sympathy. "Poor woman," he said. "In some ways tonight has been worse for her than for any of us. I'll go now and speak to Meredith. He can give one of the maids something to take up to her."

SEVENTEEN

The others had gone to their rooms. Bridie lingered, undecided, in the huge, shadowy entrance hall. Her great-aunt had set her a task. But she was tired out and it was after midnight. Surely she could safely leave things till morning? She collected her candle and went up to her bedroom. Afraid that a night's sleep might drive the old lady's words out of her head, she sat down at once and spelled them out on the typewriter: *Listen to me carefully. . . . Come along now. . . . Concentrate. . . . I'd like to know. . . . It's really not difficult. . . . Not if you do your best. . . . Just be quick. . . . It's really not difficult. . . .*

She stared at the words. "Trigger phrases", her great-aunt had called them. Each one of them meant something. And the meaning was to be found in that book hidden in the glass table in the old lady's sitting room. Or wherever else it might be, after Peggy's violent depredations.

A knock came on her door, and it opened a crack. She snatched the piece of paper from her machine and stuffed it into a drawer.

"Bridie?" Andrew stood there, candle in hand. "I was going to my room and I saw the light under your door. I don't think I'll be able to sleep much tonight. Do you mind if we talk a bit?"

At the sight of him her tiredness disappeared, and she leaped to her feet, and hurried to embrace him tenderly. "I'm so glad you've come. There's . . . there's one last thing we can do together for your mother. . . ."

She needed somebody to help her: somebody she could trust. And if not Andrew, then who else in the whole world?

She took the paper from the drawer and showed it to him, explaining what it was. He read the phrases over, wrinkling his brow. "I've seen Mama do her mind-reading trick with old Peggy, of course—but I never guessed how it was worked." He stared blankly at the paper. "If we ever decipher all this, what d'you think it'll tell us?"

"I'm not sure. Where the memoirs are hidden, I expect."

"You truly believe she wrote them, then?"

Bridie nodded. He seemed so tired and bewildered. There was so much she needed to tell him . . . about his mother's supposed drunkenness, about Dr. Macnab's long-kept secret. But not *now*—not with this new puzzle clamouring for a solution. If he could not sleep, then neither could she. How better, then, to pass the long hours?

They went softly through the darkened castle. In the devastated sitting room Andrew lit a lamp, gazing around him in amazement. Trying not to think of the thin, pathetic shape lying silent in the next room, Bridie found the glass specimen table, surprisingly undamaged, and brought out the book.

Together they spread out the paper with Lady Otranta's message on the table and opened the book beside it. *Listen to me:* Andrew found the phrase, number nineteen on Mr. Houdin's alphabetical list, standing for the letter S. *Come along now:* Bridie remembered that from her great-aunt's explanation. It represented A. *Concentrate* and *I'd like to know* were easily discovered: F and E respectively.

S-A-F-E . . . so the memoirs were undamaged. That much, at least, was clear.

The next two phrases presented more of a problem. On the alphabetical list they stood for R and B, numbers eighteen and two. Andrew stared at the letters blankly. "I'll swear there's not a single word in the dictionary that begins RB," he said.

Bridie racked her brains, remembered the other lists Lady Otranta had mentioned. She flicked through the book, found list eighteen. It was a list of prepositions: inside, outside, behind, through . . . Number two on that list was *under*.

Safe under . . . it seemed a promising beginning, so they went on to the last two phrases. These turned out to represent V and R.

"Victoria Regina." Andrew closed the book. "So there we have it—Mama's memoirs are in some manner 'safe under' the late Queen. Yet I don't really see how that helps us."

Bridie frowned. Somewhere at the back of her mind a memory lurked. "There's not a statue of the old Queen anywhere on the estate?"

Andrew shook his head. "There's a memorial down in the village. But—"

"A portrait, perhaps?"

Somewhere in the castle a clock struck two. Andrew nodded. "There are plenty of portraits. In the big drawing room, for example. That thing done by Winterhalter."

"In the big drawing room? I'm sure that can't be right. . . ." Suddenly Bridie looked up excitedly. "*Safe under VR* . . . don't you see? She meant *the safe* under VR!"

Andrew frowned. "I'm afraid I don't see."

"The green safe under the portrait of Queen Victoria. In the office up at the sawmill. . . ." She clutched his arm. "And that explains the other thing that was worrying me—how the memoirs got to wherever they were hidden. Duncan took them! He took them every morning, in that leather Accounts folder he always carried."

"Then Duncan helped her?"

"Someone had to, and who would she be more likely to turn to than Duncan?" She hurried to the window, pulled back the curtain, looked out. "Come on. We must find the memoirs at once. I can't rest till we've got to the bottom of this whole extraordinary business."

Andrew didn't argue. He went downstairs to procure cloaks and a lantern and met her by a side door.

"It's as black as pitch outside, although it's stopped raining," he said. "Are you sure you want to go through with this?"

There was a movement behind them. A rat, perhaps, or one of the many castle cats. Bridie took the lantern from him and lit it at her candle flame, holding it high, revealing nothing but the empty, stone-flagged corridor.

"We're going up to the sawmill," she said quietly but firmly.

The climb through the woods in the dark was difficult.

Repeatedly Bridie stumbled in the muddy cart-ruts, but Andrew trudged stoically along beside her, his uneven stride never faltering, the lantern in one hand, the other supporting her.

They came to the bridge, then on up the last steep curve of the track. Suddenly Andrew stopped, and pointed. Away among the trees a light flickered in the wind that gusted across the hillside.

"Someone's lighted a bonfire in front of the sawmill," he whispered. Then his grip on her arm tightened. "Unless it's the mill itself that's burning—"

He hurried forward. She ran after him and together they breasted the slope and came to the edge of the forest clearing.

In the middle of the open space a fire was burning. Over it leaned the cloaked figure of a man, his back towards them. Suddenly Bridie realized he was tearing pages from a pile of large notebooks and feeding them carefully, one by one, into the fire.

Uttering a low cry of protest, she started forward. At once a dog emerged from the shadows, snarling and tugging ferociously at her skirt. The man turned, the light from the fire playing on the heavily-bearded features of Duncan Symonds.

"Noble! Come here this instant, sir!" The dog backed away. Mr. Symonds peered in their direction. "It's Mistress Bridie, is it? And Sir Andrew? So I maun apologize for the behaviour of my dog, it seems . . . though I'm thinking mebbe he did no more than his duty, warning me of intruders at this ungodly hour."

"Hardly intruders, Duncan." Andrew limped forward into the firelight. "And as to the ungodly hour, may I ask exactly what you're doing here now?"

"Aye. You may that." He nodded judicially. "It's your right, y'ken, now that her ladyship's gone." Then, stepping back a pace, he ripped decisively at the remaining pages and threw them into the centre of the fire.

Helplessly Bridie watched them blacken and shrivel, then finally burst into flame. Was this what all Lady Otranta's work had come to? Andrew caught angrily at Duncan's arm. "You realize that's a criminal act you've just committed, man. And before two witnesses. Burning the property of—"

"Criminal act, is it? No disrespect, sir, but to my way of thinking 'twas her ladyship who was the criminal in this wee matter."

Bridie found her voice. "But how could you, Mr. Symonds? Her memoirs—you must have seen how hard she worked. Yet you—"

"*Her* memoirs?" Duncan Symonds laughed comfortably. "It's clear we're talking at cross purposes. This is no' her ladyship's work I've been setting beyond the reach of prying eyes. That's in the office safe, fine and dandy. Untouched and unread, the way I made my promise—her ladyship will have told you of that, no doubt, seeing she's told you where to come for it."

Bridie stared at him in bewilderment. "Then what. . . ?"

"Stolen property, Mistress. Stolen by her ladyship. . . . Stolen by myself now as well, I grant you—though I reckon you'll find that mighty hard to prove."

Andrew stood over him angrily. "Speak plainly, man—and be careful what you're saying. My mother may be dead, but as long as I'm alive no one shall slander her good name."

Duncan stood his ground. "Aye. . . . Weel, mebbe stealing's a bit strong. I've no way rightly of telling how she laid her hands upon the old Queen's papers. All the same—"

"*The old Queen's papers?*" Suddenly Bridie remembered what Robert had told her, down in the castle library. "Her diary, you mean? The one that was never published?"

"You've the right of it there, Mistress." Duncan held out the empty bindings to her, finely-tooled leather. "They were never published, and wi' good·reason. John Brown and her . . . she wore her heart too much on her sleeve, puir soul. Besides, there were those who said she filled her court too much wi' foreigners—Germans, that Indian secretary . . . and Scotsmen." He chuckled. "It came to Sir Henry Ponsonby to tell her so. Him and the Dean of Windsor. She didna' like it. But she bowed to their superior wisdom." He looked thoughtfully down at the bindings. "And Lady Otranta telling me times were different now. Weel, mebbe they are and mebbe they aren't. . . ."

Andrew stepped back a pace. "My mother planned to publish the diaries as part of her memoirs?"

"I'm no saying that. But she planned to use them, that's for certain."

"So you burned them? You burned priceless historical documents?"

"You can say that, Sir Andrew. But you'll no be proving it." With a final quick movement he tossed the bindings into the fire. "Let them rest easy, her and her faithful servant. I tell you, Brown was more a gentleman than the half of her court. And the gossips may say what they like—there was never a thing between them as wasna' right and proper." He began to walk away.

"Then why burn the proof of it?" Bridie asked.

His placid laugh came back at her out of the darkness. "Words prove nothing, nothing at a'. Words are what you make of them. And I ken weel what those wi' malice in their hearts might have made of the words of that puir wee lonely wumman."

Duncan whistled to his dog. "Good night to you, Sir Andrew. And to you, Mistress. If there's more to be said, we can say it the morn. Her ladyship's dead, and I maun go and pay my respects."

He whistled again, then called in anger. Finally the dog came to him from the shadows, and the two of them went slowly away out of the firelight's circle.

Andrew sighed. "He's probably right. Anyway, it's too late now. The diaries are gone—with no proof that they ever existed."

Bridie turned from the fire. "At least the memoirs are safe."

Together they made their way to the mill building. A small pass door stood open and they went in past the silent machinery and into the office. In the lantern light Bridie saw the safe gaping wide. And above it the portrait. Behind them the door to the building banged savagely in the wind, and banged again.

Bridie knelt in front of the safe, her heart pounding. It was empty save for an untidy stack of closely-written sheets of paper. Bridie drew this out with trembling fingers.

She took the top sheet and held it close to the light. The writing was small and spidery, but clear. *It's no use at all, sitting down to write one's memoirs,* she read, *and then trying to fudge them. One must be prepared to be utterly truthful. . . .* She lowered the paper. The effect was eerie, like listening to the sound of the dead woman's voice there in the shadowy office. She shivered slightly. Andrew touched her shoulder. "I don't think you should read it." His voice sounded strange.

"But Andrew—"

"It should be burned, Bridie, along with the diaries."

271

"No, Andrew. It was your mother's wish that—"

"Burn those papers, Bridie. *Please!*"

He stooped to take them from her. Instinctively she resisted. "You're wrong, Andrew. . . . What is it you're afraid of?"

His eyes wild, he stared down at her. Out in the machine shop the door banged again. His gaze flickered sideways, and he backed away. "Don't move," he hissed. "In a minute that door'll be off its hinges. Don't move till I get back."

He left her crouched on the floor by the safe. Uneasily she riffled through the pages in her hands. A suspicion had formed

in her mind. Perhaps, of all the people in the castle, it was Andrew who. . . . She couldn't believe it. Not of *Andrew*.

The door had stopped banging. She waited, listening for his return, hearing only the rushing water in the mill leet above, and the restless murmur of the wind. Finally she got to her feet and, tucking the manuscript under her arm, picked up the lantern and went in search of him. She retraced her steps the length of the machine shop, shadows fleeing before her, the great blade of the saw glinting evilly as she passed it. She reached the door, found it closed.

"Andrew?" she called. "Andrew, where are you?"

Her voice seemed tiny in the vast enclosed spaces all around. No answer came. She tried the door. It was locked.

Up until that moment she had not been afraid, only bewildered. She knew Andrew loved her. She knew he'd do nothing to hurt her. Now, suddenly, nothing was certain, not even that.

She beat upon the door, but it didn't yield. She swung round, holding the lantern high. Somewhere, out in the surrounding darkness, a tiny movement told her she wasn't alone. If Andrew was there, why didn't he answer? She called his name again and again. And received only silence in reply.

EIGHTEEN

Footsteps rang out, clicking on iron stair treads. They seemed to fill the darkness, echoing from every direction. Bridie cowered back against the door. Abruptly, on the gantry high above her, the footsteps ceased. A voice came down to her.

"Bridie? I can see you very well, you know. Those papers under your arm—I understand what they are. Are you going to give them to me?"

Horror flooded through her. She'd known it all along, really. But *why?* He was mad. He had to be.

"Robert?" She tried to sound calm, tried to treat the whole thing like some harmless joke. "Come down. Don't be silly—you had me frightened half out of my wits."

He laughed. "You'd be wise to be frightened, fair coz. For I mean to have those memoirs, you see, come what may."

Now, at last, Bridie understood a lot of things. She remembered Robert's ceaseless curiosity about the memoirs. Right from the start he'd never wanted them written. And he'd seen her, therefore, as someone to be frightened off, even—if necessary— killed. The car that had nearly run her down, the message in her typewriter, the trap set for her in the woods, they had all been directed to the one end: that somehow his mother should be prevented from writing her memoirs.

But *why?* And what of his kindness to her at other times, his

274

youthful high spirits? Had they all been simply a part of his madness? She couldn't believe it. Surely she could appeal, even now, to his better nature. "A joke's a joke," she said firmly. "Of course you must read what your mother's written. So must Andrew. But—"

"Read it? I've no wish at all to read it. I know what she's written all too well. She's written the truth. She always said she would. I did my best to stop her, but she got round me somehow. She got round the lot of us." He laughed again. "A wily old bird, the Incredible Madame Otranta. . . ."

Anxiously Bridie stole a glance over her shoulder. *For God's sake, where was Andrew?* She must play for time.

"What is this *truth*," she said, "that you and your brother are so afraid of?"

The footsteps moved in the darkness above her, then stopped again.

"I love my brother dearly, coz, but I'm afraid he's a fool. He's always had the crazy notion that somehow Mama contrived the death of the first Lady Tantallon and was hell-bent on a full confession of her sins. . . . It's utter nonsense, of course. It has to be, you see, since the old witch was alive and kicking until four or five years ago. She died in Baden Baden, I believe. And would you believe it, our noble Papa had actually paid her an *allowance* down all those years? The woman who tried to kill him? That's how I found out all about her, you see. I picked up an old account book after his death. Regular payments to a Mrs. *Wilkinson*. Mama caught me at it, so I had to ask her."

He lowered his voice. "And the ridiculous thing is that even then she could have lied to me. She could have said this Mrs. Wilkinson was some fancy woman." He moved restlessly. "But that wouldn't do for Mama, of course. No fancy woman for the honest Sir James. Anything was better than that—even the truth. The truth that the first Lady Tantallon, a murderous creature if ever there was one, had been a millstone round our necks down all those years. And for why? All because. . . ."

Bridie was too confused, too terrified to understand much of what he was saying. But that last phrase caught her attention: *a millstone round our necks.* . . . That, then, was what the conversation she'd overheard between Robert and his mother had been referring to. The first Lady Tantallon, and not Melissa at all. The first Lady Tantallon, who was supposed to have been dead for—

Robert was still speaking. ". . . So I'm coming down there now, and you're going to give me those memoirs. For Andrew's sake, you understand. So that no one shall know of his bastardy, his and mine both. . . . There'll be enough of Duncan's fire left to deal with them, if we're careful. He's a man after my own heart, that Duncan. I followed you up from the castle, you see, so I had a grandstand view of your meeting. Except that that wretched dog of his nosed me out and would have chewed my leg off if I'd moved a muscle."

Bridie thought of poor Noble's reluctance to leave with his master.

"Well now, coz, you've been quiet a long time. Are you going to give me those papers? Or am I going to have to take them. . . ?"

His footsteps began to descend the iron ladder. "Not that destroying the memoirs will do *you* any good, of course. You'll know the truth—" His voice rose hysterically. "And you'll never marry Andrew then, will you? Knowing he's a bastard, knowing the entire estate should by rights go to poor silly 'Lissa."

"Where *is* Andrew?" she demanded. "What have you done with him?"

The footsteps paused. "*A wee tappit tae th'head*, as dear old Meredith would say. Nothing serious, I think. But he'll be out of the way a while yet."

She crept sideways. She thought that she remembered a second door out of the building, away on the far side. "Of course I'll give you the memoirs, Robert. If you'll just come down here quietly and—"

"You know something, coz?" His tone caused her to freeze. "I'm afraid I don't believe you." His footsteps pattered upwards and across. "What's needed, I think, is a small inducement."

There was a metallic scraping sound. Outside the building the sound of rushing water changed. She recognized the change. Desperately she made a dash to reach the far side, but in an

276

instant Robert had slithered down the ladder, heading her off. With the lantern in her hand he could see her every movement. Yet without it she dared not budge an inch. She backed away from him, into some massive piece of machinery.

Already the water wheel had begun to turn, and with it axles, pulleys, gear shafts within the building. In the machine behind her something stirred, a faint whining sound, and she recoiled, screaming in terror. All about her wheels began to whisper. And Robert, visible now hardly ten paces away, was coming slowly nearer.

She turned again and ran, gathering her heavy cloak closely to her, and looking back over her shoulder. Robert wasn't hurrying. As long as he kept her from the far door she could run where she liked. Run until she made a mistake. . . . While behind his head the blade of the circular saw spun in a steely blue arc, singing higher and higher.

"Are you ready to hand them over yet, little Bridie? I've often heard how wonderful it is, the way a little danger focuses the mind."

She dodged between masses of equipment, and circled the big central table, putting the spinning saw-blade momentarily between her and her pursuer. If she could just dodge round the end of the table.

But Robert had guessed her intention. With a powerful thrust he set the whole table moving on its well-greased track, rolling silkily past the evil blur of the saw-blade, closing the gap between itself and the great double doors at the end of the building.

Bridie stopped, turned, put the lantern on the ground beside her, and stood at bay. The noise in the machine shop rose. Pulley belts flailed shrilly, the shimmering saw-blade keened its strange, hypnotic lament. And still Robert advanced unhurriedly upon her.

Why should she not give him the memoirs still clutched under her arm? Were they worth all this?

It was then, when she was at the end of her resources, that a dark shape rose suddenly up behind Robert, and the next moment he reeled and fell sideways across the still-moving table. He lay stunned, inert, as it carried him on towards the saw. She screamed then, her eyes tight shut against the horror.

Abruptly the saw's shrill keening stopped. She waited, shuddering, until a touch on her arm set her shrieking again. Sense returned to her only slowly, and she saw Andrew, a thin trickle of blood running down his forehead from a dark stain in his hair. His voice in her ear, shouting above the noise of the machinery. "It's all right, Bridie my love. It's all right. . . ."

Wildly she stared past him. Robert was unsteadily sitting up. And beside him, not six inches away, the saw-blade rested upon its bearings, its pulley disconnected, the searing teeth motionless.

She wept then, safe in her lover's arms.

After a while Robert eased himself off the table and went up onto the gantry to close off the flow of water outside and stop the machinery. He came down to stand shamefacedly by Andrew's side.

"It seems my 'wee tappit' wasn't quite hard enough," he murmured. "A triumph for brotherly feeling, no doubt. . . . As was yours, Andy, when you saved my life."

He put out a conciliatory hand, but Andrew drew back. "It's no use, Robert. This time you've gone too far."

Abruptly Robert's face crumpled. "Don't say that, Andy, I did it all for you. You're the one who'll suffer most, when we're both disinherited. You're the one I really care for."

"And Bridie, what of her?" Andrew held her close. "No, Robert—the trap in the woods was worse than I'd ever have believed of you. But this—"

"Bridie?" His brother's voice grew shrill. "Do you never think of anyone else but your damnable Bridie? Weren't we happy before she came along? You kept me safe, Andrew—safe from those terrible thoughts and compulsions. All my life. . . . Until that wretched meddling girl appeared."

Andrew hit him then, a calculated blow that sent him staggering back against the wall, and Robert's wildness faded as quickly as it had flared. He stood for a moment, dabbing at the corner of his mouth where a smudge of blood had formed. Then, to Bridie's shame, he began to cry.

Andrew went to him. "Go back to the castle, Robert. We'll talk

278

again in the morning. But make no mistake—life will never be the same again for you and me. You must see that." He put his arm round his brother's shoulders. "Let us be thankful we have Dr. Macnab in the house. Perhaps he can help you. God knows, I can't."

Robert straightened up, and, the tears still flowing down his cheeks, walked to the little pass door, inserted a key in its lock, and opened it. He paused, the wind gusting through his shock of silver hair.

"Macnab is a fool," he said, and laughed softly. "You know, I can't wait to see 'Lissa's face when she learns she's the mistress of Castle Tantallon." He went out.

Bridie took Andrew's arm. "Shouldn't you have gone with him?"

"Dear Bridie. . . ." He bent to kiss her. "No, he's best left to himself at times like these. I know so much about poor Robert— and yet, it seems, so little. I thought I could control him. But I didn't understand the depth of his feelings. Even after he set that trap in the woods I still thought it was all somehow a mistake. I could *not* believe he had really meant to harm you. . . ."

"If you guessed it was he up in the woods, why, oh why did you not tell me?"

"I was wrong. Terribly wrong. But I thought that with my help he would master his jealousy. And it's not easy, confessing that you have a brother who . . . who is prey to such wild imaginings."

Who is *mad*, she thought, supplying the truer word. "Did your mother know about him?" she asked.

He shook his head. "Only I knew. We were always so close, you see. And what he said was true—always I'd been able to save him from himself. Always, that is, until you came to the castle." He took her hands in his. "Dearest Bridie—can you forgive me?"

Of course she forgave him. She loved him—she would forgive him anything in the world. But there was still so much left unexplained. Robert's wild talk about the memoirs. The first Lady Tantallon . . . the estate . . . Melissa.

They walked rapidly back through the woods, speaking little. Then, as they were approaching the castle drawbridge, there came a sudden explosive clatter from within the courtyard. The engine of the yellow Argyll.

Andrew quickened his pace. "God, Robert can't be intending . . . not at this hour . . . not on these roads. . . ."

A second later the motor car swept out through the castle entrance, its headlamps casting a brief glow upon them as it thundered past and down the road towards the bridge.

Andrew took her arm again. "It doesn't matter," he said. "In fact, it's probably just about the best thing he could do. He'll drive around the lanes a bit, and when he comes back all the fire will have gone out of him. It's happened before. He—"

But at that moment from down the road came a sound, hideous, unmistakable—a tearing, splintering crash that seemed to go on and on. . . .

Convulsively Andrew thrust her forward. "Run, Bridie. Fetch Macnab. I'll go to Robert—he's skidded on the bridge. . . ."

Obediently Bridie ran. Even though she knew with utter certainty that Robert was dead.

NINETEEN

Dawn came late and reluctantly, bringing with it a strange calm: the calm after the storm. At long last Bridie dragged herself wearily up to bed. Robert lay in his room, at peace now for ever. Andrew had found him lying in the wet grass on the bank of the stream, thrown some distance from the twisted wreckage of the car. His neck was broken, and he must have died instantly.

The household, roused from slumber, had received the news of Robert's accident with bitter sadness, but without surprise. Robert had been unpredictable always, and much given to sudden jaunts in the yellow Argyll. Even Melissa suspected nothing of the night's drama, and, still stunned by her stepmother's death, simply retreated more profoundly into sorrow.

And Andrew . . . Andrew moved through the necessary business with an almost frightening calmness. Only once, briefly, when he and Bridie were left alone in his study, did he emerge from his trance.

280

Earnestly he met her gaze. "We mustn't grieve, my dear. It's hard to say this, I know, but Robert's death was all for the best. After tonight we could not have gone on as before." He bowed his head. "We must be thankful his tortured soul is at rest."

Now, wearily, Bridie flung herself down, fully dressed, upon her bed. And only then, as the faint dawn glow filtered through the curtains, did she remember her great-aunt's memoirs. They lay where she had put them, in an untidy pile on the table beside her typewriter. There would be time enough for them later. She was exhausted beyond all caring. . . .

She woke at noon, disturbed by an urgent tapping at her door. It was Agnes, her eyes red-rimmed from weeping, bearing, incredibly, a visiting card upon a silver tray.

"I'm gey sorry, Mistress Bridie. I ken weel that the Laird said ye were on nae account tae be bithered. But there's a gentleman tae see ye. An' wi' the Laird awa' in the village, speaking wi' the dominie. . . ." She choked on the words, controlled herself. "He's an *English* gentleman, I'm thinking. All the way frae London."

Bridie took the card. *Benedict Pugh-Hennessy Esq. MA Cantab. 5 Cheyne Court.* Fully awake now, she felt uneasy.

"Ask the gentleman to wait, Agnes. Tell him I'll be down immediately."

Mr. Pugh-Hennessy was waiting for her in the small drawing room. He seemed not at all the impressive figure she had thought him in his London office six weeks ago. But then, a great deal had happened since that time.

"My *dear* Miss Tantallon. I come to you upon a sad day, it seems. A *sad* day indeed." He paced distractedly to the window and back. The wind and rain had passed, and pale autumnal sunlight was shining on the castle walls. "I only heard from Macnab a couple of days ago how *sick* your poor great-aunt was. And now not only she but her younger son also have—"

"You've been to see Dr. Macnab, Mr. Pugh-Hennessy?"

"Certainly I have." His fingers were fussing with his over-long cuffs. "You *mentioned* the good doctor in your *letters*. So I—"

"You had wanted to see Lady Otranta?" This was no time to chide him for saying nothing to her first about this visit.

"See Lady Otranta? Not . . . exactly." He eased his neck

within its stand-up collar and peered round the room. "Dear me, how *grand* it all is. I had quite forgotten. It was like this in my *own* day, of course. But that's all so *dreadfully* long ago."

"You were here before?" she asked, seeming to remember that Andrew had once told her so.

"The *briefest* of visitors, you know. My people had rented a neighbouring estate." He sucked at his ill-fitting teeth. "The . . . ah, the *memoirs*? There's no news of them, I suppose?"

Bridie temporized. "I did write to you about them, Mr. Pugh-Hennessy."

"Precisely so. And now the poor woman's dead. And her son also. What a *tragic* circumstance." He wrung his hands. "And her remaining children—how are they taking it? There is a step-daughter as well as the elder son, I believe."

She was puzzled. So far she had not discovered any clear reason for his visit. She answered shortly. "Much as any other two people who have suffered a double bereavement."

"And how about *you*, my dear? I gathered from your letters that you and your great-aunt had become very close."

"I. . . ." Suddenly she felt utterly bereft. A great source of comfort and wisdom had gone from her life. She sank onto a chair and covered her face with her hands. "Forgive me, Mr. Pugh-Hennessy. I . . . I. . . ." And there, at last, she allowed herself to weep. Tears of sorrow for a dear person, kindly, witty, sometimes cruel, always surprising, whom she would never see again. . . . And even for Robert: for all the wasted promise of his youth and fickle brilliance.

Slowly she grew calmer. She had cried in Mr. Pugh-Hennessy's presence once before, she remembered. After the death of her father. It was as if he was a man who encouraged such confidence.

She dried her eyes. "I must ring for Meredith. You'll be staying at the castle, of course?"

"Not at all, Miss Tantallon. I wouldn't *think* of it." He hurried to the door. "I must return to London tonight. I came really because this is my last day north of the border."

"You'll take lunch with us, surely, before you go?"

Again the protestations. The hire car was waiting. He wouldn't for the life of him intrude.

She gave in, glanced up at the clock upon the overmantel. "I'll see you to the door, then. There'll be a ferry back to Edinburgh in about an hour."

They stood together in the pale sunlight on the steps outside. She decided to be bold. "Mr. Pugh-Hennessy—you still haven't told me your reason for coming all this way."

He flapped embarrassedly at the long skirts of his travelling cloak. "Why else should I come, except on account of the *memoirs?* A publisher will go anywhere, do anything, for the sake of the book he's set his heart on."

She didn't wholly believe his answer. But it made her feel guilty all the same. "Perhaps they'll turn up after all," she suggested tentatively.

His embarrassment increased. "I . . . I don't suppose your great-aunt talked much about the *first* Lady Tantallon?" he said at last.

"I don't think she ever mentioned her."

"No. . . . Well, it's all a long time ago. But I never *quite* understood the *extraordinary* circumstances of Lady Margaret's death." Mr. Pugh-Hennessy fiddled with his tall hat. "I was acquainted with the first Lady Tantallon, you see. Only *slightly*, of course. . . . They were quite wrong for each other. Quite, quite wrong. It was very sad, really. . . ."

The hire car waited now below them, jogging on its springs. Mr. Pugh-Hennessy held out his hand. "Well, Miss Tantallon, I'm really *most* grateful to you for all your efforts. You did your best . . . I'll instruct Mr. Thwaite to settle with you to the end of the week."

She knew she shouldn't accept his money. But she could think of no convincing way of refusing it.

As he was climbing laboriously into the car, Melissa emerged from the stables on her bicycle and pedalled sombrely by in the direction of the village. He beckoned Bridie out to him.

"Tell me, my dear, would that have been Miss *Melissa* Tantallon, by any chance?"

Bridie nodded. "She's very upset. I expect she's gone out just to be on her own."

"Yes indeed—*very* understandable. Poor thing, poor thing. . . ."

283

He rammed his hat firmly down on his head and beat with the knob of his stick on the outside of the car door, as if alerting a coachman. "You may drive on now, my man," he commanded.

Bridie caught the driver's eye and smothered a giggle. As the car lurched away across the drawbridge, she returned indoors. With Andrew not yet back from seeing the minister in Kincardine, and Melissa out also, she lunched alone, with her great-aunt's memoirs to keep her company.

They didn't take long to read. When she had finished she sat for a long time, staring at the last page. The words ended in mid-sentence. Bridie's eyes filled again with tears as she pictured the agonizing final moment when Lady Otranta's pen would move no further. And faithful Duncan taking even this fragment and depositing it, punctiliously unread, with the rest. . . .

Time had run out—but not before the first and most important part was written. The rest, the evidence of the old Queen's diaries, might well have ensured the memoirs' commercial success—indeed, the promise of this was undoubtedly what had attracted Mr. Pugh-Hennessy—but it was not what had mattered to Lady Otranta.

She'd held out against death. She'd held out against all human opposition also. The hints were there in the text, clear enough for all to see. Yet the fears that had driven her even to the bizarre pretence of drunkenness—Bridie felt sure they'd been the exaggerated anxieties of a mortally sick old woman. Nobody would have harmed her, not even Robert. He might bully her, frighten her even, but he'd do no more than that. Not to his own mother.

No, it could only be that her years with the conjuror Salvador had left their mark. She had become so fascinated by the dangerous magic of lies and illusion that in the end it had quite distorted her reason. . . .

Bridie riffled back through the pages. She sighed. What with the story's shortness, and its unfinished state, there was surely nothing fit for publication. There need be no conflict of interest between Mr. Pugh-Hennessy and the Tantallon family. But she had no idea what the legal situation might now be. Obviously, for Melissa's sake, the truth must be made known. But only—at first, at any rate—to the discreet world of solicitors. The public scandal that the memoirs' publication would have caused could be avoided.

Lady Otranta had indeed been a strange, wilful old woman. But it comforted Bridie to know that in the end her marriage to Andrew had been what her great-aunt wanted. At first, no doubt, all the impediments to the match—her son's illegitimacy, his penniless state—must have loomed large in her mind. But as the days went by something, the telling of her own story, perhaps, had reminded her that when two young people were in love, nothing else mattered. Andrew and she would face the future together come what may.

TWENTY

When Andrew returned at last he looked pale and wretched. If Bridie could have spared him further distress that day she would gladly have done so. But the memoirs were waiting. So she kissed him lightly on the cheek, then led him through into the library, and indicated the neat small pile of his mother's manuscript.

"I love you," she said. "Whatever you read, just remember that."

She then left him and sought refuge in the garden, turning in the direction of the arcaded terrace.

Old Peggy was there, hunched on one of the benches. She looked so desolate that Bridie walked on and seated herself beside her. Peggy pulled her shapeless dress close about her, and said not a word.

"You were quite right about the memoirs," Bridie said gently. "Lady Otranta *was* secretly writing them."

When this gained no response, she went on, "I think you ought to know, Peggy, that there are going to be changes here at the castle. But none will affect *you*. . . . It was one of Lady Otranta's last wishes that you should be made welcome here for just as long as you care to stay."

Peggy didn't react. Bridie cleared her throat. "Perhaps it's not for me to say this, but I know how grateful the family is for everything you did for Lady Otranta." She leaned forward and took the old woman's hands in hers.

Suddenly Peggy began to cry. "I was proud to, miss. Proud to. . . ." She groped for a handkerchief. "Folks thought as it was the drink y'see. But it was them drops, the laudanum that doctor give her for the pain—that was what really got to her. Oh, the poor soul. . . ."

Bridie stared at her, suddenly understanding the painful memory she had of her great-aunt's snoring, graceless figure, and Peggy's fierce, protective gentleness. *Laudanum*—the last resort of a dying woman.

Peggy blew her nose. "Nasty, sneaky stuff. Honest, miss. I'd never of give it to Master Robert, God rest his soul, the day of the party, not if I'd known the wicked use he was going to put it to."

"You gave Robert laudanum?" Bridie was confused.

"That's right, miss. For a toothache, so he said. And him with never a day's toothache in his life. . . ." She began to cry again. "He wasn't really wicked, Miss. Just that his head was all in a muddle. I knew what he'd done, mind, the moment I heard about Sir Andrew. Drunk, indeed—and in front of all the grand company. Not him. I spoke to Master Robert about it the very next morning and he didn't deny he doctored his brother's drink—just said it was all a joke. And then he laughed. I couldn't be cross with him—I just couldn't."

Bridie leaned forward and hugged the tearful old woman, both to comfort her and out of sheer happiness. Andrew's seeming drunkenness had been Robert's doing, no more than a part of his stupid campaign of dark hints begun that day on the croquet lawn. At last the final piece of the puzzle had slipped into place.

She left Peggy then, and went slowly back to the castle.

In the library Andrew was sitting with his mother's manuscript face-down on his knee, staring blankly into space.

When he heard her enter the room he lifted his eyes. "I can hardly believe it, that Robert should have known the truth and tried to conceal it. Poor Melissa—she must be told at once, of course." He got slowly to his feet. "Naturally I wouldn't think of holding you to our engagement, my dear. You'll want to leave for London in the morning, no doubt."

Bridie crossed quickly to his side. "But I *told* you—"

"I know what you told me, but you could say nothing else. You're loyal, Bridie. But this, my dear, on top of the way I deceived you, came near to bringing about your death . . . I can never forgive myself."

"But I *love* you, Andrew—I won't let our engagement be over." She checked. "Unless you yourself truly want it to be, of course."

He looked down at her, his face agonized with uncertainty. Before he could speak the door behind them burst open. Melissa stood there, breathing fast, her jaw set.

"I'm sorry to barge in like this," she blurted out, "but I've a confession to make." She squared her shoulders. "And don't either of you try to stop me. I've been screwing myself up to this all day."

She was in deadly earnest as she strode forward into the room. "I know very well," she said abruptly, "that dirty linen's best washed in private. But now, with Mama's will to be thought of, and me supposed to be her stepdaughter, I frankly don't see how—"

Andrew interrupted her. "Mama didn't make a will. She always refused—I thought you knew that. It seemed inexplicable at the time, but you'll see her reasons clearly enough if you read this." He picked up the manuscript.

"Will or not," Melissa insisted, "there's still something I want to get straightened out." She flung herself into a chair, then got up and moved over to the large terrestrial globe by the window and spun it slowly. "That wretched shooting accident—" she began.

"I won't let you dig that up, 'Lissa. It's all over and done with long ago."

"But it's *not*. Can't you see? For God's sake, Andrew, you've covered up for me long enough!"

"You—you were overwrought, 'Lissa. I simply did what was necessary, that's all."

"Overwrought? Of course I was overwrought. But did you never think to ask me why?"

"That was your business," Andrew's glance was wary. "You'd

just come back from visiting that lawyer. I thought you were. . . .
Look, do you really want to bring all this out now, of all times?"

"Dear Andrew. . . ." She smiled at him. "Yes, I do. I must."

She turned to Bridie, her hands clenched and her eyes closed
momentarily beneath their steeply sloping brows. Then she
opened her eyes again, and looked directly at Bridie.

"Andrew says I was overwrought. He's quite right. I was so
overwrought that I wanted to kill myself. I went to the gun-room.
He followed me just in time to stop me. We struggled with the
gun. It went off. . . ." She pointed at Andrew's injured foot.
"I've lived with that reminder of my wickedness ever since. He
saved my life—and crippled himself in the process."

The room was suddenly silent. Bridie looked away, appalled.
And Andrew, her Andrew, would have kept the secret all his
days.

Melissa leaned forward over the globe. "I fetched his mother.
Typically, they both insisted that the whole thing be hushed up.
An unfortunate accident, they said. And, bless them, they never
demanded to know my reasons. The visit to the lawyer, they told
themselves. A foolish, hysterical girl—and tactfully left it at that.
And I, for my sins, let them."

She lowered her voice. "It was my eighteenth birthday, you
see. The day when I inherited a small trust fund from my mother.
I had to go in to Edinburgh to sign some papers. . . . And the
lawyer had a letter for me. A letter from my mother. A letter from
the first Lady Tantallon." She spoke the words with sudden
venom.

"It was a horrible letter. She'd written it soon after my birth,
and it was full of wicked things about her husband. Things that
I knew from my lifetime with him must be untrue. One thing,
however, was true enough. Not even she, not even my *mother*,
would have been brazen enough to invent that—"

Her voice broke, and she bent her head. When she spoke again
it was in scarcely more than a whisper.

"Whatever happened, my mother said, I wasn't to worry.
She'd had her revenge on him. He was a cruel monster, but he
wasn't my father. She wrote it with pride. The man she was
married to was not my father.

288

"In the event, of course, it was she who died. And he who lived—to be the best father in the world to me." She pushed back a strand of dark hair from her face. "Is it any wonder," she asked, "that I wanted to kill myself? When I learned that I had no right whatsoever to his love? To his generosity? No right to anything? And is it any wonder that I should be ashamed to this very day? Accepting so much, and myself not even a Tantallon?"

Andrew broke the silence. He was smiling. "You and me together," he said softly. "You must believe me, dear 'Lissa, when I tell you that the only true Tantallon in this room is little Bridie."

It was a situation close to farce—yet, for those involved, utterly, painfully serious. Explanations followed, lasting well into the evening. Who Melissa's real father had been the first Lady Tantallon had never disclosed, except that he was a nonentity; a passable enough agent for her vengeance on Sir James.

Bridie, however, could make a good guess as to his identity. So many things added up. The dark hair and sloping eyebrows . . . the enthusiasm for Lady Otranta's memoirs, nothing to do with the old Queen after all . . . the "personal reasons" for insisting on their completion . . . and the final, wistful visit to the castle, the cautious questions as to the real manner of the first Lady Tantallon's death and the eager interest, quickly veiled, in her daughter Melissa. . . .

Mr. Pugh-Hennessy, she knew, had never married. Possibly he carried in his heart to this very day a romantic picture of that woman long ago who had beguiled him and used him. The truth would hardly help him—nor, Bridie decided, would it help Melissa. The shy old man who had left the castle only a few hours ago was a father no one need feel ashamed of. But the advantages to either side in acknowledging him were doubtful. For Melissa he would be tainted by her judgement of the woman who had used him. And for himself—well, he'd been a bachelor, a solitary, far too long.

Eventually their discussion was interrupted by the sound of the dinner gong. Melissa had been dipping incredulously into sections of Lady Otranta's memoirs. Now she looked up at Bridie.

"Well, Bridie," she said, quite without rancour. "Little did my stepmother know what she was landing in your lap."

"In *my* lap?" Bridie gaped at her.

"Of course. Don't you see. . . ? Castle Tantallon, the estate— it's all yours now, every stick and stone of it."

Bridie was aghast. The thought simply hadn't entered her head. "But—"

"'Lissa's quite right," Andrew confirmed. "I expect there'll be all sorts of legal difficulties, but we'll get them sorted out, I promise you."

Slowly Bridie crossed to the fireplace, where a log fire was smouldering. She needed time to think. "I believe Sir James left the Tantallon estate to you, Andrew," she said.

Andrew nodded. "With a substantial legacy for Mama. But I couldn't possibly be his legitimate heir."

"I see." Bridie contemplated the flames. "And since Lady Otranta left no will, her inheritance would be divided among her family?"

"I . . . I imagine so."

Bridie made up her mind. She turned to Melissa. "Did you keep that letter from your mother?"

Melissa shifted unhappily in her chair. "It's locked away in my bedroom."

"Would you fetch it, please?"

Her cousin seemed about to protest, then changed her mind and hurried from the room.

Andrew cleared his throat. "Is this necessary?"

Bridie cut him short. "That letter's the only proof we have of her story."

"I hardly think she'd have invented it."

Bridie didn't answer. He shrugged and they waited in uneasy silence. While Melissa was upstairs the gong sounded again in the entrance hall. They both ignored it.

Soon afterwards Melissa returned, an envelope in her hand. She gave it to Bridie without a word. Bridie then picked up Lady Otranta's memoirs, and faced Andrew and Melissa.

"This letter and these papers—you don't mind my keeping them?"

"Of course not," Andrew answered, a little sharply.

"Then you'd say they're mine? By rights my property, to do with what I like?"

"I . . . I suppose so."

"Good." In one quick movement Bridie went to the fire and flung the letter and the first half dozen sheets of the memoirs into the flames.

Behind her no one moved. The paper burned sluggishly at first, but soon began to flare. She added more of her great-aunt's manuscript. The light of its burning cast flickering shadows round the room, on the bewildered faces of her cousins.

She stacked the last of the memoirs in the fire's centre, watched the blackened husk of Melissa's envelope rise and dance away up the chimney, then straightened her back.

"Two of the most improbable stories I've ever heard," she said, "And without one single scrap of evidence to support them." She looked fondly from Andrew to Melissa. "The law," she said, quoting Mr. Dickens, "is an ass. It's not bits of paper that make a family. It's what people *are* that counts."

An agitated tap came upon the library door. Andrew didn't notice it. "Bridie, dearest. . . ." He held out his arms and she went to him. He would never, she knew, burden her with his gratitude. Gratitude wasn't for lovers.

Behind them the door had opened to admit a distracted Meredith. "Sir Andrew, please . . . if you're no wantin' your dinners, then mebbe you'd be good enough to break the news to cook. Meself, I daresn't."

It was Melissa who roused herself first. "Of course we're wanting our dinners. And please apologize to cook on our behalf for keeping her waiting." She moved to Meredith's side. "You can tell her too—and I don't give a hang whether it's suitable or not—you can tell her that life at the castle has just taken a decided turn for the better."

The old man looked from her to Andrew and Bridie, still locked in one another's arms. "I'll tell her that, Mistress Melissa. She'll be gey pleased, I'm thinking. We all will."

He held the door open. Briefly Melissa glanced back and then was gone. Tactfully Meredith followed her.

Bridie turned her face up to Andrew, and he kissed her. "No doubts?"

"No doubts."

"You've changed, my dearest." He cupped her head in both his hands. "You looked so small and frightened the first time I saw you, standing at the foot of the stairs, your bits of luggage at your feet. . . ."

Tears welled suddenly but she didn't care. She remembered that evening too. Well, if she'd changed there was only one reason.

"I do love you, Andrew," she said.

"And I you, my dear."

With grave formality he offered her his arm. She took it and together they walked slowly out, across the entrance hall to a dining table lit with the last golden light of the setting sun. To a dinner—hardly the first and certainly not the last she would eat at Castle Tantallon—of oatmeal in all its most Scottish permutations.

Frances Lynch

Frances Lynch inherits her love of Scotland from her proudly Scottish grandmother. The theatre, too, has featured largely in her life, for both her parents were on the stage. And, as possibly a final influence in the writing of *A Dangerous Magic*, she remembers vividly a holiday spent as a child in Portobello, beside the Firth of Forth, while her mother played a summer season in an Edinburgh theatre. In those pre-war days there were still children running barefoot in the road, and lollipops as big as dinner plates to be bought on Princes Street, where the trams rattled terrifyingly past on either side of traffic islands seemingly scarcely wide enough for a rather plump little girl to stand upon.

It was in Edinburgh, too, that she was given her first dog— appropriately enough a tiny black Scottie puppy.

After the war Frances Lynch herself worked briefly in the theatre. But she admits she wasn't much of an actress, so when marriage and children claimed her she was quite content to settle down and pursue in her spare time her second lifelong ambition: that of becoming a writer. She wrote plays at first, but when these received little success she turned, in the late 1950s, to books.

Since then she has published many successful novels, using several pseudonyms, and her work has been translated into all the major European languages. She lives now in a little Berkshire village on the Kennet and Avon canal, within easy reach of London and the libraries so necessary for her historical research.

In connection with the writing of *A Dangerous Magic*, she was lucky enough to find a 1907 Scottish steamship company's brochure, illustrating the picturesque beauties of paddleboat excursions on the Firth of Forth. Sadly, when later she travelled to Leith to see for herself, the industrial realities of 1977 were a bitter disappointment to her. Sometimes, it seems, a writer can be just *too* thorough. Far better, she thinks now, to have stayed at home and preserved intact her belief in the rustic, romanticised world of those Edwardian etchings. . . .

THE FOREST DWELLERS

a condensation of the book by **STELLA BREWER**
Published by Collins

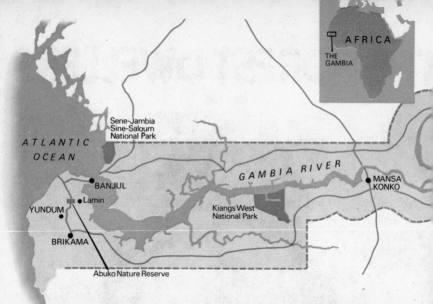

When William, a baby chimpanzee, was first brought to Stella Brewer, he was tied up in a crate far too small for him, and was desperately thin and frightened. As she nursed him to health, other neglected captives arrived at the Brewers' house in The Gambia, and it soon became clear that a permanent home must be found for them.

With the permission of the Senegal authorities, Stella Brewer camped with her chimps in the Niokolo Koba National Park, and began her exciting and rewarding venture in teaching captured or zoo-born apes to live self-sufficiently in their natural surroundings. She learnt with them how to build nests, alerted them to the danger of lions and snakes, even ate termites herself to encourage them to try this form of food! By 1972 her first three chimps were ready for complete independence.

The story of Stella and her charming, amusing and maddening companions will delight animal-lovers and all who admire a pioneering spirit.

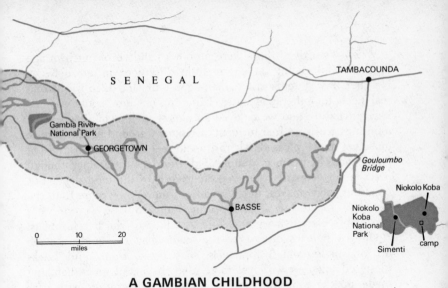

A GAMBIAN CHILDHOOD

I cannot remember a time when there has not been an animal to share our home with us. I grew up with Pal, my father's golden labrador, and my older sister Lorna's stray cats.

In the Seychelle Islands, where I was born in 1951, we lived next door to the botanical gardens. Here my nanny taught me to ride the giant tortoises. Here also I carried out my first animal rescue operation. Nanny and I were walking back to the house when I spotted a small brown bird flapping about on the path. I carried it home where I placed it in a cardboard box on the kitchen table and hurried off to call my mother. As we entered the kitchen we were just in time to see one of Lorna's cats leaving with the bird in his mouth. I gave chase, which only served to make the cat run faster and I quickly lost him and my little bird. I returned to the house so upset I could scarcely speak. My mother comforted me, and impressed upon me that I should not blame Jackie for what had happened, for to him eating a bird was perfectly natural. It was a lasting introductory lesson on the laws of nature.

When I was six my father, who is a forester, was transferred to The Gambia, where I have lived most of my life. Our ex-army bungalow is fifteen miles out of Banjul, formerly Bathurst, on Yundum Agricultural Station.

297

When we arrived there were no other children of our own age in the vicinity, but there was little difference in age between Heather, my younger sister, then aged four, and I, so we had no real need for other playmates. Exploring our new home was one long adventure and we enjoyed an almost idyllic childhood. Most mornings we were free to roam the country around us, and amuse ourselves as we pleased. There was no real danger in this, for big game had long since disappeared from The Gambia, though occasionally leopards were reported. Perhaps the most dangerous creatures were snakes, but normally we never saw more than the last few inches of a disappearing tail. So long as we were reasonably alert, we were as safe as children who live in towns.

One by one we discovered the small villages around us, made up of single-roomed rondavels constructed from mud bricks plastered together with yet more mud. Layers of grass thatching made up the roof and these were held to the rafters with bark rope or palm leaves. The influential members of the village had a more Western style of house, made from corrugated iron and far less picturesque.

We soon learned how to recognize the edible fruits and berries in the countryside, also how to plait and weave baskets. At the same time we began accumulating animals. Ginger, a marmalade kitten, came first, and to keep him company we accepted Shot, a short-haired German pointer puppy. As the first of our animals, they viewed the various other species that came to us with an aloof cordiality. They were a perfect pair, and until Shot died five years ago, they demonstrated an unusually deep affection for one another. Ginger, at twenty years old, is today as fit and as independent as ever.

After Ginger and Shot, we acquired a number of birds. One morning, after a particularly violent storm, Heather and I chanced to pass a large tree, laden with weaverbird nests. During the storm several of these intricately woven nests had fallen to the ground. Many of the small occupants were already dead, but we found twelve still alive. We took off our shirts, and wrapped the survivors in them. We took some nests too, so that the young birds would feel at home, which we dried and lined with cotton wool. Under Mummy's guidance, we fed the little birds several

298

times a day, placing the food in their ever-gaping mouths with match-sticks. Two of the fledglings died but the remaining ten survived and eventually flew away.

Our interest in animals was noticed, and more and more of them, usually orphans, were brought to us. From an early age we were experimenting with different milk formulae to suit each of the species.

One pet I particularly remember was Olly, an African barn-owl. At first, because of his formidable beak, we fed him with a pair of tweezers, but we soon found that it was safe to use our fingers. He would gently take the food and hold it for a second in his beak. Inclining his head a little, he would blink his huge, dewy eyes as he gulped, and the food would disappear. He seemed to enjoy having his head and neck stroked gently with a finger and would perch on our shoulders for hours. When the time came that he could fly confidently, we would take him out into the garden in the evenings and he would circle the house and return to us. Gradually, his flights became longer and, finally, the night came when he did not return. A couple of evenings later, there was a screeching call from the sill of the sitting-room window. It was Olly, demanding entrance and some supper. For years he kept visiting us.

Every Sunday morning my father would take us as a treat to the airport woods, an isolated patch of forest close to the airport at Yundum which harboured a rich variety of Gambian animals. Heather and I would grin at each other in silent excitement when we came across a troop of Western Red Colobus monkeys. These were always high up in the trees and their rope-like tails hung down to become indistinguishable from the mesh of dangling vines. Sometimes, we were able to watch them feed, but it was rare that we could enjoy this luxury for long as they would spot us and flee.

Of all the animals with which we were familiar the monkeys held a special fascination. We wove fantasies about them, and some of the baskets we made were taken home to our parents as gifts from "the monkeys". We would save scraps from meals and take them out into the bush as payment, in much the same way, I suppose, as some children feed fairies. Then one day the fantasy became reality. I was presented with Kim, a tiny Red Patas monkey who had lost his mother.

The joy I felt at having my very own infant to feed and look after was indescribable. From the time he arrived, we were almost never apart. While he was still relatively helpless, he would cling to the front of my shirt and I would wrap a piece of cloth around my middle to support him. In this position he would sleep for hours, only waking briefly for his bottle of milk. It was always difficult leaving him at night but here my mother was adamant: no matter how much I begged, he was not allowed to sleep with me. Then Trixie came, a Green Vervet monkey which belonged to Heather. Kim and Trixie took an instant liking to each other and shared a box at night.

IN 1960, MY PARENTS sent Heather and me to boarding school in England and for eight years we returned home only for brief holidays. Each time things were never quite the same as they had been before. The village had grown and the farms had spread farther into the bush, destroying favourite places and special trees. Perhaps the saddest thing of all was the gradual disappearance of the airport woods; by the time we left school they no longer existed. I wondered what had happened to the mongooses, the antelopes, the leaping Colobus monkeys and all the other creatures whose home they had been.

The last few letters from home that we received while still at school were full of news about new animals. Charlie, a serval cat, had been given to my father by one of the forest workers. He was a small bundle of soft fur when he came and resembled a spotted Persian kitten with over-sized ears. Two days after Charlie had come, Daddy was given another spotted infant. Tim was a genet, with a weasely little face, small, bright brown eyes and a thick, short coat that was covered with chocolate-brown spots and blotches. His long tail was ringed in the same rich colour. The new arrivals, being so young, were sharing the same nursery. Mummy had her hands full with Bambi and Booful, two Harnessed antelope fawns that lived in the back garden. Unlike most of the other animals, they rarely came into the house, as they found it difficult to walk on our polished tiled floors.

300

*Stella with the
Royal python, Percy*

Tim, the genet

*Stella, aged seven, with
Kim (left) and Trixie (right)*

Heather and I left school at the same time. I had just finished my A levels and Heather her O levels. It was a glorious feeling of freedom when we realized that we had finished with school for ever. The rest of our lives seemed like one long holiday, stretching ahead of us.

My return was made still more happy by the gift, just before I left, of a Dalmatian puppy, Duff. I brought it with me on the plane and at the airport handed the basket to Daddy. Tess, our little mongrel, was waiting at the gate and gave us all a typically warm welcome. Daddy proudly introduced us to Tim and Charlie, who were still young enough to accept us without too many qualms. Then Mummy led us into the garden to meet Bambi and Booful. Surprisingly, they came over immediately and began nudging Mummy for a bottle, even though Heather and I, two complete strangers, stood beside her.

Heather and I soon fitted into the routine and relieved our parents of some of the responsibility. We would often feed Tim and Charlie. The latter grew from a scruffy kitten into a beautiful animal. It was like a circus on the lawn in the evenings, as each of the animals, including two young hyenas who had recently been deposited with us, played out their youthful energy.

Charlie began to spend longer in the bush in the evening, and by the time he was mature he had formed a regular pattern for his activities. During the day he chose a comfortable cushion in the house and would curl up asleep. Each evening he would make his way to the kitchen where his meat and milk would be waiting for him. Having eaten his meal, he would spend an hour or so with us all in the sitting room. Gradually one could see him become restless, till finally he would walk to the dog door and disappear into the night. Each morning he would have returned by the time the household was up and would wait expectantly for his bowl of milk.

One evening I watched as Charlie decided it was time to leave for his nocturnal wanderings. He paused by the door to glance farewell at us. "Goodnight, Charlie boy," I replied. "Happy hunting."

Some time during the night there were two explosions in the bush just behind our house; undoubtedly shots fired from one of

302

the homemade muzzle-loaders still used by the local hunters. Next morning the bowl of milk on the kitchen table remained untouched. Charlie did not come home.

Heather and I spent the day in the bush calling for him. At four o'clock that afternoon, we turned for home and about a hundred yards from the house, we heard the buzzing of flies. We found Charlie lying on his side beneath a tangle of vegetation, stiff and dead. He had been shot in the hindquarters. My vision blurred as I picked up his crumpled body. Heather and I carried him home. That evening, we buried him in the corner of the garden beneath his favourite tree.

WILLIAM

It was shortly after Charlie died that William, our first chimp, arrived. He was brought to my father's office by a man whose tribal scars suggested that he was not a Gambian. As my father and I approached, the man bent and began to untie the pieces of string and rag that bound a grimy box beside him. A nauseating odour wafted up as he lifted the lid, and rough hands pulled out a rigid little body. It lay quite stiff on the concrete, bony arms and legs drawn close to its body. Its small, pale face contorted into a fixed and terrified grin, only its chest moved as it emitted a harsh choking scream over and over again. The sparse, dark hair that covered its emaciated frame was matted with filth and pus. Its belly protruded, alarmingly swollen and taut.

William had made the three-week journey from Guinea, where he had been captured, in the twelve- by fifteen-inch prison in which he had arrived. For part of the journey his box had been tied to the top of rolling, jolting, African buses. He had been secured in his box by a piece of red flex which was fastened around his groin. This had been threaded through a hole in the back of the box. William had then been folded like a rag doll, till his face touched his knees, and the flex had been drawn from behind, dragging him into his confining quarters.

He was for sale: a murdered mother and weeks of indescribable misery for the sake of a few shillings. We were overwhelmed with pity for the pathetic creature at our feet. After some hurried bartering, money was placed in the outstretched hand. We little realized what the consequences might be.

I wrapped the chimp in a sack and, gently cradling the cringing body close to mine, walked back to our home. A spacious crate was lined with clean packing-straw and placed on the veranda. Then William was wiped with cotton wool, which we had soaked in a mild antiseptic, and his sores were carefully cleaned and treated. We spoon-fed him a small amount of baby porridge, liberally sweetened with glucose, most of which he refused. Then we placed him on the bed of clean straw. Gratefully he cuddled a bundle of his bedding and fell into an exhausted sleep.

For six weeks he did little else. At first, whenever we approached, he would huddle against the back of the crate, as far away from us as he could get. Clutching his mat of straw he would whimper or scream. Tess, our mongrel, was fascinated by William from the first, and as she was of such a gentle disposition, we allowed her to visit him. Whenever she could she would slip out onto the veranda and lie in front of William's crate, occasionally giving a whimper when he stirred.

As the days passed William's attitude changed from fear to mild irritation. He would shake his hand at her or wave her away with a sweeping upward movement of his thin arm. Eventually, however, Tess's patience was rewarded. William had been in the house almost six weeks when one day, during one of Tess's vigils, he awoke. He gazed at Tess, then cautiously extended spidery fingers and touched her face. Tess whimpered and wriggled closer. William withdrew his hand instantly, but shortly afterwards the tentative touch was repeated. All seemed to be going well, when Tess burst forth in a mighty sneeze. William let out a squawk and retreated to the back of his crate.

Finally, however, he began to relax. The grin of fear on his face disappeared. He began to cast glances at Tess, then flicked pieces of straw in her direction. Slowly he inched his way towards her again, until he was close enough to pick off a piece of straw that dangled from her ear. By the end of the afternoon he had become confident enough to finger her ears and face. From that day on their friendship flourished.

William also began to come forward eagerly for his small but frequent meals. On hearing our footsteps, a drowsy little face would peek round the edge of the crate, and thin hands would extend gravely to accept our offerings. When we left him he would whimper and take a few wobbly steps after us.

Mummy became a premature but perfect grandmother to him. Shortly after he became active, she arrived home laden with brightly coloured plastic bricks, floating ducks, and other toys. She would kneel patiently on the carpet, chatting brightly to him and building a block of colourful little houses which William took a delight in demolishing. When they had tired of playing bricks, William might lead Mummy round the house on a treasure hunt. His favourite place was the bathroom: in William's opinion there was nothing so refreshing as washing yourself with toothpaste. He could even eat it, and toilet rolls made fascinating material for interior decorations. A toilet too was an ideal paddling pool.

His second favourite place was my parents' bedroom. He would play trampoline on the bed, and wrap himself up in the candlewick spread. As children we had never been allowed to bounce on the bed-springs or dress up in bedspreads, but as my mother always insisted, William was different. Whenever he approached the dressing-table, though, she was quick to distract him. Consequently, the dressing-table remained a tempting mystery, until one day Mummy made the mistake of becoming too engrossed in her flower arrangement. It was at this point that I came in through the back door.

"Mum," I asked, "where's William?"

She froze, her hand poised above the vase. "Isn't he by the door, playing with his duck?" she hesitantly inquired.

No, he wasn't. As we stood gazing at the floor where William should have been, there came, from down the passage, the sound of a bottle being broken. We hurried in the direction of the bedroom and collided with William in mid-passage. He looked like a hairy little Indian brave, face decorated with a stunning pink lipstick, the remainder of which protruded from the corner of his mouth like a rosy cigar. On one knee he had daubed nail varnish, which had run down his leg in pearly rivulets, and his coat

305

had been liberally dusted with powder. The cold cream had not gone unnoticed either and to complete the effect he stank of scent. Quite unconscious of the spectacle he presented, William climbed up my leg, put his oily arms about my neck and tightened them in an affectionate hug.

The duty of wiping up puddles was assigned to Heather and me. Every time William was seen gazing benignly ahead, legs slightly splayed, he was whisked up and placed outside on the lawn. Usually the signs were recognized too late. A puddle would form, or worse still a glistening trail would be left in the wake of whoever was hurrying William into the garden. On these occasions Heather or I would fetch the cloth from its usual place in a bucket of disinfectant on the back veranda and wipe up the puddle. Having watched this procedure several times a day, William was seen one day struggling out of the kitchen dragging a sodden cloth behind him. He approached an undetected puddle and, with an expression of grave determination, proceeded with all his tiny might to rub the cloth backwards and forwards in it. By the time he had exhausted himself, not only was there a trail of disinfectant from the back veranda to the sitting room, but the relatively small puddle had been liberally spread to cover at least ten times its original area. He looked up at us triumphantly, and dumped the dripping cloth in the seat of a nearby chair.

One evening when I was on my way to feed Bambi and Booful, Heather called me urgently. I reached the kitchen to discover that William had drunk some paraffin. None of us knew how much the bottle had contained nor how much William had drunk. I reasoned that it must taste so awful that he would only have taken a mouthful or two at the worst. However, William reeked appallingly of paraffin and not long afterwards crawled onto the couch. He seemed to be feeling very sick indeed so I rang up a doctor friend, who volunteered to come over immediately. While I waited for him to arrive, I cradled a pathetically limp little chimp in my arms. Occasionally he struggled to open his eyes; then, gripping my shirt with both fists clenched, his body would contract as if in awful pain.

The doctor's assurances that all would be well comforted and relieved us. I was recommended to feed William as much milky ·

306

tea as he could drink, but this was easier said than done. He refused even to look at his beaker and I only managed to get some of the liquid down by using a feeding-bottle, on which he sucked lethargically. He spent that night on the couch with a thick towel tucked beneath him. I stayed with him and gradually he seemed to fall into a peaceful sleep.

During the early hours of the morning I dozed off too. I was woken at five thirty by Heather, who had come to see how William was getting on. William stirred, sat up, reached for the feeding-bottle, which stood on the table beside us, and sucked on it greedily. The relief I felt was overwhelming; but the incident impressed upon us that we would soon have to decide what William's future was to be.

ABUKO

Just as we were becoming desperate about finding any solution, the unexpected happened. We discovered the Abuko Water Catchment Area, two miles away from our home. The catchment area was completely enclosed by a fence, which was partially hidden by dense vegetation. A pumping station stood at the nearest point to the road within the fence. Nailed to the gate was a large sign which read, "No admittance except on business", so we had obediently passed the area hundreds of times without stopping to look inside. Then one day Daddy was approached by Kalilu, a farmer from nearby Lamin Village, who complained that a leopard had been killing his pigs. He offered to show us the remains of one of his animals as proof, and drove us to Lamin. There he led us a quarter of a mile to the catchment area fence. After following this for a few hundred yards he dropped on all fours and wriggled through a large hole.

I compare that hole, in many ways, with Alice's looking-glass, for beyond we discovered an incredible world we had not known existed. With each step, we became more enchanted by what we saw. We were walking from the familiar savannah into the cool, damp atmosphere of a tropical rain forest. Having been protected as a catchment area since the early part of the century, the vegetation had been left relatively undisturbed and gave us a glimpse of what The Gambia must once have looked like. Lianas festooned the tall trees, and vines formed intricate patterns against the blue sky.

When finally we came to the carcass of the pig, Daddy seemed to find it difficult to concentrate on the matter we had come about. Finally, he turned to an exasperated Kalilu and said there was nothing he could do about the leopard so long as the pigs were in the prohibited catchment area. If it began killing in the village, then there might be a case.

On reaching home, Daddy sent a memorandum to the Central Government, outlining the area's need for permanent protection and suggesting that it should be given the status of a reserve. The memorandum was sympathetically received, prompt action followed, and the Abuko Nature Reserve was established only a few weeks later. We were overjoyed. Although a full-time forest officer, my father took on the additional responsibility of running the reserve, needless to say with all the assistance his family could give him.

The reserve is rectangular in shape and covers an area of 180 acres. The Lamin stream runs roughly through the centre from top to bottom and ends in a small lily-strewn lake. Because of the size of the reserve, it is impossible to allow vehicles to enter, so visitors have to explore it on foot. A narrow path meanders up one side and down the other in a rough semi-circle.

Owing to the dense vegetation the fauna of Abuko is not readily visible. The easiest animals to observe are the monkeys, because they are arboreal. These include the Green Vervet, the Red Patas, and my favourites, the graceful Western Red Colobus. Occasionally, in the earlier days, we would catch a glimpse of Abuko himself, that pork-loving leopard to whom we owed so much. The year after the reserve was founded, however, he disappeared for good.

IN ORDER TO publicize the reserve and raise money for it, Daddy began giving slide shows in the local hotels. If we happened to have any suitable animals in our care at the time, then we would take these along with us to win over our audience. Percy, a beautiful five-foot Royal python, made regular and impressive appearances at Daddy's talks, until his release into the reserve. At one time we were able to take along two heart-winning serval kittens; under our guidance, a member of the audience would be allowed to come out and feed them with a bottle.

As the reserve became more popular and received an increasing number of visitors, we found it was taking more rather than less out of the already strained family coffers. It was officially a government project so all the entrance fees were government revenue; but even if the government had been able to allocate all these funds to the upkeep and development of the reserve, it would still have been skimpy fare in those early days. There were periods when at least twice as much as the official allowance had to be found from somewhere to meet the food bills. The donations received from the lectures helped, and many of our friends would send us their excess garden produce for the animals, but even so most of the additional funds came out of Daddy's very ordinary government salary.

Then Scandinavian visitors began discovering The Gambia and tourism started to develop in a big way. For us, this seemed a double-edged weapon. On the one hand there were obvious economic advantages for the country in developing a tourist industry. Certainly it helped to support Abuko. On the other, tourism contributed to the destruction of the wildlife. There were tourist hunters, who shot anything that moved. Happily these were soon banned by the Gambian government.

It was not sufficient to have Abuko as a protected reserve on paper. For the first couple of years we could not afford to employ guards, so we thought the best policy was to encourage the people of the villages close by to understand what we were trying to do. Our biggest hazard was the local hunters. One of them, named Doodou, we knew quite well. Doodou hunted for meat, which he sold in the village. We had no complaint about this; hunting for food was acceptable. It was when they began killing for skins that we became worried. My father called at Doodou's house one evening and asked if he could arrange a meeting of all the hunters in the immediate vicinity. Then, during the meeting, my father explained exactly why he wanted Abuko protected, and asked for the hunters' help. Strangely, they all agreed with him and many of them swore on the Koran that they would not attempt to hunt in Abuko. Some of them went even further and agreed to act as voluntary protectors, promising to inform us if they heard of anyone poaching there. They have kept their word, and to date no one has violated the undertaking.

THE CHIMPS ARRIVE

It was a few months after the discovery of Abuko that Ann, a young female chimp, arrived. Chimps do not occur naturally in The Gambia and we could not understand why they had suddenly begun to appear. Later we learned that, just before William reached us, a male chimp had been bought for an exorbitant price in Basse, a village 200 miles up the river, close to the Gambia/Senegal border. The news had obviously reached Guinea, which is where we believe William and Ann to have originated.

Unlike William, Ann found it difficult to accept the whole family as foster-parents. She was quiet and self-sufficient, and it took me a long time to win her confidence. When she did accept me, I felt almost honoured.

She was the answer to our prayers. With the discovery of Abuko we realized that we had a perfect home for William; however, to put him there by himself, after he had become used to being a member of a crowded household, would have been unfair. With Ann as a companion there seemed a chance that they might make the change. Until Abuko was ready, we built temporary accommodation for them in the garden. This was a large, airy cage which we filled with tyres, ropes, complicated climbing apparatus and a box full of William's toys.

As long as someone remained with Ann and William in the cage they would amuse themselves for hours. However, if we tried to leave them alone they were desperately unhappy. Gradually, however, I tried to accustom them to spending more time by themselves. William's crate was moved from the veranda and raised on poles in the cage. Their supper was served near the newly-sited sleeping quarters. At first I remained with them until

310

they slept, usually both of them remaining steadfastly on my lap as dusk approached. With stomachs round and full they would fall asleep in my arms. Carefully, I would try to place them in the crate without awakening them. As a rule I was only partially successful. They would both half-wake, but on seeing my face and hearing my voice, they would clutch the nearest warm thing to hand, which happened to be each other, and promptly fall asleep again. Before long, it became possible to leave them as soon as supper was over.

WE HAD DECIDED that in the centre of the reserve we would fence off an area of twenty acres which we would call the orphanage. Once the animals in the house were weaned, they could be accommodated in this more natural environment while still under close supervision.

We made plans for an enclosure of half an acre for the chimps within the orphanage. This would be surrounded by eight-foot, plastic-covered, chain-link fencing, surmounted by sheets of corrugated iron. In this way, the chimps would be able to climb to the top of the chain-link fencing, but no higher. William took an active, if ineffectual, part in the work. By the time it was finished he had mastered the use of the hammer and pliers and was well on his way to conquering the spade. Though he understood the basic principles of this, the spade was almost twice as tall as he was and too large and cumbersome for him to manipulate easily. I bought him a child's beach spade which would have been more his size but he insisted on using the tools of his workmates.

The enclosure took months to build but we all felt that it had been a job well done. Large trees close to the fence had to be removed to prevent escape, but otherwise the enclosure was left with as much natural plant-life as possible. A complex of play-apparatuses was constructed, and at either end of the enclosure stood a square wooden hut on stilts with an overhanging slatted roof. One hut had no walls and would serve as a shady resting place, the other was enclosed on three sides and had a wooden ladder leading to the fourth, open side. Inside were two hammocks for sleeping. Between the huts we dug two circular pools which would serve as drinking places. Beside one of the pools a solid wooden feeding table and two benches were cemented into the ground.

At this time we discovered three young chimps for sale in the market at Banjul. They were in terrible physical condition and I knew that if they were not rescued and looked after properly they were going to die. Daddy was just as concerned as I was, but even if we could have afforded them, purchase was not the answer. We would merely be encouraging the trade.

My father decided to appeal to the Inspector-General of Police, who reacted quickly. Any chimpanzees for sale in The Gambia were to be confiscated and sent to Abuko Nature Reserve. We rushed back to Banjul market, but only one of the chimps had survived.

We called him Albert. He had not long been captured and was still very wild. A fresh scar curved over his upper lip, which I suspected to be the result of human maltreatment. In spite of all our efforts he remained a distrustful and pathetically lonely figure, who showed not the slightest inclination to interact with William and Ann. As soon as the enclosure was completed, we tried to move him into it but, during the process, he escaped into the dense cover of the main reserve.

Soon after Albert's escape, a store manager who kept two chimps behind his shop in Banjul telephoned us. The female had died. He thought the four-year-old male too dangerous to be interesting and asked us if we would take him. When we reached the shop I went round to the back to see the chimp. His coat was long and abundant and he had protruding ears which seemed unusually large and rather flaccid. He looked a solid individual. His name was Cheetah.

He was driven straight to the reserve and this time we successfully managed to get our chimp into the enclosure. He took a brief drink from one of the pools and watched from a distance as his old cage was taken away.

That evening I took Ann and William, who were still living at home with us, to the reserve, impatient to see Cheetah's reaction. He started grinning the moment he spotted them and extended his hand trustingly through the wire. The introduction looked so promising that I decided to take Ann and William into

312

the enclosure. Cheetah seemed nervous when I entered and, though showing desperate curiosity, he kept well away until I sat on the feeding-table bench and William climbed off me and onto the ground. Ann remained on my back, clinging tightly to my shirt.

Despite being somewhat larger, Cheetah approached cautiously, alternately panting his submission and drawing his lips back to squeak uncertainly. William was equally nervous but, reassured by the fact that I sat right behind him, he fluffed out his sparse coat to look as large as possible and bravely advanced towards Cheetah. For an instant they stood inches apart, both with nervous open grins, screeching in uncertain excitement. I knew that one aggressive sound or gesture from either of them could wreck the new relationship and cause a fight but fortunately William half turned round and presented his white-tufted bottom in a sign of submission. Cheetah immediately responded by embracing William.

At this point, Ann climbed off my back and stamped her feet on the bench in a state of anxiety for William mixed with general excitement. Her coat bristled but, as Cheetah began to groom William, she plonked herself on my lap and, firmly gripping my hand, regained her usual wide-eyed expression and became a passive audience once more.

Throughout the ensuing week, I took Ann and William into the enclosure whenever opportunity arose. Once Cheetah felt confident about them, he began approaching me. Each time he would take one or two extra liberties, testing to find how far he could go towards dominating me. At first his intentions were disguised in play. He would pull my hand, pinch my leg and pretend to bite me. Gradually the play became more serious. I had watched the same tactics being used by William and Ann when they met new people, so I was not surprised when the time came for me to assert authority.

Cheetah had been in the reserve just over a week when, one afternoon, I gave the chimps some bananas. William and Ann were given four each but, as Cheetah was bigger, he got six. He wolfed down his fruit and had finished them all by the time Ann was delicately beginning her third. Cheetah strode boldly towards her. She guessed what he had in mind and grasped her remaining banana firmly in one foot. Thwarted, Cheetah began to whimper, then scream harshly. Ann hurriedly took refuge on my knee. With scarcely any warning Cheetah leapt at my leg and bit it hard. Instinctively I kicked out. Cheetah fell backwards but he sprang to his feet and leapt at me again, this time ripping my shirt and sinking his teeth into my arm. Almost without thinking, I found I had leant forward and bitten Cheetah equally hard on the shoulder. He released my arm and ran screaming to the end of the enclosure.

I allowed Cheetah to scream for a moment and then approached him. He looked up at me, confused and frightened at my sudden violence. I squatted down in front of him and held out my arms. I could almost see the struggle in his face. Would I attack him again or give him the comfort he now so badly needed? The more undecided he became, the greater grew his need for reassurance. I reached out and touched his head and he responded by throwing himself against me and hugging me tightly. I returned his embrace and spoke soothingly to him. For the first time I lifted him. He panted good-naturedly as I carried him to the table and gave them more bananas. It was that afternoon that the seeds were sown for the deeply affectionate relationship we later shared.

Three days later I took William and Ann to the reserve for their usual afternoon play session with Cheetah and left them there for the night. There were dreadful protests when I tried to leave them in those strange sleeping quarters and it was well after dark before I was able to creep away. The next morning I found to my delight all three chimps engrossed in play. Even quiet little Ann was rolling around in the rough-and-tumble.

Despite all the amenities in the enclosure, we felt that it would be boring for the chimps to have to spend all their time in it. A routine was established whereby each morning I would take all three of them into the main reserve for at least three or four hours. I never had the slightest worry that I would lose any of them, for the moment I moved away from where they were playing, all three would rush to my side. At first I used to take a picnic basket of fruit and drinks but I quickly abandoned this and concentrated on trying to teach them to make use of the abundance of foodstuffs that the reserve contained.

*Baby William,
soon after his arrival*

*William, as he is now, at
work with a toothpick*

ONE MORNING when I was exercising the chimps in the reserve, Abduli, our warden, came in sight. "Stella," he burst out, "I've just seen Albert."

"Albert?" I echoed. "Are you certain?"

He assured me that he was. We hurried down the path to where the chimp had been spotted and there, high in a large mampatto tree, sat Albert. He looked healthy and well-nourished and, in fact, sported quite a paunch. Cheetah, William and Ann were openly curious but I could detect no excitement or curiosity in Albert's manner—he merely sat and serenely surveyed the group below him. Cheetah was the first to approach him but as he drew close, Albert made an expert aerial crossing into a neighbouring tree and vanished. It was six months since his escape and there was no way of telling how many times he must quietly have watched us.

From then on we all kept a look-out for him but it was another two months before he chose to reveal himself again. Throughout the whole of his first year in the reserve he never once attempted to approach William, Cheetah or Ann.

One day, while shopping in the market, I was told that another chimpanzee was in town. I was ushered into a gloomy corrugated-iron shack, in one corner of which a wooden box was resting, smelling strongly of chimp dung. Peering through a crack in the crate I saw a weeping eye staring back at me.

It took little time to arrange for the crate to be confiscated and removed to Abuko. We discovered the chimp was a female; the biggest that we had so far acquired. Tina, as we called her, had already lost her incisor milk teeth and the large white permanent ones were in the process of erupting to replace them. We guessed she was about six years old. She had unusual orange eyes and one of her front top teeth was markedly larger than the other which gave her an odd gappy-looking grin. Apart from being thin and having a slight infection in one eye, there seemed little else physically wrong with her, so we decided to release her directly into the enclosure with the others.

She must have been confined in her crate for at least a week for when the slatted lid was removed, she did not leap for freedom but merely drew her legs back and screamed her fear at the other

316

chimps. At last, in a painfully stiff manner, she made her way to a small tree and sat beneath it in the shade.

An hour later she managed to climb into the crown of an oil palm, where she made an enormous nest, and there she remained for the following three days. She watched when I fed the other chimps that evening but showed no inclination to come down and retrieve any food for herself. I tried throwing some oranges up to her and these she ate immediately.

On the fourth evening, she timidly descended and attempted to share the food on the table with the other chimps. Though she was bigger than any of them, Cheetah had only to bristle his coat and stamp his feet on the table to make her withdraw screaming. To my disappointment, neither William nor Ann were friendly towards the newcomer. Finally, after much hesitating, she managed to grab a loaf of bread and stiffly climb back to her nest at the top of the palm.

That evening over our own supper we held a family conference as to what the best solution for Tina would be. We came to the decision that since she was unhappy in the enclosure, we should risk giving her the freedom of the reserve. Being so timid, she would cause no problems with tourists. Also, she was potentially an ideal companion for Albert, whom we still occasionally saw. The question was, would she remain in the reserve?

On the fifth morning after her arrival I left the enclosure door open when I took out the others. When we returned Tina had gone, but a couple of evenings later she was sitting in a tree close to the back of the enclosure. I piled a tray with tempting fruit and some bread and placed it on the ground as close as I dared to where she sat. I then retreated to the rest-house to watch.

Slowly, and with extreme caution, she began to climb down to the ground. In a series of hurried dashes she approached the tray, then proceeded to load up with as much fruit as she could carry. She placed an orange in her neck and held it there by leaning her cheek against it, pressed some more fruit between her thighs, put a loaf in her mouth, filled her arms to capacity, and gripped a banana in each foot. Thus laden she hobbled back towards the safety of the dense vegetation. Pieces of fruit kept dropping, and as fast as she recovered one, another fell. She finally reached her refuge and settled down to eat.

From then on she appeared faithfully in the orphanage each sunset to receive her quota of fruit. Bambi fell into the habit of sharing the meal with her and, even after a special elevated feeding-table had been built and the antelope could no longer reach the food, the two of them were frequently seen together in the reserve. Bambi would stand beneath the tree where Tina fed and eat all the fruit she dropped. Tina would also groom Bambi and keep her ears and face free from the ticks which attach themselves to antelopes. For Tina in those first lonely months, Bambi was a valuable companion.

Another new acquisition was Happy. He was an exceptionally pretty chimp with a thick, long coat. The hair on his legs almost covered his feet and gave the impression that he was wearing a pair of bell-bottomed trousers. He had a round, pale face with enormous soulful brown eyes. Probably he was about eighteen months old. He was terrified of humans and shunned any attention from us. When he was used to drinking milk from a bottle, we took him to the reserve and presented him to Tina. To our great relief the introduction worked like a dream. For Tina and Happy it was love at first sight; and Tina turned out to be an exception-ally attentive foster-mother. She carried Happy around for short periods and when she grew tired, he walked beside her, clutching a handful of the hair on her back. Each evening when she came to the orphanage for her supper, we were able to give Happy the milk which he still required, before he followed Tina into a tree and settled down beside her in the nest she made.

IT HAD BEEN WELL over a year since I had left school, and I was still entirely dependent on my parents. I knew I was being useful in helping Daddy look after the reserve, but somehow I had to earn a living. I decided to accept a job at the Woburn Wild Animal Kingdom in England. Stupidly I did not realize that I had already begun my chosen career and that the year I spent there was only to serve as an interruption. However, I learnt a lot while I was away. My job was taking care of three baby African elephants, all under three years old. They were endearing, highly

318

intelligent creatures and followed me around like shadows. I became extremely attached to them, but I missed the chimps and home. When Daddy sent me an air ticket as a birthday present I returned to The Gambia immediately.

Our group of chimps had grown to eight. There had been two new arrivals during my absence, Pooh and Flint. Pooh lived free in the reserve, but Flint, having been adopted by quiet little Ann, lived in the enclosure. He was out-going and independent and reminded me in many ways of William when he'd been younger. William was if anything more confident and roguish than ever, but grinned and hugged me affectionately. Cheetah was even more demonstrative on my return. He seemed beside himself with excitement and groomed my face and hair with frenzied enthusiasm.

While I had been away, Tina and Albert had made friends. They were seated in a low branch of a tree close to the enclosure, and as Abduli approached with a tray of fruit they grunted eagerly and descended. Neither of them paid any attention when young Happy and newcomer Pooh were given their milk. It was clear that Happy, however, was still very reliant on Tina, for having finished his milk he went straight to sit beside her.

Pooh worried me. He had hair that stuck up like a golliwog's, and a permanently startled expression. Mummy later told me that he had been conspicuously quiet in the house when he had first arrived. He had been living with a French couple in their flat in Banjul and though they had doted on him, they had preferred him to act like a human child, rather than a chimp. He had not been allowed to climb trees, or do the normal things small chimps do. Consequently he had become disturbed and deprived. Put into the enclosure, he had been an outcast from the first. William and especially Cheetah had bullied him. He had been dragged about, bitten and allowed nowhere near the feed table. As a last resort he had been introduced to Tina. She had been gentle with him but he had wanted nothing to do with her. Nevertheless it was felt that, if we were too soft with him, he would never accept other chimps so, much against his will, he had been left with her in the reserve.

The day following my return I automatically took over the chimps again. I felt sorry for Pooh, and he seemed to sense my sympathy immediately. At first, I carried him or allowed him to sit on my lap and hug himself to me. Gradually, he began to lean on me more and more and, while we were out on the walks, he would constantly remain close to me. He was a finicky feeder and therefore rather thin and scrawny but, with new confidence, he began to improve. He took a more lively interest in what was going on around him and, if I played with him or tickled him, I would be rewarded with a few husky pants of laughter and the open-mouthed play-face common to all chimps. The game "this little piggy" was one of his favourites and even after the little piggy had gone "wee wee wee all the way home" for the twentieth time, Pooh would still stick his pink toes in my face for more.

Each day I would take the group of eight chimps for a walk. I began to notice that Cheetah was showing an increasing amount of interest in Tina. It didn't take me long to realize that Tina had reached puberty and that the small pink swellings that periodically appeared around the ano-genital area made her extremely attractive. Cheetah became possessive and jealous. Tina did not seem to mind for Cheetah was her favourite suitor and she would follow him without hesitation when he led her a little way off from the main group. When she was in this condition she was far less attentive and protective towards Happy, who consequently spent more and more time playing with Pooh and Flint.

Frequently, when Cheetah mated Tina, Happy, Pooh and Flint would become very excited and rush over to the pair. Cheetah was tolerant to a degree, but should they persist too long, he would chase them off.

Sometimes, while following the winding path that runs through the reserve, the leading chimps would round a corner, then all suddenly reappear, either climbing trees or gripping some part of my anatomy for protection. If I quietly crept forward I would usually find a snake stretched across the path or coiled around a branch. Snakes were the only real danger in Abuko, and the chimps showed a healthy respect for them.

William was the only chimp in the group to show any tendency to attack snakes. During one peaceful walk Tina suddenly screamed and leapt up the trunk of a nearby oil palm tree. From

320

there she repeatedly made loud "whaa" barks of alarm. I walked cautiously in the grass but could not at first see what was causing Tina's distress. Then I heard a powerful exhalation of air. Just ahead of me, stretched along a fallen tree trunk, was about twelve feet of African python.

As I began to retreat, William suddenly charged into view with the base of a dead palm frond in his hand. This he flung with all his might at the python—whaaing as he did so. There was a chorus of excited calls from the rest of the chimps. I picked up William and carried him till I considered we were a safe distance away from the snake.

PROBLEMS AT THE RESERVE

During their time at Abuko the chimps came into contact with hundreds of tourists, many of whom were children, but there were only a few cases of their actually biting a visitor and in all these cases it was the human's fault. One such instance occurred when someone gave Happy a sweet. I did not like people to feed the chimps, but occasionally they were given sweets without my realizing. On this occasion Cheetah saw a visitor slip a sweet to Happy. He ran over to her and asked for one too. She gave Cheetah a sweet and took the opportunity to place a second one in Happy's hand. Cheetah immediately reached over and took the sweet from Happy. The woman, incensed at Cheetah's unfairness, snatched it and tried to give it back to Happy. It was only when the screaming started that I realized what had happened. It took me a long time to explain to the woman that she had almost asked to be bitten.

Although the chimps were rarely aggressive towards visitors they were quick to realize that they could take more liberties with them than with me. Visitors simply did not know what to expect and the chimps quickly learnt this and took delight in misbehaving. They had been taught that it was wrong to steal objects from a pocket or a bag that was being held. I often took a shoulder-bag out on the morning walks and the chimps understood that to remove anything from it was forbidden. Should I catch them trying they could expect punishment in the form of a scolding or a slap.

Despite my warnings to visitors to hold tightly onto their possessions, people would often respond to William's polite request to peep into a basket or handbag. As his backside vanished into a thicket with their purses or sandwiches, they would look amazed at how such a polite little fellow could change so quickly into a thieving rogue.

I remember once hurrying off in pursuit of William, to discover an overweight Swedish lady crawling on her hands and knees beside the path. Looking somewhat dishevelled, she straightened up and smiled self-consciously. At the far end of a tunnel through a particularly dense patch of vegetation I could hear William's squeaks. As I crawled along I found a trail of objects; banknotes, address book, cigarettes, a lighter, a broken compact, a semi-eaten lipstick and finally William with an empty handbag beside him. He had a small comb stuck behind his ear and was busy playing with the zip fastener of a purse. As I approached he moved farther down the tunnel and I realized that I would have to use subtle tactics if I was to recover the rest of what he had stolen.

In my shoulder-bag I kept a small supply of sweets for such emergencies. I offered William a sweet with one hand whilst holding my other hand out towards him. He was interested in the sweet and offered the equivalent of a twopenny piece for it. I shook my head and pointed at the purse. William understood and to my relief picked up the purse but, before giving it to me, he opened it and tipped the contents in front of him. I handed him a sweet, amazed at his good business sense. Six sweets and much bargaining later I had retrieved almost all that William had taken and was able to wriggle back to where the Swedish lady stood waiting.

Pooh was sitting on her shoulders, carefully taking the hairpins out of her bun.

ALMOST EVERY DAY while out with the chimps, we would meet Colobus or Green Vervet monkeys, and I noticed that Colobus-chasing was becoming an increasingly popular game. The Colobus

322

were not timid and would allow the chimps to get quite close before soaring away confidently through the leaf canopy or leaping easily across the enormous gaps into a neighbouring tree.

One morning I saw Tina suddenly leap forward and run into some dense undergrowth, followed closely by Cheetah and Albert. There was much rustling of dry leaves and I thought the chimps were chasing a pack of mongooses. The sudden high squeaking seemed to confirm this, till I heard an outburst of loud excited screaming coming from the hidden chimps.

William raced forward and all the other chimps followed. As I crawled through the tangle of thick vegetation to where they were, I thought they were having an almighty fight; everyone was screaming hysterically and seeming to dive in and bite or pull at Tina's stomach. As I approached Tina leapt clear and ran, still screaming, into a small tree. All the others were still very excited and I couldn't understand the frenzy till I saw that Tina held in one of her hands a very young Green Vervet monkey that was still alive and squeaking. I stood paralysed for a moment, then ran to Tina's tree and asked her in a shaky voice to give me the baby monkey and held out my hand. I had looked after several Vervets and found them loving little creatures; that this mob should want to hurt one was unbearable. I ordered Tina again to drop the monkey and flung a small branch at her. She climbed higher, then brought the monkey to her mouth and bit into its head, ripping off an ear. The squeaking stopped and Tina began to eat.

I couldn't watch. Feeling thoroughly sick I fled back to the path. The younger chimps followed but I wanted nothing to do with them. Supposing that chimps were strictly vegetarian, I was shocked and angry. Where would you all be, I cried, if, when you had arrived on the doorstep as helpless babies, I had picked you up and bitten your heads off?

A few days later, I read a book called *In The Shadow of Man* by Jane Goodall. She had lived amongst a group of wild chimps in Tanzania. One of the most significant things that she had discovered was that wild chimps hunted small mammals in order to eat them.

The book was a revelation in other ways. It made me realize

that, though we had been able to give our chimps a far more natural life-style than most such captives, they were still very deprived.

ONE MORNING when I got to the enclosure, I found it empty. The surrounding area looked as if a tornado had hit it. The sad wilted heads of bougainvillaea flowers littered the yard, the toilets had been invaded and yards of toilet paper lay strewn all over the gardens. On examining the enclosure I could find no possible place where the chimps could have escaped. The doors were all still locked and there were no holes or other clues.

I discovered the chimps somewhere near the middle of the reserve. Somehow I had to find out how they had escaped. For a week I arrived at the reserve before dawn and waited, but nothing happened to shed any light. Then the time came round for Tina's swelling and once more she and Cheetah became inseparable. Tina spent much more time near the enclosure and it was not uncommon to see Cheetah trying to mate her through the mesh. One morning when I arrived, Abduli rushed down the path to meet me and told me he had found out how the chimps had made their mysterious escape. He had just seen Tina climb up the outside of the enclosure, which was easy as all the supports were on the outside. She had then gripped the top of the corrugated iron and hung down on the inside, bridging the barrier. Cheetah had raced up the wire, jumped to catch Tina's feet and climbed up her body to the top of the fence. Abduli had prevented the others from escaping in the same fashion but Cheetah, he said, had run off with Tina.

All that morning I thought about how we could prevent Tina from releasing the chimps but I could not come up with any satisfactory answer. To modify the enclosure would cost more than we could afford and to enclose Tina would be more or less impossible. She might enter the enclosure once but, having found herself locked in, I was sure she would never consent to do so a second time. I knew that it was only a matter of time before the chimps would escape again and create another series of disasters.

Tina, Cheetah and Albert had grown fast during the past two

years and often startled me by their tremendous feats of strength. Cheetah had succeeded in ripping the orphanage gates right off their hinges, and the stout mahogany benches which were placed at intervals along the path were frequently overturned. Most alarming of all, when we returned to the orphanage after a walk one day, Cheetah played truant, refused to re-enter the enclosure, and succeeded in ripping the padlock off the hyena enclosure, almost letting our two hyenas out into the reserve.

Things could not be allowed to go on like this indefinitely. I had sworn to myself that, whatever happened, I would rather die than allow any of the chimps to be sent to a zoo. The only alternative was to release them somewhere in the wild. I had not heard of anyone trying to do this before and wondered just how feasible it would be.

NIOKOLO KOBA

My father had visited a large national park called Niokolo Koba in Senegal the year before and had thought it a beautiful place. He told me of a small mountain there, called Asserick, to which he had driven in the hope of seeing or hearing the wild chimpanzees that were sometimes observed there.

Niokolo Koba National Park, just over four hundred miles away by road, would be the obvious place to release the chimps. For a second I allowed my imagination to wander and envisaged all eight of the Abuko chimps climbing, feeding and playing with a group of friendly wild chimps. But I knew how many difficulties and hazards would have to be overcome before that dream could come true.

Perhaps the chimps would not be able to survive alone in a strange place. Tina and Albert, I was sure, would be able to manage and perhaps they would teach and look after the others, but I would have to stay with them until they became familiar with the new area, and possibly with new foods. How was I to do this? I didn't possess any equipment, not even a tent, and having spent the last two years working voluntarily, had no money of my own.

I decided to begin at the beginning. The help and permission of Mr. Dupuy, the Director of National Parks in Senegal, would be essential. I wrote my first letter to him, my second to Jane Goodall, asking if she could help.

I got Mr. Dupuy's reply first. I had permission to release the chimps in Niokolo Koba and to remain with them so as to make observations on their release and post-release progress. I would have to stay at the guard camp in the park as the roads to Mount Asserick were cut off in the rains and he could not take the risk of allowing me to remain there alone.

Jane's reply arrived a few days later. It was a warm, informal letter, saying she would gladly help me in any way she could. I was to write and tell her how much money I thought I needed and she would do her best to find it.

Next weekend Daddy arranged for a driver to take me in his Land-Rover to Niokolo Koba camp, sixteen miles from Mount Asserick, so that I could have a look at the area, meet the people staying there and make arrangements for bringing the chimps. It was a long, rough journey and we reached Niokolo camp, dusty and weary, late the following morning. On the slopes of the hills and plateaux and in the small gullies that led into the river, the vegetation resembled closely that found in Abuko.

Before leaving, we decided that the following Friday I would return with the three older chimps: Tina, Cheetah and Albert. These were the main trouble-makers in the reserve and also would be the most likely to adapt to a truly wild existence. If all went well, the others could follow when I was better equipped. On the drive home, I realized that the saddest separation would be that of Cheetah from William. For four years they had been close friends. I reflected a while and decided that I would take William with us.

Friday evening arrived and, with the aid of a large bunch of bananas, I managed to persuade the chimps who lived outside to enter the enclosure. The tranquillizing drug they had given me at the local veterinary department was carefully measured out and given to the chimps in some fruit-juice. I sat and waited. Fifteen, then twenty minutes ticked by and not one of the chimps looked less lively than they had before we'd treated them.

The following afternoon, I once again gave the chimps their drug, this time increasing the doses slightly. This second attempt was also a dismal failure. They all looked drowsy and their movements were uncoordinated, but I was sure that Tina and Albert were still sufficiently aware of their surroundings to make it impossible to confine them in a travelling cage without a terrible struggle.

I had always been uneasy about the effect of tranquillizing the chimps and no one could persuade me to subject them to a third session. I let Tina and Albert out of the enclosure and cabled Mr. Dupuy that we were going to be late. The following day I sat on a log close to the travelling cage and struggled to find another solution. The fruit I'd put into the cage for the journey was still there so I went over and took out a mango to suck on while I thought.

Tina was beside me before I noticed her, Pooh, Happy and Albert followed her into the clearing and sat around me, staring intently at my mouth while I ate. "There's a whole pile of fruit over there," I said aloud, and absent-mindedly waved a hand in the direction of the cage. Tina without any hesitation walked directly into the cage and gathered an armful of fruit. Albert, Happy and Pooh followed her. Each took some fruit and returned to sit near me.

It took me an instant to realize what I'd seen. I had assumed that, having spent days in filthy boxes before they arrived at Abuko, they would be exceptionally wary of entering a confined space again. However, either their unpleasant memories had been erased; or the chimps had learnt to trust us completely.

We decided to try to trap the chimps on the following afternoon, and to start travelling in the cool of the night. John Casey, a young man who was working at Abuko on Voluntary Service, was coming with me, together with a driver for the Land-Rover. They had to return as quickly as possible. I hoped to be back in five or six weeks as Daddy was due to go to England for an operation on an arthritic hip, and I was needed at the reserve during his absence.

The next afternoon we tied the fruit inside the cage so that the chimps could not immediately come out with it. The plan worked perfectly. There was a sharp sound as the door of the cage slammed down, trapping all four chimps inside.

I sat close to the wire and spoke to them. William seemed perfectly at ease and sat eating, with Cheetah's arm wrapped around his shoulders. Tina and Albert huddled as close to me as they could get. Occasionally Tina would reach out, take my hand and guide it towards where the padlocked bolts were situated on the door. Then I hugged and reassured her through the bars, trying to tell her that there was nothing to worry about.

That evening, as I watched Abduli and the family saying goodbye to the chimps, the reality of what was happening struck me. A huge sense of grief and panic welled up and I had to use all my self-control to avoid breaking down in front of everyone.

WE ARRIVED AT Niokolo camp the following evening. As we could not set up our own camp, we would have to release the chimps near the main camp, a long way from where the wild chimps were usually seen. I chose a spot about three miles out, on the banks of the river Niokolo so that there would be no problem for the chimps in finding water.

Next morning we drove the Land-Rover to the spot and the crate was opened. The chimps had hated every minute of the journey. Now that they were suddenly out of their prison they rushed about hugging each other. The three of us took them down to the river. William and Tina seemed afraid of so much water, but Albert and Cheetah took a drink. Tina then led off along the bank, and we followed. We came to some fallen palm fruits, but the chimps only smelt them before moving on. They looked bored and listless and kept asking us for food and water.

I sent the driver back to camp to bring the remaining mangoes. William ate very little and seemed to be getting more listless as the day wore on. The others, though, were slightly refreshed by the meal. William, normally an energetic bundle of mischief, trailed farther and farther behind. The grass was tall and I kept losing sight of him, so I went back to pick him up.

The fact that the chimps were eating made me feel a little brighter, but I kept wondering miserably if I was doing the right thing. Was I expecting too much to hope that they could make

328

Pooh, about one year old

Daddy with Tina

such a big break? And yet what would become of them if they couldn't? The word "zoo" loomed up and made me shudder. Slowly we climbed the slope. William sat close to me while the others explored. As the evening drew in they wandered off along the edge of the plateau and disappeared. William stayed beside me and eventually I picked him up and followed the others. I came across them sitting round a water hole from which they all drank except William. I filled our empty water bottle from the pool and offered him that; he drank greedily, almost emptying it. By this time the others had moved on again. I stood and waited with William at the edge of the clearing, hoping he would follow them. Albert left the other two and came back to us. He wrapped an arm about William, who placed his hand on Albert's back, and two little white bottoms moved off slowly into the gloom. I should have been relieved—but I cried instead. We waited to hear the sounds of nest-making, then crept away.

The second day was slightly better than the first. All save William tucked into the mangoes I had brought; William ate one or two but with little enthusiasm. By eight o'clock we were on the move, Tina leading. She was by far the most competent amongst us. She blazed the trails, tried the new foods first, chose the nest sites and generally gave us all a little confidence, of which we were badly in need—perhaps I more than any of the others.

We explored the plateau thoroughly that day. William was really miserable and kept lagging behind. I began to feel that the adjustment was going to be almost impossible for him—he was too young and too unused to fending for himself. I decided that he should return to Abuko with John when he left the following day.

EACH DAY RENÉ, a labourer at Niokolo, would accompany me into the bush, as it was considered dangerous for me to wander about alone. The chimps seemed well aware of the need to take precautions. Their nests, constructed of leaves on a foundation of branches, were well-made and the sites carefully chosen high in the trees to give as wide a view as possible.

One hot morning there came a low warning hoot from Cheetah

330

who was standing up, hair raised, staring hard at the other side of the clearing. Tina and Albert were soon beside him. I was behind a boulder and remained there. I couldn't see what was holding their interest at first, but then out from the vegetation stepped a solitary male Kob antelope. Tina and Cheetah took little further notice once he was in the open, but Albert climbed out onto a branch that jutted out into the clearing and shook it vigorously, giving a single hoot as he did so. The Kob stood stock still, staring, until even Albert lost interest and climbed down again. As he reached the ground the Kob whistled once or twice and then daintily melted away into the bush.

It was heart-warming to watch the chimps meet neighbours; the slight initial hostility, then the realization, on both sides, that there was no danger, and the casual passing on. I really began to feel that this was where the chimps belonged.

By the time we had been in Niokolo Koba about a week, the chimps were finding their own food and water and, although I still hadn't seen any signs of play between them, their initial depression seemed to be lifting a little and their awareness of the bush was increasing. Tina was exceptionally alert and wise, avoiding, if possible, open spaces and keeping to the trees. If startled by a noise she was up on a branch in a flash, from where she decided her next move. Fortunately the others heeded her every move and warning.

Unfortunately for the peace of our existence a safari park in France had sent eight unwanted lion cubs to Niokolo Koba for release into the wild as soon as they were ready. The cubs, which were in an enormous enclosure next to the camp, now decided the time had come and released themselves.

On several occasions one afternoon, whilst feeding, Tina or Albert stared down the slope, hair rising slowly then relaxing again, without having uttered the alarm hoot. Suddenly, they both swung into a small tree, seeming nervous, and disappeared.

I was getting up to see what they were doing when Tina came into view. Every hair on her body was erect and as she stood upright she looked enormous. Her shoulders were hunched forward, her chin tucked in, and she held her arms slightly away from her body, looking, for all the world, like a cowboy in a western about to draw his gun. The sight of her made me stop in mid-crouch. I spun round so fast that, instead of finding myself on my feet, I was on my hands and knees staring, horrified, into eight pairs of curious kittenish eyes.

Rooted to the spot, I watched a magnificent Tina advance slowly. One by one the young lions turned and retreated into the vegetation. Finally Tina sat down and hooted at their vanishing tails. The lions were recaptured not long afterwards.

The return to the wild produced a curious shift in relationships. Once I saw Tina dig down through our ground-nuts and biscuits to extract the last mango. Holding it in one hand, she tentatively picked at the skin with the forefinger of the other. Albert, who had always been very much an underdog when compared to Cheetah, watched her intently then, much to my surprise, calmly stretched out his hand and took the mango. There had been no hint of tension or aggression between them.

I began to realize that in this, and other ways, Albert was making the most of a sudden advantage over Cheetah, who was losing a lot of his former self-confidence. Quite simply, Niokolo Koba wasn't as strange to Albert as it was to Cheetah. Whereas Albert had always fended for himself in the freedom of the reserve, Cheetah had lived in the enclosure and had become far more dependent upon people.

By the time it was necessary for me to return to The Gambia, however, I felt confident that all three chimps had made the adjustment from the semi-captive state of Abuko to true independence in Niokolo Koba. Even so it was a desperately sad moment for me when I had to leave them. I wondered when, if ever, I would see these very good friends of mine again.

Shortly after my return to The Gambia I received a letter from the park authorities telling me that ten days after my departure Cheetah had returned to camp alone, and remained for four days. He had evidently left Tina and Albert and was going it alone. The park warden had driven him towards Mount Asserick and left him there. Despite my responsibilities at Abuko I returned to Niokolo Koba at once and spent a week searching for Cheetah and the others but with no success.

During the next year I visited Niokolo Koba whenever I got the opportunity but I was never able to stay long enough to make a really thorough search and I found no trace of my chimps. All that was left was the hope that Cheetah would some day meet wild chimps and tag along with them until he was accepted. As for Tina and Albert, well, at least they had each other.

DEATH COMES TO ABUKO

A week after my initial return, Daddy left The Gambia for England. There were many half-finished projects to complete. The Abuko staff had just begun to dig an extra pool for some Sitatunga antelopes. The rainy season growth had to be cut back from the paths, a new photographic hide had to be finished near the lake, and in a particularly swampy area of the reserve a small wooden bridge needed to be constructed. There was also the varied collection of animal orphans to attend to: three antelope fawns, two more young hyenas, three wart-hogs, two baby monkeys, four civet kittens, and a Milky Owl chick, all with their own special diets.

Luckily for me, Nigel Orbell, who had worked with me during my stay at Woburn, came out to The Gambia to replace John Casey. As soon as possible I drove him out to Abuko.

We walked up the path so that he would get an impression of the vegetation before entering the orphanage. The chimps began to hoot and scream excitedly on seeing us, and I took Nigel over to meet them. Happy and Pooh lost no time in clambering up my legs to their usual positions from where they extended the backs of their wrists to Nigel. Ann sat slightly aloof, but Flint left her side to hurry over to us, his coat bristling with excitement. Hooting, he gripped Nigel's leg. As Nigel stooped to return the greeting, William leapt off a high cross-bar and landed heavily on the newcomer's back. Nigel lost his balance and had his face pushed firmly into the soil. He picked himself up from the ground, trying to remain composed, but William quickly snatched his glasses and fled. I gave chase but on the next circuit around his floundering victim, William efficiently whipped the wallet from the back pocket of Nigel's shorts, ecstatic over his easy success.

During the following weeks, Nigel spent much time with the chimps. Soon he was able to take them on walks into the reserve whenever I had something else to do. Having learnt what he could expect from William he never gave him the chance to repeat his performance at their first meeting. He was strict but fair, and William quickly found that he could take few liberties.

One day Nigel came back from the reserve to report that Happy and Flint had developed coughs and runny noses, and seemed very lethargic. That same evening they refused to eat anything and had high temperatures. I took them home with me and put them on my bed, giving them warm milk and aspirin.

During the night, their condition deteriorated rapidly and I realized that they were suffering from something far more serious than a cold. They lay beside one another, still and listless, their breathing fast and shallow, their temperatures high. When I roused them for warm milk with honey, Happy's eyes were bright with fever. On seeing the cup, he turned his head away weakly and closed his eyes in silent rejection. Flint could only be persuaded to drink a few mouthfuls.

Late as it was, I telephoned a paediatrician friend of ours and to my relief he said he would drive to Yundum straight away. At the end of his examination he diagnosed virus pneumonia. He told me to keep them under close observation and gave me antibiotic drugs and some tablets to help their breathing.

At daybreak, Flint looked as if he had improved; he would take drinks, so getting him to swallow the bitter drugs was not too difficult. He still had a bad cough, though, and scarcely any appetite for solid foods. Happy was no better; he lay limp and on the verge of unconsciousness.

When the doctor returned, he advised that we use injections, but, despite them, Happy did not improve. He looked pathetic lying on my bed, his dark head propped up on a great white pillow, his eyes reflecting the extraordinary effort required to breathe. Every few hours during the night I would check on them both and each time I would approach their bed with mounting dread until I had satisfied myself that they were asleep and as comfortable as I could make them. In the early hours of the following morning, Flint stirred a little at the sudden brightness and then went back to sleep. Happy was unconscious. His silky lashes half masked his upturned eyes, and from his sagging mouth came the rasping sound of his laboured breathing. There was little I could do other than change his position in the hope it would make breathing easier. In desperation, I took one of his limp hands and tried to will the health I possessed into his body.

The bedroom was a hushed, depressing place. I followed the doctor's instructions, and when I could do no more, simply sat beside Happy and waited. By early afternoon, I thought I could detect a slight improvement in his breathing. A little later he began to stir, and closed and opened his parched mouth. I took his hand again and called his name softly. Hesitantly, his eyes opened and he gazed about him wearily. I continued whispering to him in case he should be afraid. When his attention drifted to my face, I saw his lips pout to form an "ooh" of recognition.

When the doctor called again that evening, Happy was sleeping. I woke him for his injection and he held his arms out weakly to be lifted. For the first time he seemed to feel the injection, for he gripped my hand tightly and pouted. He accepted a drink and then fell asleep again. Flint was well enough to accompany us on to the veranda, where he had a cup of lime juice and honey, and some sandwiches.

Two mornings later I woke to find Happy sitting up in bed chewing on the remains of Flint's supper, most of which was smeared all over the blanket. He greeted me with a few nasal grunts. Flint was missing. I checked the open wardrobe without success, then noticed that the bedroom door, usually kept closed, was ajar. In the kitchen, the refrigerator door was open and most of its contents splattered liberally over the floor. Flint was sitting on the kitchen table, chirping and grunting to himself over the last of a large jam flan. I salvaged all that I could, and carried Flint and his piece of flan back to the bedroom. By the end of the week I thought him well enough to return to Abuko.

When Happy's series of injections finished he was noticeably more active. Soon he too returned to the enclosure. I was thankful that the anxiety-filled days were over. But less than a week after Happy's return, I noticed that Ann had become listless. She had a runny nose, and Flint looked very subdued as well. I began to treat them with the oral antibiotic that Flint had been receiving previously, but by evening they were coughing and seemed worse.

I arrived at the reserve earlier than usual the following morning and went straight to the store to make up a cup of fruit juice for Ann in which to disguise her medicine. William, Pooh and Happy met me at the enclosure gate, but Ann was lying on her stomach, her face buried in her folded arms. I squatted down and talked to her but she didn't stir. Her face was hidden and, believing she was still asleep, I stroked her shoulder to wake her. As soon as my hand touched her body I realized with a sickening jolt that something was horribly wrong. She was limp and heavy as I gently lifted her up. I clutched her tightly to me for several minutes before I could understand that she was dead.

I wiped her nose and mouth with my shirt, and closed her eyes. Then, almost unable to see where I was going, I carried her towards the enclosure door. Abduli met me there and took my hand. "Flint very sick too," he said sadly.

I raised my streaming face and asked chokingly, "Abduli, you knew?"

"Ann die before I come today. I find no way to tell you, Stella. I take Ann now, you go find out Flint."

Dazed I walked back to the enclosure and climbed the crude ladder to the sleeping hut. Flint was in his bunk, fighting for breath. I carried him down and he hung as limply in my arms as Ann had. Happy was waiting at the bottom of the ladder, gazing upwards. He reached out as I passed, and with slow, spidery fingers briefly touched Flint's foot.

As I approached the rest-house the Land-Rover was pulling up outside the orphanage. Nigel cheerfully got out, slamming the door behind him. He strode into the orphanage and then stopped, his expression changing as he absorbed the scene before him.

"She's dead, Nigel, and Flint's dying—and, oh God, I wish I could die as well!"

A moment later Flint began to tremble. I sat on the rest-house bench, cradling his shuddering body. It was too late to contemplate doing anything other than give him all the warmth and comfort I could during those painful last moments of his life.

At midday all those working at Abuko pushed their way through

336

a curtain of leaves and twisted vines to a small clearing which was kept shaded and secret by an ancient spreading mandico tree. Everyone stood solemnly in a semi-circle as Ann and Flint were laid side by side in their grave and buried.

The enclosure looked as painfully empty as I felt that evening. As I gave William, Pooh and Happy their supper I wept bitterly. Ann and Flint could never take part in the plans and hopes I had of true freedom for all of the chimps in Niokolo Koba.

During the depressing weeks that followed, I spent my days at the reserve with William, Pooh and Happy, and my evenings compiling a report to send to Jane Goodall. It was clear that the remaining chimps missed Ann and Flint a great deal—William especially—and more and more my mind was turning to the problems of taking them to join the trio at Niokolo Koba. Their rehabilitation would be a completely different matter to that of the earlier group. They had all been captured at a very early age and, apart from life at Abuko, had no experience of the wild. They would need a mother-substitute for some time yet. I knew I would have to spend a great deal more than five weeks on the second rehabilitation project.

It could take two years. To be able to carry out my plans I would have to find funds from somewhere. I needed a camp of my own, a vehicle, suitable equipment and somebody to assist me. I wanted to be able to make a thorough search for Tina, Albert and Cheetah. They would be experienced in the ways of the bush, ideal tutors for Pooh, Happy and William.

In reply to the report I sent her, Jane Goodall wrote inviting me to visit Gombe Research Centre in Tanzania. I spent two and a half of the most exciting months of my life there and gained valuable insight into the lives of wild chimpanzees.

I talked to Jane and her husband, Hugo van Lawick, about the plans I had for the remaining chimps at Abuko. We discussed all the practical details and difficulties of setting up a camp. They told me that I would need a sturdy cross-country vehicle. Hugo helped me to draw up a budget for the whole project. It seemed an enormous sum of money would be needed.

My stay was drawing to a close when I got news that Cheetah had returned to Niokolo Koba camp; alone and suffering from serious diarrhoea. He had been fed and treated with human medicines, and after four days appeared healthy once more. On the morning of the fifth day, he had left, and, when last seen, was already a good two miles from camp.

It seemed incredible that after a year of living independently in the bush, Cheetah should reappear at a camp full of people when he was feeling sick. Furthermore, I was immensely encouraged to know that he had successfully survived his first year in the bush. Only one thing worried me, and that was that he was still alone. I was sure, though, that it would not be long before I would be back in Niokolo, properly equipped to relocate him and offer him the company of William, Pooh and Happy.

WHEN I LEFT GOMBE I spent a couple of weeks in London, trying to find the funds I needed. Hugo van Lawick was there at the time and helped me a great deal, and my future publishers, Collins, had been sufficiently impressed by what I was doing to risk putting up an advance that would finance the first year of my project. Hugo decided that he would like to make a film of it, and the advance on film rights was sufficient to cover the cost of a second year. The excitement I felt was indescribable.

I shall never forget the delight of buying my first car; an ex-Irish police Land-Rover. Until then I had not realized what affection an inanimate piece of machinery can arouse. I fondly christened it Felicity.

Then came some bad news. Daddy telephoned me from The Gambia. Some weeks ago, while out on a walk, Happy had touched one of the electricity cables that ran across the end of the reserve and had been electrocuted. Miraculously he had survived; his left hand, though, had been badly burned. With intensive nursing he had seemed to be recovering well, his hand had healed and he had begun playing normally with the others. However, he had begun to lose his appetite and the vet could not tell what was wrong with him. Then, during the last week, Daddy and Nigel had noticed he was having difficulty in co-ordinating his hands so as to pick up the small amount of food he ate.

After a short silence, I heard Daddy's voice continue softly: "Stella, Happy is almost totally blind. If he doesn't begin eating

338

soon, I don't think he's long for this world. Come home quickly, the little fellow needs you."

I flew back by the first possible plane and a little over an hour after arriving at the airport I was at the reserve. Abduli told me that Happy spent most of his day lying in a bunk in the sleeping quarters. I went into the enclosure and walked quietly to the ladder leading up to the entrance of their dormitory. Happy had heard someone arriving and was sitting on the first rung. He was a shocking sight, small, thin and thoroughly dejected. I spoke his name. His response was deeply touching. His pinched face broke into a grin and, almost screaming, he half-slid, half-climbed down the ladder towards me. I noticed his left hand was little more than a rigid claw which he kept pressed to his chest.

I climbed a few rungs to meet him and we embraced. I sat and spoke to him for a while, stroking and caressing him. His eyes were as large and brown as ever, only at certain angles could I see the milky whiteness that was obliterating his vision. His gaze was distant and vacant. Already Happy's world was one of vague shadows, for he made his way about by feel and memory.

I took him out of the enclosure to the rest-house and offered him the fruit I had brought from England for him. He seemed to like the grapes most of all and Abduli and I were hopeful that at last we had found something he would take. Our satisfaction was short-lived, for about half an hour later he vomited up all that he had so slowly eaten.

While sitting in the rest-house with us he seemed to be constantly listening for something and facing the entrance. Suddenly he grinned and gave his throaty whimper. A few seconds later I heard the orphanage gate open as the other chimps returned from their walk. I carried Happy out to meet them. Pooh and William greeted me warmly. Happy panted and held out his hand and I guided it till he was able to touch Pooh and William.

It was essential that we should take blood samples from Happy as quickly as possible and send them to England for analysis. He was not at all cooperative. Unable to see what was happening around him and hearing a stranger move nearby made him suspicious and frightened. Finally the vet suggested that he should be tranquillized. Nigel and Abduli held him for the injection and immediately it was over I picked him up. He stopped screaming and clung to me while I walked round patting and soothing him. Minutes later he rested his head on my shoulder and slept. The blood samples were taken and rushed to the airport.

An hour after his injection Happy was still soundly anaesthetized. I drove him home carefully and, for the second time in his short life, he lay unconscious on my bed. Long after the plane had left The Gambia with the blood samples, Happy was showing no signs of waking. Worried, I rang the vet and asked his advice. I was told that, because Happy was weak, the drug might take longer than usual to wear off. Darkness fell and there was still no improvement. By ten o'clock I was sufficiently alarmed to bring Daddy to Happy's bedside. Daddy placed his large square hand over Happy's chest, then slowly moved it up to stroke his head. With startling suddenness Happy sat bolt upright, opened his eyes and coughed once, then fell back on the pillow. I quickly leant over and began speaking to him, but Happy made not the slightest gesture in answer. Again I saw my father's hand carefully cover the small, still chest. I felt rather than saw him become motionless in his concentration to listen and feel. Even before he relaxed again, I knew Happy was dead.

The following day there was a cable from England. Happy had had diabetes. Had he lived, he would always have been blind and would have needed insulin injections every day of his life. The memory of his wide-eyed innocent face was painful, but when I read the telegram I no longer wished that Happy could have survived.

RETURN TO NIOKOLO KOBA

It was the end of 1973. Preparations now quickly went ahead for my return to Niokolo. I planned to set out at the beginning of January, search for Tina, Cheetah and Albert till March, and then come back to Abuko to collect William and Pooh. Momadou, our gardener, was to accompany me.

For the whole of January we searched unsuccessfully in the vicinity of Niokolo camp. In February we began to explore the region of Mount Asserick. We discovered a wide valley, shady and green. When we stopped the Land-Rover, I could hear the musical sound of running water. A few yards farther on, dripping and splashing around fern-covered rocks, ran a crystal-clear stream. In the trees directly above us were five fresh chimpanzee nests. At that moment I couldn't imagine paradise being any more inviting.

We spent the day exploring and I saw my first wild West African chimp—or rather his bottom as he fled into the vegetation at the sight of us. Much farther down the valley, where it opened out and became wider and less forested, we surprised a group of three elephants close to the water.

In the next few weeks I explored most of Mount Asserick on foot and found nowhere more suitable as a camp than the valley. Though I had still found no sign of Tina, Cheetah and Albert, I began to get impatient to start the rehabilitation of William and Pooh. At the beginning of March I set off for The Gambia to collect them.

Nigel accompanied me on the return trip. We piled the back of the Land-Rover with cushions and foam mattresses and the chimps travelled comfortably. We camped for one night and the next day arrived at the place which I already thought of as my valley. We quickly hurried out to explore. We found plenty of fresh buffalo and elephant dung but no more signs of chimpanzees.

That evening it was difficult getting the two chimps to settle down—both refused to have their cushions in trees and insisted on bringing them to the ground to sleep. Lying on my camp-bed, I looked up into the branches of the huge netto tree. Before I fell asleep, I chose two parallel branches on which to build a sleeping platform for William and Pooh. I was sure that once they got into the habit of sleeping high up, they would no longer feel secure on the ground.

Next morning we decided to begin building the sleeping platform immediately. As we were starting work we suddenly saw, on the other side of the gully, a group of wild chimpanzees filing down to the stream. As quietly as I could, I picked up Pooh and pointed towards the wild chimps but, by the time he understood that I was trying to show him something, the wild chimps were already almost hidden amongst the trees.

Just as we were settling down that evening, the news came that a female chimpanzee had been observed several times in the area of Simenti, sixty miles away by road. She had been seen alone, frequently on the periphery of a troop of baboons. Sometimes she moved around by herself, covering remarkable distances in a day. She was relatively unafraid of cars and used the park roads a great deal when travelling. Could she possibly be Tina?

We repacked Felicity in record time and spent that night overlooking the Gambia River near Simenti. William and Pooh, despite the long journey, were full of mischief. They were in and out of the Land-Rover, stealing, eating and creating near-chaos, before I was finally able to persuade them to sleep.

Next day we spoke to the driver of a safari bus who told me the female chimp had been seen the previous evening only three or four miles from where we were.

As we approached the place, we found a set of well-defined tracks leading down the middle of the sandy road. We followed these to where they turned off the road into a small forested depression. We got down from the Land-Rover. Barely five minutes later we reached a thicket of bamboo. As we entered it Nigel froze. "Did you hear that?" he whispered. I shook my head. "A chimp's alarm sound; it came from over there."

We came to a wide dry waterway. As I was scrabbling up onto the other side I saw her. Not twenty yards away amongst the dry bamboo stood a large chimp. Every hair on her body was erect and she was swaying slightly from side to side. Unusually bright orange eyes glared past me at William. She looked splendid. William stood frozen in his tracks. Slowly Tina rose, a slim stick of bamboo swaying in her hand. William also stood upright, his coat erect and bristling. He took a branch in his hand, and shook it vigorously. For a few seconds they faced each other.

William, still upright, advanced towards Tina, slowly at first but with gathering speed. Tina stood her ground until William picked up a piece of dead wood and flung it at her. She dropped to all fours and dodged it; ran for a few yards, then stopped, screaming harshly. She was in oestrus and she sat down on her pink swelling as William approached her. The screaming changed

342

to a hoarse panting as he neared her. William, walking now on all fours and with his coat looking sleeker, replied with the same panted greetings.

Tina, bobbing slightly, extended the back of her wrist to William's face in a friendly, submissive gesture. William took her wrist in his mouth, at which Tina immediately swung round and presented her back-side to be mated. William, still panting loudly, didn't hesitate a second. Pooh rushed over, hooting, laid his hand on Tina's shoulder and began grooming her. She turned, a wide grin on her face, and making small squeaking sounds, began to groom William. They remained thus for a few minutes while I pinched myself to make sure I wasn't dreaming.

The three chimps groomed each other for about fifteen minutes, then Tina led the way to a large netto tree in fruit and William and Pooh followed her into it.

Since we had been in the park, the only wild food I had seen William and Pooh feed on had been kenno leaves. Now, having watched Tina eat for a few minutes, both of them began to chew netto pods with relish.

Tina had given no indication that she recognized me so I remained at a distance, anxious not to approach closely in case I should disturb the freshly refounded comradeship. I wondered why Albert was no longer with her and if I would ever see Cheetah again. Most important, what was I to do next? Wild chimpanzees were rarely seen in the area. The sparse, scrublike vegetation and flat terrain were unsuitable for them. It provided ideal country for antelope, however, and the density of large predators such as lion and leopard was consequently higher than in other parts of the park. For this reason, and because of the hotel at nearby Simenti, it was the area most frequented by visitors to the Niokolo Koba Park. Moving my rehabilitation camp to Simenti was unthinkable, so I was left with the alternatives of moving Tina to Mount Asserick with William and Pooh, or leaving her behind.

Tina had been released about eighteen months before and had coped admirably. I wondered whether I was being unfair by interfering in her life again. However, when I considered that she was entirely alone, and how much she seemed to appreciate

William and Pooh's company, it seemed worth interfering just once more.

The problem of how to move her was quickly solved. On a trip into Simenti I had met Claude Lucazeau, an enormously strong and stocky man with bright blue eyes in a sunburned face, who promptly volunteered to give me a trailer as a travelling cage. It would however be a couple of weeks before this would be available, so we settled down to make the best of things in the meantime.

The time was spent following Tina, William and Pooh around, taking notes. Each day the relationship between them seemed more firmly cemented. Tina was exceptionally possessive of them both. While her swelling lasted, William tried to make up for his previous bachelorhood and mated Tina at every possible opportunity. Pooh shared more of a platonic friendship with Tina and spent hours playing with her. She was so anxious to keep William and Pooh with her at first that she resented humans approaching too closely. Several times she charged at me aggressively.

Eventually Claude arrived with a small zebra-striped trailer with iron-mesh sides and roof. We wired the door of the trailer open and began to feed the chimps from it. Tina was highly suspicious at first and would go nowhere near it. Gradually, through watching Pooh and William feed and play in it safely, she began to lose her fear and at the end of the second day she was entering the trailer briefly to snatch a few mangoes.

On the morning of the third day we rigged up the door of the trailer with a long cord which would enable us to slam it shut from a distance. I placed a pile of mangoes at the far end of it and waited. Pooh and William were in the trailer the moment they woke up and Tina, still timid, followed quickly and grabbed a few. Unfortunately, William was sitting in the doorway with his legs dangling over the edge so we couldn't close the door. I had to keep replenishing the food stocks in the trailer till finally the opportunity arose to trap Tina. She went wild when she found she was locked in. We piled Pooh and William into Felicity and Nigel and I set off. As soon as we were moving, Tina was quiet, sitting in the trailer and looking around at the passing landscape.

We reached Mount Asserick just before midday. I was worried

344

*Stella and John Casey, with Flint,
Pooh, William and Cheetah*

*Raphaella Savinelli teaches Bobo
to hammer open a pod*

that, after such indignities, Tina would run away, never to be seen again; but though she ran out of the trailer, she soon slowed to a walk, climbed a laden fig tree in the corner of camp and fed. William and Pooh joined her.

LEARNING TO BE FREE

Before leaving Simenti, I had employed Charra, a tall young Bassari tribesman, to help me once Nigel returned to Abuko. On our first day back, Nigel and Charra helped me organize the camp. We cleaned out the trailer and stacked it with food supplies. A little orange tent served as another store, and Felicity made a passable wardrobe. Charra chose a site for the kitchen and made a small fireplace with a crude rock shelf next to it. That evening we slept on camp-beds grouped around the netto tree; William and Pooh were on the Land-Rover's roof-rack while Tina made a nest in a tree at the bottom of the gully. I slept soundly that evening, content that the project had really begun.

The following morning, Nigel left. I had come to rely heavily on his help and companionship during the past weeks and I felt dreadfully alone. Charra passed the day working on the sleeping platform that Nigel and I had begun before leaving for Simenti.

Within twenty-four hours the platform was finished, the cross-pieces of wood were securely lashed down with rope, bark and wire and the rungs to the ladder had been similarly lashed onto the uprights. It was about thirty-five feet high and looked like the beginning of the Swiss Family Robinson's tree house.

That evening when Tina went to her rest, I placed Pooh's and William's cushions up on the platform with a bunch of leaves and sat with them till it was almost dark. They both stretched out and I was hopeful that they would stay. However, five minutes after I had descended I found Pooh sitting on the camp-bed beside me. I tried to put him up again, but each time I left, William pushed Pooh down again and stole his cushion. Finally I was obliged to make another bed for Pooh on top of the Land-Rover. It was not until Charra had made a second platform, near the first, that both of them were prepared to sleep off the ground.

In the next few days the chimps and I began to go for walks in the valley near the camp. On these first walks I could never really relax, but I had to pretend to for, if William and Pooh sensed I was afraid, they would become uneasy too. For their sakes, I never walked in the middle of open spaces, if I could help it, even if it meant having to take a longer route. In an open space, the chimps were vulnerable to predators so I wanted them to be wary, to walk cautiously if they ever had to cross one and to keep to the tree lines whenever they could. If I ever had to cross open ground to get to the car, I exaggerated the nervousness and caution of every movement. I was gratified to see that they understood and also looked around and moved cautiously.

Gradually, I was able to relax much more. I was not constantly alert for sounds and movements. I was still aware, but aware of everything, not just the dangers—aware of the peace, the strange beauty of the place, the dappled shapes made by the sun through the leaves; aware of the colours and distortions of the heat haze hovering over the bare rocky plateaux, of my own small place in this wild kingdom.

AT THE START OF the rainy season Claude Lucazeau arrived with two Senegalese assistants. He announced that he was going to build me a hut.

"Claude," I begged. "I don't want to spoil this beautiful wilderness with some permanent hut. Please, I can manage, I assure you!"

Claude ignored me. He knew that some sort of shelter was necessary whether I liked it or not. That very night I would understand why.

Thunder was already rolling, and finding shelter for everyone to sleep was a problem. The orange tent was only big enough for Charra. Claude's two assistants slept in Felicity. Claude placed two poles against his Land-Rover and set a tarpaulin over them to form a ramshackle lean-to, beneath which he and I put our respective camp-beds.

I was woken at about 2:00 a.m. by the force of a tremendous wind. The little orange tent was flapping wildly and the trees all around camp were bending and swirling in the gale. I went out to see how William and Pooh were reacting. I was soaked within seconds. Poor little mites, I thought, they'll be dripping, but they must get used to the rain. Thunder and lightning they knew, but at Abuko there had always been shelter from the rain.

The rain was so heavy that even when lightning illuminated the camp, I could not see the platforms. Suddenly through the sounds of the storm I heard Pooh begin to scream. I ran to the ladder and met him crying at the bottom. As soon as he was safely in my arms he stopped crying and buried his face in my neck. William was also coming down. His growing independence forgotten for a moment, he clung to me too. I kept talking to them through chattering teeth, trying to impress on them there was nothing to fear.

After a quarter of an hour, I was shivering uncontrollably and felt very cold. William and Pooh kept shuddering spasmodically too. When Claude called to me, shouting that I should get them and myself out of the wet, the temptation was too great. Chatting as brightly as I could through locked jaws, I carried William and Pooh to the lean-to. Claude gave me a towel and I rubbed them both as dry as I could, then changed out of my wet clothes. Pooh was already under the covers and William was lying at the bottom of the camp-bed. There was not really enough room for me but we managed. All three of us slept comfortably till the morning.

It was grey and still drizzling when I awoke and my bed was plastered with muddy chimp-prints from the midnight adventure. After the dust and dryness of the dry season, it was almost possible to see things revive and grow and there was a beautiful smell of damp earth and cleanness in the air. Pooh and William's coats looked fluffy but shiny and healthy after their obligatory bath.

Early one morning after our second stormy night, William climbed into a tree and made a crude nest. I was delighted. Finally he lay down to dry off in the sun in the same way as Tina did.

Claude left behind him a neat little hut with a tarpaulin roof. I ungratefully christened it "the shack". The orange tent lasted only a month before the storms and William reduced it to shreds but a strong frame tent arrived in time to give Charra shelter and the shack became my cosy, much-loved home.

Pooh became an enthusiastic carpenter. He seemed to get most pleasure out of hammering. In camp he used a length of bamboo to hammer down the heads of the nails which held the shack together. He hammered pieces of wire into the ground. He made a drum from his tin food bowl by hammering it. The more noise his hammering made, the better he liked it. Later he learned to put his hammering to practical use and hammered open fruits too hard for his milk teeth to cope with.

Pooh also loved looking through my binoculars though I always held them as I didn't trust him to handle them with the care they required. Invariably I got tired of holding them before Pooh got tired of looking and when I put them away, Pooh would play pretend binoculars by placing small pebbles in his eye sockets and screwing up his face to hold them there.

ABOUT A MONTH after the beginning of the rainy season, Daddy and Hugo van Lawick drove up to visit us. I think William and I recognized my father's Land-Rover at the same instant. William leapt onto the vehicle, pushed through the window and embraced my father—squeaking and grinning his intense pleasure and excitement.

Hugo had come for the first of several visits he was to pay in order to get the material he needed for the film. He was exceptionally patient and considerate, and spent hours following the chimps with his heavy camera.

I worried a great deal about Tina. With all the activity about camp she appeared less and less frequently and was missing completely for several days. When Hugo and my father left, Julian—a willing helper who had recently replaced Charra—and I set out as usual with William and Pooh. We had gone only a few yards from camp when I saw William stand erect and, with arms held away from his body, begin to advance with curious "fairy steps" towards the dry stream bed at the side of camp. Expectantly I followed his gaze. Tina broke cover, also standing upright with her coat fluffed out and swaying slightly from side to side; then she too advanced towards William. She grinned submissively and squeaked her excitement as they met and embraced each other. Tina had a small pink swelling which she presented almost immediately to William. He responded by mating her, then both of them disappeared into the stream bed.

During the comparatively short time since we had left the reserve, William had steadily shown less need for human affection. At six years old, he was now clearly adolescent. In Abuko, he would look for excuses to be picked up and cuddled. Now not only did he refuse to allow anyone to carry him, but he shunned demonstrative affection, turning his face away if he had the slightest suspicion I might plant a kiss on it and firmly disentangling my arms if I gave him the usual goodnight hug. I can only explain his actions and expressions as embarrassment.

I knew that a wild chimp of his age would be starting to leave his mother for short periods to travel on the outskirts of all-male groups and gradually to introduce himself into the hierarchy. That William was beginning to do the same pleased me but at the same time I worried slightly. How capable was he of taking care of himself after only a few weeks in this new home? I wasn't sure whether he was aware enough of the dangers. Then I shut off such thoughts. He was with a far more experienced lady than I, a far better teacher and that was what we were here for, after all.

Tina's swelling increased that night and William's interest in Tina increased with it. Again that morning they both disappeared but this time I continued the walk with Pooh, determined not to go on worrying about William's safety. Before midday I returned to camp. We found William sitting with a small tin of milk in his hand and several packets of soup in each foot. He was either full, feeling decidedly guilty, or both, for he bobbed and coughed submissively as I approached him, and handed me all but one packet of soup and the tin of milk. When I tried to take these he got up and ran to Tina, who was sitting in the fig tree. She swayed dangerously at me as I approached them. It was obvious that, should I attempt to force the issue, she would take William's part. As I was unwilling to take the risk of being attacked by ninety pounds of angry chimp, I had no alternative but to retire gracefully.

It was at a similar tense moment, with Tina sitting in a tree above the kitchen, that I watched William add another item to his extending list of surprises. I was sitting by the fire having a cup of coffee when the chimps came over from the tree where they had been feeding. The kettle was simmering on the fire and coffee, sugar and a cup of milk were sitting by the side of the canteen. William wanted my coffee. Looking at Tina, he placed his hand on my cup, slyly glancing back at me. He began to pull gently. To have a chimp that I had raised take advantage of me in this way, made me feel really angry. I tightened my hold on my cup and in as deadly a voice as I could muster said: "Willie, you dare! Tina or no Tina, I promise you'll be sorry!" Almost immediately his hand and his eyes dropped.

He stalked off to the fireplace. As he leant over to reach the kettle, his lips curled back in a grimace at the smoke. He touched the handle of the kettle repeatedly, then drew his hand back, till he found that the handle was not too hot to hold; then, carrying the kettle well away from his body, he went to the canteen. In the mug which was already a third filled with milk, he placed two spoonfuls of coffee, then four spoonfuls of sugar. Finally he filled the mug to overflowing with the scalding water from the kettle. He had my full attention, for the perfectly reasonable way in which he had made himself a cup of coffee left me speechless.

It was a tin mug and too hot to be lifted, so William crouched over it, making extraordinary grimaces well before his lips were near enough to suck up any of the coffee. "Be careful, William," I said, "it's hot." He glanced at me, his lips still curling away from the heat of the cup. Then he reached for the spoon and spooned some out, bringing the brimming teaspoon to his mouth. Finally he took a quick sip. The liquid was still hot enough to make him jerk his head backwards and drop the spoon. He promptly looked around, picked up several marble-sized stones and dropped them into the coffee. Surely, I thought, he can't realize that by dropping cold stones into the cup, he's going to cool the coffee? If he realizes that, what else does he know?

He placed the spoon in the coffee and stirred it, then tried to sip from the cup again. The drink was still too hot. He went to the jerrycan, took a bulging mouthful of cold water, and spat the water into the cup. It overflowed and he quickly sipped some of the liquid as it ran over the brim. The coffee was now hot but

351

bearable. He lifted the mug and walked carefully to a shrub just beyond the kitchen; there he leisurely drank his coffee.

William also became surprisingly ingenious at treating his own minor ailments. When he got an ear infection, he would frequently clean his ears with twigs and bird feathers, twisting them back and forth between the side of his forefinger and thumb. When something was irritating his nose he would pick tiny pieces of grass stem and push them up his nostrils, where he would leave them till he sneezed or snorted them out again. He frequently used twigs for picking his teeth.

I was able partially to overcome the problems of William's increasing strength and size by using a small alarm pistol that I had been given. The pistol fired blanks, so couldn't in any way harm him, but he was terrified of the bang it made and the small flame which shot from the end of the barrel. In really dire situations, I could take the pistol out of my pocket and show it to him and he would immediately behave better.

When William and Tina were not present, Pooh reverted to being very dependent and whimpered a great deal if I made him walk. Each evening when the two older chimps came back to camp, he was obviously pleased to see them—patting them both in his excitement. William was usually callously off-hand with him, but Tina would respond to his excited greetings.

The night came when Tina and William did not reappear at all. Pooh was reluctant to go to bed and came down to sit with me by the fire three times before he finally settled to go to sleep.

The following morning, I heard branches moving in the trees behind the hut. I leapt out of bed and saw William and Tina walking towards me. William looked exhausted, his belly very flat, and when I opened the trailer to get out some food, instead of racing over and food-grunting, he merely managed a grin as I passed him his plate. I squatted beside him and placed my hand on his back. "Tina wearing you out, Will?" I asked. He looked at me wearily, then put his arm round my shoulder and patted me with an open hand in the same way as I pat the chimps when comforting them. It was such brief moments of complete communication with William that made up for all our squabbles and differences.

352

SHORTLY AFTER THIS Tina left camp for an entire week. William was distraught. He looked for her everywhere but never dared to go far from camp entirely alone. To pass the time he and Pooh devised what they considered a hilarious tease: unscrewing the caps on the inner tubes of Felicity's tyres and, with a long fingernail, pressing the valve and releasing the air. If I chased them, they ran round and round the vehicle, always keeping out of reach, and if I got too close it was simple for them to slip underneath to the other side. Being so close to the ground, they could also keep a good eye on my progress. If they considered that they had a few seconds' lead, I'd hear a loud hiss as another blast of air was released from the vehicle's already sagging tyres. I finally had to wire all the valve caps onto the car and cover them with Sellotape.

Eventually Tina returned. I was, of course, delighted, yet twenty-four hours later I was almost wishing that she would disappear again. William changed instantly from being a peace-loving, if somewhat irritating young chimp, into his more typical role of tyrant. The morning after Tina returned, he tried to overturn the frame tent, then leapt up and down on its roof till it threatened to tear. I managed to catch him, slapped him hard and told him to stop it. He punched me back, then somersaulted his way halfway across the yard. Suddenly he leapt up, charged the kitchen table and, as he cantered past it, skilfully grabbed the tarpaulin table cover and hauled the whole thing off. He cantered on a few more yards, then stopped, panting. He sat in the middle of the tarpaulin, and laughing heartily to himself, began to roll himself up in it.

I strode over to him, looking so purposeful that normally he would have at least sat up to take notice. Instead he just carried on laughing and rolling about. Tina was on the edge of the gully when I reached William. I hissed at him to behave. There was not the slightest reaction. I began to think that he was high on something. I held his shoulder and shook him as hard as I dared in front of Tina. "William, what's the matter with you?" He looked at me lazily, shrugged my hand away and somersaulted backwards, still keeping hold of a corner of the tarpaulin. I gathered up the rest and pulled. William pulled back and picked

353

up a rock in his other hand. I felt confused. There was nothing aggressive in his relaxed, floppy posturing, yet I had the feeling that if I continued to pull, William was going to sling his rock at me. Ever since we had left Abuko, I had been waiting for William to choose his moment for a real fight to prove which of us was dominant. This was to be it.

I was not afraid of William—I had known him too long—but I didn't want a showdown right under Tina's nose, because I *was* afraid of her. She was big and powerful with a formidable pair of canines. Slowly I took the starting pistol out of my pocket. The ruse worked. William dropped his rock and let go of the tarpaulin.

Julian and I spent the next half-hour wiring the tarpaulin on to the table. As we finished, William walked to the shack. The door was unlocked; he opened it, then slammed it back. I heard an ominous crack as some of the wood splintered around the hinges. "William, stop it or I'll thump you!" I shouted.

Tina swayed, William sat—his coat semi-erect—and glared at me. I strode over to him, anxious to avoid his deliberate provocation while Tina was around, yet determined not to lose face. I closed the door and locked it. William got up and punched my foot. By this time I was finding it difficult not to react. His insolent taunting I found unbearable. When he swung round, grabbed my ankle and neatly flipped me over, I could stand no more. The next time he came, I kicked out hard and caught him in the thigh. He screamed, his arrogance flown with the wind. I walked over to him and cupped his chin in my hand. "Now then, will you stop bugging me, you brute!" He listened, then pulled away sulkily and walked towards the edge of the gully. I had maintained my position of authority.

All three chimps remained out of camp for the remainder of the day. When William returned that evening, he greeted me affectionately and though he continued to be boisterous, he had lost all trace of his insolent, provoking manner.

THERE WAS PLENTY of ripe fruit in the gully so Tina stayed close to camp the next day and William and Pooh were able to be with her constantly. I watched them through binoculars from the gully edge so as to interfere as little as possible. In the evening Pooh sat at the top of a high tree and watched Tina make a nest. Minutes later he descended into the thicker foliage and I heard branches being broken. Pooh was either making his own nest or renovating an old nest of Tina's or William's.

The next morning Pooh drank his milk quickly and rushed off to join the others. I took the binoculars and walked about a mile down the main valley to see if I could find the chimps. About lunchtime, I returned to camp and decided to wait for them there.

Suddenly the terrified screaming of a chimp reached me faintly across the plateau. I froze and listened with every nerve tensed. The chimp screaming was Pooh. I could recognize his voice among thousands. I ran out onto the nearby plateau with Julian, and in the distance I saw William loping towards me. When I reached him, he hugged me. I left him with Julian and ran on to where Tina was swaying in an isolated wild cherry tree. I looked frantically into its branches for Pooh—he was nowhere to be seen. Farther up the gentle slope baboons were barking.

I thought I knew what had happened. Pooh had seen the baboons, had run out into the plateau to chase them, so engrossed in his daring that he was heedless of the open terrain. The lion, one we had heard calling the night before, was probably lying in the tree line. Pooh would have been easy prey.

Tina swung out of the tree and ran up the slope, then stopped, looked at me and hurried on. I followed her up a slope, down into a steep basin and into long grass, where she disappeared.

I tore after her through the grass, too worried to be cautious. I called and called Pooh's and Tina's names. I was hoarse, my lungs ached from running and it hurt me to shout but the worst pain of all was the agony of believing that I might never see either of them again.

After three hours' searching Julian returned dejectedly to camp. Hopelessly, I stumbled back to the tree where I had first seen Tina. In my aching head I heard again Pooh's voice screaming fear. Embracing the cherry tree I prayed with an intensity and fierceness I didn't know I possessed. As if in answer, a lion roared.

Suddenly William was standing beside me. He touched my leg, holding out a dry leaf to me. William, of course, William. Of all the hopes, the plans, the achievements, only William and I survived. I had failed.

William perhaps could sense but could not comprehend my uncontrollable sobbing. He handed me small stones, a twig, and finally patted my back. Then he moved away, striding out for camp. I struggled to my feet and followed him.

Julian was standing in front of camp, waving to me. I wiped my face with the bottom of my shirt and stared. He was holding something. My heart began to hammer so hard that I could feel its vibrations in my head. I lifted the binoculars; Pooh was sitting on Julian's hip. As I approached, Julian put Pooh down and he ran towards me. It seemed a miracle to be able to hold him, to see his wrinkled gnome-face again. I examined him minutely for injuries. Apart from a fresh graze on his thigh, he was perfectly all right. I held him tightly and he occupied himself by licking the salty tears off my face and neck.

Minutes later, Tina also returned to camp. She was exceptionally affectionate, panting and holding out her hand. To this day I do not know why Pooh ran off and screamed or where he and Tina had been during the time we spent searching.

PASTIMES AND PRACTICES

One day I decided to take the chimps exploring to a large basin at the foot of Mount Asserick. I remembered it as being full of fig trees and they would probably be fruiting. Julian and I left camp at seven o'clock with a packed lunch.

We followed the valley to its head, stopping periodically to allow William and Pooh to feed as we went. We were just coming onto the floor of the basin, heading for the orchard of fig trees, when a rumbling sound made me swing round to my right. Three elephants were quietly browsing about thirty yards away from us. There were two young ones and an adult with long straight tusks. William and Pooh sat down with us and watched, intensely interested. When the elephants began to walk towards us, browsing as they went, we crept away.

William led us to a large baobab tree and he and Pooh climbed it and fed on the flowers, constantly looking around and obviously ill at ease. Suddenly I looked up. An enormous elephant was walking towards us, having just left the thickest part of the fig grove. Julian, William and I slipped away from the baobab, but Pooh seemed hypnotized by the enormous bulk ambling directly towards us. "Pooh, come here!" I hissed as loudly as I dared. Pooh didn't move. I crept on, hoping Pooh would follow, but the farther away I moved from the baobab, the less courage Pooh could find to leave it.

The elephant strolled closer, then reached up with his trunk, broke off a kenno branch and began to eat the young leaves. Pooh's lips drew back in a silent grimace of fear. I told Julian I was going back for Pooh. I duly crept towards the baobab, keeping the tree between me and the chewing elephant. Every rustle in the grass seemed magnified and I was sure that at any second I would be discovered.

I got to within about ten yards of the baobab and held out my arms for Pooh. He hesitated for a brief second, shot a glance at the elephant, then quickly but silently slid down the smooth trunk of the tree and ran to me. As we made contact, he gave a high-pitched squeak of relief, then clung to me tightly.

We both looked back to the elephant. His audible chewing had stopped. He was standing like a statue, listening, the tip of his trunk exploring the air for alien scents. I froze, certain that at any second he would smell me or hear the thudding of my heart.

He stood suspiciously for what seemed an eternity, then swung around and walked away quickly. I waited till I considered him a safe distance away, then crept back to Julian.

We had even more reason to be disturbed by our next encounter. We had scarcely set off again, when a tremendous crashing of vegetation, a scream from William and Pooh gripping my neck, seemed to happen all at once. Julian was almost as fast as William to get into a tree. I stood rooted to the spot, Pooh clinging desperately to my back. Then about ten yards ahead I saw the fattest, roundest buffalo I'd ever seen. His head was lifted and his moist eyes stared stonily in my direction.

A few yards behind me a vine hung from a high branch. I leapt onto it but with Pooh's extra weight on my back, it took every ounce of my strength to get even halfway up. Then I knew I was going to slide down again.

When I reached the ground my thighs and hands were burning, my fingers ached and refused to open. However, I heard the buffalo snort and, without hesitating a second, I made a mad dash for Julian's tree. He hauled me and Pooh up into the first branch. I was shaking all over and my knees felt like water. As I looked down, the buffalo spun round and stampeded into the undergrowth.

IT HAD BEEN OVER a month since anyone had visited the camp to replenish our supplies which were getting very low. Occasional mushrooms helped, but our evening meal was usually a rather miserable affair of dried fish and boiled rice. As the sugar had been finished and milk was strictly rationed, there wasn't even a good cup of tea to liven it up.

Then one evening I was dozing off when Pooh, who was sleeping in a nest above the hut, began to pant-hoot. Tina and William joined in. I got up and walked outside with the torch. In the distance I could hear the sound of a vehicle which gradually came closer, till a Land-Rover pulled into camp. It was impossible to tell what colour it was, since it was literally caked in mud. An equally muddy Claude stepped out. It had taken him all day to travel the last sixteen miles to the camp.

When Claude went off again next day our little fridge was bulging with fresh vegetables, meat, cheeses, eggs and, greatest luxury of all, a pound of butter. Best of all, Claude had brought with him René, who had helped us at the time of the first release and was now to stay and keep us company.

Over the next few months, Tina taught us that, in fact, there was always an abundance of food if only we cared to look. There were edible leaves and grasses, flowers and bark, some of which I found very palatable. She introduced us to seven different varieties of edible seeds, and also impressed on William and Pooh that vegetable matter was not the only source of food. As she passed a sprawling bush she paused briefly, but not to feed; instead she picked a long, thin, green stalk and stripped the leaves from the stalk by pulling it through her closed hand.

She walked purposefully to the base of a termite mound. With

Lessons: making a nest and fishing for termites

the nail of her forefinger, she flicked away a small mound of damp-looking soil, exposed the opening to a termite passage, and efficiently pushed her stalk into the hole. Almost immediately she pulled it out—there was nothing attached to the stick. She tried again and the sixth time she withdrew the stalk there were two large termites clinging to the end. Tina quickly lipped them off and chewed them. From then on there seemed an endless supply of termites to be fished from the passage. She worked quickly and efficiently, drawing her fishing tool across her wrist each time as she extracted it. Some of the termites came off on her wrist, but they had to crawl through her coat before they could bite her with their powerful pincers and this gave Tina plenty of time to eat those on the stalk, then deal with those on her wrist.

Each time Tina bent her stalk while inserting it into the mound she nipped the bent piece off. Eventually her tool became too short to use efficiently so she strode off, picked another suitable stem, stripped the leaves off and came back. Pooh picked up the abandoned stalk and tried poking it into any small openings he could find. Eventually he seemed to give up. I wanted Pooh to learn to fish for termites so I decided to teach him. I walked to the same bush as Tina was using and stripped the leaves off in exactly the same way as she had. Pooh watched me with growing interest. Then I tried Tina's first hole, using the same grip to hold the stalk as she did. After several attempts I pulled out the twig to find two termites were clinging grimly to the end.

I picked one off, pinched it, and, once I had rendered it harmless, offered it to Pooh. He looked very sceptical despite my "good-food" grunts. There was only one course of action left—I had to pop the wretched termite in my mouth and chew it, all the time making the appropriate grunts of appreciation. I expected it to taste foul, but surprisingly it didn't taste of anything much. I pinched the second termite, popped that one in too and continued fishing like Tina. Eventually I got Pooh to taste one but he did not appear enamoured with the flavour and spat it out. There was a limit to how many termites I was willing to eat to persuade my reluctant pupil and finally I gave up.

The green, damp days of the rains grew into weeks and then months. The chimps were healthier and more content than they had ever been and they were slowly acquiring a sound knowledge of their new home. They always had the camp as a secure base from which to explore and this I felt was still essential.

Without their really noticing, their cups of tea became fewer and fewer and they learned to find long drinks of cool water from the stream just as refreshing. They became tougher and more alert and came to rely on the valley for food.

During the later part of the rains we had a huge crop of golden-yellow grape-like fruit in our valley. These were oval in shape and hung in massive clusters from the trees. They were juicy with a strong, slightly sour flavour, and the chimps loved them. During the weeks that the trees fruited the valley resembled my idea of the Garden of Eden. Near the waterfall, there was a grove of about ten of these trees, all laden with fruit. Each time we approached, the chimps would pant and hug each other in excitement, then hurry towards the trees, food-grunting frantically.

One day they had been in the trees for an hour when Tina climbed down and disappeared silently into the valley. Her behaviour puzzled me, so I got up. Then I heard wild chimps pant-hooting, but they seemed a long way away at the base of Mount Asserick. Pooh and William were still in the trees but looking out intently over the plateau behind us. Suddenly there was a tremendous chorus of pant-hooting right above me on the plateau and the soft thud of running feet. William and Pooh quickly but quietly climbed to the ground. Pooh stood a few yards ahead of me, staring up to where the excited chimp food-grunts were coming from.

There was only time to hide behind a tree before a young female chimp, just a little smaller than Pooh, entered the clearing below the fruiting trees. She had a pale, flat, little face with slightly slanted Oriental eyes. She stopped a few yards in front of Pooh, then walked straight towards him. Pooh didn't move. At that instant an adult female came into the clearing with a young infant clinging to her belly. She walked past me, then turned and grinned nervously in Pooh's direction. I tried to keep absolutely still but she turned her head and we looked into each other's eyes. She bolted, running back the way she had come. Pooh gave a short startled scream as she tore past him. The little chimp followed her. I almost cried. I had spoiled Pooh's first real chance to meet wild chimps. They had certainly seemed friendly.

I walked up onto the plateau with Pooh and William hoping that, if the wild chimps were watching, I would present a harmless picture. Then we returned to the grove. I was almost certain that I had scared the chimps right away but, just in case not, Julian and I sat in a natural hide of tangled bushy vegetation. A path ran through it onto the plateau, so if the chimps came again and accepted Pooh and William, Julian and I could move away unseen.

William moved into the open and began to eat grass stalks and Pooh climbed into one of the fruit trees and began to feed. Suddenly just behind me I heard chimps food-grunting. William came to me, his coat bristling. His lips drew back nervously and he held my hand, looking from me to the first chimp that came into sight. Just below the hide we sat in there was a grape tree full of fruit. Five chimps were walking along the fallen tree through the tangle of vines. All were food-grunting and some of them began to scream with excitement. Pooh began to scream too. The first female chimp saw him and the excitement-screams got louder. William moved out into the open and to my joy reacted beautifully. He was grinning and bobbing down submissively.

At least one chimp was approaching William, who continued to react respectfully but stood his ground. Suddenly a young chimp in the vines began to scream as if he had been threatened. Pooh gave the threatening whaa bark. Then all the chimps, now about ten of them, began to whaa. William and Pooh insolently whaaed in turn, confident that I was close by to protect them. I began to tremble, the noise was terrific and some of those chimps looked enormous. I could hear the screams get more and more frenzied and was certain there was going to be some sort of action.

The hide began to feel like a cage. If we were attacked we'd be easy to catch. I told Julian to move out slowly, keeping the bush between him and the wild chimps, and to sit in the long grass a few yards away. The noise around us was now deafening. I waited for Julian to get clear, then began to climb out too. I scrambled clear and got to my feet just in time, for what seemed to me the biggest chimp I'd ever seen charged into the hide and out the other side. He stopped abruptly less than three yards in front of me and charged back the way he'd come. I was terrified, my knees were knocking. Pooh and William were sitting beside me holding my trouser leg. Almost immediately there was wild pant-hooting and thudding of feet as another chimp careered through the hide.

The chimps all around us seemed in a frenzy of excitement. A few seconds later two more adult chimps, dragging branches, rushed down the path but, as they cleared the hide, the sight of me standing a jump away halted them in their tracks. They both ran back. Suddenly the cries abated and the sounds of fleeing chimps replaced them. I looked up to see three of them standing on the edge of the plateau peering down at me, but they immediately disappeared.

My knees felt so weak that it was difficult to walk but I wanted those wild chimps to get a good look at us all and to see that we meant them no harm. If only Pooh hadn't whaaed like that, things might have been different.

The following morning, Julian and I were sitting in the hide and William and Pooh were eating some grass stems close by, when there was a sudden distress cry from a young chimp halfway down the slope. Then I heard a branch being broken.

William climbed onto the plateau, stepped round the hide, and walked down the slope in the direction of the cry, making the pant-cough greeting. I strained hard to catch each sound. Suddenly, there was the excited, high, screaming sound of a female or a juvenile, reacting uneasily to the presence of a stranger. Pooh listened with interest but remained near me.

A moment later there was a burst of excited, aggressive screaming from several chimps and William ran onto the plateau. He sat down and grinned nervously in the direction of the hide. No one followed him. He sat for only a minute or two, obviously ill at ease, then walked out of sight towards the sounds again. There was silence for ten minutes and I thought the chimps had fled. Then William began his respectful greeting coughs and pants again and another bout of screaming exploded.

William entered the hide and didn't venture out again for two hours. During this time I didn't hear any chimp vocalization but the occasional snapping of small branches indicated that they were

363

still present. William was hesitant at first. He walked along the edge of the plateau, past the place where the chimps were feeding below, and climbed into a fig tree about twenty yards away from the hide. I pointed out to Pooh that William was feeding on ripe figs and urged him to do the same. He obligingly sauntered over to the fig and climbed it. William was now frequently glancing down the slope. As Pooh began to feed, William began his pant-grunting. It seemed a chimp was approaching.

Pooh gave a nervous grin and a squeal and hurried out of the tree. William followed. He reached the edge of the plateau and retreated slowly for a few yards, bobbing all the time, squeaking, grinning, torn between a desire to meet this invisible stranger and doubts about his reception. Three times William approached and retreated, then, as he went forward the fourth time, another chimp began an excited, nervous squeaking and squealing. Though I could not see what was happening I could tell from William's behaviour that the wild chimp was walking towards him. Fortunately William was backing out into the plateau and not towards me.

Then I saw an adult chimp, his coat partially erect, closing in on William. He seemed wary and unsure. William stopped, still bobbing submissively. Then the wild chimp did a strange thing— he seemed to put his face right up against William's. William grinned and squeaked but stood his ground. A second male chimp walked out on to the plateau and stood glaring at William and Pooh. Eventually the two wild chimps climbed into a fig tree. They remained there for three minutes, looking far from relaxed, then descended and walked out of sight the way they had come. I hugged William several times and whispered my praise of his courage and persistence. Then we left to go home.

BOBO AND RAPHAELLA

It was towards the end of September and six months since we had made Niokolo our home. I had been expecting a visit from Daddy or Claude for several weeks but no one came and the food supply was once more down to almost nothing except rice. I decided to risk going to Niokolo to see if there was any mail or news of an impending visit. It was a nerve-racking twenty miles; the grass obliterated the road and I left it on several occasions—fortunately never hitting boulders large enough to damage Felicity.

There was a stack of mail waiting for me, including a telegram a couple of weeks old from Italy. An Italian girl called Raphaella Savinelli had cabled to ask whether she could bring her three-year-old chimp Bobo to my camp. He had lived with her for two years but it had become impossible to keep him any longer. Before returning to camp, I wrote to say that she and Bobo were to come as soon as they liked.

Over the next week, the rains eased and finally stopped. Mount Asserick changed from flourishing green into its mellow autumn colours. The grass of the plateau looked like a huge field of ripe golden corn and many of the trees changed to yellow, then orange, and finally shed their leaves.

One day I took Felicity to carry some supplies for a gang of labourers who were working on the park roads a few miles away. As I drove back, I noticed a huge cloud of black smoke billowing up into the sky near Mount Asserick. It was the first of the bush fires. The closer I got to home, the more anxious I became about the smoke—it seemed precariously near the camp. I hoped the chimps had had the sense to keep in the gully or down by the stream—places that were unlikely to burn.

I drove Felicity as fast as I dared. The fire was roaring its way up the steep slope to the plateau and the camp.

When at last I arrived, René and Julian had already begun to cut a firebreak. For half an hour we burned the surrounding grass, beating it out as soon as we had made a large enough border to protect us.

Once the camp was reasonably safe I had time to worry about the chimps. Tina, I knew, would have experienced a bush fire; I was sure William would keep close to her and heed all she did. I held Pooh who, once secure in my arms, peacefully watched the spectacle. The firebreak worked well and the fire roared and spat all round us, then passed on leaving us hot and smoky but undamaged. The plateau, which only an hour before had been a swaying sea of golden-orange grass, was now a charred wilderness.

The dry season was truly here. Until the next rain storm seven months away, most of Niokolo would take on a barren appearance. Only the hidden valleys would remain green. Tina and William came out of the gully into camp. Neither seemed particularly perturbed. William sneezed frequently but that was due to the smoke that still hung low on the ground.

A few days after the fire I received a message that Raphaella and Bobo had arrived. I drove to Niokolo and took to Raphaella from the start. She had a strong angular face and dark fiery eyes and gave the impression of a beautiful, determined and tough young woman. Bobo strutted down the veranda towards us, very erect, and climbed into my arms. He seemed to exude the same determination and self-confidence as Raphaella.

Bobo began the journey back to camp on Raphaella's lap but was soon climbing around the Land-Rover. As we drove along, he came to sit on my lap. Looking solemnly into my face, he pinched my arm. I didn't respond. Still looking at me, he pinched a little harder. I glanced at him and slowly pinched him back. Bobo moved away and continued his playful scrambling in the back of the Land-Rover.

I was thrilled that Pooh would have a playmate. I imagined him and Bobo becoming firm friends. But how would William and Tina react? It was dark when we reached camp and the introduction to William, Tina and Pooh was carried out in the light of a hurricane lamp. Bobo was tense, so, to give him time, I gave William, Tina and Pooh half a loaf of bread each. Bobo got a smaller piece that I hoped he would finish eating at the same time as the others. He looked tiny in comparison with them.

When the bread had been eaten, Bobo began to play with William. Then Pooh, who had patiently been waiting his turn, rolled and tumbled with Bobo. He was so gentle and considerate with the tough little stranger that it brought a lump to my throat. There would be no more lonely days for Pooh while William courted Tina. Here was the perfect companion for him.

Having watched intently, Tina left and went to her nest. Finally Raphaella took a very tired Bobo and tried to settle him on a cushion on top of the Land-Rover. William and Pooh reluctantly went back to their nests in the gully. Bobo finally slept in the same bed as Raphaella. There was plenty of time ahead for him to learn about nesting. He had experienced enough of his new life for one day.

As was true of Pooh, William, and countless other baby chimps, Bobo's mother had been killed when he was still a helpless infant. Confined in a crate with others of his age and kind, he had been exported from his native Africa to Europe. Finally he had found himself in a small, cold cage on the shelf of a scruffy Italian pet shop. It was from here that Raphaella had rescued him.

For two years he had lived happily. He had never been confined, and as a result, Raphaella's house had been pulled to pieces. She got tired of buying new lavatory seats, so did without. She replaced the wash basin twice. She no longer bothered with curtains or the smudgy marks all over the walls. Her whole life had to be changed to suit Bobo. Yet the day came when she knew that, for his own sake, she could keep him in Italy no longer and began to consider taking him back to Africa and reintroducing him to wild chimpanzees. She was prepared to live in the bush with him till he was old enough and capable enough to live without her. Then she had heard what I was trying to do and the rest had followed naturally.

The following morning, Pooh and William were outside the shack earlier than usual. I had hoped to get Bobo out before either of them knew he had slept there, for they would not be able to understand why this new chimp was allowed to enter and they were not. As I was about to carry Bobo through the door, William tried to slip past me. I bent down and took his arm to prevent him. He flew into a rage, and for the first time in his life, bit my hand and then threw me to the ground with amazing ease. He was furious. I also was furious, and indignant. I ran at him with such determination that he began to scream and run away. I caught him, grabbed a handful of hair at the back of his neck, and bit him as hard as I could on the arm. He ran screaming into the valley. I lay where he had left me, shaking with exertion and spitting out the hair in my mouth. I knew though that I had regained his respect.

Later, I decided to take everyone into the valley. The new

sounds unnerved Bobo slightly, so Raphaella carried him. When we reached the stream Bobo was too bemused by his new surroundings to feel like playing. Surprisingly William whimpered for his attention, then, when Bobo still did not respond, attacked Pooh and ran on to drum out his frustration on the root of a mendico tree.

We came across some dry afzelia pods. Raphaella opened them by holding them on their sides on a rock and banging them with a second rock till the pods split with an explosion, spilling their black beanlike seeds on the ground. Each seed had a bright orange cap that fitted over one end, attaching it to the sides of the pod. They were attractive but as hard as small stones, too hard for the chimps to break with their teeth. Raphaella promptly ingratiated herself with William by pounding them into tiny pieces which he and the others could chew. Finally the chimps were wandering about picking the pods and queueing up beside Raphaella for her to open them. Before we moved on all three chimps were trying to imitate the methods Raphaella had used to make the food in the pods both accessible and edible.

ONE MORNING A National Parks Land-Rover drove into camp with a message that Mr. Dupuy, the Director of National Parks, was in Simenti for a few days and had asked to see me.

Raphaella and I drove the sixty miles to Simenti, and when we pulled up in the forecourt of the Simenti Hotel a young Frenchman, Alain, ran out to greet us. "Thank God you've arrived," he said and, gripping my arm, dragged me towards the dining room. "We have a problem here we don't know how to handle. I hope you can help."

We stopped in the middle of the dining room and Alain looked round expectantly. "*Toto, où es tu?*" he called and from behind one of the tables emerged the smallest baby elephant I'd ever seen. She walked quickly towards Alain and began to search all over him for a nipple to suck. Raphaella and I walked slowly towards the small creature and touched its bristly little body.

Alain squatted down and let the baby elephant suck his fingers. He asked anxiously, "Do you think we can save her? Her mother was killed by poachers about twelve kilometres from here; she

368

wandered into the hotel by herself two days ago. She has adopted me, but tomorrow we are going on a week's patrol. Mr. Dupuy and I hope you can take her. . . ."

The elephant interrupted Alain's words with a noisy jet of liquid diarrhoea. I knew that young elephants were almost impossible to hand-raise. Diarrhoea diminished the chances still further.

Despite my fears, I was aware of terrific excitement at the prospect of trying to look after her. It was vitally important to me that she should survive and grow up.

My thoughts flew back to the diet that three baby elephants had been started on at Woburn: a gruel of cooked maize meal, milk, glucose and calcium. They had been much older than this tiny infant, which was probably not much more than a week old, but their diet was the only one I knew and there was no one else around who had more or even as much experience.

It soon turned out that the only ingredient of that diet to be found at Simenti was milk. I decided to substitute cooked rice for the maize meal and honey for the glucose and arrange the rations as best I could. In camp we had stacks of calcium.

I asked Alain not to feed it any milk for the rest of the day but to give it warm water with honey and a trace of salt. It was an attempt to give her stomach a rest and to clear whatever was in it already before starting her on a new diet.

After lunch I saw Mr. Dupuy, then Raphaella and I set about equipping Felicity for the ride home. The guards gave us a straw mattress and cut a pile of springy green leaves to put on top of it. We collected some old curtains in case it got draughty, filled a plastic jerrycan with boiled water, and commandeered the hotel's supply of honey and several plastic water bottles. Alain made teats from the fingers cut off a pair of rubber gloves.

Before setting out I sent a cable to Daddy and Nigel with a list of other requirements for the young elephant. I also asked them to phone zoos in England that had successfully raised elephants and to ask for suitable diets.

Finally at four o'clock all seemed ready. I bent down and, with surprising ease, lifted the little creature into the back of Felicity and climbed in after her. She was strong for her size and it was quite a job holding on to her. I spoke to her constantly, trying to soothe her, and Raphaella drove at about 5 m.p.h. in order to give her as smooth a ride as possible. After struggling to keep her balance for about half an hour, she lay down with her head cushioned on my thighs. We had taken three hours to reach Simenti that morning; it took over nine hours to get back to camp. I was covered in diarrhoea and the honey water which I had had to give to her every hour.

When we lifted her down from the Land-Rover she followed us into the shack, nudging us for a drink. I put some rice on to cook and half an hour later gave her half a litre of rice, milk, honey and calcium gruel. She drank it all down, sucking on the improvised teat—her eyes half-closed with satisfaction. She seemed perfectly at home in the shack and, when she had finished her meal, climbed up on the double camp-bed beside Raphaella and lay down to sleep. I made up another feed which I put in the fridge and climbed into bed with both of them.

Fifteen minutes later, just as I was dozing off to sleep, the baby elephant stirred, got up, walked over my stomach and stepped down onto the floor. Then she began to sniff my face with her wet, rubbery, little trunk. Finally she knelt down, rolled back her trunk onto her forehead, and began to slobber all over my neck and shoulders with her tongue, searching for a nipple. I sat up and allowed her to suck on my fingers. I looked at my watch. It was barely twenty minutes since her last feed. I wasn't sure how much an elephant of her age could safely drink at a time. I didn't want her to go hungry, yet on the other hand I knew it was dangerous to overfeed her—especially when she already had diarrhoea. So I sat up and tried to soothe her the best I could.

It took her about ten minutes to realize that the fingers I kept giving her to suck produced no nourishment, and she then began to butt me hard with her forehead. Soon she began to rumble and finally she screamed. I sat through half an hour of buffeting and then warmed up the feed I had in the fridge.

She sucked strongly till there was only about half an inch of milk left in the bottle then, apparently satisfied, climbed back onto the bed, flopped down and fell asleep. I cooked some more

370

Stella and Pooh

A game with the baby elephant

rice and made up two more bottles which I stacked in the fridge.

It had taken me almost an hour to prepare the two new feeds and, as I edged my way into our now rather soiled bed, the baby elephant woke up. Refreshed by her doze, she seemed desperately hungry and once again began to suck and nuzzle any part of me she could find. I almost woke up Raphaella and told her it was her turn to baby-sit, but she was so soundly asleep that I decided against it. I tried to ignore the elephant, hoping she would go to sleep again, but instead she trundled round the room knocking everything over, then came back to me in a slight panic at having lost contact for a few minutes and began again the eternal nudging and slobbering for food. Finally, out of sheer desperation, I had to surrender and give her another feed. After that we both fell asleep for one glorious hour, until the whole process began again.

Next morning, after a cup of strong coffee, we led the elephant outside. The two young chimps had seen her in the house and were extremely curious, also rather afraid. However, Bobo came forward, took hold of her tail and sniffed it. I watched carefully to make sure that he didn't pull or bite it, but when the elephant turned around, Bobo let go and backed away. Finally Pooh came to sit in my lap, calmly pushing the wet trunk away each time it blew or snuffled at him.

When I saw William entering camp, I slipped my alarm pistol out of my pocket and held it hidden in my hand. I spoke to him, introducing the baby elephant, and tried to act as if everything was perfectly normal. He approached cautiously and I allowed him to sniff the elephant and to look behind her ears and under her tail. Then he gripped her trunk and probably squeezed it because the elephant began to shake her head. I took William's hand and, chatting brightly, firmly lifted it away. Without being aggressive, I was making sure that he understood the elephant was as much part of me as my bag and my camera and that—although he could touch her—she was mine. Surprisingly, William accepted all this very casually and, after another brief inspection, left her alone.

The baby elephant followed Raphaella and me around like a shadow. If we weren't together she seemed in a dilemma as to

which one of us to follow. Soon, so long as she was close to one
of us, she seemed content. We took her for short walks with the
chimps to visit some fruiting tabbo trees close to camp and in the
evening she would come down to the stream with us.

A week went by and Nigel arrived with all the things I'd asked
for in the cable. With glass bottles and proper teats, it was much
easier for René and Julian to keep things sterile. Nigel also
brought something less welcome, a telegram which meant
Raphaella had to leave with him to return to Italy. She was very
distressed about having to abandon me but I assured her I would
manage somehow.

After they had left the following morning, I walked back into
the house with the elephant. Very rarely in my life had I felt
quite so lonely and depressed. There was little time for brooding,
though, and I quickly got my boots on and took the elephant and
chimps out to the tabbo trees. I could not go too far from camp,
for every two hours I had to go back to the shack to give the
elephant a drink. Her diarrhoea seemed to be improving. Instead
of ejecting a stream of water, she now passed something of about
the consistency of a pudding. I began to hope that the impossible
had happened and that she was going to live after all.

The next two nights I slept little and, as the elephant would
not remain with Julian, there was little chance of rest during the
day either. Nor could I completely rely on Julian to measure out
the ingredients for a feed; it seemed impossible to impress upon
him that every quantity had to be exact. Rather than risk upsetting
the elephant's stomach again, I made all the feeds myself. The
third night I felt so desperate for sleep that I strung up a
hammock in the room so that she could not trample all over me.
A feed every two hours was still essential but I could rely on her
to wake me up for that.

One evening, about a week after Raphaella had left, I sat out
on an ant-hill in the yard till all the chimps had nested, then went
into the house for supper. The baby elephant got her bottle first
but kept trying to find out what I was eating and put her trunk
into everything on the table. When I pushed it off, she walked
round the room confidently, clumsily sniffing here and there and
knocking what few things remained on the shelves onto the floor.

I strung up the hammock and at 9.30 p.m. gave her a feed and went to bed. She climbed onto the camp-bed and settled down too. I fell into a sound sleep.

I woke with a start. Everything was so quiet. I switched on the torch and looked at my watch—it was a quarter to four. Oh God, the feeds! The baby elephant, where was she? "Baby elephant!" I called, and shone my torch frantically round the room. The bed was empty but just below the hammock I saw the elephant lying on her side. I leapt out and crouched beside her. She was unconscious. I yelled for Julian and a few minutes later he came rushing in. "Light a fire and warm up as much water as you can," I cried. "Then fill all the empty bottles you can find."

I covered the elephant with blankets to try to warm her. My insides were a tangle of guilt. I had overslept; she had missed three feeds and I was responsible for her collapse. Her breathing was slow and laboured, as if each breath was held for seconds before it was exhaled. Torn with anguish and feeling helpless I cradled her head and prayed for her recovery. She stopped breathing but, unable to accept what that meant, I began to pump her chest and lift her front leg alternately. After forcing air in and out of her several times, she began to breathe again. We packed hot bottles wrapped in towels all round her and I rubbed her body all over with my hands in an attempt to keep the circulation going. If only she could regain consciousness and I could feed her, give her some nourishment, I felt there might be hope. My elephant couldn't die. I loved her too much.

In desperation I gave her a tablespoon of brandy. Whether it was the result of the hot water bottles, the brandy or an iron will to live, about a quarter of an hour later she opened her eyes and seemed to focus. Her trunk wriggled feebly. Julian ran to the kitchen for her bottle and gave it to me. I held the teat on her tongue but she was still much too groggy to drink. I put the bottle down and continued to talk to her and rub her. Her eyes closed, her trunk went limp and she relapsed into unconsciousness. For an hour we rubbed her and kept her warm, then her breathing began to falter again and when it stopped, there was nothing I could do to make it start. I felt for a pulse and found nothing but stillness. My baby elephant was dead.

IT WAS NOT TO be too long before this sadness was made up for. One afternoon I heard René calling my name. His voice was high with urgent excitement, as he careered towards me at top speed. His face was split in an ecstatic smile.

"Come quickly! Tina has just come into camp with a baby!"

I screamed with joy, then ran outside to where Tina was sitting near the hut. William, Pooh and Bobo were staring curiously at her but she kept moving round, protectively cuddling her new-born baby to her stomach. As we approached, she climbed into a low tree. She had to use both her hands but she pinned the tiny infant to her stomach by crossing a leg over its back. I was able to see a tiny red fist clutching the hair on her side.

The baby was covered in a soft-looking dark down, his head set in a silky cap of black hair. His face was dark and screwed-up, his mouth was a bright red line, and his eyes, when they opened, were unfocused and a light beige-brown. Already his small ears stuck out like those of his father, William. I felt delirious with excitement. I asked René and Julian to bring bread and rice. I gave the others rice and, when they were all occupied, I gave Tina a large loaf of bread which she loved. As she leaned forward to take the loaf from my hand, I saw the baby was a boy. Any fears that I had secretly harboured about Tina being an in-adequate mother soon vanished. She appeared so tender and proud of her baby. While she was eating, he began to move his head jerkily from side to side on her belly and she considerately hitched him up higher so that he was nuzzling the area around her nipple. After a few seconds he found what he was looking for, fed, and then fell asleep again.

René and Julian made a special supper that evening and while we ate we thought of names for the new addition to our family. Finally we decided on "Tilly", a combination of the names of his parents, Tina and Willie.

Tina kept to the valley and remained with the other chimps most of the time. No one was allowed to touch the baby but on his third day in the camp I saw William's hand move closer and closer to a small red foot as he groomed Tina's back. Finally he gently lifted the minute toes with his thick calloused forefinger and stared at them, then quickly continued to groom Tina.

EPILOGUE

Of the original trio which I left behind in Niokolo Koba in 1973, only Tina's progress has been followed. Albert's and Cheetah's whereabouts still remain a mystery. It is not unreasonable to hope that they continue to live somewhere in the park.

As I look around camp today, I cannot help feeling enormous satisfaction at what I see. We are more organized now as a rehabilitation centre than we were in our pioneering days. The shack has made way for a larger, more solid building in which we are able to cook and keep our supplies.

Tina's motherhood has proved the success of one vitally important aspect of the project; that a chimpanzee, having spent years of her life in captivity, has not only been reintroduced to the wild, but has mated and given birth there. Her son Tilly is now a strong, healthy infant.

William, that undernourished scrap of life that we bought so long ago, is now over ten years old. He has become the dominant male of his own small group of free chimpanzees. He is entirely independent in every way and spends most of his time in the valley with Tina and Tilly.

Pooh, once the insecure baby of the group, has grown into a sociable and confident juvenile. Bobo is his closest companion. Though perfectly able to feed himself, Bobo does not as yet have the confidence to wander far into the valley alone. He still requires the security of the camp and occasional reassurance from one of us. He will probably continue to require to do so until he is about seven or eight years old, when like a wild chimp at that age, he will naturally acquire the independence needed to wander out alone.

Some time ago we acquired two zoo-born chimps from London. Cameron, a confident young male, has already left the camp. On four occasions since he left, however, a young male chimp has been sighted that could well be him, each time in the vicinity of wild chimps. Yula, the other zoo chimp, is still with us. She climbs, feeds, and interacts as easily and as normally as any chimp in the group. The fact that she has succeeded from scratch in adapting herself to the wild so well proves triumphantly that, even though a chimp is born in captivity, it can still learn to live the life of its wild ancestors.

It now appears that our remaining chimps are unlikely ever to become part of an existing wild chimpanzee community and so it is more realistic to aim towards creating a self-sufficient group. Our present members are an ideal foundation and at the time of writing three more confiscated infant chimps are enjoying the sanctuary of Abuko in preparation for the wider, wilder life here at Mount Asserick.

Finally for me there is no longer the sense of loneliness which used to mar the harmony of camp. Raphaella has returned to be my partner and together we will continue with the work. My dearest hope is that not only will our present group of chimpanzees continue to prosper, but also that our efforts will inspire others to follow our example in other parts of Africa.

Tilly

TALK DOWN

a condensation of the book by BRIAN LECOMBER

Illustrated by Pat Owen
Published by Hodder & Stoughton

Ann Moore is suddenly, horrifyingly alone in the sky: beside her in the tiny Cherokee aeroplane the pilot lies unconscious. . . .

Fifty miles away, Tony Paynton, teaching an airsick pupil, hears Ann's panic-stricken screams over the radio. But with fuel running low, there's little he can do to help. . . .

Keith Kerr, ace pilot and instructor, takes over the search. If he can find the runaway plane, he just *might* be able to talk Ann down to a safe landing. . . .

As Ann's plane drones south in the gathering darkness, emergency forces all over England swing into action, and events move towards a heart-stopping climax.

1

At forty minutes past noon on a bright January day, the coldest place in the world was the open cockpit of a Stampe SV4B biplane.

At two thousand feet the blaring gale of the slipstream was like a solid force, invading the cockpit with a million icy knives. Keith Kerr could feel his nose, cheeks, and the exposed strip of forehead between the goggles and leather helmet going tingling numb in the rawness of it.

It had been cold before, on the ground. Breath had puffed like smoke in the crystal air, and heavy boots had squeaked on frost as they'd pulled the red and yellow pre-war biplane out of the hangar. But that had been nothing but a gentle foretaste of what was to come.

Beneath the fabric wings, the East Riding of Yorkshire was a vast patchwork of fields, bright and new-looking in the dewy glare of the winter sun. Here and there tendrils of morning mist still lingered, while the sun bounced occasional flashes of light off windows in the scattered villages. Above the land, the sky was cold and clear and enormously blue; one of those rare winter days when a low-flying airman's world is pure brilliance, the visibility brittle-sharp and unlimited. On such a day a young man in an old biplane may believe that he can see for ever.

Kerr felt the familiar happy-frightened fluttering in his stomach as the Stampe growled up into the blue dome.

Two thousand two hundred feet.

He lowered the long nose to just below the horizon and eased back the throttle. The hollow feeling in his stomach deepened as he yanked all seven strap-tails of his safety harness one by one, trussing himself so tightly into the seat that it was difficult to take a deep breath. Then he pushed the red mixture-lever into lean cut-off. The engine died abruptly, windmilled for a few seconds, then picked up its steady blaring again as his numbed fingers pushed the blue handle, labelled INVERTED SYSTEM.

Now he was ready. He wheeled the biplane into a steep left turn, head twisting this way and that as he searched the sky for other aircraft. The sky was empty.

Kerr rolled out of the turn, craning his neck to look over the side of the cockpit, and watched the runways of Sherburn-in-Elmet airfield sliding back towards the edge of the left lower wing. He was aware of his attention narrowing down, the way it always did at the start. The night, Maggie, the letter from the airline in his pocket, the clutter of everyday life, even the cold, were all forgotten. His strong-featured face and pale blue eyes behind the goggles were very still, lost in total concentration. His arms were the wings, his fingertips the ailerons and elevators.

The far boundary of the airfield disappeared under the wing. He opened the throttle fully and pushed the nose down hard, nearly to the vertical.

The solid blast of engine and airflow wound up rapidly in the dive, thundering and tightening. His blue eyes flicked steadily from ground to instruments and back to ground again, while his brain clicked over calmly in the maelstrom of wind and noise. 1,200 feet and 140 knots.

He pulled the stick back smoothly, checked for a moment in level flight, then pulled back again.

The Stampe reared up. The long scarlet engine cowling clubbed through the horizon and on up into the blue. Kerr's helmeted head twisted right to watch the angle between wing-tip and horizon. As the wing reached the vertical, he checked and held it, keeping the biplane pointing straight up into the endless sky.

Then he slammed the stick over to the right.

The Stampe pivoted in a vertical half roll. The shadows of struts and wires flickered across his face as the wing traversed round the horizon. The howl of the airflow waned, the engine labouring. . . . A distant wood slid out from under the right wing-tip. Kerr snapped the stick central to stop the roll, held the biplane balanced straight up for the space of a further two heartbeats, and then kicked on full right rudder.

For an instant, nothing happened. The Stampe seemed to hang motionless in the sky, suspended by the flat snarl of the engine. Then, quite slowly, the red and yellow wings pivoted round towards the earth in a perfect stall turn.

Hanging vertically downwards, the wind-roar swelling again around him as the plane dived, Kerr found time to grin. The fluttering in his belly had subsided to a small hard knot of concentration. It was being a good day. . . .

KERR TAXIED the Stampe slowly off the tarmac and stopped in front of the hangar. One of the sparking plugs had packed up. He wriggled round in the cockpit, pulling off his helmet, and then clambered slowly out onto the catwalk on the right lower wing and down to the ground.

The concrete apron at Sherburn was quiet and momentarily deserted; everyone was either in the clubhouse or up in the air. His movements awkward with the cold, Kerr pulled off his gloves, walked to the tailplane and pushed the Stampe round and back into the hangar. Behind it, in shadow, the usual interlocking gaggle of Cherokees and Cessnas looked shabby and uninteresting; mere aerial motor cars where the romance of flight had been sacrificed for dull efficiency.

He grinned. Planes like these were his livelihood—for the moment, at any rate—but on a golden day like this you could keep them: they were insensitive hunks of ironmongery, and an insult to a flying man's art. On a day like this, happiness was a morning off and a pre-war biplane. Even if that biplane had just burned out a plug on the left-hand bank.

Kerr squeezed past the Stampe's tail to get to a row of lockers up against the hangar wall. He rooted out four new plugs in their polythene wrappers, then collected up a canvas bag of tools and made his way back to the biplane's nose. Opening up the aluminium engine cowling, the thought occurred to him, *This is where I came in.*

He blew on his hands for a moment, remembering back fifteen years. A very young and eager Keith Kerr then, on a small airfield not unlike this one. Serving fuel, polishing wings—and changing plugs—in exchange for precious, carefully hoarded minutes of flying time. And then the day when an instructor walked away from a clattering Tiger Moth and left that same young man to the jittery elation of his first solo. . . . That day in the Tiger Moth seemed a very long time ago, now. A long time and a lot of distance.

His first full-time flying job had been instructing, which is the way it usually is for an impecunious young man seeking to make a living in the sky. Big-time aviation concerns are disinclined to trust their equipment to newly-qualified barbarians, whilst the world's flying schools are notoriously willing to employ any applicant prepared to fly long hours for low wages. Kerr had worked for a Sussex flying school for a year, and then been offered another instructing job in Kenya.

He could remember those mornings, up at five in the muggy light of dawn so as to get started before the heat of the day wound up. And then, in the stifling four-hour midday break, listening to old Piet van den Hoyt, the enormously fat flying school owner-cum-chief-instructor, as he sweated out gin and told Kerr over and over again to quit instructing and get into the airlines.

High above, a jet was drawing a sharp white contrail across the icy blue sky. His airman's instinct made him look up, and he took a step towards the open front of the hangar to get a better view. Bundled up with layers of sweaters under his jacket, he resembled a short blocky teddy bear. Deep crowsfeet wrinkled the corners of his eyes as he stared up at the sky, puckering a short jagged scar alongside his left eye.

Maybe I should have listened to Vandy, he thought. Maybe if I had, I'd be in that cockpit at this very minute. . . .

But at that time, ten years ago, he hadn't wanted to be in a jet cockpit. At twenty-two years old there had seemed to be plenty of time for a chunky young man with a commanding manner and a smooth touch with an aeroplane: years ahead in which to see something of the world. Everyone knew that airline flying was a bus driver's job, best suited to pilots approaching middle age. . . .

Kerr fingered the scar unconsciously, flexed his left leg, then turned back to the engine.

The years had passed quickly in some places, more slowly in others, counted by logbooks filled and aircraft flown. Instructing and crop-spraying in Australia: a total of 3,000 hours. Chartering and instructing in Canada: the time up to 4,000 hours, and the number of forced landings up to five. Dusting and instructing in Florida; and at somewhere around the 5,000-hour mark a brief but disastrous marriage, followed by instructing in Puerto Rico.

And then the island of St. Lucia. The Caribbean paradise. Up at four a.m. in the trilling velvet darkness, filling the plane's spray-hoppers while you waited to go banana-spraying in the calm heat of first light. And then the morning when the last thing you could remember was the engine dying as you tried to pull up out of a valley at the end of a spray-run.

Kerr unscrewed the last of the four plugs. The scar near his eye was itching again, the way it did when it was getting ready to eject yet another tiny fragment of splintered Perspex. Still, at least the leg was all right this winter. When he'd first come back to England thirteen months before, the left knee had locked every time the weather went damp.

England had needed some adjusting to, this time round. Quite apart from the stiff leg. Now, all of his old flying friends were married. Some were with the airlines. Some had quit professional aviation altogether, and most of them seemed more concerned with children and mortgages than they were with looping speeds and stalling angles. When he visited their homes he was awkward and out of place; a vivid stocky stranger with an indefinable accent and the weathering of faraway winds in his face.

The airlines had felt the same way about him. To corporation minds he was an anachronism, a barnstorming albatross, a good flier, perhaps, but a dangerous individualist. Rides a powerful motor bike instead of driving a Ford. More single-engine time than multi. . . . No line experience . . . no turbine time; such qualifications are unlikely to make a good company man.

After six weeks of idleness he'd gone back to instructing, because there'd been nothing else available. The Leeds Aero Club had been delighted to get him as their chief flying instructor, of course: any 6,000-hour pilot who is still prepared to teach is a rare catch indeed. And Kerr was an excellent flying instructor and ran the school with bantam-rooster aplomb. If one or two of his fellow instructors suspected that his knack for teaching the apparently unteachable was founded in a deep inner streak of sensitivity, they were careful not to say so in his presence.

For his own part he quite enjoyed the job—apart from heartily disliking Edward Tomms, the current owner of the Aero Club, who fortunately rarely bothered to turn up there—but as the months went by he'd found himself increasingly conscious of its lack of future. As an anodyne he'd turned back to an old love; aerobatics. During his working days he flew sober Cessnas and Cherokees, and in his spare time he rode his motor bike twenty miles to Sherburn's small grass field and practised vertical rolls and inverted spins in the Stampe. But aerobatics cannot fill all the gaps in a life, and against his will he'd found himself secretly yearning for the roots he'd once despised. A house of his own, a wife, a career instead of a job. . . .

And now, suddenly, it was happening. As Kerr tightened the last plug, the movement rustled the letter in his back pocket. He knew the wording by heart: *British Island Airways are pleased to offer you the position . . . report at Gatwick Airport for the commencement of conversion training at 0900 hours on Monday February 16. . . .*

It felt very good. He whistled loudly as he collected up the tools and carried the bag back to the locker.

And then there was the other thing, too. Last night had surprised them both. The letter had come yesterday morning, he'd suggested a drink in the evening because he'd been bursting to tell someone—and things had just sort of gone on from there. And after knowing Maggie for five months and never an inkling. . . .

He smiled into the raw sunshine, his face taking on an unusually tender expression in place of the usual mischievous grin. A small voice of caution warned that last night could have been a passing thing to be enjoyed and then forgotten. But it hadn't felt like that, somehow. There'd been a sort of . . . kindness about it. As if both of them had come in from the cold and found something warm and happy and totally worthwhile.

Like . . . coming home, he thought. Like coming home when you didn't even know you had a home.

After a minute he turned his back on the sun, and went to check the Stampe's oil and close up its cowlings before setting out on his motor bike for a long day's instruction at Leeds-Bradford Airport.

FIFTY MILES to the north of Sherburn-in-Elmet, in one of the buildings of the Cleveland Flying Club at Tees-side Airport, Tony Paynton blew chalk dust off his hands and stood with his back to the blackboard, facing his student.

"So much for the forces in the spin, Jules," he said. "In a minute we'll deal with the practical aspects. But first, do you have any questions?"

Jules Martin swallowed. Forty-one next week, learning to fly in a last-ditch attempt to recapture a youth he'd never really had, there were times when he secretly doubted that he would ever make a pilot. The prospect of the spinning exercise had been worrying him for the past month, but up to now a prolonged patch of bad weather had put the ordeal off.

Today, the weather was perfect. The January sun streamed in through the windows, and the sky over Tees-side Airport was clear and blue. Martin looked at the spidery flight diagrams on the blackboard and felt slightly sick.

He said, "No questions. That's clear enough."

"Fine. The Chipmunk's a lovely aeroplane, but it can be reluctant to come out of a spin so we have to be sure of getting the recovery action dead right, then there's no problem. That means first, power off. Then full opposite rudder, pause, and control column forwards. Is everything quite clear?"

Martin swallowed again and said, "Yes."

"Right. Good. So now let's nip out and have a go at it, then. You go and pre-flight the aeroplane, and I'll come out when I see the engine running. O.K.?"

Martin nodded and scraped his chair back. Paynton watched him as he walked out into the cold sunshine.

AT TEN MINUTES to two in the afternoon, the same moment that Tony Paynton and Jules Martin were lifting off the runway forty miles away at Tees-side, and Keith Kerr was closing the hangar doors at Sherburn-in-Elmet, Roy Bazzard and Ann Moore arrived at the Tyne Flying Club. The club was housed in a dingy wooden hut sandwiched between two hangars, a quarter of a mile from the terminal of Woolsington Airport, Newcastle.

Ann, who had never been in a flying club before, found the place mildly unnerving. The inside of the hut was dusty and well worn. There was a small counter in one corner behind which sat the club operations-manager-cum-receptionist, king of aircraft bookings, flight sheets, and all the other paperwork of a six-aeroplane flying school. Along the counter was a large noticeboard covered with terse little typewritten memos signed by the chief flying instructor, and the rest of the walls were plastered with diagrams of aeroplanes and electrical systems. The whole building had the air of lived-in neglect which comes from a lot of people passing through, but never stopping.

Ann perched on the edge of a tired leather chair, while Roy went to the counter and came back with a Passenger Membership form for her to sign. The wording covered half a sheet of foolscap and included the sentence, *"No claim shall arise out of any accident involving club members or club aircraft."* She read it through twice, then filled it in and scribbled her name on it.

"There you are." Her voice was a shade over-casual as she tried to hide her nervousness. "I've signed away all my rights."

"Splendid." Bazzard was six-foot-one, with an easy smile. "You didn't even notice the cheque underneath it, either."

Ann smiled back, grateful for the joke. "Oh yes, I did. I signed it 'R. Bazzard' and kept it. I'll fill the rest in later."

For the next ten minutes she sat leafing through an old copy of *Flying* while Roy busied himself with maps, clipboard, and his small navigation computer. As a nursing sister in a large hospital, Ann was accustomed to the rigmaroles surrounding the use of precision machinery but, nonetheless, the preparations for flight seemed to be incredibly complicated, and somehow increased her nervousness. After a while she got up and went into the Ladies Room, where she renewed her lipstick unnecessarily.

Looking at her face in the mirror, she found herself searching for the telltale signs of strain that had been there recently. It was an attractive face, with blue eyes and bushy neck-length blonde hair—but still the signs were there. The corners of that rather wide mouth, for instance; they were pressed together again, prim and disapproving; Ann saw the beginning of that intangible aura of severity which she'd noticed in other nursing sisters. Too many long hours in the casualty ward, perhaps, with not enough relaxation in between. Too much efficiency. . . .

She smiled tentatively, watching the effect. It created a minor transformation, widening the eyes, making the mouth warm and friendly, and giving the slightly tipped-up nose a cheeky air. The sternness and tension were gone, which, she told herself, was the way it should be for a healthy twenty-five-year-old girl at the beginning of a long weekend off.

She went back to applying the lipstick, resolving to smile more often over the next three days. Forget the Royal Infirmary and its pressure-cooker workload, stop worrying about going in the plane, and most of all, stop worrying about Roy. It was ridiculous, worrying about whether you were in love with someone after you'd only known him three weeks. Quite ridiculous. Flying down to stay with his parents in Buckinghamshire for a weekend didn't mean a thing: nothing except that they enjoyed each other's company. And if it should end up in bed before she'd got it all neatly thought out and diagnosed—well, maybe that was just exactly what she needed before she got a shade *too* well-balanced, a little too much the super-organized senior nurse.

She found she was blushing, embarrassed by the sudden strength of her feelings. She waited until the colour had subsided, smiled again briefly at the mirror, and went back into the clubhouse.

ROY BAZZARD bent over his map: the track he needed to fly from Newcastle to the aerodrome of Denham, just above London, was almost due south. Irritably, he massaged the back of his neck. In spite of the prospect of the long weekend with Ann, he was feeling stale and waspish: he'd woken up that morning with all the symptoms of a hangover, although he'd had nothing to drink the night before, and his neck was wincingly stiff with the same apparent lack of cause. He'd put the malady down to overwork—at thirty-six he was the junior partner in an old Newcastle firm of accountants, pushing hard to establish his footing—and told himself that he'd feel better as the morning went on. But beneath his outward cheerfulness he still felt sluggish and used-up.

He rubbed his eyes with his knuckles, wondering for a moment whether he really ought to fly. He was basically a cautious man, still mildly nervous of the air after ninety-two hours of piloting and he was very aware that his one-year-old Private Pilot's Licence was a flimsy guarantee against the occasional error. But then there was Ann. He'd told her that if the weather was good they'd fly down to Denham instead of driving, and she'd seemed to like the idea. And the weather indisputedly *was* good. . . .

He shrugged his shoulders, then jabbed his Chinagraph pencil down on the wind-scale and began to calculate his heading.

A few seconds later Ann came back into the room, and he looked up smiling.

THEY WALKED OUT to the aeroplane at a quarter past two, carrying their weekend luggage. Outside the clubhouse the sunshine was cold and brittle, with patches of frost still blanketing the tarmac in the shadows of the hangars. The line of parked aircraft were all sleek and modern-looking, except for one: a tiny, chunky biplane, garishly painted in chocolate and yellow. Ann blinked at it as they walked by.

"Is that one of the flying-school planes, Roy?"

Bazzard glanced round. "No, not that one, love. That's a thing called a Pitts Special. Specialist aerobatic job. I expect Barry Turner's got it out to do a bit of practising. He's the chief flying instructor here." He glanced up at the brilliant blue sky, streaked now with wisps of high cirrus. "Nice day for it, too, if you like turning yourself upside down."

She said, "Can you do that, Roy? Stunts and things?"

Bazzard grinned. "I can just about do a loop, but anything else makes me go a delicate shade of green." He gestured towards a sober blue and white Cherokee Arrow parked next to the biplane. "This is more my line. Nice American airborne motor car, easy to fly, enough navigation equipment for a small airliner, and room for the prettiest nurse in Newcastle to sit beside me!"

Close to, the Arrow was bigger than Ann had expected. The white platforms of the wings were wide and thick, and she couldn't see over the body at all. In spite of her thick-knit sweater and jeans, she stood shivering in the January breeze while Roy walked all round it, moving the control surfaces and kneeling to see the undersides.

When he'd finished his inspection he stepped up onto the walkway on the starboard wing root and opened the cockpit door. Ann handed up the luggage and he leaned in and stowed it behind the front seats.

Then the pain hit him.

It came very suddenly, like a red-hot skewer behind his eyes. Vision blurred. For a few seconds it seemed as if his head was about to burst. He wanted to cry out but couldn't. . . .

And then it was gone.

Bazzard blinked in astonishment. For a moment he wasn't even certain there'd been any pain at all. He moved a little, and felt a renewed twinge across his stiff neck and shoulders. Ah—that was it: he must have put pressure on a nerve or something while he was reaching in with the second case. Stiff shoulders at thirty-six, for God's sake! He'd have to get more exercise.

Folding himself into the cockpit, he twisted round and called to Ann to come up. He shifted over to the left-hand seat as her legs arrived in the doorway.

"Sorry I couldn't help you in, love. But I have to get in first since they only put one door on these crates. Chivalry seems to be dead in the Piper Aircraft Corporation."

Ann smiled a little shakily, and lowered herself into the right-hand seat beside him. Bazzard stretched across her and swung the door to, then reached up and twisted the top clip above her head to the locked position. As he brought his arm down he rested it lightly across her shoulders and leaned over and kissed her quickly on the cheek.

"Don't, Roy—there are people watching in the clubhouse."

Bazzard smiled and withdrew his arm. "Then I'll wait until we're in the air," he said.

"No, you jolly well won't. You'll be busy flying the plane, or the passengers are going to start complaining."

"Aha." Bazzard waved a hand, ignoring the twinge across his shoulders. "That's all *you* know—this little buggy caters for that. Once at altitude, the gallant aviator sticks it on autopilot and then has both hands free for chasing young ladies around the cockpit."

Ann burst out laughing. "Has it really got an autopilot, Roy?"

"Sure it has—two axis wing-leveller and heading-hold, if you're interested. What's so funny?"

"Oh . . ." Ann subsided into giggles. "It's just that my flatmate was talking about autopilots this morning, before you came. She said your plane was bound to have one, and that I'd have to fight for my honour all the way to Denham."

Chuckling, Bazzard showed Ann how to strap herself in; then he turned his attention to the chores which had to be performed before starting the aeroplane's engine. While his hands moved across the controls, Ann took her first good look around the cabin. The quality of the trim and décor surprised her; she'd vaguely imagined that a small plane cockpit would be coldly functional, like the fighter cockpits she'd seen in films. The whole inside of the Cherokee Arrow was finished in blue and white, matching the exterior, with neatly-fitting carpets and leather and broadcloth seats. The overall impression was like being in an expensive, if slightly antiseptic, motor car; even the two half-wheel control yokes, one in front of Roy and a duplicate in front of her own seat, were reminiscent of car steering wheels.

Forward of these wheels, however, the similarity ended. The curved blue nose of the aeroplane was so high that she had to crane her neck to see over it, and the instrument panel was covered with hundreds of dials, switches and levers.

Ann stared at the array in bewilderment. "How on earth do you know what all these things are for, Roy?"

That question was familiar to any pilot.

"Oh, it's not as bad as it looks. You're never using everything at once, for one thing. Most of the time you're just keeping track of speed, altitude, and heading—and then glancing down occasionally to the engine instruments to make sure the clockwork hasn't fallen out. Then the rest are mainly radio navigation aids, which you only use when you need them. Once you've got everything divided into sections in your mind, it's not difficult."

Ann shook her head. "It would be for me. I'm hopeless with mechanical things." She groped for something intelligent to say, then added, "So how fast will we be going, Roy?"

"Once we've finished climbing we'll cruise at about 155 m.p.h. We'll get to Denham in an hour and a half."

Impressed, Ann said, "Is that fast for a small plane?"

"Yeah. For a single engine job, anyway. This thing's a Piper Cherokee Arrow. Two hundred horsepower engine, with fuel injection, constant speed prop, and retractable undercarriage."

"Retractable undercarriage? You mean the wheels go up? What happens if they don't come down again?"

"Don't worry about it, love. For one thing, they always *do* come down. And for another, this particular kite's designed to take a belly landing without too much damage."

Bazzard had finished the checks. "I'm going to start the engine now, O.K.?"

Ann nodded. Bazzard twisted the key. The propeller churned over tinnily on the starter, then vanished· suddenly as the engine burst into life. The Arrow nodded on its nosewheel, and then the noise settled to a steady rushing rumble as Bazzard throttled back. Ann watched his hands and eyes moving round the cockpit, checking mysterious gauges and switches. She felt out of her element, slightly silly in her total ignorance of what he was doing. Her stomach felt hollow, and for an illogical moment she caught herself hoping that he'd find something slightly wrong; just wrong enough so they'd have to get out and go down by car. . . .

A voice from somewhere in the cockpit bellowed suddenly: "CALEDONIAN ONE-SEVEN-FOUR CLEAR TAXI RUNWAY TWO-FIVE . . ." Ann jumped, and Bazzard's hand whipped up to the radio to turn the volume down.

"Sorry about that, love. You never know if you've got it too loud until somebody talks. It's easier to tell if you're wearing headsets, but all ours are in the training aircraft today, so we're stuck with the hand-mike and the cabin speaker."

Ann nodded, not understanding a word. "That was the radio, was it? The one you talk to the people on the ground with?"

"Eh? Oh—yes." Bazzard glanced at her, surprised by her pale face: she was normally so calm and collected. "This is what you talk into," he said, smiling encouragingly. He brought the microphone up to his mouth, and pressed the button.

"Newcastle, good morning. This is Golf Alpha Yankee Whisky Tango, pre-flight check and request taxi."

The speaker over their heads replied immediately, talking fast. To Ann, it sounded like total garble. She looked at Roy, wondering how anyone could understand the high-speed metallic voice, but he was calmly making notes on his clipboard. After a moment he lifted the microphone and replied.

"Whisky Tango fives also, runway two-five, QNH one-zero-one-four." The speaker click-clicked in return.

Bazzard turned his head. "Sounds impossible the first time you hear it, doesn't it? Everyone thinks they'll never understand a word, then suddenly you get it." Then he added: "I'm going to start taxiing now, all right?"

Ann smiled nervously. The rumble of the engine seemed to be shivering in her stomach.

Bazzard reached down and released the parking brake, added a little more power, and the Arrow started to move. He screwed his head round to make sure the taxiway was clear, and the movement shot a bolt of pain through his neck.

"Here, Ann, do you know anything that's good for neck-ache?"

"Why, have you got one?"

"Yes, just a bit." Bazzard yawed the Arrow gently right and left as he taxied, checking the movement of the turn needle and the compasses. "In the muscles, it feels like."

Ann was immediately sympathetic. In the alien world of the small cockpit, a muscular pain was something she could understand.

"Is it bad? How long have you had it?"

"Woke up with it this morning. Must be getting old, y'know."

"Dreadful, isn't it?"

"Sure is." He glanced at her. "Not too old to appreciate having my neck rubbed by you, though. At the right moment, that is."

Ann smiled, relaxing.

At the end of the taxiway, Bazzard turned the Arrow into the wind, ran up the engine, and checked the propeller and magnetos. With the engine-run completed, he throttled back and started on the pre-take-off checks. The last item was "controls full and free", and he wound the half-wheel back and forth, looking out at ailerons and elevators to check their movement. Ann watched the duplicated control yoke in front of her own seat moving in unison.

"Is this dual controls, Roy?"

Bazzard nodded. "Yep. Everything I've got you've got on your side as well. You can have a go at flying it when we're in the air, if you like."

"N . . . no thanks. I'd rather you did it, this time."

Bazzard grinned again. "Me and the autopilot, love—I've got better things to do once we're under way."

The Arrow pulled out onto the runway and growled into the air at 1423 Greenwich Mean Time.

2

Tony Paynton was frozen. Crouching behind Jules Martin, he tugged at the fur collar of his flying jacket in a futile attempt to shut out the draughts whistling under the trainer's cockpit canopy, then gave it up and went back to staring moodily forwards.

The view ahead was less than inspiring, as were several other aspects of his tiny world aloft. For one thing, the engine of a de Havilland Chipmunk is unsilenced, its flat blare dinning into your bones. For another, the seating is arranged in tandem: in effect, two entirely separate single-seat cockpits, each with its own set of controls, one behind the other under a single long canopy. So, at this moment, with Chipmunk G-BCYL climbing through 6,500 feet, Paynton's forward vista consisted of the back of Martin's head, and then nothing but the wide brilliant sky and a vague brown line above the wings which was the distant horizon.

He watched the altimeter as the aircraft levelled out clumsily from the climb, and waited while Martin settled down to level flight. Then he raised his left hand and moved the headset microphone closer to his lips.

"Jules." His voice was calm and stolid with its Midlands accent.

"Jules, that last one was better, except you still didn't get the stick far enough forward. So now we'll do another one, to the left this time, and we'll hold it in a bit longer. Got that?"

In front of him the shoulders under the head hunched slightly, as if their owner was trying to scrunch down still farther in the seat. Jules was feeling apprehensive and a little airsick; he swallowed hard and tried to settle the butterflies in his stomach by keeping his eyes on the instruments in the cockpit. It didn't help very much. The all-pervading roar of the engine seemed to boom through his body, turning his bones to jelly and numbing his brain. He was very conscious that he was sitting on a few thin sheets of aluminium 7,000 feet up in the sky.

"Yes. O.K.," he mumbled.

"Right then, me old mate. So go. . . ." The voice in Martin's ears suddenly dissolved into a clashing crackle, and became a new voice, speaking slowly in a north-country accent.

". . . Charlie India's estimatin' Tees-side in, eh, abowt five minutes," it said. "Requestin' roonway in use an' . . . or . . . Quebec Fox Echo. Eh, ah . . . over."

Paynton stayed silent while he waited for the approach controller at Tees-side Airport to reply to the pilot of Charlie India and get the radio conversation over with. It was a nuisance having the air-to-ground radio and the front-to-rear cockpit intercom all going through the same box of tricks; for the hundredth time he wished there was some way of cutting out external transmissions while he was talking on the intercom.

The headphones said distantly, "Aircraft calling Tees-side approach; say again your full call sign."

"Eh . . . er . . ." The north-country voice hesitated. "What was that?"

Paynton raised his eyes to heaven. "Switch over a frequency or two, Jules. This dumb beggar'll be yapping away all day on this one!"

"Oh. Yes—roger." Martin leaned forward to reach the radio, and twisted the frequency knob from 118.85 M.h.z. to 116.85. He didn't know it was 116.85, and he didn't care. Getting rid of the distraction meant that he was going to have to spin the aeroplane, which he didn't want to do. On the other hand, though, the sooner

396

it was over with the sooner they could get down from this dizzy height and land. He sat back, his hands feeling hot and prickly, his feet trembling on the rudder.

"O.K. then, Jules. Let's do a clearing turn and then go into our spin. . . ." Paynton started giving instructions, his voice clattering over the intercom. Martin sat in silence, not taking it in. His brain was whirling and he was feeling ill. The only thought he had was that he wanted very much to be back on the ground.

AT THE SAME MOMENT, fifty miles away, Cherokee Arrow G-AYWT was passing through 1,000 feet. With the wheels and flaps up, Bazzard reduced power to the en-route climb setting and then glanced across at the girl for the first time since take-off. Her face was pale. He watched her anxiously for several seconds.

"You all right, love? If you really don't like it, just say. We can always go back and drive down instead."

"Oh, no. I'm all right." Ann swallowed. "It's just a bit . . . strange at first, that's all. It's not like a big plane at all, is it?"

Bazzard nodded, his eyes sliding back to the instruments. "That's true," he said. "This is real flying. Those big jets are like riding on the Underground." He looked at Ann again, and waved a hand at the left side window. "We picked a lovely day for it. You can see the whole of Newcastle. Look."

Ann twisted her head. The city was spread out far below, vast and toy-like in the brittle winter sunshine. Outside the window, the wing-tip marched slowly backwards across the miniature landscape as the aircraft turned. It felt as if they were just hanging in space, suspended at a dizzy height and not moving forwards at all. She swallowed again, and forced herself to keep looking out.

"You're lucky today," Bazzard said. "All you usually see this time of the year is a blanket of industrial crud."

Ann licked her lips, then said, "Why's that?"

"The smoke and vapour from all the factories." Bazzard rolled the Arrow out of its turn, and maintained the climb. "All the muck gets into the air and forms a big smoggy bubble over the place. You don't know what pollution is until you see it from the air."

Ann nodded, and turned her head again, shading her eyes. She was amazed at the way the plane didn't seem to be moving; she

397

had to look directly down before she could be sure that the ground was sliding backwards at all.

"How fast are we going, Roy?"

"A hundred miles an hour at the moment. I'm climbing up to four thousand to get over the top of all the military zones down south, particularly Leeming; they give you a right old run-around if you get into their airspace."

"A hundred! It doesn't feel as if we're moving at all."

Bazzard smiled. "It always feels like that. It's because of the height. The only time you get any impression of speed's when you're flying very low. Then the scenery fairly scoots by." He glanced at the altimeter and added, "I'm going to level out from the climb, now. When we're level you'll be able to see something out of the front."

Ann gripped the armrest beside her seat. Bazzard eased the nose down gently from the climbing attitude, then sat making small adjustments to the trim wheel and listening to the changing engine note as the airspeed crept up to 150 m.p.h. Easing the throttle back, he made a tiny adjustment to the propeller pitch to settle the revs at exactly 2,400. Then he lowered the nose a fraction and watched the altimeter as the hands slid down to precisely 4,000 feet. He checked the descent there, and carefully trimmed both elevator and rudder for straight and level flight.·

The speed settled at 155 m.p.h.

Experiencing the small superior glow that every pilot feels when he's successfully put his aircraft "on the step", he set about going round the cockpit doing all the after-climb chores which ought to be dealt with before switching in the autopilot. His neck twinged as he turned his head to Ann again.

"Better now we've finished climbing?"

Ann smiled at him. She was still pale, but not so tense as she had been. "I'm fine. Just beginning to get used to it."

Bazzard studied her for a moment. She looked as if she'd be all right after all. He grinned suddenly and said, "Right, Miss Moore. Time for the autopilot!"

He pressed the two white buttons on the bottom left-hand side of the panel, and let go of the control yoke with a flourish. The tenor of the Arrow's flight immediately underwent the subtle change which comes over all light aeroplanes when they go onto automatic stabilization; the aircraft made a tiny course correction, then droned on steadily. Ann watched the two unattended control wheels, momentarily fascinated. Their miniscule corrective movements as the wing-leveller operated were too small for her to see.

Bazzard said: "Now then, Madam. The time has come, I think, for a little in-flight entertainment!" He reached out and squeezed her hand.

"Oh, sir! No, sir. . . ."

They both laughed. The Arrow snored on placidly, the sunshine warm in the cockpit. After a minute Bazzard let her hand go and picked the microphone off its hook.

"Got to call Newcastle to say goodbye." He raised the mike to his lips and pressed the button. "Newcastle, Whisky Tango; leaving your area to the south, flight level four-zero, switching to Tees-side Approach."

The speaker clicked and replied, "Roger, Whisky Tango; and good day to you."

Bazzard clicked the transmit button twice in acknowledgment, then put the microphone down in his lap while he reached up to change the radio frequency. It was on Newcastle Approach, 126.35, and it had to be switched to Tees-side on 118.85. He started by twisting the decimal knob from .35 to .85 . . .

And then passed out.

It happened in an instant, so quickly that he himself was hardly aware of it. There was a split-second bolt of blinding pain in the back of his head, and then consciousness blacked out. His body slumped forward against the diagonal shoulder strap.

It was several seconds before Ann realized that anything had happened. She heard Roy make a small grunting noise, and turned to look at him. He was sitting more or less upright, with his eyes closed.

"Having a nap, are you?" she said jokingly.

Bazzard didn't say anything.

Ann stared at him for a long moment, the smile fading from her face. Even then she didn't realize the calamity. Conscious of a strong feeling of disappointment—she hadn't thought Roy was the sort to play vicious jokes—she said icily and distinctly, "You beast. That isn't even a tiny bit funny."

Bazzard didn't move.

Suddenly furious and frightened, Ann twisted in her seat and slapped him twice round the face with all her strength. Bazzard stayed upright, eyes still closed.

The Arrow flew on. The burring rumble of the engine seemed to fill the cabin. Realization trickled through.

Ann's eyes dilated. Her face changed from anger to terror, colour draining away, as she stared at Roy. The implications hit her one by one; slowly, then in a rush. After a long moment she swung wildly round, staring at the far reaches of the empty horizon, panic welling up in her throat.

Then, because she'd seen Roy using it, she snatched the microphone from his lap and pressed the button.

She screamed.

JULES MARTIN wiped a hand over his face, fumbled with the boom-mike, then said abruptly, "D'you mind if we go back, Tony?"

In the rear cockpit, Paynton was instantly sympathetic. Like most flying instructors, he'd suffered from airsickness himself.

"Certainly, Jules. Soon as you like. You have control. Turn to a heading of—er—zero-two-zero, and we'll be home in ten minutes. We're not far away from Tees-side."

Martin nodded. The Chipmunk made little uneasy lurching movements as he took over the controls. The first thing an instructor always does if a student feels ill is to make him fly the aeroplane; it gives him something else to do apart from sit there feeling sick.

Paynton reached up and forward, twisted a yellow handle on the inside of the canopy roof, and hauled backwards. The noise of the airflow deepened immediately to a booming open roar, and the cockpit became colder than ever.

"That better, me old mate?"

"Uh . . . er . . . yes." Martin was past thinking about whether it was better or not. The hollow feeling in his gut had become a nasty churning sensation. Cowed by the naked blast of the gale

400

and the thunder of the engine, he just wanted to get down. He wondered blearily how far it was to the airfield.

"Can you take her again please, Tony?"

Paynton took the controls.

"O.K., I've got it. Not feeling so good, Jules?"

The head in front of him waggled miserably, then scrunched down as Martin bent forward and fumbled in the map pocket for a sick-bag. Paynton leaned left and then right, looking down. A railway line was sliding under the left wing, the town of Darlington was about five miles ahead, and the River Tees meandered through the fields directly below. That made the aerodrome under the nose and about four miles away.

"Nearly home now, Jules. Just two or three minutes. Will you switch the radio back to 118.85, please?"

Martin stretched forward and reached for the radio. His hand was shaking as he found the main frequency selector, and turned it quickly and clumsily. Too far. The figures in the frequency window flicked from 116.85 right through to 129.85. As they went, there was a momentary screeching in Martin's headphones. He winced and turned the knob back again quickly.

"That's it," he said, with a grunt of relief. "118.85."

Paynton was frowning. That split-second screech had been an odd sort of sound, somehow unlike the usual sort of interference. It wasn't the time to start mucking around with the radio—not with Jules about to bring his guts up—but all the same, it *had* sounded strange. . . .

"Hey, Jules," he said suddenly. "Just flip back to that frequency you hit a moment ago, will you?"

Martin groaned. Slowly he leaned forward again and twisted the knob. The movement made his head swim. The frequency figures clicked round to 119.85, 120.85, and on.

At 126.85 the noise came back, piercingly loud. For a few seconds it sounded like nothing but feedback screech—and then, all at once, it resolved into a young woman's voice, screaming and almost incoherent.

"*Oh GOD . . . please ANSWER! He's PASSED OUT! Somebody . . . anybody . . . PLEASE HELP me . . . !*"

At that moment Martin vomited. The spasms squeezed through

401

his whole body, filling his head with a huge dull roaring and leaving him clawing for breath. He slumped forward.

Paynton didn't even notice. He just sat, frozen with shock, while the blood-curdling shrieking in his earphones went on without break or pause. The raw panic in the woman's voice seemed to paralyse his brain: dimly he knew he ought to be doing something, but he couldn't think what.

"Oh *God!* Won't someone *answer! Please* help me . . ."

Paynton snapped back to life in a rush.

Reaching up to the yellow handle, he slammed the canopy shut. Then he opened the throttle to full power, pulled the nose up towards the cold blue sky, and bent the Chipmunk into a gentle climbing turn: the first essential was not to lose the transmission, and more altitude meant more radio range.

The Chipmunk blared upwards in a slow spiral. Paynton re-trimmed for the climb and wondered what to do next.

The problem was horrible in its simplicity. From the distorted words he could pick out among the screams and sobs it was fairly obvious what had happened, but on the face of it there seemed to be nothing that he could do. For the moment, at least, he couldn't even talk back to the woman. An aircraft radio is so designed that it cannot transmit and receive simultaneously; pressing the transmit button automatically cuts out the receiver. So until she stopped screaming and let go of her transmit switch, Paynton couldn't get through, even if he yelled his lungs out.

Not that it would make any difference one way or the other, he thought. Because whatever happened, the woman was going to die within the next few minutes.

The reason for this was simply that no aeroplane, left to its own devices, will continue to fly straight and level for very long. If a pilot takes his hands and feet off the controls, after a short while the aircraft will adopt a banked attitude, and this bank will cause a turn. The turn itself will then create further bank in a self-perpetuating process, until the machine ends up in a steeply-descending spiral dive. This phenomenon is no problem to an experienced pilot, since preventing a spiral dive while flying is as instinctive as steering a straight line in a car—but the chances that someone who didn't have the faintest idea about flying would stumble on the correct recovery action before the aircraft hit the ground were so small they just didn't exist.

And the one thing that was clear was that this woman didn't have the faintest idea about flying.

So he waited for her to die, as the voice went on pleading, the words blurring into wild sobbing. And meanwhile Jules vomited again, shaking his head from side to side in his helplessness.

Paynton was sweating in the freezing cockpit. Listening to the

403

woman crying was somehow like an intrusion; nobody had the right to listen to another human being panicking through the last seconds of her life. He wanted to yell at Jules to switch frequencies again, so he wouldn't have to hear the final terrible screams and the aching silence that would follow.

But he kept his mouth shut. For some reason it didn't seem right to let the woman die alone, either. He waited, desperately trying to think of something he could try.

Maybe she was on autopilot.

The thought came with sudden clarity, halting his racing brain in its tracks. Cursing himself for not thinking of it before, he examined the possibility. It could well be right, at that: he'd been listening to her now for about four minutes, and yet here she was, still in the air. *And* it was reasonable to suppose that any pilot who thought he might be going to pass out would switch in the autopilot if he had one.

He drew in a deep breath, finding he was shaking with tension. She certainly *could* be on some kind of autopilot. And that made a difference. In that case something might be done. He ought to switch back to Tees-side, get out a Mayday call. . . .

The crying in his headphones suddenly stopped.

TERROR, complete and undiluted terror, is a violent physical force. Unless it can be channelled into action, it feeds on itself. And for Ann Moore, suddenly alone in the roaring cockpit with its thousand alien controls, the only outlet for her terror was the microphone; and when nobody answered, panic grew like a spreading fire.

How long she screamed and sobbed she had no way of knowing: it was actually about five minutes, but to her it could have been seconds or hours. She struggled against her seatbelt, shouting half at Roy and half into the microphone, imploring him to wake up.

Bazzard sat unheeding, eyes closed, head stiffly upright. The Arrow droned on smoothly, the autopilot holding it rock-steady in the calm winter sky.

In the end, Ann crumpled. Crying wildly, she buried her face in her clenched fists, trying to shut out the sight of the cockpit and the terrifying emptiness all around. No one was listening, no one was going to do anything.

The microphone slipped down as she released it, clunking softly onto the carpeted floor. Immediately, the speaker in the cabin roof crackled and broke into slow deliberate speech.

"Aircraft in trouble. Do not do anything, and do not *attempt to reply to me yet. I repeat, do* not *attempt to reply to me yet."*

Ann jerked in her seat, shock making her shriek in new fright. Then she screamed and laughed all at once, unable to stop herself. Her hands went to her ears to shut out the horrible sound of her own hysteria; then, slowly, the screaming began to subside. You've *got* to pull yourself together, she thought desperately. You're a nurse; you're supposed to be cool, sensible, reasoning. . . .

The voice started speaking over the radio again.

"Aircraft in trouble, I say again." The words were clearly pronounced, matter-of-fact. "Do *not* attempt to reply to me until I tell you. Up to now you have been holding your microphone button down all the time. When you do that, you cannot hear me talking to you. Now, in a moment, I want you to speak to me again. But this time, just press the microphone button, say 'yes', *and then release it again,* so that I can talk some more. If you understand that, say 'yes' now; if you do not, then do not say anything, and I will explain it again."

For God's sake, where was the microphone?

Ann looked wildly round the cockpit, panting. The mass of dials and switches and levers seemed to mock at her helplessness, hiding the black matchbox-sized cube amongst them. If she didn't find it the voice would go away. She'd had it just now; it'd been hooked under the bulge where the coloured levers were. . . .

Then she saw the curly black lead it was connected to. She grabbed the lead, and a second later she had the microphone in her hands. She snatched it up to her lips and squeezed the button with all her strength.

"Yes. *Yes!*" It came out in a muted, terrified croak. It was several seconds before she remembered to let the button go.

". . . Tell me calmly and clearly what has happened, without speaking for too long, and remember to release the microphone button when you stop talking. Tell me now."

Ann took a deep breath, feeling her whole body shuddering. However crazy, however incredible it was to be talking to a disembodied voice speaking in the cockpit out of thin air, she *had* to calm down, had to answer.

"I'm . . . in a plane. Roy—the pilot—he's passed out." The words sounded hollow and strange; disconnected, as if somebody else a long way away was saying them. "He passed out suddenly, and I can't make him wake up. I don't . . . don't know . . ."

It was another long moment before she took her thumb off the transmit button; this time, the man seemed to have been waiting for her.

"All right, miss. Just relax, and we'll get this sorted out. Now first of all, do you happen to know if the aeroplane's flying on autopilot? I say again: is it flying on autopilot?"

For a moment, Ann blinked—and then the memory came suddenly. Of course it was. There'd been all that talk about it. Roy had switched it on, and then they'd held hands.

She felt the trickle of new tears on her face. She *had* to stop being stupid. . . .

"Come on now, miss." There was a trace of urgency in the voice this time. "I need to know that now."

Ann raised the microphone and said hoarsely, "Yes." She cleared her throat. "Yes, it is. He put it on before . . . before it happened."

"Ah. Good." Paynton's relieved tone was lost in the distant hiss of the Chipmunk's transmitter. "That gives us plenty of time, then. So first of all I want you to sit back and relax, get a grip on yourself, and just listen."

The voice was unruffled and masterful: Paynton was a good instructor. Ann squeezed her eyes shut and leaned back, gripping the sides of her seat, trying to still her fluttering muscles. Just pretend it's a hospital emergency, she thought lightheadedly; calm down and think sensibly. She stared at the radio panel directly in front of her, and raised the microphone. It quivered in her hand.

"I'm . . . all right, now."

"That's good." The slow disembodied voice seemed to fill the cabin. Its matter-of-fact, Midlands accent was somehow steadying. "Now, my name's Tony Paynton. I'm a flying instructor, and I'm

406

in the air at the moment over Tees-side. I'm going to help you, and I want to start off by asking you some questions. First of all, you'd better tell me your name."

Ann pressed the button and said, "Moore. Ann Moore."

"Good, that's fine, Ann. So first off, let's just make sure I've got everything straight. You're in an aeroplane, on autopilot, and the pilot has passed out. He's unconscious. Is that right?"

Ann looked at Bazzard's still figure beside her. His face was deathly white and immobile, lips slightly parted. His shirt-front moved in slow irregular jerks as he breathed. She wrenched her eyes back to the radio, feeling herself trembling. She *must* think only about answering the questions . . .

She swallowed stickily, and pressed the microphone switch.

"Yes. Yes . . . that's right."

"O.K. I see." The voice paused for a moment. "Now the next thing is, have you been talking to anyone else—was I the first person to answer you?"

"You were . . . you were the only one."

"Right. Now, have you tried to revive your pilot at all?"

"Yes. I did slap his face." Ann felt more tears starting down her cheeks. "But there was no reaction."

"All right, Ann." In spite of the radio static the voice was somehow soothing, reassuring. "Forget that for the moment; we'll come back to it later on when we've got a doctor lined up on the ground. Now, I've got one or two questions about the aeroplane you're in and where you are. O.K.?"

Ann took a deep, shuddering breath. "Yes. Go on."

"Right. First, do you know what kind of aeroplane it is?"

She bit her bottom lip, trying to think.

"I don't know. He—Roy—said, but I don't remember. It . . . um . . . the wheels go up and down, I remember that, if that's any help . . . I mean . . . I've never been in a small plane before . . ." She tailed off, hopelessly.

"Aye, I'd rather got that impression." The voice was deliberately droll and unconcerned. "What you *can* tell me though, I expect, is the pilot's name."

"Bazzard." Ann rubbed her eyes. "R-Roy Bazzard." She spelled it out.

"Fine. And now, would you tell me where you took off from, and where you're going to?"

"We went from Woolsington Airport, in Newcastle. We were going to . . . er, Denham. Near London."

"Good. Now, how long ago did you take off from Newcastle?"

Ann tried to cast her mind back. She hadn't noticed the time before they left, and like most nurses she didn't wear a wristwatch. The watch she had was pinned to her uniform, back at home. She cleared her throat and said into the microphone, "I don't know. It was after lunchtime. About . . . half an hour ago, I suppose. I don't know."

"All right, not to worry. Now, can you tell me where the sun is in relation to you? It may sound silly, but it'll tell me which way you're heading, you see."

The sun . . . ?

Reluctantly, she raised her eyes to the windscreen. The huge emptiness of the sky and the vast distance of the horizon brought on a new rush of fear, like cold water in her stomach.

"It's to the r-right. Ahead and a bit to the right."

"Good. And now, lastly, it'll help if you can tell me whether your aeroplane has one engine or two. In other words whether it's got two propellers, or just one on the nose, in front of you."

"J-just one, on the nose. Roy said it was s-single engine."

"Ah, that's fine. You've done very well, Ann." The voice hesitated, then carried on. "Now, I'm going to leave you for a moment while I talk to the people on the ground. I'll be back to you in a minute or two, so just sit tight. And don't touch anything. O.K.?"

Ann nodded. The idea of touching anything in the cockpit filled her with horror.

"Yes. O.K.," she said dully.

"Good. All right then, I'll leave you now. You just relax."

Ann nodded for the second time. With the man's voice gone, the steady burr of the engine seemed to close in, pressing on her ears. She suddenly felt terribly alone. She clenched her teeth to stop them chattering, and gripped the microphone tightly in her right hand, as if it were something infinitely precious.

The Arrow roared on, serene and steady.

408

"Jules!"

His thumb off the transmit button, Paynton was talking over the intercom to his pupil in the front seat of the Chipmunk. Martin didn't respond. He'd stopped listening to the voices in his earphones some time ago; they'd just become part of the background to an interminable nightmare.

"*Jules!* Come on! Switch the radio to 118.85!"

Martin coughed, then leaned forward laboriously and twisted the main frequency knob. He didn't know what Paynton was doing, and felt too ill to care, his body swept by alternate waves of hot and cold. All he wanted was to get to his feet on the good earth and never, never get into an aeroplane again.

Paynton, on the other hand, was just cold. Cold and worried and trying to assemble the important factors logically in his mind before he started talking to Tees-side Approach. He screwed his head from side to side, searching the empty sky. There was no sign of anything, which was about what he'd expected: an aircraft out of Newcastle half an hour ago and heading south should be *somewhere* in this area—but *somewhere* covered an awful lot of sky. And even if by some freak of chance he did see it, he wouldn't be able to catch it up; if it had a retractable undercarriage and an autopilot it was certainly something a damn sight faster than any Chipmunk.

And then there was the other problem, too: fuel. Because he'd wanted the Chipmunk light for Martin's spinning exercise, Paynton had taken off with considerably less than full tanks. Now, the port fuel gauge read just under two gallons while the starboard one indicated between 0 and two—and even that wouldn't be accurate, since Chipmunk gauges are somewhat optimistic when the aircraft is climbing. The more likely figure was a total of two gallons or a fraction more in both tanks. And a Chipmunk burns six gallons of 100 octane an hour.

Paynton frowned at the instrument panel, pursing his lips. Then he pressed the transmit button on top of his control stick.

"Mayday, Mayday, Mayday," he said calmly. "Tees-side from Golf-Bravo-Charlie-Yankee-Lima, d'you read?"

The radio crackled, hesitated, and then the flight controller at Tees-side replied.

3

Two and a half miles north of Heathrow Airport, in a road called Porters Way, West Drayton, is a large concrete and glass building constructed on the graceless lines of most modern industrial architecture. At first glance it looks like any one of a thousand office blocks in and around London: the only obvious differences are the police guardhouse on the gate and the soaring tower of radar dishes alongside. There is nothing else to indicate that the staff of this ugly block are the guardians of most of the airspace over England.

The building is known as the London Air Traffic Control Centre —abbreviated to LATCC and usually referred to as "Latsie" by everyone concerned in aviation. And here, under one roof, practically every inch of the country's airways network is monitored and controlled minute by minute, twenty-four hours a day. Radar pictures and radio links are "piped in" from fifty or sixty ground stations all over the country, and over a hundred licensed air traffic controllers are on duty at all times. Thus an aircraft flying between Prestwick and Manchester will be talking to a controller at West Drayton. This system means that as an airway's flight progresses through different radar areas, the aeroplane is "handed off" through a number of controllers sitting within yards of each other instead of hundreds of miles apart.

LATCC's responsibilities, moreover, do not end with en-route airways' control. Two corridors away from the main centre control room, with its eighty-odd radar screens, is another much smaller room; dim-lit, cluttered with sophisticated equipment, it is known throughout aviation circles simply as "D and D": Distress and Diversion. The correct name for this room is the Emergency Cell.

The role of D and D is as the title suggests: to provide and co-ordinate action in the event of an airborne emergency. The service is run by the RAF (as opposed to most of the rest of the centre, which is operated by the Civil Aviation Authority) but its function is by no means restricted to military aircraft alone. Any aeroplane in any kind of trouble in the skies of England may be assisted by D and D—and assisted with considerable power, since the drawing-room-sized Emergency Cell has at its immediate call every facility of every aerodrome, military or civil, throughout the land.

On this Saturday afternoon, it looked as though that power might come in useful.

The call from the chief controller at Tees-side Airport was taken by Flight Lieutenant John Peterson, the number-one D and D controller on duty. As the Yorkshire voice talked in his headphones, Peterson made brief notes in his log: time and nature of emergency.

When the man had finished, Peterson sat silent for a moment. A tall, wiry man, full of nervous energy, his natural impulse in any emergency was to act immediately. But his years of experience had taught him that whenever there was even a little time to spare in an aircraft incident, it was invariably worth using that time to think things over. He frowned at the foot-round radar screen on the console in front of him for nearly half a minute while he examined the problem. Then he swung round suddenly in his chair.

"Corporal!"

His corporal assistant was just entering the room. "Sir?"

"Listen. We've got a civilian instructor in a Chipmunk over Tees-side, who's picked up a transmission from a woman on 126.85. Apparently she's in an aeroplane with the pilot passed out or possibly dead. She doesn't know anything about the kite except that it's a single engine retract, on autopilot, heading more or less south, and it took off from Newcastle bound for Denham about half an hour ago. The Chipmunk pilot's talking to her again now, and he's going to call Tees-side back in five minutes."

The corporal said quietly, "My God!"

"Quite. Now one thing I want to know is, what ground station radios operate on 126.85? See if you can find that out bloody quick, will you?"

The corporal crossed the floor in three paces to the shelves of reference books at the back of the room.

Peterson chewed a fingernail. Finding out who had the 126.85 frequency was important—ground radio installations cannot switch frequencies like aircraft receivers, which meant that his only

411

chance of talking to the woman directly was if some station within her range already had the frequency—but far more urgent was the problem of locating the runaway aircraft and getting a doctor organized to advise on bringing the pilot round.

He leaned forward and dialled the code for Woolsington control tower on the Mediator private telephone network between air traffic controllers. Five seconds after he'd finished dialling, Peterson heard a northern accent answer briefly, "Newcastle, Woolsington; go ahead."

"D and D, Drayton here." Peterson visualized the Newcastle controller snapping to sudden alertness as he swiftly described the situation to him and spelled out Bazzard's name. "That's all we know about it at the moment, so I want aircraft type, callsign, the owner or operator's name and anything else you can give me."

The voice in the receiver sounded shaken. "Stand by, D and D. I'll check."

Peterson heard muffled sounds as the controller shouted for someone to check the logbook—which is legally required at all British control towers to record details of every landing-away flight.

The man was back in under a minute.

"Got it, Drayton. Bazzard's flying a Piper Cherokee Arrow, Golf Alpha Yankee Whisky Tango, VFR to Denham. He took off at 1423 hours. The Arrow's one of the Tyne Flyin' Club's planes—they're on Newcastle 72876."

"Thanks." Peterson wrote fast on his notepad. "Now, do you have 126.85 up there at all? Apparently that's what the woman's transmitting on."

"Negative. Nearest would probably be one of Tees-side's: their Approach is 118.85, and they've got radar on 128.85."

"Right. Much obliged. One last thing: d'you happen to know what an Arrow cruises at?"

"About 150 knots, I think. 150 or 160."

"O.K. Thanks again."

Peterson broke the connection, and glanced at the clock on the wall. The time was 1441, which meant that the Arrow had now been airborne for just about eighteen minutes. Less than the woman had said to Paynton, but that was hardly surprising: it

412

probably felt like eighteen years to her. He chewed the end of his pencil for a moment, calculating. Reckon on an average of 130 m.p.h. . . . call it thirty-five miles. Between thirty-five and forty.

He reached forward and gripped the butt of a swivelling device mounted on the top edge of his radar console. Squeezing the trigger produced a small cross of light on a sheet of milky glass which covered a wall ten feet in front of him. Painted on the glass was a simple outline map of England, showing the position of aerodromes, major control zones, towns, and radar stations. Flexing his wrist, he traversed the light-cross to Newcastle, then slowly down again, due south, for a distance equal to roughly forty miles. The cross came to rest about fifteen miles north of the RAF Master Airfield of Leeming, in the North Riding of Yorkshire.

Well, that was a start, anyway. If the runaway *was* somewhere around there, then it should already be painting a trace on Leeming's radar screens, and possibly Tees-side's as well. . . .

Peterson leaned back, chewing his pencil, and thought about what they were going to do when they *had* found Whisky Tango. If the pilot was dead or otherwise unrevivable, there would obviously have to be some sort of attempt made to talk the woman through flying and landing the aeroplane. And that raised the question of how the hell to do it.

A pilot himself, he had no illusions about the chances of successfully talking down a non-pilot from the ground. That idea was strictly for adventure comics and film producers: in real life, it simply couldn't be done. If the person in the aircraft knew enough to circle over you so you could watch the results of your instructions it *might* just work—but if she was flying in a straight line a couple of hundred miles away then there wouldn't be a chance. Telling her to pull back a little on the stick might produce a two-degree change in angle or it might send her screaming up into a loop, and sitting in front of your radar screen you'd have no way of knowing which. So that seemed to leave interception by another aircraft as the only possibility: get the talk-down pilot sitting in formation with her where he could follow her progress second by second.

But the first thing was still to get the search under way and a doctor available, and time was passing.

Peterson looked up expectantly as the corporal reappeared at his elbow.

"I can't find anyone with 126.85, sir. It seems to be a spare frequency, unless some company's got it privately."

Peterson said, "Blast!" very softly. Then he looked down at his pad. "You know what could have happened," he said slowly. His finger tapped on the scrawled page. "Our pilot could've been switching from Newcastle to Tees-side when he went out. He'd have been on 126.35, so if he'd switched the decimals first, and then passed out, he'd have ended up on his 126.85. See what I mean?"

The corporal sucked his teeth. "He'd have to have passed out jolly quick for that to've happened, sir."

"That's true." Peterson shrugged. "But there's no use thinking about the why of it: if no one can get her to change frequencies it means we're stuck with relaying through other aircraft, and that's that. Now then: I want you to get me the Tyne Flying Club, Newcastle 72876. Get the chief instructor—full priority—and hold him until I can speak to him. Right? Then get Leeds-Bradford Approach on the Mediator."

"Yes, sir." The corporal looked slightly stunned. He snatched a headset over his ears, and reached for the telephone switches.

Peterson glanced down at the small panel of buttons on his console which controlled the direct ground-link to all RAF Master Aerodromes. His finger hovered for a second and then stabbed the one marked LMG, for Leeming.

THE APPROACH CONTROL ROOM at RAF Leeming, thirty-five miles north of Leeds, is a quiet place on a Saturday afternoon. With British service flying cut back to a minimum over the weekends, the controllers simply keep a general eye on civil aircraft and issue occasional Military Air Traffic Zone clearances to aeroplanes en route below 3,000 feet. Flight Lieutenants John Myers and Mark Trowbridge, manning the Approach and Director screens respectively, had very little to do.

Myers was bored. He had his chair tipped back on the point of balance, his knees nearly up to his chest, his feet on the edge of his control desk. He kept half an eye on his radar screen, noting almost subconsciously the various traces within the sweep. There was quite a lot about this afternoon: the unexpected fine weather had brought out all the weekend birdmen.

Suddenly, the red telephone on his desk rang.

Myers whipped his feet down. The red telephone was a direct ground-link to Distress and Diversion and nowhere else. Every RAF Master Station in the country had a similar red phone, and when it rang it meant *move*.

"Leeming Approach Controller," Myers said crisply. "Go ahead." He looked round his control desk, then snapped his fingers urgently. Trowbridge handed him a ballpoint pen.

The voice on the telephone started speaking rapidly. "We have a civilian light aircraft in your vicinity with the pilot dead or passed out, and a woman on board who can't fly. She's talking to the pilot of a Chipmunk overhead Tees-side Airport. This Chipmunk will be handed off to you in about three minutes, and he's requesting a doctor on hand to relay advice. Can you get your Medical Officer on the spot?"

Myers snapped, "Stand by," and passed on the order to Trowbridge. Trowbridge grabbed for the internal telephone.

"O.K., Drayton, that's in hand. Is this aeroplane in my area?"

"Affirmative. It's a Piper Cherokee Arrow, Golf Alpha Yankee Whisky Tango, off Newcastle at 1423 for Denham. According to the woman it's on autopilot, and it's cruising more or less southerly at around 150–160 knots—so it ought to be about fifteen miles north of you now. The woman's transmitting on 126.85, so you won't be able to get a DF on her unless the Chipmunk pilot can get her to switch. But we've got to find her somehow, so in the meantime start trying to sort her out on radar. O.K.?"

Myers's initial reaction was one of hopelessness: the D and D man must know that sorting out one unidentified blip from all the others was going to be next to impossible. His radar screen was sweeping a thirty-mile radius, and at the moment he had eight or ten traces of civilian aircraft en route or on training flights. Only one, a Piper Apache from Norwich on its way to Carlisle, was in radio contact. The rest could be anything.

The voice in the receiver said, "I know it'll be difficult, but we've got to try. Flight Information'll be switching their known traffic in the area to you to identify, and we'll be calling the light aircraft fields to get their pilots to contact you as well. You should be able to eliminate most of them, anyway. Call me back when you've got anything, and also when you've spoken to the Chipmunk. O.K.?"

Myers said, "Roger." He clapped his headset on, and reached for a Chinagraph pencil to start tracing the echoes on his screen.

As PAYNTON put out his Mayday call to Tees-side, Ann Moore was making Bazzard as comfortable as she could.

The realization that up to now she'd practically ignored him penetrated her fear like a shock of cold water. And she a senior nursing sister. . . . She set to work. Twisting in her seat, she pulled his tie loose and unbuttoned his shirt collar. It made no visible difference: he went on breathing slowly and erratically, each breath rasping through his slightly parted lips. She undid his seat belt, her fingers shaking and clumsy, and unfastened the top of his trousers to relieve the pressure on his abdomen. Then she struggled with the buckle end of his lap-strap until the adjuster slackened off, and pulled the limp body forwards until it rested against the diagonal shoulder strap. With Bazzard's neck rigid, it was the only way of getting his head far enough forward to ensure that he wouldn't choke on his tongue.

After that she sat back, trying to think what to do next. Her mind seemed to be a woolly blank, every thought disjointed and spaced out. There must be *something* else she ought to be doing . . . At least she should examine him.

She picked up his right hand. It was a large hand, very masculine and capable-looking, which somehow made its flaccidness all the more frightening. His skin was cool under her fingers as she felt for the pulse; the beat was thin and erratic. She put the hand back in his lap after half a minute and, reaching up to his face, raised his eyelids, first one and then the other. The eyeballs were rolled upwards, but the bottoms of the pupils were still visible. Both were dilated.

That ought to add up to something, she thought. Neck muscles in spasm, pupil dilation, irregular pulse and respiration. . . . The words squirrelled round in her mind, repeating themselves in a

416

mocking rhythm. Somewhere, dimly, they seemed to ring a bell, as if she'd heard them before. She tried to catch them, to wrench the meaning out of them, but they wouldn't stand still.

Sudden collapse; neck in spasm; irregular pulse and respiration . . .

It was no good. She couldn't remember. It was like being drunk, or only half awake. She shook her head and whispered hopelessly, "Please be all right, Roy. *Please* be all right . . ."

After a long moment she twisted round as far as her seatbelt would allow and reached back to where her thigh-length overcoat was lying on the rear seat. She opened it out and draped it over Roy's shoulders like a cloak, pushing it down behind his back. It wouldn't make much difference, but it might help a bit. Body temperature was very important. . . .

Paynton's voice came over the speaker with startling suddenness.

"Hello there, Ann. You still with us?"

She gasped with shock, then fumbled in her lap and snatched the microphone up to her mouth.

"Yes." She cleared her throat. "Yes."

"Good. Just keep your voice loud and clear, O.K.?"

"All right."

"Fine. Now, I want you to tell me about—er, Roy, isn't it? So that I can pass it on to a doctor in a minute. Just answer as many questions as you can. Are you ready to do that?"

Ann glanced nervously at Bazzard. The stillness of him suddenly frightened her more than ever, making her stomach sink and her face hot and tingling. She swallowed hard.

"Y-yes," she said. "Yes. I'm ready."

AT 8,000 FEET, still climbing in a slow spiral, Paynton was frozen to the marrow. His hands and feet were almost totally numb, and he was shivering constantly. But he wasn't thinking about the cold. Or about Jules, huddled miserably in front of him. As the Chipmunk's nose slowly traversed the winter horizon, his entire concentration was focused on the urgent need to ask the girl the right questions . . . and on the fact that her radio signal strength was fading.

It was the first thing he'd noticed when he came back to her after talking to Tees-side; her voice was markedly fainter than it had been five minutes before. He could just about make out what she was saying at the moment, but if she continued to fade she was going to become unreadable within a very short time. Perhaps he should ask a ground station to take over. Except that he couldn't think of a single one with 126.85. . . .

He pressed the transmit button again and spoke slowly and loudly, keeping the anxiety out of his voice.

"Let's start off with any advance symptoms, Ann. Tell me if Roy was complaining of anything at all before he passed out."

The girl's voice came back blurred and distorted. "He had . . . muscular pains this morning . . . thing apart from that."

It's the distance, Paynton thought. She was flying away from him, down south, lengthening the radio range. The obvious answer was to quit making small circles over Tees-side and follow her. He wouldn't catch her up, but at least he'd be slowing down the rate of separation, which would keep her in radio contact for as long as possible. The only thing was, one didn't normally turn one's back on a known airfield with only fifteen or twenty minutes' fuel left.

Paynton wavered, undecided. His teeth chattered in the freezing cockpit. Then he thumbed the transmit button again.

"O.K. Ann, I've got that. Now, can you tell me just *how* he passed out? How sudden it was, whether he moved his hands to any part of his body, that sort of thing. O.K.?"

". . . didn't see him . . . pass out . . . heard him grunt . . . then unconscious. It . . . ve . . . sudden. As if . . . been hit."

The voice in his headphones was almost inaudible. Suddenly losing patience, Paynton abruptly slammed the stick to the left and pushed the throttle wide open.

"*Jules!*" he shouted into the intercom. "We're going after her. Turn the radio volume up full, and re-set the squelch—*get on with it!*"

After a moment, the head bent slowly forwards. A few seconds later the carrier-wave hiss in Paynton's headset abruptly increased, and then backed off again as Martin filtered out interference with the squelch knob.

"Thanks, Jules. Sorry about all this, but we won't be at it much longer."

418

Paynton eased back the throttle a little as the airspeed crept past 110 knots, and pressed the transmit button again.

"Hello, Ann. Sorry about going off for a moment there. Now, can I confirm that Roy passed out very suddenly with no warning signs? Speak up nice and clearly."

This time the girl's voice was louder, although more distorted than before. Paynton had been expecting that; he only hoped that his turn to the south would keep him in radio range for long enough to achieve something useful.

"It . . . very sudden. He grunted . . . then . . . unconscious."

"O.K., I've got that. Now you said you slapped him, Ann. So can you confirm that that produced no response at all?"

"No. No response."

"Oh. Hmmm." Paynton tried to think what to ask next. Even as he thought, part of his brain was worrying about his own immediate destiny. If he kept up this course for another five minutes he was going to have to forget about going back to Tees-side. So maybe he'd best think in terms of lobbing into RAF Leeming, fifteen miles to the south. They might not like him pitching up out of the blue, but . . .

He cleared his throat and thumbed the button again.

"What about now, Ann? What is his breathing like?"

The girl's voice came back, hesitant and faint.

"It's . . . irregular . . . depth and timing. Pulse is . . . irregular. His neck . . . scles . . . in spasm. Pupils are . . . dilated."

Paynton blinked, startled by the phraseology. On impulse, he said, "Are—er—are you in medicine at all, Ann? You seem to know what you're talking about."

"I'm . . . nurse. A n . . . ing sister."

"Oh." Paynton hesitated, finnicking with the trim wheel and looking out at the sun glaring on the wings. Then he squeezed his eyes shut for a moment. Concentrated. "Respiration and pulse irregular. Neck in spasm. And the collapse was sudden. O.K., I've got that, then. Do you have any idea what it might be, yourself, that I could pass on?"

There were a few seconds silence. Belatedly he wondered if he might have said the wrong thing. If the pilot wasn't going to recover it might not be a good idea if she realized it suddenly.

419

Then the girl came back, slower and fainter than ever.

"I can't seem . . . think properly. It's like . . . oh, *God!*" Her voice rose suddenly, almost to a scream. "Oh *God.* . . ."

Paynton took a fast breath, pressed his own transmit button, and spoke calmly and soothingly.

"Well, don't worry about it any more, Ann. I'm sure I've got enough now to pass on to a doctor and get some help. So you just relax for a bit and don't worry about it. O.K.?"

For a time, there was nothing but the frying-pan sizzle of the radio. Then the voice came again, slow and wavering with terror, catching on the words.

"I think . . . he's had a s-subarachnoid haemorrhage."

SQUADRON LEADER DR. JOHN OSCOTT, Medical Officer at RAF Leeming, arrived in the Approach Room at fourteen minutes to three. Trowbridge's telephone call had caught him in his garden on the married quarters estate, and he'd come straight away. Large and florid, wearing an old tweed jacket and muddy Wellington boots, he looked more like a country gamekeeper than the senior medical officer of a major RAF station. He swept into the dim-lit radar room in a gust of cold air, then stood breathing heavily while he waited for someone to speak to him.

Trowbridge and Myers were busy on the radio, trying to eliminate as many radar echoes as possible. The Flight Information Service was obviously hard at it, too; aircraft after aircraft was coming onto the Leeming frequency for identification and instructions. Myers was following the tracks of ten aircraft traces on his screen, occasionally marking one off after it had been positively identified. He was speaking into his boom-mike almost non-stop.

"India Oscar, Leeming, I have you identified four miles east of Sutton Bank on a southwesterly heading, confirm . . . ?"

"Affirmative for India Oscar."

"Roger. Break, break . . ."

He turned to another aircraft trace. "Golf Whisky Delta, Leeming—we have an emergency here: would you intercept an aircraft for me for identification?"

"Certainly, sir."

420

"Thank you, Whisky Delta; turn left heading two-four-zero and stand by for further steers. Break, break. . . . November four-zero Tango, say your heading . . ."

It was another two minutes before the call they were waiting for came through. Tony Paynton in the Chipmunk.

"Mayday, Leeming; Golf Bravo Charlie Yankee Lima."

The other traffic shut up instantly; a Mayday call has priority over everything. Myers turned his volume up and replied, "Yankee Lima, Leeming has you strength three. Go ahead."

"Roger, Leeming." Paynton's voice was a little louder. "I have been handed to you from Tees-side. Confirm you have my details, and do you have a doctor there?"

Myers said, "Affirmative, Yankee Lima; but stand by for the doctor, I have some information for you."

"Go."

"Roger. D and D says your target aircraft is a Piper Cherokee Arrow, Golf Alpha Yankee Whisky Tango. Confirm you're still in radio contact with it?"

"Ah—not sure about that, Leeming. I've just been in contact, but she was getting very faint so I may not be able to get her again. I'm on a southerly heading at 110 knots, now about eight miles south of Tees-side passing four-five, and I think she's ahead to the south, going faster than me."

Myers glared briefly at his radar screen. Three of the blips on it were holding approximately southerly headings. One—a Cessna 172—was identified, and another one, coming in from the top of the screen, was probably Yankee Lima. That left only one remaining, a little way below Leeming . . .

Myers's breath caught with excitement. He said quickly, "Thank you, Yankee Lima. Couldn't you get her to change frequency? Speak to the doctor herself?"

"Negative, Leeming. She doesn't know anything about anything, and she's pretty upset. If she starts trying to switch we'll probably lose her altogether."

Myers hesitated. The Chipmunk pilot was right. The girl would be fiddling with a panel of at least four different radios. "Roger, Yankee Lima; stand by to talk to the doctor."

"O.K." The voice buzzed with static. "Put him on."

Myers swung round to Oscott, who was still waiting patiently. Slipping the left earphone of his headset back from his ear, he spoke fast, outlining the situation.

"We can't talk to the girl, but I'm in contact with another pilot who's been on to her. Would you speak to him and see what you can make of the medical side?"

Oscott nodded and stepped forward, pulling a plugged-in headset over his head.

"Yankee Lima, Squadron Leader Oscott here." His voice was deep and reassuring. "I'm the Leeming MO. What can you tell me about this man who's passed out?"

In his racketing cockpit ten miles away Paynton collected his thoughts, not wanting to miss anything out. "The girl in the aircraft's a nursing sister. First, she says the pilot was complaining of muscular pains in his neck this morning. Then when he passed out, it was very sudden. Now she says his breathing is irregular and so is his pulse. His neck's in . . . in spasm, and his eyes are dilated. She's tried slapping him round the face, but nothing happened. She says she thinks it's a—ah—suberanoid haemorrhage. I think that was it."

Oscott's face went blank. Myers, watching him, was suddenly reminded of another doctor a year before, telling him his mother had just died. His face had looked like that.

"Would that word be *subarachnoid* haemorrhage?"

There was a pause. Then, "Yeah, that's it. Subarachnoid."

"All right, Yankee Lima; that's a very lucid report. Just wait a moment now, please." Oscott released the transmit switch and stared unseeingly at the radar console, thinking. After half a minute, he seemed to come to some sort of conclusion. He pressed the transmit switch again and said, "Yankee Lima, I think you must proceed on the assumption that the girl is right. That means you must not expect the pilot to recover sufficiently to fly the aircraft. Over."

There was a few seconds silence. Then the tinny voice said, "There is *no* chance of the pilot recovering, confirm? Nothing at all the girl can do to bring him round?"

Oscott frowned, and then said distinctly, "That is correct. On the data you have given me, it sounds very much like a subarachnoid, or possibly a cerebral haemorrhage. In either case, there is no chance of recovery for a minimum of twelve hours or so, and probably a lot longer. There is nothing the girl can do apart from keeping him warm and making sure his breathing is not restricted. Over."

"Roger. Understood. Can I have the controller now, please?"

Myers nodded briefly to Oscott and pressed the transmit switch.

"Leeming controller here, Yankee Lima."

"Roger." The voice paused for a moment, then came back. Even through the poor transmission it sounded weary. "Look, there doesn't seem to be anything more I can do, now. I'm low on fuel and I need to land at your field, and I've already told the girl to expect someone else to take over from me. I'd advise an instructor in another aircraft to get up there and try and talk her down, and pretty quick, too, because I had to leave her in a bit of a state, what with her radio fading."

Myers said, "Roger, Yankee Lima. That's understood, and thanks for all you've done. Do you want a steer for Leeming?"

"Be appreciated."

"Right; stand by." Myers glanced across at Trowbridge, who nodded quickly and reached for his transmit switch to give the bearing.

Myers leaned back and looked up at Oscott.

"Is that what I should tell D and D, sir? That this pilot probably isn't going to recover?"

Oscott pulled off his headset and put it on the table.

"Well, obviously I can't be sure, not without seeing the patient. But as an off-the-cuff opinion I'd have to say yes; I don't think you should expect a recovery in time to be any use. The symptoms as described are right for a subarachnoid, and a nursing sister would probably know one when she saw one anyway."

Myers nodded. "All right, sir. Er—could you explain what this haemorrhage *is*, please? D and D might want to know."

"Well, briefly, it means an artery bursting within the subarachnoid cavity, the small cavity between the brain and the skull—not uncommon in men of thirty-five to forty. Blood pumps out of the leak and increases the pressure on the brain, restricting the blood supply into the brain itself. This causes unconsciousness

423

and possible brain damage. It's largely due to a congenital deficiency in one of the artery coatings. The patient sometimes gets a stiff neck beforehand, and then when the artery bursts they go out like a light. The best indication that it's happened is that the neck muscles go into spasm, so that the neck's as rigid as a board in spite of the person being completely unconscious."

"I see, sir." Myers finished scribbling notes and looked up. "So if that's what's happened, then there's no chance at all of bringing him round long enough to land the aircraft?"

"Oh, no." Oscott was quite definite. "It's a very serious condition, you understand. If this man isn't wheeled into a neurosurgical centre very soon, he may not come round at all."

Myers reached for the red telephone.

WHILE PAYNTON was talking to Squadron Leader Oscott, the chain reactions to the emergency were spreading out from the Distress and Diversion Cell like ripples on a pond. Radar controllers at Leeds-Bradford Airport, Manchester and Northern Radar at RAF Lindholme were notified and told to begin eliminating as many unidentified echoes as possible on their screens. Telephones rang at five RAF aerodromes and urgent questions were asked about aircraft availability. The answers, on this Saturday afternoon, were less than helpful.

At the same time, a total of seventeen police stations were alerted to the possibility of an air crash within their parishes. They in turn notified fire and ambulance services to stand by. Five light aircraft fields were called with the request that their off-the-circuit traffic should report to Leeming by radio, and similar instructions were given to six individual aircraft on the Flight Information Service frequency en route over Yorkshire. Altogether, within fifteen minutes of Paynton's first Mayday call, more than three hundred people had become either directly or indirectly involved in the fate of Whisky Tango.

THE TELEPHONE RANG in the Tyne Flying Club at fourteen minutes to three.

Peter Castlefield, the club receptionist, picked up the receiver as Barry Turner came into the clubroom.

424

"Barry; phone for you. Bloke wants to speak to the chief flying instructor."

Turner was running late. He had two more lessons to fly before the end of the day and he needed to get a move on. "See if you can deal with it, Pete. Or ask them to hang on a mo'."

Castlefield spoke into the phone again. His expression changed to sudden surprise. "Barry! It's Distress and Diversion. They say it's important."

Turner brushed through the clump of people standing around the reception desk, grabbed the receiver, and snapped, "Chief Flying Instructor."

A neutral male voice said, "Distress and Diversion Cell, West Drayton, here. Hold the line please."

Flight Lieutenant Peterson came on the line after thirty seconds.

"D and D number one controller here." The voice was brisk. "Am I speaking to the chief instructor?"

"Yes. Barry Turner."

"Right, sir. Does your club operate a Piper Cherokee Arrow aircraft, Golf Alpha Yankee Whisky Tango?"

Turner said, "Yes," feeling his face going stiff.

"Can you confirm that it took off from your aerodrome about twenty-five minutes ago for Denham, pilot's name Bazzard?"

"Yes, affirmative. Why? Has something happened to it?"

"I'm afraid so, sir. It appears that the pilot's passed out in the air. We have another aircraft in radio contact with a woman on board, and we're trying to locate your machine on radar."

Peterson paused to let the news sink in. Turner stared sightlessly at the club noticeboard, tingling with shock. After a moment he swore softly and emphatically.

Peterson said dryly, "Quite so. Now, I need some facts as quickly as possible. First, can you confirm that the aircraft has dual controls, and also some form of autopilot?"

Turner roused himself. "Yes. Full dual except for the toe-brakes. It's on auto, is it?"

"The woman says it is, and it would've fallen out of the sky by now otherwise. Now; do you know this woman at all?"

"Negative. All I can tell you is she's about twenty-five and blonde. I'll have her membership form dug out and give you what

I can on her." Turner spun round and snapped an order. Then he spoke into the phone again. "Go on."

"Next, can you confirm the aircraft's cruising speed at 150 m.p.h., and do you know what its fuel state is?"

"Cruising's nearer 160, true air speed. Stand by on the fuel." Turner took Ann Moore's Passenger Membership form from Castlefield and said to him, "Check the fuel book and the flight sheets on Whisky Tango, pronto." Then, into the receiver, "I've got the girl's details now."

"Go ahead."

"Right. The name's Ann Moore. Miss. Her address is 19 Wallsend Road, Jesmond, Newcastle. Occupation, nursing sister, Newcastle Royal Infirmary."

"O.K., got it. Any idea if she has any flying experience?"

"No idea. Hang on a mo'." Turner conferred swiftly with Castlefield. "We don't think so: her passenger form's newly dated so I doubt if she's been up here before, anyway. . . . Hang on a minute, I'm just getting the fuel figures." Turner frowned for a few seconds, calculating. "It should have at least three and a half hours' fuel on board. Maybe a bit longer, but call it three and a half hours for certain."

"Roger," Peterson replied. "That's all for the moment, but I'd be obliged if you'd stay by the telephone until we've got the aircraft down, in case we need anything else."

Turner ran a hand through his red hair, thinking fast. After a few seconds he said, "O.K., sure. But just how *are* you going to get it down? Try to bring the pilot round, or what?"

"I'm not sure yet, sir. We haven't even got the aircraft located yet. I've got a doctor at Leeming talking to the relaying pilot now, though, so we ought to be getting some idea soon of the chances of the pilot recovering. If that isn't possible it will have to be some sort of talk-down."

"Yeah, right. What d'you have in mind for that, if it comes to it? You're not thinking of doing it from the ground, are you?"

Peterson was in a considerable hurry, but he also realized that in Turner he was talking to a pilot who probably had more overall experience than himself, and was furthermore in current instructional practice on the particular aircraft involved.

426

He said quickly, "No sir, I don't think it'd be possible from the ground. Once we've got it located I'm thinking of getting something else in the air to sit behind her and talk to her from there. If you can add anything to that, though, I'm listening."

Turner stared blankly out of the window at the winter sunshine for a moment. Then he said, "Well, that's about the only thing you can do. But you say you don't know where it is, yet?"

"That's right. It's transmitting on an unused frequency, so we can't use any direction-finding equipment on it. We're working on the assumption that it's more or less on a straight line from Newcastle to Denham, and that it's between forty-five and fifty-five miles out from your end. If we're right about that we ought to find it before too long."

"That sounds reasonable." Turner pondered for a few seconds. "Who're you going to get up when you do find it? I'd go myself, but I certainly haven't got anything here that'll catch an Arrow with a half hour start."

"I'm checking service aircraft availability now."

Turner frowned. "I shouldn't have thought any of the small RAF kites would be any good. You won't catch an Arrow with a Bulldog, so it'd have to be something like a Jet Provost. And then you'll have a pilot who doesn't know what an Arrow's cockpit's like or what its speeds are or anything. You'd be better off with a civvy instructor who knows the aircraft, flying something similar himself."

Peterson went silent for a moment; this instructor had a good point. The RAF had fast aircraft and it had slow aircraft—but it *didn't* have a single-engined retractable with a 160 m.p.h. cruise. Nor did it have any pilots who were used to flying that sort of American light aircraft.

"You could be right about that, sir," he said slowly. "Can you think of anywhere in particular who might help, off the cuff?"

"Not . . . um . . . not offhand." Turner realized that time was wasting. "I'll think about it and call you back if anything occurs to me, shall I?"

"Right, sir. It's West Drayton 44077. Thanks."

"God, I should thank *you*, man. That's one of my pilots up there."

Peterson said, "O.K., sir. We'll try and get him down." He broke the connection.

Turner put the phone down and stood staring at it, oblivious to the silence that had fallen in the clubhouse. The news of Bazzard's emergency had shaken him considerably. Like all good chief instructors, he felt a deep-seated responsibility for every pilot, experienced or beginner, who flew the aeroplanes belonging to what he regarded as *his* school. His instinctive reaction was to jump into the first aeroplane he could find, chase after the Arrow, do the talk-down himself. . . . Except, of course, that he could never catch it. Not if Bazzard was forty or fifty miles away and heading south towards Leeds and Bradford.

He suddenly swore loudly, and spun round abruptly to the reception desk. "Pete! Get me the Leeds Aero Club on the blower, quick. I want the chief flying instructor if he's there, guy called Keith Kerr. Then get D and D back."

Castlefield grabbed for the phone with one hand and the club contacts book with the other. "Is that your mate? The aerobatic bloke?"

"Yeah. He's also one of the best instructors in the business, *and* he's got an Arrow down there. He's the one to catch this bloody aeroplane for us."

4

At 1446, while the call from D and D was going through to Barry Turner, Keith Kerr was doing 100 m.p.h. on the A6120 between Sherburn-in-Elmet and Leeds-Bradford Airport.

Winding the twistgrip hard open against the stop, he blared the Norton past a gaggle of slow-moving motorists and laid the bike over into a long, sweeping right hand bend. As the road straightened he pulled upright and snatched a quick glance back over his shoulder. The bend behind was empty; no sign of any flashing blue lights.

Kerr held the throttle open, tucked his elbows in, and scrunched down over the tank. He grinned into the gale, elated. *That should have lost them. . . .*

The chase had started ten minutes before, as he'd zipped past a police Granada parked in a farm entrance. He'd been doing seventy at the time, and he'd only seen the car for a split-second. But in that moment he'd also caught a glimpse of a blue uniform and the car starting to move.

That was enough. He'd dug his knees into the tank and opened up harder still, riding as fast as he could. The cops might not be following at all, of course, but if they were, they were going to have to sprout wings to catch him before he nipped off into the airport.

Kerr's ideas of the rights and wrongs of speeding were simple. Blanket speed limits were some inane politician's whim, not to be taken seriously. If you didn't get caught you were in the clear.

When Kerr reached the airport, there was still no sign of the police car. He pulled in alongside the low straggling buildings that house the Leeds Aero Club, hauled off his crash helmet and strolled towards the clubhouse, whistling as he went.

It didn't occur to him that the police in the Leeds area might be getting to know a certain distinctive black-and-chrome Norton 650SS rather well by now. . . .

Inside, the place was the usual crowd of milling instructors and students. Kerr shouldered his way through the door marked "Instructors Only", dumped his gear, and then walked through into the area behind the bookings counter. The counter was being managed by an attractive black-haired girl in blue jeans and a red sweater, currently dealing with half a dozen students who all wanted to sign in, pay, and book their next lessons at once.

Kerr watched her for a moment, his blue eyes softening, then said quietly, "How goes it, Maggie?" His voice was deep and carrying, with a trace of a transatlantic accent.

Maggie looked round and saw him for the first time. She blushed in momentary confusion, and then shyly returned his brief conspiratorial smile.

"Fine, thanks. Very well." She was unable to keep a note of relief out of her voice as she added, "How did the aerobatics go?"

"Not bad." Maggie made as if to speak—and then suddenly flicked an apprehensive glance over his shoulder, and bent her head quickly back to the bill she was writing out.

A grating Yorkshire voice behind Kerr said, "What sort o' bloody time d'you call this, then?"

Kerr's smile faded. He hadn't noticed that Edward Tomms was sitting behind the counter, and the realization didn't please him.

Tomms had purchased the Leeds Aero Club from its previous owners seven months before, and he and Kerr had disliked each other on sight. Tomms had had a brief career as a bomber pilot in the Second World War, but he'd acquired the flying school solely as an investment, and his only interest was the financial return. He paid badly, expected his staff to work long hours, and quibbled constantly at what he referred to as Kerr's "namby-pamby" reasons for grounding machines with technical faults. The antipathy between the two of them had deepened over the months until it was ready to erupt into an open row; up to now Kerr had avoided a showdown with uncharacteristic patience.

Today, however, things were different. The letter crinkling in his back pocket made all the difference in the world. *British Island Airways are pleased to offer you the position....*

He paused deliberately and said, "I'd call the time sort of just before three, chum. Unless my watch is badly out, of course."

Tomms heaved himself off his stool. He was fifty-nine years old, short and tubby with a mop of iron-grey hair cut close to a bullet head. He wore thick-rimmed spectacles which exaggerated his aggressively staring eyes.

"Eh!" He confronted Kerr at a range of three feet. "An' you were supposed to be here a bloody hour ago!"

"Very true." Kerr grinned savagely into his employer's face. "Except that according to my contract, chum, *you* don't tell me when I take my time off anyway. For your information, I checked in just before lunch and found that my first booking was three o'clock. So I figured that since I'm night flying until eight tonight, for which I don't get paid anything extra, this was a good time to take half an hour off instead of twiddling my thumbs in here. O.K.?"

Tomms was momentarily taken aback. Then his temper, never far under the surface, boiled over.

"No, it's *not* bloody O.K.! I don't pay people to saunter in this time o' the afternoon just 'cos they feel like it! An' furthermore—" his eyes flicked down to Kerr's motor-cycle boots and back up again "—I don't pay my instructors to turn up lookin' like ton-up boys. When you coom in 'ere I want you in a shirt an' tie, or you'll be bloody *out!* Got it?"

"Right, chum," Kerr said deliberately. "If that's the way you want it, then this is your lucky day. Because I quit. I'm giving you a month's notice as of now, or you can fire me and give me a month's money. Either way, I want you to know that you're the worst niggling bastard I ever worked for, bar none."

Tomms's eyes seemed to go almost black behind the thick glasses. Twenty years in a tough business had taught him to count three before letting himself go, and he counted three now. Then he took a deep breath. . . .

The telephone rang, shattering the electric silence. Maggie picked up the receiver. "Keith! Someone called Barry Turner. He says it's an emergency."

Keith ignored her and so did Tomms. His face suffused with fury, he said heavily, "Right then, young man. *I'm* giving *you* bloody notice, an' you'll work out the whole month. . . ."

Maggie waited. "Keith! It's an aircraft emergency!"

Kerr spun round, took two steps across the room, and snatched the receiver. Tomms started forward angrily, but the instructor had his back to him as he started speaking.

"Kerr here. What's the problem?"

"Keith—Barry Turner. Listen, I've got to be quick: one of our guys has taken off in our Arrow to go down to Denham, and passed out in the air. He's left the kite on autopilot with his bird in it, and she's screaming for help on the radio."

Kerr stiffened. He'd known Barry Turner for years, and it didn't occur to him to ask time-wasting questions. If there was nothing to be done, Barry wouldn't have called him. It took less than twenty seconds to absorb the problem and its implications.

"Where is the plane?"

"Nobody knows yet. Our man got off from here at 1423, so if he's on a straight line for Denham he ought to be about fifteen or twenty miles northeast of you by now. D and D are looking for him on radar. Can you get into the air and try and talk the girl down for me if it comes to that, Keith? I haven't got anything here that'll catch the damn thing."

Kerr thought for a few seconds, calculating and juggling possibilities. Then he snapped, "Right. The only plane I've got that's fast enough's our own Arrow, so I'd better get moving. You stand by the phone and I'll get someone to call you and relay to me; I'll want a lot more gen once I'm in the air."

"Roger, will do. Thanks, Keith."

Keith crashed the phone down and whirled round, the problems of the emergency racing through his mind. Speed was vital. The first requirement was to catch the plane. That ought to be possible providing he got into the air while the runaway was still heading towards him, but once it had passed abeam Leeds-Bradford he'd be stuck chasing it. And with two Arrows of similar performance it could take him half an hour to close a gap of even five miles. He had to get off the ground *now*, immediately. . . .

"Eh! Look! What the bloody 'ell's goin' on . . . ?" Tomms's face was still suffused with fury.

Kerr stepped round him and snapped, "Maggie! Call Distress and Diversion. Tell them I'm getting up in Romeo X-ray to try and catch their runaway from Newcastle. They'll know all about it. Ask them to get on the Approach here—I'll be talking to them first and I'll want information. O.K.?"

The girl flustered. "What *is* it, Keith? What's going on?"

Kerr was scanning rapidly down the board where the aircraft keys were hung. "Haven't got time to explain, love—just *do* it. Tell D and D to call Leeds Approach."

Maggie caught the urgency in his voice and reached for the phone, wide-eyed. Kerr located the keys to Cherokee Arrow Romeo X-ray and snatched them off their hook. He spun round towards the door.

And found Edward Tomms standing solidly in his path.

"Where the 'ell d'you think you're going? You don't go gallivantin' off in one of my planes wi'out a word of explanation!"

Kerr snarled, "Get out of the way, you fool!" and made to push past. Tomms grabbed his jacket, livid with fury. Kerr pulled against his grip for an instant, then suddenly swung back and punched him in the stomach. Tomms reeled, collided heavily with the wall, and then slid down onto his knees.

The whole thing had taken three seconds.

432

The clubhouse went dead still, suspended in shock. There was total silence, broken only by a groan from Tomms as he fought to suck air into his winded lungs.

Kerr stepped round him and ran. He pounded up the taxiway that led to the light aircraft hangar, making straight for the Arrow, and arrived at it panting and coughing with exertion. He jumped onto the walkway, flung the door open and plumped into the right-hand seat; no time for pre-flight inspections, he slammed the door and slid the seat forward in one continuous flurry of movement. Then his hands were darting round the controls.

Ten seconds after the door had closed, the propeller moved jerkily, the blades chunking over, then disappearing as the engine blared into life. As the Arrow started to move, Kerr's hands and eyes ran automatically through the after-start routines. Radio and beacon—on; oil pressure—coming up; fuel pressure—in the green; tank contents—between a quarter and a half on each side . . .

He swore aloud.

A third of a tank a side meant a maximum endurance of an hour and a half even if he left nothing in reserve. For a few seconds he thought about stopping to re-fuel, and then realized suddenly that it wasn't going to matter anyway: it was already three o'clock—in an hour and a half's time it was going to be dark.

The radio warmed up with a small fizzing noise. Kerr pulled a headset over his ears and thumbed the transmit button on the control yoke as he swung the Arrow onto the taxiway, rolling fast.

"Leeds, Mayday traffic Golf Bravo Charlie Romeo X-ray, at the Aero Club. I am attempting to intercept an aircraft heading down from the north with the pilot incapacitated. Request taxi and immediate take-off runway one-zero."

"Roger, Mayday Romeo-X, cleared taxi. Leeds Approach is working on this emergency at the moment. Confirm you intend to talk the woman down if necessary?"

Kerr said briefly, "Affirmative."

"Roger. Runway one-zero clear. QNH one-zero-one-two, QFE nine-eight-niner, wind, two-four-zero at twelve knots." Kerr pushed the throttle open a bit more and bowled down the taxiway at 30 m.p.h. checking magnetos as he went. In the background of his attention he heard the tower ordering a British Airways

Viscount on final approach to overshoot and break right immediately. The Viscount acknowledged calmly, with no trace of annoyance: in the air, emergency traffic takes priority over all. He grinned briefly, realizing that at that moment he had precedence over everything up to and including a Concorde. God bless the British Air Traffic Control Service.

Engine husking, scuttling fast on its three ungainly legs, the Arrow taxied past the airport's western entrance. Kerr didn't notice the police Granada nosing in from the road outside; he was too busy in the cockpit.

He swung onto the runway at exactly one minute past three, and opened the throttle.

NOT MANY YEARS AGO, a single-engined private aeroplane was a comparatively simple piece of machinery. It would have the basic flight controls, perhaps five or six instruments on the panel—and that was that. Nowadays, however, a modern four-seat single like a Cherokee Arrow is capable of operating in practically any conditions. It frequently has equipment and weather-beating systems equal to those carried by many multi-engined transports: there are fifteen major flight and engine controls and a total of twenty-five instruments keeping track of flight attitude, navigation, and engine performance. Bazzard had had to set nine separate controls before switching in the autopilot, and twenty-one dials were now providing a continuous flow of information concerning the Arrow's performance and progress.

To Ann Moore, who had no way of understanding that in a less sophisticated aeroplane she and Bazzard would already have been dead, the machinery was nothing but a low steady hum pervading her prison cell in the sky. The huge emptiness outside the flimsy windows seemed to press in on her with a physical weight, producing a peculiar effect of claustrophobia in the tiny plastic room. Her stomach ached as if an iron fist was gripping her insides.

She clutched the microphone in her lap, and tried to think about flying the plane.

No one had told her that she would have to do it. But she was well aware that people who suffer a spontaneous subarachnoid

434

haemorrhage slip into a deep coma which lasts a minimum of twelve hours, even under intensive care in a neurosurgical unit. So, quite simply, there was no alternative: she was going to have to fly the plane.

The realization that Roy *had* had a subarachnoid had been instantaneous and appalling; in the moment of saying the words she realized with sudden clarity that she'd actually known it for several minutes. Her body had shaken uncontrollably and her stomach had tightened, squeezing the acid taste of panic into her throat. Paynton's voice had pattered on out of the speaker, but the only thing she'd taken in had been the words, *"Someone else will be talking to you next."* Then the voice had gone, and she was alone again.

For what had felt like a long time, she could do nothing but fight her terror. It seemed to lap and recede in waves, dimming for a moment and then welling up again through her body. She clenched her teeth, tightened every muscle in her body in an attempt to still the shivering; eventually, panic had died down to a steady background throb of fear. And in its wake had come the peculiar lassitude which accompanies drawn-out terror, where the brain refuses to concentrate for more than a few moments. She yawned, and wiped her face with the sleeve of her sweater.

Somehow she had to fly the plane.

Dully, she wondered about it. Roy had said it was dual controls. That would be the half-wheel thing in front of her. She supposed they'd tell her what to do over the radio: how to turn it and when to do it, and which gauges to look at. Unless they just abandoned her, of course: decided there was nothing anybody could do, and just forgot about her. They could be doing that at this moment: shrugging helplessly, pretending she and Roy had never existed.

The engine snored on, solid in the silence of the sky.

Ann turned her head and looked at Bazzard. He was still and pale, breathing raggedly in his unconsciousness. For a moment she found herself thinking in a vague way about what might have happened between them in the future, but somehow the familiar questions seemed utterly disconnected from reality. Whether you were in love, whether you should go to bed with someone—these were half-remembered conventions of some other world,

435

incredibly distant. Even the unfaced question of whether Roy would live or die held no shock, no impact. He was just . . . there; a part of a nightmare which she couldn't get to grips with.

The plane. Come on, now—think about the plane. Force. yourself to think.

She shook her head and ground the heels of her hands up and down her face and across her eyes. When she stopped it took a long time for vision to clear and re-focus. She frowned at the instrument panel—it didn't mean a thing to her. It was hopeless, impossible; the cockpit was a jungle of things she didn't even begin to understand. She felt herself beginning to sob again and buried her face in her hands, feeling the wetness of tears between her fingers. She hadn't known it was possible to be so frightened; the fear just kept welling up, blotting out thought, everything. And in a minute they—someone—would be talking to her. Then she'd *have* to get a grip on herself, *have* to face up to it. . . .

After a moment she took a deep breath, raised her head, and looked deliberately out of the side window.

Four thousand feet below, the North Riding of Yorkshire was a cold patchwork in the harsh winter sun. The hills were flattened, the fields an irregular mosaic. Most still bore a white threadbare tracery of last night's frost. Nestling in a fold in the patchwork was a tiny grey-brown village, incredibly detailed in the bright afternoon. Wisps of smoke ambled away from the toy houses, and model cars made pinpoints of colour in the miniature streets. She'd been born and raised in a village like that, in Northamptonshire. For a moment she remembered the smell of the winter country and the swish of the Saturday cars as they turned into the pub opposite their house.

Then the village slid under the wing, and there were just the fields, stretching away to the wide horizon in every direction. And above the horizon-line the sky, endless and towering and coldly blue: the naked yellow glare of the winter sun and the sparse high streaks of cloud seemed to emphasize the limitless expanse of nothing. The Arrow's quietly-droning cockpit seemed very small and puny against the vast indifference of the sky.

Ann looked back in at her trembling hands. Two fresh tears rolled down her cheeks.

TEN MILES TO THE SOUTH, Keith Kerr was climbing up into the same sky. As Romeo X-ray roared up through 3,000 feet, he wriggled himself into a comfortable slouch in his seat and anxiously rubbed the scar near his eye. Beneath him, the sunlit clutter of Leeds spread away in all directions; the usual noise-abatement rule of not overflying the city was ignored in the emergency.

Kerr moved the control yoke with tiny flexings of his right wrist while his left hand pulled a Gold Leaf out from the packet on the empty seat beside him. His light blue eyes, narrowed against the glaring sun, casually surveyed the familiar vista of sky above and earth far below. He leaned back, picked the cigarette lighter from the panel as it popped out, and blew smoke at the windscreen. The debâcle with Tomms was temporarily forgotten, pushed out of his mind, as were thoughts of the previous night or of his new career with British Island Airways. All of those things were ground matters, which have a way of receding in importance once an airman has returned to his element.

His headphones made a small pipping noise, then clattered metallically in his ears.

"Romeo X-ray, Leeds; say your passing level."

Kerr glanced at the altimeter as his right thumb pressed the transmit switch on the control yoke.

"Romeo-X passing three five. D'you have this runaway aircraft located yet?"

"Not sure, Romeo-X. We have a suspect trace nine miles north of you, moving approximately south at about 160 m.p.h. We're trying to get some identification on it."

"Sonofabitch!" Kerr muttered excitedly. Then he pressed the switch again. "Can you head me towards it?"

"Affirmative, Romeo-X. What is your present heading?"

"One-three-zero."

"Roger. Turn right now to one-four-zero."

Kerr repeated the new course and made a brief climbing turn. Then he trickled smoke through his nostrils while he considered the odds against this unidentified radar echo being the right one. A lot of aircraft go up and down England every day, and this route was a good alternative to flying through the complex of industrial control zones to the west. *Could* this be the runaway? If the aircraft he intercepted turned out to be the wrong one, he'd have used up his vital ten-mile lead for nothing. On the other hand, if he did draw a blank they'd have had it anyway; the only possible conclusion would be that the runaway was miles away in some unguessed-at portion of the sky, or that it was too low to be picked up on radar at all. In either case, the chances of anyone finding it would be non-existent.

The Arrow droned on up into the blue, passing 5,000 feet. Kerr glanced at his fuel gauges, then eased the mixture lever back towards the lean position, reducing the fuel flow; his endurance *could* become a factor, however unlikely it seemed at the moment. The cylinder head temperature crept slowly up and stopped just below the red danger line at 260 degrees centigrade. He frowned, and tapped the glass of the dial with his finger. Cylinder head temperature gauges were nowhere near accurate enough for optimum fuel economy in a Lycoming engine. He'd been asking for months for an exhaust gas temperature gauge in the Arrow, but Tomms had overruled him. One day the engine would overheat and seize solid. . . .

Drumming the fingers of his left hand on the throttle quadrant, he surveyed the streaks of high cirrus beyond the invisible propeller. After a moment his lips formed an O, and he whistled soundlessly into the snore of the engine.

AT THAT MOMENT, forty miles to the north, Tony Paynton was waiting for his engine to stop. Level at 2,000 feet, with the Chipmunk slogging along at its best economy cruise of 65 knots, his eyes were flicking across constantly from his fuel gauges to the distant sunlit criss-cross of Leeming's runways.

The runways were three miles away, almost hidden under the nose. The fuel gauges both read zero.

In spite of the cold, Paynton was aware of a hot prickle of tension in his face and the clamminess of sweat on his palms under his gloves. In front of him Jules Martin's head lolled mute and miserable. Every now and then Paynton glanced down at the fields below, where he would have to attempt a landing if the fuel ran out. They all looked terrifyingly small, and every one of them

438

seemed to be bounded by hard grey lines, the low stone walls which are a feature of North Yorkshire farmland. His throat tightened every time he looked at them; if you hit one of those during a forced landing you were going to write off the aircraft at the very least. . . .

His headphones said, "Yankee Lima, Leeming; you have two miles to run, join right base for runway three-zero."

Paynton pressed the stick-button and acknowledged; his tongue seemed large and clumsy in the dryness of his mouth. He looked at the fuel gauges again. ".One more minute, pal," he muttered. "Just keep running for one more minute."

A minute went by. The hangars on the north side of the aerodrome crept slowly under the wing's leading edge. The engine was still running. . . .

The Chipmunk rolled its wheels onto runway three-zero at Leeming at five minutes past three. It made one stiff-legged little bounce, settled, and finished its landing roll abeam the first taxiway. Paynton turned off the runway, braked to a standstill, switched off the magnetos, then reached up and slid the canopy all the way back. The cold January air smelt incredibly sweet as he stepped gingerly down to the ground.

Martin staggered out of the cockpit behind him, half-fell, and sank down on the taxiway, both hands flat on the cold concrete as if he needed reassurance that it was real.

"God—" He coughed, his head hanging feebly. "—Thank Christ . . . that's over . . ."

Paynton leaned against the fuselage. For a moment he had a vision of the girl, still trapped in the Arrow's cockpit as it droned on southwards, still terrified.

"It's not over, Jules," he said slowly. His teeth chattered in the cold. "It's not over at all, yet. Not for that girl."

"Romeo X-ray, Leeds?"

Kerr slapped the headset-mike closer to his mouth and snapped, "Romeo-X, go ahead."

"Romeo-X, continue chase for presumed runaway. Turn right heading one-eight-zero, and continue climbing to flight level seven-zero. Also, we have some information for you. D and D now have a doctor's opinion on the pilot's illness. They are not expecting any recovery, and advise that you proceed on the assumption that the girl will have to land the aircraft. D'you copy that?"

Kerr's left hand, holding a cigarette, ground to a halt halfway up to his mouth. After a long moment he pressed the transmit button and said deliberately: "Roger. Copied."

"O.K., Romeo-X; stand by for further steers."

Kerr said "Roger" again. The radio double-clicked in acknowledgment, then went silent.

So it was really happening. For several seconds Kerr just stared out over the nose, blind to the empty sky and the dwindling earth far below. Up to now, his role in the emergency had been nebulous; *if* the aircraft was found, and *if* the pilot didn't come round, then he might have to try and do something. He had recognized the possibility—but deep down, he now realized, he hadn't expected it to come to that. It was too melodramatic—the sort of thing that only happened to other people, never to you.

Except that now it *was* happening.

He took a deep drag on his cigarette and applied himself seriously to the problem of how to teach someone to fly and land an aircraft in the ninety minutes between ten past three and nightfall on a winter's afternoon.

On the face of it, landing an aeroplane is one single exercise, flowing and straightforward. You merely line the machine up with the runway, descend, and then just before the moment of touchdown pull back to check the descent so that the landing is gentle.

Delving a little deeper, however, that seemingly simple operation breaks down into a hundred separate elements, all demanding prerequisite skills for their proper execution. In order to get to the runway at all you must first be able to turn the aircraft within fine limits of accuracy; and as any flying instructor is only too well aware, a normal student requires a solid hour of his airborne course devoted solely to turns before he achieves anything like an adequate performance. And then there was setting up the descent: even the crudest of landing approaches requires the pilot to make an accurate power reduction, a careful adjustment of the nose position to achieve the correct airspeed, and finally a resetting of the elevator trim. This aspect of the aviator's art usually requires at least five hours of detailed practice.

And Kerr had an hour and a half to go before dark.

Then there were all the other factors. Flying straight and level; slowing down so she could put the undercarriage down; locating the manifold pressure gauge and the throttle for the power changes; switching off the autopilot; making the all-important landing flare-out itself. . . .

An hour and a half.

Well, the short answer was that it simply wasn't possible: no one could teach any person to fly and land an aeroplane from scratch in ninety minutes. The only way it might be done was to forget any notion of *teaching* in the normal sense, and concentrate instead on achieving blind parrot-fashion obedience, so that *he* flew the aircraft through the girl's hands. The flying time would have to be devoted to just that; getting her to carry out the minimum of manoeuvres using the minimum of controls, with the accent on immediate response to every command he gave her.

Kerr sucked hard on his Gold Leaf, breathed out slowly, and frowned at the instrument panel through the swirling smoke. For the moment, there were more urgent things to be considered.

One of them was that he didn't yet know what sort of autopilot the other Arrow had. It was probably the same as the unit fitted in his own aircraft—but *probably* wasn't good enough: if the engagement buttons were in a different place he could make a very serious mistake.

He was frowning at the sky when the radio jerked him to attention. "Romeo X-ray, Leeds, d'you read?"

Kerr pushed his transmit switch and said briefly, "Go."

"Romeo X-ray, turn right heading one-niner-zero for interception with the target's extended trackline. You are about four miles ahead of the aircraft."

"Roger: one-niner-zero." Kerr banked to the right for a moment. "Leeds, what's the registration of this aircraft?"

"Er—G-AYWT, sir. Golf Alpha Yankee Whisky Tango."

"Thanks." Kerr craned his head round, resting it against the cold Perspex of the side window as he looked over his right shoulder, searching the depths of the sky below and behind. Four miles was a long range to spot another light aircraft, but you never knew.

After a moment the voice in his headphones came back.

"We have more information for you, Romeo-X."

"Go."

"First, the aircraft is transmitting on 126.85. I say again 126.85. Apparently it's an unused frequency."

Kerr raised his right eyebrow. "Roger; 126.85."

"Next, the fuel state. The aircraft took off at 1423 Zulu, with fuel on board for three and a half hours flying."

Kerr mentally crossed "fuel" off the list of problems: he might have fuel troubles himself, but Whisky Tango was all right.

"What about the autopilot?" he asked.

"The aircraft operator says it's a standard Piper Autocontrol Three. The engagement buttons are under the left-hand corner of the instrument panel, and there is no altitude hold."

Kerr stretched his neck to see his own autopilot panel past the left-hand control yoke. It bore the black-printed legend "Autocontrol III": exactly the same as Whisky Tango.

He said, "Roger, copied. Standard Autocontrol Three."

"O.K., Romeo-X. You are converging on the target's extended trackline now, range from you three miles. Suggest you begin a slow circle to the right now."

"Roger." Kerr tilted the horizon twenty degrees with a small pressure of his fingers, and added, "Can you tell me anything about the girl?"

"Affirmative, Romeo-X; just coming to that. D and D say she's a nurse, name Ann Moore, no known flying experience. The pilot's name's Roy Bazzard. An RAF doctor has confirmed his illness as serious—a probable subarachnoid haemorrhage, a haemorrhage in the brain. According to the pilot of another aircraft who's been speaking to her, the girl is aware of this. D'you get all that O.K.?"

"Got it. What's my range from the target now?"

"Just under two miles, Romeo-X."

Kerr stared until his eyes smarted, willing himself to see the tiny speck which was out there somewhere, crawling towards him. His eyes quartered the cold blue sky and the patchwork quilt of the earth, searching in vertical strips. Nothing. The sky was clear as a bell, visibility nigh on perfect—and nothing in sight.

The cabin-pillars and then the port wing dappled shadows across his face as the Arrow turned across the low afternoon sun. The horizon, tilted over to eighty degrees, streamed past the curved red engine cowling for several seconds and then pivoted back as Kerr rolled off most of the bank. He stared out again, this time across the empty left-hand seat and over the left wing. Still nothing.

"Romeo-X, your target range now one mile."

The controller's calm was maddening. Kerr snapped, "Negative contact," and went on looking. Without taking his eyes away from the void, he reached out his left hand and increased power.

"Romeo X-ray, target range now half a mile. Target bearing about three-five-zero from you."

Kerr felt his temples prickling. His eyes darted urgently. He *must* be able to see the damn thing from half a mile away. Another few seconds and he'd be flying away from it . . .

"Range completely closed, Romeo-X. Single radar trace."

Kerr swore aloud, glanced at the gyro compass again, and hauled the Arrow round on its left wing-tip in another steep turn.

Then he saw it. It was almost directly beneath him, thousands of feet below. A small, scurrying beetle with straight white wings, inching across the brown-green earth.

"Got it! Going down for a look." His own voice sounded tense in the feedback through his headphones.

Leeds said something in reply, but he wasn't listening. Keeping his eyes on the beetle's white wings he twisted the control yoke round to its full left deflection and pulled the throttle all the way back. The Arrow's shining red cowling clubbed upside down into the panorama of the landscape till it was pointing directly towards the other aeroplane, and rolled right-way-up as Kerr reefed into a steep curving dive. He stared over the nose, eyes narrowed and still, as the noise of the airflow rose to a solid thrumming roar as the speed wound up. 180 m.p.h. . . . 190 . . . 200. . . .

The white beetle floated up and back, becoming a model aeroplane swimming in space. Details grew rapidly obvious.

Square-cut wings and tailplane; blue nose.

At a range of a quarter of a mile, Kerr was diving at nearly 220 m.p.h. He banked slightly left to come down alongside the other machine, then pressed the transmit switch and said, "Romeo X-ray closing on the target now. It's certainly a Cherokee."

The Leeds controller suppressed his own excitement in careful formality. "Roger, Romeo-X; advise when you have the aircraft positively identified."

At 200 yards, Kerr began flattening out of his dive. The aeroplane ahead seemed to rise out of the depths. When it was above him Kerr pulled back hard on his control yoke, eyes watching the target's underbelly. The wheels were retracted. And the only square-winged retractable in the Cherokee range was the Arrow.

Using the speed of his dive, he pulled up until his height matched the other aircraft as the gap between them closed. At a range of a hundred yards he straightened up abruptly, moved the throttle to keep him in station three or four wingspans to the left and slightly behind, and stared out of the right window.

The other Arrow floated serene and steady, completely oblivious. He could read the registration letters on the side of its fuselage without even squinting. They were G-AYWT.

5

Ann Moore was looking at the dust in the cockpit. The top of the dashboard was very dusty, and motes of it danced in the small flow of air from the windscreen de-mister. It was like the dust in the tiny ward office at the hospital: you could sweep and clean, but as soon as the winter sun shone in, there it was again.

She clenched her teeth together, and rubbed her eyes hard with her knuckles. She *must* concentrate on something useful. Look at the dials again, for example. Look at the dials and try. . . .

Without warning, the radio speaker over her head came to life. Ann started violently. The voice was a new one, clear and slow and sounding incredibly close, almost as if the man was in the cockpit with her.

444

"Good afternoon, Ann. My name's Keith Kerr, and I'm going to help you. Can you hear me all right?"

She fumbled, snatched the microphone out of her lap, and said, "Yes!" It came out low-pitched and hoarse, and she cleared her throat. "Yes. Yes, I can hear you."

"Great. That's fine. Now, I'm in another aeroplane, just like yours, and I'm right alongside you, on your left. If you look out of the window you'll be able to see me."

Ann's head snapped round, eyes wide with shock. And there it was. Another plane, hanging in the void alongside and slightly behind. It looked incredibly close, as if it had been parked alongside in the sky. She couldn't hear it; it was just *there*, rising and falling gently beyond the left wing-tip, the sun glaring white on its body. She could even see the pilot, inside the cockpit, clearly enough to see that his face was turned towards her. He was watching her, talking to her. . . .

She suddenly found she was laughing and crying all at once, tears rolling down her face. Someone was here! The man in the other plane might not be able to do anything but he was *here*; she wasn't abandoned, wasn't alone.

The voice said calmly, "Can you see me all right, Ann?"

Still staring at the other plane, she brought the microphone up to her mouth. "Yes. Ye-yes." Her voice caught on a sob, and she released the mike button.

"Great." The man's speech was deep and unhurried, with a slight American accent. "Now first, I want to talk to you. I'll be staying here all the time, so you just sit back and relax. O.K.?"

Relax. Ann was twisted round in her seat, straining against the lap-and-diagonal belt. Slowly, reluctant to lose sight of the other plane, she turned to face the front again. This was where she *had* to pull herself together; *had* to be sensible. . . .

After a moment she opened her eyes and raised the microphone. She pressed the button. "O.K. I'm all right." The calmness of her own voice surprised her.

"That's fine, Ann. You sound as if you're bearing up very well. Now, I understand you're a nurse. Is that right?"

"Yes." The question was unexpected. "I'm a nursing sister."

"Good for you. That's a job I'd never be able to do in a hundred

445

years. Now, I gather you've got some idea of what's wrong with your pilot. Roy. Is that right?"

"Yes." She shot a frightened glance at Bazzard. "I think . . . he's had a subarachnoid haemorrhage."

"Well, I understand a doctor on the ground agrees with you: he thinks you could be right. So to be on the safe side, we ought to consider what we're going to do just in case Roy doesn't come round for a while. You with me?"

Ann took another deep breath, then said, "You mean flying the plane. I've got to fly the plane."

"Yes, that's right." The man's matter-of-factness surprised her; it was strangely reassuring. "You've obviously thought it through for yourself. I'm going to be sitting here in formation with you until you're safely back on the ground, so the most sensible way to use our time is to have you work on controlling the aeroplane in case it's necessary. O.K.?"

"Yes." Now it was actually happening she suddenly felt very still, nerves poised on a razor-edge of calmness.

"Right then. Now, am I right in thinking you've never flown in anything at all before?"

"No. I've only been up in a big passenger plane, once."

"I see." The voice sounded unperturbed. "Do you drive a car?"

"Yes." Ann stared at the instruments, not looking out.

"Right. Well, what we're going to do is actually easier than driving a car. For what we need to do today, which is just to descend, turn and land, there isn't any great problem at all. The only controls we'll need to touch are the steering wheel in front of you, the throttle, and two other small items which I'll be telling you about later. All the rest you can forget. You with me all right?"

Ann blinked in astonishment. This wasn't what she'd expected at all. "You mean . . . just the wheel, alone?" She could hear the doubt in her own voice. "You don't need anything else, at all?"

"Just about." The voice from the speaker was calm and confident over the drone of the engine. "As I say, if I were teaching you properly you'd have to understand the instruments, watch your height and speed and so on, but since I'll be with you all the time, I can look after all that myself. All you'll have to do

446

is move the wheel and the throttle exactly when I tell you, plus a couple of other things which you'll only have to move once and then forget about. You follow me?"

Ann swallowed. For the first time, the idea of flying the plane suddenly seemed real and possible.

She raised the microphone and said, "Yes. I see."

"O.K., good. One other thing I ought to mention: I believe you know that your plane's flying on autopilot at the moment?"

Ann said, "Yes," her stomach going suddenly hollow again. He was going to tell her to switch the autopilot off. . . .

"Well, what we're going to do for the time being is to leave the autopilot switched on. You'll be able to over-ride it with your control wheel, but if you let go at any time the aeroplane'll just go back to flying on its own, like it is now. You understand that?"

"You mean it'll come back . . . by itself?"

"That's right; you've got it. So bearing that in mind I'm going to explain now what we want to do. What we'll do for a start is just raise and lower the nose a little. Just that. We need to do that because the nose must be pointed downhill a bit to descend, and then picked up again for the landing. I want you to be able to raise or lower the nose when I tell you, and hold it in its new position. You with me so far?"

"Yes." The word came out hoarsely.

"Good. Now, first we have to have some point of reference so we can see how *much* we've raised the nose. For that, we use the natural horizon. So what I'd like you to do is sit normally in the seat, just as if you were driving, look forward over the top of the instrument panel and tell me how far above the top of that panel the horizon is."

Ann swallowed, and then slowly raised her eyes. The distant horizon-line was just visible over the imitation leather crashpad on top of the instrument panel. She tilted her head back, craning her neck to see it better.

"It's—it's just above the nose. About two inches above."

"O.K., great. Now then, Ann, I want you to make a note in your mind of just *exactly* where it is, so that when we come to move the nose I can say to you 'raise the nose by an inch', and you'll have some reference to judge it by. Got that?"

447

"Ye-es."

"O.K. Now probably at some point we'll be raising the nose *above* the horizon a little bit. When we do that, you'll need to look at where the horizon cuts into the panel on the right-hand side. You see what I mean? You'll have to look *alongside* the panel to see the horizon."

"Yes. All right."

"Okeydoke, that's super." The voice paused while Kerr tried to think of something to break the tension. After a few seconds he said, "You can have a cigarette, if you want one."

Ann blinked. "No . . . no thanks. I don't smoke."

"Very wise of you. Did you give it up, or never start?"

"Er—I never started."

She was flooded with a sudden feeling of unreality. Sitting here in the middle of nothing, talking to someone in another plane about smoking.

"Pity: I was hoping you'd be able to tell me how to give up, later on. Anyway, back to work. Do you see the control wheel in front of you? The thing like half a car steering wheel?"

"Yes." Ann forced herself to pay attention.

"Great. Now, to raise the nose, we pull that wheel *back*; and to lower the nose we push it *forward*. You got that?"

"Yes—we pull back to raise the nose."

"Good. It's the logical way to it, when you think about it. The other thing to remember is that you only push or pull very lightly, over a very small distance. With me?"

"Yes."

"That's fine." The voice was the same as ever, deep and steady. "O.K. then, that's what I'd like you to do: take hold of the control wheel and pull it back, very gently. Look over the nose as you do it and just raise the nose an inch or so on the horizon. Then hold it there until I say."

Ann looked at the yoke. Her face was hot and her muscles tingling—but the raw fear was draining away, leaving a kind of fatalistic acceptance. It was almost as if she was sitting outside herself, watching her body react.

She put the microphone down in her lap, took a deep breath, then reached out and gripped the control wheel. Craning her neck to see the distant horizon, she pulled slowly and firmly backwards. Smoothly, without any hesitation, the nose canted upwards towards the brilliant blue canopy of the sky.

KERR WATCHED the Arrow anxiously as its nose tilted upwards, wondering if Ann would be able to maintain the climb. He shook his head irritably as the nose began to droop down again. In a little while he'd have no choice; he'd have to hustle, push her along, prompt her non-stop against the kind of mistake she was making now. But at the moment, at this initial stage, instinct warned him that the girl was stretched near to breaking-point. Urgent as the time factor was, the first vital requirement was to let her alone for a few brief moments to build up her confidence: too much pressure now and that confidence would shatter.

Ahead and to the right, the other Arrow was slowly levelling off. Kerr followed suit, allowing himself to drift down slightly lower. He glanced at the clock on the panel; it said 1521.

"Hey, you did that all right, Ann." He kept his voice light as he uttered the oldest confidence-booster in the book. "You *sure* you haven't done this before?"

There was a very long pause. Then the girl's voice said in his ears, "No. N-no, I haven't." Beneath the tension there was an undertone of surprise, almost relief.

"Well, you must be born to it, then. Nice natural touch; real gentle. How did you find it, yourself?"

Another pause. Then, "It's heavier than I'd expected, I think."

"Yes, it is heavy. Mr. Piper makes a very easy aeroplane to fly, but he does seem to think that all pilots are built like Russian weight-lifters." Kerr paused, then allowed his voice to become fractionally more brisk. "O.K., then. So what we need to do now is the same again, only this time with the emphasis on *holding* the nose up after you've raised it. You let it drop down a bit last time. You'll have to keep pulling back on the wheel, and you'll find that the trick is to keep your eyes on the horizon all the time. You understand that?"

"Ye-es. I'll try."

"Good lass. Now while you're doing that, in your own time, I'm just going to talk to the ground for a moment. O.K.?"

"Yes."

For a moment, nothing happened. Then, very slowly, the other Arrow's nose lifted up. It began to climb gently, a tiny white bird crawling upwards into the vast blue dome of the heavens. Kerr gave it half a minute, then pressed his transmit button.

"That's lovely, Ann. Just go on holding the nose up there, where it is now. I'll be back to you in a moment."

The Arrow climbed on steadily.

Kerr reached out to the radio panel, and flicked the frequency to Leeds Approach. When he spoke, the gentleness was gone from his voice; the words were snapped and urgent.

"Leeds, Mayday Romeo X-ray."

At first there was no reply. Then a new, calm voice said in his ears, "Mayday Romeo X-ray, from Dan-Air Boeing 724. Leeds are replying to you, sir. Would you like me to relay?"

"Ah—affirmative, 724; I can't hear 'em—they seem to be out of reach. I just want to know who I'm being handed off to, please."

"Roger. Stand by." A pause, then, "O.K., copied. Romeo-X, Leeds says switch to Northern Radar, 131.05. Good luck with your problem."

Kerr acknowledged and double-clicked the transmit switch, thanking a benefactor somewhere in the sky whom he'd never met. Then he changed the frequency to 131.05.

"Northern Radar, Mayday traffic Golf Bravo Charlie Romeo X-ray."

"Romeo X-ray, this is Northern Radar. We have you strength five, radar identified, and we have your details."

"Roger." Kerr spoke fast. "What's my position, please?"

"You're fifteen miles northeast of East Midlands Airport, Romeo X-ray. The big town ahead on your right is Nottingham."

Kerr whistled soundlessly; no wonder he hadn't been able to hear Leeds. He glanced down, found the sprawl of Nottingham about five miles away up-sun, and then thumbed the transmit switch again.

"Roger, Northern Radar. I'm going to need some help on this: there's some things I need done. Ready to copy?"

"Go ahead, sir."

"First thing is aerodromes. We're going to be flying straight for

450

the next forty minutes, so I need details of the biggest aerodromes within our reach before dark after that time. I'm going to need the longest and widest available runway that has flush landing lights, no obstructions either side; also I'd like details of the largest available grass airfield where we can land in more or less any direction. I'll make the decision on which to go for when I know what's available."

"Roger, Romeo X-ray, understood." The voice hesitated for a moment. "Ah—be advised your present track will take you into the London Control Zone in about forty minutes, sir."

Kerr frowned for a couple of seconds, and then shrugged to himself. If he had to go through Heathrow's patch, he had to. "Roger; I'll worry about that later. I'll be calling for radar steers when I can—I haven't got any maps here, and anyway I'll be too busy to navigate." His voice changed suddenly. "Stand by."

The other plane was sinking down, dropping gently below the horizon into the drab brown depths of the distant landscape. Kerr held his position, squinting into the sun as he watched the other aircraft. The girl had done much the same thing as before; allowed her nose to sink back down instead of holding it up. It wasn't her fault: earthbound eyes are simply not accustomed to considering the immutable horizon as variable. Three-dimensional awareness is something which has to be taught.

Kerr thumbed the transmit button.

"Northern Radar, Romeo-X; sorry about that."

"O.K., Romeo X-ray. D'you want to squawk 7700 now?"

"Affirmative." Kerr reached for the transponder. As the figures clicked up his face creased in a brief grin. A transponder is an electronic radar reflector capable of painting up any four-figure code for easy identification on an air traffic controller's screen. Most codes do just that and nothing else—but 7700 is special: it is known as the "Mayday squawk", the international transponder code meaning "I am in distress". At this moment his trace on Northern Radar's screens would be changing from the single short dash of a normal transponder echo to the four-lines-in-a-row of a Mayday signal; at the same time an alarm bell would ring. It was a perfectly sensible thing to do in the circumstances—but it also appealed to a streak of showmanship in him. Like a man who has

451

always wanted to dive into a phone box and dial 999, he had long harboured a small secret desire to squawk Mayday just once.

He said evenly, "Romeo-X squawking Mayday."

"Roger, Romeo X-ray. We advise you come up on 121.5 for transmissions, sir. That'll save you bothering about hand-offs."

Kerr thought for a few seconds. If he stayed on the normal frequencies he'd have to change every time he passed from one radar area into another, whereas if he used 121.5, the universal aircraft emergency frequency, he could be picked up by any major control tower in the country.

He said, "Good idea, sir. Thank you."

"O.K., Romeo X-ray. Call us back on 121.5 when you can."

Kerr said, "Roger, thanks," then reached out and changed back to Ann Moore's frequency again.

The time was twenty-four minutes past three.

BACK AT THE Leeds Aero Club, Edward Tomms's stomach seemed to be on fire. The pain pulsed up every few minutes, agonizingly, growing into a red-hot dagger which stabbed right through to his backbone.

Slumped in a chair facing the club counter, he felt very ill indeed: he badly wanted to get to the lavatory a little way down the corridor, but didn't want to ask for help. So he stayed where he was, hiding his agony behind a thickly-mumbled monologue concerning Kerr's ingratitude. He was bitterly aware that he had provoked the quarrel, but the knowledge only served to increase his anger and frustration.

Most of his employees were conspicuously ignoring him. Ian Mackenzie, the deputy chief instructor, was bent over the counter filling in a student record form. The only person taking any notice of him was Maggie, who kept darting scared little glances over her shoulder in between flustered attempts to deal with the crowd of students at the counter.

The two policemen walked in on the scene at twenty-five minutes past three.

They paused just inside the threshold while the silence spread through the room. After a moment they walked over to the counter. Tomms looked up.

"Eh, I'm glad you coom," he said thickly. "'Oo called you?"

The younger of the two policemen said coldly, "No one called us, sir. We're looking for the owner of a Norton motor cycle parked outside, number XTM 817."

"'Ere . . . Tha's bloody Kerr's! He's bloke who 'it me."

The older policeman said, "Hit you, sir?"

"Aye, damn right!" Tomms was aware of a stillness all around him. He started to stand up, winced, and plumped back into the chair, clasping his stomach. He jerked his head at the Instructors Only door. "Coom round. I'll tell you. I been assaulted."

The crowd of instructors and students began to melt away. Maggie shrank back nervously as the blue uniforms filled the small space behind the counter with their presence. Only Mackenzie seemed unaffected; he stayed where he was, ignoring the police completely.

The older policeman took off his black leather gloves and started unbuttoning the top pocket of his jacket.

"Do you want to tell us what happened, sir?"

"Aye, that I do!" Tomms stared up at the policemen through his thick spectacles. "My bloody chief instroocter 'it me, tha's what. Punched me in the bloody stomach!"

The older policeman looked at Maggie and then back at Tomms. "There's a lady present, sir," he said woodenly.

"Oh. Aye." Tomms glared at Maggie for an instant and then back at the policeman, not sounding sorry. "Well, what you goin' to do abowt it?"

The policeman regarded him stonily. After a moment he said, "Well sir, if you want to make a complaint . . ."

"Aye, I bloody do!" Tomms jabbed an angry finger at the air and then grabbed his stomach again as another wave of pain hit him. "Punched me in the gut . . . I'll 'ave 'im . . . put away."

"Mr. Kerr is the man you say assaulted you, sir?"

"Yeh. Keith Kerr. My bloody chief instroocter."

"Is Mr. Kerr here now, sir?"

"No, he ain't. Bastard went off in one o' my planes, wi'out my permission."

Both policemen stiffened. The younger one said sharply, "Without your permission, sir?"

"Aye! He grabbed keys to one o' my planes, an' when I asked 'im what he were doin' he just punched me an' went off in it. Tha's bloody stealin' it, in't it?"

There was a shocked silence. Tomms became aware that Maggie was staring at him with an expression of horrified disbelief and that Mackenzie was slowly turning round.

The older policeman said, "Stealing means taking something with intent to permanently deprive the owner of the use of it, sir. Are you alleging . . ."

"Don't give me that!" Tomms stabbed the air again with a stubby forefinger. "Bloke took that plane wi'out my permission: that's got to be stealin', ain't it?"

"Rubbish!"

Four cold official eyes pivoted round to look at Ian Mackenzie.

"I'm the deputy CFI," Mackenzie said quickly. "I'm not involved in this, but I ought to make a couple of things clear. The first is that Keith's the chief flying instructor here: that means he doesn't need *anybody's* permission to fly—he's the one who *gives* flight authorizations, not receives them. The second thing . . ."

Tomms exploded. "Eh, bloody hell!"

". . . and the *second* thing," Mackenzie went on loudly, "is that Keith was going off on an emergency flight, and Mr. Tomms was obstructing him and delaying him."

Tomms shouted, "You're bloody fired an' all . . ."

"All *right!*" the older policeman said loudly. He looked at Mackenzie. "Now; what's this emergency flight?"

"There's a pilot been taken ill and passed out in an aeroplane flying down from Newcastle. He's left a woman on board who doesn't know how to fly. Keith's gone up to talk her down if the guy doesn't come round."

The policeman turned his impassive face to Tomms.

"Does that information conflict with anything you know, sir. Do you agree that Mr. Kerr is engaged on an emergency flight?"

Tomms weaved his head about, like a bull looking for someone to charge. "I know he's on soom sort of urgent flight. But that in't th' point. The thing is, he . . ."

"All right, sir." The policeman's voice was flat, commanding. "I just want to get this straight. Would I be right in thinking that

454

this assault took place during an argument between you and Mr. Kerr, about Mr. Kerr's going on this emergency flight?"

Tomms felt the pain coming again, and gripped his stomach. "Aye . . . but I didn't know it were an emergency flight, not then. He just bloody 'it me. Just like that."

The policeman watched him impassively. After a pause he said formally, "All right then, sir. Now if you want, I can take a complaint from you on assault. Do you want to make a statement now; or leave it until you've—ah—calmed down a bit?"

Tomms hesitated, and at that moment his stomach twisted in a fresh stab of pain. His face mottled as his temper boiled over.

"Too right I want to make a statement—assault *an'* stealin' bloody plane! That bastard 'ad been fired when he took that plane: he weren't employed 'ere no more, so he din't 'ave no authority to take anything! I'll see the bastard in jail."

Maggie said, "N-no. It . . . it wasn't like that."

All four men turned to look at her. The older policeman said, "What wasn't like what, miss?"

Maggie said, "Keith. Keith being fired." She looked nervously at Tomms. "He . . . they . . . had a row, when Keith came in. Keith said he was quitting, or that Mr. Tomms could fire him on the spot and give him a month's pay. Mr. Tomms said he was fired, but that he'd have to work the month out. S-so Keith was still employed when he . . . went off."

"Eh! Damn lies!" Tomms strained forward in his chair. "You lyin' little cow. . . ."

Maggie backed away as far as she could, looking pale but determined. "I'm *not* lying," she said. "Mr. Tomms said Keith'd have to work the month out. I heard him."

Tomms jerked suddenly in his chair. His face was putty-white, his breath coming in harsh agitated gasps.

The pain smashed into him, and he fell.

The two policemen got to Tomms a split-second too late to stop his rag-doll tumble to the floor. They both went down on their knees beside the still figure. Tomms's eyes were open and staring, glazed with shock.

The older policeman glanced up at Mackenzie. "Dial 999," he snapped. "Get an ambulance here, quick."

Mackenzie wheeled suddenly on the girl, who was staring at Tomms in wide-eyed shock.

"Maggie! Get Doc Munro! He's in the lounge waiting for a lesson with me." Then he started dialling.

Maggie ran out of the room, and came back followed by a tall man in his early forties. Munro knelt quickly beside Tomms and started checking the pulse. Keeping his eyes on the second hand of his watch, he said, "What happened?"

For a moment, nobody replied. Then Maggie said hesitantly, "Keith . . . hit him in the stomach."

"I know that. But what about afterwards? What did he say?"

"He just kept holding his stomach as if it was hurting."

Munro nodded, and finished taking the pulse. Working quickly, he unbuttoned the heavy overcoat and jacket and loosened the collar and tie. He fumbled under the sagging stomach to loosen the trousers, and then took the bottom front of Tomms's shirt and yanked it apart. He probed the artery below Tomms's stomach with one hand and the base of his neck with the other.

"Was he suffering from anything before this, anyone know?"

Mackenzie and Maggie looked blank.

Munro glanced quickly at the older policeman. "Go through his pockets, will you—I want to know if he was carrying any medicines." Then, to Mackenzie, "Hold your watch in front of me. I'm checking the pulse again."

For what seemed to be a very long time the only sound in the room was the ragged gasping of Tomms's breathing. Finally Munro nodded, and took his hands away from the two arteries. His face was impassive.

The older policeman said, "Ah—here we are, sir," and held up a small round pill-box.

Munro shook half a dozen yellow pills out into his hand. His jaw tightened as he looked at them.

"What are they?" Mackenzie asked.

"Aldomet," said Munro absently. "For blood pressure."

Tomms groaned, and started mumbling. Maggie dropped to her knees close to him, reached out and touched his forehead. His skin felt cold and clammy against her fingers, and she turned her frightened face to Munro. "Can't you *do* something?"

456

Munro shook his head.

Tomms didn't see the gesture—but even if he had, it wouldn't have registered. Everything seemed to be fading now, slowing like a broken-down old film. The whole world had come down to a narrow, soundless cone of vision in which grey shapes moved sometimes and then were gone. Then the tunnel of vision faded quite suddenly into blackness.

His breathing stopped.

Munro stood up swiftly, caught Maggie's right arm, and pulled her up after him. The girl resisted for a moment and then staggered to her feet, sobbing wildly.

"God . . . he's *died!* You've got to *do* something!"

Munro led her to a chair. He said gently, "There's nothing I can do, I'm afraid."

Both policemen were staring at the body as if they hadn't yet accepted the evidence of their own eyes. The older one looked up sharply and said, "Artificial respiration . . . ?"

"No." Munro's voice was quiet but definite. "No point. He's had a burst aortic aneurysm—a split in the main artery from his heart. I'm afraid there's nothing we can do."

The two policemen scrambled up; for a moment they both just stood there. After a few seconds the older policeman said awkwardly, "You *are* sure, sir . . . ?"

Munro glanced at him. "In my own mind, yes. There'll have to be a post-mortem, of course, but I'm in no doubt." He looked at Mackenzie. "Have you got a blanket or something you can put over him?"

Mackenzie seemed to shake himself. He pulled his eyes away from Tomms's body, and turned to a steel filing cabinet. The sound of Maggie's crying diminished a little as Munro sat her down and handed her a handkerchief.

The older policeman seemed to pull himself together with a visible effort. He looked at Munro. "I don't want to press you, sir. But could you give me some idea what might've caused this aneurysm? It might be important."

Munro looked at him impassively for a moment, then gave a small shrug. "Well, the aorta is the big main artery running down from the heart. An aneurysm is localized dilation in it, rather like a weak spot in an inner tube. It develops over months or years and may eventually start to leak, or even burst altogether, as this one did. Since you say he was complaining of stomach pains before he died, I should think the process started with a leak, which must have developed suddenly into a major split."

"How can you be sure?"

"Well, you can feel a massive aneurysm like that with your fingers, you understand. The aorta's only just under the flesh and the weak spot's very obvious."

"I see." The policeman paused for a moment, then added in exactly the same tone of voice, "So would you think that a blow to the stomach might have any effect on an aorta bursting under these conditions, sir?"

The room went suddenly very quiet. Maggie's head jerked round, wide-eyed, and Mackenzie halted in the act of pulling an old army blanket out of the filing cabinet. Everyone looked at Munro, who thrust his hands into his trouser pockets and frowned at the floor.

"Well, yes." He spoke reluctantly, obviously picking his words. "When a person has a severe aneurysm, it's pretty obvious that a blow in the stomach could precipitate a burst. Equally obviously, it won't help if the patient has high blood pressure and remains in an agitated state." He looked up at the policeman. "You understand that is only a *general* inference, not a proper medical opinion on this particular case. I won't stand by it in any way."

"I appreciate that, sir." The policeman turned to Mackenzie. "You say Mr. Kerr is in the air now, sir?"

Mackenzie tore his eyes away from Munro. "Yes. He's trying to talk that woman down, the last I heard."

"Would you know the registration of the aircraft and where it's going to land, sir?"

"It's G-BCRX. I don't know where he's landing."

"I see." The policeman swung round to his companion. "Get out to the car and call in, Chris. Say what's happened and make sure it goes through to CID double quick."

Maggie stared at him in dawning horror while the younger policeman walked out. Her voice trembled as she spoke.

"You're not . . . *after* Keith?"

The policeman looked at her steadily. "He'll have to help us with our inquiries, miss. I'm sure you can see that."

Mackenzie said sharply, "What *are* you inquiring into?"

The policeman looked down at Tomms's body and then back up at Mackenzie's face. "A man has died after an alleged assault, sir," he said formally. "I can't say whether there'll be any proceedings or not, of course. But I'm afraid we have to treat that as a murder investigation."

6

In Whisky Tango's cockpit, Ann Moore was trembling with the effort of concentrating. Moving the plane's nose up and down was more difficult than she'd imagined: there seemed to be so much to watch out for in an apparently simple task. She'd assumed, vaguely, that when you did anything the plane would respond and then the manoeuvre would be over and done with: she hadn't counted on the difficulty of *sustaining* each adjustment.

The voice was speaking again, a metallic clatter against the steady background snore of the plane.

"That last try wasn't bad at all, love. You've still got a bit of a tendency to lose track of your nose position after a while, but you're doing very well indeed. So this time we'll lower the nose again, about three or four inches below the horizon: lower that nose now, and concentrate on what I say."

Biting her lip, Ann pressed forward on the wheel. Gently but firmly. The floor and seat tilted downwards under her, and the hazy horizon slid up the windscreen. She made herself hold it there. Ignore the frosty patchwork fields all that way below, and just hold it. Forget the arms aching with strain, the hands trembling. . . .

The voice said calmly, "Make a careful note of where it is on the centre windscreen pillar and *hold* it there."

The windscreen pillar. The horizon about *that* far up it, above the top of the dashboard. Watch it; keep it there . . .

"Letting the nose come up a bit, love. Watch that horizon. Keep it where it is . . . That's better. Now hold it."

Ann forced herself to concentrate on the horizon, ignoring the sinking pit of coldness in her stomach. Just watch the nose position, shut out‘everything else. . . .

"You're holding that nicely, Ann. Now, we want to come back to level flight. So just relax your pressure on the wheel a little, so that the nose comes back up to its original position."

Relax. Let the nose come up. Muscles trembling, feeling watery. The nose rising. Reaching the horizon. Concentrate on holding it there, holding it for an endless time. . . .

"O.K. Ann, that's very good. We're back in level flight now. Have you got any particular problems you can think of, about raising and lowering the nose?"

Ann blinked. Then she pressed the mike button. "No—not really . . ."

"Fine. In that case then, we'll carry on and take a look at controlling the engine power." The metallic voice paused for a second, then went on. "The first thing we need to do is identify the throttle lever, which is what you move; that's on the quadrant which sticks out of the dashboard, in between the two control wheels. It's got one lever with a black T-handle, rather like a car's automatic transmission lever, and two slightly smaller levers with knobs on. One of the round knobs is blue, and the other one red. Have a look."

Ann looked, trying to shut out the sight of the staring dials. The sound of the engine seemed to drum through her bones. Black, blue and red . . .

"I think I've got it."

"Good. Now the one we're going to be moving is the throttle, which is the black one. To increase power we push it forwards, and to reduce we pull it back. Right?"

"Forward to . . . increase power. Back to reduce it."

"Fine. Now we'll leave that for the moment, and turn to the manifold pressure gauge. This is basically a measurement of power. We need it so I can tell you how *much* to reduce power by. Now; it's one of a pair of dials at the bottom of the panel, just above where Roy's knees are. One of them says RPM on it, and the other one's for manifold pressure. So have a look for that, and tell me when you've found it."

460

Ann turned her head and looked at Roy. He was leaning forward on the diagonal shoulder strap, his rigid neck holding his head nearly upright in a weirdly natural position. His face was ashen, his breathing irregular and shallow.

She shivered and looked down at the panel. The two dials were there, the half-circular scale of the left one labelled MANIFOLD PRESSURE. She lifted the microphone and said, "Yes, I've got that. The needle's on, um, twenty-four."

"That's great. Now, when you *increase* power that gauge'll show a higher number, and when you reduce it, it'll show a lower one. So what I'd like you to do now, when I tell you, is reduce power just by a little bit. Bring the throttle back so that the power goes down to about twenty—and then, a little later on, increase it back up to twenty-four. You with me on that, all right?"

Ann cleared her throat. "Yes. Yes, I understand that."

"Fine. Now, there's just one other thing: as you reduce power, the nose will tend to drop down a bit, and I want you to hold it up, to prevent that happening. You follow that O.K.?"

Ann repeated mechanically, "I've got to hold the nose up, as I reduce the power."

"That's it, love. Right on the ball. O.K. then, let's do that, in your own time. Don't bother to reply to me from now on."

Ann put the microphone down in her lap and wiped the palms of her hands on her jeans. After a moment she took hold of the wheel with her right hand, and with her left, she moved the throttle backwards a fraction of an inch.

The burr of the engine immediately muted a little, frightening her. She bit her lip and tried to shut the sound out, to concentrate on what she had to do. She looked down at the manifold pressure gauge: the needle was halfway between the twenty and twenty-four. She pulled the throttle back further, very slowly. The needle slid down until it touched twenty.

The voice from the speaker said matter-of-factly, "You're letting the nose drop a little there, Ann."

She looked up, letting go of the throttle and jerking back on the wheel with both hands. The nose bucked, the floor pushing up against her feet for an instant. Shivering from head to foot, she forced herself to concentrate on the horizon.

461

"O.K. Ann, you're doing great. Now let's open the throttle again until the power goes back up to twenty-four."

Power. More power.

She reached out to the throttle lever again, and edged it forwards. The engine note deepened, swelling up to its previous full-bodied snore. She went on looking forwards for half a minute, and then glanced down at the gauge. The needle was a couple of sub-divisions over the twenty-four. She hesitated, and then pulled the lever back a tiny amount. The needle settled a fraction over twenty-four.

"Watch that nose position, Ann."

Her head jerked up. The horizon had disappeared. She pushed sharply on the wheel. There was a horrible sinking sensation, the nose dropping away. . . .

"Steady now! Slow and easy!"

She bit hard on her lip, forcing herself to hold the wheel still. The nose was below the horizon, the engine cowling pointing into distant toy fields. She waited a few seconds, breathing quickly, then pulled back gently and held.

The Arrow stabilized in level flight and flew on smoothly through the winter afternoon.

KERR SAGGED BACK in the seat and puffed out his cheeks in a huge sigh of relief. She'd done it.

She'd followed his instructions slowly and sloppily—but she had followed them. While the power had been reduced her life had been in her own hands for the first time, and she'd come through it.

But she still had a lot more to learn.

Kerr ran his hand through his hair, pushing the headset down round his neck like a collar. What he wanted to work up to was practice descents and mock-landings in the air, but before that could be begun, there was the problem of the aircraft's speed to be considered. Practising landings from high-speed cruising flight would be dangerously misleading: the first thing was to get the runaway plane slowed down in level flight to somewhere near its normal approach speed.

Except that slowing an aircraft in flight is a complex operation. Perhaps too complex for her to manage at this stage.

Kerr chewed the inside of his cheek, frowning out at the aeroplane crawling across the distant landscape beyond his right wing. He wished that he had some idea of what the girl was like—whether she was short or tall, pretty or plain, timid or self-confident. Without sitting beside her and seeing her react he was robbed of the subtle tools of his trade, left shouting into the empty sky.

The clock on the panel said 1544: less than an hour to go before sunset. He shook his head angrily, irritated at his own time-wasting thoughts. At forty-four minutes past three o'clock the question of whether she was *ready* for a speed reduction was neither here nor there.

Kerr frowned, looking doubtful. Then he glanced at his fuel gauges, pulled the headset back over his ears, and started speaking cheerfully into the microphone.

IF A PERSON meets his death after being assaulted, the British police are obliged to treat the matter as a murder investigation. This does not mean the end result will necessarily be a murder *charge* (the eventual outcome may be almost anything); it is more a question of the urgency with which the police conduct their inquiries. The investigating police officer's job is not to formulate the charges, but to present the Director of Public Prosecutions with a complete report of the facts at the earliest possible moment. And in order to achieve this end, the rule book states that in all such cases the full murder investigation procedure be carried out.

Detective Chief Inspector Neville Lauder of Leeds Horsforth Station was determined to follow the rule book to the letter.

Seven minutes after the call from the Aero Club, Lauder was being driven rapidly through Leeds's Saturday congestion in a police XJ6. He sat exactly upright in the front passenger seat, a tall thin man in his mid-forties with a gaunt face and still, suspicious eyes. Lauder had been promoted to CID from the Traffic department six weeks before. He knew that he was regarded by the rest of the CID staff as being pedantic, humourless, and a stickler for regulations. This reputation was accurately founded: he *was* a rule-book man, and always would be. He saw nothing wrong with that, especially in an instance like this: this was his first murder investigation, and the rules were a comforting bulwark against any possibility of an embarrassing error.

Watching the Kirkstall Road roll past as the XJ6 swished towards the airport, he went over his duties again in his mind. Standard rule-book murder investigation procedure, and nothing left out. No loose ends, no room for awkward comebacks.

He relaxed a fraction in his seat. After a moment his left hand came up and unconsciously checked the straightness of his tie.

AT THE SAME MOMENT, a hundred miles to the south, Ann Moore was staring dazedly at the cold blue sky over Whisky Tango's nose. Her back was aching, her throat was parched, and she was too hot to think. Which was a pity, because the man on the radio was explaining something which sounded important.

She was trying to listen, trying hard, but her brain seemed to have lost its ability to concentrate. Her thoughts kept squirrelling off down idiotic sidetracks all the time: looking at the plastic trim over the windscreen pillar and thinking it cheap and nasty; looking out at the sky, and thinking how out of place this tiny plastic box was in the enormous blue reaches of nothing. . . .

". . . down in between the seats. Ann: d'you understand me all right, about the trim wheel?"

The trim wheel . . .

She looked down beside her left thigh. Sticking out of the curved blue plastic runnel between the seats was the top rim of a wheel about six inches in diameter, with finger-grip serrations around its edge. At the back of its slot were the printed words NOSE UP, and at the front NOSE DOWN.

She lifted the microphone and cleared her throat. "Could you . . . sorry . . . could you say what I've got to do with it again? Please."

"Sure." The voice clattered on. "When we've reduced power and speed and raised the nose a little I'll be telling you to wind it back. It'll take the pressure off the main control wheel; otherwise you'd have to keep pulling back all the time, which'd make it impossible to fly accurately. You with me there?"

"Yes. I understand."

"Fine; you're doing really great. One thing more. I want you to look at the small red lever beside the throttle. It controls the fuel mixture and it needs to be right forward. It may already be forward. I want you to tell me if it is."

Ann stared at the lever. "Yes," she said. "Yes, it is right forward."

"Great. I thought it might be. Now, if you're ready, we can start the slowing-down bit."

She rubbed her eyes, hearing her breath rasping in her dry throat. A small shrinking part of her wanted to scream, *No! I'm not ready! I didn't understand what you said!*—but you couldn't do that. It was like doing things you didn't want to in hospital. You just had to shut your mind, make yourself into a sort of machine, and get on with them. Be efficient, detached . . .

She looked forwards, into the vast blue emptiness beyond the windscreen. "Yes. I'm ready."

Straining upwards in her seat, she took hold of the control yoke. With her neck craned and her head tipped back she could just see the top surface of the engine cowling in front of the windscreen. She reached out to the throttle. She took a shaky deep breath as the engine note lowered from its steady drone. She went on pulling the lever back.

"That's good, honey. Have a glance in now and check that you've got the power at twenty."

Her eyes darted down. The gauge read 20. She looked up again —and the nose was dropping. Pull it up, hold it . . .

"That's it; you're in great shape, love. Just stay with it. I'm going to assume you've got the power at twenty now, so if you haven't, you tell me."

For a long moment there was just the muted rumble of the engine. Ann stared forwards, her back aching with tension. Hold the nose up. Concentrate. Then the voice came again.

"O.K. then, that's cool. Now, we want to raise the nose a bit; raise it by about three inches."

Pull back. Hold the nose up. It was like being in one of those dreams where you keep on doing the same thing interminably, running away or falling, and you can't stop it. *Just keep pulling, keep the nose above the horizon . . .*

The Arrow's wings, pitched upwards to a slightly steeper angle of attack, generated both more lift and more drag. The control yoke became heavier than ever, requiring more and more back-pressure to keep the nose up. On the panel, the climb/descent needle wavered languidly, then stabilized on the climb side of the zero figure.

After an age the voice chattered out of the speaker again, loud and deliberate in the new quiet.

"That is magnificent, Ann. Perfect. Now just hang on there, hold the nose exactly where it is, and listen to me carefully. I want you in a moment to reach down with your left hand to the trim wheel, and, turn it, roll it back by about five inches. Remember that the pressure on the main control wheel will change as you move the trim, so you'll have to concentrate hard on the nose position."

Very slowly, Ann took her left hand off the control yoke. Still staring forward at the horizon, she reached down and groped between the seats. She took hold of the wheel near the front end of its slot, hesitated for a moment, and then revolved it backwards in one movement—much too quickly.

Instantly, the nose reared up. Seat and floor pushed hard up underneath her, and the earth disappeared. The cowling was suddenly pointing into blue emptiness and streaky clouds, the engine starting to labour.

"Push the nose down, Ann! Down, gently!"

She pushed forward on the control yoke, and the plane dropped away from under her, leaving her stomach behind like an express lift.

"Hold it *there!* Just hold it! Steady!"

She held the yoke still, gripping it desperately with both hands. The sound of the engine began to wind up in the dive, like a car accelerating ponderously.

"That's good, love." The voice was quick, urgent. "Now raise the nose up, but do it very slowly and gently."

Raise the nose. . . .

Trembling, not knowing whether she was pulling back or merely relaxing a forward pressure, she brought the nose up. The landscape marched downwards in front of the propeller for a moment and then suddenly there was the horizon, lowering itself into place on top of the panel. The control yoke felt lighter, somehow, as if it wasn't doing so much as it had been before: she didn't seem to be pulling back so hard.

"That's fine." The man's voice was back to normal. "Now just hold her nice and steady, as she is now. You moved the trim a bit too quickly there, that was all. But no harm done. Just hold her steady, and don't worry about a thing."

Ann went on staring at the horizon.

"All we need to do now, then, is establish whether that trim movement you made was adequate. If it was, then if you were to let go of the wheel, the nose ought to stay more or less where it is now. I'd like you to do that now: let go, but be prepared to take over again immediately if the nose goes up or down."

She hesitated, then she slowly unclenched her fists, holding her trembling hands just clear of the yoke.

Very gently, almost imperceptibly, the nose pitched up an inch or so higher against the horizon. Then it remained steady, and the Arrow hung stable in the sky.

THE MUSCLES in Kerr's neck were aching sullenly from having his head turned constantly to the right. His eyes never left the streamlined shape of the other Arrow, floating serenely alongside.

After half a minute his headphones made a small whistling click, and the girl's voice spoke in his ears.

"I've let go. I'm not touching it."

Kerr stared, astonished. She'd done it! Relief flowed through his body like the warmth of a stiff drink. His face split into a sudden grin, and he let out his breath in a long slow *whoosh*. Then he thumbed the transmit button again.

"That's great, honey!" He could hear the lift in his own voice, feeding back through his headset. "You've got the aeroplane slowed down, and you've done it very well indeed. That was the most difficult thing you'll have to do, and now it's all finished with. So sit back now and have a rest for a couple of minutes."

Then the voice said tonelessly, "Yes. All right."

The remains of Kerr's grin faded. He frowned, then said gently, "How do you feel, love? Everything going O.K.?"

467

Again the time lag; again the peculiar flatness when the headphones eventually spoke, "Yes. I'm all right."

Kerr said, "Good, fine," forcing heartiness into his voice to cover the sudden coldness in his guts.

The girl's wooden response was a danger signal as clear as a red flare. When a student sounded like that it meant that you were pushing too hard, exceeding their ability to cope—and if you continued piling on the pressure, something was going to break. He *had* been pushing her too hard, of course. He'd swamped her with too much talk, introduced new tasks before she could cope with the old ones—but he hadn't any choice. And with the clock on his instrument panel reading seven minutes to four, the pressure was mounting. He became aware that his scar was itching furiously, and rubbed it with the knuckles of his left hand.

"O.K. then, Ann." Kerr kept the anxiety out of his voice, striving to sound relaxed. "Now while we're having our rest, I guess we might as well use the time by putting the wheels down. That doesn't mean we're going to land for a while yet—we've got plenty of fuel still—but if we get our wheels down good and early then it'll be out of the way. You understand?"

There was another long silence. Then the girl said, "Yes."

Kerr frowned suddenly. His own words had jogged something in his mind, some forgotten detail which clamoured for attention. Too experienced a pilot to ignore a subconscious warning, he stopped short and glared across the void at the other Arrow. What had he said? Undercarriage? Fuel . . . ? *Fuel* seemed to ring the warning bell again, but it couldn't be that: he had his own fuel state constantly in mind, and Whisky Tango had enough for two and a half hours or more.

His frown deepened and he glanced at the instruments, eyes flicking over the dials with the speed of long habit. All O.K.—but the nagging feeling of having forgotten something persisted. His eyes passed over the clock, nestling in the corner of the panel. As he watched it the second hand completed a sweep and the time was three fifty. Whatever it was bothering him, however important it was, there was no more time for it.

He cleared his throat, pressed the transmit button again, and began to talk Ann through lowering the undercarriage.

468

DIRECTLY ABOVE the manifold pressure gauge, unnoticed by Ann, one small rectangular dial looked out of place. Alone out of all the instruments on Whisky Tango's panel its needle was far over to the left, nearly covering a thin red line at the bottom of its scale.

Underneath it were the printed words FUEL LEFT TANK.

7

As air traffic radar consoles go, the ones in the Distress and Diversion Cell at West Drayton are not immediately impressive. There are only two of them, one for each controller, and each is no bigger than a small television screen.

They have, however, one or two unique features. The most important of these features is their versatility. Whilst normal radar screens are limited to one or two transmitters, the D and D sets are able to roam the whole of England: the flick of a switch can "pipe in" a picture from any of the ten major route-surveillance radars in the country. This picture then goes through the LATCC computer, with the result that the presentation appearing on the screen comes complete with illuminated transponder codings and the special symbols triggered by anyone squawking Mayday, Hi-jack, or Communications Failure.

Right now, the D and D number-one controller, Flight Lieutenant Peterson, was watching Kerr's Mayday squawk, which appeared as a pulsating circle-and-cross of orange light with the letters SOS beside it. The trace was creeping southwards towards Denham, and within a short while it would be penetrating the complex block of controlled airspace which is the London Air Terminal Approach Area. Two minutes before, Peterson had taken over direct control of the flight from the Bedford Radar controller.

Peterson watched the squawk for a full minute, chewing a fingernail thoughtfully. Then he reached out and made a small cross on top of the light symbol with a Chinagraph pencil. The mark was the latest in a line of similar crosses, made at three-minute intervals, which plotted Kerr's passage over the ground.

He pictured the instructor in Romeo X-ray, hard-pressed and

sweating as he fought against time. In many ways Peterson's job now was to act as a kind of alter-ego to that instructor: to anticipate the problems which the man in the air had no time to consider, and have the answers ready to hand. The first of these problems was the emergency's position and track.

Northern Radar had reported that Romeo X-ray was intending to rely on ground assistance for his navigation; so at this moment the pilot probably didn't know his present location. Peterson, however, was better placed. By mentally extending the line of crosses a few inches on his screen he could calculate with considerable accuracy the position of the two aeroplanes in eighteen minutes' time, assuming they made no attempt to turn. In eighteen minutes' time they would be more or less slap over the top of London's Heathrow Airport.

Air traffic-wise, this was not a problem. Contrary to the popular notion of white-faced controllers scattering jet airliners like minnows at the hint of an emergency over Heathrow, the actual juggling of traffic was already being accomplished with the minimum of fuss. The three London director controllers at Heathrow Tower were calmly preparing to "knit a hole" in their constant stream of arrivals and departures so that their Control Zone would be completely free of traffic at the appropriate moment. The net result of clearing a passage for the runaway would be a delay of ten or fifteen minutes for perhaps 10,000 passengers and airline staff, but for the controllers it was no problem. Air traffic was the least of Peterson's worries.

He pulled his headset back from one ear and twisted round to look at Squadron Leader Lyle, who was sitting in a spare chair behind his left elbow.

"What do you think, sir? About the built-up areas?"

The officer commanding D and D removed his pipe from his mouth and blew a cloud of smoke. His permanently quizzical face looked as if he were about to utter some gem of sarcasm.

"I think," he said slowly, "that there's probably very little we can do about it anyway. Where does he actually look like coming through?"

"Right over the top, sir, I reckon. The Uxbridge, West Drayton, Sunbury sort of area."

Lyle swung round in his chair and stared intently at the topographic map of England which was pasted up on the wall behind him. As the chief emergency controller, his duty very definitely included taking all reasonable steps to prevent the possibility of the machine going down in a heavily populated area. He studied the map, thinking hard.

"It could be a lot worse, you know. If he was a bit left of his present track he'd go smack over the centre of London, and if he was right he'd hit Slough or Guildford. If he's got to come down over here at all, at least it's not the most densely populated district in the area."

Peterson twisted and looked at the map himself. "I suppose so," he said doubtfully.

Lyle had made up his mind. "When he comes on, John, ask him if he can make a turn, but don't make a big thing of it. If he can't make at least a ninety-degree turn and then hold his heading, I'd rather he kept going as he is."

Peterson nodded slowly and went back to watching his radar screen. For the moment, there was nothing else he could do. The police, fire and ambulance services on the emergency route had already been alerted, the air traffic side was well in hand, and he had in front of him a list of runway data and surface winds for every aerodrome which the pilot of Romeo X-ray might conceivably wish to consider for the landing attempt. Now, the only thing left was to wait for the instructor to say something.

They waited until two minutes past four. Peterson had 121.5 switched through to the loudspeaker as well as his headset, so that the disembodied voice boomed suddenly loud in the small smoky room.

"Emergency controller from Mayday Golf Bravo Charlie Romeo X-ray, good afternoon."

Peterson jerked in his seat and said quickly, "Romeo-X, this is Distress and Diversion Drayton Centre, go ahead."

"Roger, D and D. I'm still in formation with Whisky Tango, and I've now got her slowed down with the wheels lowered. Have you got some airfield information, please?"

Peterson said clearly, "Affirmative, Romeo-X. But first, sir, be advised that your present heading will take you directly over

Heathrow. Do you intend continuing on your present heading, or is there any possibility of making a turn?"

Kerr's metallic voice came back immediately.

"Negative, D and D: I'm working on pitch control and throttle with her, and I don't want to interrupt that yet."

Peterson frowned, but said calmly, "Roger, Romeo-X. Can you confirm you'll be maintaining your present heading until south of the London Control Zone then, sir? That'll take you about twenty minutes at your present airspeed."

"Probably, D and D." Static hissed for a moment. "I'll advise if I'm thinking of any major course changes before then. Now, have you got that airfield information? This will be a wheels-down landing, no foam required."

"O.K., Romeo-X. Now the longest hard runway is Greenham Common: the runway is one-one two-niner, three thousand metres by sixty metres wide, no significant obstructions to the sides in the immediate vicinity. Surface wind at Greenham is two eight zero at fifteen knots. We could refer you for a straight-in on two-niner beginning with a right turn off your present track in about twenty minutes time."

There was a few seconds' pause. Then the voice said, "Roger, D and D; copied. What about the grass fields?"

Peterson flipped a page in his notepad. "Romeo-X, the best I can do on grass airfields within your reach before dark is Lasham. They have a grass area to the north of runway one-zero two-eight, which is one thousand eight hundred metres long. Otherwise

there's White Waltham, with twelve hundred metres east-west. White Waltham has a built-up area on the eastern boundary, and I believe the Lasham grass area may have obstructions on the north side—I can check that for you."

"Negative, D and D. Don't bother checking Lasham if it's no more than eighteen hundred metres—I'd hoped there was something a bit longer. I'll take Greenham Common, I think. Can you confirm they have full crash facilities there?"

Peterson said, "That's affirmative, sir. The US Air Force have just moved there from Upper Heyford. Three squadrons of F1-11s and all the equipment."

The metallic voice said dryly, "That ought to be enough. Confirming landing at Greenham Common, then. I'll call you around the south boundary of the London Zone—switching back now to 126.85."

"Roger Romeo-X; good luck, sir."

Lyle was the first to break the sudden silence. He took the cold pipe from between his teeth and said quietly, "All right, John. You speak to Greenham, and I'll talk to Latsie about the routing." He glanced across at Peterson. "And we'd better start using up our prayer quotas: because that woman's going to need all the help she can get."

473

THE CALL FROM LEEDS came in two minutes later, and was taken by Peterson's corporal assistant.

"It's the Leeds police, sir. The bloke says it's urgent."

Peterson pressed a button to connect the telephone into his headset. "Yes? Number one controller."

"Detective Sergeant Barnes here, sir, Horsforth Police Station. Are you controllin' an aircraft registration G-BCRX at the moment, sir? It's a Piper Cherokee Arrow plane."

"Yes, I've got it. But the emergency passed out of your area hours ago. . . ."

"Aye, I know that, sir. But can you confirm the pilot of it's a Mr. Kerr, sir? Mr. Keith Kerr?"

Peterson blinked at the unusual question—controllers deal with aircraft callsigns, not pilots' names—then glanced down at his notes. "That's affirmative," he said into the microphone. "Why do you want to know?"

"We want Mr. Kerr to help us with some inquiries, sir. So I'd be obliged if you could tell me where and when the aircraft will be landing if you can."

Peterson glanced at his radar screen and said, "Well, he'll be landing at Greenham Common, near Newbury, some time before dark, as far as we know. What sort of inquiries do you want him for?"

The Yorkshire voice hesitated for a moment, then said evenly, "We want him for questionin' in connection with a murder investigation here, sir. My instructions are to find where he's landing an' arrange for his arrest."

"*Arrest!*" Peterson literally couldn't believe his ears. Then he swung round in his chair and spoke urgently to Lyle, oblivious of the fact that the man on the line could still hear him. "There's a copper on here, sir." Peterson swallowed. "He says they want the pilot of Romeo-X in connection with a murder investigation."

There was dead silence. The other men in the room froze for a moment in shock, and then Lyle seemed to shake himself. He tapped the headset connecting button and barked, "Squadron Leader Lyle here, Officer Commanding D and D. Now tell me what this is all about."

There was another pause. Lyle's features tightened, shocked out

474

of their normal quizzical expression. After half a minute he said, "Well, that isn't enough for me, I'm afraid. I want to speak to the senior officer handling the case. Where? Well, we'll get on to him there."

Lyle broke the connection and then rounded on Peterson.

"John. Phone Horsforth cop-shop double quick and confirm the call actually did come from him; I want to make sure it isn't some stupid joke. I'm going to get on to the Leeds Aero Club—the copper in charge of the case's supposed to be there now."

"Yes, sir." Peterson's hand reached out for the main switchboard button and then hesitated, hovering. He said awkwardly, "Silly question I expect, sir. But . . . do you think this actually *affects* this emergency?"

Lyle ran a hand over his head.

"Well," he said slowly, "we could hardly pull Romeo-X down at this stage even if we wanted to." Then he added: "All the same, if we've just cleared a homicidal maniac to command an emergency flight right over the London Control Zone, then I *would* like to know about it."

On the steadily scanning radar screen the illuminated Mayday symbol crept towards London.

IN THE BRIEFING ROOM of the Leeds Aero Club, Detective Constable Ivor Jones sneezed violently. He wished the Mobile Control Room would hurry up and arrive: it might be cold and cramped, but at least it was free of chalk dust. When he spoke his voice was thickened by the stuffiness of a heavy cold.

"Going to 'ave to tread softly on this one, sir."

"Oh? Why?"

Detective Chief Inspector Lauder, sitting beside him at the battered instructor's desk, was regarding him stonily.

"Well . . ." Jones shrugged. "I mean, this bloke Kerr—seems he's a bit of a hero, up there talking that woman down. Been some Sunday papers on the phone about it apparently."

Lauder's expression remained unchanged. He said coldly, "Yes, I heard. Does that make a difference, then?"

Jones hesitated, suddenly wary. "Well, no sir," he said. "What I mean is, it doesn't seem like the usual run of murders, that's all.

Like, we'll probably end up dropping the murder charge and accepting a plea of manslaughter, won't we? And under the circumstances I shouldn't be surprised if he gets off with a suspended sentence or even a discharge."

Lauder raised one eyebrow. "Thank you, constable," he said acidly. "So you suggest *tread softly*, then?"

"Well, we hardly need to call the cavalry out, do we?"

There was an ominous silence as Lauder leaned back in his chair. "Listen, constable," he said deliberately, "I want you to understand this. I carry out my investigations according to the book, and I am not in the habit of *treading softly* just because a few newspapers are sniffing around. I will not have this investigation performed in a casual manner just because you've got it into your head that you know all the answers. Is that clear?"

Jones felt his face going red. After a long moment he took a slow, deep breath and just said, "Sir."

8

Ann pulled the throttle back another half an inch. The snore of the engine subsided still further, becoming a low hissing ruffle of propeller and airflow. The plane was sinking.

She could feel the sinking as if she were in a descending lift. But the weird thing was that there was no other evidence of going down: the frosty earth a mile below the engine cowling still looked exactly the same, not coming up to meet her at all. It was somehow like a nightmare she used to have where she was teetering on the parapet of a tall building. There was no reason not to take half a step forward into emptiness and be falling, falling. . . .

The speaker clicked and came to life again.

"That's great stuff, Ann. You're in a nice gentle powered descent, just like you will be when you come in to land. We could do with the nose an inch or so higher, that's all."

Part of her mind seemed to be curiously detached from her body, sitting somewhere behind her shoulder and watching the girl at the controls as if she were a stranger. She felt contemptuous in a distant sort of way, because the girl was reacting very stupidly. Her body was rigid with tension when she should have been thinking calmly and clearly. She ought to relax, this silly girl. . . .

"Come on now, love." The voice was clear and commanding. "You want the nose higher than that. An inch or so higher."

There! The stupid girl at the wheel had let the nose drop, even though the man had *told* her she'd have to keep holding the nose up because of the reduced engine power. Now she was pulling harder, knuckles white. The floor tilting gently. . . .

The cowling lifted soggily. It was difficult to tell exactly how far because the horizon was becoming hazy, misting in readiness for the early winter evening.

"That's fine, honey. Now, we want to increase the rate of descent. So bring the throttle back about another half an inch, and keep holding the nose position."

Bring the throttle back.

She saw the girl fumble for the lever with the T-handle, and pull it backwards a fraction further. A small rhythmic cycle of vibration started up, quivering gently through control yoke and seat. The feeling of sinking increased.

"Good. Now we'll pretend we're getting low, and we're going to make the landing. We'll say we're at second-storey building height. So raise the nose a bit *now.*"

She watched the girl shudder. The nose was heavier than ever, trying to drop down . . .

"*Now*, Ann! Raise the nose *now!*"

The girl pulled back. The cowling popped up above the horizon, pointing suddenly into blue sky.

"Right—now close the throttle completely. All the way back. Expect the horn I told you about any moment."

The girl reached out to the throttle pedestal again. Her hand seemed to be moving in slow motion as she pulled the T-handle back to its stop.

The engine immediately died right down to tickover; ahead of the windscreen, the propeller hazed into a nearly-visible disc. The wind-hiss backed down the scale, dying.

The detached part of her brain watched dispassionately. The phenomena of the power-off glide and the aerodynamic stall were completely unknown to her, but the lowering sigh of the wind and the nose-high attitude a mile above the ground *felt* wrong. The plane needed the engine roaring to keep it in the sky, and now the roaring was gone.

The stall-warning device chirruped suddenly like a faulty car horn, then stayed on in a solid electric bleep.

The girl quivered from head to foot as she kept up the back-pressure on the wheel. A trickle of blood started down her chin from where she was biting her lip. The cabin was balanced on an invisible knife-edge in space, sinking faster. . . .

The voice came again, urgent over the bleating horn.

"Right—now we'll overshoot. As if we're going round again off a bad landing. Hold the nose where it is and give her full power."

The girl still had her left hand on the throttle lever. Without taking her eyes off the misty horizon she pushed it forwards. The nose tried to lift up by itself; she snatched her left hand back to the control wheel. The plane was wriggling, not steady any more. Some unseen force jostling the controls, taking over, trying to pull the nose up. . . .

"Ann! Give her *full* power! Throttle *all* the way forwards!"

Push the throttle more. More. The lever suddenly hard against the stop. The engine noise huge after the quiet. The voice again, tinny now over the roar.

"O.K., love, good. Now, push the nose down a bit. Gently, down to level flight, like before. You're doing fine."

The horizon floating up over the crashpad. The girl holding it steady, sitting numb in the engine roar.

"That's great. Now hold the nose there, and bring the power back to twenty. Take your time: you've got it made."

Bring the power back to twenty. . . .

Her left hand flexed, moving the throttle slowly backward. The hand stopped and she turned her head, staring dully at the manifold pressure gauge. Her hand moved again, and the roar of the engine slid back to a background drone. The manifold pressure was 20. She took her hand away from the throttle.

The voice came again, calm and clear.

"Honey, that was very, very good. You've just been through a descent, a landing, and overshoot, and brought yourself back to

478

level flight. The aeroplane will fly itself again now, so you can sit back and have a rest. That was very good indeed."

For nearly a minute Ann went on sitting upright, still holding the wheel. Then, when the words sank in, she unclenched her fingers, collapsed down in the seat, and buried her face in her hands. The small, lonely sound of her sobbing was lost under the monotonous rumble of the aircraft.

KERR FOUND that his feet were shuddering on the rudder pedals. Every muscle in his body was knotted and aching, straining with the effort of trying to reach out across the void to the other aircraft. If only he could transmit his will and his skill through the girl so that *he* flew the aeroplane, *he* fed in the small pressures and responses on control yoke and rudder. . . .

He wiped a sweaty hand over his face and made himself relax, untensing his leg muscles with a conscious effort. His feet were hot and slippery, and after a moment he leaned forward awkwardly and pulled down the zips of his motor-cycle boots, leaving the uppers flopping loosely around his shins.

He breathed deeply, thinking hard. When it came down to it the girl had done as well as could be expected considering the barrage of instruction she'd been getting. All the same, the past ten minutes had been a non-stop running battle, slamming his own controls around to stay in station and at the same time trying to identify the other Arrow's mistakes as it rose and fell. The main difficulty had been the slowness of her reactions, particularly on the simulated overshoot: if that had been a genuine go-around-again off a bad landing she'd have flown into the ground half a dozen times over.

Kerr wondered whether he should abandon the idea of a go-around altogether, and concentrate on getting her on the ground any-old-how off the first approach. So long as the wing-leveller was still switched in, even quite a serious landing accident probably wouldn't kill her, whereas attempting an overshoot and then flying the aircraft into a tree almost certainly would. It is one of the oldest axioms of aviation that it's preferable to have a crash sliding along the ground rather than hitting something when airborne.

After a moment he shook his head tiredly, pushing the question out of his mind. At this time there was no possible answer: it would have to be decided in a split-second during the actual landing attempt, and then lived with afterwards.

He lit his last but one Gold Leaf, and sat back to think about his other problems.

His diminishing reserves of time, fuel, and daylight had been on his mind ever since he'd first turned on his back and plunged down after Whisky Tango: the difference now was simply that bankruptcy was that much more imminent. The clock on the instrument panel said four twelve in the afternoon. In a quarter of an hour the sun would have set, and fifteen or twenty minutes after that it would be dark. That meant the landing attempt would have to be made within the next thirty minutes—and *that* dictated that the final descent from their present altitude should commence within the next quarter of an hour.

Kerr looked at his fuel gauges for the twentieth time in half an hour, and shook his head.

When he'd first seen his fuel contents, before taking off, he'd reckoned he had enough to last until dark and then a little beyond —and under normal circumstances he should have had. But instead of droning along steadily at economy-cruise, he'd been slamming his throttle around to stay in formation with the runaway plane. And that sort of treatment meant that fuel consumption would have gone up, just as when a car was being driven in traffic. Now, the left tank read between a quarter full and empty, while the right tank showed a fraction less.

Kerr dragged in a deep lungful of smoke, then reached out and clicked his undercarriage switch to UP. Retracting his own gear would make it more difficult to hold station with the other aircraft, but on the other hand the dangling wheels meant burning precious extra fuel to overcome the drag.

His fingers drummed on the throttle quadrant for a moment. Then he leaned across the cockpit and twisted the fuel tap to the left tank position. He'd stay on this one until the needle was nearly on the zero, switch back to the right tank and run that dry, and after that assume he'd got a final ten minutes remaining on the left. It wasn't a good plan, but it was the best thing he could

480

think of. It was far too late to get someone else up to take his place now.

He looked ahead. With a flying man's eye for the cities that pass beneath his wings, Kerr had always liked London: where so many younger urban areas of the world are drably laid out in neat chequerboard squares, the capital of England is refreshing in its refusal to conform. Now, in the sunny late afternoon, he saw a huge undulating carpet of civilization; a carpet speckled with red, brown and green, decorated in its distant centre with the cake-icing towers and spires of the inner city.

Kerr frowned, ignored the ten million people who would shortly be sliding under his wingspread, and concentrated on the simple arithmetic of time and distance.

He had seven or eight miles to go to the northernmost tentacles of the built-up area. Then he'd be over-flying the London Control Zone with about ten minutes to run to the southern boundary—by which time he'd damn well better be ready to get the girl turned due west for Greenham Common. So he was going to have to start teaching right now: turns first, then more pitch and power practice later if there was time.

Keeping his eyes on the other Arrow, he blew a slow jet of smoke at the windscreen, planning the moves ahead. The first step would be to get her to disengage the heading-hold of her autopilot: with that out of the way she'd be able to make turns simply by banking the aircraft, overriding the wing-leveller. The result would be sloppy flying, but if he taught her to use the rudder it would mean introducing a new control. A snag about *not* introducing the rudder was that without it she'd have no way of steering once she was on the ground, but with an aerodrome the size of Greenham he was prepared to accept that: running off the side of the runway after landing was the least of her dangers.

He wiped his mouth with the back of his left hand, feeling the prickle of a nine-hour stubble on his chin. It suddenly occurred to him that he'd have to shave again when he got back to Leeds. He had a date tonight with Maggie. . . .

For a moment his face softened, the lines of tension dissolving. Then he shook his head briefly and concentrated on the floating shape of Whisky Tango. His thumb pressed the transmit switch.

481

"How're you doing there, Ann?"

For ten or fifteen seconds there was no reply. Then there was a metallic click, and the girl's voice spoke in his ears.

"I'm all right, thanks."

Kerr frowned, worried by her tone, then pressed his own switch again.

"O.K. then, honey. What we're going to do now are one or two gentle turns. But before we can do that, we need to locate the heading-hold button of your autopilot and disengage it. That will mean we can make our turns without the magic box trying to pull us back onto our present course all the time. You with me so far?"

His headphones hissed for a moment. Then the girl's voice said dully, "Yes."

He paused, groping for something to say to make her relax. But there wasn't anything.

"Right, then. Now, the autopilot control buttons are on a small white panel on the bottom left-hand side of the instrument panel proper. It has two buttons, and it's labelled Autocontrol Three. Don't touch it yet; just get it located."

After a long pause the voice said flatly, "I've found it."

"O.K. then—you should find that the right hand button has the letters H-D-G written under it. They stand for heading. Now, I want you to press that button once, firmly, and then release it. If you understand that then do it now, and let me know when you've done it."

Nothing seemed to happen. The runaway hung immobile in space, pinned in the pale blue sky above the yellow glare of the setting sun. Kerr watched it intently. Switching out the heading-hold *shouldn't* make any difference, of course—the Arrow's natural directional stability should still make it fly straight—but on the other hand, if that particular aeroplane had a tendency to hold a slightly asymmetric flight configuration . . .

For some reason the word *asymmetric* jarred in his mind, ringing the same half-subconscious warning bell he'd been aware of earlier. Asymmetric: out of balance. What could be out of balance?

The radio interrupted his thoughts.

"I've done that." The girl's voice sounded more strained than ever. Kerr winced, stretching his lips back against his teeth. Every instructing instinct screamed that he was swamping her, pushing on remorselessly far beyond her capacity to take everything in. At the very least he ought to provide some casual chatter to help her relax as far as possible.

But there was no time. The sunlit clutter of London's suburbia was already creeping under his wings, and the Control Zone south boundary was only eight or nine minutes away.

He made his voice brisk and businesslike. "Good lass. Now we'll do a left turn, to start with. All you have to do is take hold of the control wheel and turn it a little to the left, like a car steering wheel. It'll be rather heavy to move, because you'll be overriding the part of the autopilot which holds the wings level. But if you just put a steady pressure on it the aeroplane'll bank gently to the left, which'll make it turn. Then, when we want to come out of the turn, all you'll have to do is relax the pressure on the wheel and the autopilot'll bring the wings level again, as they are now. All right?"

"Yes." It was little more than a whisper in his ears.

Kerr said firmly, "Fine. So let's try a left turn now, then. Make a small turn to the left."

The other Arrow banked suddenly towards him, showing the top surfaces of both wings against the evening sky. Kerr twisted his own wheel sharply to turn inside its radius, following. The horizon and sky stayed tilted for a few seconds—and then the runaway's wings abruptly flattened out. Kerr followed suit, treadling the rudder pedals and adjusting the power to stay in position. He started speaking quickly.

"Well, that's the general idea all right, Ann. You were a little bit rough with it, but you can certainly see how it all works and how the autopilot brings you out of the turn when you want. So now let's do it again; only this time be a bit more gentle, and hold it in the turn until I tell you."

A mile in the sky above the town of Uxbridge, Whisky Tango banked hesitantly into a shallow left turn. The time was seventeen minutes past four. In the yellow blaze of light to the west, the bottom rim of the sun touched the hazy line of the horizon.

THREE MILES to the northwest of Uxbridge, on the dividing line between Middlesex and Buckinghamshire, lies the broad grass field which is Denham Aerodrome. On the south side of the field are the Denham Flying School, the visiting aircraft park, and the aerodrome's small public car park.

On this January Saturday the couple inside the yellow Rover 3500 were noticeable only because they were outside the usual age group of aeroplane spotters and wistful spectators. The man was in his late fifties, with thinning brown hair and a neat brown moustache. The woman beside him was about the same age, dumpy, pleasant-faced and grey-haired. They were watching the steady stream of landings with interest, looking in vain for a blue-and-white Piper Arrow.

Breaking a long silence, the man said abruptly, "These people are damn awful. They just seem to *drive* the planes on, as if they were cars. We'd never have got away with that in my day."

The woman picked up the knitting in her lap and bent her head over the needles. She didn't care to remember her husband's flying days. The sleepless nights while the Lancasters were out over Germany, the terrible waiting for the click of the door after a raid had come back. . . .

A police car nosed into the car park. It paused for a moment, then drove slowly in between the two rows of cars, coming to a halt behind the Rover. A uniformed constable got out and walked round to the driver's door. The man wound down his window, eyebrows raised questioningly.

The policeman stooped, looking awkward. "Mr. and Mrs. Bazzard . . . ?"

AT THE SAME MOMENT, in the D and D Cell at West Drayton, Flight Lieutenant Peterson was sipping tea from a chipped mug while he watched his commanding officer losing his temper.

For the past three minutes Lyle had been talking on the phone to a Detective Chief Inspector Lauder at the Leeds Aero Club, and it was obvious that the conversation was not exactly proceeding well. Lyle's face was tight with rare anger, two bony knobs in his jaw working as he listened to the tinny rattle from the receiver. He took a slow deep breath before replying.

484

"I quite appreciate your position, Chief Inspector," he said coldly. "But the man you want to arrest is at present in command of an emergency flight under my control; and in order to make the correct decisions from this point onwards, I *must* be informed if there is any reason to suppose that this pilot is in a dangerous mental state. I should also point out that if you won't co-operate with me I shall be obliged to contact the Provost Marshal's office immediately to present a formal order to your superiors."

The receiver rattled again. "I most certainly *do* have the authority," Lyle retorted, "and I assure you I won't hesitate to use it. I've already told you what I want: simply the brief facts of the case. I trust I have made myself quite understood?"

There was a pause, then a quieter tone from the receiver. "I see." Lyle made quick notes on a pad. "So it looks as though there was no intent to kill. Correct? *Thank* you. And as far as you know, Kerr is unaware of the death and the fact that the police are looking for him? Right . . . good . . . then I wish you a very good afternoon, Officer."

He crashed the receiver down and swung round to the watching Peterson.

"It seems that our bloke thumped his boss in the stomach during an argument about this flight, and accidentally ruptured a weak artery. The man died half an hour later, after our chap got airborne. At least there's nothing to suggest this bloke Kerr might do anything stupid. We don't have to think about trying to pull him off, or anything like that."

"Oh, I see. Yes, sir." Peterson glanced automatically at the radar screen, where Kerr's Mayday squawk had just crossed the London Control Zone northern boundary. He found himself wishing that area radar gave height information as well as position: it would somehow be comforting to know that there was still plenty of airspace under the runaway plane as it passed over the built-up areas. He chewed a fingernail, waiting. The trace, which had started swinging round to the left, straightened up two or three miles inside the Zone. That meant Kerr must be starting the girl on turns.

One minute later the loudspeaker on the wall crashed into life with shocking suddenness.

"Mayday Romeo X-ray! Whisky Tango has just gone into an uncontrolled dive, passing 4,000 this time. Expect a crash—she doesn't look like recovering."

9

When the power unit of a single engine aeroplane ceases to function in flight the machine does not fall out of the sky like a stone; the usual result will be a fairly steep power-off dive with a rate of descent of perhaps 2,000 feet a minute.

Whisky Tango's engine failed at exactly nineteen minutes past four, at 6,000 feet over the London Borough of Ealing. One moment it was snoring away evenly and the next it hesitated, then cut out altogether: the propeller slowed to a gently shuddering idle, leaving the only sound in the cabin the ominous hiss of the airflow. In the silence the nose swung down, smoothly but inexorably, into a thirty-degree gliding dive.

Ann blinked in surprise. The ghastly sinking feeling as the nose fell away seemed unreal, too sudden to be accepted. It couldn't be anything *wrong*; when the engine came back on the instructor would tell her about it.

The radio was silent. The moan of the wind swelled in volume as the Arrow began to accelerate in the dive. Ahead of her the engine cowling steadied, pointing steeply down into a crisscross vista of tiny streets and buildings far below.

Shock finally penetrated. She brought her fists up to the sides of her face and screamed continuously.

With no reason to think in terms of an engine failure, Kerr's first reaction to the other Arrow's sudden dive was also blank disbelief. The girl *couldn't* be doing something crazy now: not over London. She must have just knocked her control yoke or something: in a moment the nose would lift up again.

His flying sense came back in a rush. He shoved his own nose down to follow Whisky Tango, belatedly thumbing the transmit button.

"Hey, Ann! C'mon! Get your nose up!"

There was no response.

As he dived the runaway plane appeared to float up and back towards him. He found he was overtaking too fast, and yanked his throttle all the way shut.

"Ann! Come *on!* What's happened?"

No reply. Just the other Arrow bobbing and sliding ahead of him like a jiggled camera projection. He snatched a glance in at his instruments. The speed was 140 m.p.h. and increasing, rate of descent about 1,500 feet a minute, altitude passing 5,000. He shouted into the radio again. Still nothing.

Fear was hot in his stomach. What had *happened?* Had she fainted? Accidentally wound on a handful of forward trim? The man beside her stirred and jammed the stick? Engine failure . . . ? An engine failure now wasn't fair, wasn't reasonable. . . .

The speed was 150. The altimeter winding through 4,500.

So O.K.—forget the chances against it happening and think, look for the cause of the failure. . . .

155 m.p.h.; passing 4,000 feet.

She was going to crash. On London.

Kerr felt sweat pouring down his face and into his roll-neck collar. He snatched his left hand up to the radio, twisted the knobs, and snapped out his Mayday call, switching frequencies immediately to try the girl again.

Still nothing. Just the mounting roar of the air, and the plunging shape of the other Arrow alongside.

Passing 3,500 feet, he looked straight ahead for a moment as he pressed the transmit button again. Over the red curve of the nose was a calm solid toy-town of inner suburbia, roads and houses and factories expanding slowly up to meet him. He had a vivid split-second image of the bobbing aeroplane alongside his right wing ploughing into that toy-town, smashing through buildings and people and finishing up in a raging ball of fire as the remainder of the fuel went up. . . .

Oh, God—FUEL! That was it! He'd forgotten to have the girl change fuel tanks!

The realization hit him like a physical blow. For seconds he seemed to be paralysed in the shuddering cockpit.

He'd been so pre-occupied with his own fuel problems that he'd committed the incredible, unforgivable error of forgetting to tell her to switch from one wing-tank to the other. He'd even half-thought of it—the words fuel *and* asymmetric *which had nudged his brain—and ignored his own warnings. So she'd flown for two hours on whichever tank she'd started from Newcastle on, and now that tank had run dry. The other one might be full to the brim, but unless she could find the fuel tap and switch it over, its contents might as well be on the moon. . . .*

Passing 3,000 feet. The airspeed clawing past 160.

His thumb was slippery on the transmit switch. "Ann! Listen to me! All that's happened is we've run one fuel tank dry, so we need to switch to the other one! Do you hear me?"

The only response was the whistling howl of the dive. Whisky Tango seemed to be diving into a vast brown bowl, a bowl whose edges were expanding steadily upwards to engulf them as the horizon-perspective shifted. Eyes fixed on the other cockpit, he pressed the button again and went on talking, urgently and continuously.

In Whisky Tango's cabin the instructor's voice, crackled loud out of the speaker over the howl of the wind.

"Come *on*, Ann! Reach across to the wall behind Roy's left leg and turn the fuel tap. Just *turn* it! It doesn't matter which way."

The words lapped and receded in her head, without meaning. Now that her screaming had stopped she seemed to be stunned, trapped in a dull acceptance of the inevitable. The plane had taken over. The thought formed in her mind, weirdly calm, that these were the last few seconds of her life.

"Ann! Turn the fuel tap! Behind Roy's left knee. Then the plane'll recover!"

Recover . . . ? The words vaguely registered. *Recover* beat like a gong, penetrating the barrier of shock. She had to turn the fuel tap. . . . The detached part of her consciousness watched herself reacting in dreadful slow motion, wasting endless moments in confusion as the plane went on down.

"Turn the fuel tap, behind Roy's left knee!"

She twisted sideways, reaching over the cockpit across Roy's lap. There was something on the side wall of the cockpit, down near the floor: a red-painted circular thing with a lever in the middle of it. Straining against her lap-strap, fumbling to hold Roy's knees out of the way with one hand, she stretched down and tried to twist the lever backwards.

It wouldn't move.

She tugged frantically, distantly feeling pain in her fingers. The lever still didn't move. She made a small animal noise of terror and tried it the other way, forwards.

It revolved smoothly round through ninety degrees, and as it stopped the engine bellowed into life.

It came back even more suddenly than it had stopped, an explosion of thunder running immediately up the scale to a huge roar. And the nose started to lift, pitching slowly upwards in the normal reaction to engine thrust.

Ann pushed herself back off Roy's lap. Over the roaring she could hear a thin high screaming sound, on the edge of hysteria. It was several seconds before she realized she was making it herself. She clapped her hands over her ears.

The altimeter unwound past 1,000 feet. Below, the streets and houses and cars were very clear, cold and long-shadowed in the last minutes of the winter sun.

The radio yelled, *"Ann! Pull back! You're still diving. Pull back on the wheel!"*

She didn't hear it. The pull-up, mild as it was, seemed to be pressing her into her seat like a huge weight on her shoulders. She was trapped, powerless.

At 600 feet, still going down and with the speed passing 180, the port undercarriage door gave way, a quick *snap-bang* almost lost under the roar of engine and slipstream. Two seconds later the engine r.p.m. hit 2,850 on the rev-counter. The figure had no special significance—except that at that particular combination of barometric pressure and temperature, 2,850 happened to be the revs at which the outermost tips of the propeller blades reached the speed of sound. The prop went supersonic in a drawn-out bandsaw scream which was heard ten miles away. Down in the streets below, a thousand people looked up at the sky.

Whimpering in terror, Ann pressed the palms of her hands hard against her ears and squeezed her eyes tight shut.

Its automatic pilot stopped Whisky Tango going down at 300

feet above the ground, doing 190 m.p.h. It passed gracefully through level flight and continued pitching gently nose-up into a shallow climb, dissipating its excess speed.

By TWENTY-ONE MINUTES past four, Flight Lieutenant Peterson was convinced that the D and D electric clock had slowed to a fraction of its normal pace.

Initially, Kerr's Mayday call had sparked off a burst of feverish activity, alerting the emergency services to the new imminence of disaster. Then, quite suddenly, it had all been done: the police, fire, and ambulance services would be flashing the information along their own lines of communication, but for the Emergency Cell the task was over. Silence settled in the room, deepening as the seconds ticked by. Every eye was glued to Peterson's radar screen, switched now to its minimum range to cover only the immediate environs of London. Kerr's Mayday squawk moved slowly across Ealing and Brentford. There was no trace of the runaway plane; if it was still in the air, its radar echo was being swamped by the proximity of Romeo X-ray's transponder-return.

Peterson breathed softly, waiting for the Mayday squawk to stop flying straight and start circling. There could be only one reason for such a manoeuvre. That Whisky Tango had gone down.

Outside in the corridor, someone clattered teacups.

The minute hand of the clock made a tiny movement to twenty-two minutes past the hour. The second hand went on crawling round the dial. Twenty-three minutes past.

Peterson stirred and said softly, "Might just make Richmond Park." Nobody replied.

The radio speaker clacked suddenly and blared into life.

"D and D, Romeo-X. Whisky Tango has recovered from the dive. Climbing away now, passing 800 feet this time."

For a second, no one moved. Then Peterson jerked forward in his chair and almost shouted into his microphone.

"*Roger*, Romeo-X! What happened?"

There was a moment's pause, then Kerr's voice came back. Even through the metallic reproduction of the speaker it sounded suddenly tired and old. "She didn't change fuel tanks, and ran one dry. I forgot to tell her. My fault."

490

Peterson made a silent *ouch* with his lips, glancing at Lyle. Then he said calmly, "Not to worry, sir; these things happen. What are your intentions now?"

"She's levelling off now at about 1,000 feet. We'll maintain that altitude, and I'll try to get her turned due west and then call you for steers to Greenham Common."

"Roger, Romeo-X. We'll be standing by for that. Will you be making a straight-in approach at Greenham?"

"Affirmative." The speaker crackled for several seconds, then cleared. "I want to intercept the Greenham centre-line as far out as possible. Whisky Tango will be landing without using rudder, and will almost certainly run off the side, so tell Greenham to keep their crashwagons well clear of the runway. Lastly, please advise them I may be landing behind her myself."

Peterson frowned, then said, "You'll be landing *behind* Whisky Tango, confirm?"

"Affirmative—I've a small fuel problem myself. I'll want to land as soon as possible once Whisky Tango's down, maybe behind her."

Peterson drew breath to speak, then hesitated as he caught sight of Lyle shaking his head furiously. He gave a tiny nod, and said matter-of-factly into the microphone, "Roger, Romeo-X, that's understood. I'll pass it on."

The speaker double-clicked and went quiet. In the sudden hush Lyle ran a hand over his head and said "Ph-ew!" in a long drawn-out sigh. As an afterthought he added, "No point in following up about his fuel. Just waste time."

Peterson nodded; half nod, half helpless shrug. Then he said flatly, "Not good, though. I'm worried about this bloke Kerr. First the coppers want him, then he nearly crashes the woman in the middle of bloody London, then he hasn't taught her to use the rudder, and now he says he's low on fuel himself. You know what I mean . . . ?" His voice trailed off.

Lyle leaned forward in his chair and picked up his pipe. He stared at it thoughtfully, turning it over in his fingers, then looked up. "Forget the fuel for a moment, and look at what he's done. He's only had an hour or so and he's got her slowed up, climbing and descending, making turns, and got her wheels down.

Whatever he might have missed out, I reckon that's bloody good going."

Peterson was still frowning. "But what about her not using rudder? How's she going to steer on the ground?"

Lyle shrugged. "So what if she doesn't? A Cherokee's pretty stable in a straight line. No, I reckon our lad's got his priorities right: he's having her turn on ailerons alone, probably over-riding the wing-leveller, so that all she'll have to think about's the control wheel and the throttle. If you ask me, I reckon he's a bloody good instructor."

Peterson nodded. After a few seconds he leaned forward and reached for the Mediator phone. While the Greenham Common number burred in his ear he glanced at Lyle again.

"I hope you're right, sir," he said softly. "I hope you're right."

AT THAT MOMENT, one person who would not have agreed with Lyle was Keith Kerr.

Closing on Whisky Tango as the runaway plane settled back into level flight at the top of its climb, he was trembling from head to toe. His fault. His ridiculous error of omission which had nearly killed two people as well as an unknown number of others on the ground. He couldn't stop thinking about it.

In his own mind, the final avoidance of catastrophe had been purely a matter of luck. Luck that the modern Cherokee Arrow fuel tap can switch the feed from one tank to the other without turning it off altogether—and still more luck that the girl had reacted when she did, and not a few seconds later. He remembered the scream of the supersonic propeller as he'd waited, agonized, for Whisky Tango to explode into the streets and houses below.

The other Arrow was steady now, swimming smoothly over the tight-packed roads and buildings of London. He knew he should be talking to the girl, but the words wouldn't come. What *could* you say when you'd nearly crashed someone under your command . . . ?

Suddenly, he saw old Piet van den Hoyt—when was it, ten years ago?—slumped in his cane chair in the torpid Kenyan heat, talking about the art of instructing in his hoarse Afrikaans accent. "*Remember you will make mistakes often, Keith. Admit the mistake in your mind, then put it behind you and start again fresh. The real danger is carrying on when you are angry with yourself and thinking wrong. That is what kills people."*

Kerr lifted the lighter to his last cigarette, aware that his hand was shaking. He tilted his head back and exhaled slowly.

Put the mistake behind you . . . start again fresh. One of the unteachable disciplines which a professional instructor must acquire the hard way over the years.

He brought his head down, and looked round the sky. Greenham Common was twenty miles away or more to the west. With full dark in twenty, twenty-five minutes it would be a tight thing. And then there was his own fuel situation. . . .

He hunched his shoulders once, then reached out and twisted the radio knobs from 121.5 back to Ann Moore's frequency.

IF THE HUMAN BRAIN is subjected to extreme fright for an extended period of time, it eventually reaches saturation point. Unable to cope any longer, the conscious mind cuts out into a state of confusion. This syndrome is commonly called shock.

As Whisky Tango settled gradually into level flight at the top of its climb, Ann's crying ceased. She stared out of the windows, the pupils of her eyes hugely dilated; streets and buildings slid smoothly under the wings, 900 feet below. Existence on the ground was something in the past, like a film once seen or an old memory; the whole world now was this little burring room in space, Roy's unconscious body, and the vast empty sky all around.

The cabin smelt rather like a hospital: plastic and metal and disinfectant.

She thought about her own hospital.

In the casualty ward she had seen people brought in, mangled and broken, after a car crash or an industrial accident. The blood and dirt, the careful desperate haste, the quiet scurrying of the nurses and doctors. Maybe we'll be like that, she thought vacantly. After the plane crashes. It would be strange to see it all from the other side; watch other nurses going through the hopeless motions of trying to save your life.

Over her head, the radio speaker said something.

"How're you doing then, love? O.K., now?"

Moving in a daze, without knowing why she did it, she reached for the microphone and said blankly, "Yes. O.K."

The man said something else, but she didn't bother to reply. Time seemed to be expanding and contracting. One moment the plane seemed to be racing over the ground and the next, everything appeared to be going on in slow-motion. But then, that was a symptom of shock and nervous exhaustion. It was funny how you could recognize symptoms in yourself, as if it was somebody else. It didn't seem to help, though. It was easier just to let go, let your mind drift.

"Come on, Ann! *Answer me!* How's Roy doing?"

Roy. The man she'd been falling in love with.

She turned her head slowly to look at him. The only sign of life was his chest, moving in shallow, irregular gasps. She thought mechanically *pressure in the subarachnoid cavity affecting the respiratory centre in the brain.* When he came round—*if* he came round—he might be all right, he might be partially paralyzed or he might be nothing but a vegetable for the rest of his life. The fact that his condition had stayed unchanged for nearly two hours could be a good sign, but you could never really tell. Not until he was in hospital.

But he wasn't going to get to hospital, of course. The plane was going to crash.

I could have fallen in love with him, she decided in a detached way. He's kind and he's warm, easy to be with. And now he's dead. Quite certainly. Still breathing, but because of the crash to come, he's dead.

Two big tears rolled down her cheeks. Ann reached out slowly, picked up Roy's limp right hand, and held it in her own.

The speaker said urgently, "Come *on*, Ann! Let's hear from you!"

She twisted her head so she could see the other aeroplane through the cabin window. It was floating close alongside, rising, falling, and weaving gently all the time, with the city sliding past below. She could even see the pilot: funny to have someone so close and talking to you, in the middle of the sky. There he was, so near, and he was just a voice. She knew nothing about him. And now she never would.

The radio said again, "Come *on* now, Ann! Pull yourself together. Will you please answer me!"

The voice was loud and commanding. She lifted the microphone and said tonelessly, "Roy's . . . the same. Still the same."

The voice clattered back immediately, sharp with relief.

"Good. I'm glad to hear that. Now listen; I'm sorry about that dive just now. But it's all over now and nothing like that'll happen again. In fact, it actually helped us in one way, getting rid of all that excess height. Anyway, we'll forget it now and carry on, making a gentle turn to the right, so that we start heading towards the place where we're going to land. All right?"

Turn.

She let go of Roy's hand and looked dazedly at the control yoke. It wasn't fair, telling her to do this now. She'd do it in a minute, when she'd rested. That was it. In a minute . . .

"Hey, Ann!" The voice was hard, almost angry. "Let's not give up now! It'll be dark in twenty minutes. And we've got to get Roy down. So let's have a simple turn to the right."

Dark in twenty minutes. . . .

For some reason the words were important. The sky ahead of the windscreen was changing with the sinking of the sun, taking on the huge electric-blue coldness of a clear winter evening. The cold seemed to reach suddenly into the cockpit, making her shiver.

She had to go on. Just go on trying, for a little while longer. Just until it got dark.

She reached out and took hold of the wheel. Straining upwards to see over the nose, she twisted it slowly to the right.

Holding formation, the two Arrows pivoted gently round. As they turned, the top rim of the sun sank finally below the horizon, leaving an orange glow at the base of a fading sky.

The time was twenty-seven minutes past four.

10

The left fuel gauge read empty.

Kerr glanced at it for the hundredth time as the runaway plane rolled stiffly out of its turn ahead of him. There was no doubt about it; the needle was sitting rock-steady on the bottom of the scale.

He dragged the back of his hand over the sweat on his face. He'd been running on the left tank for fifteen minutes, and with luck it might still have enough in it for another five or ten. With luck. So now was the time to switch to the starboard tank, leaving the last few pints in the left tank as a reserve.

Stick to the plan, he decided. He thumbed the boost pump switch, leaned across the cockpit and twisted the fuel tap to the RIGHT position, then clicked the pump off again. He thought for a few seconds, then pressed the transmit switch.

"That was a good turn, Ann. We're heading just about right. Now I'm going off the air for a moment while I talk to the people on the ground. I'll be back to you right away. O.K.?"

There was a pause. Then the girl's voice said "Yes" in his earphones. He hesitated for a moment, then reached out and switched the radio frequency to 121.5.

"D and D, Mayday Romeo X-ray."

A new voice boomed in his ears immediately: an American voice.

"Romeo X-ray, this is Greenham Common Approach. You've been handed on to us by Distress and Diversion for approach control."

"Roger, Greenham. Confirm you have me on radar?"

"That's affirmative, sir, got you identified bright and clear. You've got fifteen miles to run to Greenham, heading two-eight-five for runway two-niner."

"Roger, Greenham. I want to intercept your extended runway centre line about eight miles out, for a very long final approach. Can you give me a heading for that, please?"

"Roger, sir. Heading for that'd be—ah—two-eight-zero, sir."

"Understood. Request your runway lights on, please. I want to see you as far out as possible."

There was a tiny pause. "You've got runway and approach lights on now. Confirm this'll be a straight-in approach?"

"Straight-in first time. And please keep your crashwagons well clear of the runway. The emergency aircraft will be coming in fast and might go anywhere once it's on the ground." *If the* emergency aircraft managed to get on the ground as anything other than a ball of scrap.

"Yes sir. We already know that."

"Fine. Thanks for all you're doing."

"S'O.K., sir," the American voice replied. "Wish you luck."

Kerr double-clicked the transmit button and then switched back to 126.85. For a time he stared out sideways, watching the floating shape of the other Arrow while he forced himself to concentrate on what was ahead. This was his last chance to get the approach plan perfectly clear in his mind; think of the hundred and one things he might have forgotten.

He mentally ran through the pre-landing checklist, trying to think himself into the girl's cockpit. The first essential was a long, straight approach, exactly lined up with the runway as far out as possible. That meant turning her onto the course he'd just been given.

Then at the same time he'd have to start her on a gentle descent. No flaps, because she didn't know how to use them; it meant she'd be coming in fast of course, but with 10,000 feet of concrete to play with that shouldn't be critical. Even if she slammed it on the ground at 100 m.p.h. and then let it roll to a standstill without using the brakes at all she shouldn't have a distance problem.

So use of the brakes wasn't vital—but getting her onto the ground good and solid was. The best bet was probably to aim to get her levelled off about ten feet up, let the Arrow fly itself onto the ground, and then have her let go of the wheel at the moment of impact. The result would be a hell of a heavy landing, but safer than trying to talk her through "holding off" just above the ground for a proper nose-high touchdown. Letting go of the wheel should make the nose nod down, and keep the aircraft pinned to the runway during the ground-roll.

So. A long straight approach, a gentle descent, and then slam it on the ground and let go. Right?

Kerr shook his head. Below, as the daylight began to fade on the ground, the first lights of evening were appearing, grim reminders of the night soon to come.

He swallowed, tasting the sourness in his mouth. The false

confidence in his voice rang in his ears like a cracked bell as he started speaking.

"Right, Ann. Back again, and you're doing great. Now all we need at the moment is a small turn to the left. Then, after that, we'll be starting a very gentle descent towards an aerodrome called Greenham Common."

GREENHAM COMMON has one of the largest runways anywhere in the United Kingdom: the paved area is two miles long and 200 feet wide. The world's biggest bombers and transporters are capable of stopping in half the available distance, and light aircraft have occasionally been landed *across* the runway without undue difficulty.

Normally Greenham Common is closed. Functioning as a reserve base for the American NATO forces in Britain, it is empty of aircraft for most of the year and manned only by a skeleton staff. Occasionally, however, need arises and Greenham becomes activated for a brief period.

This winter the tenants were the 20th Tactical Fighter Wing of the US Air Force, transferred from their normal base in Oxfordshire while its main runway was being re-surfaced. Three Fighter Squadrons had moved in ten weeks before, bringing with them a number of F1-11 swing-wing interceptors as well as a stream of trucks, tow tractors, crashwagons, radar wagons and ambulances. Along with the equipment came hundreds of personnel, ranging from engineers, cooks and controllers through to their own Military Police.

At 4.32 p.m., the chain of events for the arrest of Keith Kerr had come to a halt at Greenham Common's main gate.

Parked alongside the guardhouse, the Ford Escort from Newbury police station looked small and out of place, dwarfed by the square Dodge trucks which rumbled past. Inspector Philip Wylie stood warily on the guardhouse step, somehow feeling like a supplicant whining for entry into some superior foreign country. Behind him, the gate guard put down a telephone and spoke to his back.

"Ah . . . sir, I can't get either Sergeant Bowman or Lieutenant Ricker right now. They're gonna call me right back."

Wylie turned round. The guard stayed where he was. Wylie stared at the man coldly, aware that the constable in the driving seat of the Escort was watching him. "Very well. Who's your base commander? I want to speak to him immediately."

"Colonel's out on the field, sir. Seems they got some kinda emergency out there. But his secretary'll have him call soon as he gets in."

Wylie felt his face going red. He said, "My business is concerned with that emergency. I suggest you find somebody immediately, who *can* authorize my entry." He was aware of sounding pompous even as he spoke, and the realization made him angrier than ever.

"Yes, sir." The guard remained completely indifferent. "I guess I won't reach anyone now till the emergency's over, but I'll sure try the police post again for you. If you wanna wait in your car I'll have a police escort pick you up soon as I can, O.K.?"

Wylie seethed. After a long moment he stalked round the front of the police car, snatched open the passenger door, and threw himself violently into the passenger seat.

In the guardhouse, the hands of the clock moved to 4.34 as the sentry picked up the telephone.

HALF A MILE AWAY across the aerodrome, Staff Sergeant Karl Haff wiped a gloved hand over the windscreen of the Oskosh P4 foam-and-water tender. Like the other three men chatting quietly in the large cab, he resembled a bulky silver spaceman in his one-piece asbestos suit. He shifted his body slightly, causing the fireproof material to rustle like heavy canvas, and looked across the expanse of concrete in the direction of runway two-nine.

Twenty minutes earlier there had been twelve F1-11s parked to the south of the runway; now there were only three left. Squat tow-tractors were pulling two of them towards the hangars, and a third tractor was hurrying back to the line. At this distance it looked like a nervous beetle scurrying among the mantis shapes of the fighters, and the notion so pleased Haff that he chuckled out loud.

Suddenly, the tender's dashboard radio stilled the chatter of the crash crew.

499

"Attention all crews. All crews from Crash One, attention. The two emergency airplanes have now commenced their final descent for landing. Arrival time is approximately five minutes. The pilot has just warned that the first plane is not likely to make a successful landing. It may also be off one side of the runway. Drivers to be ready for collision avoidance, but otherwise no driver to move till both airplanes are past his position. I say again, no driver to move till *both* planes have passed his position. Rescue Ten onto breathing apparatus in two minutes. Crash One out."

The cab of the Oskosh was suddenly quiet apart from the rhythmic idling of the engine, kept running according to regulations for the duration of the emergency. Haff looked along the vast empty plain of the runway, stretching away until the two lines of yellow lights converged in the cold grey shadows of evening. The last F1-11 crawled away behind its tow-tractor, leaving the aerodrome still and waiting under the fading turquoise sky.

KERR FIRST SAW the runway lights from five miles away. They materialized quite suddenly out of the dimming landscape ahead, two short strings of glittering yellow beads in the grey haze.

They lay off to the right, dammit. An S-turn right-left to get lined up was certainly something they could have done without . . . Especially since the girl was going to pieces.

Even as his thumb hovered on the transmit button, Whisky Tango's fuselage tilted abruptly downwards; the third or fourth time that had happened since he'd started her on the final descent three minutes before. The Arrow dropped away ahead of him and he pushed his own nose down to follow, thumbing the button at the same time.

"Letting the nose drop again there, Ann." He heard his voice strain with the effort of speaking calmly. "Pick the nose up now to where it was, and we'll be doing fine."

Slowly, very slowly, the runaway plane's nose lifted. The white silhouette seemed to swim lazily upwards, then steadied. Fields and hedges unrolled 500 feet below.

"Right! Great. Now just concentrate on holding it. Stare at the horizon, all the time."

500

The runway lights crawled nearer, maybe four miles to run. Still off to the side.

Kerr dragged a shaking hand across his mouth. The air in the cockpit was stale and cold now, but his body was crawling with sweat. Doubts jostled in the back of his mind in the thrumming of the slow descent. He should have had her re-trim for the approach; he should be landing her wheels-up after all; he should have talked to her differently, handled the whole thing a different way. . . .

Beyond his right wing-tip the other aeroplane flew on, bare winter trees and fields sliding faster and faster under its wings in the twilight. Kerr knew the impression of speed was an illusion, but for a moment he nonetheless had the eerie feeling that the Arrow was accelerating, rushing headlong towards its end as the last few minutes of flight drained away. He shook his head irritably and forced the notion out of his mind, willing himself to concentrate, to find the right words to get the girl turned without pushing her over the final edge of panic.

He pressed the transmit switch.

"O.K., love, that's fine. Lovely and steady. Now, still holding it steady, we want a gentle right turn. Come along, Ann, a small turn to the right."

The Arrow banked suddenly, showing its exhaust-streaked belly. At the same time its nose dropped.

"Good, but hold the nose *up!*" Kerr increased power, following. "Hold the nose *up*, keep the turn going till I say."

The Arrow pitched sharply up, the wings twisting level as the girl forgot the turn. Kerr followed: she'd rolled out of the turn early, but it would do. Two miles to run, height passing 400 feet, and intercepting the centre-line. Ready to start bending left in a few seconds to line up.

"All right, love; now turn *left*." His voice fed back clipped and urgent in his earphones. "We need a little turn left. *Go*."

The wings wobbled, then tilted into a twenty-degree bank. The Arrow paused for a second or two, then seemed to slide sideways across the horizon in front of him, so that Kerr had to juggle yoke and rudder to keep station on the inside of the turn.

"Good . . . that's great . . . just keep it going, now. We've got to keep turning till we're pointed at the runway." The wings rolled suddenly level and the nose dropped.

Kerr released the transmit button and yelled aloud in frustration. He wrenched his own wings level and pushed forward to follow.

"Hey! Pull the nose up, Ann! Pull the nose up and keep the turn going. Nose *up* and turn *left* . . ."

Whisky Tango's nose jerked up. The aeroplane soared above the hazy horizon, steadied, and the wings canted left again.

"Great! Keep it going! Hold that turn as you are!"

The Arrow crawled round the horizon, maintaining a shallow bank. Kerr flicked his eyes between the aircraft and the light-studded ruler on the ground, judging. If she kept going as she was she ought to be just on the centre-line, just about right. . . .

"*Now* straighten out, Ann! Let the wings come level *now*."

The shark-shape flattened abruptly out of its bank, appearing to skate upwards and away. Kerr slammed on full throttle, flying in a powered side-slip to get a better view forward and down. His eyes darted between the Arrow and the lines of lights, gauging, judging. . . . As far as he could tell, Whisky Tango was pointing directly down the runway. A mile or so to run, height 250 feet, and lined up.

He blinked in surprise. The realization that there was a chance now was somehow shocking, like a renewed fright. Just a chance. . . .

Without taking his eyes off the girl's cockpit he reached out and snapped his undercarriage switch to DOWN and the fuel boost pump on. Then he took a fast, shaky breath and started talking once again.

DOWN HERE the trees looked very close. Ann watched numbly as they slid past below her; a small scrubby wood of dark brooding evergreens and the bare winter skeletons of beech and elm. The tops looked soft and yielding, almost inviting, as if you could settle in them and sit until someone came along to let you out.

The sense of unreality was stronger than ever. Every second seemed to be spaced out. The little droning room *couldn't* be about to be smashed and buckled against the ground. She *couldn't* be about to try and land it. . . .

The voice came again, speaking fast.

"O.K. Ann, we're beautifully lined up. Great. Now, just lower the nose a touch. Let the nose come down a couple of inches."

The voice had been going on since the beginning of time, urgently demanding.

"*Lower* the nose, honey. Just a couple of inches."

Lower the nose. She relaxed her back pressure on the wheel, holding it with both hands.

"Bit too much, there. Pull it up a bit, now. *Up* a bit."

She pulled back again, arms quivering. The plane felt different, quite suddenly, sinking around her like a lift, with the ruffle of wind and engine increasing.

"Right! Now hold it! Look alongside the nose, and just hold it."

She shifted her eyes, blinking. The runway looked enormous, stretching away for miles like a discarded motorway section in the middle of nowhere. There were white numbers and markings on it, and ambulances waiting alongside in the winter dusk. Waiting for the end, just moments away. . . .

The Arrow snarled on down, bumping nervously in the turbulence over the trees. Kerr's voice came again, brittle with urgency: "Getting low, now. Raise the nose a little and open the throttle about half an inch. *Now.*"

Cockpit sinking again. Pull back. Nose bobbing and lifting.

"*Now, girl—power! POWER!*"

Power. Throttle lever forwards. Hold the nose, one-handed. Engine winding up, nose bucking, lifting up. Hold it. Row of orange lights on posts whipping by below. . . .

The Arrow cleared the second row of approach lights by ten feet and clawed away upwards, climbing slowly.

"O.K.! You're O.K. Hold the nose steady and bring the throttle *back* an inch."

Passing a hundred feet in a shallow climb, the two Arrows slid over the threshold of the runway. At 90 m.p.h. it takes around one and a quarter minutes to cover three thousand metres of concrete.

Kerr yelled, "Ann! Throttle *back* a couple of inches, and *lower* the nose. *Now!*"

She jerked her left hand backwards, partially closing the

throttle. The roar of the engine diminished, sending tremors of vibration down the fuselage.

"Lower the nose!" The voice crackled in the cabin, desperate with urgency. *"Do as I say—lower the nose!"*

Ann whimpered, and relaxed her pull on the wheel.

The nose dropped into a steep gliding attitude; over the blue engine cowling, the runway suddenly filled the world. It rushed up at her, vast and wide and endless. For a split-second she just stared, petrified. Then she hauled back on the wheel with both hands.

The Arrow wallowed and then ballooned upwards, stall-warning horn blaring, an uncontrollable toy on an invisible aerial switchback.

Kerr bawled into his microphone: *"Get the nose down to the horizon! Now; immediately!"*

Gasping, Ann relaxed her pressure on the wheel. The sinking sensation was suddenly less, and she could see the horizon over the crashpad. The horn wavered, gave a final blip, and then stopped. The voice was yelling over the burr of the engine.

"Hold it! Hold it there!"

The two Arrows growled past the number-three turnoff point, halfway along the runway. They were fifty feet up, running off to the left of the centre-line, and descending slowly.

"Hold it steady and reduce power slowly. Hold it just like it is and bring the throttle back slowly. All the way back."

At 80 m.p.h., engine still rumbling, Whisky Tango sank down through 50 feet, 40 feet, 20 feet. The port wing-tip passed over the number-four turnoff board, to the left of the runway. Six thousand feet out of ten thousand gone . . .

"Bring the power OFF, Ann! Throttle back all the way! Then RAISE the nose a little!"

The power command didn't register. Ann pulled the nose up a fraction, straining her head up to keep sight of the trees over the engine cowling. She had to concentrate on the nose position, not jerk it, keep it steady . . .

The Arrow hit the ground.

The impact was shocking in its suddenness: Whisky Tango simply flew into the ground, walloping on with a hollow *b-bonk* and a screech of tyres. The shock threw Ann hard into her seat-belt and snatched the yoke out of her hands. The nose tried to bounce up for an instant then smashed down again as the mainwheels slammed on. Something hit her on the forehead with a faint *thack* as the cockpit contents cannoned all around her. . . .

Then the Arrow was on the ground and running at 80 m.p.h. The aerodrome rushed past, jarring and unstoppable, as the engine growled on almost casually at low cruise power.

The end of the runway came into sight, five hundred yards ahead. Ann clapped her hands over her ears and waited to die.

KERR YELLED, "You did it! Dear God, you did it!"

He was flying fifty feet up and out to the side, overtaking the other Arrow as it rocked and swayed along the ground. His own chance of landing behind her was gone, but that didn't matter—he had fuel to spare and the girl was down, she'd made it.

Whisky Tango was bumping along the grass behind him, to the left of the runway. Still doing at least 60 m.p.h.

The elation froze on his face. Even without brakes she ought to be slowing down quicker than that . . . A few hundred feet in front was the large flat concrete pan of the holding-point at the end of the runway, and then the scrub and bushes of the over-run area.

"*Ann!*" His voice rasped dry in his throat. "*You've still got some power on! Close the throttle now! Pull it hard back!*"

There was no sign of response, nothing at all. Whisky Tango nodded over the edge of the grass, its speed barely diminished.

"*Ann! Listen! Throttle back and then go for the handbrake, sticking down under the panel! Throttle back first . . .*"

It was useless, and he knew it. From a hundred yards out to the side he saw the Arrow run off the apron into the over-run area, wings rocking sharply as it bumped off the smooth concrete. It was still doing 40, 50 m.p.h. Bushes and leaves exploded, swirling round the propeller as it ploughed on. The over-run area was about 500 feet long before it ended in trees.

The end came suddenly. The port wing-tip hit a steel fence post, the Arrow spun round abruptly through ninety degrees, and the undercarriage collapsed.

Kerr hauled into a steep climbing right turn, staring down helplessly. With the deliberation of a slow-motion film the Arrow skated sideways on its belly for fifty yards, ploughing up a moving tangle of bushes and fencing as it went.

Then it stopped. Intact. Just a skid and sliding to a stop. . . . *Survivable!*

Kerr thumped his fist on the crashpad and bellowed, "You did it!" The words were absorbed into the urgent snarl of the engine. He was pointing upwind, away from the runway, but it didn't matter because he still had his reserve of fuel in the left tank. Just take it in a tight right-hand circuit and. . . .

The engine noise developed suddenly into a loud grating which went on for a second or two, then ended in a huge metallic *clang*. The propeller stopped dead, one blade pointing straight up in front of him like an accusing finger.

For an instant, he just felt mildly surprised and somehow tired. He thought stupidly, *The damn thing's seized because you ran it too hot trying to save fuel.*

His left hand reached out and slapped the mixture lever into full rich, instinctively and uselessly.

Then he was flying for his life.

He had 80 m.p.h. and 150 feet: maybe enough to turn back and land downwind. He slammed on right yoke and rudder, then saw that the near end of the runway was cluttered with the

moving shapes of the crash vehicles, beacons flashing in the twilight. He cranked the wings level again and glided away from the aerodrome. Over the nose were trees, the light-coloured crater of a gravel pit, and then a large ploughed field. Ought to make the field, just about. . . .

He yanked the flaps up, reached out and switched the magnetos and master off, and tightened his lap-strap. The field floated up towards him in the hush of the glide. He was going to make it, just creep in over the hedge. . . .

A huge structure loomed up suddenly in the dusk; a conveyor gantry towering out of the gravel pit.

For a split second he thought he'd pass over it, then realized he wouldn't and started to turn.

THE SILENCE was the deepest that Ann had ever known. The windscreen was splattered with mud, which somehow seemed shockingly unnatural. Over the nose and the bent propeller blade, the winter trees were cold and still in the fading daylight. There seemed to be things she ought to be doing; but all that really mattered was the

stillness and the silence and the frozen ground outside the windows.

A large blunt-nosed lorry slithered to a stop alongside, crushing bushes underneath itself. Eerie blue lights flashed round regularly, illuminating the white dirt-smothered wings.

The door at her elbow flew open. There was a big man in a bulky silver overall crouched in the doorway. He was saying something. . . .

Sergeant Haff said, "You all right, ma'am?"

Ann blinked at him.

A huge silver arm reached into the cockpit, round her waist, and unclipped the seatbelt. Then there were other faces . . . hands at her elbows and under her armpits. . . .

Suddenly she was outside the cabin, standing on the wing. Hands were supporting her, voices talking. The lorry engine roared steadily in the dusk. A long blue station wagon with an AMBULANCE sign on it lurched over the rough ground and stopped a few yards away. Doors jumped open and figures leapt out.

In the distance, another crashwagon and ambulance roared round the perimeter track and off down the road outside the aerodrome. The *wow-wow-wow* of an American siren rolled over the Berkshire countryside.

"P'raps you'd like to get on the stretcher, ma'am. Doctor'll be with you in just a moment."

Ann looked round the crowded faces. Two men in green fatigues were holding a stretcher, looking at her.

"No." Her voice seemed to come from a long way off. "No. I'd like to . . . just sit. . . ."

The scrub was whipping round her ankles. People were helping her walk, saying things to her while she tried to think. . . .

They sat her in the front seat of the Dodge ambulance. Someone put a blanket round her shoulders, and someone else got in behind the wheel to sit with her. A radio on the dash panel squawked and blattered with voices.

"Rescue Six ten-eight to Structural . . ."

"Ten-four Chief Two, negative the field ten-eight the quarry . . ."

"Ten-four One, Crash Two goin' in . . ."

The white shape of the plane lay on its belly in the scrub, speckled and streaked with mud. There was a torn-off wheel lying

twenty yards away in a long gouge of fresh earth. Rusty barbed
wire lay over the right wing, and there was a mass of fencing and
undergrowth underneath the nose.

Three men were standing on the wing, by the open door. While
Ann watched dazedly a fire-axe flashed up and down, and the door
swung right back against the engine cowling. One man in a silver
overall dived into the cockpit, while another reached in after him
and started pulling.

Roy.

They brought him out head first, turning him sideways so that
he wouldn't choke on his tongue. They laid him on a stretcher
alongside the wing, and a big man with red crosses on his sleeves
knelt down beside him.

Ann fumbled for the door handle of the ambulance.

The man beside her said, "Hey, you don't have to go out there,
ma'am. The Medical Officer is doing all he can."

Ann barely heard him. She started to clamber out, her arms and
legs weak and slow to respond. She stumbled, got her feet on the
frozen earth, shrugged the blanket off her shoulders, and pulled
herself upright.

Suddenly, the man with the Red Cross armbands was in front of
her. "Lieutenant Troy, ma'am. I can tell you your fella's still with
us, all right. He may be out for some while yet, but his breathing
and pulse are mighty good, considering. Looking at him, I'd say
he's got a good chance of recovery."

Ann nodded. She heard herself say, "Yes. Thank you."

Then she put her head in her hands and wept.

KEITH KERR was alone in the gravel pit for five minutes before
they found him.

He didn't feel as if he could move, and he didn't try to. The
Arrow had hit the gravel conveyor with its right wing, and brought
the whole structure crashing down onto a man-made hill of shale.
The plane had gone with it, tangled up in the crumpling
framework, and in the final impact the engine had smashed nearly
two feet backwards into the cabin.

Kerr's legs were underneath the engine.

The cockpit was buckled and smashed around him, windows,

windscreen shattered, jagged edges of Perspex in front of his face. The raw January wind blew in, smelling of countryside.

He breathed softly, because breathing hurt, and listened to the ticking of cooling metal in the cockpit. Something tinkled quietly on the far side of the crumpled instrument panel. He looked across and saw that it was the broken glass of the clock, fallen out onto the seat. The dial was undamaged, its second hand still going round: it read exactly four fifty-two.

It was getting dark. Dark and quiet. Above him the remains of the gravel conveyor frame were twisted spidery lines against a black-purple sky.

The noise must have been fantastic. Funny how he didn't remember hearing anything.

Maybe you didn't, when you crashed.

He thought about Maggie, and the airline job.

From somewhere in the distance came the *wow-wow-wow* of a siren.

Brian Lecomber

Journalist, flying instructor, aerobatic pilot, and now a writer, Brian Lecomber has packed a lot of living into his thirty-two years. His first job, at sixteen, was as a motor-cycle mechanic; then for several years he worked as a journalist. In his spare time he learned to fly, and qualified as an instructor. It was at this stage that he became a wing-walker in a flying circus, performing stunts that were to cost him several broken bones.

Then impulse took Lecomber to the tropics, as chief flying instructor in a West Indies flying school. His career was glamorous, but also crippling hard work: in one year he remembers totalling more than 1,300 hours in the air–and the average airline pilot is limited to around 750!

To get away from the cockpit Lecomber retired to a tropical bungalow to write his first novel, *Turn Killer*. When it was published in England, to be followed by *Dead Weight*, he was amazed to find himself a professional author.

"So far as the literary world is concerned," he says honestly, "I have to admit to being a fish out of water. I don't see my writing as an art form: I think the novelist's job is to entertain— to pick the reader up from his or her life and make them live something different for a while." Nevertheless, a lot of work goes into his books. "I *know* aeroplanes and the people around them—and when I take you into a cockpit or onto an aerodrome, you can be sure that the cockpit is real and the aerodrome is there. The scene has got to be exactly right," Lecomber maintains. "If I can then also make you hear the engine and feel the turbulence through your seat and straps—then I figure I've achieved something worth while."

Writing doesn't claim all his time nowadays. As well as running his own flying school, Lecomber is a regular performer in British airshows: in 1977 he won four major aerobatic contests, and also became the only pilot to fly a World War I fighter (the cumbersome Sopwith Camel) in competition. And his pride and joy is his own pre-war Stampe SV4C biplane.

QQ98